THE FATEGUARD
TRILOGY

GALLOW
THE FATEGUARD
TRILOGY

NATHAN HAWKE

The right of Nathan Hawke to be identified as the author
of this work has been asserted by him in accordance with the
Copyright, Designs and Patents Act 1988.

First published in Great Britain in 2013
by Gollancz
An imprint of the Orion Publishing Group
Carmelite House, 50 Victoria Embankment, London EC4Y 0DZ
An Hachette UK Company

This collected edition published in Great Britain in 2014
by Gollancz

3 5 7 9 10 8 6 4 2

A CIP catalogue record for this book
is available from the British Library

ISBN 978 1 473 20838 4

Typeset by Deltatype Ltd, Birkenhead, Merseyside

Printed and bound by CPI Group (UK) Ltd, Croydon, CR0 4YY

The Orion Publishing Group's policy is to use papers
that are natural, renewable and recyclable products and
made from wood grown in sustainable forests. The logging
and manufacturing processes are expected to conform to the
environmental regulations of the country of origin.

www.orionbooks.co.uk

CONTENTS

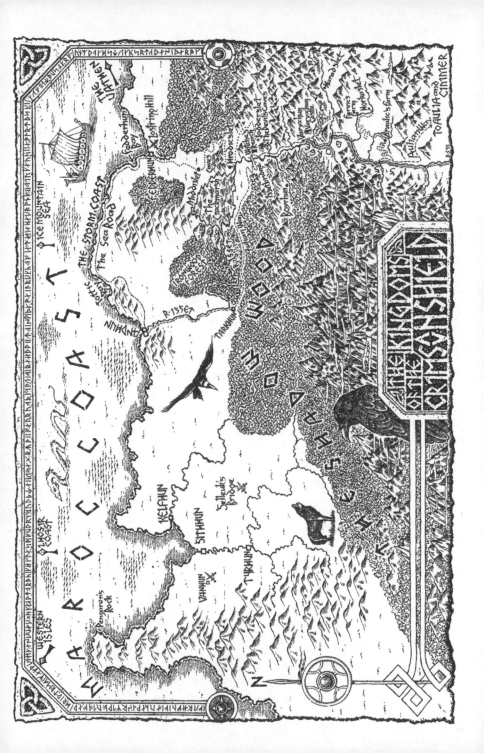

MEDRIN AND THE MAGICIAN

The man on the table in front of the Aulian was dying. The soldiers with their forked beards crowded around, full of anxious faces, but they knew it: he was past any help. The Aulian shook his head. 'I'll do what I can. I make no promises. Leave him with me.' And when they did leave, that too was a sign of how little hope they had. A prince of the Lhosir left alone with an Aulian wizard. The Aulian opened up his satchel and his bag and set about making his preparations. The dying man's eyes were open. The skin of his face was grey and slick with sweat but there was a fierce intelligence behind those eyes. And a fear, too. A prince of the Lhosir who was afraid to die, but then who wouldn't be when dying looked like this?

'Who are you?' The Aulian didn't answer, but when he came close the Lhosir still had enough strength to grab his sleeve. 'I asked you: who are you?'

'I'm here to heal you. If it can be done.'

'Can it?'

'I will try, but I'm … I am not sure that it can. If you have words to say, you should say them now.' The Aulian lifted the Lhosir's head and tipped three potions into his mouth, careful and gentle. 'One for the pain. One for the healing. One to keep you alive no matter what for two more days.' The Lhosir let go. He was trembling but he seemed to understand. The Aulian unrolled a cloth bundle and took out a knife and started to cut as gently as he could at the bandages over the Lhosir's wound. The room already stank of putrefaction. The rot was surely too far gone for the Lhosir to live.

'I left him. I left my friend. I abandoned him.'

The Aulian nodded. He mumbled something as he cut, not

really listening. The Lhosir was fevered already and the potions would soon send him out of his mind entirely and nothing he said would mean very much any more. 'If you survive, your warring days are over. Even small exertions will leave you short of breath. I am sorry.'

'I was afraid. I am Lhosir but I was afraid.'

'Everyone is afraid.' The Aulian lifted away a part of the bandage. The Lhosir flinched and whimpered where it stuck to the skin and the Aulian had to pull it free. The stench was appalling. 'I'm going to cut the wound and drain it now. It will hurt like fire even through the potions I've given you.' The Aulian dropped the stinking dressing into a bowl of salt. He forced the Lhosir's mouth open as delicately as he could and pushed a piece of leather between the Lhosir's teeth. 'Bite on this.'

The Lhosir spat it out. 'The ironskins took him.'

The Aulian paused, waiting for the potions to take the Lhosir's mind. 'Ironskins?'

'The Fateguard.'

The Aulian looked at the knife in his hand, razor sharp. 'Then tell me about these iron-skinned men while we wait.'

'The guardians of the Temple of Fates in Nardjas, magician.' The Lhosir tried to rise but his strength failed him. 'I know I'm dying. I know the cure for flesh-rot.'

'I must cut out the rot. All of it.'

'And it's spread too far and too deep for you to do that without killing me. And if you do *that* then the men who brought me here will murder you.'

'Perhaps.' The Aulian frowned. 'Someone should have tended to you sooner.'

The Lhosir spat out a laugh and shook his head. 'I'm the son of our king. No one dared and so they brought me here flat on my back in a cart. Corvin the Crow thinks it's bad luck to have his prince die in the middle of his army and so he sends me away to die alone instead. Oh, he said he was sending me back to my father but we both knew I'd never live to cross the sea. Away, that was all that mattered. Flat on my back, and I a proud Lhosir prince.' He coughed.

'Tell me,' said the magician again, 'about the iron men.'

'They serve the Eyes of Time. What, magician, did you not see them when they crossed the sea last summer after the Crow took the Crimson Shield from Prince Yarric's corpse? They took it away from him and brought it back to to Nardjas.' He coughed again. 'And that's how I earned this end.'

'No, I did not.' The magician looked at his knife. The Lhosir was slipping into the trance of his potions. Another few minutes and he wouldn't feel a thing. And the Lhosir was right, too – he probably wouldn't ever wake up again. 'Speak your peace to your gods now, Lhosir.'

'The Fateguard. Skins of black iron.' The Lhosir closed his eyes. 'Iron masks and iron crowns. What they are beneath, who can say? Men, I suppose, but there's plenty who believe otherwise. No one ever sees them without their iron skins, no one outside the temple. Stupid rumours that can't be true, that they never eat or sleep or rest. Dead men brought back to life to serve Fate.' The Lhosir closed his eyes.

'Smoljani?' The word came out of the magician like an unforeseen breath of wind, lingering a moment and then gone. His face, his voice, everything about him changed as though he was suddenly a different person. A chill went through him. 'There was another like that that came before them,' he said, as much to himself as to the Lhosir. 'Long ago. We buried it far away from here under a place called Witches' Reach. It was a terrible thing made of old pacts with ancient dusty gods. Its power was very great.' The Aulian touched a thumb to the Lhosir's face and drew back an eyelid. The eyes beneath had rolled back. 'Smoljani.' He shook himself and took up his knife again, opened the Lhosir's wound and started to drain it. The stench was enough to make him turn away and gag, and when he turned back the Lhosir's eyes were open again.

'Is that one of your potions?' The Aulian didn't answer, and after a moment the Lhosir sagged and his eyes rolled back a second time. 'They took my friend and I didn't stop them. I've heard of you, magician. They say you have a fine house, a palace almost, yet none of the Marroc will go near it. They say you're a witch.'

'I will cut away the rot and fill the wound with maggots and honey. Do you understand? Maggots to eat away the bad flesh I cannot reach and honey to help with the healing. Where do they come from, these iron-skinned men?'

'The Eyes of Time makes them in frozen halls of the Frost Wraiths.' The Lhosir's lips drew back in something that might have been an effort at a smile. 'Maybe there's no flesh under that black iron at all. Maybe they're the wraiths themselves.'

'Oh, there is flesh,' said the Aulian.

'You know them?'

'I do.'

'And the Eyes of Time?'

'By another name, yes, I think my people knew it once.'

'They took my friend. I am responsible.' The Lhosir's words were slurring.

'Yes, yes.'

'How do I kill the Eyes of Time, magician?'

'Salt and fire and the Edge of Sorrows.' The Aulian took the Lhosir's hand. Maybe that would ease him on his way.

'They took my friend. I should have ... I should ... I was afraid ... I was ... I ...' The Aulian listened until the Lhosir's words broke into senseless mumbles. The potions were taking hold. He turned his knife back to the Lhosir's wound and the Lhosir screamed. He screamed like a man having his soul torn out of him piece by piece. Like a man slowly cut in two by a rust-edged saw. The Aulian worked quickly. The wound was deep and the rot had spread deeper still and the stink was enough to make him pause now and then and breathe through a scented cloth. He cut it out as best he could, drained the seeping pus, cut until blood flowed red and the screaming grew louder still. When he was done he placed a bowl over the wound and tipped a hundred wriggling maggots over the dying Lhosir's bloody flesh, then fresh warm honey.

The door flew open. Another Lhosir, with the dying prince's bodyguards scurrying in his wake. They ran in and then stumbled and turned away, hit by the reeking air. The Aulian didn't look up. He wrapped cloth over the wound as fast as he could, hiding what he'd done. The first of the soldiers was on him quickly, gagging. The dying prince was quiet now. Fainted at last.

'Wizard, what have you done?'

The Aulian cleaned his knife and began to pack away his bags. 'If he lives through the next two days then he may recover. Send someone to me then.' He looked at the forkbeard soldier. 'Only if he lives.'

But the Lhosir wasn't looking at him, he was looking at the wound and at the cloth over the hole in the dying prince's side. He was looking at the blind writhing thing that was trying to wriggle free from under it. The Aulian frowned. He'd been careless in his haste. He turned back to the soldier. 'It will—'

'Sorcerer!' The forkbeard drove his sword through the Aulian. 'Monster! What have you done?'

The Aulian tried to think of an answer, but all his thoughts were of a different monster, the monster with the iron skin that he'd thought long buried and gone. And as he fell to the floor and stared at the dying Lhosir's hand hanging down from his table, how the Lhosir seemed to have too many fingers.

THE CRIMSON
SHIELD

Honour has not to be won, it must only not be lost

The Vathen rode slowly through the ruins of the village. There was little left. Burned-out huts, not much else. They stopped at the edge, at what had once been a forge, and one of them dismounted and poked through the rubble. Whatever had been done here, it had been a while ago.

'The forkbeards call themselves men of fate.' She said it without much feeling one way or the other, as if noting that the clouds had turned a little darker and perhaps more rain was on the way.

'This is a Marroc village,' said one of the others with a voice that was keen to push on.

'Yes,' said the first. 'But a forkbeard lived here once. They called him Gallow. Gallow the Foxbeard.'

SCREAMBREAKER

1

THE VATHEN

Beside him Sarvic turned to run. A Vathan spear reached for him. Gallow chopped it away; and then he was slipping back and the whole line was falling apart and the Vathen were pressing forward, pushed by the ranks behind them, stumbling over the bodies of the fallen.

For a moment the dead slowed them. Gallow turned and threw himself away from the Vathan shields. The earth under his feet was slick, ground to mud by the press of boots and watered with blood and sweat. A spear point hit him in the back like a kick from a horse. He staggered and slipped but kept on running as fast as he could. If the blow had pierced his mail he'd find out soon enough. The rest of the Marroc were scattering, fleeing down the back of the hill with the roars of the Vathen right behind. Javelots and stones rained around him but he didn't look back. Didn't dare, not yet.

He slowed for a moment to tuck his axe into his belt and scoop up a discarded spear. The Vathen had horsemen and a man with a spear could face a horse; and when at last he did snatch a glance over his shoulder, there they were, cresting the hill. They'd scythe through the fleeing Marroc and not one in ten would reach the safety of the trees because they were running in panic, not turning to face their enemy as they should. He'd seen all this before. The Vathen were good with their horses.

Sarvic was pelting empty-handed down the hill ahead of him. They'd never met before today and had no reason to be friends, but they'd stood together in the wall of shields and they'd both survived. Gallow caught him as the first Vathan rider drew back an arm to throw his javelot. He hurled himself at Sarvic's legs, tumbling them both down the slope of the hill. Gallow rolled away, turned and rose to a crouch behind his shield. Other men had dropped theirs as they ran but that was folly.

The javelot hit his shield and almost knocked him over. Another rider galloped towards them. At the last moment Gallow raised his spear. The Vathan saw it too late. The point caught him in the belly and the other end wedged into the dirt and the rider flew out of his saddle, screaming, the spear driven right through him before the shaft snapped clean in two. Gallow wrenched the javelot from his shield. He forced another into Sarvic's hand. There were plenty to be had. 'Running won't help you.'

More Vathen poured over the hill. Another galloped past and hurled his javelot, rattling Gallow's shield. Gallow searched around, wild-eyed and frantic for any shelter. Further down the hill a knot of Marroc had held their nerve long enough to make a circle of spears. He raced towards them now, dragging Sarvic with him as the horsemen charged past. The shields opened to let him in and closed around him. He was a part of it without even thinking.

'Wall and spears!' *Valaric?* A fierce hope came with having men beside him again, shields locked together, even if they were nothing but a handful.

Another wave of Vathan horse swarmed past. The Marroc crouched in their circle, spears out like a hedgehog, poking over their shields. The horsemen thundered on. There were easier prey to catch but they threw their javelots anyway as they passed. The Marroc beside Gallow screamed and pitched forward.

'You taught us this, Gallow, you Lhosir bastard,' Valaric swore. 'Curse these stunted hedge-born runts! Keep your shields high and your spears up and keep together, damn you!'

The Vathan foot soldiers were charging now, roaring and whooping. As the last riders passed, the circle of Marroc broke and sprinted for the woods. The air was hot and thick. Sweat trickled into Gallow's eyes. The grass on the hill had been trampled flat and now gleamed bright in the sun. Bodies littered the ground close to the trees, scattered like armfuls of broken dolls where the Vathan horse had caught the Marroc rout. Hundreds of them pinned to the earth with javelots sticking up from their backs. There were Lhosir bodies too among the Marroc. Valaric pointed at one and laughed. 'Not so invincible, eh?'

They reached the shadows of the wood and paused, gasping. Behind them the battlefield spread up the hill, dead men strewn in careless abandon. Crows already circled, waiting for the Vathen to finish so they could get on with some looting of their own. The moans and cries of the dying mixed with the shouts and hurrahs of the victors. Before long the dead would be stripped bare and the Vathen would move on.

'Got to keep moving,' Gallow said.

'Shut your hole, forkbeard! They won't follow us here.' Valaric picked up his shield. He kicked a couple of Marroc who'd crouched against trees to catch their breath, glared at Sarvic and headed off again at a run. 'A pox on you!' he said as Gallow fell in step beside him. 'They'll move right on to Fedderhun and quick. They don't care about us.'

But they still ran, a hard steady pace along whatever game trails they could find, putting as much distance as they could between them and the Vathen. Valaric only slowed when they ran out into a meadow surrounded by trees and by then they must have been a couple of miles from the battle. Far enough. The Marroc were gasping and soaked in sweat but they weren't dead. There wouldn't be many who'd stood in the shield wall on Lostring Hill who could say that.

The grass was up to their knees and filled with spring flowers and the air was alive with a heady scent. 'Should be good enough,' Valaric muttered. 'We rest here for a bit then.' He threw a snarl at Gallow. 'This is the end of us now, forkbeard. After here it's each to his own way, and you're not welcome any more.'

'Will you go to Fedderhun, Valaric?'

Valaric snorted. 'There's no walls. What's the point? Fedderhun's a fishing town. The Vathen will either burn it or they won't and nothing you or I can do will change that. If your Lhosir prince wants a fight with the Vathen, I'll be seeing to it that it's not me and mine whose lives get crushed between you. I'll be with my family.'

There wasn't much to say to that. Old wounds were best

left be. Gallow's own children weren't so many miles away either. And Arda; and they'd be safe if the Vathen went on to Fedderhun. He touched a hand to his chest and to the locket that hung on a chain around his neck, warm against his skin, buried beneath leather and mail. He could have been with them now, not here in a wood and stinking of sweat and blood. 'I'm one of you now,' he said, as much to himself as to Valaric.

Valaric snorted. 'You're never that, forkbeard.'

Gallow set down his spear and his shield and took off his helm, letting the air dry the sweat from his skin. 'It's still your land, Valaric.'

But Valaric shook his head. 'Not any more.'

2

VALARIC

'Not any more.' Valaric spat. Four hundred men. King Yurlak had sent four hundred forkbeards to fight ten thousand Vathen, and no one, not even a crazy forkbeard, was that terrible. The fools on the hill were always going to break. He'd seen that from the moment he'd seen the Vathen and how many they were – and it grated, thinking that if every man standing on the top of Lostring Hill this morning had been a Lhosir forkbeard then they just might have held the line, even outnumbered as they were, and maybe it *would* have been the Vathen who'd broken and fled. Maybe. Because Yurlak hadn't just sent four hundred men. He'd sent the Screambreaker, the Widowmaker, the Nightmare of the North, and the Widowmaker had called the Marroc to arms and Valaric had been stupid enough to believe in him because a dozen years ago Valaric had been on the wrong end of the Widowmaker and his forkbeards four times, one after the other, and each time the Marroc had had the numbers and Valaric had been certain that the Widowmaker couldn't possibly win, and each time he had. A man, he reckoned, ought to learn from a thing like that.

Out of the shadows of the trees a Vathan rider stepped into the clearing. Valaric froze for a moment but the rider was slumped in his saddle. He had blood all over him and he was clearly dead. Half his face was missing.

'Well, well. An unwanted horse. Now there's a blessing.' He grinned at the other Marroc around him. He'd picked them carefully, the ones who'd fight hard and long and keep their wits. Torvic, the three Jonnics, Davic, all men who'd fought the forkbeards years ago and lived, even towards the end when the forkbeards had hired Vathan mercenaries with their plundered gold and sent them in after the Marroc lines broke. The Marroc were used to running away by then, but not from horses. Thousands of men dead. And here he was not ten years later: same forkbeards, same Vathen, only now the forkbeards claimed they were his friends. Valaric was having none of it.

The other Marroc were on their feet now. They were all thinking the same thing. All of them except the forkbeard Gallow, who'd keep quiet if he had any sense. Valaric got to the horse first. He took the reins and hauled the dead Vathan out of the saddle.

'So let's see what we've got, lads.' He left the body to the others and started going through the saddlebags. Food and water they'd share since none of them carried any. A rare piece of good fortune. Someone else's horse and saddle were fine things to carry away from a battle even after a victory. They'd have to divide it somehow. Needed a care that did. He'd seen men kill each other over spoils like this, men who'd fought side by side only hours before.

'There are more.' Gallow was pointing off into the trees on the other side of the clearing.

Valaric growled. He let go of the horse and slipped his sword into his hand and picked up his shield where he'd left it in the grass. 'Men? Or just horses?'

'Horses.'

Horses was more like it. But still ... He looked around the other Marroc. They all had a greedy look to them, but nervous too. 'Right. You lot stay here. Keep on the edge of the trees. Shields and spears ready in case. Me and the forkbeard, we'll go see what's there.' He took a long hard look at Gallow. He was tall – certainly compared to a Marroc, and maybe even tall among his own kind – and broad. His muscles might be hidden beneath mail and thick leather, but the man had been a soldier for years and worked in a forge before and after, and there was no such thing as a weak-armed smith. His face was strong-boned and weathered. Valaric supposed there'd be some who'd say it was handsome if it hadn't been for the scar running across one cheek and the dent in his nose that went with it. He didn't have the forked beard of a Lhosir any more, but Valaric's eyes saw it anyway. *Demon-beards.* Thick black hair that didn't mark him as anything much one way or the other, but eyes of the palest blue like mountain glaciers. Lhosir eyes, cold and pitiless and deadly. Valaric cocked his head. 'You man for that?'

Gallow didn't blink, just nodded, which made Valaric want to hit him. They stood face to face. Gallow looked down at him. Those ice-filled eyes *were* piercing, but Valaric didn't see the things he was looking for there. Forkbeards were merciless, filled with hate and rage – that's how they'd been on the battle-field – but Gallow's eyes were just sad and weary. They had a longing to them.

'You can go back to your own kind after this,' he said shortly and brushed past on into the trees, eyes alert for the horses Gallow had seen. He picked up two of them straight away, two more Vathan ones, riderless this time. Probably they'd followed the first. If there were more, so much the better.

'I have a family, Valaric,' said Gallow. 'A wife and an old man and two young sons and a daughter. Those are my people now, and yes, I'll go back to them. I don't know these Vathen but they'll head west for Andhun. If that falls then who knows what they'll do? Maybe they're set on making new kings and cities and will leave my village alone. Or maybe they're the sort to swarm across the country with their horses and their swords, with burning torches, sweeping everything before them until nothing is left.'

'Two young sons and a daughter, eh?' Valaric couldn't keep the bitterness out of his voice. 'Sounds like you've been busy since you finished raping and murdering and settled to the business of breaking our backs for the pleasure of your king.'

Gallow didn't answer. Didn't care, most likely, and the thought flashed through Valaric's head to kill him right there and then while the two of them were alone. None of the others would think any less of him for doing it. They'd all lost some-thing when the forkbeards had come across the sea in their sharp-faced boats. He had no idea why Gallow had stayed. Married a local girl, a smith's daughter, and that alone was enough for Valaric to hate him. *Our land, not yours.* Nine years ago that was, when everyone had hated the forkbeards and everything they stood for; but over those years the world had slowly changed. Everyone in these parts had come to hear of the forkbeard who hadn't gone home. Maybe he even had friends now, but for Valaric time had healed nothing. Gallow wasn't welcome. None of them were.

'There.'

Among the trees in the shade Valaric saw the shapes of more horses. A dozen maybe, one for each of them to ride and a few spare. Good coin if they could get to a place where they could sell them. Changed things, that did. Not so much chance of a squabble over the spoils. The battle was going to give him a decent purse after all – which wasn't why he'd come to fight it, but a man still had to live.

Gallow pressed ahead through the trees to the horses, his hand staying close to his axe. He moved quickly but with cautious feet. Valaric let him go ahead while he tied up the first two animals and then ran after him. Couldn't let a forkbeard take the best of the pickings, but by then Gallow had stopped. When Valaric caught up, he saw why.

'Modris!' Cursing the old god's name was the only thing left to do.

There were bodies everywhere. More horses too, a lot of them with their Vathan riders still slumped on their backs. The bodies on the ground were mostly forkbeards. Valaric took it all in and nodded to the dead. He pointed through the trees, roughly back towards the battlefield. 'Forkbeards were riding through the forest. The Vathen got ahead of them. They encircled them and took your friends from the front and from behind.'

Gallow nodded. 'The Lhosir made a stand rather than run. They dismounted because that's how we like to fight. Like you, with our feet on the earth. The trees made that work for them. No one ever thought of running. Not our way.'

'The Vathen stayed in their saddles. Maybe that wasn't so clever of them.' There were a lot more dead Vathen than forkbeards. One of them had an arrow sticking out of his chest. Valaric saw it and frowned: the forkbeards almost never used bows in battle. Arrows were for hunting or for cowards, but someone had used one here. For once not losing had mattered more than how they fought.

'They were protecting something,' he whispered.

Gallow was staring around the corpses of his own people. He nodded. 'These were the Screambreaker's men.' He walked slowly among them, axe drawn, eyes darting back and forth among the shadows.

'A pretty sight. Forkbeards and Vathen killing each other. My heart soars.' Valaric didn't feel it though, not here. He'd told himself that he and Gallow were enemies from the moment they'd met, reminded himself that one day they might face each other in a different way, iron and steel edges drawn to the death. He hadn't bothered much about that though, because they both had to live through the Vathen first for that to ever happen, and Valaric had been in enough battles to know when victory lay with the enemy. The Marroc were mostly too stupid and too fresh to fighting to see it, but the forkbeards must have known too, yet they'd faced the enemy anyway. They'd stood and held their shields and their spears and roared their cries of battle. 'Is he here then, your general?'

Gallow crouched beside a man with blood all over his face. He nodded. 'Yes, Valaric, he is.' He stood up. He still had his axe, and the way he was looking made Valaric wonder if that day when they'd face each other wasn't so far off after all. 'He's still alive.' Gallow's eyes were right for a forkbeard now. Merciless. Valaric took a step back. He let his hand sit on the hilt of his own sword. The Nightmare of the North. The man who'd led the forkbeards back and forth across his land and stained it black with ash and red with blood. Whoever killed the Widowmaker would be a hero among the Marroc, his name sung through the ages. And here he was, helpless, and there was only one forkbeard left standing in Valaric's way.

Gallow met his eye. 'Now what?'

Valaric couldn't draw his sword. Simply couldn't. Not that Gallow scared him, although it would be a hard fight, that was for sure. Or he could have called the other Marroc and told them what he'd found, because no forkbeard ever born was strong enough to face nine against one. But he didn't do that either. The honest truth was that the Nightmare of the North hadn't done half the things people said he had. What he *had* done was stand with two thousand Marroc against the Vathen in a battle he must have known he couldn't win. He'd done that today. Valaric turned away. 'They say things about you, Gallow.'

'I'm sure they do.'

'Tavern talk, now and then. They say you're good to your word. That you work hard. Decent, they say, for a forkbeard. Always with the same words at the end: *for a forkbeard*. Which is good. Doesn't serve a man to forget who his enemies are. Why did you fight beside me and not with your own people, eh? Would have been safer, after all. Likely as not they were the last to break.' The words were bitter. *Bloody forkbeards.*

'You're my people now, Valaric.'

Valaric spat in disgust. 'No, we're not. A forkbeard is a forkbeard. Shaving your face changes nothing.' He stared at Gallow and found he couldn't meet the Lhosir's eyes any more. They were the eyes of a man who would stand without flinching against all nine of his Marroc if he had to because it would never occur to him to do anything else. Valaric shook his head. 'I tell you, I got so sick of running away from you lot. Must be a first for you.'

'Selleuk's Bridge, Marroc.'

'Selleuk's Bridge?' Valaric bellowed out a laugh. 'I missed that. Beat you good, eh?'

'That you did.' Gallow's hand still rested on the head of his axe.

Valaric turned and started to walk away. 'I've done my fighting for today. Best you be on your way. You take more than your share of these horses and we'll come after you like the howling hordes of hell. Go. And be quick about it.'

3

DEAD WEIGHT

Gallow saw to the horses first. Two of them, one for him and one for the Screambreaker. That was fair. A man took what he needed and no more when times were hard. He chose Lhosir mounts over the Vathan ones. Stamina over speed. He couldn't see he'd be needing to win any races today but it was a long ride home and there wouldn't be any stopping while the sun was up.

He grimaced as he lifted the general across his shoulders. The Marroc called him the Widowmaker and the Nightmare of the North. To the Lhosir he was Corvin Screambreaker. He was a heavy man, full of muscle, but old enough to have a belly as well, and nearly ten years of peace had done him no favours there. In his armour he was almost too much; but for all Gallow knew, the Screambreaker was already knocking at the Maker-Devourer's cauldron, and a Lhosir died in his armour if he could, dressed for battle with his spear in one hand and his shield in the other. That was a good death, one the Maker-Devourer would add to his brew. Once Gallow had the Screambreaker on the back of his horse he strapped a shield to the old warrior's arm and wrapped his limp fingers around a knife and tied it fast with a leather thong ripped from a dead Vathan's saddle. A sword would have been better, but swords were heavy. Chances were it would fall out and be lost and then the Screambreaker would have nothing. A knife was at least something. The Maker-Devourer would understand that.

The Marroc were still back in the clearing. He ought to lay out the other Lhosir dead and speak them out, tell the Maker-Devourer of their names and their deeds, but he couldn't. He didn't know them. He put swords and knives into empty hands, knowing full well that the Marroc would simply loot them again as soon as he was gone. With the Screambreaker's horse tethered to his own, he whispered a prayer to the sky and the earth, mounted and rode away.By the time he was free of the woods, the sun was sinking towards the distant mountains of the south. Varyxhun was up there somewhere, up in the hills, surrounded by its mighty trees and guarding what had once been a pass through the mountains to Cimmer and the Holy Aulian Empire, but that was an old path. Nothing but the odd shadewalker had come from the empire for more than fifty years now, while the castle overlooking Varyxhun itself was said to be haunted, full of the vengeful spirits of the last Marroc to hold out against the Screambreaker. It was said to be the home of a sleeping water-dragon too, but the Vathen wouldn't bother with it, dragon or not. They'd stay north and move along the coast to Andhun. If Valaric and the other Marroc wanted a fight, that's where it would be. *I'll be with my family*, Valaric had said, but Valaric's family were six wooden grave markers in a field near a village by the coast, far away to the west, and had been for years. Everyone knew that.

He watched the sun finish creeping its way behind the distant horizon. As the stars came out, he stopped and eased Corvin to the ground and gently took away his shield. He let the horses cool and took them to water; when he was done with that he searched their saddlebags for food for both of them and blankets for Corvin. The Screambreaker's breathing was fast and shallow, but at least he was still alive. Gallow forced one of his eyes open. It was rolled back so far that all Gallow could see was white. He made a fire, forced some water into the old man and ate from what he'd found on the stolen horses.

'If you die on me I'll make a pyre if I can. I'll miss a few things when I speak you out, I reckon. Forgive me. The sky knows there's enough that I do know.' He took the Screambreaker's hand and held it in his own. *Talk to a troubled spirit. Helps it to remember who it is.* Some witch had told him that, not long after he'd crossed the sea. 'They say you were a farmer once, no better than anyone else. The old ones who knew you before. Thanni Thunderhammer. Jyrdas One-Eye. Kaddaf the Roarer. Lanjis Halfborn. We listened to all their stories. You were one of them, and you were their god too. Even then people knew you because of what you'd done, not because of a name you carried when you were born. "That a man should somehow be better than his brothers simply because his father was rich? A Marroc nonsense. Lhosir will never stomach it." You said that. Do you remember? I think we'd been talking about Medrin.' He let the Screambreaker's hand go and poked at the fire. 'Things were changing even before I crossed the sea. Some of these Marroc ideas were taking root and a dozen and more winters have passed since then. Was it all different when you went back? Is that why you sailed again? Or was it simply too hard to resist? One last glorious stand. A battle you couldn't possibly win. A hero's death for a hero's life.'

He shifted the Screambreaker closer to the fire and settled down on the other side, gazing up at the stars. 'We weren't all that far from here when we last parted. Andhun opened its gates to us, do you remember? You gave your word not to plunder it. We honoured that. By then we just wanted to go home, to get back across the sea and eat proper food again. Drink water that tasted of mountain ice and marry some big-boned woman who'd bear us lots of sons and sleep in a longhouse with all our kin and not in those stinking Marroc huts. That sort of thing. We talked about it all the time in those last weeks. Was it all there waiting for you just as we remembered it? It must have gone well enough for you and the others, what with bringing old Yurlak home and every ship laden with loot and plunder. But I can't say it's been too bad here.'

The Screambreaker moaned and shifted, still wandering the Herenian Marches where the lost spirits of those neither alive nor dead were cursed to dwell, spirits like the Aulian shade-walkers. Gallow patted his hand. 'I wasn't going to stay. I was as eager as the rest of you. But then Yurlak fell ill and everyone was sure he was going to die before you reached home and Medrin would be king in his place. I'm not so fond of Medrin. So I got to thinking that maybe I'd stay and I watched you all go, ship by ship. You took Yurlak back across the sea so he could die in his own house and among his own people, only then he went and didn't die after all. If I'd still been in Andhun, I'd have come home when I heard but, as you see, I never did. I left. Back to the mountains and the giant trees of Varyxhun. I was going to cross the Aulian Way. Go south, to lands we can hardly name, but on my way I found a forge and an old smith who needed a strong arm to work it, and one of his three dead sons had left a wife behind him and a girl he likely never saw. It was us who left her a widow, us who took the old man's sons, so I won't say they were happy with having a forkbeard around the place. But it felt good to be making things again. I wonder if you can understand that.' He took a deep breath and touched his hand to his chest, to the place where the locket lay next to his skin. 'I took a lock of her hair while she was sleeping. A little luck to carry into battle. I know what you'd say about that, old man. Laugh and scoff and tell me I was daft in the head, tell me that a man's fate is written for him before he's born. But here we are, so perhaps it worked, in its way. No one would have her, see, because she was another man's wife and she came with another man's child to feed when both men and food were scarce, and she was ... Screambreaker, you'll understand if you meet her. The Marroc prefer their women a little more docile.' He rose and looked up at the stars. 'A fine woman, Screambreaker. We have two sons of our own now, and another daughter. You'll like her if you last long enough to see her. Fierce and speaks her mind as often as she likes and doesn't give a rat's arse what anyone else thinks. She won't like *you*, sorry to say. Not one bit. Arda. That's her name.'

He lay down beside the fire and pulled his cloak over himself. 'Maker-Devourer watch over you, old man. Don't get yourself lost in the Marches. And don't tell Arda about the hair. I'd never hear the end of it.'

Gallow closed his eyes. The Screambreaker was mumbling to himself. He hadn't heard a word.

4

THE ARDSHAN

Gulsukh Ardshan's horse shifted beneath him, impatient to move. From where he sat, the battlefield looked as though the Weeping God had reached down from the sky and picked the Marroc legion up to the clouds, shaken them fiercely and let them go, scattering them to fall as they may. The light was fading but he still watched from where the Marroc line had stood and looked down the gentle slope of the hillside. His riders swarmed over the dead, the dark litter of mangled shapes that had once been proud Marroc men. Looting mostly, but it served a purpose. His horsemen needed their javelots, those that could be thrown again. There were spears and axes and shields and helms and perhaps even a few swords and pieces of mail for the soldiers of the Weeping Giant, the ones who fought on foot. And, too, he was looking for someone.

In the failing light a dozen riders emerged from the trees at the bottom of the hill. Their horses looked tired, Gulsukh thought. They trotted closer up the slope and he saw that one of them had a body slung over his saddle. Watching them weave their way in and out of the piles of naked corpses and the fires that were just being lit, he felt a hungry thrill of hope, but it died as they approached. The lead horseman stopped in front of him, clenched his fist across his chest and bowed his head.

'And what did you find, Krenda Bashar?' Gulsukh peered at the body. A Lhosir, yes, but from a distance there was no telling who, other than it wasn't the man he was looking for.

The bashar kept his head bowed. He spoke loudly and quickly and a little too abruptly. 'Ardshan! Beymar Bashar is dead. We followed his trail. He caught up with the Lhosir and tried to take them but he was beaten. The men with him were killed. Most of the Lhosir too.'

'But not the Widowmaker.' The ardshan turned away. Failure was in the bashar's voice.

'The Widowmaker wasn't there, Ardshan. But ...' Krenda Bashar looked up with a furrowed brow. 'Ardshan, I would like to pursue this further. The tracks are unclear but the Lhosir bodies were left where they fell. Whatever happened, too few survived to take their dead with them. I ... I think the Widowmaker may have been killed too, and the last of his men took the body with them. They must have been in a hurry.'

Gulsukh shrugged. 'It means nothing without his body.'

'And so I beg your leave to pursue. Ardshan, the Lhosir don't leave their dead, not like this. At the very least they would lay out the bodies and leave weapons in their hands. There were no weapons at all. Further ...' Krenda's frown deepened. 'There is this.' He turned and led over the horse with the dead body across its back, bringing it close so that Gulsukh could see the dead Lhosir's face. 'Lanjis ...'

'Lanjis Halfborn.' The ardshan stared at a face he hadn't seen for ten years.

'We found him. Lying dead as he fell. The Widowmaker would not have left him so if he was alive to do otherwise.'

Gulsukh nodded. 'They were like brothers.'

'We found a handful of horses but most were gone. The trail leads inland. We followed it a short way. They weren't heading for Fedderhun.'

The ardshan closed his eyes. Even one last Lhosir would have laid out their fallen, and they surely wouldn't have have left one like Lanjis Halfborn behind, even dead. They must have had a very good reason to leave in haste and he could only think of one. To take the Widowmaker out of danger.

Krenda coughed. 'I think we weren't the first to find the Lhosir. Some of the Marroc fled through the same woods. They would have followed the same trails. It would explain the looting.'

The ardshan opened his eyes. 'Marroc aid the Widowmaker? I doubt *that*.'

'They'd most likely kill him. Or ransom him, Ardshan, and even his body would be worth a great deal. Perhaps they know that. Or perhaps they simply took him to strip him later, in a quieter safer place.'

'Yes.' Gulsukh smiled and nodded. 'Yes, and even dead they might do that. Then go and follow and see if you can find them, and make sure that every Marroc knows there's a price on the Widowmaker's head, dead or alive. Take some silver to show them. That should make them happy to see you.'

Krenda Bashar nodded. They might have talked more, but Gulsukh's son, Moonjal Bashar, was riding up the hill at a gallop now. The ardshan rolled his eyes. Krenda bowed. 'The Weeping Giant calls again?'

The ardshan nodded. 'Doubtless to debate when we shall press on to Fedderhun. Go. Perhaps while you're looking you could save us all some bother, Bashar. You could probably seize Fedderhun yourself while the Weeping Giant muses.'

5

FORKBEARD

The sun rose. Gallow shook the dew off his blanket and fetched water up from the nearby stream. He pissed on the last smoking remnants of his fire and checked to see if the Screambreaker had died in the night; but the old man was still breathing so he sat and ate breakfast and waited. The sky was a cold blue but the late spring sun was already warm on his skin and chasing away the chill of the night. The sun would have to be enough. Out here on the open downs the smoke of a fire would be seen for miles and the Vathen he remembered had been a restless people. Always with their horses and they liked to roam.

'My helm, man! My helm!' The cry jerked Gallow away from burying the traces of their camp. The Screambreaker was sitting up and staring blankly at the sky, one hand on his head. He looked at Gallow. 'Who are you? What have you done with my helm?'

Gallow took his own off the ground and offered it but the Screambreaker threw it away. 'That's not my helm. Where's my helm? Where is it?'

'Fell off your head when someone whacked you one, I'd say. Wasn't anywhere near when I found you. Probably some Marroc has it now. Glad you're awake.' Gallow rummaged among the saddlebags and pulled out a piece of dirty cloth, something used for polishing saddle leathers by the looks of it. It would have to do. He dipped it in water and crouched in front of Corvin. 'You've got blood all over you. I'm going to wash it off. Should have done that last night.' Except last night it had been dark and he'd half thought the Screambreaker wouldn't live to see the morning.

He leaned forward but Corvin lunged and pushed him away. 'Get off me!'

'Suit yourself.' Gallow squeezed the water out of the cloth and hung it over his saddle. 'There's a horse there. It's yours now.'

The Screambreaker didn't move. He lay where he was, panting with his head twisted to one side. 'You're not a Vathan. You're not Marroc either. I don't know you. Who are you?'

'I was with you at Vanhun.' Gallow stood up. 'Most of the times afterwards as well, for that matter, until you went back across the sea. Gallow. No particular reason you'd remember me.'

'Gallow?' The old man wrinkled up his face. 'Where are the Vathen? This isn't Fedderhun! Where's the sea? The Marroc won't last the first charge! Where are they? They need their spirit!'

Gallow pointed to the rise behind them. 'See that hill? Good view from up there. I'm going to go and have a look and see if anyone's following us. Doubt it, but you never know. You led us against the Vathen yesterday, Screambreaker. The battle's been and gone. The Marroc held the first charge but it was never going to last. The second one broke them. You don't remember, do you? Thump round the head can do that.' He walked away, leaving the general to gather his thoughts, to sort his memories and get up off the ground and maybe come up and look too, but Corvin did none of those things. When Gallow came back the Screambreaker was asleep again, snoring loudly. Gallow lifted him up and flopped him into his saddle. 'There's smoke a way to the north. Probably not Vathen on our tracks but best be on our way.' Corvin didn't wake. The wound on his head was oozing again. At least the old man still knew who he was.

They rode through gentle hills down into the sweep of the Fedder valley and forded the river. The shape of the land grew more familiar. Gallow started to see places he knew – a lone tree here, the crook of a stream there, a particular hilltop – until early in the afternoon he looked down on the little Marroc village that had been his home for the last nine years. He left the horses beside Shepherd's Tree, a tall old broadleaf that stood on its own at the top of the hill where Vennic the shepherd watched his flock. There was no sign of Vennic today, nor of his sheep. There was no one in the village either, no fire lit in the forge, not even any animals, no clucking and snuffling of chickens and pigs wandering free. He walked back to Shepherd's Tree and climbed into the lower branches and peered out across the hills but there was no sign of anyone for miles. *Strange.* Something had made the villagers run but there was no trace of it now.

Corvin was still asleep as Gallow led the horses round to the forge yard. There were no stables in Middislet but Nadric had his workshop, one side open to the sky, big enough to tie up two horses and keep them at least half out of sight. He hauled the Screambreaker down and laid him on the hard earth and set to work on the old man's armour, one piece at a time, laying each carefully out beside the horses. A man could hardly lie in his sickbed all dressed up in mail and leather, not unless he had one foot already in the Herenian Marches and his eyes already set on the Maker-Devourer's cauldron. He smiled to himself. Nadric would rub his hands with glee if he ever saw all this metalwork. 'Better come out from wherever you're hiding then, eh?' He loosened the buckles on Corvin's leather undercoat and slowly eased him out of it. When that was done he lifted the general over his shoulder as gently as he could and carried him into the house, into the tiny night room where he and Arda slept. It was just a corner close to the hearth fire with curtains of rough-spun wool hanging around it to separate it from the rest of the house, but it would do. In the gloom with the curtains closed no one would see the Screambreaker as long as he was quiet. He set the old man down on the bed of straw and furs, shook him and offered him water.

'Do you remember it now?' Gallow asked him. 'The battle?'

The Screambreaker looked off into the distance, right through the walls and far off beyond. 'The Marroc broke. I remember that. Afterwards there wasn't much to be done. A few hundred of us would never turn away so many Vathen.' His eyes narrowed. 'Who are you?'

'Gallow, old man. I told you that already.'

'You're no Marroc. So who are you, Gallow?' He rolled the name around his mouth, frowning, savouring it as though in

some lost corner of his memory maybe it meant something.
'I came from across the sea. I'm one of you. I'm Lhosir.'

'No, you're not.' Corvin stared and Gallow knew exactly
where he was looking. At the bare shaven skin where Gallow's
forked and braided beard should have been.

'Yes, I am, old man. I cut it off.'

The Screambreaker didn't say anything. A Lhosir cut his
beard because he was ashamed, or else someone cut it for him
because he was a coward or a liar or a thief. A Lhosir without his
braided forked beard wasn't a Lhosir at all. He was a ghost to be
ignored and shunned. Until it grew back he didn't exist.

Gallow shrugged. He fetched a blanket and covered the
general. 'I have to see to the horses. I'll come back when that's
done.'

'Where's my mail?' Corvin didn't turn to look at him but
spoke to the wall.

'Cared for and out of sight.'

'I want it here. My sword too. And my shield.'

Gallow hesitated. 'I'll bring you your blade, Screambreaker.'
He could hardly deny a man his sword. 'The rest is best hidden
away. There are Vathen roaming the land.'

'I'll not hide from them!'

Gallow brought the Screambreaker his sword and his shield
too and then returned to the horses, ignoring the complaints
that followed him. The horses had been worked hard and they
needed some kindness. He lifted off their saddles and bridles
and set to work grooming them; when that was done, since
he had no hay or feed for them, he turned them loose in the
fields. They were Lhosir horses so they wouldn't go far. Then he
went back to the workshop and set about cleaning the general's
armour and then his own, wiping every piece with an oily rag
and hanging them in the shadows at the back of the workshop
among Nadric's old tools, the broken ones that he never got
around to fixing but couldn't bring himself to throw away. He
hung up his axe and then took both swords and cleaned those
too, hiding them under a pile of sacking. The Vathan javelot he
propped up in the darkest corner of all. Then, stripped to the
waist now, he started on the saddles, cleaning the leather and

polishing it. He'd never had a horse so he didn't know what he was supposed to do with all the bits and pieces that came with one, but he knew about caring for leather. Spit and polish and a bit of beeswax, although that was usually something Arda tended to.

When he was done with the saddles he wrapped them in sackcloth and hid them at the back of the workshop. They were clearly Lhosir-made and too decorated to be from anything but a rich man's horse, and too big to properly hide too. He wondered about burying them, but the Screambreaker's beard would give him away if any Vathen came by, and if they didn't then only Nadric would see them where they were, tucked away in the shadows of the forge.

The sun was still high. The village was empty, but if something had spooked them then Gallow knew where they'd be. They'd be up on the edge of the Crackmarsh, hiding in the waterlogged caves that riddled the hills. A couple of hours on foot, but on a horse he could easily be there and back before dark. He'd look for them tomorrow, he decided, if the Screambreaker was up to the journey, but for now it was useful to have the place to himself. He wondered what had scared them away.

With the swords and mail and the animals cared for, Gallow walked to the well and drew a bucket of water. He threw a few handfuls of it over himself and carried the rest back to the workshop. Nadric always kept a few rags about the place – he was forever on the lookout for shirts that were so worn and torn that they couldn't be patched and repaired. Gallow took one and went back to Corvin. One way or another that wound was getting cleaned, even if he had to punch the old man out to do it.

The thought made him laugh. Punching out the Scream-breaker. How many people had tried that all those years ago? A lot, and he couldn't remember any that had succeeded. 'I need to—'

He stopped. The curtains were drawn back. The Screambreaker was sitting up, propped against the wall. He had his sword in his lap and the blankets around his feet and he was staring across the house. He didn't move or even look at him as Gallow came in. Gallow followed the Screambreaker's eyes. The village wasn't as empty as he'd thought. The Screambreaker screwed up his nose. 'I don't think this Marroc likes me,' he said, and Gallow couldn't have stopped himself from smiling even if he'd wanted to.

'Well I did tell you she wouldn't.'

6

ARDA

Vennic had been keeping watch up in the Shepherd's Tree. As much as anything it was something for him to do, but then he'd come running back late in the morning and said there were riders coming. The villagers had sighed and rolled their eyes. They knew what to do: take everything that mattered and hide, let the soldiers come through and be on their way, and then start again once they were gone. The forkbeards had taught them that. Burned-down houses could be built again. People and animals, they were what mattered, and so the men and women of Middislet had run out into the fields and called everyone back and gathered the animals that could be gathered and scattered the rest. The Vathen would come and go, and for most of them life would go on.

But not for all. The forge and Nadric's workshop weren't things you could simply pack up into sacks and throw over your shoulder and carry or herd up to the Crackmarsh. Without them Nadric had no living, and Arda had four children to care for and her man was off to war. Again. It made her furious because it was always *her*. Why did *she* have to suffer the most?

'I'm not having it,' she told Nadric. 'They come here, they'll burn us down over my dead body.'

Which, Nadric pleaded, was almost surely what would happen, but Arda was done with wars and fighting and running away. She took a knife and shut herself in the cellar, and nothing Nadric could say would make her come out. If Vennic was right and a band of soldiers came by then she'd plead with them. The forkbeards admired courage like that, didn't they? Maybe the Vathen would too. So in the end Nadric gave up and took the children away to hide in the Crackmarsh caves with everyone else and left her.

For a long time she sat in the quiet and in the dark and all alone. Trouble with that was it gave her time to wonder. What if the Vathen were different? What if they didn't care? Twice she got up, ready to climb out of the cellar and head after the rest of the village, and twice she stopped herself. Maybe the Vathen, the forkbeards or whoever it was that Vennic had seen had passed on by. Or maybe the riders were actually a herd of deer or simply figments of his imagination. There was no real telling with Vennic. That was what she was thinking – that Vennic was an idiot and there was nothing at all coming their way from the hills – when she heard the first noises above.

Footsteps. No voices. She froze, crouched in a corner, a lot less sure of herself than when she'd argued with Nadric. Vathen? She sniffed the air for smoke. *And if it is, what are you going to do?* She looked at the knife clutched tight in her fingers. *Stupid woman. What were you thinking?*

The footsteps came and went. For a while there was quiet. She was about to slip out of the cellar to see what was happening when they came back again, heavier this time, above her head through the wooden floor. They stopped by the night room and there was some quiet talking and then one set of footsteps left and everything fell still again. It certainly didn't *sound* like a gang of rapacious soldiers burning and looting and smashing everything in sight. More the patient unhurried paces of someone going quietly about their business. Whatever that was in *her* house.

Someone had slipped back from the Crackmarsh! Was that it? A thief? So when the footsteps didn't come straight back she opened the cellar door and crept up and pulled back the curtain from the night room. And there right in front of her was a forkbeard she'd never seen before, lying on her bed for all the world as though he was asleep. She let out a yelp and he lurched blindly awake, sat up, grabbed a sword and then swayed sideways as though he was drunk. She held her knife at him, arm stretched out, backing away, afraid for a moment but only until she saw that the forkbeard's face was covered with old dried blood, that his beard was matted with it. As soon as she saw his weakness, her fear turned to anger. A forkbeard in her house!

'Get out!' she hissed. She took a step forward and waved the knife at him. He shuffled back against the wall. He still had his sword in his hand but he looked so weak she doubted he could even lift it.

'Who are you?' His words were slurred and heavy with that savage forkbeard accent. She held out her knife as though he was a snake. He didn't look as though he could even stand. She had no idea what to do.

The yard door opened. Gallow! The relief was like a sudden dive into a river. The forkbeard kept looking at her. 'I don't think this Marroc likes me,' he said.

'Well, I did tell you she wouldn't. Hello, Arda.' He was grinning, the clothead! He had no idea what he'd done to her. Relief turned quickly to a flare of anger. She was scared, and Gallow didn't look surprised at all by the half-dead man lying on his furs. 'What's this?' she yelled at him and jabbed her knife at the forkbeard. 'What's this in my house? In my *bed*?'

Gallow sat down beside the wounded man with a bucket of water in one hand and a rag in the other. 'I need to clean that wound,' he said. 'You have to lie down, old man.' He was ignoring her in that deliberate *not-now* way he did sometimes. She ground her teeth in frustration. It made her so furious!

The forkbeard didn't move. He didn't look at Gallow at all, just glared at her. Arda hissed: 'Get him out of my house or I swear I'll stab you both!'

Gallow looked up. 'Where is everyone?'

'Where do you think they are, you sack-headed oaf? Hiding up at the Crackmarsh of course! Vennic saw horsemen in the hills, coming this way.'

'Horsemen in the hills?' Gallow wrinkled his nose.

'Vathen? Forkbeards? Who knows? Does it matter?' She scowled. 'Maybe he saw a cloud with a strange shape that frightened him!' She looked away and snorted. Vennic. Useless fool.

'Well there are no horsemen, I'm sure of that.' Gallow reached towards the wounded man but the forkbeard pushed him away.

'Get him out of here!' Gallow was trying to ignore her, and by

Modris she wasn't going to have it. She brandished the knife at him now instead. '*Get him out of my house!*'

'Be quiet, woman.'

'Don't you *quiet woman* me, you tree stump!'

The forkbeard's head swayed from side to side. He groaned. 'Give me back my horse and I'll be gone. I spurn your hospitality, clean-skin.' To Arda he looked ready to drop dead at any moment. And he was welcome to do just that, as long as he did it outside.

Gallow shook his head. 'Don't be stupid, old man. You'll be lucky if you get to the edge of the village.'

Arda folded her arms. 'You heard him. He doesn't even *want* to stay. So, we're all done here now and he can go.'

She watched as the man she'd married took a deep breath. He sat back and looked at her at last. Properly, eye to eye like he should have done in the first place. 'Wife, he's a soldier! I found him like this after the battle, beside his horse. I could hardly leave him to die.'

'He's a forkbeard! And we've got children to feed.' She spat on the straw at the wounded man's feet.

'You mean I should have taken his horse and come back on my own?' His eyes narrowed and grew suddenly cold. 'I'm a forkbeard too, or had you forgotten?'

He had what she thought of as his fighting face on now, the one where he stopped listening. She didn't care. She'd been looking for a fight from the moment Vennic had come running into the village. 'Forgotten? Tch!' She might have thrown something at him, but at that moment the forkbeard's head slumped onto his chest and his eyes slowly closed. Arda peered at him. 'So is he dead now?'

'No.'

'Pity. Why are you back here so soon?' She winced at the anger in her own voice. Not anger that he was back, far from it, but at the way he'd come, at the fright he'd given her. At … at … She looked at the furs where the two of them lay together at night, at the battered old forkbeard lying there instead. 'Is it over then?'

Gallow's face fell. He shook his head. 'We broke and ran. The Vathen will come.'

A thrill ran through her along with the inevitable dread of war. *Forkbeards, beaten!* 'So much for your great Widowmaker then.' She spat out his name. 'Murdering bastard. I hope the Vathen slaughtered him.'

Gallow glanced at the wounded man. He was asleep now. 'Where are the children?'

'Where do you think? Nadric took them into the hills.' Her grip on the knife eased. A part of her would always hate Gallow simply for being from across the sea, but she'd dealt with that part and told it to shut up often enough to know how. It was better to have him than not, that was the long and the short of it. Better that he was back than dead. 'You're such a thistlefinger! The Vathen are coming? What if they come here? What if they find *that*?' She pointed at the forkbeard again. 'Do you *want* to see your children killed in front of you?'

His eyes flashed. The children were the chink in his armour, but they were the chink in hers too. Made him hard to hate even on her bad days. 'The Vathen won't come this way,' he said.

She stuck her chin out at him. 'Did you stop to ask while you were busy running away from them, then?'

'They've gone to Fedderhun.'

'Really? Vennic was in the Shepherd's Tree. *He* said there were riders coming. That's why we left. You forkbeards taught us that.'

Gallow cocked his head at her. 'But *you* didn't leave.' She caught a smile flicker across his face and frowned even more deeply. Later, when they were making up again, he'd tell her how he liked her spirit. How it reminded him of home. Every time he said that she punched him. Hard, but he kept on saying it anyway. She pointed her knife at the sleeping forkbeard. 'I don't want him here.'

'He'll go when he can ride again.'

She threw back her head in disbelief. 'You're going to let him keep his horse?'

'It's *his* horse.'

Arda threw the knife she was holding hard into the floor in disgust. It struck the wood and stuck, quivering. Right there was the thing between them that would never go away. Family first.

'You cloth-mouthed scarecrow! There's four children to be fed here. Hungry ones, and it won't be the Vathen that feed them. Soldiers only take, whoever they follow.' She'd lived it once. Never again. 'You'd get silver for a horse in Andhun, even an old nag. In Tarkhun too.' She shook her head. 'You're still one of them. You just pretend you're not because they wouldn't have you any more.' Now she was being nasty. His fault. He drove her to it.

Gallow looked away. They both knew she was right, though: the other forkbeards wouldn't even look at him, not with his bare face. He'd done that for her, years ago when she'd thought it would change him, but of course it hadn't changed anything at all. 'I ran away,' he said, 'with a band of Marroc who were as brave as anyone else. We found horses in the woods with dead men sitting on their backs. This one was alive. We shared the horses between us. I have another.'

'You got two?' Her eyes flashed. 'Where are they?'

'Out in the fields.' Gallow shook his head. 'There are no riders in the hills, Arda. I came that way myself. Vennic probably saw the two of us in the distance and panicked. You know what he's like.' He must have seen the uncertainty in her face. Yes, she did know what Vennic was like, the whole village knew. He looked away. 'Someone should go to the Crackmarsh and bring the others back.'

'Someone should get those horses brought into the yard before they're eaten by wolves!'

Gallow cocked his head at the man asleep on their furs. 'His wound should be cleaned and stitched closed in the way of the Aulians.'

'And are *you* going to tend to him?' Arda let out a scornful laugh. 'Yes, and I should let you! A fine way that would be to help him on to the Marches. Might as well just use that knife on him.' She sighed. She didn't want this other man here but she didn't want him dying under her roof either. A lot of bad luck that was, and she certainly wasn't going to open his throat in her own house, however much a part of her would have liked that. 'Fine then. Since you say he must stay then let him get well or die quickly. When Nadric comes back we'll see. Until then at least let someone who won't stitch his eyes shut tend to him. I'll do it. Go and get those horses and keep them safe!'

They looked at one another. It was hard to be angry with Gallow for long. He'd never been cruel or unjust, he just didn't *think*, that was all. Flesh and blood, children and household, all that came before anything else, and if it hadn't been that way for her then she would never have married him, never even taken him into her home. 'I won't cut his throat,' she snapped. 'Much as I'd like to.'

He gave her a hard look. She threw up her hands in disgust. 'I swear by Modris and by Merethin's ghost! Happy?' Merethin had been Nadric's son and had fathered Jelira, her oldest. The forkbeards had killed him. She hadn't thought much of him before he'd gone off to war and had roundly cursed his name ever since, but she always held him up to Gallow whenever she was angry. She scowled. For being from across the sea, that was what it came to. That's what he'd done wrong. Nothing else.

Gallow nodded. He put a hand on her shoulder and squeezed. He could be kind when he wanted to be, and kindness was something she secretly craved. She didn't flinch away. 'I'm sorry I scared you.'

'I wasn't *scared*, you idiot! Modris and Ballor! Will you get on and do what needs to be done!' Scared? Maybe she had been, but she'd die before she'd admit it to a forkbeard, even him. When he'd cut his beard, perhaps he'd thought it would mellow the hardness she wore like armour, just like she thought it might change him, but it didn't change either of them. It wasn't fair. She knew that. But it wasn't fair to see a husband and a brother killed and a home burned by the forkbeards either. The only time she let him see any other side of her was at night. Women had their urges as much as men.

He squeezed again and then let her be when she almost kicked him away from her. 'Stupid man!' Ah, Modris! If he'd seen how she'd squirmed inside when he'd told her he was going to fight the Vathen ... The thought of losing him, that *had* scared her, and it had turned out to be a far deeper fear than she'd thought it would be. She'd never admit it though, just as she'd never admit she was pleased to see him back. It all turned to anger instead.

'Off with you!' She shooed him out of the house and then went to look for her bone needles and some thread. She wouldn't be too careful, stitching this unwanted forkbeard back together. It would hurt and he'd have a scar. Both would please her, but she'd keep her promise. He wouldn't die.

7

NIOINGR

Gallow saddled one of the horses and rode it out to the Crackmarsh. In spring when the streams ran fast off the mountains and the Isset was deep and strong the Crackmarsh was fifty miles of water meadow criss-crossed with swamp paths and pocked with smooth bare boulders and little hillocks crowned by stands of stunted trees, a thousand tiny islands breaching the shallow water like the backs of petrified whales. Later in the year it dried out to a huge flat swathe of soft boggy soil between the litter of giant stones and the tufts of trees. Fine growing land if it hadn't been for the ghuldogs.

Around its eastern edge rose a line of low hills scattered with crags and thick groves of trees, guiding the Isset and the Crackmarsh westward out of the Varyxhun valley and the pass that led to the old Aulian Way across the mountains. There were caves here, lots of them. Whispers told stories that the deeper ones ran right across to the mountains, but the deeper ones were always flooded so no one really knew. Gallow found the rest of the villagers there, as Arda had said and he had guessed, bored and fractious and already arguing among themselves about whether they should go back. None of them was pleased to see him. Even Nadric was barely civil. Old wounds had opened with the coming of the Vathen.

It was almost dark by the time he got back to the forge. Arda had finished with Corvin. Her face was furious.

'You said he was a soldier.'

'He is.'

'I saw his sword. He's not just *a* soldier.'

He could have lied. Men picked up whatever they could find after a battle, after all, but sooner or later she'd find out. The old man would tell her if she ever asked. He shrugged. Better to hear it from him. 'He's Corvin Screambreaker.'

Arda hissed at him, bearing her teeth. 'The Widowmaker himself? Are you mad? You bring the Widowmaker into *my* house?'

'I bring a man who is hurt, woman!' For a moment he almost lost his temper. Arda was good at that. 'Should I leave him to die?'

'The Nightmare of the North? Yes, you surely should! If I'd known who he was before I stitched his eye ... Get him out of here!'

'When he's well enough to travel on his own.'

'No! Now! What if the Vathen come?'

'I told you, woman! The Vathen have moved on Fedderhun. And why would they come here? Unless someone told them of a very good reason.'

'Don't you *woman* me, foxborn!' She leaned into him, red with rage. 'Never mind the Vathen then – what if anyone else finds out who you've got here? The rest of the village. They'll burn the place down around us!'

He met her gaze, eye to eye. 'Then you'd best not tell them.'

She stormed away out to the workshop and Nadric. In a while Nadric would come inside and tell Gallow that the Screambreaker had to go, and Gallow would say no, and then they'd argue and drink and drink and argue, and eventually Nadric would give in, just like he always did, and Arda would storm away and disappear into the fields just like *she* always did when they argued and she lost, and then she'd come back in the middle of the night and tear the furs off him and they'd make love like dragons. For a moment, after they were done, he'd see the gentleness that was buried so very deep inside her. But only for a moment. He touched a finger to the locket under his shirt. Maker-Devourer, what scorn she'd pour on him for *that* if she knew! 'He stays until he's well,' he called after her.

At the open door little Feya and Tathic peered up at him with their big child eyes. Pursic was probably out in the yard crawling in the mud. Jelira would be watching Nadric in the workshop. Gallow smiled at them and knelt down. 'Listen to me, little ones.

When boys grow to be men they may carry swords or they may not, but every man and every woman carries their own heart-song. It's not a thing you win in battles. It's a thing you're born with and you must always listen to it. It will tell you what is right and what is wrong. You must look after it too, because if you don't then one day it might go away, and when it goes it won't come back. More men lose their heartsongs in their own home than lose it in a wall of shields.'

They kept staring, too young to understand. Gallow took their hands, one in each of his. 'There's a stranger here, in the night room. A man who helped me fight. He was very brave but now he's hurt. He'll stay until he's well. You must leave him alone and you mustn't tell anyone that he's here. He'll be gone soon.'

Tathic nodded, his face serious. Feya smiled and yawned and reached out to pull Gallow's nose.

'Do only boys have heartsongs?' asked Tathic. 'Jel says girls have heartsongs too, but they don't, do they?'

'Oh they very much do, little man. Everyone has a heartsong. Boys and girls, men and women, Marroc and Lhosir.'

'Does Ma have a heartsong?'

'Of course she does. Do you not hear it? It's the strongest heartsong in our house.'

'See!' Feya pushed Tathic. 'I do have har-sow!' She scampered behind Gallow to hide. Gallow ruffled her hair and shooed them back into the yard to chase each other in the twilight. When they were gone he drew back the curtains to see what Arda had done to Corvin. The Screambreaker was sitting up against the wall. His face was ashen but his eyes were clear. He had a gash over his temple and around his forehead as long as a finger and swollen up like an egg. Blood oozed from it. Arda's stitching hadn't been kind.

'She said I was cut to the bone.'

'You were lucky to live.'

'Where am I?'

Gallow sat down beside him. 'You're in the house of Nadric the Smith in Middislet. About three days' walk inland from Fedderhun.'

Corvin closed his eyes. He took a deep breath and moaned. 'Marroc.'

'Yes.' The pain must have been bad for Corvin to let it show. 'No one outside this house knows you're here. Best it stays that way. The Marroc still curse the name Screambreaker.'

'I thank you for your hospitality.' The words were forced between his lips, empty of feeling. 'Send your wife to me. I will thank her to her face even if she spits at my feet. In the morning I'll take my horse and be gone.'

'To where, Screambreaker? Fedderhun is surely fallen and Andhun is a week's ride across unfamiliar country along paths you won't remember. You'll not get any help from any Marroc, not looking as you do. You'll die before you get there. You're feverish already.'

The Screambreaker snarled. 'Who are you to tell me what to do, no-beard? I'll be gone in the morning and that's the end of the matter, and if I die before Andhun then that's my fate and the Maker-Devourer will have me. I'll not lie here like some invalid in the bed of a downy-cheeked *nioingr*.'

The blood rushed to Gallow's face. If he'd had a knife he might have pulled it. As it was, he grabbed Corvin's head in his hands and forced him to meet his eye. 'I didn't save your life to kill you here, but your tongue will not travel with you to Andhun unless it learns some manners. You're in my house, under my roof. I followed you into battle for years. I've fled from the enemy twice and twice alone. At Selleuk's Bridge and now from the Vathen, and so you'll take those words and swallow them!'

The Screambreaker met his eyes and bared his teeth. 'I will eat them when you show me your beard, clean-skin. I still remember some of those who never came back across the sea. *Nioingr*, all of them.'

'I didn't stay because of any shame, Screambreaker.'

'Then why?'

Corvin didn't flinch from him. Gallow let go. 'Because Yurlak was sick, that's why. We all thought he'd die. Medrin would have followed him, and I'll not serve a king I've seen turn and run while his friends stood fast.'

The last words earned him a glare. 'You call the king's son a coward?'

Gallow shrugged. 'It was fourteen summers ago that I crossed the sea. The Medrin I left behind, yes, I call him a coward. Perhaps he's changed. He must have a beard now.'

'Long and fine, unlike yours.'

'If you say it's so then I shall believe you.'

'What you believe is nothing to me, clean-skin. Send your wife so I may thank her for her attentions. I *will* be gone in the morning.'

Gallow rose and left. Outside the door Arda took his arm and pulled him away across the yard and into the workshop where Nadric was sitting by his anvil.

'We've decided.' She looked him in the eye. 'We'll ransom him.'

Nadric nodded slowly. Gallow shook his head. 'No.'

'Yes!' Arda hissed. 'He's nothing but grief and another hungry mouth, and we can barely feed the ones we have. What happens if anyone finds him here? The Vathen will kill us all and burn our homes. They'll burn the whole village! If any of the others find out he's here, *they* will go to the Vathen. *They* will be rewarded and *we* will be killed. There's no other way that makes sense. We sell him to the Vathen. It's decided.'

'No.' Gallow looked at them both. 'If you do this then I'll burn our home myself with both of you inside it. He means to leave in the morning. No one will know he's here and he'll be gone before any Vathan could get here. Think on how *that* will seem. No. He'll leave us a fine horse and the spoils it carries to keep us fed and we'll have done what was right. Let that be enough.'

'Your Prince Medrin is in Andhun,' said Nadric. He tried, when Gallow and Arda set against one another, to be the voice of reason, always a thankless task. 'Could we not ransom him there instead?'

Arda spat. 'Why, when we could give him to the Vathen and he could get what he deserves?'

Gallow turned away. In their eyes he'd brought an enemy into their house. He understood that. They were Marroc, and Corvin was the Screambreaker from across the sea who'd led armies against their people and conquered their king in the name of his own. What they thought hardly mattered though. The Screambreaker had said he would be gone, and so he would, and that would be that and he'd either reach Andhun alive or he wouldn't.

They slept in the main part of the house that night, leaving the Screambreaker the night room with the curtains closed around him. In the early hours before the dawn he woke them all with a scream, wild with fever. He was not gone in the morning, nor the one after, nor the one after that. Each night Gallow thought he would die. Each day Arda prayed for it, and yet she tended to him as she would have tended to her own children, even as he denied her and his heart kept beating. As far as Gallow could see, no one said a word of it outside his walls. The Marroc of Middislet looked at him just as they always did. With disdain, a sneer and a little fear.

8

VIDRIC

The Vathen gathered around the dying Marroc. There wasn't much left of him. Just a bloodied sack of flesh and bones hung from the branches of a tree by his wrists and ankles. They'd tortured him, beating and flaying him with bundles of wiry sticks. They'd been doing it for hours. The sticks were vicious, splitting the skin like whips as often as not.

'He's done.' Gosomon threw his bundle away. 'He's got nothing more to say.'

The rest of them nodded. The air among them changed. Hostility ebbed and a question grew in its place. Eyes shifted from the dying Marroc to Krenda Bashar. *And?*

'The Screambreaker isn't with them.' Krenda Bashar nodded to himself. Nodded to the gods who'd dealt him this pot of shit. He grabbed the dying Marroc by the hair and pulled up his head. 'There was a Lhosir with you when you fled the battle. You found a clearing and the remnants of a skirmish.' The Marroc had had a gold-handled Lhosir knife tucked into his belt when they'd taken him. Krenda waved it under his face. 'You found Beymar Bashar's ride, all of them dead, and plenty of dead forkbeards too. You had a fine old time looting the bodies. Afterwards the Lhosir who was with you suddenly wasn't there any more. You have no idea whether he took a horse. You have no idea if he took anyone with him. You have no idea whether he found another forkbeard alive or took away one of the dead. You don't even know who he was except his name. Gallow. You have no idea where he went or why. Am I missing anything? Oh, and this all happened two whole days ago, so by now he could be pissing *anywhere*!' He didn't wait for the Marroc to answer. With a sudden jab, he stabbed the Lhosir knife into the

Marroc's neck and let him bleed out. 'Mollar and Feyrk!' he cursed. 'Gosomon, take your ride and go after the rest of these Marroc. Maybe one of the others knows more. Find where this Lhosir went and who he is.' *Andhun, surely. Where else?* 'If he's gone to ground, it'll be in the Crackmarsh. That's about a day's ride straight south. Huge mess of a place. Mostly under water this time of year. You can't miss it, but if he's hiding in there and you somehow manage to find him then I'll have you made the next ardshan.'

Gosomon snorted as Krenda Bashar climbed back into his saddle. 'Going back to Fedderhun are you, Bashar? Back to your woman? A couple of soft nights while *we* sleep in the mud?'

Krenda Bashar's face turned sour. 'I'll join you again in a few days, Gosomon. Gulsukh won't like it, but if the Screambreaker is on his way to Andhun then maybe he can get there first if he moves fast. He'd want to know that. But find him for me, Gosomon. Make me look less stupid that I am, eh? I tell you what – you find him, you can have Mirrahj for your own wife, if she doesn't knock you out first, and I'll take a woman who's still got a use to her – how about that? Oh, and if you pass any Marroc, have the sense to ask.' He patted the little bag of silver hanging from his saddle. 'Show them a little of something that shines.'

He kicked his horse into a canter and turned for Fedderhun.

9

THE FESTIVAL OF SHIEFA

Vathen or no, Fenaric the carter and his sons headed off for Fedderhun as they did every year before Shieftane. The whole of Middislet came out to watch them go, clapping their hands at their bravery or else shaking their heads at such foolishness. Gallow thought they were stupid, so of course Arda thought they were brave and pointedly went out to tell them so before they left. A week later they were back, alive and well. They even had what they'd gone looking for, barrels of Fedderhun beer. Fenaric drew up his cart in the middle of the village and stopped and waited while everyone gathered around him.

'Well they haven't burned it down!' He sat calmly on the back of his wagon, used to being the centre of attention.

'There's Vathen everywhere!' His sons were more wide-eyed. 'They look so strange. Short and faces the colour of Harnshun clay and eyes as dark as a forkbeard's soul.'

'Hundreds of them! Thousands!'

'There's people running away too. The roads are full of them.'

Fenaric patted the barrels and nodded sagely. 'Aye. But these Vathen prefer their own brews over good Fedderhun beer and they haven't gone burning anything down, not yet. There's a few folk keeping on—'

He wasn't allowed to finish. 'They're marching on Andhun!'

'They're eating all the food and—'

'That's where the real fight's going to be.'

'I heard the Sword of the Weeping God is coming! Out from the swamps far to the east. They're bringing the red curse back!'

Fenaric looked from side to side, drawing his audience in. 'They do say that, yes.' He looked sombre.

Later on Gallow passed the news to Corvin. The fever had

broken but it had left the Screambreaker as weak as a child. 'Another two or three days and you'll be strong enough to ride. I'll go with you to Andhun.'

'No need, bare-face. I'll leave tonight.'

He said that every day, when he was conscious enough to say anything at all. Gallow shrugged. For once he might actually mean it. 'Then I'll leave your horse saddled for you, because you won't be managing that without help and tonight you *will* be on your own. It's the festival of Shiefa. Fenaric has brought ale back from Fedderhun. You'd stand a better chance if you waited a few days more. I'm sure you know it. But ...' He paused. 'If you don't want to be seen then tonight is a good night for slipping away.'

The Screambreaker's brow furrowed. 'Ale back from Fedderhun, did you say? Your carter must be an unusually brave man. Are you sure it's not horse piss?'

'The Vathen never had much taste for Marroc beer. They ferment milk, don't they?'

'They do. Sour stuff.' The furrows on his brow wouldn't leave. He let out a long sigh and shook his head. 'If I were you I might ask him how he paid the Vathen. I think I *will* leave tonight.' The Screambreaker spat. 'Shiefa? Some Marroc god?'

'The lady of the summer rains.'

Corvin shook his head. 'You have a god for everything. I never understood the need for so many. The Maker-Devourer is enough for me.'

'It's their way.' Gallow gave the Screambreaker a long look. 'They'll be celebrating tonight. If your heartsong says you have to go, I'll make it easy for you. No food, no water, no shelter, no help, riding into a battle from the wrong side, all of those will be trials enough. The house and the road will both be empty tonight. Everyone should be in the big barn. Wait until dark and no one will see you, or if they do then they'll be too drunk to be sure you're not a ghost. For what my words are worth, I ask you to wait. I'd come with you to guide you there. I know this country better than you, and if Andhun falls then Yurlak will need you.'

The Screambreaker roared, 'Maker-Devourer! Andhun has

walls and the sea! It won't fall to a horde of bloody Vathan horse lovers no matter how many of them there are!' He turned away with nothing more to say. Gallow went out to Nadric's workshop and finished off a few simple jobs that the old man was working on. Better to let Nadric get himself ready. The Marroc grudgingly let Gallow into the big barn to drink ale with them these days, as long as he kept to the shadows and didn't bother anyone, but they certainly didn't want him dressing up and dancing and singing like he was one of them. So he stayed in the workshop, pottering from one thing to another until after dark, when everyone else was gone and Arda would be dancing with the village men and Nadric would be swaying back and forth with a happy ale-smile on his face and the children would be asleep in a corner with the other little ones. Perhaps Jelira might still be awake this year, yawning as though she was out to catch flies.

Before the forge fire died he lit a torch and took it into the fields, calling the two Lhosir ponies. The old general wouldn't have the patience to stay. *Lhosir pride over simple sense.* Arda's words those, said about him, and when she'd said them he hadn't understood; but now he did and they made him laugh because they were sometimes so true. In the workshop he saddled a pony ready to go. He filled a couple of skins from the well and put cheese and some bread and some eggs into the saddlebags. Arda would see they were gone straight away and they'd have another fight, but the Screambreaker was a guest under his roof and a Lhosir never sent away a guest without at least a first meal for the journey. He took down the Screambreaker's armour and laid it out piece by piece beside the horse. Last of all he left his own helm. The Screambreaker would leave a proud warrior. If the Vathen weren't heading south with torches to burn Marroc villages then he had no need of the helm for himself. He was a smith now, a father, living as a Marroc even if he wasn't. He could let Arda have that much. Peace.

He left the fire to die and walked slowly to the big barn and the bonfire outside. Music and singing and dancing filled the night. He kept to the shadows around the edges, avoiding the other villagers as best he could. They tolerated him – just barely

– throughout most of the year, but festival days were bad and today would be worse. They'd be drunk tonight and ugly. A good few had once lost kin to a sword or a spear from across the sea and the Vathen were making them remember all over again. He waved a cup at Fenaric and took an ale from him. The carter seemed to dislike him less than the rest, perhaps because he travelled and saw Lhosir traders now and then in Andhun and sometimes even in Fedderhun, or perhaps because he and his sons hadn't been born in the village and he was something of an outsider himself. Or maybe none of those things. Maybe he simply hid it better.

'Might be better if you go home early tonight,' murmured Fenaric. Gallow thought he was right, but he stayed for a drink because Marroc ale was a pleasure and one of the few things that no Lhosir could reasonably say was done better across the sea. He waved his cup at Fenaric again. Drink always brought out the sea in him. He saw more clearly now: he *had* spent too long living among the Marroc. The Screambreaker would go tonight because that's what any Lhosir worth his beard would do. And he'd go alone, because Gallow would stay here. Because this was where he belonged. And it would be a shame, he thought, not to share a last toast with the Screambreaker after all the years they'd fought side by side.

He held the cup carefully in front of him as he walked out of the big barn. Share a few memories and a few mouthfuls of Marroc ale with the old warrior. Have their own little festival and then help him onto his horse and watch him go. Better for everyone that way. And besides, a man couldn't bring a stranger into his house and call him a friend without sharing his bread and ale.

As he reached the yard a horse snickered somewhere behind him. Lit up by the embers from the forge, a shadow flitted across the back yard. Gallow chuckled. The Screambreaker moved quickly for an old man emerging from the grip of a fever. Maybe he wasn't as weak as he'd seemed.

The Screambreaker's horse was where he'd left it. The other Lhosir horse was standing beside it. Gallow froze. Then the horse he'd heard behind him wasn't one of his. And that shadow *had* moved too quickly.

Maker-Devourer! He burst into life, dropping Fenaric's cup and racing for the workshop, low and quiet and glued to the shadows. To where he kept his sword hidden. Men creeping about his house? Someone who'd somehow found out about the Screambreaker? Who? The whole village was up in the barn! Who was missing?

He took up an axe instead of his sword and snatched his helm, still lying on the ground beside Corvin's armour. For a half-second he hesitated, wondering whether to take his shield. A Lhosir always fought with his shield, even though it was a cumbersome and clumsy thing inside a house. He cursed himself as he reached out and grabbed it.

A man came out the back door and began to cross the yard. From the shadows of the workshop Gallow blinked and shook his head. He could see the man clearly in the moonlight and this was no villager. This was a Vathan soldier. A rider!

The Vathan stopped in the middle of the yard. Gallow readied his axe. Two more came out, dragging the Screambreaker between them. The fever made his struggles feeble and turned his curses into groans, but he was fighting them as best he could. Gallow watched them go, waited until they turned away and had their backs to him, and then he charged, his heavy footfalls lost beneath the raucous songs from the barn. He crashed into the soldier on Corvin's left, shield rammed into the man's back, sprawling both him and the Screambreaker forward. Gallow swung his axe at the other Vathan's neck just beneath the line of his helm. The blade hit hard and bit into the mail draped from the back of the bassinet, twisting in Gallow's hand, almost wrenching itself out of his grasp before he jerked it free. The soldier let out a startled grunt. Gallow stumbled over the Vathan he'd sent sprawling to the ground, fell, landed on top of him, straddled his back, pinned him, took his axe in both hands and brought it down as hard as he could into the back of the man's head. The Vathan helm split open and the soldier's brains spilled over Gallow's hands. The other one lurched towards him, sword drawn, staggering from side to side, blood running down his shoulders. Gallow jumped up, casting his eyes around for the last of the three and not finding him. The lurching soldier walked straight into Corvin, prone on the grass, and stumbled. His movements were jerky and full of twitches. Gallow scooped up his shield, let out a roar and swung, whirling the axe, but the soldier didn't move, didn't even seem to see it coming. The axe shattered the Vathan's jaw and left the bottom half of his face a ruin of pulpy flesh and fractured bone. Blood poured down his hauberk. He sank to his knees and pitched forward, face first.

'Get up, you sickly dog!' swore Gallow at Corvin. 'Get up and take his sword!'

An arrow struck his shield. A stroke of luck that he'd lifted it to look down at the Screambreaker. Gallow let out a bellow and ran at the last Vathan, but the rider was already on his horse and galloped into the dark and was gone. At least the Screambreaker was getting to his feet.

'Let him get away, did you?' Gallow ignored him. He sat on his haunches for a while, trying to think. The old man's breathing was hard and he dragged his feet, but at least he had *some* strength. 'They'll be back,' he said.

Gallow stared at him. 'They knew you. Didn't they?'

The Screambreaker gave him a sour look. 'Of course. They knew before they came, bare-skin.'

'Then this village is dead.' Gallow glanced back at the horse and the armour he'd laid out on the ground. 'The mare's all ready for you. I have to go back to the barn.'

'Why?'

'Because I have to warn the Marroc. The Vathen knew who you were. One of them got away. So they'll come back, and when they find you're gone they'll burn my village and kill everyone here. Would you, the Widowmaker, have let this pass?'

The Screambreaker thought. 'No,' he said. 'But they brought this on themselves, no-beard.'

'I would spare my wife and my children.'

The old man shrugged. 'One of them has spoken out of turn. One of them told the carter.'

'The carter?'

'I told you to ask him how he paid the Vathen for his ale. And for his life.' The Screambreaker shook his head. 'I've dealt with these horse-lovers before. I know how they are. Your kinsmen have made their own fate now, bare-skin.'

'They've made yours and mine too.'

The Screambreaker shrugged, indifferent. 'I was going to leave in the night anyway. *My* fate isn't changed at all.'

'Yes, it is. You were going to leave alone. You would have left a small trail that would be hard to find. Now, when the Vathen come, the tracks will be those of two Lhosir, more if I can make it seem that way, and the trail *I* will leave will be so glaring that even the blind couldn't miss it.'

The Screambreaker looked at him for a long time. 'You think you'll spare these Marroc who betrayed you by drawing the Vathen away? They'll simply split their numbers.'

'But if I don't try then there's no hope.'

Corvin kept staring. He started to laugh and then nodded. 'Then I have a proposition for you, clean-skin. I'll leave your trail. Go back to your Marroc. They might actually need you now. Which is more than I do.'

10

FENARIC

Gallow was gone from the festival for a long time. Fenaric drank his own pale ale and grew pleasantly drunk, relieved that the big forkbeard had found something else to do. He should really stay away from these festivals – they weren't his place and no one wanted him. What he should really do was go home, back across the sea.

He fidgeted, unable to relax. Gallow made him nervous tonight more than most nights. He couldn't settle. He looked over the empty space of the big barn to where Arda was dancing with Nadric since she had no husband to join her and he had no wife. It was a shame, and he wished it could have been him with her tonight, but it couldn't. It was a shame she hadn't been patient eight years ago. Others would have taken her, even with another man's child to feed. She hadn't had to lie with a forkbeard, but now that she had, no Marroc would touch her when Gallow finally left her. Four children, and three of them half-breeds? Even Vennic had more sense. Yes, a shame.

I'd have taken you with a child from another man. It wasn't as though Merethin had been a thief or a layabout or had simply run away. He'd gone bravely to fight the forkbeards and he'd died on their spears with other decent men. There was no shame in that. *You should have waited for me.* But Fenaric had been languishing in a forest full of outlaws a hundred miles away and they'd never heard of King Tane's death or the fall of Varyxhun and Andhun or that the fighting was done with until six months after Yurlak and the Screambreaker had gone back across the sea. It was almost a year before he'd come through Middislet again, and for all that time he'd had no idea that Merethin was dead. He'd seen Arda and he'd smiled and waved and she'd smiled back, and it was only later he realised she was married to the forkbeard now, and he was, again, too late. He glowered at Nadric. He had pushed her into it. Nadric, who was getting old and needed someone who knew his way around a forge. Well now maybe he was going to be short-handed again.

The music faltered and stopped as two soldiers rode into the barn. For a moment Fenaric was confused. The soldiers weren't Vathen from Fedderhun. Both wore mail hauberks and carried burning brands taken from the fire outside. The first one didn't have a helm but he had the terrible forked beard and a brutal scar from his eye to his ear. The second one was Gallow.

'Fenaric!' Gallow pushed through the barn. The dancing petered out; drunken villagers staggered away from Gallow's horse. Fenaric looked for somewhere to run but he was stuck in a corner beside his own cart and his barrels of beer. Gallow levelled his sword. 'You! You sent the Vathen to my house!'

'No!' Fenaric tried to shake his head but he couldn't. Couldn't even move.

'Who else, Fenaric? You went to Fedderhun; you came back. The Vathen came back with you. Did you show them which house it was? Brave of them to wait until dark.'

'No! No, I didn't!' Fenaric backed into the corner. He cringed as Gallow advanced.

'Yes, you did. Someone told you he was there. Someone sent you. How did you know?'

Fenaric glanced at Nadric. He shook his head and fell to his knees and clasped his hands, begging. 'Modris have mercy!' He should have known better. Never cross a forkbeard. His bladder suddenly felt very full.

'I did it,' said Arda. She stood proud in the middle of the barn, pushing past the others to stand across from Gallow, hands on her hips. 'I told him to do it.'

The look on Gallow's face was murderous. 'Why, wife? Why would you do that?'

'I told you I didn't want that man in my house. I said that many times and you never listened.' She pointed at Corvin and turned to the Marroc around her. 'Do you know who this is? This is the Widowmaker, the Nightmare of the North. In *my* house.'

She rounded on Gallow. 'You said he'd be gone in the morning. And he wasn't. So yes, when Fenaric went to Fedderhun I told him to bring the Vathen, that I had a forkbeard from Lostring Hill in my house if they wanted him. I never said who, and I told no one else. Bluntly, I thought he'd be dead by the time they came and that would have been fine for all of us.'

Gallow turned on Fenaric. 'Did they pay you?' Fenaric shook his head but he couldn't help looking at the barrels of ale. 'If they did then that's blood money, and you give whatever they gave you to Arda and let it hang around her like a curse.' He backed his horse away and looked at them all. 'Do you know what you've done?'

'*You* brought him here!' snapped Arda. Sometimes she was the only one of the Marroc who wasn't afraid of him.

'I came from fighting the Vathen with a soldier who was hurt, defending our land!' roared Gallow. 'Does it matter who he was?'

Arda matched him, thunder for thunder. 'Yes! When it's the Widowmaker, yes, it does!'

Fenaric stared at Corvin. 'I didn't know who it was.' *Oh Modris. The Nightmare of the North! He'll kill every one of us.* Gallow's eyes were on him, hard and narrow. 'I swear! I didn't know!'

'And that makes it somehow better? That you betrayed a man without even knowing his name?' Gallow snarled and growled and turned his horse. 'Listen well, Marroc!' he cried. 'The Vathen have come to Middislet. You did that, not I. Now two of their soldiers are dead. That? *I* did that. And Fenaric, you may not have told them who was in my house, but someone did. The Vathen know that the Screambreaker was here and more will come. Go! Hide in the Crackmarsh! Stay there this time and don't wait for Vennic to see ghosts up in the hills – they *will* come. If they burn your homes, let that be all you lose. You're fools, all of you.' He jumped off his horse, grabbed Fenaric and dragged him towards Arda. 'Screambreaker, if anyone leaves the barn before I come back, kill them!'

The forkbeard nodded. He looked distant, as though he was

barely listening. His eyes were half closed. Fenaric whimpered as Gallow hauled him along. *Modris, but he's strong!*

Arda looked at Corvin in disgust. 'He's half de—'

Gallow slapped her before she could finish, hard enough to knock her down. Fenaric tried to pull away, certain now that Gallow meant to kill them both as soon as they were outside, but he couldn't break free. He knew, because Arda had told him, that Gallow had never struck her in all the years they'd been married.

Gallow didn't break stride. He tossed his torch among the cringing Marroc and bent down as Arda started to rise. He grabbed her arm with his free hand and dragged them both out of the barn like a pair of naughty children, walked them past the bonfire, threw Fenaric to the ground and drew his sword.

'No!' Arda at last sounded scared. Fenaric couldn't find his voice.

Gallow pointed his sword at Fenaric's face. 'Now listen to me. I'll leave with the Screambreaker tonight. I'll take the Vathan horses and everything they had. There'll be no sign they were here but that won't save you. How far away were they, Fenaric? Closer than Fedderhun?' Fenaric shook his head. 'Then you have two days, perhaps three. Arda, for once in your bloody-minded life, listen and do what I say: Fenaric will take you south in his wagon. You'll take the children with you. You'll go to Varyxhun. There are two horses tethered beside the workshop. They're Lhosir horses. Take them.' He ground his teeth, staring at Arda. 'Take everything you can from the forge. Take Nadric and his tools. You and Nadric can ride the horses. Fenaric will take the children and whatever from the forge that can't be replaced in his cart. The Widowmaker thanks you for your hospitality.' He threw a purse at her feet and shook his head. 'Why, woman? Why couldn't you simply do as you were told for once?'

Arda stared up at Gallow with burning eyes. 'He's half-dead. How do you think he'll stop anyone from leaving the barn?'

'He won't need to. They won't dare to try. You told them who he was and that'll be enough. You'll wait for me in Varyxhun. Keep my sons safe. I'll deal with you when I return.' His glare fell on Fenaric and his sword touched the skin of the carter's throat.

Fenaric scrabbled away but the sword point simply followed until he gave up and wept. 'I'll not kill now you, carter, because Arda has need of you, but let it be clear in your mind – that's all that saves you. I've seen the way you look at her. You'll take her to Varyxhun. You'll do whatever you must to look after her and her children, all of them. When I return, and I will, I'll judge you by how well you've done this. And if you run from me, Fenaric, or if you touch her, I'll hunt you. I'll find you and I will sever your ribs from your spine and pull out your lungs like wings and sprinkle salt on you as you die.'

Fenaric gagged. The way the forkbeards had hung King Tane's huscarls along the roads to Sithhun after Tane was driven to the mountains.

'Do you understand, Fenaric?'

He nodded, weeping with fear. Arda spat at Gallow's feet. '*Now* you care about your family? Now, when it's too late?'

'Stay here if you'd see what *your* caring has done!'

She turned from him. 'Go! Take your Widowmaker. Don't bother coming back!'

Gallow fixed her with icy eyes. 'My sons will need a mother a few years longer. Be thankful for that.'

'You never changed, did you? Cut your beard and pretended to be meek, but the forkbeard was always there.'

He nodded. 'Yes, Arda. As well you know. And neither of us would have had it any other way.' For a long moment Gallow stared at her. The look on his face was a strange one, impossible to read. His hand strayed to his chest as if touching his heart. Then he turned back to the barn. 'When the Screambreaker and I are gone, go and be with our children. They'll wonder what's happening. They'll be afraid. And if you must tell them anything at all, be sure it's the truth. All of it.'

He left. Fenaric watched him go. 'I'm sorry ...'

She hissed at him and glared. 'So was it Nadric who told you, was it?'

He nodded hopelessly. 'He said ... I thought ... Why did you say it was you?'

She rolled her eyes at him and shook her head. 'Pull yourself together and be a man, Fenaric. Go and get your cart ready.'

He lay still, too weak to move. When he finally found his strength again, he lifted his head in time to see the shadow-shapes of two horsemen vanishing into the night. Arda got up and left him there, and the look on her face was every bit as sharp as Gallow's sword.

11

THE CRACKMARSH

Years of living among the Marroc put the words on Gallow's tongue: *You did well in the barn.* He bit them back. Sitting on a horse while Gallow put the fear of the Maker-Devourer into Arda and that idiot of a carter? Nothing for a Lhosir to feel proud about, no matter how hurt he was.

'Since you're not about to die, I suppose you might stay on that horse as far as Andhun,' he said instead.

'I don't want you riding with me, clean-skin.' The Scream-breaker's words were weak, his voice at the end of its strength. 'You want to leave a trail for the Vathen to follow, you do that. I'll make one too. I'll make my own.'

'You'll have to speak louder,' said Gallow.

'You heard.'

Gallow sniffed the night air. The trail towards the Crackmarsh was easy enough to follow in the moonlight. He still carried a burning branch from the festival fire and he'd walked the path a dozen times. 'I think I must have taken a blow to the head in the battle too. Hearing's been here and there ever since. You'll have to shout to be sure I don't misunderstand you. Probably not a good idea in the middle of the night.'

'Go away! I do not want you with me,' growled Corvin. It wasn't exactly a shout.

'I think,' said Gallow, as if he hadn't heard, 'that if I were to go back, I might just kill my wife.'

'Do you need me to do it for you, bare-face? For a betrayal like that I'd hang my own brother. You should have dragged her by the hair back into that barn and whipped her to death in front of the rest of them!'

'Your brother's at the bottom of the sea, Screambreaker, and when he was alive, I think most of us were surprised with each day that passed when one of you still hadn't killed the other. The Marroc aren't like us.' He wouldn't kill Arda, not for trying her best to look after what was hers. Couldn't. But Fenaric was a different matter. Fenaric he wanted to hurt. Badly. His blood was up, his axe had tasted the enemy and that's what Fenaric had made himself: the enemy. 'Maker-Devourer. I have two sons by Arda and a daughter. They're too young to ride with us.'

'Good. Then go back and watch over them and leave me be.'

'No, better I ride with you, Screambreaker. I'll save my rage for cracking Vathan skulls, not Marroc ones. You can show me the road to Andhun, which I might not find were I alone, and remind me why I should grow my beard again. And I'll return your generosity by hunting food and water for you.' If he put it like that and made it sound like somehow the Screambreaker was the one guiding them and not the other way round then maybe Corvin would at least shut up about being left to manage on his own.

'That woman took your beard. Is she why you stayed in Andhun?'

'Not at first.'

'But she's why you never came back.' The Screambreaker screwed up his face. 'I've seen how you look at her. And how she looks at you. Women like that make men weak. You forget who you are.'

'You're wrong, Screambreaker. I've not forgotten. I chose to be something else.' They rode in silence after that. Gallow watched Corvin's shoulders start to sag and then the Screambreaker slumped in his saddle. They were only a few miles from Middislet but the Marroc wouldn't start for the Crackmarsh until dawn and probably not for hours afterwards. Gallow reined in his horse. 'It's been a long night and I don't trust these Vathan beasts not to trip and throw me. I'll stop here and make my camp. I have food and water if you choose to join me.' He half expected Corvin to refuse, to insist on riding on alone until he fell off his horse, but the Screambreaker didn't answer. When Gallow stopped, Corvin's horse stopped too. The old man was asleep. Gallow lifted him down and got a fire going. It had been a long night.

He rose again at dawn. The fire was down to embers but they were enough to light some kindling and start a new one. He roused Corvin with warm water and soft bread and the smell of roasting meat. 'Breakfast, Screambreaker. Make the most of it. We won't eat like this again until Andhun. I've got food for another day and then we'll be foraging in the Crackmarsh. You'll not get another fire either, not with Vathen on our trail.'

'Go home, Gallow.' That was all he said, but he didn't spit out the water or throw Gallow's food away. Arda would howl about the meat, the only piece of it they'd had for weeks. She wouldn't have forgotten when he found her again in Varyxhun either, but they'd be doing well if that was the worst they had to scream about by then.

'We'll be at the edge of the Crackmarsh long before the sun peaks,' he said as they rode. 'We'll head west when we reach it. Once the sun is high we'll rest a while. We'll make it as obvious as we can which way we went. Maybe the Vathen will be too eager for our blood to stop and hunt for a handful of Marroc.'

The Screambreaker laughed. 'Shall we scare away the wolves and the bears and the bandits for them? Perhaps the foxes and the badgers too? Their teeth are sharp, after all, and their claws can leave a nasty scratch.'

Gallow ignored the scorn in the Screambreaker's words. 'Outlaws might lurk in its fringes, but the Crackmarsh is no place for food and shelter. The wolves and the bears know that and yes, the foxes and the badgers too. The only things that hunt there are the ghuldogs. You can try to scare *them* away if you like. Likely as not they'll come for us.'

They rode hard through the morning; when they stopped, Corvin didn't so much climb off his horse as fall. The Scream-breaker waved Gallow away, made angry noises and then fell asleep. While he snored, Gallow wandered the edge of the woods and the broken stones alone. The Marroc would go to the closer caves a few hours east of here, but if the Vathen came in any numbers then caves and trees wouldn't save them. He'd left a trail that anyone could find so far. Later he'd take that trail into the Crackmarsh. They'd disappear – almost impossible not to in the marsh – but the Vathen would know by then exactly where they were going. Andhun. He had a two-day start, at least, given how long it would take for the Vathen to find reinforcements. Easy enough.

'Why did you face them in the field, Screambreaker?' he asked when the Screambreaker was awake again. 'Why make your stand on Lostring Hill? They were five times our numbers, maybe ten.'

'More than ten,' Corvin said. 'But Fedderhun has no walls, bare-beard. The battle would have destroyed the town and the Vathen would have won all the same.'

'They're only Marroc. Isn't that what you used to say?'

'I did, and there's little enough glory in hiding behind Marroc soldiers on the battlefield, never mind their women too.'

'Little enough glory in riding your enemy down from the back of a horse or slaughtering them with arrows from far away,' muttered Gallow, 'but the Nightmare of the North did both in his time.'

'The Marroc got too good at running.' The Screambreaker spat. 'They wouldn't face us any more. As soon as a man runs, he's no longer a man. Makes him the same as an animal and there's neither honour nor dishonour in killing an animal, it's simply a chore. A bear or a boar, they're a different matter, but they won't run if you fight them one against one and don't hide behind an army of spears and shields.' He turned away. 'Yurlak kept falling ill. See how his strength came back when he returned across the sea to his home? These Marroc sapped the life out of him. The fighting had to end. We needed to go home.' A thin smile settled on his lips. 'Andhun will be different. Andhun has walls and even the Marroc can fight if you give them a wall to hide behind. Varyxhun showed us that. The Vathen won't get past Andhun. We'll smash them in the field and the Marroc will hold the walls.'

Gallow helped him onto his horse. That was the Scream-breaker. He'd let the Marroc hold the walls of Andhun because he didn't trust them in the field, but give him a few thousand Lhosir and he'd face the Vathen in the open no matter how great their numbers. Five thousand Lhosir had beaten an army of Marroc said to be thirty thousand strong. That had been the

height of the war before Sithhun fell, before Gallow had crossed
the sea, and so all he'd heard were the stories. Corvin had earned
his names that day. Widowmaker to the Marroc, Screambreaker
to the Lhosir.

They reached the edges of the Crackmarsh. In the distance
mountains darkened the southern horizon. Varyxhun nestled
somewhere on their edges where the River Isset emerged into
the hills. A canyon channelled the water, funnelling its energy,
and then spat it into a great flat plain two score miles wide
and circled by hills. The Crackmarsh, and here it was. Water
everywhere.

It rained that night and they rose stiff and miserable in the
morning. Corvin's face was glassy-pale. He didn't complain but
then he wouldn't, not until he fell off his horse stone dead and
probably not even then. As soon as they set off, Gallow steered
their course deeper into the water meadows. The changes came
slowly. The ground became wetter, the undergrowth darker and
denser and more tangled. Their horses' hooves began to sink into
the earth. By the middle of the day they were walking through
ankle-deep water that stretched ahead as far as either of them
could see. Islands hunched out of it – hundreds of them – some
bare, most clustered with dense stands of trees. Here and there
some grew out of the water itself. They stood on thick tangles of
roots and their branches were twisted and ancient. They looked
sickly.

'That Vathan who escaped, he'll have reached Fedderhun by
now.' In the distance, away from the mountains, Gallow could
see the hills on the far side of the marsh where the land rose and
then sloped towards Andhun and the sea. 'With luck we'll be
across the marsh before they get here.'

He tied Corvin to his saddle in the afternoon when the old
warrior finally lost his battle with sleep and succumbed, and
pushed them on hard and far. One night in the Crackmarsh
would be more than enough. As the daylight began to fade he
chose an island that looked big enough to shelter two men and
their horses. He tried to light a fire, but between the rain and the
marsh everything was too wet.

'The Marroc have a story about this marsh,' said Corvin.

Gallow grunted. He'd thought the old general was asleep.

'They have several.'

'They used to tell me that the marsh was cursed and haunted. They told me there were hills here once long ago. The Aulians crossed the mountains and built a great city in the middle of it. They catacombed the hills with tunnels to bury their dead, just as the Marroc do now. They liked to dig, the Aulians. Then the city was struck by plague and there were so many dead that the living couldn't make new tunnels quickly enough, and so one night the dead got up and dug tunnels of their own. They dug an enormous labyrinth, huge and vast and so far and so deep that one day they reached the river. The water rushed under the hills and brought their tunnels down, and the hills and the city on top of them as well, but the dead didn't know any better and so they kept on digging. They're still there. Still digging. The ghosts and spirits that haunt this place are Aulians.'

'The Aulians never built a city here and there aren't any ghosts or spirits.' Gallow lay down and closed his eyes. 'The Marroc around Fedderhun say there used to be a fine valley here until a witch came to live in it. The witch was so wicked that the one day the river changed its course to wash her away and scour the land of every trace of her. That's why nothing good grows here. Witch's taint.'

'That's quite a witch then.'

'Oh, she was a very powerful witch and very wicked.' Gallow laughed. 'Aren't they all? And have you ever met a real one?'

'If a witch is an old crone then I've met many. But one who talks to the spirits of the Herenian Marches?' The Screambreaker spat. 'Witches or the dead of some ancient plague scratching away under our feet? Ghosts and goblins. Stories for frightening children.'

'The ghuldogs are real enough.'

'Then you watch for them, bare-beard.'

'I will.'

By the time he'd stripped the horses, the general was already snoring again.

12

IRON AND STEEL

For the third time in as many hours Sarvic's boot stuck in the mud of the Crackmarsh and he couldn't pull it out. The water on top was only ankle-deep, but the mud would swallow a man whole if he stood still for long enough.

'Shit on a stick, Sarvic!' hissed Valaric. 'You're worse than a forkbeard. Special shoes, is it?' He crouched low in the swamp, motionless amid the tree roots. Sarvic took the bow off his back and handed it to Angry Jonnic. Every movement had to be painstakingly slow. The Vathen on their horses were close. Trouble was, slow and careful wasn't going to get his boot out of the mud. Angry Jonnic wrinkled his nose.

'Swamp stink gets worse every time you move.'

Valaric was watching the Vathen. 'I wondered why that fork-beard saved your worthless hide back on Lostring Hill. Now I know. Make my life miserable, that's why.'

Angry Jonnic braced himself against a tree. He and Sarvic wrapped their arms around each other and heaved. The swamp let go of Sarvic's foot with a deep belch and a pungent stink of marsh gas. Valaric shook his head and winced at the splash. Jonnic settled himself against a tree. When Sarvic had done the same, Jonnic handed him his bow.

'Wait on me,' growled Valaric. 'And Sarvic, for the love of Modris, show me it was worth it.' It was already clear as the sky on a summer's day that the only reason Sarvic was riding with them at all was because the filthy bastard demon-beard who'd saved his skin when the line broke on Lostring Hill hadn't left any of them with too much choice. But he was here *now*, soaking and mud-covered instead of still on the back of his nice new horse, because he'd said he could shoot a bow. And that, at least, he could.

Luck was a fickle thing in war. He'd been lucky to live through Lostring Hill. Lucky to find a dozen dead forkbeards and their horses – some good looting there. Not so lucky that twenty-odd Vathen had been following them for a day now. Valaric had ridden off the road and into the Crackmarsh to see if they'd go away but they hadn't. So now it came to this. Twenty Vathen probably thought they had the easy beating of a dozen Marroc, but that was because they hadn't met Valaric the Wolf until now. The Wolf made his own luck.

Valaric let fly when the nearest Vathen were some fifty paces away. He didn't shoot at the ones at the front. His first arrow flew wide, must have missed the Vathan at the back by a finger. The rider jerked, startled. Angry Jonnic put an arrow in his neck. Sarvic shot the lead rider's horse neatly through the ear.

'Rat's piss!' Valaric strung another arrow. The Vathen were confused but they wouldn't stay that way for long. One in the middle must have found his helmet uncomfortable and had taken it off. Sarvic cleaned out his ear with a shaft of wood and tickled his skull with a tip of iron. The Vathan was dead before he even started to fall.

Jonnic and Valaric went for the horses now. The Vathen had worked out where the arrows were coming from, but Torvic and Stannic and Silent Jonnic were leading the rest of the Marroc out from where they'd hidden behind the largest of the nearby islands, splashing their own horses out towards the Vathen while arrows tipped rider after rider off into the swamp. The Vathen had good armour and carried shields, so Valaric had said go for the horses as soon as the first volley was off – drop all that nice heavy armour into the water and the mud and watch it flounder. Now he cursed as each one fell. A fighting horse was worth a good purse.

One of the Vathen was looking right at him. Open helm. Sarvic shot him in the face. Down three men already, with five more thrashing in the water, the rest of the Vathen thought better of it, turned and fled.

'Save your arrows.' Valaric watched them go. He unwrapped

himself from his tree and strode with slow deliberate steps out into the water. Stannic and the rest got there first. Sarvic was last but at least he didn't get stuck again. By the time he caught up, Valaric had taken his axe to two of the Vathen and Torvic was in the middle of riding down a third. A fourth was face down in the swamp and hadn't moved. Which left the fifth. The one who'd been at the front. Valaric picked him up right out of the water, armour and all. 'And who by the tears of the Weeping God are you?' He didn't wait for the Vathan to answer, just threw him back into the water and then went and pulled him out again. 'I'm Valaric. Every bit as mean and every bit as much of a bastard as any forkbeard. I piss on your name, horse-lover, and I wouldn't give the wrong half of a dead rat for you or anything about you. Why are you following us?'

Took a while and a good bit of beating, but it turned out the Vathen were looking for the Screambreaker. Sarvic stood in the water meadow, soaked and smelling of swamp-rot without the first idea what they were talking about, but once the Vathan came out with that, Valaric threw back his head and roared with laughter like he'd just been offered the throne of Aulia.

'Whey-faced weasel!' He gave the Vathan a kick. 'Does it look like he's here?'

'But you found him. Didn't you?'

A chill ran all over Sarvic as he remembered the dead Lhosir in the wood, and Valaric was still there, laughing away. 'Yes, horse-lover, we did. We certainly did.' And then Valaric spun some wild-arsed story about the forkbeard who'd dragged Sarvic down the hill and the two of them finding the Widowmaker still alive and Valaric letting the forkbeard take him – didn't ask where and didn't care – but most likely they were nicely on their way to Andhun by now. And then after all that, after they'd stripped the Vathen of anything they might sell, Valaric kicked the last one up the arse and let him go, and they all watched and laughed as the skinny little viper splashed and ran and splashed and fell his way across the Crackmarsh, getting himself away from them as fast as he possibly could.

'They do look *different* when they're not on the back of their horses,' muttered one of the Jonnics.

'Was any of that true?' Stannic and Torvic didn't look too pleased at the thought. Valaric nodded and Stannic rolled his eyes. 'Sweet Modris. The *Widowmaker*? We had the Widowmaker and you let him go?'

Valaric shot a look at Sarvic. 'A life for a life,' he said. 'Now shut it!' He bared his teeth at them all and swung himself back onto his horse. 'If you're all done stripping the bodies, boys, we'd best be gone before it's dark and the ghuldogs come sniffing.' No one was going to argue with that.

When Sarvic tried to move, his foot was stuck again.

13

THE ROAD TO ANDHUN

It was a quiet splash at the edge of the water that woke him, but Gallow had his axe in his hand even before he'd finished opening his eyes. In the gloom a shape was crawling out of the Crackmarsh. It had arms and legs like a man, scrawny and thin, but it crawled out of the water on all fours and its head had a pointed snout like a dog. It crouched where Gallow had guided their horses onto the island and sniffed. Behind it another snouty head poked out of the water. A second creature emerged and then a third.

Ghuldogs. Gallow let out a shout, half fear, half fury, and charged through the trees. Three heads whipped round to stare at him. The nearest sprang, leaping straight at him, jaws wide to rip out his throat. Gallow smashed the beast with his shield and battered it away. The other two crouched and stared. Moonlight shone in their dead eyes; then one jumped for the arm that held his axe while the other snapped at his feet. He blocked low with his shield, twisted out of the way and brought his axe down on the creature's skull. Bone crunched and blood and brains spattered his arm.

The first ghuldog was up again; it threw itself at his throat; he dodged, but not enough and its teeth clamped down, tearing at his shoulder through his mail. The second one seized his shield; he dropped that and let out a gleeful howl and swung again, shearing the creature's spine between the shoulder blades before it thought to let go. It fell twitching at his feet.

The last one still had his shield arm. He bashed it with the haft of his axe, cracking its nose. It shrieked and let go, snarled, and before it could think to spring again Gallow split its head in two. He stood over the corpses, fighting for air, watching the light fade from their eyes and looking around for any more. His shield was at his feet, the hand that would have held it pressed to his chest, to the locket and the little piece of Arda he still carried with him.

'Stupid, stupid ...' Who or what, he didn't know. When no more ghuldogs came, he picked up the shield. His arm hurt, aching and throbbing. The bite of a ghuldog was poisonous and rumoured to be cursed, but he didn't dare take off his hauberk to see if its teeth had broken his skin, not now.

The Screambreaker was still snoring where Gallow had left him. Gallow sat beside him, rested his axe across his knees and leaned his shield against his arm. There'd be no more sleep tonight. He touched the locket again and looked at the old man sleeping. 'You'd never understand, old man. You just wouldn't. It was a convenience to start with, that's true. Nadric was growing too old to wield the hammer. Arda with a child by a man lost from the fighting. And I ... Well, I had my reasons for not sailing back across the sea with the rest of you. I was off to Aulia across the mountains, but truth was I just needed a place and a thing to be. We sheltered each other.'

The Screambreaker mumbled something and shifted in his sleep. Gallow pressed the locket hard against his skin. 'I wish you hadn't broken that, old man. I was happy with that life.'

He sat watch until dawn and then shook Corvin awake. 'Ghuldogs,' he said shortly. 'Guard yourself.' The bodies by the shore were gone when he looked. There must have been more then. They'd be out there in the water now, watching and waiting for the next twilight. He went back to Corvin once the old general was up and moving and took off his hauberk and the leather jerkin underneath. The mail had held. His shoulder was sore and scraped from the mauling but the ghuldog's teeth hadn't found a way through. There'd be bruises and some stiffness but nothing worse.

The Screambreaker glared at him. 'I'm hungry.'

'Good. You've hardly eaten for days.'

They shared the last of the food from the village and set off again through the marsh. In places the water was still ankle-deep but more often now it came to their horses' knees and sometimes they were almost swimming. Late spring – the Isset was in full flow and the marsh water was as deep as it would get. Ghuldog territory, although in daylight the ghuldogs wouldn't trouble them as long as they kept going. He stopped them once around midday to let the horses rest a while – Corvin was asleep again – and after that they pushed on until dusk. They were slow, though, and as the light began to fail they were still in the marsh. He'd hoped to be out by now – between the Ghuldogs and the Vathen they weren't short of reasons to press on hard – but it was what it was.

'You sleep; I'll watch. In the middle of the night we'll change.' He gave the Screambreaker the harder watch, the one through the small hours before dawn, but the Screambreaker didn't complain, and he didn't mention it when Gallow didn't wake him up until the sky started to lighten again. There were no ghuldogs this time, at least. He slept for an hour while the Screambreaker sat beside the horses, grumbling on about being hungry.

They reached the edge of the Crackmarsh in the early afternoon, pushed on over the first brow of the wild grassy hills until they were out of sight of the wetland, and there they stopped. Gallow dismounted and fell into the grass with a smile and a sigh. 'The horses need to rest,' he said. 'They haven't eaten for two days either. They need to graze and so do I.'

Neither of them would say it but the Screambreaker needed to rest too. He was already taking off his boots and rubbing his feet. 'So have you *got* any food?'

'No, and you know it.'

'Fat lot of use you are then.'

'How about *you* find us some.'

'*You're* the Marroc. Have you not got a bow? Didn't they teach you?'

He wasn't a Marroc and he hadn't learned much since he'd crossed the sea, except how, maybe, it didn't matter as much as he'd always thought whether you were Marroc, Vathan, Lhosir, Aulian or what. But the Screambreaker could barely move and so he took a Vathan bow and a quiver of arrows from one of the horses and lost nearly all of them shooting at rabbits until he got one. More a stroke of luck than skill, but he wasn't going to shake his fist at it. After the last few days he reckoned he was due a bit of luck. With the rabbit in his hands, he walked back up to the crest of the last hill and looked out across the Crackmarsh. Miles and miles of water glittering still in the sun, pockmarked by islands like boils on a pox victim's skin. The wind blew in his face, bringing the smell of rot. The Vathen, if they were following, would be on the other side of all this by now. From here that looked pleasingly distant. With a bit of luck they wouldn't be ready for the ghuldogs either.

He stretched his aching back. Eight years working in a forge and his muscles had forgotten all about riding a horse.

Corvin was asleep and the horses had strayed when he returned so he skinned the rabbit and let it hang for a while and dozed. As darkness fell he set a fire. The rabbit was cooked and eaten and he and the Screambreaker sat licking their fingers.

'I remember days like this,' Gallow said. 'Scouting these hills, looking for traces of the Marroc so you could fight them.'

'You were a scout?' Corvin snorted.

'Sometimes.'

'I do remember a Gallow,' he said after he'd stared at the flames a while. 'A good fighter.' He tugged the braids of his beard. 'Why did you shame yourself?'

'I chose to stay.' Gallow shrugged. 'I thought cutting my beard would make me more a part of them.'

'But in the name of the Maker-Devourer, why would you want that? They're sheep! The man I remember didn't belong here. I remember a warrior. Fierce. A whirlwind and a wolf. Men looked up to you. Or maybe I have some other Gallow in mind. Gallow Truesword, he used to be called. Killed a lot of Marroc. Never wavered.'

'I did kill a lot of Marroc.'

'How many?'

'More than I can remember.'

The Screambreaker lay back and stretched out his arms. 'So why *did* you stay, Truesword?'

'I told you – I didn't care for Twelvefingers and it looked like he was about to become our king.'

'You were wrong.'

'Yurlak was stronger than any of us thought.'

The Screambreaker stretched again and groaned. 'It did him good to be home. The air is different here. Stifling. The air across the sea is cold and crisp and smells of mountains and the ocean. It tastes of salt. Here it tastes of nothing. See?' He sniffed. 'Medrin made mistakes when he was young, that's true. Coming across the sea to fight the Marroc changed him. That wound he got. Everyone thought he was going to die, but he didn't. Made him stronger on the inside as well, when he finally got over it.'

Gallow sniffed. 'They'll need you in Andhun.'

'There are already two thousand of us in Andhun and more on the way.' Corvin laughed. 'They don't need me.'

'The Vathen still outnumber you ten to one. You saw how many there were.'

'It didn't help King Tane.'

'Perhaps not, but the Vathen aren't the Marroc either.'

They sat in silence for a while, watching the fire die. 'Grow back your beard, Gallow,' said Corvin. 'Stay in Andhun. Fight with us.'

'I have a wife and family who'll be waiting for me in Varyxhun.'

'You still have a wife?' The Screambreaker snorted. Gallow couldn't answer that, not easily. Yes. He did. But . . .

He shook his head. 'I have sons, Screambreaker. I should abandon them?'

'Tell me, Gallow, would you see them grow up as Marroc or as Lhosir?'

He had no answer to that. Both.

'Go and fetch them. When the Vathen are broken, bring them back across the sea and raise them as they should be raised. *We're* your people, Gallow, not these sheep. You can't escape that. I saw you fight the Vathen outside your home. You made me proud. You were a warrior.' He laughed. 'I'll not quickly forget how we sat on our stolen horses, mailed and with sharp iron in our hands, the two of us and all those Marroc circled around, scared out of their wits. I could barely keep my head up. Sheep, Gallow. You live among sheep and yet you remain a wolf.'

'They do make a good ale though.'

'That they do.'

They slept under the stars. In the morning Gallow carefully lifted a sod of turf and buried the remains of their fire and the bones of the rabbit beneath it. He pushed them on as hard as he dared, stopping only for water and to hunt with the last of the Vathan arrows. Another day took them to the edge of the hills. The Screambreaker was getting stronger. Three or four more would see them to Andhun, and then ... And then to Varyxhun. To Arda. He'd have to face her and face what she'd done. He dreaded it.

At the top of the last rise before the plains he stopped. Andhun was out there somewhere, beyond the horizon haze. 'I tell you one thing, Screambreaker. There's simplicity to battle. Sometimes having a family feels like having to run kingdom in a court where no one listens to a word I say.'

The Screambreaker laughed. 'I can't offer you any kingdoms but I can find you a fight or two if that's what you're after.' He pointed out over the plain to a plume of smoke a few miles away, too large to be a campfire. 'What's that?'

Gallow squinted. 'There are Marroc farms and villages here. Nothing else. Andhun is that way.' He pointed off into the haze. 'Another three nights.'

'And will these Marroc farms and villages have food for us? My belly rumbles and you've used up all our arrows with your poor shooting.'

'The Screambreaker I remember could catch a rabbit with his bare hands.'

Corvin laughed. 'I could never do that. I did see a man kill a rabbit with his axe once. A fine throw.'

'A lucky one.'

'I thought so, but it was Jyrdas One-Eye back when he had two, and so I chose to hold my tongue.'

They sat on their horses, watching in silence as the smoke rose.

'That's too big for a campfire. That's a house burning, or else a barn,' said Corvin. 'That means Vathen. How many down there, do you think?'

'More than two.' Gallow wrinkled his nose. What were the Vathen doing this far from the coast?

'There might be some of your precious Marroc to save.'

'Doubt it. For all we know the whole Vathan army could be between us and Andhun by now. The wise thing would be to avoid them. Stick close to the edge of the hills and circle round. Come at Andhun along the valley of the Isset.' Then again, the Isset valley itself could be crawling with Vathen looking for a place to cross the river.

The Screambreaker shrugged. 'There's only one way to know, Gallow, and I *am* hungry. When it's dark, we'll go and look.'

14

GOSOMON

Duvakh stepped over the body of the Marroc farmer who'd been stupid enough not to run away and looked the other man up and down. Shivering, starving, dull-eyed and with nothing to his name except a shirt. He couldn't have been in the hills for more than a few days, yet he was half-dead. Still, he was definitely Vathan. Duvakh even knew him. 'Gosomon? From Krenda's ride? Why, Gosomon of Krenda's Ride, are you hiding in a Marroc barn?'

Gosomon told him. By the time he was done they were inside the farmhouse, eating some of the dead Marroc's food and drinking his beer. Duvakh's head was buzzing. The rest of his ride sat around, scratching themselves and patting their bellies. Good food was to be cherished. There were only five of them – six if you threw in the ghost he'd found in the barn – and the Marroc here had a good larder.

'I reckon we'll stay here another day or two.' He pointed to Gosomon. 'You might want to stay here a bit longer. Get your strength up.'

Gosomon shook his head. 'Krenda Bashar and the ardshan are waiting on my news. I need one of your horses.'

The other riders laughed but Duvakh didn't. The sun was setting. The flames from the burned-out barn had largely died away. The glowing embers would keep his riders and his horses pleasantly warm through the night. He looked at the gash on the back of his hand and then sucked at it. The wound was still weeping. 'Krenda and the ardshan? I'd go right back to your swamp if I were you.' He shook his head. 'Hai Frika!'

The laughter died. Duvakh scowled. Gosomon's expression made him uneasy. He helped himself to some more of the dead farmer's ale and made a face. An unpleasant drink, but it did the job. 'We smashed those Marroc at Lostring Hill to pieces, eh?' he said. 'Broke their line and slaughtered them.' He'd killed three men by his own count, charging down from the crest of the hill, cutting them down before the Marroc managed to reach the woods. 'No one thought the forkbeards would be at Fedderhun, but they were and they broke like the rest. So you were one of the ones who went chasing off after the runners, eh?'

Gosomon looked up. His face was hollow and haunted. Even in front of the fire with a couple of blankets wrapped around him he was shivering. A sheen of sweat covered his brow.

'Scatter them far and wide,' Duvakh said. 'We learned that when we took gold from the forkbeards. The Marroc are good at running but not as good as our riders are at chasing, eh?' He poured himself another cup. '*While* you were off chasing, you might like to know that the ardshan and the Weeping Giant had a falling-out. Next thing we knew we were on the move again.' He puffed his cheeks, remembering the disappointment of Fedderhun, small and worthless, and how eager the bashars and their riders had been sink their teeth into something worth plundering. 'Someone put it in the ardshan's head that the forkbeards at Andhun weren't ready for us. We thought we'd get in quick and have the place to ourselves for a few days before the Weeping Giant and his foot-sloggers could catch up with us. Load of toss that was. Not ready? Forkbeards looked plenty ready to me.'

'Wasn't so bad, though,' chipped in another rider. 'At least we didn't have the Weeping Giant looming over us all the time telling us what we couldn't do ...'

Gosomon's head jerked sideways, staring at the wall as though if he looked hard enough, he might see right through it. A hand, sharply raised, drew silence. For a few long seconds they sat there frozen. Then Gosomon relaxed. 'Thought I heard a noise.'

Duvakh got up. 'I'll go and look. Need a piss anyway. Dansukh, tell him what happened at Andhun, eh? Let him know why he's just a little bit too late with that word he's carrying to Krenda and the ardshan.'

'You took it? You took Andhun?'

'Not exactly.' Duvakh laughed, shook his head and got up, leaving Dansukh to pick up the story. Outside, he walked around the farmhouse in case someone was out there but he couldn't see anything except the dying flames from the barn and the shadows they cast. He belched loudly and stamped away from the embers for a piss. The forkbeards had come out from behind Andhun's walls. Duvakh reckoned the ardshan had had the numbers by about two to one and everyone who'd fought with them said that the forkbeards knew squat about fighting against mounted soldiers; then again everyone who fought with them knew they were crazy too. Well, there wouldn't be any Vathen coming back from Andhun saying the forkbeards knew squat about fighting horsemen any more. Turned out they knew perfectly well with their wall of shields and their long spears and their Marroc archers. Still crazy, though.

He sighed as the pressure in his bladder eased. Say one thing for the Marroc – their beer tasted rotten but it did the trick. Oh, and say another thing for them – they could shoot. An arrow had torn through his gauntlet and ripped open the skin across the back of his hand. He counted himself lucky it hadn't been a lot worse. The forkbeards, when they'd charged, had hit the ardshan's lines like a battering ram. The ardshan's foot-sloggers had simply folded and crumbled. Duvakh wasn't sure the forkbeards had ever actually stopped moving.

He kicked the dead Marroc farmer one more time, wondering why this one hadn't run like the rest when he'd seen Vathen coming over the hill. Marroc always ran. That was the joy of them.

Quiet footsteps came up behind him.

'Suppose we'll have to cross the hills or make our way back to the coast and the Weeping Giant,' he muttered to whoever it was who'd come out to join him. He laughed. 'And then listen to the foot-sloggers' jibes and taunts.' He spat. 'Maybe we should stay out here on the edge of the wild, helping ourselves to whatever comes our way. Tempting thought, eh?'

Some sixth sense suddenly made him wonder if the footsteps behind him weren't another one of his ride out for a piss after all. His sixth sense was right too, just not quick enough. By the time he turned the axe was already coming down.

*

The Vathan turned at the last moment. His mouth fell open and he reeled back in surprise. Gallow's axe blade went straight through his face, opening him from cheek to cheek and smashing his jaw. He made a hooting noise and then the backswing caught him cleanly on the nape of his neck. Gallow caught him as he fell. He dragged the dead Vathan into the shadows and crouched beside him, listening. There were five horses tethered outside the farmhouse. Four more Vathen inside then. With luck the others were drunk too.

The house fell quiet. A voice called, 'Duvakh?' Gallow crept back around the walls, bent almost double as he passed each window, to where the Screambreaker stood with an ear pressed against the stone. He held up four fingers and pointed inside. Trying to get Corvin to stay a half-mile away with the horses was like talking to the tide, asking it not to ebb and flow. He'd given up.

The Screambreaker shook his head and held up another finger.

'They heard me,' Gallow whispered.

The Screambreaker yanked him close and hissed in his ear. 'Didn't they just. Clumsy oaf. Should have let him go back inside.'

'I want to take them where there's space.'

'And *I* wanted to hear what happened at Andhun.' He spat. 'Still, too late for that now. They heard something and now they're nervy as virgins in spring. Get on with it and call them out!'

'No.' He wished he'd kept some of the Vathan arrows now. When they were on their horses, the Vathen preferred bows or their javelots, spears light enough to throw but hefty enough to run a man through. The quivers on the horses here were empty. 'They'll come out soon enough, looking for their friend.' Gallow pointed to the edge of the shadows cast by the embers of the barn. 'I want you to stand there. They'll see you when they come out. Don't move when they challenge you. I'll take them from the side.' He'd have to be quick too, before they could get to the Screambreaker. The old man was getting stronger but he was in no shape to fight.

'That sounds like Marroc talk. We should stand together and call them out.'

'And if you were at your strength, Corvin Screambreaker, I would like nothing better. But you're not, and so a Marroc strategy must suffice if you want to eat bread and not steel tonight.'

The Screambreaker stiffened. A Lhosir was either fit to fight or useless.

'Oh, the wound to your head,' muttered Gallow. 'I dare say it impedes your sight. It's not a fair fight.' He looked at the old man, but all he got was that word on his lips. Silent but there. *Nioingr.* 'Fine then! Do it your way and die. In fact no, I'll not give you the pleasure of killing any of them.' He stalked back past the house, openly this time, shaking his axe arm loose and gripping his shield. 'Hoy!' he shouted. 'Vathen! Are you listening? There's more of us out here but none of the rest can be bothered with fighting you. They say it's too easy!' He reached the door and kicked it in. The farmhouse was a typical Marroc dwelling, one big space with a curtained-off night room. The Vathen were on their feet and ready for him with their heavy leather riding coats, long knives and axes. Not one of them had thought to put on his helm. And he was right – four not five, although there was an odd-looking Marroc cowering in a corner wearing nothing but a shirt. They had food too. It reminded Gallow how hungry he was.

Two of the Vathen rushed him together. The other two bolted for the back door. Gallow met the charge with his own, buffeting one away with a great blow from his shield. He caught the swinging axe from the other with his own weapon, barged on with his shoulder and head-butted the next Vathan in the face, cracking the man's nose. As he staggered back, Gallow turned and brought his axe down, shattering the first Vathan's collar and splitting him to his breastbone. A torrent of blood exploded over both of them and the man went down. Gallow turned. The Vathan with the broken nose dived through the curtain to the night room. Gallow ignored him, went for the two who'd run outside and caught them at their horses. The first was vaulting into the saddle – Gallow threw his axe, catching the man in the ribs and caving in his side. The horse bolted and vanished into the night, the Vathan lolling lifelessly on its back. The last one jumped at Gallow with his knife. He pulled Gallow's shield aside and stabbed. Gallow twisted sideways. The blade skittered off his mail, hard enough to spark; then he caught the man's arm with his own and gave a vicious twist. There was a crack of breaking bone and the Vathan screamed. Gallow twisted more. The man fell, writhing; before he could get back up, Gallow had his sword out and drove it through the back of the Vathan's neck.

He paused for an instant. Inside the house he saw movement – the Vathan with the broken nose bolting for the other door. He jumped up and gave chase but he needn't have bothered – the last Vathan ran straight into the Screambreaker's sword. The old man staggered. The Vathan stumbled on a few more paces and then toppled to his knees and fell to the dirt. Gallow made sure he was dead.

'That's a strong arm you have there, Screambreaker, to drive a sword through all that leather,' he said as he came back.

Corvin looked at him. He was breathing hard. 'You'll not give me the pleasure of killing any of them, eh?' He pointed. 'You missed one.'

Someone was bolting for the horses. It was the man Gallow had taken to be a Marroc. From the way he landed in the saddle and sped away, he was a Vathan after all. A Vathan with no weapon, no armour, nothing but a shirt. The Screambreaker had been right. Five, not four. Gallow reached for a stone to throw, but the old man held his arm back.

'Let him go,' he said. 'He saw my face and he knows who I am.' He bared his teeth. 'And that, Truesword, is a knife in every Vathan heart.'

15

ANDHUN

They ate what the Vathen had left and made themselves comfortable. In the morning when it was light Gallow found the first Vathan soldier who'd tried to flee lying on the ground with his horse standing beside him a hundred yards away from the farmhouse, Gallow's axe still stuck through his ribs. Gallow pulled the axe free and set about cleaning and sharpening it.

'We've missed the battle,' grumbled Corvin. 'You should have let me leave sooner.'

'You were welcome to leave whenever you wanted,' said Gallow. 'Debate that with whoever thumped you on the head after Lostring Hill. How do you know we missed it, anyway?'

'Listening to their talk before you made such a mule's arse of killing them. But look. Quivers on their saddles but no javelots, so they used them already. And the horses – they've been ridden hard. The first one you killed, he's got the sash of a ride leader. He should have sixteen men with him but he's got four. Got a fresh wound too, a cut on his hand. There's blood on one of the saddles that hasn't been cleaned. If they were scouts then their quivers would be full and they'd have bows. If they were foragers then they should have a cart or some mules. This lot were on the wrong end of a fight not long before we came. Look at the way they ran from us. No spirit left in them.'

Gallow shrugged. 'Doesn't mean they came from Andhun.'

'Well they did, no-beard. Where else?'

They took the Vathan horses and rode on towards the coast. The farms and hamlets they passed were deserted. A few were burned-out but most were intact. The Marroc had fled, fearing the coming of the Vathen, but the Vathen had followed the sea road and now the land was deserted. Even the fields were empty, the animals taken or gone.

'Twelvefingers must have sent them across the Isset.' Corvin nodded approvingly. 'Take away everything the Vathen can eat and Andhun is the only crossing.'

'Not so, old man. If you know the paths, a man – a whole army of men – could cross the Isset through the Crackmarsh. Still, I doubt the Vathen know that.'

The Screambreaker stopped and looked at him long and hard. 'They may not know it now, but sooner or later they'll find a Marroc to tell them.'

Gallow shrugged. 'Good luck to them if they try it. About time someone cleared out the ghuldogs.'

With each day the Screambreaker grew stronger. As they started at last into the line of hills before Andhun, a band of riders came over a crest heading the other way. Lhosir, eight of them. When they saw Gallow and Corvin they stopped and one rode forward apart from the rest.

'I'm Tolvis of the Black Mountain,' he called. 'Sworn blade to King Yurlak. Name yourselves.'

'I know him,' muttered Corvin.

'The man I ride with is Corvin Screambreaker,' cried Gallow. 'Known among the Marroc as the Widowmaker and the Nightmare of the North. He too is a sworn blade to King Yurlak. I am Gallow of Middislet, sworn to no one.'

'You're sworn to the king, bare-beard, whether you like it or not,' snapped Corvin.

'Corvin Screambreaker?' Tolvis of the Black Mountain took off his helm and cocked his head. 'Now there's a thing. See, we'd heard the Nightmare of the North was dead. The Marroc have been quietly drinking to that for a week now. When they think we won't see and with one eye cast over their shoulder in case they're wrong of course.' He grinned.

'Someone at Lostring Hill was kind enough to land the Screambreaker a good blow to the head and render him senseless just long enough for me to drag him away. Come see him for yourself if you don't believe me.'

'I'll do that.' Tolvis of the Black Mountain rode closer. He was cautious, more so than Gallow would have expected, but as he came close enough to be sure of Corvin's face, a smile spread across his own. 'Maker-Devourer! It's true!'

The Screambreaker grunted. 'Tolvis of the Black Mountain is it now? You fought with me years ago but you weren't called that back then. It's a Tolvis Loudmouth that *I* seem to remember.'

The smile broadened. 'Pardon my caution, Screambreaker. You're on Vathan horses.'

'Their previous riders forgot their need of them. I'd hoped to aid you in the fight here but I hear the Vathen have already come.'

'They have, but not in all their numbers.' Tolvis turned his horse. 'Very obliging of them it was, and so we obliged them right back. I'll ride you to Andhun. We'll pass the field on the way. You'll know it when you see it – it'll be the one that's mostly the colour of Vathan blood. They were five or six thousand and a lot of them on horse, and we smashed them.'

The Screambreaker curled his nose. 'Five or six thousand? That all? There were five times that number at Fedderhun. Did they have the Sword of the Weeping God with them? The red sword Solace?'

Gallow looked at Corvin, curious. Fenaric had said something about the same thing, words he'd heard at Fedderhun, but Gallow had never repeated them to the Screambreaker. Something he overheard from the Vathen at the farm, then?

Tolvis shrugged. 'The Comforter? They didn't have it here, no.'

'You haven't seen the main Vathan force yet.'

'Oh, we know *that*.' Tolvis laughed. 'But let them come in bits and pieces – we'll chew each one up and spit it back at the next.'

An hour later they began to see bodies. Dead Vathen, most of them speared from behind.

Corvin frowned as he passed them. 'They look like they were killed by their own horsemen.'

A black cloud of rooks or crows circled ahead of them past a stand of trees. Tolvis put on a face as though he'd eaten a mouthful of something rotten. 'Prince Medrin had those of us with horses mount up and ride them down, same as the Vathen used to do for us against the Marroc.' He laughed. 'I'll tell you, the Vathen are a lot better at it than we are. Spent more time collecting spears that had missed than we did riding.'

'*Medrin* had you do that?'

Tolvis wrinkled his nose. 'Can't say as any of us much liked it. Or were much good at it. But he *is* Yurlak's heir.'

Through the trees on the open ground Gallow could see the walls of Andhun and the valley of the Isset, which flowed through the middle of it to the sea beyond. He could smell the city in the air, the stink of human waste and fish. The battlefield was in front of them now. The bodies of the fallen had been cleared away but there were looters on the field still, nervous Marroc folk scouring the trampled grass for swords, shields, helms, anything that might have been dropped in the fight and somehow missed in the three days since. There couldn't be much left by now.

The Screambreaker rode a little further, then turned away from the walls of Andhun. He looked hard at the ground. 'The Vathen came from over there.' He pointed away from the city. 'They had horses.' He climbed down and picked up an arrow half buried in the mud. 'You had archers?'

Tolvis grunted. 'Marroc,' he said, disapproving. 'But then they came at us on horseback so they deserved that. We fought them properly after their riders fled.' He grinned. 'And we destroyed them. There were a thousand Vathan corpses here when we were done and a few hundred more scattered where they ran. Vris, Ironfoot and Igel lost a few dozen each and Jank took a thumping on the flank. Didn't get his spears and his shields sorted properly when the Vathen started throwing their javelots.'

'Vris is here?' For a moment the Screambreaker looked up and grinned. 'And Ironfoot? Jank was always a bit dim when it came to horses. Whoever put him in charge of anything, *he's* the one who needs to be thumped.'

Tolvis laughed. 'You can thump Twelvefingers then.'

'Oh, so he's here at last, is he? Then I will.'

They walked their horses slowly across the battlefield. There wasn't much left: the broken shaft of a javelot here, a few arrows in the ground, bloodstains in the mud and the grass. Three crows picked at the remains of a hand and half an arm already stripped to the bone. On the far side Gallow saw half a dozen corpses hanging from the trees. Closer and he could see what had been done to them. They hung, arms and legs dangling loose, each man drooping over a wheel with two stakes driven right through him and emerging from his back. A bolt fastened the stakes together. They were suspended like this from ropes. Below the stakes, ribs had been cleaved from spines, the lungs drawn out and with twine sewn into them and tied to the branches of the trees so the ragged sails of dead flesh seemed to rise like wings. Corvin wrinkled his nose. The men had been hanging there for days; birds had already pecked at them and strips of dried red skin and muscle dangled from gleaming bone.

Blood ravens. Gallow couldn't say whether they were Vathen or Marroc, or Lhosir who'd first had their beards cut.

'Deserters?' Corvin frowned.

Tolvis shook his head. 'Vathen. The wounded horsemen. The ones who couldn't get away. Pretty, eh?'

'What did they do to deserve this?'

Tolvis shrugged carelessly. 'Lost.'

'Medrin ordered this, did he?' asked Gallow.

'Couldn't say. I was off discovering how hard it is to throw a spear into the back of a man who keeps dodging out of the way.'

They passed the hanging men and soon came to another cluster of corpses, this time bound upright to the trunks of trees. The bark around each one was scarred with the marks of spears and Gallow understood at once: the Lhosir had taken Vathan captives and used them for spear-throwing games. He'd seen it done with the Marroc once before, years ago, before the Screambreaker put a stop to it.

In the fields closer to Andhun small companies of Marroc were digging pits and erecting wooden poles. Dozens already stood surrounding the city. Each had a dead Vathan hanging from it. More blood ravens, like the ones around the battlefield.

'Something for the rest of the Vathen to think about when they get here, I suppose,' said Tolvis.

The Screambreaker frowned. 'This is for *nioingr*.'

'Apparently they're all *nioingr* for staying on their horses and throwing javelots at us instead of doing things properly and getting nice and close where we can chop them up with our axes and stab out their eyes with our spears.' Tolvis shrugged.

'No.' The Screambreaker's lips tightened. 'No. This isn't right.'

'Well you won't be the only one who doesn't think much of it, but Medrin wants it done and there's a lot of the younger ones who see it his way. Might be for the best. Maybe the Vathen are sheep like the Marroc, easily scared.' He laughed. 'Pity if they are though. Be a shame to come all this way only for them to go running back home again.'

They crossed another field, turned onto a road churned to mud and passed two open burial pits. The bodies, Gallow saw, were neither Vathan nor Lhosir. They were mostly Marroc.

'And this?' Corvin asked.

'Some trouble with the Marroc when we first came off the ships. Apparently a few of them weren't too pleased at having the son of their king come to visit. They learned to be happy about it soon enough.'

Close to the city walls black patches of earth and charred stumps of wood scarred the roadside. There had been huts outside Andhun's gates once but now they'd been burned. Gallow supposed it made sense. If it came to an assault on the walls then the slums here would give cover to the Vathen. Today, though, the gates stood open, inviting them in. Six bored and sour-looking Lhosir lounged around them, picking their noses and sharpening their axes. Over them a row of spikes stuck out from the stonework. The spikes looked new, the mortar around them fresh and lighter than the rest. Each spike had a head on it. The heads wore Vathan helms.

Tolvis rode up to the guards. 'Still scratching, Galdun? If it's a dried-up piece of turd you're looking for, you're poking at the wrong end.'

One of the guards looked up at him and rolled his eyes. 'Ha ha. At least you're not riding your horse backwards today, Loudmouth. You're not supposed to be here until dusk. What happened? Get lost again?'

'Oh, several times.' Tolvis jumped off his horse. 'Then I found the Screambreaker and he was kind enough to set me right. Thought I'd better come back with him in case he mistook you lot for a Marroc rabble.' He punched Galdun on the arm. Galdun puffed his cheeks and palmed Tolvis away.

'You're full of air, Loudmouth.' Galdun peered at Gallow and found nothing interesting, and then his eyes settled on Corvin. He frowned and took a step closer and then grinned. 'Maker-Devourer! Welcome to Andhun, Screambreaker. I knew you wouldn't be as easy to kill as they said.' He looked back to Tolvis. 'And Holy Eyes of Mother Fate, Loudmouth, you actually did something useful. You'd best run along now and make sure everyone gets to hear so it gets remembered. It'll be first on the list when someone finally has to speak you out. One of your greatest deeds, right up with that one bright day you managed to recognise your arse from your elbow. Pity it didn't last, eh? Off you go now. See if you can find the Fedderhun road this time.'

'Where's Twelvefingers?'

Galdun laughed. 'Do I look like a soothsayer? He's either somewhere in Andhun or else he's not. If he's not then he didn't leave this way. Probably he's in the keep like he always is, but I'd try the square first. I hear him and his Crimson Legion were hanging Marroc again this morning.'

They rode together through Andhun's gates. Gallow looked around him. After the Screambreaker had sailed back across the sea with King Yurlak, he'd wandered these streets and taverns, drinking his way through what he'd plundered from the Marroc in five years of fighting. He hadn't been the only one. Hundreds of Lhosir had stayed at first, helping themselves to whatever they wanted. Every day a few of them had turned up dead, stabbed during the night. The rest drifted away over time. Back across the sea mostly, or else across the Isset, until Gallow had been almost the only one left. When he'd turned his own back on the place at last, down to his last few scraps of silver, it was for the mountains. The Aulian Empire, or the shattered remains of what was left of it. He'd kept his mail and his axes and his sword, kept them all neat and clean and sharp, not traded them for ale like a lot of the others, and he'd never found a home for the hunger that five years of fighting had given him. Aulia. Plenty to do for a man like him, mired in blood, and the Marroc from around Varyxhun had said there was a pass that was mostly forgotten but still there, impossible when the winter snows closed in but not too bad in the summer.

His hand went to the locket under his mail. A tear stung his eye. The salt sea air, probably. Across the sea they'd flog Arda and hang her for what she'd done, but he wouldn't do that. Couldn't.

He'd never reached Aulia, nor the mountain pass, nor even got as far as Varyxhun. He'd managed as far as Middislet on the fringes of the wilderness and found his Arda instead, and it was all so unexpected and unlooked-for. He closed his eyes and squeezed them tight. Varyxhun. What would he do about her when he went back to Varyxhun? Couldn't do nothing. Did she hate him now? It had always been a fine line between them.

They crossed the open cobbled space beyond the gates. More of the wooden frames like the ones in the fields hung over the streets. Dead Marroc dangled from them like grotesque winged gargoyles. The corpses here were fresh, and there were more as they rode up the hill towards the keep and the town square. Marroc townsfolk scurried back and forth, keeping well out of the way of the mounted Lhosir. Their eyes, when they looked at Gallow, were filled with fear.

Halfway up he stopped. He took two of the riderless Vathan horses and left the other two for Corvin. He would have turned and simply ridden away but the Screambreaker stopped him.

'Two for you, two for me. I killed the man whose horse you're sitting on,' said Gallow. 'Seems fair. I've done what I said I'd do.'

'You killed six men. I killed one. You should have five of the horses, not three.'

Gallow thought about that for a moment. 'All right.'

'You should stay and fight the Vathen too.'

'I'd like that, and I envy you. But no.' Gallow looked around at the Marroc dangling from their gibbets. 'You'll do well enough without me.' He took the Vathan horses the Screambreaker had offered, turned and rode away.

*

Tolvis watched him go. He shook his head and spat. 'Bare-beard.'

Beside him the Screambreaker shook his head. 'No,' he said. 'Not him. We called him Truesword once, and he was a terrible thing to see. He might have changed his face, but all the rest is as it always was.'

And he whispered something in Tolvis's ear.

16

MEDRIN

Prince Medrin Twelvefingers, first son of King Yurlak, Scourge of the Seas and Prince of the Marroc, stared out of a window high up in Andhun keep. The shutters were flung wide, letting in the crisp salt air of the sea. The smell of it soothed him when the wind blew right and wasn't tainted by the stench of death.

Below the window a few Marroc dangled in the wind, dead and ripped open, an example to the others. They were a drop in the ocean, but if the Marroc were so determined to hate him then they'd damn well fear him too. When the followers of the Weeping God came he would have the Marroc of Andhun up on its walls, fighting for their city, whether they wanted it or not. Yurlak and the Screambreaker had thought a few hundred Lhosir at Fedderhun would turn the horsemen back. Stupid pride and they'd paid dearly for it. The Vathen had seen a Lhosir army beaten for the first time in more than ten years. Worse still, the Marroc had seen it too, the ones who survived. Some of them had started on the idea that maybe the Vathen weren't such a bad thing. A chance to rid themselves of their unwanted king from over the sea. Medrin meant to crush that idea into dust.

A heavy fist banged on the door. Medrin stayed where he was, staring out at the sky. 'I told you to leave me be.'

'Loudmouth's here.' He'd picked Horsan to guard his door because Horsan was huge, about as big as a Lhosir ever got, tall enough to go nose to nose with even old Jyrdas One-Eye, and he didn't think too much either, just did as he was told. Mostly.

'He's supposed to be sweeping the roads to the south for Vathan runaways. Tell him to get lost.'

He heard Horsan chuckle. 'Lost? He probably already is. Hey, what are you— Whoa!' The shuffle of feet at the doorway dragged Medrin away from his window. Horsan was backing in, all furrowed brows and confused, and there was Tolvis Loudmouth, a head shorter but shoving him on, poking him with the head of his axe.

'Is the castle on fire, Loudmouth?' Medrin shook his head. 'It had better be.'

A third man emerged from the shadows, stopped Medrin's ire and killed it dead. If anything he felt ... he felt afraid. He stared at the old man with grey in his beard. Corvin the Screambreaker. Nodded, working out in his head all the things this might mean, and most of all whether the Screambreaker likely meant to kill him. Probably not, but with Yurlak getting older every year, he was never quite sure that the Screambreaker didn't mean to make himself the next king.

No. He hadn't come here with death in mind. Medrin relaxed a notch. 'I see you're not dead after all.' The Nightmare of the North. With the Screambreaker here the Marroc *would* be afraid, and they'd fight too – he'd managed to get a legion of them together at Fedderhun after all, for all the good it had done. *So it's good to have him back then. Isn't it?*

The Screambreaker glowered at him. 'No.'

Isn't it? He wasn't sure. Yurlak and the Screambreaker were of an age. They understood one another and saw things the same way, and neither was afraid to use blunt words with the other when what they saw didn't please them. Yes, he'd be useful for keeping Andhun and the Marroc in line, but in the larger scheme of things Medrin found he was happy enough for the Screambreaker to have been dead.

He paused for a moment and then marched to the door, punched the Screambreaker firmly on the shoulder and clasped his arm, welcoming him as a friend.

'Found him coming up the road from the south,' said Tolvis, 'so I brought him back here. The Vathen are long gone.'

'Thank you, Tolvis.' Medrin tried to smile. It was hard with Loudmouth. And there was another thing: the old ones who called the Screambreaker a friend and thought that made them special. Thought that meant they could say whatever they liked. 'Now go back and watch the roads, Loudmouth. I won't have the Vathen slipping through the hills and coming at me from the south.'

'No, you won't, because there aren't any of them there,' grumbled Tolvis.

Medrin glared. 'See it stays that way!'

Loudmouth left, sulking, down the stairs. Medrin was getting a lot of that. Stupid men who wanted nothing more than to fight and get drunk and gave no thought to where the Vathen would strike next.

'And they will, won't they,' he said as soon as Tolvis was gone.

The Screambreaker stared at him. 'Who will what?' Two months ago, when Medrin had seen him last, the Screambreaker had been about to set sail in the vanguard of the Lhosir army. He'd been getting fat and had a sleepy look to him, but all that was gone now. *Now*, if anything he looked thin, as though he'd wasted away in this filthy Marroc air. He had a great gash on his head, terribly stitched and with a bruise that reached around his eye and down to the top of his cheek, all purples and yellows. His mouth twitched with impatience and he didn't look sleepy at all. Medrin stared at the bruise.

'And what happened to you?'

'A Vathan.' He stood there, still and at ease as if he was already bored.

'Well, that's who and what. You don't need to tell me it wasn't their full strength we faced.'

The Screambreaker shrugged. 'Tolvis said you faced five or six thousand so I'll assume it was more like four. They have another twenty or twenty-five thousand men and horse somewhere between here and Fedderhun. Unless they've had enough and gone home.'

Medrin clenched his teeth. *Unless they've had enough and gone home.* His father had had enough ten years ago. Yurlak and the Screambreaker had conquered a whole country and now, give it another few years, the Marroc would have it back. Not because they'd fought and pushed the Lhosir into the sea, but because his father and the Screambreaker and everyone like them simply couldn't be bothered with keeping the place in line. Medrin would have had them crossing mountains to Cimmer and the Aulian Empire and yes, the Vathen too, but Yurlak wanted none of it and the Screambreaker would be the same. He could already see it in the old man's face, the disapproval.

The frown flickered to half a smile. 'You bloodied them well, Twelvefingers. Better than I did.'

The compliment took him off guard. 'So did they have it with them at Fedderhun?' he snapped.

'Did they have what?'

'The sword. What do they call it? Peacebringer?' Although it had other names, as he'd come to learn not all that long ago. Much more important names.

'Solace. No, they're waiting for it. When it reaches them they'll come.'

'To Andhun?'

The Screambreaker gave him a hard look. 'Unless they mean to carry the Sword of the Weeping God all the way from where Tarris Starhelm buried it just to see how it looks in the sunset over the sea at Fedderhun instead then yes, of course to Andhun. Where else?' The old man sniffed. 'I see a lot of winged corpses hanging over the streets. Marroc giving you trouble?'

'No.' Medrin couldn't hide the sharpness in his words. 'Nor will they.' He clenched his teeth and pressed a hand to his chest, to the old Marroc spear wound.

The old man was smirking at him. 'I met another soldier after Lostring Hill. One who never came back from the last time. Gallow.'

'Gallow?'

'Gallow Truesword. I remembered him, eventually, from Varyxhun and other places. Fierce in his time but he's shaved his beard and lives with the sheep now. He seemed to think he knew you.' The hardness was still there in Corvin's eyes. 'I think perhaps he did.'

Gallow! Medrin pursed his lips, trying to keep his thoughts out of his face. 'Gallow? I thought he was dead. I thought he died in your war. But yes, I did know him, or *of* him at least.' He put on a grimace for the Screambreaker. 'Maker-Devourer, but that was a long time ago. Before either of us crossed the sea. You'd taken Sithhun.' His eyes narrowed. 'You'd taken King Tane's palace. You remember his shield?'

The Screambreaker nodded slowly. Medrin felt the old man's eyes watching him hard. 'They thought it made them invincible.' He laughed. 'Turned out it didn't. Don't think they ever got over that.'

'You remember what happened to it?'

The Screambreaker's eyes blazed. 'I know very well indeed what happened to it. My brother the Moontongue happened to it, and good riddance to both of them.'

'I mean before.'

'Before? You mean when the Fateguard sailed out of Nardjas for no discernible reason and demanded I hand it over. Yes, I remember that too.'

'And you gave it to them.'

The Screambreaker shrugged. 'A shield's a shield. I let them have it.'

Medrin grinned. 'I mean in between. You were still here, banging Marroc heads together.' His lips pinched to a smile as the old bitterness crept up inside for a moment and every word was a razor between them. He shook it away and looked hard at the Screambreaker. 'Everyone knows about what happened with Moontongue, but this was before. Before they sent it off to Brek. Beyard Ironshoe tried to steal it too, or so they said. I don't suppose the name means anything to you. The Fateguard always said he'd had an accomplice or two, but Ironshoe never told them who. There were whispers that Gallow was one of them. The two of them were friends.' He cocked his head. 'Whispers were enough to ruin his family though. The Fateguard took Ironshoe and no one ever saw him again. Killed him, I suppose. I wasn't pleased. Ironshoe was a friend, a good one.' He cocked his head. 'What was it like, the shield?'

He'd managed to take the Screambreaker off guard. Corvin frowned as if trying to remember. 'Big. Red. Heavy. Round.' He shrugged. 'The Marroc reckoned it was unbreakable so we had a go at it with some axes. Didn't scratch it. Wasn't too sorry to see it go after that, but in the end it was just a shield. A red one.'

'A shield that doesn't break. I was thinking we should try and get it back.'

The Screambreaker's face soured. 'Yes, I heard you've been looking. Ever since One-Eye came back with his daft stories. Why? Why not let it lie? It never did any good for anyone.'

'The Marroc still believe it's the shield of their god Modris, don't they? They'd follow it, Screambreaker.'

'It's just a shield, Medrin.' The Screambreaker snorted. 'The Fateguard weren't happy when I took it from Sithhun. I doubt they'd look well on you following my example. Why in the name of the Maker-Devourer would you want to cross them?'

'Because the Marroc would *believe*. The Vathen have their sword. Let the sheep have their relic too.' For a moment the venom and the anger that Medrin Twelvefingers had spent the last dozen years trying to hide spilled through. He hissed, 'And if it's just a shield then why do the Fateguard care? I tell you, if they demand the Vathan sword, I'll give them the sharp end!' He raised an eyebrow, catching himself. A moment to find his calm again. 'Just a shield that an axe can't mark, eh?' He smiled as the Screambreaker scowled. Lhosir were ferocious enough in battle, but wave a touch of supernatural under their noses and everything changed. 'At the least I was hoping it might give the Marroc some spirit.'

Corvin nodded slowly. 'It just might do that.'

'We'll take it away again after the Vathen are defeated. Let the Eyes of Time and the Fateguard have it back if they want it so much.' He bared his teeth. 'I'll take it to them myself.'

'So were One-Eye's stories true then? Does he know really where it is? I thought it went to the bottom of the sea and the Moontongue with it. A good place for both if you ask me.'

'It did.' Medrin laughed and shook his head. 'You know the story as well as anyone. Wouldn't surprise me if you'd even been there. Blood being thicker than water as it is.' He paused and waved a finger, revelling in the cloud of anger on Corvin's face. The Screambreaker looked ready to smash something. Then he let out a long breath.

'Tread carefully, Twelvefingers. I know the same as the rest of you. Moontongue stole it from the Fateguard on Brek.

Some Marroc paid him to do it and then they killed him. The Moontongue's men got to hear of it, caught them and sent them to the bottom. Drowned the lot, shield and all. Years later, One-Eye comes back with his stories that the shield has washed up on one of the western isles. So what more do *you* know?'

'I know that One-Eye was right. It's spent the last years in a monastery on Gavis.'

'One-Eye!' The Screambreaker snorted a laugh and shook his head, and for a moment all the tension between them was gone. 'I suppose you want me to get it for you?' There was an eager gleam in the Screambreaker's eye. Up against the monks of Luonatta, relishing it already. Medrin shook his head.

'You're the Nightmare of the North. The Widowmaker. I want you here where the Marroc can see you. I know you don't like all my ravens – I saw *that* look on your face from the moment you came in. Well, deal with Andhun your way then. However suits you. It'll probably go down better than mine. I'll get the shield myself.'

'And if the Vathen come while you're gone?'

'You'll stay in Andhun behind the walls and wait for me.' He could see how much the Screambreaker didn't like *that*, even more than being left behind in the first place. 'We'll need some Marroc legions to fight beside us when the time comes. Archers to counter their riders. You won't have them ready before I get back with the shield.'

The Screambreaker growled. 'Two thousand Lhosir broke ten times that many Marroc. We'll break the Vathen too.'

Medrin smiled. 'You can go now, Screambreaker. It's good to have you back.' He paused as a last thought crossed his mind. 'Gallow. What's he like these days?'

'He's cut his beard off, but he's still one of us.'

'When you go down you'll find Loudmouth still skulking in the yard, I expect. Tell him to go after Gallow and get him back here. If the whispers about him and Beyard Ironshoe were true, perhaps he'd like to finally see it. Make sure they both understand their prince commands it.'

He watched the Screambreaker go. *Gallow.* Of course he remembered. How could he not?

THE TEMPLE OF LUONATTA

THE TEMPLE
OF LUONATTA

17

AN EXCHANGE OF GIFTS

Gallow rode slowly out through the gates of Andhun. The dead Vathan heads watched him go while the bored Lhosir guards gave him sour looks. A Lhosir with no beard, dressed as a Marroc, riding a Vathan horse and leading four others. He must look strange. He felt a freedom though, unexpected and unsought, and also a sadness. A part of him wanted to stay. He'd tasted what it felt like to be among his own people again and now he yearned for them, for their strength and their simplicity. The Vathen were coming. The surge of battle, the fire inside, yes, he remembered all that, all buried and half forgotten, boxed away because he had a new life now where such things had no value, but not gone, and now he wanted it back; and he might have stayed if it hadn't been for all the dead Vathen and Marroc, gazing down at him with their blind empty eyes. Another week, maybe two, maybe three before the Vathan host came. Varyxhun could have waited that long. Right now he still didn't want to go back. For nine years Arda had been a good wife, strong-boned and strong-willed, not like the other Marroc. Now she'd betrayed him to his enemies. There was no forgiveness for that. Across the sea he would have killed them both, would have had no choice about it. Fenaric with a sword, Arda by cutting off her hair and strangling her with it.

He laughed at himself. Strangle her? The idea was absurd. He patted the Vathan horse he rode on the neck. 'Maybe I should stay, eh, horse?' There were a hundred and one reasons why he shouldn't strangle her, but they were all by the by really, since he'd open his own throat first. Love didn't have much place in a marriage, Marroc, Lhosir or any other, but sometimes it came anyway in the most unlikely places. A mutual desire that sustained, never expected and never sought, but there nonetheless.

Stupid doubts – *they* had no place in a Lhosir. And he still didn't know what to do about her, because there really was no forgiveness for what she'd done. That lecherous *nioingr* of a carter, now *he* needed to be punished. Killing him would be too much for the Marroc. Send him away and take his wagon? Arda would shout and beat her fists but she'd see that he was right, wouldn't she?

Wouldn't she?

No, she probably wouldn't.

'Gallow! Gallow Truesword!'

Maker-Devourer! He hadn't been paying attention to where he was going, just aimlessly following the way he'd come. And *Truesword*? No one except the Screambreaker had called him that for years. He stopped and looked back, and there was Tolvis Loudmouth, slowing to a trot. He looked angry.

'Well then, bare-beard. Seems you're not going off to Varyxhun after all. Seems I'm to bring you back to Prince Medrin. So turn your horse around again, eh, clean-skin.'

There were ways of asking a man to do a thing, and then there were ways of asking a man to break your face for you. Gallow turned his horse. His hand fell off the reins. 'But Loudmouth, if I'd wanted to see Medrin, I'd have stayed in Andhun and seen him, wouldn't I?'

Tolvis bared his teeth. 'Well I certainly shan't be going back to Andhun on my own to tell him you said that. Our prince commands us. Both of us.'

Gallow shrugged. 'Not my prince. I turned my back on him years ago.'

'And took off your wolf pelt and dressed up as a sheep, but the Screambreaker says you're still a wolf underneath that fleece.' Tolvis grinned. 'Me? I'm not so sure. But either way, Yurlak is king of the Marroc too nowadays, or had you forgotten? So Medrin *is* your prince after all, and I don't give a goose whether you like that or not, and he wants you back in Andhun, and so now that's where you're going.'

'If that's what he wants then he can come and tell me himself.'

'Another thing I won't be going back to tell him. Are you coming with me freely, sheep-lover, or do I have to carry you over my shoulder like some old woman?'

With careful, almost bored movements, Gallow leaned forward. He swung his leg over the saddle and jumped to the ground. 'I was wondering which road to take. Me and my horse were having a good long talk about it, whether Varyxhun was the right place to be heading, back when the road was pleasant and peaceful. Now there's a bad smell in the air that seems to have set my mind for me. Can't put my finger on it but I think I'd like to be on my way. Since you ask so kindly, I'm going to Varyxhun, Tolvis Loudmouth. You have anything to say about that, I'll happily put you right.'

'Oh ho! I'm definitely sure you said Andhun.' Tolvis dismounted and pulled his axe from his belt. He gave it a few practice swings. 'This looks like it'll be some fun, eh? Twelvefingers wasn't clear about how many pieces he wanted, but I'll try not to break anything. I know how fragile you sheep lovers are.'

'Varyxhun.' Gallow drew his sword and settled his shield. It felt strange to face down another Lhosir again after so many years. But comfortable.

Tolvis glanced at the sword and shook his head. 'I'm not so sure the old Screambreaker's right about you at all.'

Gallow swung his arms back and forth, loosening his shoulders. 'I use the axe for killing, Loudmouth. There's six Vathan corpses between here and Fedderhun can testify to that.' Now he gave the sword a few twirls. 'Mostly I use this for spanking my boys when they've been naughty. Mind you, they're only little. Shall we talk some more about kings and how little I care for them, or shall I spank you too?'

Tolvis let out a howl and ran at Gallow, shield first. Gallow met his charge, springing forward at the last moment before they collided. Both of them staggered away. Tolvis swung his axe at Gallow's head, the blade passing a few inches from his nose.

'You hit like my wife,' said Gallow. They circled each other now, half crouched and hidden behind their shields, eyes peering over the top.

'Yes, I've heard which one of you carries the axe in your house, Gallow Cripplecock.'

Tolvis danced closer and rained a flurry of blows on Gallow's shield, easily blocked. Gallow lunged once, poking Tolvis hard in the side. Tolvis's hauberk turned the point but Gallow saw him wince. 'Nasty bruise you'll have there.' They jumped apart. 'You can stop if it hurts too much. Take your time. Catch your breath if you need to.'

'Filthy Marroc!' Tolvis charged again, the way Lhosir often fought one another, trading shield blows until one of them was dazed enough for a swing of the axe to finish the fight. Gallow met him hard. The shock of the impact jolted his arm all the way to the shoulder and they stumbled apart. Gallow jumped right back at Tolvis, thumping shield against shield, pulled back and battered at him again. Tolvis took two steps back and now Gallow leaped once more, smashing the two of them together for a third time and pushing with all his strength, poking his sword over Tolvis's shield, stabbing at Loudmouth's face and driving him back. He gave one great heave and Tolvis staggered and almost lost his balance. For a moment his shield swung away from his body as he tried to catch himself. Gallow lunged again, a huge blow that caught Tolvis in the chest and knocked him down. He reversed his sword, ready to drive it down into Tolvis's face like a knife, and then stopped. The fire in his belly still burned but he didn't really want to kill this man.

'Fine,' he said. 'Andhun.' Varyxhun could wait. 'Was settling on staying to fight the Vathen anyway before you showed up. I make no promises when it comes to Medrin though.' He stabbed his sword back into its scabbard and offered Tolvis his hand. 'When I said you hit like my wife, I suppose I should tell you she's a giantess who fells trees with a flick of her fingers.'

Tolvis stayed where he was for a moment. The surprise on his face turned into a deep frown. He dropped his axe, took Gallow's hand and let Gallow haul him back to his feet. 'And when I said she carried your axe, I think I clearly meant she brings it for you when you go to fight your enemies.' He looked Gallow up and down. 'I may simply have been mistaken about you being filthy.'

'No, that was fair.' Gallow grinned. 'I've travelled a long way in these clothes. They *are* filthy.' He bent down and picked up Tolvis's axe and offered it back, haft first.

'Yours,' Tolvis wrinkled his nose. 'You won it fairly.' He was breathing hard, still bemused he was alive. Gallow looked at the axe. It was a decent piece, similar to his own and no small thing to give away.

'That's a fine axe and a fine gift then. I wish I had something that was its equal to give.' He pulled his own axe from its loop on his belt and slid Tolvis's in its place. Then he held out his own. 'Suppose I won't be needing this one any more. It's Marroc made but it has the blood of six Vathen on it.'

Tolvis stared at Gallow as if trying to read his mind. 'I can't take a gift from you, Truesword. I'd like to, but I can't.' He shook his head.

Gallow shrugged. 'I have enough things hanging off my belt. Anything more would be uncomfortable. You can carry it for me, if you prefer.'

Tolvis took a deep breath and puffed his cheeks. He took the axe. 'All right then.'

'Do you know what Medrin wants?'

'Not really. The Screambreaker said I should bring you back. Said something about there being something you needed to hear.' He spat. 'I know Medrin wants to go off looking for the Crimson Shield of Modris. Maybe it's something to do with that.'

Gallow laughed. 'Well now, if you'd said all that at the start, we'd be halfway back by now.'

'Wouldn't have been half as much fun though, now would it?' Tolvis laughed too, then shook his head and looked Gallow over. 'Gallow Truesword eh? I remember him. You I'm not so sure. Are you one of us or not?'

Gallow shrugged. 'I suppose I'm a bit of both.'

18

THE OTHER JONNIC

Some days it seemed that every other Marroc in Andhun was called Jonnic. The harbour was full of them. There was Angry Jonnic and Laughing Jonnic and Fat Jonnic and Thin Jonnic and about a dozen others. Now and then Grumpy Jonnic wished he'd been bald or red-headed or something else more obvious, but fate had endowed him with a dour demeanour and an unremarkable unkempt appearance, and so Grumpy Jonnic he was, like it or not. It was little consolation that he was right about how often things turned out worse than they looked. The Vathan horde drawing the forkbeards back from across the sea, there was a thing. He'd seen *that* coming clear as the sun, and now here they were. He did his best to avoid them but it wasn't always so easy.

'Well?'

Valaric sat across the table. He had more scars than Jonnic remembered, most of them on the inside. The men with him were the Marroc soldiers from Lostring Hill. Years ago they'd all fought the forkbeards together and lost. Jonnic reckoned you got a sixth sense for that sort of thing. They ought to have been friends, but something about them unsettled him. And then the Vathen had come.

He took a deep swig of ale and glared at the other two Jonnics beside Valaric, Angry and Silent. 'There's a lot of them. Two thousand or so and more coming every day. They're eating everything and drinking the place dry.' He spat on the floor. 'This lot are demon-whores, that's for sure. With the demon himself living in our whore of a duke's keep.'

'Turns out the Widowmaker didn't die at Lostring Hill after all, and never mind what—'

'You think that's news here?' Jonnic hawked up a gob of phlegm. 'You're getting slow, Valaric. The Widowmaker came through the gates this afternoon.'

The look Valaric gave him after that was odd. Shifty, maybe. Troubled. 'The Vathen are looking for him,' he said after a bit. 'I was wondering whether to help them, or whether that was a bad idea. What's this Medrin like?'

Jonnic spat again. 'Twelvefingers the demon-prince? Worst of the lot.' He looked around, nervous. You never knew who was listening. There were good Marroc, the ones like Valaric that you could trust. Then there were the bad Marroc, the ones who'd sell you out for a handful of pennies. Most of the men sitting and drinking in the riverside tavern were men he knew, but there were always a few strangers. He leaned forward. 'He's the one who's been hanging people up in the square. So fond of his bloody ravens you'd think he was married to one. Even his own kinsmen don't seem to like him that much but they still do what he says. Don't know if the Widowmaker's any better but he can't be any worse. Funny, him showing up. Even the demon-beards thought he'd died at Fedderhun. Been drinking toasts to the end of his damned soul all week, we have.'

Valaric twitched. 'Turns out he didn't die after all. How many men here you trust?'

'In Andhun?' Jonnic shook his head. 'Fifty, maybe. Don't know they'd take up arms against the Widowmaker though. Don't know that I would either.'

'You've seen what they're doing to us,' snarled Valaric. 'You happy with that?'

''Course I'm not bloody happy!' Jonnic growled right back at him. 'But what are you going to do with fifty swords, Valaric?'

'Make it two hundred.'

'And then what? Against two thousand forkbeards led by the Widowmaker?' He laughed. 'I don't mind swinging an axe for you, Valaric, but not when there's no point. You'll get us killed for nothing, and then this prick Twelvefingers, he'll decimate the city. He'll not baulk at murdering women and children, this one. You'll have the streets swimming red with his bloody ravens.'

'You get your men ready for the call, Jonnic, and then we'll see. There might be two thousand of them now but there won't be so many when the Vathen are done.'

Jonnic shook his head. 'They smashed the Vathen already, Valaric. You're too late.'

'No. I've seen their army and that was just the start.' Valaric got up. 'My money would be on the Vathen, if I had any. Doesn't really matter though, does it? Whoever wins, you don't suppose they're just going to wave and go home? That's not what they do. And this time it'll be worse, because if it's the forkbeards, we'll just let them shove sticks up our arses and then ask for more. Like we already do.'

Jonnic watched him go. *That's not what they do.* He was right about that. Valaric had had a family once. Wasn't the forkbeards that had killed them either. Just a winter that had been sharp and harsh, a wasting disease among the animals, and the whole village had simply frozen and starved to death, every last one of them. There were whispers of an Aulian shadewalker but Valaric blamed the demon-beards. If he hadn't been off fighting them, he'd have been in his home. He could have saved them or else died with them, one or the other.

Jonnic finished his drink and got up. When three forkbeards followed him out it didn't seem that strange, not with so many of them in the city these days. Not until he turned down an alley to the river and they still they followed him and then stopped to watch while he took a piss into the Isset. By then he knew he was going to die.

He turned. 'So what do you three ugly *nioingr* want then?'

They closed around him. All three had knives at their belts and Jonnic had nothing, so he lunged at the nearest, pushed him back and pulled out the man's knife for himself. The other two grabbed him as he did it, one from each side. He stabbed backwards with the knife and one of the forkbeards shouted and fell away. 'Maker-Devourer! He cut me!' The other pulled him hard, spinning him around, and head-butted him. Jonnic staggered. For a moment the night was filled with stars.

Arms tackled him from the side, lifting him up and throwing him down. He stabbed out with the knife again but this time they pinned his arm.

'Maker-Devourer! The little mare's killed me! Turn his face inside out!'

He caught sight of a flying boot in time to turn his face away. It smashed into the side of his head in an explosion of noise and light and pain. Someone stamped on his hand and he dropped the knife. He screamed as they broke his fingers. When he looked up he could see that one of the three demon-beards was clutching his side, blood seeping through his fingers. After that he lay curled in a ball while they kicked him and stamped on him and cursed. *Traitor! Bare-face! Nioingr! Feeble-finger! Mare!* Caught one last glimpse of the stars as one of the forkbeards lifted a lump of wood and brought it down, and then nothing until a shock of cold water roused him again.

They'd thrown him into the river. Into the Isset. He felt the pull of the water dragging him towards the sea, dragging him down and sucking him under.

And then the darkness again.

19

GIVEN TO THE RIVER

Tolvis and Gallow rode back to Andhun together. Gallow made sour faces at the burial pits and the Marroc hung up over the streets of their own city. Tolvis pursed his lips. 'We never used to do this,' he muttered. 'The Screambreaker would never have had it.'

Gallow snorted. There were ways of saying things without having to put them into words. The relief at having the Scream-breaker back was a solid thing among the few Lhosir he'd seen in Andhun, real enough that Gallow could almost have reached out and grabbed hold and shaken it. Maybe that was why he hadn't left Tolvis on the road.

The blood-streaked corpses looked down, mocking. *Stupid, coming back here.* Stupid, thinking he could make some difference to the Marroc. Stupid to have left his old life at all. He almost turned right back round again. *Go home*, the bodies said. *Put things right with Arda. Go home and shout and scream and then hold each other tight and forget about us.*

Tolvis sniffed and stretched his arms, cracking his shoulders. 'I'm in your debt, Truesword. Don't particularly want to be but here we are. Stuff Twelvefingers – the Marroc make good beer. You want ...' He chuckled and shook his head. 'What am I saying? You already know that. Those Vathan horses – Medrin will take them if he sees them. He's seized almost every horse in the city. Don't see why he'd make yours an exception.'

'You tell me that now?'

'Well, I didn't think I'd mention it when you had me flat on my back in the road, no. Didn't seem the time, if you see what I mean. You want Medrin to have them or not? Because if you don't then now's the time to say.'

'Do I have a choice?'

Tolvis roared with laughter. 'With the Vathen coming, I'd have have a hard time showing you a man who wouldn't take them off you. It's finding someone who's still here but who has the coin, that's the trick.' He jumped out of his saddle and curled a beckoning finger, pointing off the wide Gateharbour road and into a side street so narrow that Gallow had to dismount and lead his horses in a line and Maker-Devourer help anyone who wanted to come the other way. 'Benelvic the Brewer. We drank him dry, but he's got a few carts he uses to bring in beer from wherever he can get it. Twelvefingers tried to take his horses and Benelvic made like he was happy enough to give them up. Just wouldn't be any more beer, that was all, and so we told Twelvefingers where to stick it right there and then.' He laughed. 'Benelvic does favours for some of the other Marroc. Sort of thing that would have him hanging from a wheel over the street if Medrin ever knew. Some of us do, but we don't tell Medrin because we like our beer. We have an, ah ... *understanding*. So he owes me a favour or two.'

'That sounds very Marroc of you.'

Tolvis didn't rise to that. He pushed open a gate and led the way into a big yard filled with barrels, most of them empty. There was another gate on the other side, wide enough to take a cart. As Gallow led his horses into the space, Tolvis pushed him gently back again. 'Go on down to the river. There's a tavern at the bottom of the street. I'll meet you there.'

'Why?'

Tolvis kept pushing. There was a pained look on his face. 'Because you look like a Marroc, and Marroc don't have any money, and if he sees you and thinks you're not one of us, I won't get as much for them, that's why. Grow a beard, Gallow.' He closed the gate with Gallow on the other side, left to the sounds of the Isset rippling its way to the sea at the far end of the alley.

Benelvic turned out to be more than happy to have a handful of Vathan horses come his way for a fraction of their worth. Tolvis finished their business and sauntered down the alley towards the river, leading his own horse and with a nice fat purse on his belt, smiling to himself but also a little wary. He found Gallow quickly enough, not in the tavern like he was supposed to be but outside, standing on the river path over a dead Marroc, both of them soaking wet.

'Can't leave you alone, eh?' Tolvis put a hand on his shoulder. 'I was wondering where you'd gone. I suppose I should have warned you. There's Marroc here who see a Lhosir alone at night and don't think too much about the consequences of a quick knife in the dark.'

'Can you blame them?' Gallow sounded bitter.

'You hurt?'

'Me?' Truesword laughed, full of scorn. 'I just caught the end of it. Three of our brothers from over the sea. They beat him half to death and then threw him in the river. No idea why.'

Tolvis shrugged. 'Marroc say stupid things to get themselves killed every day.'

'*I'm* Marroc now.' Gallow spun to face him.

'No, you're not.'

They stood by the water for a while, watching the Marroc, but he didn't move. Drowned, by the looks of him when Tolvis knelt down to see. 'You hauled him out again, did you?' Stupid question. Who else? 'Why? Thought you could save him?'

'One of ours went away with a hole in him.' Gallow was staring down the path as if he had half a mind to go after the three Lhosir, whoever they were. Tolvis caught his arm and pulled him towards the warmth of the tavern.

'Come and share a cup or two with me before we go up to the castle, Gallow. Medrin won't notice. Best you know how things are just now. Leave this be. Not your business.'

'Then what *is* my business? Why did we come across the sea?'

'To kick the sheep and make them bleed and take their women and their gold and drink their beer, that's why! Maker-Devourer, maybe you *are* one of them after all.'

'I thought we came because we were better.' Gallow spoke softly.

'We were!' Tolvis put a hand on his shoulder, steering him away. 'We were better than them every time apart from Selleuk's

Bridge. But only because I wasn't well that day. Something I ate. If I'd been myself then it would have been a different story.' He rolled his eyes. 'Could have ended it all there and then, I reckon.'

Gallow spat. 'I should have kept on to Varyxhun. I don't belong in this war.'

'Don't belong in this war?' Tolvis shook his head and guided Gallow inside. 'Choice tavern this. Feel the air! Lhosir come here; Marroc come here. Both want the others gone. Good place for a fight later, if that's what you need, but I'd suggest you choose your side before you start laying about with those fists.' Tolvis tossed him the purse. 'For your horses. I sold them all. You didn't want to keep one, did you?'

Gallow weighed it in his hand and looked inside. He wrinkled his nose. 'Not really. No use for one in Varyxhun.'

'That's a lot of silver, that is. A good price in these times, I promise you.' Tolvis flicked some pennies at a Marroc, who ran away and came back a moment later with two foaming cups of beer.

'Mind you, I could have gotten twice this if I'd taken them with me.' Gallow tied the purse to a string and tucked it under his shirt. 'Ah well. Arda's not to know how many there were.'

'Arda your woman?'

Gallow nodded, although with a pause as though he somehow wasn't entirely sure. 'She looks after the money.'

Tolvis raised his cup and laughed. 'Don't they all. That should be enough to put a greedy smile on her face though.' He stopped. Gallow was staring over his shoulder through the open doorway at the riverside. When Tolvis looked, the drowned dead Marroc was hauling himself up off the dirt, not quite as drowned and dead as Tolvis had thought. He glanced back at Gallow but the big man made no move. Just watched, and so they watched together until the Marroc was gone. He didn't come inside. Tolvis shrugged and turned back. 'She's a Marroc then is she, your woman? She why you stayed?'

Gallow looked dour. 'With the Marroc, everything is coin.' He shook his head. 'That's one thing about them I'll never understand. There's a carter who comes through our village. Fenaric.' As he said the name a flash of something dark crossed his face. 'Sometimes he needs work done at the forge. I tell him he doesn't need to pay, that I can give him a list of things we need and he can bring them the next time he's passing through. Or else a keg of Fedderhun ale when the chance arises. But he never does. He smiles and nods and then he goes to see my wife and pays her his money anyway; and then when he comes through with a keg of ale or a new hammer for the forge, or whatever else we need, we pay it back to him. I ask Arda sometimes: if Fenaric came to us and he had no money and all he could offer were promises, would we send him away? She calls me a fool and says no, of course not, the carter is our friend. So I ask her are his promises worth more when he has no money? And if they aren't worth more, why are they not good enough when he has coins in his pocket? She tells me coins are better than promises, that coins can't be broken. But coins can be lost or stolen and the Marroc are as much people of their word as we are. I've lived among them for nine years but I don't think I'll ever understand their fascination with money.'

All the while he talked, Gallow stared at the table, at the floor, anywhere that was down. He held one hand pressed to his heart as if trying to keep something safe. Then he suddenly stood up. 'You know, I have half a mind to ask everyone here about that Marroc I pulled out of the river. Who he is. And why—'

Tolvis pushed Gallow gently back onto his stool and put his cup back in his hand. He raised his own. 'To the crazy Marroc. May they find the strength to defend their homes against the Vathen. Leave it, Gallow. You saved him, or maybe he would have lived anyway, but he's gone now, and, Marroc or Lhosir, no one here wants you to ask questions.' He steered the talk to the old days then, to the fights against the Marroc and the Screambreaker's campaigns. Turned out they'd both been at Vanhun and at Varyxhun and Andhun and half a dozen other places, even on the bridge together at Selleuk's Bridge. Then later Tolvis had gone back home like most of the other Lhosir when the fighting was done, and now he filled the evening with stories of all the other soldiers they'd known and what had happened to them. Grown fat on all the plunder they'd carried home and made lots of children, mostly. 'It's strange,' he said, 'to see this place again. It's not how I remember it. It was filthy back then and the Marroc were so terrified of us.'

'They're not now?'

'Not like they were. But then we never touched Andhun. They must have been waiting for the Screambreaker to turn his eyes on them for more than a year. They knew he'd come for them one day, sooner or later. And then Tane died out in the middle of nowhere and ...' He paused. 'What did happen at Varyxhun in the end? I heard all sorts at the time.'

'We found the castle empty, the gates open, the last of the Marroc huscarls already dead. They killed themselves rather than be taken.' As he spoke, Gallow touched a finger to his scar, to the small piece missing from his nose.

Tolvis shook his head and chuckled into his cup. 'That's so ... *Marroc*. No wonder they all looked so terrified when we got here at last. They must have thought we'd burn the place down around them.'

'It wouldn't have been the first time.'

'I remember all those stories about Varyxhun. The river flooding to wipe away anyone who attacked it and those other curses the Aulians left behind. How we laughed.'

'No curses. Just dead men.'

Tolvis stretched his neck and looked around the tavern. There were other Lhosir here but not so many Marroc tonight. Maybe they'd finally settled whose drinking place this was going to be. 'I always liked a good burning. Pretty stuff, fire. Twelvefingers would never hold with it though. Too much waste. Empty their houses and then burn them down, that's how it was at the start. Then the burnings stopped and we just emptied their houses. Now Twelvefingers acts like he wants to be some sort of king and we just empty their pockets instead. I suppose he *will* be king when old Yurlak goes, Maker-Devourer help us.' He looked Gallow up and down. His eyes narrowed. 'There's a lot of us are going to miss Yurlak. Some would say it's the Screambreaker who should follow him.'

Gallow met his eye. 'Do they say it to Medrin's face?'

Tolvis threw back his head and roared. 'Not unless they want to end up like those Marroc sheep strung up over the streets!'

'So who *do* they say it to, Loudmouth? I fought with the Screambreaker and so did you. He was never one to take cowards to his cause. Men spoke their minds freely in those days. Have things changed so much?'

Tolvis flushed. His brow furrowed and then he paused and looked confused for a moment. 'Strong words, Gallow Truesword. Be careful with them.'

'I ask if things across the sea have changed, Tolvis Loudmouth.' Gallow shrugged. 'The Screambreaker judged men by their hearts. Marroc or Lhosir, it never mattered. If you showed courage, he kept you. If you were weak then he threw you away. He was the finest we had, and that's why we followed him. Strong as an ox and sure as the sea, but the men around him weren't ever afraid to tell him when he was wrong. If men are scared to speak before their prince, the Screambreaker will have naught but scorn for them.'

'Would *you* tell the Screambreaker he was wrong?'

'I did so on the road to Andhun, and more than once. I don't say he listened, mind!'

They both laughed. Tolvis wiped the spit from his mouth. 'Did he ever go any way but his own?'

By the time they left the tavern, night had long settled over the streets. Clouds scudded across the moon like ghosts. A fresh wind blew in from the sea, warning of storms on the way. Tolvis was too drunk to even walk straight and Gallow was little better. They staggered up the steepness of the hill, holding on to one another, leaning on Tolvis's horse, both of them still dressed in their mail and carrying their shields and with their swords and axes at their belts. Here and there they had to walk up wide steps, or detour around sheer sides of rock that jutted out from among the houses.

'Need to keep your ears open down there,' muttered Tolvis. 'Docks aren't far. Marroc there aren't like the ones up near the castle. Got more balls.' He turned and roared into the night. 'More balls, I said! Eh?' He looked back at Gallow and laughed. 'Don't like our sort down in the docks, not at all.'

Gallow picked his way up the next flight of steps, weaving precariously from side to side. 'After Yurlak and the Screambreaker left, those of us who stayed started to show up in the river. Every day one or two more.' Gallow shook his head. 'Andhun and the Isset probably killed more of us than Tane did when we took Sithhun from him.'

'So what was it made you stay, eh? Why didn't you come home? Your Marroc woman?' Tolvis peered at him. 'No? Something else then.'

Gallow grunted. 'Is every bastard Lhosir I ever meet going to ask the same thing? Thought Yurlak was going to die. Didn't like Medrin. That's why. Good enough?'

Tolvis hooted with laughter. 'No one *likes* Twelvefingers.'

'Then perhaps I didn't like him more than the rest of you.' He stopped. 'He wants to go off chasing after the Crimson Shield, does he? You remember we had it once? It was in the Temple of Fates in Nardjas for a few days. Someone tried to steal it, or that was the story that went round.'

Tolvis nodded. 'I was with the Screambreaker, killing Marroc, but we heard eventually, yes. Don't remember the thief's name. Bard or something. I know the Moontongue did the job not long after. Always supposed they were together, somehow.'

'Beyard, not Bard. And Medrin was the king's son. He should have said why Beyard was really there. But he didn't, and Beyard died. He was my friend.'

Gallow fell quiet and they walked in silence up the last winding road to the castle. Tolvis led the way to the keep. The doors were open, warm stale air wafting out between them. A pair of Lhosir soldiers waved them inside, yawning.

'Who's the Marroc, Loudmouth?' one of them called. Tolvis ignored him.

'For the love of the Maker-Devourer, grow your beard, Gallow. Cut it off again when the Vathen are gone if you must go back to living with the sheep.' He took them into what had been the Marroc duke's feasting hall before Medrin had come and the Lhosir had filled it up with furs and straw and snores. He sat against a wall in the gloom, pulling off his mail, his head already spinning, his eyes starting to close. 'Sleep where you can,' he mumbled. 'Like being back home. One big longhouse.' He lay down on the first piece of floor he could find, a smile on his face. 'Why did we come across the sea, Truesword? Truly? Marroc beer, that's why. It's certainly why I came back.'

20

THE WEEPING GOD

Gallow lay down. Loudmouth was right: the smell of the air and the sounds of men breathing brought old memories out of hiding. This was how it was when he'd been a child out in a homestead somewhere on the coast. One longhouse and a dozen barns and sheds, and at night they'd all slept together. He'd never counted, but there must have been nearly thirty of them. One big extended family, and in winter they'd have the animals inside as well for their warmth. The Marroc did that too, but the Marroc didn't have winters like the ones Gallow remembered. He closed his eyes. The memories were strong, the smell of straw, of sheep and horses. He could see his father again, as he'd been when Gallow was young, before they'd gone to Nardjas. Yurlak had wanted smiths to hammer the swords and armour for his raids against the Marroc. It had seemed to Gallow that the Lhosir had always been at war, but for a moment he wasn't so sure.

His thoughts lost their focus. They wandered, drifting past the edges of the Herenian Marches and he found himself standing in a great stone hall, far larger than the one in Andhun where he slept. The hall was filled with soldiers, shouting, waving swords and burning brands, but their cries seemed small and helpless, and when he looked to see what it was that made their blood burn so fiercely, he saw another warrior had entered the hall, striding through great gates streaming with sunlight. The newcomer was a giant, head and shoulders above the rest. He strode through them, cleaving left and right with the great rust-red sword he carried. His mail dripped with the blood of those he slew. He carried no shield and yet no blade touched him, and where the red sword swung, shields and mail split and tore apart. He walked and slew with deadly purpose, yet slowly and sorrowfully too, and when the last of the warriors fell to his sword he lifted his helm and surveyed the bodies. Gallow knew him, for the giant's eyes wept tears of blood. He was the Weeping God, and the sword he carried was the blade the Marroc called Solace, the Vathen called the Comforter, and the Aulians had always named the Edge of Sorrows.

Gallow saw that the giant wasn't alone. Beside him was a boy clothed in a golden shift. Diaran the Lifegiver. The boy-god came to stand beside Gallow instead, unafraid as the giant stepped slowly forward.

I am sorry, the Weeping God seemed to say. *I am sorry but there is no other way. All life ends in slaughter. I see it always. Let it end.* He lifted his sword to strike the boy-god down. Gallow drew his own, but in his hand all he found was a sapling branch.

The boy-god beside him looked up and Gallow saw he was Tathic, his own son.

Don't be afraid. But how could he not be? He launched himself at the giant but the Weeping God swatted him aside. In his dreams Gallow watched, broken-boned and helpless, as the old-blood blade of Solace swept down, but the blow didn't land. At the last moment another god stood beside the boy, Modris the Protector with his Crimson Shield, and his shield caught the Edge of Sorrows and turned it away. The old story, as it had always been.

21

THE LEGION OF
THE CRIMSON SHIELD

On the next high tide two Lhosir ships eased their way out of Andhun harbour through the many that had come from across the sea and the more that were still coming with band after band of raucous Lhosir eager to fight the Vathen. Medrin had taken only a few dozen warriors in each ship, the rest left with the Screambreaker in case the Vathen marched before Medrin returned with his precious shield. The monastery where the shield was kept wasn't guarded by an army, just a few crazy monks.

Medrin captained his own ship, filled with young Lhosir who'd been children when Gallow had crossed the sea. Medrin's men they called themselves, young and full of vinegar and so desperate for a fight to show their strength Gallow wondered how many would survive. The prince had chosen them and they'd sworn themselves to him as his own Fateguard, the Legion of the Crimson Shield, with their shields painted red. Gallow's ship was much the same. He looked at the men around him and found few faces he knew. The old soldiers, the ones who'd fought with the Screambreaker that last time round, they'd all stayed in Andhun. These were more of Medrin's men, all except for Tolvis and their captain, Jyrdas One-Eye, who'd been the one to find the shield in the first place. The young ones had an air to them, an arrogance. They looked at Gallow askance, wondering at his lack of a beard, their eyes filled with a cold disdain even as they pushed the ships into the water and set Andhun behind them. Gallow watched it diminishing, the two hills shrinking away, the castle on top of the taller, the sharp valley of the Isset between them and the line of Teenar's Bridge slanting over it. Most Lhosir thought the bridge had been built by the Aulians but Gallow knew better.

The Aulians had never come this far. The Marroc, when they were left to get on with things, were good at building. The huge trees that made the bridge had come from Varyxhun less than a hundred years ago, floated down on the river. Maybe the library the Aulians had left behind there had told the Marroc how to do it, but the bridge was Marroc-made.

'Gallow, is it?' Jyrdas loomed over him as he pulled at the oar. Jyrdas was a hand taller than even he was, barrel-chested and, from the grey streaks through his beard, a good ten years older. His hands were scarred and his face looked as though it had been clawed by some beast long ago. A scar ran across one eye, which was now milky white. The two braids of his beard were long and there were blades woven into the ends. Gallow nodded.

'Jyrdas One-Eye. I remember you.' Someone like Jyrdas, once you saw him, you were hardly likely to forget.

Jyrdas spat on the deck. 'Well, I don't remember you. You Marroc all look the same to me.'

Beside Gallow, Tolvis looked up. 'He's one of us, Jyrdas. Gallow. Gallow Truesword.' He nudged Gallow. 'Jyrdas is rolling in Twelvefingers' favour right now on account of accidentally stumbling into some Marroc plot or other while he was bashing heads for the fun of it.'

'Huh.' Jyrdas laughed. 'You've got two eyes to my one, Loudmouth, but I say my one works better. I know a sheep when I see one. Gallow Truesword? *Him* I remember. *You* I'm not so sure.'

Tolvis shrugged and turned back to Gallow as Jyrdas left. 'See? Please the Maker-Devourer, Truesword. Grow your beard.'

They rowed hard, pushing against the wind, which kept everyone busy for a while, and then One-Eye held up a finger to test the air and scowled and waited a while longer than he really needed to before he called in the oars and raised his sails. As the wind caught them and Andhun drifted into a haze on the horizon, Gallow felt a hollowness inside him. He wandered to the stern, watching the land fade, and touched the locket around his neck.

'I will come back,' he whispered to the wind. 'On my word. On my life. Tell her that.'

'Missing the stink of your city already, Marroc?' A Lhosir

whose name he didn't even know shoved into him. 'What's a sheep doing here, eh?'

Gallow couldn't pull his eyes off the horizon. 'You've chosen a bad time, friend. Go away.'

'Marroc *nioingr.*'

A savage fury stabbed him. At the word, yes, but more at being pulled away, at the shattering of his thoughts of home. He spun round and shoved the young Lhosir away and then looked him up and down. Painfully young, an untried blade full of bile and piss like most of the rest of them, but there wasn't really any going back from this. '*Nioingr?* Do any of you even understand what that means any more? Eat your words, boy, before I cut your beard and shove it down your throat.'

'Kyorgan!' One-Eye had spotted them. There was plenty enough warning in his voice, but the young Lhosir chose not to hear.

'You can try, *nioingr.*' Kyorgan snarled and laughed, but he glanced around too, looking for allies, checking to see who was with him and who wasn't. The other Lhosir had quietly stopped what they were doing. They'd watch but they all knew better than to intervene. Gallow felt sorry for him. He was barely a man. 'Kyorgan of Beltim,' he said loudly, as though it mattered. He looked around again. 'I've killed—'

Gallow split his skull with Tolvis's axe. Kyorgan stood looking stupid for a moment, then realised he was dead and fell over. Gallow looked down at him. Half the other Lhosir hadn't even seen him move. 'You've killed a few sheep in Andhun, is that it? Butchered a few who gave you sour looks in the street?' He shrugged and pulled his axe out of Kyorgan's head, then looked at Tolvis. 'Nice edge you put on that. Sorry if I've blunted it.'

Tolvis shrugged. 'A few scrapes with a whetstone and you'll have it back as good as ever. Keeps well that one.' He didn't even look at Kyorgan. Gallow took his time to look at the rest of the crew, to meet their eyes one after another. At least they didn't look away, but he knew now which ones were Kyorgan's friends. One in particular. When Gallow stared at him, he stared back. He had that blood feud look on his face. The rest ... most of them just looked shocked. As they should.

And then Jyrdas was standing next to Kyorgan's friend, bending down and whispering loudly in his ear. 'If you say anything, Latti Draketongue, if you even say a word, you'll answer to me.'

'I'll say—'

Jyrdas jabbed him in the face with the haft of his axe and cracked his jaw. He glared at Gallow. 'I'll be thinking I'm on a whole bloody ship full of *nioingr* soon. Waste of a good helmet that, bare-skin, and this is *my* ship and so you can clean up that bloody mess you made. Strip his stuff and hang him out. We'll burn him when we hit land. I'll even let Latti speak him out if he can make his mouth work with his head instead of his balls by then. And that's the end of it. The rest of you can watch your manners and save it for the Luonattans. All of you. Even you, Loudmouth.' He turned away, muttering to himself.

In the end Kyorgan started to stink before they reached land and so they sank him into the sea, offering him up to the Maker-Devourer. He'd died a good death, after all, cut down in battle. The Maker-Devourer didn't care if you were stupid. If anything, Gallow thought, he preferred his soldiers that way. So he watched Kyorgan sink, dressed up in his mail and with his sword and his shield tied into his hands, and felt nothing very much at all about what he'd done. Latti's jaw was swollen up so bad he could barely say a word that anyone else could make any sense of, so One-Eye spoke Kyorgan out before they dropped him in the water. Recited his deeds, what he was known for, good and bad. Not that it added up to much. Years of living with the Marroc made Gallow feel a bit sorry for him by the end. But only a bit.

'Waste of good steel and a good shield,' muttered Tolvis. 'At least it made him sink quick. Did you have to kill him?'

Gallow looked out across the sea. The other ship had stopped to watch and Gallow thought he caught Medrin staring at him from across the water. He imagined a wry smile on the prince's face. As yet Twelvefingers had managed to avoid him, or else the fates had kept them apart. Probably for the best. 'Won't say I didn't want to. But if it wasn't him then it would have been one of the others, sooner or later. Best to get it over with quick, I thought.'

Tolvis shook his head. 'Grow your beard, Truesword.'

'What if I don't want to?'

'Then go back and be with your sheep.'

Gallow laughed. 'Remind me, Loudmouth, who it was who dragged me back to Andhun in the first place.'

One-Eye, it turned out, had been to Gavis a good few times and knew where there were beaches for landing. As they sliced through the surf, the monastery was visible in the distance. It sat on the top of a rauk, a pillar of rock cut off from the land by the sea and surrounded by crashing waves. The Lhosir were still drawing their ships up onto the shore when the first warning beacon lit up, perhaps only a mile away.

'Bollocks!' Jyrdas threw a stone across the beach as hard as he could in the direction of the smoke.

'Thought you'd have been glad,' said Tolvis. 'You'll have a fight now.'

'No, I won't. Problem wasn't ever going to be the killing. It's the getting inside in the first place. They'll all run back behind their walls and close the gates and that'll be that. We can stay outside and throw stones and call them cowards all we like, they won't come out. There's a bridge, but you won't like it when you see it.'

'We'll build a ram and smash the doors in.'

Jyrdas cocked his head in scorn. 'Been here before have you, Loudmouth? You do that. See how far it gets you.'

They left a party to watch the boats, Latti and a few others. That was Jyrdas keeping the two of them apart, and Gallow might have thanked him only One-Eye would probably have spat in his face.

'This would never have happened with the Screambreaker.' Tolvis ran with Gallow as they left. 'Would the Screambreaker need some old relic of a shield to beat the Vathen? No. He'd just go up and thump them and be done with it.'

'He already tried that once.'

Tolvis rolled his eyes in exasperation. 'Well, then maybe Twelvefingers has a point, eh? Maybe he's not stupid after all.'

Gallow looked away. 'I never said he was stupid.'

They ran at a steady pace along the coast towards the monastery, up the cliff paths and along their tops. For much of the time the headland was lost behind the ups and downs and the thick heathers that grew beside the sea. In the final cove the Lhosir reached a village in time to see the last stragglers desperately running ahead, carrying chickens and chasing pigs. Medrin let out a cry and raced after them, through the abandoned houses and on. As he closed, the last islander turned. He wasn't even armed but he threw himself at Medrin, crashing the two of them back into the others. He came up fighting, swinging his fist and landing a good blow before someone spitted him on the end of a sword and hurled him back down the path. Jyrdas took the lead and promptly took a stone to his face, splitting his cheek just beneath his helmet.

'Sheep buggerers!' he roared. 'I was only going to eat your women and rape your men until you did *that*!' The next man tried to break from the path into the heather and went down with a spear in his back. 'Fall on your knees and we'll let you live! A bit.' A pig came charging down the path into the middle of them, squealing in terror. Jyrdas brought his axe down on the back of its neck and kicked it into the heather. 'Roast hog tonight!'

They passed blankets, pots, pans, loaves of bread, squawking chickens, all thrown aside in desperation. But when Gallow ran past a small squalling bundle, he stopped. A Lhosir woman would have turned and fought them to the death for her children. Arda too.

He reached into the heather. The baby had been put there with hurried care, perhaps in the hope that the Lhosir wouldn't see; perhaps in the hope that it would somehow still be there and still be alive when the Lhosir were gone. He picked it up and unwrapped it. A girl. That made it easier. He wrapped her up again and tucked her under his arm and followed the others, past three more bodies, and then the path flattened out and widened into a field of long grass. He could see the monastery again now. Its walls weren't particularly high or thick or strong, but the twenty-odd feet of empty air that separated the rauk from the rest of the island cliffs might as well have been a steel curtain. The bridge, Gallow saw now, curved and then curved back, narrow enough that a horse would have trouble crossing it. A clever design. The gates were black and bound with iron

– still open, but a man who tried to run at them risked falling over the edge and a ram would be almost impossible.

The gates closed as the Lhosir reached the bridge. Up on the walls the islanders jeered and hooted. The Lhosir stood and laughed and cursed back. They had a few men from the village, three or four run down in the chase but not killed yet. Medrin would have them beheaded one by one in sight of the walls, daring the islanders to come out and stop him. When that didn't work they'd put the heads on spikes. Or maybe he'd make some more blood ravens. Gallow winced at the thought. He pushed past Jyrdas and Medrin and walked onto the bridge. If the islanders had had bows then they'd have used them by now; still, they surely had javelins and stones, so as he crossed he held the baby up high. When he reached the gates, he put the child down. By now both the Lhosir and the islanders had fallen silent. He looked up at the men on the walls.

'Take her back!' he shouted to them. 'The Lhosir don't make war on children.' He walked back across the bridge, daring them to try and spear him.

When he got back, Medrin slapped him on the shoulder. 'Vicious, Gallow. I didn't think you had it in you.' They were the first words the prince had spoken to him.

'It's a child, Medrin,' Gallow said. 'Let them take it in.'

'It is, isn't it? And likely as not with the mother inside.' Medrin laughed. 'Gorrin, Durlak, come with me. Bring your hunting bows and show me a place where you'll see through the door when they open it. Gorrin, you shoot the first man you see. Durlak, you shoot the next.' Medrin turned to the rest of his men and raised his voice so they'd all hear. 'You all know how it is. If they were men then they'd come out and face us, sword and axe. A man who hides behind a wall and throws spears at you, he's a man full of fear and not a man at all. The Maker-Devourer spits on them. They deserve any death they get. Don't think of these as men, think of them as sheep.' He grinned at Gallow then turned to the others again. 'Ferron, you've got fast legs. When Gorrin lets fly, you head the charge.' His eyes flicked back to Gallow. 'Very nice indeed.'

Gallow spat at his feet.

22

ENEMY AT THE GATES

The child screamed for hours but the gate didn't open. Eventually the cries fell silent. Gallow had no way of knowing if the girl had simply fallen asleep or if she was dead. The wind wasn't that cold, though, so probably not dead, not yet. He hoped.

Late in the afternoon Medrin brought the islander men he'd caught up to the end of the bridge. He slit their throats one by one and held them up by their hair until they stopped jittering and jiggling and the blood turned from a river to a trickle. After that he had Horsan chop off their heads with his big axe. Jyrdas took each one by the hair and had a go at hurling them over the monastery walls. The first two bounced off the cliffs and down into the sea. The third one made it over. The Lhosir gave a cheer. Medrin walked out onto the bridge. The islanders watched him.

'I only want one thing!' he shouted up at them. 'That's all. It's not even yours. The Crimson Shield. I know it's here. Give it to me and I'll go.' He pointed to the baby at the gates. She was crying again. 'You can just take her back.' Now his arm swept towards the cove and the village they'd passed. 'And that. Your homes. Why should I burn your homes when I have what I want? Give me the shield and no one else need die.' He smiled. 'These monks who shelter you might not care about any of those things, but ask them: will they come out and build back your houses for you after we're gone? Will they make the tools you've lost? Will they replace the animals you need to live? You had lives. Simple, peaceful lives. Why should these mad fools take those away from you for some old shield? Does it help you? Does it catch fish for you? Does it grow your crops? Does it feed you and keep your children safe? No. It's brought us, and after us it will bring others. Give me the Crimson Shield and we'll go. Or open the gates to us, if these monks will not. Let us fight it out between us. If we die, so be it. If we do not, we'll take the shield and be gone. But all the time we're out here, we have nothing better to do than make fires from your homes and feast upon your animals. What's this shield to you? And as for you, soldiers of Luonatta – can you call yourselves soldiers? Are we so many? I'd heard you were fierce! Face us then, for we are not afraid of you!'

Silence met him. Medrin stood on the bridge, alone in the failing light and the quiet. The waves below hissed and splashed over the broken rocks at the foot of the cliffs. The tide was nearly out. Slabs of stone caked in barnacles and seaweed filled the space between the shore and the rauk. When no answer came, Medrin turned back. He surely couldn't be surprised, Gallow thought. Not after what he'd done to their men.

'The babe,' he said. 'When night falls they'll come for the babe and then we'll be inside. Keep your mail on and your eyes open.'

Which made for a lot of grumbling after Medrin went back to where Gorrin and Durlak were out on the cliff with their bows. Gallow dozed, and the moon was up high when Jyrdas nudged him. 'Very quiet and still now, lad,' he hissed. He nudged Tolvis too. Others were crouched on their haunches, staring at the monastery. 'They've opened the gate a crack and now they're waiting to see if we move. But we don't. Not until Medrin says.' He gave Gallow a hard look with his one eye. 'What is it between the two of you?'

'Our business, that's what. Old business.'

'Best forgotten then.' Jyrdas's good eye gleamed. 'If any of you think you can creep up closer without anyone noticing then go right ahead. But if they see you and slam the door, I'll throw you off the cliff and then come down to stamp on the bits.'

No one moved. Gallow watched the monastery gates. A crack of orange light from the fire inside split the door. As he waited, it slowly grew wider.

'Should have crept someone out on the bridge to cling on under it,' muttered Jyrdas.

'Rather you than me,' said Tolvis.

'Not up to it?'

'Do I have eight arms and legs? Or is there something else about me that makes you think I can hang upside down like a spider as the mood takes me?'

For a moment the crack went dark as someone stepped across the light. One of the islanders had come out onto the bridge. Jyrdas tensed. It had to be now.

'Go!' screamed a voice from off in the dark. The shape on the bridge bucked and stumbled, but didn't fall. Gallow was up on his feet, running. Tolvis and Jyrdas and Ferron and a dozen others charged beside him. The orange light darkened again.

'Take him now! While he's in the door!'

Another arrow flew. This time the figure fell. Gorrin and Durlak had shot perfectly. Whoever had come out for the babe, they'd brought him down between the two gates and Ferron was already on the bridge.

Shouts went up from the wall. A javelin flew square into Ferron's chest. He fell forward, skidded and tumbled off the edge of the bridge with a scream and a splash. 'On the walls!' Gallow lifted his shield, covering himself as best he could. Jyrdas reached the gates and shoved his sword through the gap; then suddenly the gates burst open and Jyrdas flew back. He stumbled and fell and rolled and caught himself just before he went over the edge, but the fall saved him. A volley of javelins fizzed through the air. One hit Gallow's shield hard enough to spin him round. Clevis took another in the throat, hard enough to lift him off his feet and dump him off the bridge. Another Lhosir screamed and fell – Gallow didn't see who. Through the gates the javelin throwers dropped to their knees and there were more right behind them.

'Shields!' Half the Lhosir must have roared it all at once. Gallow dropped to a crouch. He was halfway across the bridge, in the open and with nowhere to run. Most of the others had done the same and this time the javelins flew over his head.

'On!' Medrin again, but now the islanders had pulled their fallen man in and the gates slammed closed.

'You've got axes!' screamed Medrin. 'Chop it down.'

Jyrdas was the first there again. He swung hard and the gates shuddered. Gallow saw movement on the walls above. 'Jyrdas! The sky!'

One-Eye dived sideways and away from the gate just in time as buckets of hot pitch rained down. The air stank of it. Medrin waved his sword. 'Smash it down! Smash it down!' He had Gorrin and Durlak with him. Gorrin ran past Gallow. He had his bow and shot up at the wall. There was a scream.

'Archer square!' shouted Tolvis. He crouched down on one side of Gorrin with his shield covering both of them. Gallow crouched on the other side. Two more quickly took up position behind them. For the men on the walls, all there was to see were four round shields with a small hole in the middle; from that hole Gorrin would pick them off one by one. Gallow had used the tactic before once or twice, when he'd had no other option, and it worked well enough when the enemy on the walls had Marroc hunting bows. Less well when they had crossbows or something as heavy as a Vathan javelot. Forming it twenty feet away from the walls, though, that was madness and desperation.

Jyrdas and two others were back to hewing at the gate with their axes. Jyrdas swore as he slipped and fell on the hot pitch. Gorrin loosed again. Another scream, but then two islanders appeared at the top of the walls, easy enough to see this time because of the torches they carried.

'Fire!' roared Medrin. 'Jyrdas! Fire!'

For the second time Jyrdas jumped out of the way. Both torches came down. For a moment they simply lay on the blackened stone, burning, and then something else came over the wall, a pot of hot fish-oil probably, and shattered between them, and the bridge in front of the gate erupted in flames. Jyrdas ran, another flailing silhouette beside him, flames rising off his back, straight at Gallow. There was nowhere for him to go – the bridge was already too narrow for the arrow square – but Jyrdas didn't stop. Gallow braced himself as the huge Lhosir, bellowing and howling, jumped straight onto his shield, onto the next and over the top of them. The other Lhosir followed the same way, knocking Gallow sideways so he almost fell off the bridge. His shield waved wildly as he fought to catch himself.

A javelin flew straight into the middle of them. It hit Gorrin and the archer let out a roar and cursed loud enough to shake the walls down.

'Back!' shouted Gallow. Picking men off the walls was pointless with the gates wrapped in flames and so they ran and limped off the bridge, out of range of the javelins, past Jyrdas rolling around in the grass to put out the last of the fire on his back, and nursed their wounds. Four men lost. Gorrin's mail had saved him from that last javelin but he had a broken arm which made him useless as an archer. Jyrdas's injuries seemed to be no more than a stink of burned pitch.

'Up up up!' Medrin was shouting at them. 'The fools have set fire to their own gates! Get down to the village! Down the path! Come on, you dogs, get on your feet. Anything that will burn. Bring it up and fire the gates!'

The Lhosir pulled themselves back to their feet and started down the path to the cove, full of angry mutterings as they ran. Gallow found himself kicking in doors, tearing down piles of thatch, anything that would burn, and then as soon as he had an armful, running back up to the top. They took it in turns to run out onto the bridge, shields up, dodging the stones and javelins as best they could to throw armfuls of straw and sticks. Later they stood at the far end, running up and throwing pieces of wood across the gap and then running back again. They kept the fire going for an hour before the islanders came up to the walls with buckets of seawater and tipped them over the flames. When the fire was out, the gate was still there. Jyrdas ran across and chopped at it but it was as solid as ever. With that, the Lhosir turned their backs in disgust and went to their furs and their blankets, too exhausted now to listen to Medrin's pacing and cursing.

23

SARVIC

Sarvic watched from the darkness of the alley in Andhun as the two Lhosir rolled up Castle Hill. They were so drunk they could barely stand and they passed Sarvic's hiding place without the first idea he was there. Sarvic kissed his knife.

'Forkbeard bastards.'

He slipped out behind them, wrapped an arm around the first one's face and ran the knife across his neck. Blood fountained over the street and over the second forkbeard too, and by the time he'd turned to see what was happening, Sarvic's knife was buried in his belly. Sarvic yanked it free again. The Lhosir looked down and the knife came up into his face and straight into his open mouth. He gagged and staggered. Sarvic jerked the knife back and tried again.

'Hoy!'

He'd been seen. He took one last slash at the stumbling drunkard, who was too deep in his cups to notice he was dead yet, and bolted down the hill.

'Hey! Filthy Marroc! Murdering sheep!' Another forkbeard was coming after him at full pelt, sober and armed this one, one of the demon-prince's guards. Sarvic dropped the knife. Easier to run with empty hands. He looked up. Couldn't help it, because this was where they hung the Marroc they murdered. Men – sometimes women – who'd said the wrong thing, or who were in the wrong place. The forkbeards ripped open their backs and snapped their ribs and pulled out their lungs and hung them on wheels from gibbets over the street, and for that the forkbeards deserved to die, all of them.

Ahead four more burst out of a tavern. The Grey Man. They were drunk and had two giggling Marroc women with them

– giggling, but their eyes were fearful and with good reason. Chosen by a forkbeard. Give them what they want, because if you don't they'll take it anyway and hang you from a gibbet afterwards; but if you do, you might just get a knife from a Marroc like Sarvic for your pains.

Whores and bastards. He raced towards them; the forkbeards looked up and saw the guard and heard his shouts and suddenly forgot about their women. They fanned out across the road and ran at him. Sarvic skidded sideways and dived into Leatherbottle Lane, narrow and lightless – maybe he could lose them here. With luck the Marroc women had had the sense to slip away, but the Grey Man? Tomorrow it could burn right down. The Marroc in there were no Marroc at all. Men who sold their own kind to these animals, and for gold the forkbeards had stolen from their own pockets in the first place.

He had five of them after him now, all shouting their lungs out and only a matter of time before another one showed up in front of him. Damn but they were fast. Even the one in mail was keeping up and showed no sign of tiring. For the first time since he'd turned and run, he started to wonder whether he'd really get away this time.

Marroc are good at running. That's what the forkbeards always said. *Good at running away. It's all they do.* A surge of anger pushed him faster. But even if he didn't pelt right into another one, there'd be a Marroc who'd sell him to them.

Ahead someone quickly got off the street at the sight of him, to skulk in an alley until the forkbeards were safely gone. That was how it was. What he really needed now were some Marroc with the spine to stand with him. Stand up to the bastards. He turned hard, crashed into a wall and dived into the same alley as the Marroc who'd skittered away. The alley was empty now, but he was only three paces into the darkness when an arm shot out of a doorway and grabbed him, pulling him into a tight space. A hand went over his mouth. 'Stay very, very quiet. And still.'

Sarvic froze. The forkbeards poured into the alley a moment later and ran straight past where he stood invisible in the darkness. A moment later and they vanished out into Sailmaker's Row at the far end.

'Move! Right now! Before they come back.' The arm around his face let go and pushed him out into the alley and back into Leatherbottle Lane, back the way he'd come.

'Valaric?'

'Yes, Valaric, you bloody idiot. Now shut your hole and move!' They ran back up Leatherbottle Lane and down another alley until Valaric stopped at a door and banged on it, three times and then another two. When it opened, the air inside smelled of food and beer, and a hum of loud voices and laughter crept through the walls. Another Marroc hurried them into the gloom of a kitchen, face lost in the shadows, but Sarvic knew him from how he moved. Silent Jonnic from the Crackmarsh.

The sound of voices rose and fell as a door opened and closed. Valaric looked Sarvic up and down. 'Squirrels' balls, but you're a dim one.'

'Valaric?' Obviously, but he couldn't think of anything else to say. He hadn't seen Valaric since they'd reached Andhun. 'I thought you were going home. Back to your family.'

Valaric pushed him away. 'Dumb Marroc. This *is* my family. Look at you!' He shook his head. 'Been watching you. A Marroc running about the streets with forkbeard blood all over him. How long did you think you were going to last?' His nose wrinkled in disdain. 'Where's your knife, Marroc? Drop it like you dropped your spear and your shield when the Vathen came over Lostring Hill?'

'I was—'

'Took a forkbeard to keep your blood on the right side of your skin back then. You remember that? How's that sit for you?'

Yes, he remembered right enough. He squared up to Valaric. '*Someone* has to do something. I see people hung up for the crows all over Castle Hill and Varyxhun Square. Mean nothing to you, does it? Might as well grow a forkbeard of your own then.'

Valaric hit him. Sarvic crashed into the wall, sending pots and pans flying as Valaric came after him, grabbing him by the shirt. 'And every time some knife-in-the-dark like you slits a throat, how many more hearts do you think the demon-prince tears out? I should turn you in. If he hasn't got you up on a gibbet by midday tomorrow, he'll take ten more of us. Doesn't bother *him* who they are. Your life to save ten? Yes, I *should* turn you in.' With a heavy sigh, Valaric let him go. 'You think about that when you see fresh blood dripping up on the square in the morning.'

'I killed two of them,' said Sarvic. 'Not one.' Ten Marroc put to death for every Lhosir murdered. The demon-prince had made sure everyone knew.

Valaric turned away. 'You want to fight them, you fight them my way.'

'And what way's that, Valaric? Sit around and wait for them to get old? They won't stop coming. It's like it was fifteen years ago, all over again.'

'Is it? And how would you know that?' Valaric turned back sharply. 'Fifteen years ago you were barely even a boy. You know nothing, Sarvic, and no, it's not like it was the last time. The last time they came we still had our pride. No, we don't wait for them to get old, we wait for the Vathen to come, you clod. The demon-prince has gone off looking for the Crimson Shield. The Widowmaker's setting his camp, and say what you will about him but the Nightmare of the North is far less fond of his ravens than that bastard Twelvefingers. Or he would be if people like you stopped to think for a bit.' Valaric's eyes glittered. 'My way is the way of letting the Vathen and the forkbeards kill each other. That's what they both want, after all. It doesn't matter to me who wins, because afterwards we finish them off, whoever they are. Vathen, Lhosir, we take our land back from both. That's my way, Sarvic, and I'll be needing an army to do it, not a handful of angry murderers. A *Marroc* army, you fool.' He pulled at Sarvic's shirt and then waved his hands in disgust. 'Look at you. Throw that away. Get the blood off you. And stay out of my sight. You'll know when it's time. Keep quiet, and if that's just too much for you, go and find others and tell them the same.' He gave Sarvic his own shirt and then looked down. 'New boots?' Sarvic nodded. 'Throw them in the river. You got blood on them.'

He pushed Sarvic back out into the alley. The forkbeards were probably long gone, but Sarvic stuck to the shadows as he made his way home. Just in case.

It was only later that he realised where Valaric had taken him. The back of the Grey Man.

24

SHADOWS UNDER STARS

The monastery gates stayed closed. In the morning light it was clear that the fire had hardly touched them. Medrin swore and cursed and had the Lhosir cutting down trees to make a ram for something to do, all of which seemed to Gallow a waste of time. Jyrdas simply shook his head, laughed and walked off while the others set to work. He didn't come back until the middle of the day.

'There's a rise a few miles back that way.' He pointed inland. 'You can see all the way to Pendrin castle.'

Medrin looked at him as though he was mad. Tolvis shook his head. 'Getting excited, One-Eye?'

Jyrdas cuffed him. 'Strawhead! There's two hundred men could come at us from Pendrin, and they saw that beacon lit as we came in, clear as I did. They know we're here. They won't know our strength and that'll make them cautious, but they'll come. Be quite a fight when they do. Glorious.' By which he meant they'd all die.

'Are they marching on us already?' snapped Medrin.

Jyrdas gave him a scornful look. 'Even with two eyes I could never see across twenty miles of hills and look inside a castle. If they're on the move, they're not close. Take them a day to sort their arses and their elbows from one another, but they'll be on the move before long, I'd reckon. Master of Pendrin castle was a fierce old sod last time I heard.'

'They'll be on us tomorrow then?' Medrin's jaw twitched. None of them liked the idea of trying to force a ram through the monastery gates, not with the bridge curved like it was and the islanders up above dropping rocks and javelins and burning pitch and Maker-Devourer knew what else on them. But the bridge was the only way in.

Jyrdas shrugged like he didn't much care either way. 'Might be. Might be they'll wait longer. Might be the old bastard's off elsewhere bashing some other heads and they won't come at all. If he *is* there, then sooner or later he'll come. I'll stake my eye on it.'

Medrin looked up at him askance. 'Which one?'

Jyrdas didn't answer. He towered and glared instead, letting his size speak for him. The two of them stood glowering at each other until Horsan, who was every bit as big as Jyrdas, came and stood beside his prince and Medrin turned away with a shake of his head.

They made their ram and carried it to the bridge anyway. Then they had a good long look at what they were about to try and even Medrin had to bow his head and agree that it wasn't going to work. With the curve of the bridge being what it was, they could get maybe six men to swing the ram, while the gates were solid wood and iron. Maybe, left to get on with it for a bit, the ram might have been enough, but six men left no one to hold shields over them and the bridge was too narrow for shield bearers to stand to either side. Whoever had built it had known what they were doing.

'Bugger to get stuff in and out,' muttered Tolvis, which didn't help.

Medrin sent them back to the woods with their axes. They'd build a cover for the ram, he told them. A wooden box on wheels with the ram hanging inside, thick and strong enough to keep out stones and javelins. Jyrdas just laughed. 'Over that bridge? I don't think so.' He watched them work, merrily telling them everything they were doing wrong without lifting a finger to help. 'It's not going to work,' he said. 'Nice as it is to get a bit of practice swinging my axe, I'd rather it was at someone's head. Even if you get it to the gate, they'll just drop fire on you.'

As the sun started to fade, Gorrin came back all out of breath from the rise where Medrin had sent him to keep watch. Someone with two eyes that actually work, Medrin had said, and it wasn't like Gorrin was much use for anything else with his arm smashed up. 'There's a force on the way from the castle. A few miles away. Can't see how many.'

'Couple of hundred.' Jyrdas yawned.

'Could be that.'

'Or could be anything else!' snapped Medrin.

'Well that's how many men he has.' Jyrdas shrugged. 'Might have killed a dragon while no one was looking and grown a few more from its teeth, I suppose. Might have.' He shook his head and rolled his one eye.

Gorrin blinked, confused. 'They're setting a camp. I can't see all of it.'

'Was here a couple of years back,' said Jyrdas, stretching and stifling a yawn. 'That was when I first heard about the shield. Just a ship of us. Thought we'd have a fine old time sacking a few villages up and down the coast. Couple of hundred men came out of that castle right quick and they were a mean lot too.'

'You fought them?' Medrin frowned.

'Nope, we hopped back on our ship and buggered off sharp-like.' Jyrdas cricked his neck. 'Weren't here for a fight. Not that time.'

'How far to this camp?'

Gorrin winced and held his arm. 'Couple of hours if they march quick. Could have been here by nightfall if they'd kept on coming.'

Jyrdas shook his head. 'Worn down from a day's march and no idea how many we are? No, and they know that no one's getting into that monastery in any hurry. Could take the fight to them, I suppose. Wait until dark and then fall on them in their beds. Make a big noise. That way they won't see we're not so many after all. Might work. Probably would if they were Marroc. Not so sure about here – ferocious bunch, these sheep-shaggers. Could be they'll hold and then likely as not they'll kick us back into the sea, but it would make a good offering to the Maker-Devourer either way.'

'We're here to get the shield,' Medrin growled. 'Fine. Jyrdas, go back to the ship. Take the men we left there. Fall on them in their beds and send them running.'

Jyrdas looked at him like he was mad. 'What?'

'You heard. Take the men watching the ships and do it.'

'I see. Well, if that's what you want, then yes, I could do that. Don't see as how it would help you. Thirteen against a couple of hundred. We'd have to be mighty terrible indeed.'

'Aren't you?'

'There's me with my one eye. Still terrible, I reckon. Then there's Latti with that jaw I cracked for him. Maybe not quite as mighty as he was right now. And Yeshk with his foot. I mean, he'll fight well enough once he gets there, but that might not be until tomorrow morning. And Dvag's got three broken fingers on account of that punch he threw at Blue Forri, and Forri's shoulder hasn't been working right ever since. But, right enough, if you want some heads broken, we'll do that. Pity about none of us getting to see the Crimson Shield in the end, but when they burn our ships and pin you to the cliffs and send you off to visit us in the Maker-Devourer's cauldron on the morrow, you can tells us all what you *thought* it would look like, eh?'

For a moment Medrin stared at Jyrdas like he was a rabid animal needing to be put down. Whatever favour Jyrdas had had, Gallow reckoned he'd just lost it. But he'd said what he'd said, and so had Medrin, and neither of them would move an inch now, and so Jyrdas and the others would march off into the twilight and get themselves killed just to prove a point, and Medrin would let it happen, and when they sailed empty-handed back to Andhun, Jyrdas would take the blame.

'There might be another way,' Gallow said. Because there was, and he'd been thinking about it all through the day.

Medrin fixed an eye on him. 'You can go with Jyrdas too. The mighty Gallow Truesword. The Screambreaker seems to like you. You can show us you're not a sheep even if you look like one.'

'I'm here, aren't I? There was another time we went looking for the Crimson Shield, you and I. Don't think I've forgotten.'

'And don't think I have, either.' Medrin glowered, poised to go on, then bit back on whatever words were waiting. Instead he laughed. 'So, what is it, this other way? Going to take some nice Marroc words with you and ask these *nioingr* to open their gates for us?' He rolled his eyes. 'If it was that easy—'

'Go on,' butted in Jyrdas. 'What's this other way that none of the rest of us have thought of then, clean-skin?'

'We climb the cliff.'

Several of them laughed. 'And how do we get there? Got an Aulian witch squirrelled away to cast some spells so we can walk across the water?'

'When the tide's right out, you can see rocks down in the water almost right across the gap. That'll be about an hour after dark.' The look on them changed right there, Jyrdas and Tolvis and a few of the others who could see where he was going. Even Medrin, but then no one had ever said Medrin was stupid. 'Won't be easy, but there's rocks to hold right across to the bottom of the cliff.'

'And some right buggers of waves in between them,' grumbled Jyrdas. 'No place in the Maker-Devourer's cauldron for the drowned.'

Gallow shrugged. 'If you don't think you can do it ...'

'Don't *you* start.' Jyrdas's one good eye burned. 'So if you get across the water, then what, clean-skin?'

'Climb the cliff.'

'And then?'

'Climb the wall. Slip inside. Open the gate.'

Jyrdas was shaking his head. 'Might as well just get that Aulian witch of yours to grow us some wings – would be a mighty sight easier than making the sea be still and making the watchers on the wall go blind and stupid. I'll grant you might climb the cliff. Don't know how you're going to climb the wall on the top of it though. Get a cloud to carry you?' He laughed.

'They'll be watching the bridge. They won't be watching the other side.'

Medrin was looking at Gallow intently. 'O One-Eye, you don't know this man like I do. Gallow here could climb that wall right enough. Always was good for that sort of thing.' He smiled. 'Jyrdas, go and get the men from the ship and bring them anyway. Gallow opens the gates for us or else you can show the *nioingr* over the hill how terrible you are. One or the other.'

'I'll want two more men with me. Climbers who aren't afraid of the sea.'

'Loudmouth,' said Medrin at once. 'He'll have to be quiet for once. Be a new experience for him and he needs the practice.' He started looking among the others for a third.

'Me,' said Jyrdas. 'I'll go.'

For a long time Medrin held his eye. Then, very slowly, he nodded. 'The Screambreaker's men. All three of you. Fitting. Even here, with a hundred miles of sea between us, he has to make his point. Go on then, One-Eye. You do that.'

'And if we bugger it up and you have to go traipsing across the hills to bring down a few nightmares on Pendrin's sleeping army, you can do that yourself. Can't think of anyone better.'

Gallow hid a smile. Medrin wore his on his face but there was no love in it, not one little bit. 'Nicely done, One-Eye. Nicely done.'

Jyrdas laughed and ran off to get the men from the ships. If someone came in the night and set fire to them both, well then that was just the Maker-Devourer's way of telling them that they weren't meant to have the shield – that or that they were meant to fight their way to the nearest fishing village and steal themselves a new boat. Gallow and Tolvis went and sat at the top of the cliff, looking at the monastery, far enough from the bridge so they didn't have to worry about the odd javelin. They watched while the islanders on the wall watched them back. Gallow's eyes traced the routes around the cliff.

'I was thinking,' Tolvis said quietly, 'that we could simply send half the men away on the ships while the rest of us hide nearby for a few days. They'd see our sails from up there. They'd think we were gone.'

'Take them a few days to feel safe enough to come out.'

'Are we in a hurry?'

'The Vathen will march on Andhun sooner or later. You have to wonder what's holding them up.'

'The sword,' said Tolvis. 'That's what the Screambreaker said. They were waiting for the sword. Their Sword of the Weeping God.'

'*I* think they're waiting for Medrin to come back with the shield. Maybe it's fate for the two to meet again.'

Tolvis puckered up his face. 'That some Marroc idea? In

which case I think it might be fate that either you or Jyrdas are going to kill Medrin if we stay out here much longer. Which would be a pity, because then the rest of us would have to tear your lungs out and stick you on a pole for old Yurlak. Medrin and the Screambreaker I can understand – they can't stand each other, and there's the whole thing about what happened to Medrin when he came to join the Screambreaker's fight against the Marroc all those years ago, and then which one of them will stand in Yurlak's shoes when the Maker-Devourer finally takes him. But you two? What happened between you?'

Gallow shook his head. He stared out over the sea at the cliff beneath the monastery. A part of him was looking at the rocks, at the waves. They'd have to make their way around the base of the cliff with the sea crashing over them, right round to the other side. The waves would hide any noise. Good chance they'd smash them to bits as well. Stupid idea, except he really thought that perhaps it could be done.

Another part of him had got to thinking about fate. About Arda and Tathic and Feya and little Pursic, and even Jelira, whom he still loved even though she wasn't his. Wondering what *their* fate would be. Wondering where they were, whether they were in Varyxhun, whether they were safe. Whether he should have stayed on the road from Andhun and left Tolvis lying there in the dirt. Whether he'd see them again and whether he was meant to. Hadn't really thought about it back then. He'd still been too angry with Arda, too desperate to see a way out, too eager for anything to delay the words that would inevitably pass between them. Kyorgan had eaten that anger. Bad luck for him to be in the wrong place at the wrong time – or was that simply fate too?

'We did something stupid together once, that's all,' he said. 'A long time ago. Didn't end well.'

Jyrdas was back as the sun set. He'd brought a great pile of wood with him and a bundle of sacks. 'Still think we'll fall off and drown in the sea,' he said, 'but if we're going to do this, we're going to do this properly.'

25

SEA AND STONE

'But I like hearing about stupid things,' hissed Tolvis. 'Puts my own many foolish deeds into a more forgiving context.'

Jyrdas hit him. 'Shut it, Loudmouth.'

They stood at the bottom of the cliff a little way from the bridge, where it was easy enough to scramble down from the top even in mail and with swords and axes hanging from their belts. They'd left their shields and Jyrdas was still muttering about that. Making them wear sacks over their mail seemed like it was his revenge.

'When the Fateguard brought the shield back across the sea, they were going to take it to the Isle of Fates. Medrin wanted to see it before it went,' said Gallow.

'Yap, yap!' snapped Jyrdas. 'Everyone wanted a look at that damned shield. Now shall we all shout and wave at the islanders on the wall while we're at it?'

The other Lhosir were making a noise up on the cliff beside the bridge, jeering and shouting. They'd made the wood Jyrdas had brought into a bonfire and then gone to get more. It was burning nicely. Give the men on the walls something to look at. Take their minds off anything else. A fire made it harder to see a man hiding off in the shadows. Jyrdas's idea. The sacks were to stop the moonlight from glinting off their mail.

'A man might think you'd done this sort of thing before, One-Eye.' Tolvis grinned. 'Care to tell?'

'Nothing this stupid.'

They crept along the foot of the cliff. Low tide exposed a litter of rocks fallen from the cliffs long ago. The three of them picked their way slowly and carefully along the shore, hugging the shadows, down on their hands and knees where they had to. Spray from the breaking waves soaked them.

'Don't look at the light,' growled Jyrdas. When they reached the pool of black beneath the bridge, he pointed to where the shadows were deepest. 'That way. Keep in the darkness.'

A half-moon shone high up in the sky. A fresh wind chased heavy rags of black cloud across the stars. A good wind for blowing them back across the sea to Andhun. They paused, waiting for the next cloud to darken the sky. The men up on the cliff had taken to singing bawdy songs, the words changed a little to give some needle to the islanders. Gallow knew these songs, knew their words. Not long ago he'd almost have wept with joy to hear them. Now they only made him sad. Truth was, he didn't belong any more, not here, not anywhere.

He touched the locket at his breast. Crazy stupid woman, pig-headed and bloody-minded. But his, and he missed her.

The moon slid behind ragged black shadow. Gallow crept out among the waves, clinging to the rocks. When the moon came out again, they stopped where they were, hugging barnacles and seaweed, heads down, sackcloth wrapped over their helms and the surf breaking over their heads. The sea tossed and churned, clawing and tearing, did everything it could to rip Gallow away and suck him under. The water came suddenly up over his head and into his nose and his mouth to make him choke and then fell away again. Wave after wave, but they all three held fast, and at last a new cloud covered the moon once more. Beside him, One-Eye growled.

'Waves looked smaller from up top.'

'It's not deep, One-Eye. Calm day, even Loudmouth could walk straight across without getting his hair wet.'

'And if we had the time to wait for one of those then I'm sure that thought would cheer me greatly. First wave hits you, it's going to knock you flat and you'll sink like a stone. Keep your lungs full and your legs underneath you, and when you feel something hard under your feet, kick and kick hard. Bit a bit of luck it might be Loudmouth.' He bared his teeth and chuckled. 'True enough, it's not that deep and it's not that far. You keep telling yourself that. I'd have roped us up, but I reckon chances are good that one of you is going to drown and I don't want the dead weight tugging on me. Go on then, Gallow. Show us how it's done.'

Gallow waited for the ebb and launched himself into the foaming water for the next boulder to break the surface. He took one step and his ankle turned. The next wave came, smashing him back against the stone he'd let go. He kicked again, pushing against it, took two steps before another wave bowled him over. The weight of his mail sucked him down at once and he couldn't help but kick and thrash as the water covered him. Another wave sent him spinning. His feet touched stone; he pushed hard against it and broke the surface gasping. The ebb picked him up and threw him a yard further and then dashed him against the next slab of rock, thumping his head and shoulder against it, the barnacles shredding the sackcloth away from his helm. His fingers turned to claws, gripping at the stone, his feet scrabbling and slipping on seaweed then finally finding purchase, heaving him up until his head was out of the water and he could breathe again.

The next wave broke over him and almost knocked him loose. It smothered him. He felt his helm slip but he didn't dare let go with either hand. As it fell, he snapped his head around and caught the noseguard between his teeth, cracking one and slashing his lip. Blood and the sea mixed their salts in his mouth. He pulled himself tighter to the boulder and hauled himself round the other side where the crash of the waves kept him pressed in place and he could put his helm back where it belonged.

He looked up. The moon was still hidden behind her shrouds. He knew where Tolvis and Jyrdas had been but they were lost now, swallowed by the darkness and the battering of the waves and perhaps by the sea herself.

Maker-Devourer preserve us! Lhosir weren't much for prayers because the Maker-Devourer wasn't much for answering them. Another gulf that lay between him and the Marroc, what with Modris the Protector and all their other gods. They believed in guiding hands and greater purposes, but the Maker-Devourer offered none of that. Each man had his own fate and each man followed it to his doom, and that's all there was.

The next wave was a big one. He didn't see it coming until it broke over him hard enough to knock the air out of his lungs and shake him loose, and then the ebb came after and pulled him off and he was sinking, everything icy and black. He thrashed wildly but found no purchase. Tried to kick towards the next stone but the swirl of the water had turned him around and he had no idea where it was. Salt and icy cold crept into his nose, making him gag. He still had the taste of blood in his mouth, and then the next wave caught him and dashed his head against stone hard enough to make him see stars. He grabbed at it but the ebb pulled him away and sucked him under once more, bouncing him across the stones under the water. Try as he might, he couldn't get his feet underneath him. He envied the Marroc for a moment, for their gods. At least if he'd believed in Modris and Diaran and the Weeping God then he could have had a last moment of hope. Wouldn't have made any difference to him drowning, but he could have hoped.

His hand caught something. Too soft for a rock. It felt like ...

Sacking. With mail underneath!

He clutched at it, swung his other hand towards it, all in the pitch-black heaving water, lungs burning now, and then another hand grasped his and was hauling him up, and at last he got his feet down to push against the bottom. He broke the surface and took a great gasp of air. Tolvis! He'd found Tolvis and they were right under the bridge, almost at the other side. They waited together for the next cloud and then launched themselves one after the other across the last foam-filled gap of water. It was easier with two. Tolvis went first and Gallow half threw him across; and then when he was on the other side, Gallow followed and Tolvis was waiting to pull him in. With a grinding effort they dragged themselves up the stones and out of the water and clung to the tumbled rocks at the foot of the rauk beneath the bridge, every limb as heavy as lead, slowly remembering how to breathe. Tolvis had somehow lost his sword. Gallow, when he thought to check, found he'd lost his helm again. At least they were under the bridge where the watchers on the wall couldn't see them.

'Right under the gate.' In the light of the stars Tolvis's eyes glittered. He patted Gallow's head. 'And you're right. Calm day,

I could have walked right across without even getting my hair wet.'

They waited another minute and Gallow was beginning to think it would be just the two of them when Jyrdas finally clawed his way out of the water. His helmet was twisted around so he could barely see with his one eye.

'Maker-Devourer's bollocks!' he spat, sitting on the stone beside them. 'I've come out the wrong end of battles easier than that. Wish I'd gone with Medrin's plan now.' He looked up at the cliff above them. 'Ah crap!'

'You can always go back,' panted Tolvis.

'Only if I can make a boat out of your bones, both of you. Mostly yours, Truesword.' *Truesword.* First time Jyrdas had called him that.

'Can't have been that bad with so much talk still in you,' said Tolvis.

Jyrdas straightened his helm and bared his teeth at Gallow. 'Go on then. Show us the way up. I'll be as ready as it gets for splitting heads by the time we're up there.'

Gallow made his way along the side of the cliff. He went slowly, each movement as smooth as it could be. Peppered with ledges and crevices, it wasn't as hard as it had looked from across the water, even in mail and with a sword on his belt. Up by the bridge Medrin's men were still singing their songs and shouting their taunts and insults while their fire burned brightly, and no one saw the three Lhosir as they traversed the cliff to the far end of the rauk and began to climb. Once they were above the water the stone was dry, even if it crumbled in places under Gallow's fingers and clumps of grass came away in his hand.

The monastery wall rose straight up from the the cliff. It was an old wall, the stones large and ill-fitting, the mortar between them crumbling and badly eroded. Gallow pulled a dirk from his belt and held it between his teeth. Where the cracks were too narrow for his fingers, he took it and widened them; where he couldn't do that, he forced the dirk itself deep into the crack until it would take his weight. His feet found what purchase they could. The wall wasn't tall, and he thanked the Maker-Devourer for that.

There were no sentries on the back wall and he thanked the Maker-Devourer for that too. Once he was over he wrapped the end of his rope around his waist, braced himself and tugged. On the other end, Jyrdas tugged back. He came up fast, jumping over the top of the wall and landing with the grace of a man half his age, sword already out and gleaming in the moonlight. Tolvis followed, and there they were, the three of them in an empty darkness. The walls curved around to each side of them, following the shape of the rauk. From the outside they'd looked taller than they were. Two small towers rose from the walls, each with a sentry on top. The walls and the towers wrapped the space around the monastery itself, a stone longhouse with a steep leaded roof and that was all. Small and shabby. Gallow had expected something grander.

The sentries on the towers and on the walls were all looking towards the bridge. So far the three Lhosir hadn't been seen.

'Right then.' Tolvis squinted across the yard. 'That was so easy that One-Eye here might possibly still be asleep.' He frowned. Close by stood a pile of wood, a beacon carefully prepared and ready to be lit. 'So now what? One-Eye shakes the ground with one of his farts and then while the islanders are screaming in horror and choking to death, you and I see if we can hold our breath long enough to get the gates open? Either of you got any idea how many people are actually in this place? Not that I suppose you care, eh?'

Jyrdas grabbed him round the throat and snarled, 'The sentries, piss-pot boy. We cut their scrawny necks.'

'Really?' Tolvis blinked as Jyrdas let him go. 'Well, I suppose. If you say so, but I thought my way sounded easier. Painful as it is to say, One-Eye, but after sharing a ship with you, I think you underestimate your prowess.'

26

LOYALTY

Gallow pulled them apart. Jyrdas took his axe off his belt and hefted it. He aimed at the sentry on the closer tower. Gallow caught his wrist. 'Even the Screambreaker couldn't fell a man from this distance, One-Eye.'

'In my prime I would have split his skull.'

'In your prime you had more eyes!' hissed Tolvis.

Jyrdas glowered, but he lowered the axe and crept toward the tower instead. Gallow watched him go and then turned his eyes to the one on the other side of the rauk. With Tolvis close behind, he sidled along the wall until he could see the gates past the dark bulk of the monastery. Torches lit the yard around them and he could see men moving there, maybe a dozen or so split between the yard and the walls. The shouting had died down, as though the Lhosir outside had given up and gone to their beds.

When he pushed gently at the tower door it swung open onto a spiral stair. Gallow climbed in silence to a small round room, empty except for a handful of crossbows hung from pegs and a ladder to the roof. He put a finger to his lips and handed Tolvis the sword and axe from his belt, then inched up the ladder until the cool sea breeze touched his head and his eyes emerged back into the night. The sentry was looking the other way and Gallow didn't hesitate: he grabbed the islander's ankles and pulled hard, falling down the ladder and into the guardroom and taking the sentry with him. The islander let out a squawk. His arms flew out as the rest of him flew back, his face smacked into the stone roof, he fell down the ladder and the back of his head hit the floor below. He might have been dead from that, but in case he wasn't, Tolvis jumped on him and twisted his neck until it snapped.

Gallow climbed up again. From the tower roof he could see the gates clearly, the bridge and Medrin's bonfire dying slowly. There was no gatehouse, just the two squat stone columns that held the gates. The gates themselves were barred, the sort of bars that would take two men to lift. And he was right: there were a dozen or so men in the yard and on the battlements, too many for even Jyrdas to hold at bay while he and Tolvis opened the way for Medrin and the others.

He went back down and took a crossbow. 'What we need is Gorrin or Durlak.' They were a Marroc thing, crossbows, brought across the mountains by Aulian traders before they'd vanished when their empire collapsed. The Screambreaker had looked down his nose at anyone who tried to learn the use of one; Medrin doubtless saw them differently.

Tolvis spat. '*Nioingr* weapons.' Arrows were bad enough.

On the south side Jyrdas had silenced the other sentry. They watched across the darkness, waiting until they saw him slipping back along the wall. Tolvis's lips twitched. 'I hate to say this and he surely wouldn't thank me for mentioning it, but One-Eye was quite a good shot with one of these once. Back when he had both eyes.'

Jyrdas climbed up through the tower. His eye gleamed at Gallow in the starlight. 'Managed to keep Loudmouth quiet enough not to give yourselves away, eh? That must be a first. So, here's what I say: stuff Twelvefingers. Half the islanders are out at the gate and the other half must be asleep. I say we slip into the monastery and find their shield and slip out again and murder anyone who opens an eye to our passing.'

Gallow thrust a crossbow into One-Eye's hands and picked up the fallen sentry's shield and helm. They made him feel whole again. 'We open the gates,' he said. 'That's what we came to do.'

Jyrdas gave him a long hard look, then shrugged and nodded. He looked past Gallow at the crossbows still hanging on the wall. 'All right then. So we load them all up. You and I get as close as we can. Loudmouth stands at the top of the tower and starts shooting. When they all start running around like frightened chickens, we throw the gates open. Anyone comes after us, Loudmouth does for them.'

'Which is fine enough,' agreed Tolvis, 'except I can't hit a barn door with one of these things.' He winked at Gallow. 'Mind you, I have got two eyes, so at least when I shoot at something there's a chance of the arrow at least going in the right *sort* of direction. So yes, probably best I take them.'

'Give me those!' Jyrdas pushed past Gallow into the tower and started cocking the crossbows. Gallow and Tolvis slipped out into the darkness of the yard. They hugged the wall, keeping in its shadows. The half-moon was heading towards the horizon now but the clouds were breaking apart and the stars were many.

'Knowing that I'm about to trust my life to a one-eyed archer, I think I'd rather have gone with Twelvefingers' plan too.' Tolvis still had Gallow's sword. Gallow loosened his axe. A small bonfire burned in the middle of the yard behind the gates. A cauldron hung over it and Gallow caught a whiff of boiling pitch.

'A javelin or two would be nice.' Gallow counted the islanders again. Four down in the yard, two of them tending the fire, the other two by the gate pacing back and forth and looking bored. Eight or nine up on the battlements, but there were wooden steps down from either side of the gates and the men up there would be down them quick enough when the fighting started. He wondered whether he and Tolvis could simply walk out into the yard and how far they'd get before anyone realised they were Lhosir. Gallow had a sentry's helm and shield. It was dark. They'd know Tolvis for what he was as soon as they saw his forked beard, but they wouldn't know *him*. Not until he spoke. Which just might be enough. He risked a glance back at Jyrdas's tower. 'Your one eye had better be a good one,' he muttered. And then to Tolvis, 'Stay here and follow my lead.'

He walked out into the open towards the flames in the middle of the yard and the two men beside the fire. They glanced at him as he came up to them, but it took a moment for the nearest to realise that under the helm was someone he didn't know.

'Reidas?'

Gallow picked up a burning brand from the fire. He nodded and grunted and shrugged.

'Reidas?' The islander was reaching for his sword. The other one had turned and cocked his head, trying to understand what was going on. Then a crossbow bolt hit him in the chest. He staggered back with a grunt and fell. 'Luonatta!' shouted the man in front of Gallow. 'They're inside!' He drew his sword but too late: Gallow gave the cauldron over the fire a mighty kick towards the nearer steps up to the battlements. The cauldron wobbled and toppled. Burning hot pitch spewed across the yard and he threw the burning brand into it. Flames jumped across the stones as he ran for the other stairs. The islander who'd sounded the alarm came after him with his sword and then stopped short and slumped, another crossbow bolt in his back. Gallow raced to the steps. He whipped his axe from his belt and swung at them. The two soldiers by the gates saw him too late. His axe split one of the wooden supports clean in two and a solid kick brought the whole lot crashing down.

'Maker-Devourer!' he yelled. Two on two in the yard, now *that* was better. The islanders on the battlements now either had to jump down with their mail and shields or walk through fire. Enough to slow them and Jyrdas would be shooting at them. He bellowed and ran at the nearest gate guard, hooking the man's shield with his axe and then slicing at his neck. The islander jumped out of the way and straight into his fellow, tripping him up, and then Tolvis was there to split the man's skull while Gallow stamped on the second soldier's arm, snapping it. His axe finished the job, smashed into the man's face.

Tolvis looked at the axe in his hand and held it up to the moonlight. 'Nice edge you keep on this,' he said. 'Six Vathen was it?' They ran to the gate. Someone on the battlement screamed and fell. Gallow remembered six crossbows hanging in the sentry tower. The first three had all counted and the other three had to count too. For a moment, though, they were the only ones alive beside the gate. The smoke from the burning pitch swirled around them, choking. Three bars held the gates closed. They reached for the top one.

'It would be helpful just about now,' roared Tolvis, 'if Medrin and the rest of them came hollering across the bridge.'

Two islanders ran down the burning steps, yelling and shouting through the flames, waving their swords. Gallow and Tolvis heaved the beam from the door at them, staggering one and pinning the other. The trapped islander screamed as the flames licked through his mail. The other one died with Jyrdas's next arrow in his back. Tolvis shook his fist at the tower. 'Don't waste them, you one-eyed clod!'

They lifted the second bar out. The men from the other battlement were jumping down now, the danger of a broken ankle less than the danger if the gates fell. Another islander howled as Jyrdas's fifth bolt took him in the leg. Two more came at Gallow. He turned to face them but Tolvis jumped in the way.

'You're the one with the arms of a smith! Get the last bar!' He launched himself at the two islanders with such savagery that for a moment they backed away. Gallow took a deep breath and grabbed the beam and heaved. Damn thing was as heavy as a man and it was stuck. Behind him Tolvis was howling away: 'Take your time, Truesword. These two aren't much sport but I'll have another couple in a moment and I'd hate for that opportunity to go to waste!'

With one last savage effort he lifted the beam away. He turned to drop it and stared straight at another islander who'd jumped through the flames on the stairs. A crossbow bolt flew between them, inches from Gallow's face and buried itself in the gate. For an instant they looked at each other, then the islander brought down his axe and Gallow did the only thing he could: he lifted the beam to put it in the way. The axe bit into the wood and stuck. Gallow dropped the beam on the islander's foot and kicked the gates open.

The bridge was empty. Medrin and the others who should have been hammering to get in weren't there. Gallow whipped out his axe and hacked the islander who'd come at him, severing his wrist. Tolvis was facing three now and there were more coming. Gallow ran to him. They stood back to back.

'Medrin!' he roared. 'Now or never, Twelvefingers!'

The three islanders circled them. Two more, the last from the battlements and the one with the arrow in his leg, came warily closer then stopped where they stood, looked at Gallow and Tolvis, and went for the gate instead. The monastery doors were open now and more islanders were running out from inside, half-mailed, helms askew, grim-faced.

'Medrin!' They'd never get it open again. But two men side by side could hold the gateway. For a while. If they could get to it. Gallow let out a cry and launched himself at the nearest islander, the one between him and the gate. The islander met him, took Gallow's axe on his shield and stabbed back, forcing Gallow sideways. A second islander lunged, slicing across his mail, driving him even further away from the gate. The men from the monastery were flooding the yard now, surrounding him and Tolvis. The islanders by the gate had it closed and now they were trying to lift one of the beams back into place. Another, a huge brute of a man, was running along the battlements to help.

Back to back, he and Tolvis held their ground, a dozen men around them now. Here was where he was going to die. Medrin had betrayed them.

I'm sorry, Arda.

'Come on then!' The huge brute from the battlements jumped down to the gates, swinging steel and bellowing. Jyrdas!

The gates swung open again. Jyrdas stood between them, towering over everything, an axe in each hand and dead islanders all around him. And there, finally, at the other end of the bridge was Medrin, the other Lhosir yelling and waving their spears and their swords and their shields and charging across the bridge. The men around Gallow backed away, wavered, then as one turned and ran towards the monastery and its flimsy doors. Jyrdas came screaming past, chasing them, and then the yard was filled with Lhosir, all shouting in triumph, and Tolvis had Medrin by the throat.

166

27

JYRDAS

Jyrdas pulled Tolvis away before one of them did something stupid. 'Get your hands off your prince, Loudmouth.' That done, he gave Twelvefingers a good shove too, enough to make him stumble and almost fall. 'And where were you? Should have been at the gates the moment they opened. Fall asleep, did you?' He turned away, not wanting for a reply. 'Would never have happened with the Screambreaker.' Didn't need to even look to see how sharp *that* cut. It would have to do, though. Merited it might be, ripping Twelvefingers to pieces, but here wasn't the time or place. *Here* he had a yard full of battle-hungry Lhosir with no one to fight but each other. 'You lot!' He pointed to the nearest group of the them. 'Go back and get that ram we built. The rest of this is going to be easy.'

Twelvefingers looked murderous but he hadn't said anything yet. Jyrdas clapped him on the shoulder and got in quick before the prince could open his mouth. 'We'll be through that gate in no time. You'll have your shield and be back on the sea nicely before that lot from Pendrin fall on us. You can hold it up high in Andhun and watch the Marroc weep.' Weep with joy or weep with sorrow? Jyrdas wasn't sure and he certainly didn't care. Sheep were sheep.

He held Twelvefingers' eyes with his one good one for a moment longer. 'You and Gallow. Whatever it is, put it away until we get back.' Anyone could see the two of them had some old feud far from forgotten between them – the mystery was why they didn't just get on with it, fight each other and then one of them would be dead and that would be the end. Because Yurlak was king and that somehow made Twelvefingers special? But Yurlak himself would fall out of his shoes laughing at that.

Jyrdas shook his head. He let Twelvefingers go and went to help carry the ram to the monastery doors. The other Lhosir were already hacking at them with their axes. There was no stopping it. For better or worse, Twelvefingers would have his shield tonight.

'Hoy! Dog-buggerer!' He grabbed Tolvis. The two of them being the oldest, veterans of the Screambreaker's first war, as far as Jyrdas was concerned they were in charge of the fighting and never mind what Twelvefingers had to say about that. *Prince?* The Marroc were the ones impressed by titles, not Lhosir.

'What do you want, One-Eye? Did you wink at someone and think you'd gone blind and get confused?'

'Ha bloody ha. The beacon in the back yard. You think of that?'

'I did.' Loudmouth made a big show of shrugging his shoulders. 'Some fool lit it. Couldn't be bothered to put it out. Seemed like it might not be such a bad thing actually. Makes some good light and gives us plenty of burning brands for setting fire to things.'

'And if the soldiers out of Pendrin see it?'

Tolvis shrugged again. 'If they see it then they already saw the fire Medrin lit by the bridge. Otherwise they won't see the smoke until dawn. Either way it makes no difference.'

'They know we're inside, they'll come quick.'

'Well then I guess we're none of us clever enough to have thought of that until it was too late.' Loudmouth laughed. 'Although *now* a clever man would surely think that we'd have to get out of here sharp-like when we're done. No time for making any ravens. Shame, eh?'

Jyrdas considered that. He gritted his teeth. 'Likes his ravens, doesn't he?' Blood ravens were for *nioingr*. Doing it to any old Marroc who happened to look at you in a funny way made the whole thing a mockery. Man called you a pig, you ripped his lungs out. Man murdered your family in their sleep? Same thing. Might as well go ahead and do the murdering then. Someone crossed you, you had a fight about it, quick and simple. Nothing wrong with a fair fight. Even the Marroc understood that much. Maybe you killed them or maybe they killed you, or maybe one of you marked the other and then you were all friends again. Ravens though, that was for something else. The Maker-Devourer would frown on them if he cared about anything at all.

Sod it. He looked about for Gallow and saw the no-beard running past the monastery towards the back yard. Maybe he wasn't quite as clever as Loudmouth and had decided to go and put out the beacon. Jyrdas shrugged. There was killing to be done here and he was eager for it. He headed for the ram.

The monastery door splintered at the first blow and fell at the second. The Lhosir let out their battle cries and charged into a hail of rocks and javelins. A stone hit Jyrdas on the helm and a spear went straight through the man beside him. Stupid not to think of picking up a shield, but too late for that now. They swarmed through, swinging their axes and swords. Jyrdas charged the first islander he saw, shoulder dropped straight into the man's shield, knocking him down. He ducked the swing of a sword and stabbed at a face. The inside of the monastery was dark, so damn dark that everything was reduced to shapes and shadows, glimmers in the feeble starlight that came in through the windows and wild dancing shadows from the burning beacon, and in the middle of all that the men and the women from the village below the cliff, screaming and shrieking and running and falling over, desperate just to get away. The kind of fight where everything came to luck, where the fearless won out over the afraid, which was fine by him.

A blow from behind caught him on the shoulder, cracking a bone. He roared in pain and spun around, lashing with his axes. His left arm hung almost useless. He caught sight of a shape and screamed, jumping at it, bringing the other axe down. The shape threw up a shield.

'For Yurlak!' He swung again, battering the man back.

'For Medrin!' The islander lunged with his sword. In the dark Jyrdas didn't see it coming and it caught him hard in the ribs, snapping at least one. His mail held, though, and he had the bloodlust on him now. A dim thought wondered why the islander trying to kill him was shouting his own prince's name.

But the man *was* trying kill him. He ducked and lashed out

with a foot at where the islander's legs ought to be. Caught something. The islander staggered and his shield dropped and that was enough. Jyrdas brought his axe down and felt the blade bite deep. The islander shrieked and Jyrdas swung again, a backhand swipe to the head that shattered the islander's cheek and tore most of his face off. Jyrdas stamped on him and looked for the next. His shoulder hurt and his ribs too and he couldn't breathe without stabbing pains, but he'd had worse and more than once.

The fight was ebbing now. Shapes in the dark, that was all he could see, curse his one good eye. The screams were mostly outside. The villagers either dead or they'd got away.

'The shield!' shouted Twelvefingers over the ruckus. 'Where's the shield? Bring it to me!'

Jyrdas pulled himself straight. 'Come on!' he roared. 'Which one of you *nioingr* wants to fight me?'

A silhouette appeared against the broken doors, darkening to the vague idea of a shape as it came inside. 'Jyrdas?'

'Who wants me?'

'Gallow. Maker-Devourer, this is madness!' Gallow ran out and came back with a burning branch taken from the beacon. 'Someone lit it,' he said, not sounding much bothered. 'Didn't get there in time to stop them.'

'I think you might want to ask Loudmouth about that.' Jyrdas clenched his good fist. 'Seemed far too smug about it if you ask me.'

'Some of the women from the village got away. Some of the men too. There's quite a few of them dead out there though.'

'Ach, let the bastards from Pendrin come. Damn but I want to kill something.'

The light from Gallow's torch showed the fight was all but over. The last few islanders were surrounded and being cut down one by one. They didn't try to surrender even though they must have known there was no hope. Good for them. The Maker-Devourer liked that sort of spirit.

'Looks like you already did.' Gallow was looking at Jyrdas's axe, at the blood still dripping off it. And at the man lying on the floor with his jaw hanging off his face by a flap of skin. The dead man was a Lhosir. Mangled beyond recognition but he had the forked beard. Couldn't be anyone else.

'Stupid shit hit me in the back with an axe.' He couldn't move that arm at all now. 'Bugger couldn't tell the difference between friend and foe in the dark. Serves him right. What kind of *nioingr* takes a man from behind anyway?'

There was an odd look on Gallow's face. 'Where's Tolvis?'

'Do I care? Where are the bloody monks?' Jyrdas clenched his teeth and snarled. Damn but that shoulder hurt.

The other Lhosir were scaling the stairs and ladders to the upper floor of the monastery, or else running outside to smash in the doors of the little outbuildings that pressed against the walls. Jyrdas pushed past Gallow, looking for Twelvefingers. 'Where's the shield, boy? I want to see it!' Every breath hurt. Not coughing up a bloody froth though, so no need to go and pick a fight with someone just so he could go to the Maker-Devourer with a weapon in his hand. He found Twelvefingers and a few of his closer Lhosir clustered at the hearth. Someone had pulled back the furs that had been scattered there. There was a door in the floor. 'Is it down there?'

Twelvefingers looked at him and laughed. Little prick. 'It may be, old One-Eye. Do you want to go and look for it?'

'Do I? Out of the way, boy.' Jyrdas pushed at him with the one arm that still worked but this time Twelvefingers stood his ground. His eyes glittered in the firelight, a flash of hostility.

'Mind your mouth, One-Eye! Looks to me like you're down to one of almost everything. Not sure you could handle a few monks right now.'

'You little ...' He clenched his fist, but before he could punch Twelvefingers across the hall, Loudmouth was beside him and had a hold of his arm.

'If the shield's down there then Prince Medrin, may his glory shine like a thousand suns, should have the honours. This is his hunt, not yours.'

Jyrdas backed away. 'Half mine,' he muttered. Loudmouth being right didn't make it any better. 'Little prick,' he muttered again. 'If Yurlak was here or even the Screambreaker, they'd put him over their knee and spank him. May his glory shine like a thousand suns? Head gone as soft as the rest of you, has it, Loudmouth?'

Tolvis laughed. 'You need to sit down, old man. Take some air.'

'No, I bloody don't. I need to stand up so I don't shove the broken end of some rib or other through a lung and bleed to death on the inside.'

'Then lie down.'

'*Lie down?* Have you lost your balls? Anyway, some shit stain smashed my shoulder. Can't lie down.' His head was spinning a little.

'Battle's over, Jyrdas. Here. Have a spear to lean on.'

'Daft bugger! Shoulder and ribs, I said! Nothing wrong with my legs!' He gripped his axe. Might be that Loudmouth had a point, though. 'Who are *you* calling old, anyway?'

Tolvis smiled. 'You got me there, One-Eye.' Medrin's men were vanishing down the hole in the floor, big Horsan at the front. Jyrdas felt a surge of envy. That was where *he* should be. Would have been too, in the old days. Wouldn't have been stupid enough to get thumped. Wouldn't have been stupid enough to fight a man in the pitch dark. Axed in the back by one of his own? Maker-Devourer! Still, no accounting for idiots. 'Children. Half of them should be back across the sea still sucking at their mothers' tits by the look of them.'

'They have their beards, One-eye. How old were you on your first raid?'

Twelvefingers and his men had all gone down to the cellars now. With a bit of luck someone would knife a few of them in the dark. Learn them a thing or two about a bit of common sense. Jyrdas sank to his knees and clutched at the spear. His head was buzzing and all the pain made it hard to breathe. 'Don't let those little shits see me like this, Loudmouth.' He could smell smoke, little wafts of it creeping in from outside where others were setting fire to the outbuildings. Like the old times. He smiled.

'Lean on me if you want.'

'Lean on *you*, Loudmouth? I'd snap you like a dead twig.' He bared his teeth and growled. 'Ah but it hurts, damn it.'

'Pain, Jyrdas? A Lhosir doesn't feel pain. You told me that. I had a Marroc arrow in my leg at the time, but I'm sure you were right.'

'Time I lost my eye? Hurt like being taken up the arse by the Maker-Devourer himself. Worse than this. I'll live.' He spat back at the dead Lhosir on the floor. 'Stupid *nioingr* crap stain piece of shit!'

One of Medrin's men poked his face up out of the floor. 'It's here! The shield! It's here!'

Jyrdas tried to get up. If there was one thing he was going to do now he was here, he was going to see the damn thing with his own eyes. The Crimson Shield, holy relic of the Marroc and their gods. The shield the Fateguard had said was too dangerous for the Screambreaker to take. Why? Because he'd have made himself king? Probably, but he could have done that anyway if he'd wanted to.

Instead of getting up, he seemed to be sliding closer to the ground, hands slipping down the shaft of Tolvis's spear.

'Loudmouth! Your spear's not working properly!'

'It's a lump of wood, you daft half-blind ...'

He caught sight of a strange look on Tolvis's face and then his one good eye wouldn't stay open and all he could hear were the monks singing from down in the cellar while a pleasant warmth spread through him.

28

THE CRIMSON SHIELD

'Since we both know you're as keen as I am, you might as well lead the way.' Medrin slapped Gallow on the shoulder and pushed him towards the ladder leading under the monastery hall. Gallow climbed down, the rest of the Lhosir pressing after him. The ladder led them into a narrow tunnel, a dank and winding thing so low that he had to stoop. He passed niches in the walls, crudely cut from the raw stone, dozens of them, in each a desiccated body wrapped in bandages. The smoke from the Lhosir torches quickly filled the air, choking him, making his eyes water so he could hardly see.

The tunnel led lower, deeper, past pits filled with skulls and bones. The passage grew narrower and uneven, steeper, until it was little more than a fissure in the rock crudely etched with steps that wound down from the crypts sunk deep in the rauk. Gallow heard the Lhosir behind him muttering, wondering where he was leading them. They were men of the sea and the mountains and wide-open spaces. Cramped dark places deep under the earth brought out the superstitious in them. Monsters dwelt in the darkness deep beneath the earth – they all knew that.

The fissure widened, spilling them out into a slanting cave that ran deep to the bottom of the rauk. He could smell the seawater at the bottom, rank and salty. The Lhosir torches barely touched the darkness of it, but it was easy to see where the cave ended and the water began because that was where the monks of Luonatta were waiting for them, fifty feet below. They stood in a circle on a tiny island surrounded by rings and rings of candles and black glittering water. A narrow wooden stair, steep and creaking, wound down the side of the rift, little more than a string of wooden pegs hammered into holes in the rock. Now and then, as Gallow shifted his weight from one to the next, he felt them flex and bend, heard them creak. There was nothing to hold on to except the damp wall of stone, pressed so close beside him that it seemed to want to push him over, down into the depths below.

As the Lhosir entered the cave the monks began chanting. Something lay in the middle of their circle, large and round. The cave was too dark to make out what it was, but there was only one thing it could be: the shield. Gallow shook his head. Monks were the same everywhere – he'd seen it enough times among the Marroc. When terror came to call they made a circle and prayed to their gods, and from when he'd followed the Screambreaker he couldn't think of a single time those prayers had been answered. What were they praying for? That Medrin and all his men would slip on the narrow steps and break their necks? Lhosir didn't pray. The best they could hope for was for the Maker-Devourer to ignore them. The closest thing the Lhosir had to people like these monks were the iron devils of the Fateguard, the soldiers of the Eyes of Time, and *they* certainly wouldn't meekly close their eyes and pray and die.

A man swore behind him and then another screamed as he slipped and plunged into the darkness below. Gallow didn't dare turn to look. A deep unease washed over him here in this dark place under the earth with strange men and their strange gods waiting for him. Maybe there *was* something to those prayers after all. Prayers to what?

The steps brought him down to a shelf of rock almost level with the water and slippery with black seaweed. A small wooden bridge led to the island. After the crudeness of the steps, it was strangely ornate, narrow but with a rail on either side and carved with fish-like figures. Water monsters. Serpents. Women who were half beast. The other men stopped behind him, waiting, none of them sure what to do until Medrin pushed past them all and came to stand beside Gallow at the bridge.

'Hey there!' He waved his sword across the narrow waters. 'We've come for your shield. It belongs to the Marroc. If you'd be so kind as to pass it over, we can be on our way. I also have some swords here that you can fall on, if you're feeling accommodating.' The shadows of the flickering torchlight had changed his face. He looked somehow monstrous. Eyes agleam, teeth bared in a hungry grimace.

The monks didn't even look at him. Their faces were glassy, chanting the same words over and over: Modris, Modris, Protector! Modris, Modris, Builder! Modris, Modris, Maker! Modris Modris...

Modris? Gallow started as though he'd been stung. Wasn't this supposed to be a temple to Luonatta the battle god? Why were the monks chanting the name of Modris?

'Oh never mind.' Medrin stepped back from the bridge. 'Gallow, since you were clever enough to get us through the gates, I give you the honour. Kill them for me.'

Gallow's feet wouldn't move at first. He touched the locket around his neck and felt it urge him to turn and leave and go home and never look back. There was something wrong with this place; but maybe that was only his old Lhosir blood and all its wariness of what lurked in the deeper places of the world where the shadewalkers were born. And then his Lhosir pride had him too, refusing to let him show his fear, and so he stepped onto the bridge, tense as a drawn knife. When nothing happened he began to walk across. His hand felt tight on the hilt of his sword, restless and twitchy, screaming at him for release. He pushed the hunger aside and merely shoved the first two monks out of his way and pushed them into the water. The others didn't move. He reached for the shield. His arm tingled as he did and his heart beat a little faster. A dozen years ago Medrin and Beyard had been transfixed by this god-forged shield and what it meant, and he'd been no better. Now he told himself what the Screambreaker had told him after he'd crossed the sea and found the courage to ask: it was just a shield and nothing more, one that happened to be red. And yet the hairs on his arm prickled as he touched it. The Crimson Shield. The invincible shield of Modris the Protector.

Not that it had saved the Marroc. Just a shield, that's all.

He pushed another monk away, set his own shield down and took the Crimson Shield instead. It was heavy. Instinct demanded that he put it on his arm but that would be to claim it for himself, so he carried it carefully back across the bridge, hairs still prickling all over his skin. The monks continued their chanting as though nothing had happened. Even the ones he'd pushed into the sea were climbing back out of the water, shaking their robes and retaking their places back in the circle. Gallow took a long look at the shield as he held it out in front of him. The darkness and the torchlight hid its colour. It looked like a simple round shield, thick wood reinforced and studded with metal. A single colour, dark grey in the cave but surely crimson in the sunlight. No design. He offered it up to Medrin. 'Here you go then.'

'Funny,' said the prince as he took it, 'to hold it after all these years. Don't you think?'

'It's just a shield.' Gallow let it go. His fingers didn't believe him and his guts didn't either, but how could it be anything else?

'You seem to have left yours behind.'

'That was some islander piece of rot. I left *mine* back on the cliff.' He shrugged and walked away.

'Gallow!' Medrin called him back.

'Twelvefingers?'

'I told you to kill them.'

'And I didn't. I got you the shield. That's what you wanted.'

'No, I wanted you to kill these thieves who took what was ours and claimed it for themselves.'

'King Tane's heir are you now?'

'My father is king of the Marroc.'

'Then kill them yourself. There's no honour in slaughter.' Where was Jyrdas when he was needed? Even bloodthirsty old One-Eye would say the same.

'There's honour in serving your prince, clean-skin.'

'Then I'm sure you'll find someone to do it for you.'

Medrin looked past Gallow to the other men. 'A village full of Marroc to whoever kills a monk. Go. Have yourselves some fun.'

No one moved, not straight away. 'Lord of a village full of sheep?' called a voice from the back. 'What would I do with them?' *Tolvis. Damn it, where was Jyrdas?*

'Probably something unnatural, Loudmouth.' The big man Horsan stepped forward, gripping his giant axe. Gorrin, the archer with the broken arm, pushed his way to the bridge too.

'If I kill two, do I get two?'

'Kill six, you get six,' said Medrin with a shrug, and with that half the Lhosir swarmed over the bridge, howling and swinging their swords. The other half stood and looked at one another, muttering uneasily. It was over in a moment and then the Lhosir fell silent and stopped to look at what they'd done: a dozen unarmed monks crumpled in a ring around the stone where the shield had been. A dark tension swirled around them.

'I don't know about the rest of you,' said Tolvis from the back, 'but I think I've had about enough of this place. I think I shall be off a-looking to see if these monks had themselves a wine cellar anywhere. Those who fancy a swill, Gallow, are very welcome to join me.'

Tolvis began to climb the steps. He wasn't the only one, but in the gloom Gallow couldn't see who else went with him. And he ought to go too, he knew it, but he couldn't quite bring himself to move. Medrin ignored them all. 'It's called what it's called for a reason,' he said, and he walked across the bridge and put the shield back where Gallow had found it. He knelt beside a dead monk and began to cut out the man's heart.

'No.' Gallow pushed his way back towards Medrin. 'No, Medrin, we do not do this.'

'Stop him.' Medrin didn't look up. 'Kill him if you have to.'

Twelvefingers took out a knife, felt for the bottom of the dead man's ribs, then drove the blade in deep and slit the monk open. He reached in, struggling for a moment before he tore out the dead monk's heart, bloody strands of flesh trailing behind it, and squeezed it over the shield. Gallow drew his sword. Three men seized him. He tried to shake them off. 'Blood rites, Medrin!'

'Let it go, Gallow,' warned Horsan. 'There's no good end to this. Our prince knows what he's doing.' He didn't even seem surprised.

Gallow broke free and readied his sword again. He surged towards the bridge, the other Lhosir moving uncertainly out of his path. 'Innocent blood, Medrin!'

'Innocent?' Medrin lifted the shield and held it high. 'These monks?' he cried. 'Innocent? Maker-Devourer, they're dead! And maybe these monks *were* innocent, but what of all the Marroc that you and the Screambreaker and all the rest put to the sword?' He bared his teeth. 'You've forgotten what you are, Gallow. You're no *nioingr* but you're no Lhosir either. You're nothing but a Marroc like any other.' He kicked the nearest dead monk, slapped the iron rim of the shield down on the stone and pointed at Gallow with his sword. 'You have no idea what this is, no-beard. You have no idea what it can do, what it means. If you did, you wouldn't ride your sanctimony so sweetly. A little ritual of thanks to the Maker-Devourer and you draw steel on me? You forget where this came from and you forget what you are! Yes, Gorrin, please.'

Gallow blinked, realised that Medrin was no longer looking at him but past him instead, and that was when someone hit him round the back of the head with the butt of an axe.

Light and noise and then quiet and dark. He was standing on a hilltop in the twilight, a steady wind blowing around him. He knew the place at once. His old home, where he'd grown up before his father had taken them to Yurlak's Nardjas to make armour for the Screambreaker. He remembered the hill. A favourite place, especially when the sun was setting. He used to go there with Kyerla, the sweetheart of his childhood. He hadn't thought about Kyerla in ten years, but he remembered now how much he'd missed her when his father had taken them away. In a different world, one where they'd stayed in their forge and their farm by the sea, he and Kyerla would have been married, younger even than when Gallow had crossed the sea. He could be there now, curled up with her softness under a pile of furs with six or seven fine sons ...

He sensed movement and turned, expecting to see her, but the woman waiting for him was Arda, arms outstretched. 'Remember us, Gallow.' He couldn't see his children, but they were there too. He felt them. Kyerla was forgotten as quickly as she'd filled him. He tried to walk towards Arda but something caught his eye to make him look away. When he looked back she was gone and all

he saw standing at the top of the hill was a long sword, dark red,
stuck fast, point down in the chalky earth.

'No, don't kill him …' Words drifted in and out. Light flickered
and came and went.

'We could just leave him.'

'Any of you want a fight about it?'

'What about him?' The pain was huge. Even blinking hurt.

'One-Eye?' The back of his head. 'Is he still alive then?' He
couldn't touch it. His hands were tied. When he moved he felt a
sharp tug on the skin at the back of his neck. Dried blood.

'He's made of granite, that one. He's bound to live.' His blood.

'Bring them both.' Deep breaths. Fighting back the waves of
nausea. 'The dead too.' One after the other. 'Put a torch to the
rest.' Too much effort. His eyes wanted to close again. To let it
all pass.

Another voice, hurried. 'Get back to the ships!' He forced his
eyes open. Took deep breaths, one after the other. He slipped
in and out of darkness a while, but by the time the Lhosir were
ready to leave, his senses were back enough that he could stand.
His hands were tied behind his back. Gorrin and two men
who'd sailed with Medrin were standing guard. A few bodies lay
around him. Off across the yard Tolvis was shouting at someone
about an axe. He had Jyrdas slumped against him, leaning hard
on his shoulder. The big man looked ready to collapse.

They'd taken his weapons. The worst humiliation. 'Gorrin!'
It had to have been the archer. 'You hit me. You took me from
behind.'

Gorrin gave him a look of disdain. 'You were heading sword
drawn towards our prince, Marroc.'

'A good blow for a man with a broken arm, I'll give you that.
You don't need me to say what sort of man takes another from
behind. You know the answer.'

Gorrin leaned into him. 'When I have my arm back, Marroc,
I'll be happy to talk about the answer to all sorts of things. Prince
Twelvefingers killed a few monks? So? You're on your own if
you think anyone gives a pot of piss about that.'

Medrin got them back on the move quickly. The Lhosir were

surly now. The fighting was done, the battle madness sated, the fires were lit and buildings blazed all around them. They had little to show for their fight; they were hungry and tired and they wanted to go to sleep, and now Twelvefingers was going to make them walk back across the cliffs to the ships in the dark and row out to sea. Gorrin turned to Gallow. 'If the soldiers from that castle catch us out in the open, I'll cut you free, but only for that.'

The moon had sunk below the horizon. Clouds hid half the stars, making every stone and every divot a hazard in the dark. They stumbled across the fields and cliff-tops in moody silence, carrying what they could, shields thrown over their backs, plunder on their shoulders, the fires of the burning monastery lighting their way. Medrin would expect them to sail as soon as they reached the ships and work the oars until the morning. As far as Gallow could see, the monks of Luonatta had hardly been rich. The spoils were meagre. A few barrels and casks stolen from the pantry but no gold, no treasures, no women, nothing worth taking home, nothing even making it worth leaving Andhun in the first place except for the Crimson Shield.

Tolvis and Gallow took turns to prop up Jyrdas. They reached the beach. No one had burned their ships, and before dawn broke the sky they were riding the sea again. A melancholy settled around them despite their victory. A sadness for the men who were dead and an uneasy sense of something changed and thus something lost. Maybe on the other ship, with Medrin and with the Crimson Shield there for all to see, things were different, but on the second boat Gallow thought he felt a creeping edge of doubt. Jyrdas hobbled around, screaming murder at anyone in his way, face screwed up in permanent pain. Wind and wave fought against them as if trying to turn them back, making them slow. With the madness of the fight cleared from their heads, the Lhosir around him remembered what they and Medrin had done. Gallow made sure to remind them.

They kept him bound, tied to the mast through wind and rain even when they could have used another strong pair of arms on the oars. 'I can row,' he told them. 'Where am I going to go?' He saw them waver but that was all. Even Jyrdas looked at him with a face full of rage. Maybe they were afraid he'd throw them all over the side and sail to Andhun single-handed.

On their third day at sea a storm hit. They took in water and almost foundered. Oars broke, snapped by the strength of the waves. The Marroc in Gallow would have said it was a miracle they didn't sink and drown, but Lhosir didn't believe in miracles. Fate, perhaps, had spared them, or perhaps they were merely lucky: Jyrdas and the others who'd been to sea before certainly thought so. When the winds passed and the waves fell, they lay about the deck and slept and broke open a cask of mead taken from the monastery and drank toasts to the Maker-Devourer, and Gallow thought nothing of it until Tivik, who might have been the youngest of them, raised a drunken horn to the clouds.

'To Medrin! It was the Crimson Shield that guided us! The shield of the Protector!'

Jyrdas, on another day, might have thrown Tivik into the sea for being an idiot, but Jyrdas was fast asleep and half dead. The other Lhosir gave Tivik queer looks and muttered to themselves, but he wasn't alone. It spread among them like some disease, slow but lethal.

'It's just a shield,' Gallow tried to tell them, but by the time they reached Andhun none of them wanted to know.

29

THE MARROC

After the storm, the wind and the waves favoured them to Andhun. The castle still sat on the cliffs overlooking the harbour. Teenar's Bridge still lay strung across the Isset. Nothing, as far as Gallow could see, had burned down, although the blood ravens hung across the docks had been cut down and the gibbets were gone. The town felt quiet and peaceful. The Vathen, then, hadn't yet come.

The Lhosir made good their ships and unloaded what was left of their plunder from the monastery. Their melancholy had gone after the storm, replaced by a strange fervour for the shield. They bound Gallow and manhandled him to the shore and then when they were standing on the beach together, they crowded Medrin, trying to see the shield more closely. Touching it. And yes, in the light of the day it was as crimson as fresh blood, and either Medrin had spent a great deal of time cleaning and polishing it, or perhaps it did have a magic to it after all.

The shield took their eyes, and that was why they didn't see the Marroc at first. Not too many, just a dozen men gradually gathering together, keeping their distance but watching from the top of the shingle beach with the air of those waiting for something to happen. As Gallow eyed them they were joined by more, and then more still, until the first dozen had become two and more were coming all the time. He saw Valaric among them, and was that Sarvic too?

Soldiers. Marroc soldiers. A cry of alarm caught in Gallow's throat. The Lhosir were still hauling their swords and their armour and everything else out of the boats, or were clustered around Medrin. Elsewhere the docks were falling still, Marroc workmen scurrying to safety or else joining Valaric and his band. Something was coming and they knew it.

'Loudmouth!' Gallow shouted. But Tolvis was still on the ship, and the devil inside Gallow wanted to wait, wait for the Marroc numbers to swell a bit. A good charge now and they'd break and scatter and that would be that, but if more came ... He wondered what Valaric was thinking, yet still the Lhosir didn't see, not until Tolvis finally started climbing out of the boat, helping Jyrdas, who kept trying to push him away, the last ones ashore.

'Get off me, you sheep!'

From across the beach a Marroc let fly an arrow. It hit Jyrdas and staggered Tolvis enough to make him jump down from the boat. He half caught One-Eye as he fell and they both stared at the arrow sticking out of One-Eye's side. Jyrdas bellowed in pain. He stumbled back to his feet and picked up the first axe he saw and looked, wild-eyed, for someone to hit. He stared at the Marroc mob and held the axe high. '*Nioingr*! Come on then, if you think you can take me!'

There were forty or fifty of them now, the same sort of numbers as the Lhosir, and the arrow must have been a sign, because even as Jyrdas raised his axe, they howled and ran down the beach, waving clubs and spears. They had shields and helms and some even had armour and swords. The Lhosir drew back around Medrin.

'Loudmouth! Cut me loose!' Gallow looked about for anyone to help him, but all the Lhosir eyes were on the Marroc now. Valaric at their van slowed and raised a hand. The Marroc stopped around him, an angry line facing the Lhosir.

'What you have there belongs to the Marroc, Twelvefingers,' he cried. 'Give it here and go back where you belong before I cut you down to six.'

Medrin burst out laughing. 'How many are you? Fifty? Sixty? And you think to throw me out of my own city.' He shook his head. With deliberate care he buckled the Crimson Shield to his arm and bent to pick up a seagull feather from the ground. He held it high. 'When this touches the ground, I'll have every Marroc still standing in front of me hung by his own spine.'

'How many are we?' Valaric laughed right back in Medrin's face. 'How many Marroc in Andhun? And how many demon-beards? Take a look around you. The Vathen are coming. Your army has moved outside the walls to face the enemy and we've closed the gates behind them. There's not one of you left inside the walls to save you. So drop your feather and let me kill you or just give me the shield and slink away like a fox before a bear. I'll have it from you either way.'

Medrin cocked his head. He let the feather slip from his fingers. The Marroc and the Lhosir watched each other as it fell. Nobody moved. Gallow howled again for Tolvis to cut him free but no one was listening. More Marroc had stopped to watch. Valaric's fifty would become a hundred the moment it seemed as though they might win. And if they did, that one hundred would become five, and then a thousand, and with the Crimson Shield Valaric would turn the whole of Andhun, and its gates would stay closed to both Vathen and Lhosir alike.

And Gallow wondered: *Would that be so bad?* 'Cut me free!' He couldn't have said, even to himself, whose side his sword would have taken. For Medrin? The thought was bitter. Turn against his own kin? More bitter still. But worst of all was to stand idly by and do nothing, to be cut down by some Marroc who saw only another forkbeard, easy and helpless.

The feather touched the beach. The stillness remained, and then Valaric howled and Medrin screamed and drew his sword, and the Marroc and the Lhosir threw themselves at one another. There was no shield wall, no tight press of men pushed together. They flew at each other, spears and swords and axes fired by fury. Gallow watched, helpless. Valaric and Medrin were trying to reach each other while the other Marroc and the Lhosir tried to protect them. He watched a score of men die on either side, then the Marroc suddenly scattered and ran back across the beach, even Valaric, and Medrin stood by his ships, blood dripping from his sword in one hand, the Crimson Shield in the other, the Lhosir jeering and waving their spears. Bodies lay scattered around them, the dead and the dying. Dozens of them. Half the Lhosir to come back from the monastery were down and no more had appeared. Valaric's words were true then: the Screambreaker had left the city.

Jyrdas broke away from Medrin's men and staggered up to Gallow, walking like he was steaming drunk. He still had the Marroc arrow sticking out of his side. His beard and his shirt were soaked in blood. He sat beside Gallow.

'I lost my sword,' he said. 'I killed two of the faithless *nioingr* and then I dropped it.' For a moment he looked scared. 'I can't pick it up again, Truesword.' Frothy blood bubbled from the corners of his mouth when he spoke.

'Cut me loose! I'll find it for you.'

Jyrdas shrugged. 'I don't have the strength. Don't have a blade. I can see the Marches, Gallow. Don't let me die without my sword.'

The Lhosir survivors were pushing Medrin's ship back into the sea now. At the top of the beach Valaric and his Marroc were gathering again. They'd run but they weren't broken, and Valaric was screaming and pointing. In a few minutes Medrin would have his ship back in the water. He'd sail away and the shield would go with him. If Valaric couldn't get enough men together with the courage to fight this last handful of Lhosir then perhaps the Marroc didn't deserve to have it. Gallow hobbled, bent almost double by the ropes that tied his ankles to his wrists, to where the dead lay. With his hands tied behind his back he groped for a sword and hobbled back to Jyrdas. Valaric and a dozen Marroc were starting back down the beach again now, but he didn't have enough and Medrin's ship was almost in the water.

'That's right!' shouted Valaric. 'Run! What's your word for it? *Nioingr!* Faithless worthless cowards, that's what you are!'

Trying to goad Medrin into another fight. Gallow managed to drop the sword into Jyrdas's lap. 'If it was you and not Medrin, you'd stop and turn and fight him for that, never mind how many Marroc there were behind him.'

'He wouldn't have to call me names. I'd do it anyway.' Jyrdas groped for the sword. The ship was in the water now, the Lhosir ignoring Valaric. 'If it was me or Yurlak or the Screambreaker, or any one of us who fought them the first time, we'd never have thought about leaving. Twenty of us, a whole city of them, so what? We fought, they ran, the city was ours. We'd have taken it. Hindhun was taken from a thousand Marroc by fifty of us. We'd win or we died trying, and either way served a purpose.' Jyrdas closed his eyes. 'Maker-Devourer take me quickly, before I see a prince of the sea driven from these shores by a rabble of Marroc.' His brow furrowed and then he stood up and turned. 'No. I'll not watch this in silence.' Up on the beach the Marroc were finding their numbers and their nerve, spurred by Valaric's taunts. 'Hoy! Twelvefingers!' Jyrdas roared. 'The Marroc's right. You're *nioingr*! You hear me? Running like a sheep? *Nioingr!*' He shouted it until the Lhosir couldn't pretend not to hear. It must have taken the last strength he had; he sat heavily down and the sword fell from his hand again.

Medrin walked quickly over, two men at his back, all of them glancing up the beach towards the approaching Marroc as the ship ground out into the surf. 'Eat your words and beg for forgiveness, One-Eye,' hissed Medrin. 'These men will witness it.'

'*Nioingr*,' whispered Jyrdas again. Medrin whipped out a thin dagger and stabbed him through his good eye. Jyrdas slumped sideways and fell without another sound.

'Was it really an accident that one of your men took Jyrdas from behind in the monastery?' Gallow asked him.

Medrin bared his teeth. He backed away, shouting as he ran into the breaking waves and to his ship, 'The Marroc can have you! Back to your own kind, clean-skin!'

Gallow watched him go. He watched Valaric and the Marroc on the beach do the same and pitied them for how it must feel, seeing Medrin get away when they had so nearly stopped him. When the only thing that stood in their way was their own fear. How it must feel for Valaric, who had the courage in himself but couldn't find it in the men around him. Or for the Marroc who were afraid, who knew it was their own weakness that brought their defeat. Terrible to be either. One day the Marroc would find their hearts. One day the sheep would become wolves.

He bent down and fumbled Jyrdas's sword off the beach and dropped it beside him. It was the best he could do, but the Maker-Devourer would understand.

31

THE PYRE

The Marroc didn't know what to make of him. The first ones looked at his face, saw no beard, took him to be a Marroc prisoner and cut him loose. When they kicked and spat on Jyrdas's corpse and Gallow knocked them both to the floor, they wondered what they'd done.

'Valaric knows me,' he said, 'and any who fought at Lostring Hill. They'll vouch for who I am. One way or the other.'

'Lock him up. We'll deal with him later,' said Valaric when they brought him to Gallow. 'He's not one of us and he's not one of them. He's half and half and you never really know which half it's going to be.' He looked Gallow up and down and stared hard at the sword Gallow held – Jyrdas's sword. 'You coming nicely or do we have to have a fight at last, you and I?'

Gallow glanced at the bodies on the beach. 'Is Marroc justice to a Lhosir any better then Medrin's was to you?'

'Maybe. Maybe not.' Valaric stared out at the sea, at Medrin's ship ploughing through the waves. 'He won't go far. And he'll be back, and it won't be long either.' He nodded to himself and then his eyes came back to Gallow.

Gallow looked down to Jyrdas. 'I'll ask one thing of you, if you want my surrender.'

Valaric laughed. 'You don't get to ask for anything, forkbeard, you get to thank me for not killing you.' But he followed Gallow's gaze.

'Give him a proper Lhosir pyre. Burn him.'

Valaric prodded Jyrdas with his boot and rolled him onto his back. 'I know him. Jyrdas One-Eye. A right bastard. I should hang him up over the gates like he did to us.'

'A proper Lhosir pyre or I'll kill every man who comes near him until you take me down, Valaric.'

'So be it.' Valaric drew his sword. There was no anger in his eyes, no glee, no joy, only a cold sadness. 'I wasn't going to kill you, Gallow, but it does make everything that bit easier.'

'Jyrdas didn't hang your people, Valaric. He hated it. But if you want a reason, I'll give you one. After Medrin broke you and he was about to sail away and you and your Marroc were standing at the top of the beach not finding the courage to do anything more than bawl names at him, did you not hear him? He called Medrin out for running away. He had an arrow in him; he could barely stand, and he shouted and shouted it for everyone to hear.'

Valaric's lips tightened. A slight nod. '*Nioingr*. Yes, I heard. What of it?'

'Until even Medrin couldn't ignore him and came and stuck a knife in his eye to shut him up. You all saw *that*.' He looked up at the houses and streets of Andhun. 'And if you'd had even one man like him in this city then Medrin would be dead and you'd be standing in front of me holding your precious shield. You know you've just brought doom on the whole of Andhun, don't you?'

Valaric glowered. 'Shut your hole, forkbeard.' He snarled, looked away and took a deep breath as though struggling with something. 'Go on, burn him then,' he said at last. 'You do it. You can make his pyre and you can light it and watch him burn and not one Marroc will lift a finger to help you. Then you can go. Get out of my city and get out of my sight. Go and fight the Vathen. I never want to see you again. If I do, you're just another forkbeard to me and that's all. Now give me your sword.'

Gallow blinked. He reversed the sword and held it out. 'It's not mine, Valaric. It's just a blade I found and it belongs to Jyrdas now. But I think he'd be happy for me to give it to you. Please take this sword, the sword that Jyrdas held in his hand as he died, as his thanks for honouring him as a valiant foe.'

Valaric took the hilt and lifted the sword. He shook his head. 'You Lhosir are demented.' He left and the Marroc moved around Gallow, collecting the weapons and armour and the food and plunder that Medrin's men had unloaded from their ships and then abandoned on the beach. Gallow took an axe to the ship that had been left behind, Jyrdas's ship. It seemed only fitting that it should make his pyre. He took its oars and chopped out its rowing benches and collected pieces broken by the storm, but he left its hull and mast alone. It was still a good ship. He worked into the night and then slept on the beach in the shelter of its hull, and in the morning, when the rising sun woke him, he took the time to carve a name onto the ship's prow: *The One-Eyed Hunter of the Sea*. He carved it deep and large. If ever it sailed again then it would take Jyrdas's memory with it.

Afterwards, as he began to build his pyre, a Marroc came down onto the beach. Sarvic. He didn't say anything, just started to help pile the wood. They worked until the middle of the day and the pyre was done.

'For what you did on Lostring Hill and the debt I owe you,' said Sarvic when it was finished. 'Not for him. *He* was a bastard.'

There were still helms and hauberks and shields. Gallow took one of each for Jyrdas and carried them to the pyre. The rest he piled beside the ship for Valaric to take away. The Marroc of Andhun would need them, one way or the other. After that he carried and dragged Jyrdas across the beach and lifted him up onto the pile of wood, then looked at the sky. Clear and bright with no sign of rain, and so he sat waiting for twilight. Jyrdas would burn as the sun went down, dressed in mail, carrying a shield. Pity about his sword, but he could take an axe with him, the one Gallow had used to chop the wood.

The sun crept lower, the day wore on and a small crowd of Marroc began to gather. They didn't do much except stand and stare but Gallow felt their hostility. Once or twice he saw Valaric moving among them, pushing and shoving and snapping at them. As the sun reddened and sank and its light began to fail, Gallow took the last mail hauberk he'd left hidden on the ship. He polished up his helm and his shield, and walked up the beach. The Marroc shouted and jeered at him, but they parted as he came.

A rock pinged off his helm. Not a big one, but he stopped and turned and stared at them anyway. Sheep, Jyrdas called them, but that was hardly fair. They were fishermen and weavers and bakers and housewives. People content to spend their time building a life for themselves, laughing and singing and making more happy Marroc. He stared at them and saw the same thing he saw in Middislet, in the eyes of the villagers. Muted after all these years but it was still there. They were afraid. Afraid of him because of what he was. Because men like Jyrdas would have tried to take an entire city from them with just a few dozen warriors and wouldn't have given a fig of a thought for how it might end.

He snatched a torch from one and walked back down the beach to the pyre and stood before it, the brand held over his head. They could shoot him if they wanted too. They'd shot Jyrdas, after all, but it didn't bother him. If that's what they did, then that was his fate. A sadness settled over him. To the Marroc he was always a forkbeard, to the Lhosir always a sheep. To Arda, he'd just been Gallow, and that had been enough and right, but she'd betrayed him and now it was gone. *Choose one or the other*, said the voices in his head, but in the final reckoning he'd always chosen her and never mind the rest. Without her he didn't know who to be any more.

Most songs for the fallen that he knew were rowdy bawdy things because that was how the Lhosir dealt with death. The Maker-Devourer cast them out of his cauldron to live a life however they saw fit to live it, and when they died the Maker-Devourer took them back again and he only ever asked one question: Did you live it well? And he'd look into the eyes of the newly dead and see into their souls and know the truth of their answer, and if they answered yes and they believed it in their hearts, he'd take them back no matter what they'd done; and if they answered no then they were cast straight back to live a new life again, one that would be harder and more testing than the last, over and over until they found their courage. The ones who answered yes but knew in their hearts that it was a lie, best not to dwell on those. *Nioingr*. The true meaning of the word. Liars of the worst sort. Self-deceivers. They were ones who were devoured, their bones and shredded ghosts left to roam the Herenian Marches. Thus was the Maker-Devourer's brew made ever richer and stronger.

He held the torch high and began to speak out the deeds of Jyrdas One-Eye, both the good and the bad as far as he knew them. He spoke them loud and clear, straight to the pyre, with the thought that they would find Jyrdas as he waited for the Maker-Devourer's question, and remind him of anything he might forget. Everything that had made him. Everything that would be remembered.

'Jyrdas will make your cauldron.' He threw back his head to the dying sun and began to sing, the 'Last Lament of Pennas Tar', until something jabbed him in the side.

'For the love of Modris, stop howling!'

He turned, ready to tear apart whoever had interrupted this moment, and there was Valaric, holding a sword. The one he'd just poked into Gallow's mail. Gallow turned back to the pyre. 'Go away, Marroc.'

'The Vathen will be here tomorrow or the day after. The Widowmaker took his men out of the city. Every single one. To save Andhun from the Vathen. They can hardly launch an assault or dig in for a siege with the Nightmare of the North and four thousand Lhosir at their backs. The duke has his castle again and he'll open the gates for whoever wins. If it was me, I'd keep them closed. I'd fight either of you. Both of you if I had to.'

'Spoken like a forkbeard, Valaric. Now go away.'

'The Widowmaker took my land from my people. Thousands of us died on the ends of his spears. Yet he came to Fedderhun and he fought at Lostring Hill. He's my enemy and I'll kill him if I can, but if he falls, I'll let you honour his corpse too.' He thumped Gallow with the sword again and then held it out, hilt first. 'You want to give him this or not?' Then he took the sword back. 'No, *I'll* do it. He really did call Twelvefingers a *nioingr* to his face, didn't he?'

'He did.'

'And you?'

Gallow shrugged. 'The Screambreaker said that Medrin had changed. He was wrong.'

Valaric walked to the pyre. He put the sword across Jyrdas's chest beside the axe. When he stepped back, Gallow touched the torch to the kindling. As the flames leaped up, he stood away.

'I'm not staying here on some all-night vigil to honour him, though.' Valaric turned to leave. 'That's what you do, isn't it?'

'It is.' Gallow stared at the flames.

'Then I'll come for you in the morning. I meant what I said. You can go and you can fight the Vathen or sail across the sea or find your Marroc wife and grow beans and cabbages for the rest of your life. I don't care. Just get out of my city and get out of my sight. If I see you again and it's not to get my horse shod or a new blade for my scythe, I'll kill you.'

Valaric left him. The sun slowly set and Gallow watched Jyrdas One-Eye burn.

32

THE SCREAMBREAKER

The Screambreaker looked out over the fires that sprang up in the fields outside Andhun's walls. His father had called him Corvin after a rock at the end of one of his fields. Corvin's Rock. He'd thought it was a strong name, hard and weathering like the stone. Turned out it had been called Corvin's Rock after an old crow that had taken to making the rock its place to watch the world back a generation, but his father hadn't known that. Corvin the crow. Mostly Corvin preferred the idea of being a rock, but there were days when he knew, in secret, that he was really the crow. Crows were drawn to battlefields, after all.

They called him Screambreaker after he shattered King Tane's army. They said his battle cry as the two sides had met had broken the Marroc. It wasn't true but it was a good story and so they called him that anyway. The other names, the ones the Marroc had given him, he supposed he'd earned them. He might, on another day, have claimed that they'd fallen on him unsought, that he'd never gone looking for them, but on nights like tonight he knew better. Battles made for widows. Wars made for nightmares. Death had danced with him with such an easy grace and for so long now that they might as well be wed. Together, the two of them in a longhouse somewhere growing old, Death and the Widowmaker. But they weren't. They were looking for each other still, finding each other now and then, and yet somehow one of them had always had another lover at the time, and so they were never joined. *Next year, when this one is gone. We both know we were meant to be.* Twenty years of it. He looked out over the fires. Would they find each other tomorrow?

The Vathen wouldn't reach Andhun until the afternoon. They wouldn't want a fight after a day of marching, and so he'd see that they got one. Tomorrow. One way or the other, his last great battle.

'General, the prince wants to see you.'

The Screambreaker didn't move. *General?* When had he become that? A long time ago, and another thing he'd never sought. A firebrand even in his own land, just like his brother, and so Yurlak had sent him across the sea. *Go and do something useful. If you have to stir up trouble, stir it with the Marroc not with me.* Yurlak had been afraid of him ... no, *afraid* wasn't the right word, because he and Yurlak were two of a kind and neither had ever been afraid of anything. But Yurlak had known well enough that Corvin, left to his own ends, was bound to break something. Better if what he broke was somewhere far away.

'I came here to be less trouble for my kin.' He was talking to the stars.

'General?'

Bring me back something pretty, and what he'd brought back was a crunching great war and a kingdom three times the size of the one Yurlak already had, and he'd given it away without a thought. There had been moments when he'd wondered about that. Set himself up as king of the Marroc? But a throne and a crown, what did he want with either of those? What use were they to a man?

He'd never married. Never raised a son. Rarely even taken a lover for long because he'd always known that death would be his bride. A tragic romance drawn out over the years, but they were bound together by fate, and every Lhosir knew better than to flout his destiny.

'General, the prince requires your ear.'

Corvin got to his feet. His knees ached from sitting still for too long. His bones creaked and groaned. He was getting old. He could have lived out his days back across the sea and taken his pick of what he wanted. Could have had Yurlak's own throne if he'd fancied it, pickling himself in mead and women until he was too fat to put on his armour, until horses screamed and bolted rather than carry him. The thought had filled him with daily horror as he'd seen the torpor of a quiet life slowly overtake him.

Only a fool prayed to the Maker-Devourer, so he'd prayed to his mistress, to death. And death had answered and had sent the Vathen for him.

'What does he want, our great prince?' The words dripped out of him. Twelvefingers had been so like the young Corvin that Yurlak had sent away. But the fates were fickle and Medrin had almost died in his first battle at Corvin's side, and the wound had taken years to truly heal, and by the time he was strong again, the war was all but done. Now look at him.

'That's for him to say, General.'

It hardly mattered. Tomorrow he'd either smash the Vathen or the Vathen would break him at last, and it would be what it would be. He followed the young soldier who'd been sent for him, a man too young to even have a full beard yet. Medrin's men they called themselves, the young ones who'd grown up seeing their fathers and their uncles sailing across the sea to fight. Who were used to tales of war and battles, used to hearing of nothing but victory, even if maybe their fathers and half their uncles never came back again. They were hungry for it, feeling they'd missed something, yet they had no idea of what war truly was. Tomorrow they'd know better.

Medrin had taken his tent. The Screambreaker supposed he was entitled. Yurlak's son, after all, but didn't he have his own?

'Screambreaker.' Medrin sat on a stool. He had a thin knife in his hand and he was using it to pick at the dirt under his fingernails.

'Medrin.' Corvin didn't bow. Medrin might expect it but that was a Marroc thing. Lhosir faced one another as equals. Always.

'You left Andhun to the Marroc.'

'Yes.'

'When I returned they tried to take the shield from me.'

'Did they succeed?'

Medrin stopped his picking and looked up. 'Clearly not, Screambreaker, otherwise I would not be here. Would you like to see it?'

'I've seen it before.' He nodded. 'It's a good thing. People will sing your saga for this. Your men will fight harder when they face the Vathen.'

'Why did you leave Andhun, Screambreaker?'

'To face the Vathen in the field.'

'But Andhun has walls.'

'It does. And a Lhosir doesn't hide behind walls.'

'And what's a row of shields then, if not a wall, Scream-breaker? Indeed, do we not call it a wall? A wall of shields?'

'A wall held by men.' Corvin closed his eyes for a moment. A headache. Yes, he had a headache coming. Now *there* was a thing that never used to trouble him on the night before a battle. Slept like a newborn, he used to. 'Do you mean to order us back through the gates, Medrin?'

'I strongly doubt the Marroc will open them for you. If the reception they gave their prince is anything to go by, I imagine they'd welcome us with arrows and javelins and anything else they can lift and throw.'

'They gave their word they wouldn't close their gates until the Vathen were in sight of the walls.'

'Have you looked, Screambreaker? Don't bother, because *I* have and they're firmly shut. I had to beach my ship a mile down the coast to get here at all.' Twelvefingers got up and walked to the back of the tent. He picked something out of the shadows, something dark and round. The shield. In the gloom it had lost its colour. 'Are we going to win, Screambreaker? Are *you* going to win?'

'Yes.' Strange to have no doubts about such a thing.

'They are ten times our number.'

'More like five.'

'They beat you outside Fedderhun.'

'Fedderhun was lost before the first blow.'

'Yet you fought it anyway?'

'Yes.' Hoping some good might come of it. Or that he might finally die.

'Me, I would have stayed behind the walls – as I was told by my prince until my prince came back and said otherwise.' He lifted the shield. 'You'll face the Vathen in the vanguard?'

'A man who claims leadership can do no less.'

Medrin put a hand over his heart, over the wound he'd taken

half a lifetime ago when he'd first crossed the sea. 'Harder for some than others.'

'Yes. But still true.'

'Should I give you this shield then, since you say you lead my army?'

'I lead those who will follow, no more. You took the shield. It's yours by right.'

Twelvefingers smiled for a moment. '*You* took it first.'

'And I lost it, and now you have it. It's a shield and I already have one.'

'I might give it to you as a gift.'

'And I will accept any gift given with a good heart, Twelvefingers. But there's no need.'

'I'm displeased with you about Andhun, so you'll get no gifts from me today. Win this battle and the shield is yours, Screambreaker. Now tell me how you'll do it.'

So Corvin told him. It wasn't any work of genius. Only the plan of a man who'd seen more of war than any other.

33

THE ROAD TO VARYXHUN

Gallow watched Jyrdas burn through the night. As the flames died, he went back to the beached ship and slept. In the morning Valaric was waiting for him. 'Give me your axe. No Lhosir carries arms in the streets of Andhun now.'

'My axe went to Jyrdas. If you want it, pick over his ashes.'

They walked side by side in silence up the beach, along the bank of the Isset and up the hill, past the castle towards the Castle Gate. The gibbets were all gone. Valaric followed his eyes. 'What, did you think we'd leave them?' Marroc soldiers fell in behind them. They jeered and threw insults, and if Valaric hadn't been there, Gallow knew they would have set upon him. They knew who he was. *What* he was.

The gates opened to let him through. Valaric turned his back.

'I fought among you against the Vathen,' Gallow said. 'I don't regret that. As for the rest, all I wanted was my family and my forge, making a life for us all. Watching my sons grow up happy and strong.'

Valaric turned his head and spat. 'Isn't that what we all wanted? A lot more of us would have had it if you forkbeards had stayed across the sea where you belong.' He walked away. The gates closed and Gallow was alone. The stumps of the gibbets remained beside the road where they'd been cut down. He stopped beside them and took the locket out from under his shirt, closing his fist around it. The Vathen had come. How could he not fight them? *Our land, yours and mine. I didn't ask for it. I didn't ask to find the Screambreaker half dead after we fled, but how could I leave him when he'd stood and fought as I had, with no reason save the doing of what was right? I didn't ask you to bring the Vathen to our home, and when you did,*

*how could I send him away alone, barely alive? O Arda, why did
you have to do that?* His grip on the locket was so tight it hurt.
His vision was swimming, tears on his cheeks. He still had the
money Tolvis had given him for the horses. A little to get him
home and plenty left to put a smile on Arda's face. If that was
what he wanted.

Fate. He walked past the ruins of homes that had once
crowded in the shadows of Andhun's walls. Was he sorry for
what he was? No. But no one had made him sail with Medrin,
chasing after the Crimson Shield. No one had made him offer
Tolvis Loudmouth his axe instead of leaving him in the road
and heading for Varyxhun with a string of Vathan horses. He
could have been beside a warm fire, listening to Arda shout and
rave at him for what had happened to their home, knowing all
the while that she loved him despite herself. He could have been
holding his children in his arms, watching them sleep. All he
had to do was forgive her for the one terrible thing she'd done.
Say it was a mistake, a moment of madness, though they both
knew it had been neither of those things.

The gibbets, the blood ravens, Medrin's murderous hunger,
Jyrdas's pyre: none of that would have been any different, but he
wouldn't have seen it. Yet now he had. And Arda would be a lie
too, however easy it might feel, and when the Maker-Devourer
whispered in his head at the end of his days, *Have you led a good
life?* what could he say? Not *Yes, yes, I have,* not any more.

He could feel Jyrdas's ghost laughing at him. *You've turned
into one of them. A sheep.* And perhaps it was true and perhaps
he was, and perhaps that wasn't so bad after all. He looked at the
locket one last time and then squeezed his eyes tightly shut as he
put it back inside his shirt.

The road towards the mountains was the one that he and
the Screambreaker had travelled after the hills around the
Crackmarsh. If he followed it far enough, it would take him to
Tarkhun, squeezed between the Isset and the Shadowwood and
the Ironwood. A boat across the water and he'd be on the Aulian
Way, past the Crackmarsh and then winding up the mountains
to the Aulian Bridge and the old fortress of Witches' Reach
guarding the entrance to the valley. And, past that, Varyxhun.

He wasn't sure how long it would take. Ten days? Twelve? Something like that. Plenty of time to think about what to say when he got there.

Away from the city gates the gibbets were still up. The bodies were little more than skeletons now, pecked clean by the birds. Further still and he passed small knots of men on the road. Lhosir. They looked him over.

'Another Marroc who wants to fight,' said one. 'Good for you. That way.' They pointed across the fields to where a haze of smoke hung over a low rise.

'What's that way?' he asked.

'The Vathen!' They laughed. 'Any more of you in there?'

Gallow shrugged. 'I'd keep out of the city for a bit if I were you, after the battle's done. Be safer out here.'

'Oh, I wouldn't worry about that. Best if *you* keep away, more likely.' They laughed again and rode on towards the gates.

'And what does that mean?' he called after them. They didn't answer but they didn't need to. If Medrin won, his anger with the Marroc for what Valaric had done on the beach would be unquenchable. Andhun would burn.

He walked on, talking to himself, muttering under his breath. Varyxhun, that was where he should be going. To Arda. To his family. To what *mattered*. And if Medrin happened to beat the Vathen and turned on Andhun and then burned it to the ground and slaughtered and raped every man and woman within its walls, was that his business? Arda would tell him no, it wasn't. And she was right, wasn't she?

Was that how to say he'd led a good life? Just let that be?

He didn't even notice that his feet had left the road until he reached the rise and saw the Lhosir army spread out on the other side of it. They'd taken him that way instead of towards his home, quietly and without a fuss, as though they knew perfectly well where he needed to go. *A fat lot of good that pledge was then.* Arda was laughing at him, mocking and scornful. *Lasted what? A few minutes?*

He pushed his hand to his chest. 'Sorry.'

Was that how to say he'd led a good life? No, it wasn't.

Can't eat sorry. But she'd betrayed him. She'd betrayed all of them. And she had no answer to that.

Smoke from the campfires – he could smell it, could see its dirty stain in the air. It was hardly suffocating, but for some reason it was making his eyes water again. He saw Arda behind him, clear as the sun, waving him away as he'd gone to fight the Vathen at Lostring Hill, shaking her head. *Stupid men. Always think they have to fight. Can't you just stay here and look after the people who matter? What about us, Gallow? What do we do when you get yourself stuck on the end of a spear?* She too had had tears in her eyes. *Going to have to find myself a Vathan now, am I?* The more she shouted and raved at him not to go, the more she gave herself away.

'I will come back,' he'd murmured, 'I swear it.'

That's what Merethin said. She turned her back on him and disappeared.

No one challenged him as he walked through the Lhosir army. He found the Screambreaker at his breakfast at the far edge of the camp, looking out towards where the Vathen would come.

'Truesword.' He didn't look up. 'When Medrin came back with the shield, I wondered what happened to you. And to Loudmouth and to Jyrdas.'

Gallow looked around him. The soldiers nearby were old ones. The Screambreaker's men, the ones who'd fought the Marroc years ago. Men he trusted. 'Jyrdas? A Marroc put an arrow in him. Jyrdas killed a couple of them anyway, just to make a point. Then he called Medrin *nioingr* until Medrin stuck a knife through his good eye to shut him up.'

'Sounds like Jyrdas.'

'The Marroc let me built him a pyre and speak him out and then they let me go.'

'Good of them.' The Screambreaker was still staring out across the fields as though none of what Gallow was telling him particularly mattered. He pointed. 'The Vathen will come from there. They won't want to fight today, so we'll take it to them.' He beckoned an old Lhosir closer and whispered in his ear. The soldier nodded and trotted away.

'I feel the Maker-Devourer more closely these days,' said Gallow. 'You and I have a grudge between us. I would have it ended before I meet him. You spoke words not fitting for a guest in my house. Or were you too gone with fever to remember?'

'I've not forgotten, Gallow. We'll settle it after the Vathen are defeated.'

'And if I want to settle it now?'

'I'll say no and remind you that you're a Marroc and have no voice here. If I call you *nioingr*, so what?' He turned sharply, before Gallow could reach for a blade. 'Hold your hand, True-sword. Fight the Vathen. Fight beside me as I know you can and I'll concede that the words I spoke were wrong.'

'Concede it now!'

'No.'

'Why?'

The Screambreaker stood up and faced Gallow squarely. 'I remember you from the old days, Truesword. You were fierce and terrible, without mercy or remorse, and I was proud to have you fight among my men. I saw you fight the Vathen on the way to Andhun and I saw the man I remembered. But you've changed. Your beard is gone. You're either more or less than the man I once knew and I don't know which it is. Do you, Gallow?'

Maker-Devourer! But this was the Screambreaker, who never gave ground, not to anyone and not for anything. Half a smile crept onto Gallow's face. 'I'm me, old man. Born every part a Lhosir but Marroc too. So yes, I'll fight beside you if that's what it takes, and if I have to kill three Vathen for every one of yours to prove what I say then so be it. But when you take back your words, you'll owe me a boon.'

'True enough.'

'Then I'll ask you for it now, so that if I die you'll know what to do. When the battle is won, Medrin will call for Andhun to be sacked. Deny him.'

'This isn't my army, Truesword. Twelvefingers can do what he wants.'

Gallow laughed in his face. 'It's every bit your army, Screambreaker, and if you give them victory today, they'd follow you even if old Yurlak himself was here to tell them otherwise.'

'Twelvefingers is Yurlak's son. You're asking me to defy my king and my friend.' The Screambreaker sniffed. 'The Marroc of Andhun gave their word that they would open the gates to us if the Vathen are defeated. If they honour that, I see no reason for any reprisal. But the Marroc who attacked Medrin and killed One-Eye, I'll not spare them. They made their fate and they'll be punished for that without mercy. They'll hang in the streets. For once I agree with Twelvefingers. I'll not move on that, Truesword.'

Gallow met his eye. 'Then if the gates open, let the punishment be theirs and theirs alone. That's the boon I ask.'

'Done.' The Screambreaker scowled and flipped a knife from his belt. He made a shallow cut in his arm a little above the wrist and offered the blade to Gallow, who took it and did the same. They clasped their arms together so their blood would mingle. The Screambreaker looked at the men around him. 'Witness this, my friends. This man Gallow Truesword claims I have slandered him. If he fights well today, he will have proved he is right and I will have spoken poorly of him and unjustly so. *If* he is right, there shall be no plundering of Andhun after the Vathen are broken, and if others say otherwise, I stand against them.' He let Gallow go. 'I'm only one man, Truesword.'

Gallow snorted. 'No, you're not, Widowmaker. You've not been that for a long time.'

'Either way, you have to prove me wrong first.'

'That I can do.'

For a moment the Screambreaker smiled. 'Yes. The man I remember could do that.'

'I have another boon to ask.'

The general laughed. 'Against what debt?'

'None.' He took the purse of silver off his belt and held it out. 'But if I die, I'd have this taken to my family. To my wife Arda in Varyxhun.'

The Screambreaker shook his head and waved him away. 'And what if *I* die, Truesword? Who will take it then?'

'You'll never die.'

A dark look crossed the Screambreaker's face. He turned away. 'Don't be so sure, Truesword, not today.' He snatched the

purse. 'But very well. I'll find a way. If you die and I live, I will
have it done. If I die and *you* live, it will find its way back to
you.' He sighed and leaned forward. 'The truth is, Truesword,
that perhaps I do owe you a boon. Do you want a reason to live
through his battle? Perhaps I have one for you. It was not your
wife who betrayed me to the Vathen. It was the old man.'

For a moment Gallow stared into nothing. 'What? *What?*'

'It was the old man who told the carter that I was in your
house. The old smith. Nadric? Was that his name?'

'Nadric, yes. But ...' All the feeling drained out of Gallow's
face and his fingers, as though his heart had stopped pumping
blood and was keeping it all to itself. 'How do ...' He shook his
head.

'How do I know?' The Screambreaker's lips twitched into a
thin smile. 'Because when you dragged the carter and your wife
out of the barn, every man and woman there, me included, was
quite certain you were going to kill them. The old man blabbed
then. Said it was him. Wailed and howled and kept clutching at
my foot until I had to kick him in the face to shut him up. Wasn't
at my best then, if you remember. I've seen a lot of begging and
wailing in my time, Truesword. I know the ones who are telling
the truth. He meant it. It was him, Truesword. Not your wife.'

Gallow couldn't move. 'And you thought I was going to kill
her, and you didn't stop me?'

'No.'

'And you didn't tell me. All the way to Andhun and you *never
thought to tell me.*'

Rage was boiling up inside him. The Screambreaker looked
him in the eye. 'For a while I thought you *had* killed her and the
carter. It's what I would have done, and if you had, I didn't think
you'd want to hear. After that, I wanted you back in Andhun.'

'You *what?*'

'I wanted you here, Truesword. I wanted you at my side
against the Vathen. And against Twelvefingers, if it comes to it.
So live through this day, Truesword, and then go back to your
Marroc wife and your sons when it's done. And ask, if you must,
why *she* didn't tell you either. But I think we both know the
answer. Now go away. Eat and rest. We have a hard day before

us. Find yourself a spear and a sword and an axe to go with that shield. We have plenty.'

The Screambreaker turned away. Gallow watched him go. *Why? Why didn't you tell me?* But the Screambreaker was right, the answer obvious: because in his anger he would have murdered Nadric there and then, and there would have been no going back from that. And so she'd lied to him and trusted to the truth that she was the one person he could never hurt.

He closed his eyes and thought of her. Arda. She hadn't betrayed him after all and everything would be as it was.

The two of you are the same, she seemed to whisper. *You dress it up in valour and glory, but really you just like fighting.* He thought that if he listened hard enough, there might have been a smile somewhere in there.

He settled himself among the Screambreaker's men, keeping among them and away from others who might recognise him. He filled his belly and armed himself as he was told, and then he sat, quietly waiting for the Vathen to come, touching the locket under his shirt.

I have to make my life a good one, he told her.

You might find it easier if you didn't try so bloody hard, she answered, and he smiled and sat easily, waiting for the Vathen to come, full of all his memories of her, of all the scoldings and the rolling eyes and the rare twinkle that now and then lay behind them.

34

THE VANGUARD

Gallow stood shoulder to shoulder with men he barely knew. The Screambreaker faced them from the back of his horse, proud and noble and fierce. He was the best. The Lhosir knew that. He was invincible, *they* were invincible, and the Vathan numbers would be no use to them. They'd stumble over their own dead as they ran and the slaughter would be terrible.

'For Andhun,' Gallow whispered to himself. 'For all the Marroc. And for you, Arda. Please understand why I must do this.' He held his shield firmly in one hand, a spear in the other. At his belt he carried an axe and a sword. He stood loose, not tense like the younger men. His mail felt old and comfortable like a long-missed friend and his helm seemed to whisper words of calm into his ear. The mail at least was still his own, good solid metal plundered from a dead Marroc a decade ago, and he trusted it now as he'd trusted it then. He'd been here before, more times than he cared to count. He remembered how it felt, the tension, the blood running fast and hot.

'Look at them!' the Screambreaker shouted. 'Look at them! See how many they are and rejoice, my warriors! Feel how it will be, for they will break upon your shields like water on the rocks and die writhing upon your spears like fish caught helpless in a net. You will stand fast and they will see you there, waiting for them with your shields held strong and your spears held high, helms bright, and they will come up this hill and every step will sap their strength. Their legs will ache and their souls will quiver. You will scream Yurlak's name in their faces and fall upon them, and they will quiver like women and they will break! And as each slaughtered rank turns and flees they will spread your terror and their numbers will count for nothing! We are

Lhosir! We have the strength of the bear, the fangs of the wolf and the speed of the hawk!'

The Vathen were crossing the bottom of the valley, the first rank now marching steadily up the hill. So many, but they'd been marching all day, and now it was the middle of the afternoon and they'd be tired while the Screambreaker's army was fresh.

The Screambreaker turned his horse and cantered away. He'd be back. Back to the centre where his own small band of Lhosir stood waiting for him, Gallow among them. The men he'd brought back across the sea with him for one more fight. *They* wouldn't break. They were soldiers who'd seen ten years of war, who'd fought in a dozen battles like this and won all but one.

Either side of the advancing Vathan centre black swarms of horse scattered towards the flanks, ready to envelop the Lhosir and come at them from the side and the rear. Pits filled with spikes waited for them, and hidden clusters of spearmen with shields and javelin throwers lurked at the edge of the trees. Archers, even a few hundred of those, from the few Marroc who'd come out to fight. There were more than Gallow had thought and Valaric would be fuming if he knew, but this was right, wasn't it? Lhosir and Marroc together, fighting for their land.

The Vathen were a hundred yards away when the Scream-breaker returned. He walked slowly between the two armies as though the enemy was barely worth his notice and took his place in the front line in the middle of his men. They made space for him with an easy movement practised for years.

Fifty yards and the Marroc archers behind the Lhosir line let fly. They were shooting long, Gallow saw, over the top of the Vathan shield wall, raining their havoc on the lines behind where men couldn't see what was happening around them. The arrows would bring confusion and despair. Men would raise their shields over their heads so as not to be scythed down, and then they wouldn't see anything except the man standing in front of them. This was how the Screambreaker fought his wars, with fear and panic as his sword and shield.

Thirty yards and the black-painted Vathen let out a roar and charged. The sky grew dark as the ranks behind both lines of shields hurled javelins, clubs, sticks, stones, anything they'd been able to carry into battle. Men screamed and fell. Gallow raised his shield, hiding his face, shielding the man on his left as well. A javelin almost split the wood right in front of his eyes. A stone glanced off his helm. The Lhosir on his right howled as blood fountained from his ripped-open neck.

'Get him out! Get him out!' Gallow smashed the javelin out of his shield and then the Vathen and the Lhosir crashed together. A spear came at his face. He ducked and jabbed his own point at a Vathan, caving in the man's teeth, slicing open his cheek and ripping the back of his throat.

The Lhosir beside him finished dying. He sank slowly down with another spear through his face, pointlessly killed for a second time. Another stepped up from behind. They'd be standing on each others' corpses soon, but better that than fall. Anyone who fell was dead. Men screamed as they tried to kill each other and men screamed as they died, and soon the screams all sounded the same. A Vathan swung an axe. It turned off the mail on Gallow's shoulder and then hooked his shield, tugging it away. Gallow stabbed the man with his spear. The crush was suffocating. He ducked another thrust. Ribs cracked from the sheer press of men. His shield was pressed hard into the Vathan in front of him, so close he could see the whites of his eyes, but the crush made them both almost powerless.

Another spear point glanced off his helm. He pushed his shield forward, hard and sudden, made a momentary inch of space and lunged his spear straight down into the foot of the Vathan in front of him. The Vathan screamed and dropped his guard and the Lhosir behind Gallow jabbed a spear into his face. Gallow watched the Vathan die, a terrible glee inside him. A dead man trapped in front of him meant he could strike more freely, and so he did, thrust after thrust. Most of the Vathen were down to knives and axes now, but the Lhosir had learned to keep their spears. The battle turned slowly to slaughter.

A horn sounded. The Vathen broke off and stumbled away. The Lhosir line took two paces forward, unable to help themselves. A few cheered, the young ones who didn't know any better. For a moment Gallow had to brace himself against his own men so as not to be pushed forward down the hill. He was breathing hard and the battle had barely started.

A cloud moved across the sun, stealing its light and its heat. He was grateful for that. He sucked in the spring air, the smell of grass and flowers and trees now tainted by the sweat of men and the tang of steel and blood. The sun was too hot for a heavy leather coat and mail but he held back the urge to take off his helm and cool his head. That was how men died. He'd seen it.

The black-painted Vathen front line melted away down the hill. The next line waited just out of javelin range, shields raised against the Marroc archers. He could see the enemy – from the brow of the hill they all could. The last ranks of the Vathen were at the bottom of the valley now, still crossing the stream there. The rest were massing on the lower slope, taking their time.

So many.

It started to rain. An hour earlier and that might have changed the battle, made the hill into a sea of mud and crippled the Vathan advance. Too late now, but the cold water was still delicious. It wouldn't last. Five minutes, maybe ten, and then the cloud would pass and he'd have the sun on his back again.

'For Yurlak!' shouted the man beside him. 'For the Scream-breaker!' The Lhosir was quivering. He still had his shield, but his spear was gone and all he had now was an axe. Gallow watched the Vathen. The next line of them was painted bloody red. They didn't move. Very slowly, without taking his eyes off them, Gallow moved his spear to his shield hand. He carefully crouched and leaned forward, reaching for a spear that hung from the belly of a dead Vathan. The rain was coming down hard now, dripping into his eyes. His fingers closed around the haft of the spear. He pulled it slowly towards him and then jerked it free and passed it to the soldier beside him.

'They bleed like any others,' he said. The rain was already easing.

'Don't they just.'

The Vathen lowered their spears, pointing them straight at the faces of the Lhosir. Gallow felt the soldiers around him tense, bracing for another fight, but the Vathen held their ground, and then through the midst of them came a giant in blood-red mail.

His shield was black, but when the giant drew out his sword, the blade was a deep red like his mail, with an edge as long as a man's leg. The air fell still, the voices of the Lhosir and the Vathen alike quiet. The giant held out his sword and swung it this way and that. As he cut the air, the sound it made was like the shivering moans of lost souls.

'The Sword of the Weeping God!' The Lhosir beside him raised an eye. 'So they really have it then.'

'And we have the shield,' said Gallow. He stared. The sword he'd seen in his dream of the Weeping God, before he'd left Andhun, and again after Gorrin had hit him on the back of his head under the monastery. 'It's just a sword, no better or worse than the man who wields it.' Today he said it as much for himself as for anyone else.

The soldier grinned. 'Aye. And that man is no Lhosir!'

The giant walked up to the Lhosir line, batting aside a hail of missiles with his shield or simply letting them bounce off his armour. When he reached them and the first Lhosir tried to stab him, he caught the spear in the sword's guard and wrenched it away. He took another blow to his shield, this time from a sword, and then Gallow couldn't see anything, but there were screams and the giant was bellowing something; and then there was the Screambreaker, out in front of the Lhosir.

'Here!' he cried. 'Here I am! Corvin the Screambreaker. Widowmaker! Nightmare of the North!' He threw down his spear, jamming the point into the ground, and drew his sword. 'I have no god-touched blade or shield, but I will still bleed you. So face me if you dare, Vathan!'

The giant turned. He pointed the red sword at the Screambreaker and roared. The second Vathan line raised their spears and charged, the hail of stones and javelins began again and the giant and the Screambreaker vanished into the swirl of swords and spears. At the front of the shield wall, crushed by friends from behind and the enemy in front, barely able to move, Gallow had no eyes for either. The flash of swords and spear points became all that mattered. He stabbed the Vathan in front of him in the foot, same as he had the last, and the man behind Gallow, a stranger, finished the job just as he had before with a sure understanding for him even though they'd met only minutes ago. Blood flecked Gallow's face and spattered his helm. His arm screamed with the effort of holding up his spear but he shut out the pain and stabbed and stabbed until this line of Vathen fell back like the last, leaving their own new litter of corpses behind.

The giant with the red sword was still standing. He prowled between the lines, bellowing challenges. The Lhosir answered him again with stones and javelins, and the giant shrugged them aside in disdain. Again the Screambreaker stepped out to face him and again the giant ignored him. The Lhosir jeered. Another line of Vathen assembled down the slope.

'Where are their horse?' muttered Gallow. The longer they took about this next attack the better. His arm was killing him. They'd all tire soon. Whatever stamina advantage they'd had taking the battle to the Vathen today, that was surely gone now.

'Not here,' said the Lhosir beside him. 'That's all that matters. I don't know your face, but you must be Gallow Truesword since you're the only man without a beard. They say you've taken to living among the Marroc.'

'So I did.'

'Well you don't fight like them.' The soldier nudged him, the closest they could get to clasping arms with their shields still held up in front of them. 'Nodas of Houndfell. I've heard of you. Some things good, some things bad. The good came from men I know and trust, the bad I'm less keen to believe now I've stood beside you.'

'Well, Nodas of Houndfell, if we live through this, you can tell me all of both over a keg of Marroc beer.'

Nodas laughed. 'More likely I'll tell it to you in the Maker-Devourer's cauldron.'

Here and there, up and down the line as the giant walked, other Lhosir stepped forward, throwing down their own challenges and laughing as they were ignored. 'What's he doing?'

'Making a fool of himself.'

And the Vathen came again.

35

GIANT

Wave after wave came, and each time the Lhosir line threw them back and held its ground. Then finally the Vathen sent their horsemen, who threw a hail of javelots and withdrew, and when they did, the Lhosir plucked the javelots from the ground and out of their shields and passed them back to those behind them, so that the next ranks of advancing Vathen felt them too.

After each wave the giant was still there. The hill was awash with the dead now, piled up to make each Vathan advance harder than the last, but the Vathen weren't the only ones dying and there were still thousands upon thousands of them on the lower slopes. Taking their time. Waiting. Slowly wearing the Lhosir down until they didn't have the strength to hold their shields tight and their spears high. When Gallow looked over his shoulder, the Lhosir line looked thin. He couldn't see much past the helms and the angry faces, but there, right at the brow of the hill, Medrin's standard still flew. Five hundred men, the Screambreaker had said, to throw into the fight wherever they were needed.

'Let them miss it all,' said Nodas. 'All the glory for us.' He was breathing heavily and bleeding from a savage cut across his cheek that must have gone right through the skin, judging from the blood dripping from the corner of his mouth.

'Medrin needs to do something with those.'

'He does. Imagine if they miss it all. They'll kill him.'

The next wave came. A moment before it broke, the Vathan in front of Gallow hooked Nodas's shield with an axe and pulled it down, and the next Vathan along stabbed Nodas squarely with a long knife. The blade skittered off Nodas's mail, straight up his chest and buried itself in his throat. Nodas looked surprised, then angry, and then nothing much at all. When the Vathen withdrew once more, he toppled forward onto the mound of bodies that lay in front of the Lhosir line. Gallow looked at the sky. A warm spring evening, the sun sinking low but not yet starting to tinge with orange. Another two hours maybe before dark. Two hours? He didn't have the strength for that.

'Twelvefingers!' The Screambreaker stepped out from the line again. He looked exhausted. 'Call our prince to the centre before we win the battle without him! Medrin! Medrin!' The shout went up, but when Gallow looked to the brow of the hill, the prince's standard never moved.

It started to rain again, a longer shower and heavier than the last. The Vathen didn't wait this time but came again, though they weren't happy about it. They slipped and stumbled among the bodies of their own fallen and this time broke quickly. On the slopes across the valley Gallow saw more movement. Men running away perhaps, chased down by Vathan riders? Or something else. But either way the battle was close to its end. The Lhosir were losing their strength and the Vathen were losing their stomach for it.

The giant was roaming in front of the next line of Vathen again. No one threw anything at him any more because no one had anything left to throw. Even the Marroc archers had fallen silent.

'Face me!' bellowed the Screambreaker. He looked as though he could barely stand. His shield sagged and he couldn't keep the point of his spear up. And now, at last, the giant stopped and turned. He faced the Screambreaker and twirled his sword. Around him the air moaned, and if the giant was worn down at all by two hours of fighting, he didn't show it. He came at the Screambreaker slowly, cautiously, while the Screambreaker circled away from his own men, inviting the giant in closer.

The giant closed the gap between them with a charge and swung the red sword. The Screambreaker didn't even try to strike back but threw himself out of the way, stumbling and barely keeping his feet. The giant whirled and swung again – this time the Screambreaker slipped as he ducked out of the way.

He rolled and dropped his shield as he scrabbled back. Gallow frowned. The Screambreaker? Dropping his shield?

The giant roared. He came on slowly.

'He's playing with him,' Gallow whispered in disgust.

'Yes,' said the man beside him, a greybeard Lhosir who'd come up to stand in Nodas's place. 'But then he's only fighting a Vathan, and the Vathan has refused him a half a dozen times already. Give the old sword his sport.'

It took Gallow a moment to understand. The greybeard thought he'd meant the Screambreaker?

The Vathan took another swing. As the Screambreaker launched himself out of the way, the giant lunged with his shield, battering the Screambreaker back and knocking him down. The Screambreaker dropped his spear now too. He rolled and barely got out of the way as the giant struck out yet again. He hauled himself to his feet and stumbled away, then staggered and tripped over a body with a spear sticking out of it and fell. The Vathan laughed. As the Screambreaker pulled himself to his feet, the giant roared and drew back the red sword for the killing blow.

The Screambreaker drew his own sword in the middle of the giant's backswing and threw it. The Vathan swatted it away with his shield but just for a moment he blocked his own sight of the Screambreaker, and that was when Corvin moved with a sudden surge of speed, rolled and snatched his spear from the ground where he'd dropped it. The Vathan took a moment to see where the Screambreaker had gone and by then it was too late. The Nightmare of the North came up into a crouch to one side of him and thrust the spear sideways into the giant's knee. The Vathan screamed. Now the Screambreaker didn't look tired at all. He picked up an axe and a shield from the battlefield and marched straight forward, whirling the axe over his head as if to finish the fight, and then dropped suddenly to one knee and let the axe fly. It caught the giant just above the ankle of his other leg; the Vathan roared and down he went, both legs ruined. The Screambreaker picked up another spear. The giant tried to protect himself with his shield as Corvin walked in circles around him, out of reach of the red sword, jabbing with his spear, but it was hardly any time at all before the Screambreaker found a way through and touched the spear point to the giant's throat. He held it there lightly.

'Yield!' he cried, loud enough for both the Vathen and the Lhosir to hear.

The giant's answer, if he gave one, was lost to the wind, but it was clear what it must have been, for the Screambreaker suddenly leaned hard into his spear and drove it through the giant's neck. Then he took another axe, cut off the giant's hand, unpeeled his dead fingers from the red sword and held it high where everyone could to see. 'Solace!' He cried. 'The Peacebringer! The Comforter! The Sword of the Weeping God! Sorrow's Edge! See! Just a sword! That's all it is! There is no god here guiding any hand to victory. There are only men.'

Cries went up from the Lhosir lines, jeering and cheering and laughing at their enemy, but if the Screambreaker was hoping for the Vathen to break and flee, what he got was the opposite. Instead of coming up the hill at a steady pace, the next wave broke into a run, howling in rage and fury, surging forward at such a fierce pace that the Screambreaker had to run to make it back to his own line. He pushed into the shield wall beside Gallow.

'Look at it,' he hissed. 'It's just a sword. Give me a spear any day.' Gallow offered his own, but the Screambreaker shook his head. 'I left the scabbard for this on the giant's body.'

'Then throw it away, if it's just a sword.'

'I'll see how it swings first.' The Vathen smashed into the Lhosir line and their first ranks were slaughtered, undone by their own fury, but more and more and more of them came, rank after rank running up the hill to pile into the back of the heaving melee, pushing and pushing. Gallow stabbed with his spear over and over. Beside him the Sword of the Weeping God sang as it cut the air. And it *wasn't* just a sword, whatever the Screambreaker said, for the red steel cut through mail and man as nothing Gallow had ever seen. From behind his shield the Screambreaker lunged and the sword point seemed to seek out the Vathen with a will of its own over and over, throats and necks and faces. And the Vathen were afraid of it, Gallow saw that too. Within the Screambreaker's reach they whimpered, eyes wild, and dropped their swords and axes and clutched at their shields, eyes on nothing else.

But beyond the circle of fear that reached to the tip of the red sword, the Vathen had become a raging horde. They pressed and howled and died at the points of the Lhosir spears but still they came on, and the push of them forced the Lhosir slowly back up the hill, a litter of dead in their wake for the Vathen to climb.

'Medrin!' roared the Screambreaker. 'Twelvefingers! We need his five hundred! We need them here! To the centre! Now!'

Gallow lost his spear, lodged in some Vathan helmet and torn out of his hand. A brief rain of arrows fell, loosed by the Vathen but falling on Vathen and Lhosir alike. He hacked and slashed with his axe, tearing at the men either side of him. His face was covered with blood, his helm, his mail; Vathan gore spattered across his shield. And always beside him the red sword lunged and lunged as if the Screambreaker's arm was made of iron and never tired. The Lhosir beside Gallow on the other side fell and another pushed up to take his place and fell in turn to be replaced by yet another.

'Where's Twelvefingers?' the Screambreaker shouted again.

The man on the other side of Gallow staggered, his helm knocked sideways by a javelin from among the Vathen. Before he could recover, an axe hooked his shield, a sword lunged and he was falling backwards. This time no one stepped forward. Gallow snatched a glance behind him. There was no one there. No Lhosir left, only fifty yards of open grass to the top of the hill. And Medrin with his five hundred. Standing fast and doing nothing.

The Vathen swarmed around him. He took a step back – had no choice or they'd be round his shield. Took another, back among those few Lhosir that were left. For a moment the Screambreaker was open. Unguarded where Gallow's shield should have been. Gallow watched helplessly as the onslaught battered him back. They were all over Corvin. A Vathan clawed at the Screambreaker's shield, pulling it away with his fingers. The red sword rose and fell, driven with such force it burst clear through the Vathan's head. Another swung an axe and the arc of the red sword cut both axe and man in two; yet as that Vathan fell, another lunged with his sword and another leaped at the Screambreaker, and then another and another and they bore him staggering to the ground. Gallow screamed and swung his own axe in great circles around him, but there was no getting through. The Vathen were everywhere now. The centre of the Lhosir line had gone. There simply weren't any of them left.

Then finally Medrin came.

36

THE SWORD OF
THE WEEPING GOD

Medrin and his five hundred swept down the hillside, spears held high, Medrin in the middle of them, the Crimson Shield gleaming in the evening sun. A minute sooner and the Screambreaker would still have stood. A minute later and Gallow would have fallen too. The Vathen around him faltered and wavered. He swung wildly, not caring whether or what he struck, thinking of nothing except to drive them away from the fallen Screambreaker. He smashed this way and that and then Medrin's Lhosir swept into the swirling melee and at last the Vathen broke and ran, colliding with their own men still marching up the hill. Gallow curled up as the Lhosir hit, and when they were past he staggered to where the Screambreaker lay still, surrounded by a ring of corpses, his face in a pool of blood. His grey beard was black, matted with it. There was no way to know *whose* blood, but he wasn't moving. Gallow crouched beside him, cradling the old warrior. The roar of the battle died away, the shouts of victory mingling with the wails of the dying. Corvin looked old now, so frail and fragile and nothing like the Screambreaker who'd stood before them at the start of the battle, telling them how the Vathen would be smashed. There was so much blood that Gallow couldn't see the wound that had finally brought him down. The Screambreaker was still breathing, though fast and shallow. Gallow had seen it a hundred times before: the last ragged breaths of a man as he set his sails and packed his axe for the Maker-Devourer's cauldron.

'He let this happen,' Gallow whispered. 'Medrin. He stood and watched with his men all around him, doing nothing, waiting for you to fall. And you very nearly didn't.'

A coldness washed through him as the frenzy of battle slowly drained. He hadn't really thought about what he was saying, but now the words were spoken he saw they had a truth to them. Medrin *had* waited, and now there was no one left to stand up to him. No one left to keep him from crashing into Andhun, from slaughtering every Marroc inside, man, woman and child.

He let the Screambreaker slide back into the bloody mud. The dead littered the hillside like autumn leaves after a storm. The sun hung low and bloated and orange. It shimmered on burnished helms, broken swords and blood-drenched mail. Solace slipped out of the old man's fingers, almost as if he was making one last wish. *You* stop him.

Gallow looked at the red sword. His hand closed around the hilt. Medrin wanted that sword, he wanted it badly. Maybe Gallow could bargain with it. The sword for Andhun? But Medrin was the worst *nioingr*, a liar and not to be trusted. Gallow stood with the Sword of the Weeping God in his hand, looking down the hill. The Vathen were streaming away down the hillside. Bodies lay scattered everywhere, trampled. In the dying light of the day the valley was stained by a tide of red. Like a beach at low tide after a storm, littered with debris, only here the sea had been a sea of blood.

A last few Lhosir were standing around him, dazed and confused and wondering what to do. The Screambreaker's men, the handful who'd survived. Old soldiers all, most of them bloody and broken from Vathan swords and spears, staggering and close to collapse. They'd fought for hours, watched the battle slowly slip away and then watched Medrin steal it back at the last. Gallow raised the red sword.

'Men of the sea! You fought for the Screambreaker. Here he lies!' He began to walk among them, pointing to the Screambreaker's body, still surrounded by Vathan dead. 'It was no Vathan who killed him. Twelvefingers did this. Your prince. He waited for us to die.'

'He gave us glory,' said one whose arm hung uselessly at his side.

'No. We took our own glory. Twelvefingers wants us gone. We who remember the old ways, who honour the Maker-Devourer.' He picked a face he knew. 'I knew you once, Thanni

Ironfoot. Jyrdas was your friend. Medrin poked out his other eye.' Another. 'Galdun. You too. At Selleuk's Bridge we turned and ran, but never again. And Twelvefingers has you guarding gates?'

But they wouldn't listen. They were too hurt, too dimmed by their wounds and dazzled by victory. He'd end it himself then. The Red Sword raised once more against the Crimson Shield. The Weeping God come at last to face his old brother and foe, Modris the Protector. He left the Screambreaker where he'd fallen to finish his dying among the men who remembered him best and started off down the hill, picking his way through the dead. There were so many, Lhosir and Vathen all jumbled together, lying on top of one another; and then further on there were only Vathen. He reached the black-armoured giant and stopped to take the belt and the scabbard of the Weeping God. On the ground the giant didn't seem so large after all.

So many dead. Did any of them even know why the Vathen had come? Did the Vathen know themselves? He saw a few of them still alive, the injured, the crippled, the ones too frightened or damaged to move. They watched him fearfully but he let them be. There was only one man left on this battlefield he wanted to add to the tally of the dead.

He began to pass Lhosir moving among the bodies, looting them while it was still light. Men who'd lost their spears and their axes, their helms, searching among the dead for weapons, stripping boots and hauberks, plucking out arrows, collecting javelins before night fell and the battlefield belonged to the wolves. The sun had touched the hills now. It would be too dark to chase the Vathen down before long, and so the Screambreaker's design had a flaw after all. The Vathen wouldn't be scattered. They'd come again in the morning, if they had the will for it.

'Medrin?' The Lhosir he passed pointed down into the valley where the last shouts of fighting still echoed; and as the sun sank behind the hills he found the prince marching back up the slope of the battlefield with Horsan and a dozen more of his men around him. They stopped when they saw Gallow. Medrin spread his arms wide.

'Truesword! Look at us! Victorious once again.' He squinted

at Gallow. 'How many Vathen came to this field today? My men say thirty thousand marched through Fedderhun. The Scream-breaker said it was more like twenty-five and my own eyes say more like twenty. But still, four or five times our numbers, and look at them, Gallow. Look! When word of this crosses the sea, more will come. We'll march across their nation as the Screambreaker marched across the Marroc!'

All the while his eyes were locked on the sword. Gallow held it up in the orange light of the dying sun. 'Is this what you're looking for?'

'We saw the Screambreaker take down the Vathan giant and take his sword, every one of us. His legend is complete. But ... how is that *you* carry it now, Gallow?'

'The Screambreaker fell while you stood at the top of the hill and did nothing.'

'He's gone?' Medrin didn't even bother trying to sound troubled or surprised.

'He is.'

'Give me the sword, Gallow.' Medrin held out his hand. 'Give me the sword. I will carry it in his name, for his memory, and you will march beside me. The sword and the shield together. No one will stand before the Lhosir.'

'*You?*' Gallow spat at his feet. 'Carry it in *his* memory?' He pointed the sword at Medrin. 'And when your father dies, shall we build his pyre from a pile of turds too? Do you imagine I've forgotten the temple of the Fates, Medrin? You and Beyard and I? The Screambreaker told me you'd changed, you were now a man whose beard was fine and strong, but I've watched you and I do not believe that to be so. Where were you when Jyrdas and Tolvis and I opened the gates of the monastery for you? How was it that one of your men struck Jyrdas in the back? And when he *still* wouldn't die, you finished the work yourself!'

'Jyrdas spoke words that could not be left unanswered!' Medrin's face darkened.

'You let the Screambreaker die. You waited for him to fall.'

'No, Gallow. I waited for the moment when the Vathen would break. And they did.'

'This victory is his. It could not have been without him.'

Medrin nodded. 'True enough.' He held out his hand again. 'Now give me the sword, Gallow.' For a moment his face changed. He looked sad, almost pained. 'I need it to put something right.' He nodded at Gallow. 'All those years ago.'

'I will not give it to a *nioingr*!'

A stillness swept over the Lhosir. They stopped whispering to each other and stared.

'*Nioingr!*' declared Gallow again. 'You're not fit to crawl across the mud he walked, Twelvefingers. You're a coward and a liar. I call you again. *Nioingr!*'

Called three times. There was no turning back from that, and now Medrin had to answer with steel, and then Gallow would kill him no matter what shield he carried.

But Medrin only laughed. Not just laughed, but threw back his head and howled while his men looked uncertainly at one another. 'And who are you, Gallow? Or what? Here are my words, then, to answer your slur, for *I* have not forgotten that day in the Temple of Fates either. Yes, I ran, that's true and shameful. But what fate befell *you*, Gallow? Nothing, though it was *your* foolishness that betrayed us. Never caught? Never punished? I've long held that against you, Gallow, for it was you I thought of as I watched a man I called a friend cast away by my own father and taken across the cold seas to the icy castle of the Eyes of Time. How was it that *you*, Gallow, didn't suffer the same fate? Yet you brought the Screambreaker to Andhun and he spoke for you. "Pay no heed to his clean chin," he told me. "This is Gallow Truesword who fought with me against the Marroc. A fine man worthy of his beard and he has not changed, not in his heart. Grown strong now by the forge of war." And so I offered you a place at my side again to see the shield we sought once before. An effort to look past the friend I lost, yet my reward for such trust? You turn my men against me. Tolvis, Jyrdas, how many minds did you poison with your lies? And when that wasn't enough, when the shield was mine for the taking, finally we all saw the truth of Gallow Truesword, the bitterness and the envy. I take your name and give you another: Gallow Foxbeard. From this time hence that is how you shall be known and remembered by those who care to remember you at all. And how is it, Gallow Foxbeard, that I left you bound among the Marroc and yet here you are? How is it that you escaped Andhun when the streets ran with traitors baying for Lhosir blood? Did you not walk openly to the gates? Did they not throw them wide for you? Why weren't you killed, clean-skin? Because you're one of them and you've turned against your own kind, that's why.'

Gallow hurled himself forward, howling. 'Nioingr! Kintraitor!' He swung the sword as he ran and the air seemed to moan like ghosts around him, but Medrin didn't step forward and the Lhosir around him moved to block Gallow's path. 'You let the Screambreaker die! Him and all those like him. The ones who would have stood up to you for the old ways. You let them all die.' He hacked at the first man to stand in his way; Solace struck the other man's blade and shattered it, sending shards of steel flying. The Lhosir lurched back as the red sword clove the air an inch from his face, but another one stepped in and lunged at Gallow.

'Let him die? And what could you see from where you stood, pressed hard up against the Vathen? What did you see of my men on the hill? Nothing! And yes, I dare say you fought with courage and strength, all the easier when you're watching your enemies butcher one another. Do you want to know what I did while you fought so hard? I sat on my horse and did nothing but watch! No, no honour or glory for Medrin Twelvefingers.' He was snarling now, his fist clenched on the hilt of the ornate Marroc sword he carried. Gallow lunged at another of the Lhosir standing in his way and drove them back, but only for a moment before they pressed around him again. 'And when my warriors wavered, I rode my men to rally the left and then to the right, because the centre held firm, always, even though that was where the Vathen pressed the hardest. And why? Because the Screambreaker was there and he had no need of this Crimson Shield or that sword you carry.' His eyes narrowed. 'I saw who was beside him at the end, Foxbeard. Whose sword was it that dealt him that fatal blow? Was it Vathan or was it yours?'

Gallow howled with rage and swung at the Lhosir around him. They kept their distance, still uncertain and wary of the red sword but not afraid of him either. Waiting for Medrin's order.

'You would have me spare Andhun for their treachery,' said Medrin mildly. 'I know the bargain you struck with the Screambreaker.' Six of Medrin's men were around him, and now Horsan stepped in front of him while the others moved to encircle him. Gallow backed away. He slashed at the haft of one man's spear, cutting it in two; the man threw it at him, catching him in the chest and winding him, then drew an axe. Gallow staggered back. They were all advancing on him now. 'But Andhun was not his to give you, Foxbeard; Andhun is mine. The Marroc who came out to fight the Vathen, they'll be honoured as they deserve. The rest? The rest burn!' He slammed the Crimson Shield into the ground and the earth shook. Gallow almost fell, while the soldiers around him paused, awed and stunned by the power of the shield. 'Kill this sheep, Horsan. I'll not dirty myself with him.'

He couldn't face this many. Couldn't and he knew it. And Medrin knew it and the other Lhosir knew it too. If he stood his ground there was only one way for this to end and, sword or no sword, he'd fought for hours against the Vathen while these men were still fresh. He turned while Horsan and the Lhosir stood there with their eyes wide, threw down his shield and ran into the twilight.

'Stop him!' roared Medrin. 'Bring me back the sword!' He heard them running after him, felt their feet shake the ground but he didn't look back, didn't dare.

'Everyone knows Lhosir don't run, Gallow Foxbeard!' Medrin again, and there was nothing else that Gallow could do.

ANDHUN

37

TOLVIS

On the day that Jyrdas died, the day before the battle with the Vathen, Tolvis stood on the beach in Andhun with a handful of dead Marroc and a few dead Lhosir in front of him, breathing hard in the moment of calm after the Marroc had run. He'd killed one of the Marroc himself. It hadn't much bothered him. Which, he mused, meant that whatever it was that *was* troubling him, it must be something else.

Not that he had much time to think about it as they pushed Medrin's ship back into the sea before the Marroc found some more courage from somewhere, but it niggled at him anyway, itching like an old scab. He watched Medrin stab Jyrdas in the eye and come and climb into his ship and push away from the shores of Andhun. As he pulled at his oar he watched Gallow too, standing on the beach over Jyrdas and a pile of Marroc bodies. He watched the crowd waving angry fists and knives, and then he looked around him at the men in the ship and realised they were all Medrin's men, every one of them, and that was the moment he understood what troubled him. The young ones Medrin had brought with him from across the sea, they knew the Screambreaker by his name but they'd never fought with him, never fought a real battle at all. Medrin had sailed for the monastery of Luonatta with sixty men. Maybe they'd only had a handful of old soldiers to start with, but now not one of that handful was left except him. Not that Medrin had done away with them, except for Jyrdas in the end, and that had just been old One-Eye looking for a clean way to die, but still, it was the sort of thing that set a man to thinking. And after that, now and then as they sailed along the coast, he caught Medrin looking at him. Looks that made him uneasy.

Damn the man! If he'd *seen* the prince do anything wrong then he could have called him out on it, but Medrin hadn't, not really. *Really* all he'd done was honour the old ones. He'd let the Screambreaker's men stand at the front of his lines where they were proud to fight. He'd let them have the glorious deaths they wanted.

But not me. Not that he was shy of a fight if a fight had to be had, but mostly what he liked was the swapping of stories afterwards over a good bottle of mead or a cask of Marroc beer.

No, he didn't like the way Medrin was looking at him at all. Couldn't have said why but it set the hairs on his back all on edge; so when they beached the boat a few miles out of Andhun, where the cliffs parted to make a little cove, Tolvis made sure he was first over the side and into the waves. He made sure he had his shield and his sword and his axe and he didn't look back, just set off along the beach away from Andhun. He didn't turn to see if anyone followed. There were a few shouts, but over the breaking waves he couldn't hear what they said, and it might just have been the others shouting at each other about making the ship safe on the beach.

He reached a headland where he had to climb over broken rocks that had fallen from the cliffs to get past. When he'd done that and the ship was out of sight, he collected a few good-sized stones from the litter on the beach, throwing stones that fitted nicely in the palm of his hand, and then he sat down to wait and to see what would happen.

He didn't have to wait long before two more Lhosir came picking their way carefully through the rocks. Treacherous out on those rocks. The broken remains of waves still reached far enough to lap at a man's feet here and there, and the lower parts were slimy with seaweed. He let them come closer, close enough that he could see who they were. Latti with his jaw all wrapped up tight and Dvag with his broken fingers. Two of Medrin's closest, shields over their shoulders, helms and hauberks and all dressed up for a fight. Tolvis sighed and wearily got to his feet, a stone in his hand. He waited on the edge of the shambles of rocks until they were a few dozen paces away.

'So this is what it comes to, is it? Twelvefingers couldn't think of a way to do it properly, so he sends you two?'

The two Lhosir on the rocks stopped. Dvag opened his arms. 'Loudmouth! Friend! We wanted to know where you were going, that's all. In case you were lost. That's the way to the Vathen.'

'You might at least try and pretend there's a good reason. I don't know, maybe say I'm in league with them or something equally stupid.'

Dvag tried to smile. 'Reason for what, Loudmouth?'

Tolvis threw his stone. It probably surprised them both when it flew straight and true and smacked Dvag in the face. He staggered on the top of his rock, lost his footing and fell out of sight between the boulders. After a moment, when he didn't get back up again, Latti cocked his head. 'Reckon that's a reason enough right there.'

The words were mashed by his broken mouth, but the meaning was clear enough. Tolvis backed away into the shingle of the beach. 'Reckon it is.'

'You going to throw rocks at me too?' Latti screwed up his face in pain.

'Only if you pretend you didn't come because Twelvefingers sent you to kill me. And if it hurts to talk, do feel free to spare us both.'

Latti shook his head. 'Not Medrin. Came ourselves.'

'Then you should have brought some men with you who can actually fight.' Tolvis backed away some more and yawned, waiting for Latti to make his way through the boulders. 'Take your time. Don't want you to slip and hurt yourself and spoil the fun of killing you.'

'*Nioingr!*'

Tolvis shrugged. 'I hear that word so much that I'm beginning to think it doesn't mean what I thought it meant. Seems to me it just means someone who doesn't do what Twelvefingers says.'

'Medrin ... our prince.' Latti jumped onto the shingle. He took the shield off his back and drew his sword, swinging it from side to side, warming up his arms.

Tolvis began to pace back and forth. 'For a man with a broken jaw you talk far too much. That bandage round your face isn't tight enough. Now learn something before you die, boy: a *nioingr* is someone who is a traitor to himself, not to anyone else. I see I'll have to teach you that.' He ran at Latti and clattered into him, shield against shield, knocking him back, then brought his axe down at his head. Latti lurched sideways. Tolvis came at him again, before Latti could find his balance, battering him a second time. This time his axe slipped around Latti's shield and Latti didn't have a hand any more. He shrieked and stumbled back, falling on the stones. Tolvis jumped on him, crushing a foot hard into his throat.

'Anything to say? No? At least you died well. No begging and pleading for mercy. Good for you.' Tolvis leaned down, pushing all his weight into Latti's throat, crushing until the light went out of his eyes. Then he went back to look at Dvag. Not much hope that a simple rock on the head had killed him, and when he found the bastard he was stuck between two boulders, eyes rolled back, muttering nonsense to himself. One of his ankles was twisted all wrong. He could add that to his mangled fingers. 'I'd wake up before the tide comes in if I were you,' Tolvis said, and left him there.

He walked a little way further along the beach until he found a way up the cliff and headed inland, looking for the Lhosir camp. Tricky, figuring out a way to get close that wouldn't lead him into more of Medrin's men or a band of Vathan scouts, and so he crept to the tops of ridges to survey the land ahead before retreating to make his way on beside hedges, along streams and ditches and, where he could, through woods. Twelvefingers would get to the Screambreaker first but that was by the way. Didn't matter much either way as long as the Screambreaker got to hear what needed to be said.

The campfires in the evening darkness were what finally led him to the Lhosir camp – not that he knew which army it was until he got close and heard the swearing and the songs. Even then he walked among the soldiers with his head down, hiding his face as best he could, keeping his shield by his side. *Medrin didn't send anyone. We sent ourselves.* Maybe that was even true. Twelvefingers had the knack of letting people know what he wanted done without ever saying, and once it was all too late he could put on that well practised look of horror he had and throw up his hands in despair and shake his head.

He reached the Screambreaker's tent only to find Twelve-fingers already in it and it was only sheer luck that no one happened to look up and see his face before he turned away and moved on. When he eventually found the Screambreaker's standard, the old man was sitting on a stool, dressed in his mail, staring out across the fields.

'Screambreaker!'

The old man didn't move. Just sat and stared. 'Maker-Devourer watch over you, Loudmouth. Medrin said you'd wandered off.'

'That's about right. Say anything else much?'

'Lots of things, but none that particularly matter save that he has the Crimson Shield. There's at least some Marroc that will fight with us now.'

'The Marroc aren't our enemy, Screambreaker.'

The Screambreaker turned and looked up at him. 'It's a wonder you need to say such a thing.' He stared at Tolvis long and hard, and it seemed the old man was looking right through him at something far away. The Screambreaker looked ... lost. Then the moment broke and the Screambreaker cocked his head. 'Whatever you have on your mind, Loudmouth, you'd best shed it. It's a stone around your shoulders as clear as the sun. Draw up a stool.'

So he did, and he told the Screambreaker about everything that had happened since Medrin had left Andhun, about Gallow and Jyrdas and Latti and Dvag, and how it was that Twelvefingers wasn't to be trusted any more. The Screambreaker listened patiently, and when Tolvis was done, he offered him a horn of mead. 'We'll fight the Vathen tomorrow, Loudmouth,' he said. 'For now that's all that matters.'

And that was all he would say while they drank together, and Tolvis talked and talked and finally walked away filled with anger and frustration, but in the middle of the next day, as the Lhosir army formed its lines, the Screambreaker called him one last time and told him how Gallow Truesword had come out of Andhun and how things were between the two of them, and how, if he wasn't alive by the end of the day, it would fall to Tolvis and to the dozen Lhosir beside him who'd fought in the last war from the beginning. He told Tolvis one other thing and then he laughed and told Tolvis what he had to do before any of that could happen. 'The woods on our seaward flank. Take ropes and shovels and fill it with traps for their horsemen. Let none of the Vathen pass.'

Tolvis looked at the men he'd been given. 'A dozen of us and you want us to hold off a thousand Vathan horsemen?'

'But you're more than a dozen. You have the trees, Loudmouth, and there are more trees than there are Vathen. And you're Lhosir so it shouldn't be too hard for you.'

He never stopped smiling and somehow he was right, and by the end of the day as the sun sank and the Vathen fled, Tolvis was still alive and he hadn't had to kill quite as many as a thousand Vathan horsemen after all.

38

THE ARDSHAN

Gulsukh Ardshan watched the disaster unfold from the top of a hill of his own. Two defeats in a row now, and the best that could said of this one was that it wasn't *his* defeat. He'd taken four thousand men to fight two thousand Lhosir and lost nearly half of them. Now the Weeping Giant had taken twenty thousand, but he'd also taken his time, and the Lhosir had kept on coming from across the sea while he'd sat in Fedderhun, waiting for the sword to tell him it was the right day to march.

'It was the right day to march when I said it was,' Gulsukh muttered to himself.

'There are more of them now?' Moonjal Bashar hadn't seen the first battle. A part of Gulsukh was disappointed – it would have been a good lesson for a young bashar to see an ardshan beaten. A larger part was relieved that a son hadn't seen his own father humiliated. 'Twice as many. Perhaps more. If we'd all marched on Andhun a month ago, we'd have destroyed the Lhosir and taken it. We'd be in Sithhun by now.'

Still, twenty thousand men should have been enough. The bashars of the Weeping Giant had conducted themselves well, sending each of the clans into battle one after the other and withdrawing each one before they turned to rout. Wearing the supposedly invincible forkbeards down, because no one, in the end, was truly unbeatable. The horsemasters were wary this time too, racing their men in to hurl their javelots and racing out again before the Marroc archers could wreak the havoc they had before. The forkbeards had chosen their field well, pitched between a steep gully lined with stakes and a light wood. From his hill Gulsukh hadn't been able to see what had happened to the horsemasters and their efforts to flank the Lhosir line and take it from behind, but they'd clearly failed.

The Weeping Giant had fallen, but even then the day hadn't been lost. The enraged Vathen fell on the forkbeards, heedless of their bashars. They pushed and pushed them back, slowly breaking them down until finally, *finally*, they broke the Lhosir line. Gulsukh had to admire whoever had held the top of that hill for the forkbeards. However many men he had there, he'd waited and he'd waited. A lesser mind might have thrown them into the fight sooner, but no, this one waited until the very last possible moment, for when the battle hung in the balance and the Vathen had taken beating after beating and yet found themselves on the point of victory, and *then* he threw them in, snatching it away again. Five hundred men, give or take, while the Vathen were still thousands upon thousands, but in that one moment he broke their spirit. The Vathan soldiers crumbled, their bashars failed, they broke and they ran, and the Lhosir cut them down. The best that could be said for what happened next was that the forkbeards themselves were too bloodied and spent to turn the rout into a proper slaughter.

He raised an eyebrow to Moonjal Bashar. 'My advice would be to have the horsemasters supply cover to our retreat.' Not that anyone listened to him any more. An ardshan in disgrace. Disobedient to the Weeping Giant, and then he'd gone and lost as well.

'I'll send a messenger.'

'Will you? I'm not sure who you're going to send it to.' He watched Moonjal send a runner anyway.

'You don't seem disturbed, Ardshan. Is there some finer point I'm missing?'

'Not really. The setting sun means the forkbeards won't be able to make the most of what they've done to us. Other than that, no.' There was a little consolation to be taken there, but the smile on his face that he couldn't quite hide was because the Weeping Giant was dead. The Sword Brothers would be in disarray and a good few of those dead too. They needed an ardshan again. There was still a horde here, if he could keep it together.

'Should we join the retreat, Ardshan?'

Gulsukh shook his head. 'Let the Sword Brothers deal with it. Let them be seen and let them take the blame. Let them cherish their defeat. An ardshan knows that defeat comes as well as victory. Time they learned it too. We'll find them later. I want to see our prisoner.' He turned his horse and rode down the back of the hill and left the fleeing Vathan army that was no longer his to whatever fate the Lhosir would find for it. He rode to his own camp in the woods, away from the main Vathan force and the onrushing forkbeards. He had a few score men now, no more. Kinsmen mostly, who still took his orders over anyone else's. The last vestiges of his old clan, before the Sword Brothers had swept through the steppes. A meagre handful, but among the Vathen the right man with the right words could make a handful into a horde with a snap of his fingers.

The forkbeard was waiting for him inside his tent, still bloody from the beating he'd taken the night before. Gulsukh's men had found this one on his own, creeping about down by the sea. He was bound so tightly that his hands had gone blue. Gulsukh cut him loose. He sat down beside the Lhosir and offered him a cup of Aulian wine. The Lhosir batted it away.

'When my men found you, they swear to me that someone had done this to you already. They tell me they were gentle and that you didn't put up much resistance for a forkbeard. So what were you doing down by the sea at the dead of night? Did you come on that ship out of Andhun? The one drawn up and abandoned on the shore?'

The Lhosir shrugged but the pinch of his lips gave him away.

'After you beat me the first time, I haven't had much else to do except stay out here watching who comes and who goes. Your prince has taken the Crimson Shield of the Marroc and that ship on the beach is his. So why weren't you with him?'

The Lhosir spat at him. Gulsukh poured another cup of wine, for himself this time, and supped it. 'In the old Aulian Empire it was understood that men might divulge their secrets and retain their honour after they were taken. Any prisoner was permitted to remain silent for one day and one night. When that time was done, it was assumed that a torturer of any skill would have reduced him to the point of revealing whatever he knew. So instead of the torturer, there was only ever the *idea* of a torturer, and of the pain and everything else that comes with such people. At the end of one day and one night, a man like me would come to a man like you. I would offer you a fine wine and a pleasant meal and we would discuss matters. It was understood to be honourable, then, for the captive to reveal everything he knew, and in return he was spared any unkindness. That's not to say that he would keep his life, but often that was the case; and even when it wasn't, death would be swift and clean and proud. I think you'd understand *that*, at least.' He poured a second cup of wine for the Lhosir. 'That was the Aulian way, but the Aulians are gone now. I simply stake my enemies to the ground, cut strips of skin from their flesh and sprinkle them with salt until they tell me what I want and then let the ants eat them. I don't know how it is among you forkbeards, but I've seen the men your prince hung up from his poles after you beat us. They were my men. I knew them. Their families. Their wives, their sons, their brothers. I was the one who led them to defeat. It doesn't make me think well of you, what your prince did to them.' He offered the cup of wine. 'I fought for your king once, so I know you well enough to suppose you'll opt for pain and heroic resistance, but I'll offer you the Aulian way anyway in case you'd prefer it.' Gulsukh moved in closer to the Lhosir. 'I won't tell if you won't. What do you say, forkbeard?'

'I say you talk too much.' The Lhosir slapped the cup across the tent.

Gulsukh nodded. 'I do. Perhaps that's why I prefer the Aulian way to this.' He rose and whistled for his torturer, the best he had among the men left to him. When the torturer had dragged the Lhosir away, he called in Moonjal. There was no reason why a father and son shouldn't share what was left of what was a rather fine old Aulian vintage.

Moonjal Bashar bowed low as he came in. Gulsukh picked up the cup that the forkbeard had refused and refilled it. 'Did he say what he was doing?' asked his son.

Gulsukh shook his head but smiled as he did. 'He thought not. He was very brave. But let us suppose that Twelvefingers left his ship where he did because he was unable to enter Andhun. Why would that be?' He didn't wait for an answer. 'How far away are the nearest bashars of the Weeping Giant?'

'A few miles, no more.'

'What would *you* do, Moonjal?'

Moonjal Bashar stiffened. 'The Lhosir have beaten us soundly but are unable to press their advantage. Many of our clans remain strong. I would rally the bashars and attack again at dawn, pressing them as hard as possible and keeping them away from the city if I could. They committed all of their men while half of ours barely fought at all. They will be tired. I would continue as we planned and wear them down.'

'Exactly right. Exactly what I'd have done if we hadn't found this Lhosir on the beach.'

'But will the forkbeards not withdraw behind their walls?'

Gulsukh smiled. 'What if they can't, Moonjal?' He laughed. 'We shall see to it that the forkbeard scouts find camps abandoned in the night. That they see us scattering and fleeing along the coast road and into the hills. We watch them and we watch Andhun and we see what will happen; and we keep all our riders close, each with a fresh fast horse to hand.' Gulsukh leaned forward. 'I also mean to send a young bashar out into the night with a few good men at his side to go looking for the forkbeards. In case they need some encouragement to see us running away.'

39

THE WOODS AT NIGHT

Horsan and his men chased the bastard *nioingr* Gallow Foxbeard right across the battlefield, hurdling the bodies of a thousand broken men, into the trees where the shadows were black and welcoming, and in the dark they lost him. Horsan supposed he must have slipped away out the other side. The Marroc were good at running. It only went to show that Medrin was right: a Lhosir didn't run and a Lhosir didn't hide. A Lhosir stood, one against one or one against a hundred. Maybe a Lhosir died, but so what?

Now they'd lost him they'd have to go back to Medrin and tell them that both the *nioingr* and the Vathan sword had slipped away in the twilight, and Medrin would have a belly full of rage when he heard and Horsan didn't want to be the one who had to tell him.

Halfway back through the trees, Durlak pointed and yelled and started to run. 'He's there! I see him!' A shape broke cover right where Horsan was looking and bolted through the bracken. The woods were full of shadows and not much else, but it wasn't the Foxbeard. Horsan wasn't sure he remembered Gallow having a helm, but it certainly hadn't had a Vathan plume on the top.

'Wait!' But Durlak was jumping and shouting and whoever had been hiding in the woods was running and plain for all to see. They chased the darting shape right through the wood and out the other end. The sky was a dim grey now, streaked with a long bruise of purple over the horizon, the last dying light of day. Enough to show Horsan that he was right.

'It's a Vathan!' And now they really had missed the Foxbeard and he'd be halfway to Andhun. Horsan pulled up. 'Leave him! It's the *nioingr* we're after.'

The others ignored him and ran on and after a moment Horsan followed too, because what else was there to do except go back to Medrin with their heads hanging to tell him they'd failed? And maybe Gallow hadn't gone to Andhun and his precious Marroc but had taken the sword back to the Vathen instead. It was a *nioingr* sort of thing to do. Maybe these Vathen would lead him right where he wanted to go.

For all his running and darting through shadows, the Vathan never quite managed to get away. It seemed ... *odd* ... and for a moment Horsan was almost inclined to stop and let him go.

'Forkbeards! Forkbeards!' the Vathan cried out to the night, sharp with fear. 'Hundreds of them! Run!'

Hundreds? Horsan laughed and forgot about stopping and ambushes and caution. *Hundreds? There's a dozen of us, you fool!*

But the Vathan kept shouting and running, and now Horsan could see fires in the woods ahead, quickly being stamped out, sparks shooting into the air like Aulian rockets. Shapes and shadows of more men moved ahead of them, and once more the cries went up: *Forkbeards! Flee!*

Gallow crouched in the dark beside the road. The moon was up and the gates of Andhun lay in sight. A handful of Lhosir stood clustered around a small fire, far enough away to be out of range of any arrows. Medrin's men. Watchers. Watching for *him* perhaps, and Andhun's gates were firmly closed. No fires burned up on the walls, no stars of torches moved back and forth. And even if he found a Marroc and called out, why would they let him in?

I have Solace. I have the holy sword of the Vathen, the Sword of the Weeping God. But the Marroc god was Modris, and Modris and the Weeping God fought their eternal battle, the Protector and the Peacebringer, the Crimson Shield and Solace. They'd never allow the red sword through their gates. More likely they'd kill the man who carried it and hurl it from their cliffs far out to sea. It was cursed. He could feel it. There was a burden that came with bearing such a sword.

Arda! He touched the locket, but he knew what Arda's words would be. He could hear them, clear as a bell. *Sell it, you oaf! Sell it and come home. Must be worth a fortune and more than we've any need for. So get what you can and think of your sons. Or throw it into the sea if you must, but whatever you do, don't you be sneaking around the bottom of the cliffs, finding your way past those walls! Just don't!*

Just don't! In the darkness Gallow laughed. That was how she did it. She went by what she knew of him, guessed what he was most likely to do and then told him to do something else. The opposite if she could find one, just so she could shake her head and wag her finger and tell him how wrong he was. It was never about what she wanted, it was about being able to scold him afterwards. Eight years of being married to the woman and he'd never seen through her until now, carrying a cursed sword and trapped between the Marroc on one side and Medrin on the other, probably with some Vathen still around for good measure and all of them wanting to kill him; and now he had to clamp a hand over his mouth to stop himself laughing aloud. He could see her, eyes rolling, shaking her head in disbelief. *And there you go, keeping on wondering why it is you can't leave me be, you great lump of wood. Now get yourself home. You can give Nadric a good shouting at for being such a thistlefinger if you need something to look forward to.*

He didn't, but there was something else to done before he could leave. 'I have to get into Andhun. I have to warn them. Medrin will slaughter them.'

Naturally I disagree, but I suppose you do. If she'd been there he would have kissed her, and if she'd shaken her head and told him that no, really, he *did* have to go with her instead, he would have gone.

Only a fool would climb the cliffs in the dark wearing mail and gauntlets, but then again, a Lhosir never abandoned his shield or his weapon, not if he could help it, and the Maker-Devourer preferred fools armed and ready for battle over wise men who came to him old and empty-handed, and Gallow had always been a good climber. It was part of what had started all this in the first place.

Once he was inside, he set about looking for Valaric.

The Vathan camp wasn't a big one, only a few dozen soldiers and their horses, and Horsan ran right into the middle of it and roared and swung his sword at the first shape he saw, and the Vathen panicked and fled. After they were gone he searched the camp, and that was when they found Dvag, or what was left of him, still alive if only barely. Dvag Bloodbeard they'd call him now, by the looks of him. As names went it wasn't so bad. Horsan and the others hoisted Dvag between them and limped him home. By the time they got back, the sun was rising and Medrin was up again. He listened to Dvag's tale as he broke his fast. To the things Dvag had heard around him while the Vathen had flayed his face. It wasn't much. Something about the sword and a Marroc in Andhun.

Medrin's eyes gleamed.

40

THE WALLS OF ANDHUN

Valaric watched the battle from a hill beside the sea. He watched the Vathen break like waves on the wall of fork-beard shields. He watched the wall waver and almost crumble, and then hold and the last forkbeards surge down the hill, and he watched the Vathen turn and flee. He didn't stay to see what happened after that but walked quickly back to the sea cliffs and down a path that ran to the shore and to the little boat that waited there. A tiny thing, hardly big enough to fit the half a dozen men it had carried out of Andhun. The others looked at him expectantly.

'Close, but the forkbeards broke them.'

The other Marroc fell to cursing as they pushed the boat out into the waves. Valaric said nothing. What difference did it make whether the invaders were Vathen or forkbeards? Both sides smashed to pieces, that was the best he could hope for. 'The Vathen are still out there.' When the waves were breaking around his chest, he hauled himself aboard. 'We keep the gates closed and the forkbeards have nowhere to go. And they can't do anything about it while the Vathen are still there.'

'And if the duke keeps his word and opens them?'

Valaric looked away. He'd felt the change in the city as soon as the demon-prince Twelvefingers had gone off looking for the Crimson Shield and the Nightmare of the North had cut down the gibbets. A few more Marroc had been hung and then the Widowmaker had moved his army out of the city. The killing had stopped. Better for the forkbeards perhaps, not to have their numbers whittled slowly down, but better for the Marroc too. It had taken Valaric a while to see that. And then the Vathen had come, and the puppet Marroc duke who ruled Andhun with Yurlak's hand shoved up his arse had promised, sworn on everything holy, that Andhun would open its gates to the Screambreaker when the battle was done.

It occurred to Valaric, as they sailed their little boat through the twilight sea and back into the harbour of Andhun, that the Nightmare of the North might be kinder to his people than some Vathan ardshan. Yet he'd take a Vathan anything over the demon-prince. Anything was better than that.

'We have to make sure he doesn't,' he said, after such a long pause that no one knew what he was talking about any more.

'We make our stand now,' said Sarvic. 'Doesn't matter who won. Never did. We keep them out until they go home.'

It wasn't a stupid idea either. When the forkbeards had first come across the sea there were good reasons why Andhun had been the last city to fall. 'Good luck telling that to the duke.'

Sarvic gave him a look as though he was mad. 'Me? *You* have to tell him! You have to make him keep them closed!'

'I'm an old soldier who fought the forkbeards and lost his family to old man winter for his pains.' Valaric spat into the sea. 'He's not going to listen to me.'

'If he won't, others will. People know you! They *will* listen to you.'

'And what would you have us do, Sarvic? Seize the gates and hold them closed? Fight among ourselves while the forkbeards laugh at us? I'll not do that. I'll not lift a blade against another Marroc. Might as well throw myself in the sea.'

'So you're just going to do nothing?'

No. Couldn't do that either, but what else was there but to take the gates and hold them shut? Words, maybe? A silver tongue might caress the duke around to his way of thinking, but Valaric was never that. Hard rusty old iron, more like, and besides, he'd never get close enough to even try.

He didn't sleep well that night. Every time he closed his eyes the shadows filled with old faces. Men he'd fought beside in the early days. Friends, killed, one after the other by the faceless forkbeard terror. And then forkbeards too, the ones he'd killed in the later days when he'd turned from battlefields and taken to hunting them in ones and twos, any who strayed from the pack and Wolf of the Wild Woods had been his name for a time. And when he finally pushed all the faces away, what he saw was the slight hump of broken earth, already covered with grass, where his family had been buried. All of them together, because the savagery of that winter hadn't left those who'd survived with enough strength to dig separate graves for so many dead.

Forkbeard bastards.

Snow and starvation and the curse of an Aulian shadewalker, but he could have done something about any and all of those things if he'd been there. Could have hunted for them. Could have found more food. Could have taken them away to another place. Somehow. Something. He didn't know what but he would never have let them die.

The forkbeards hadn't killed them though. It was his fault and his alone. His choice. No getting away from it.

Sarvic was right. The gates should stay closed. The duke was right too. He'd made a promise to open them and promises should be honoured. Who was wrong then? Who'd be wrong when the forkbeards came back inside the walls and wreaked their revenge for what he'd done when the demon-prince had come with the Crimson Shield in his hand? Him, that was who. He'd tried to take the shield and he'd failed, and now it didn't matter who led the forkbeards when they came, they'd want blood for that.

Stupid. Stupid to fail. Stupid to even try, and Gallow's words chased him like hounds after a fox. *If you'd had even one man like him in this city, Medrin would be dead and you'd be standing in front of me holding your precious shield. You know you've just brought doom on the whole of Andhun, don't you?* And he had, and Gallow was right, and all the other forkbeards too, and the Marroc were just frightened sheep and you couldn't rouse a sheep to be a wolf, whatever you said to him.

He gave up on sleeping and wandered the streets for a while in the dark, until he came to the city gates and stopped where the rows of gibbets had been.

Maybe there was a way after all.

*

And Tolvis Loudmouth watched the battle at its end too, when the Vathen had finally hurled themselves in one last madness at the Screambreaker's line. The fighting was over for him by then. Of the dozen men he'd taken into the woods, four were dead. Too few to stand in a wall of shields and spears against the Vathan horsemen who tried to come around the edge of the battle, they'd strung ropes between trees, dug trenches and set spikes in the ground. They'd thrown javelins and led the horsemen into one trap or another and then fallen upon them. A tiny skirmish when set against the battle as a whole, a hundred or so Vathen held and turned away, maybe a dozen killed and as many again wounded. A small victory. Perhaps it played some part in the greater one or perhaps not, but it would be quickly forgotten either way. But then the Screambreaker hadn't sent them to that wood to turn the battle, he'd sent them there for what would come after and they all knew that too. In the darkness of the Lhosir victory they slipped back into the camp, in among the tents, looking for the men they knew, faces they called friends. The old soldiers who'd fought at the Screambreaker's side long ago. The Screambreaker's men. They took the words he'd whispered to them and passed them along to any who would listen and quietly they gathered themselves. In the morning they spoke out his deeds, one after the other for the wind and the sun to carry away across the land and his name passed among the Lhosir like fire across a stubble field. A thousand men had seen him fell the Vathan giant. They'd seen the Screambreaker take the unholy sword and hold it high, and when they couldn't find his body in the breaking dawn light it was because the Maker-Devourer himself had come to take it, and so they made another pyre, a dozen men at once, all brothers-in-arms since that first crossing of the sea. The Screambreaker was gone but he'd left them his legend, and they took their time to honour him, even Twelvefingers. When they were done, the Screambreaker's men turned their faces to Andhun.

41

THE OFFERING

'**I**'m not a fool.' Medrin stared at the little statue of the Maker-Devourer he'd brought with him from across the sea. Outside his tent the sun was rising. 'I am *not* a fool,' he said again. 'We both know there can be no turning away from this. The Screambreaker would have known though, somehow he would have known which way to face. The Vathen or the Marroc? Which is it to be? I need a sign.' And for a moment he felt himself missing the old man who just might have been planning to steal his birthright. Missing his certainty, his presence, his assurance.

And then, waiting for him outside his tent, were Horsan and the others to tell him how the Vathen were fleeing in terror, witless and lost without their precious sword, and what was that if it wasn't a sign? 'Which isn't to say they'll stay that way,' he said to the statue of the god, 'but when they turn, we'll be ready. We'll destroy them for a second time.'

There were a few Vathan wounded who weren't dead yet. He saw to it that they were kept alive and set men to cutting wood for gibbets. Scouts rode off through the hills to keep an eye on the Vathan retreat. While they were away the Lhosir stopped what they were doing and honoured the Screambreaker and the dead who'd fallen beside him. He let the old ones do that, Tolvis Loudmouth and the rest. Let them start the pyre and, when the pyre was built, put the bodies of those they most wanted to honour on top and set it alight. He said a few words himself, because he was their prince after all, then let the old ones who'd fought with the Screambreaker against the Marroc finish speaking him out. The pyre was huge and there probably wasn't a single Lhosir who hadn't put a piece of something on it. It troubled him a little that they actually couldn't find the Screambreaker's body and the foolish whispers that spread like fire when that got out. More than likely the Screambreaker hadn't been quite dead, had crawled off to breathe his last alone in the night and didn't want to be spoken out because no one had spoken out his brother the Moontongue down at the bottom of the sea and he'd be damned if he didn't find his way to the Maker-Devourer's cauldron on his own too. But Medrin let it pass, let the old ones who'd known him stay staring at the flames until his scouts came back to tell him what he already knew: camps abandoned, Vathen flooding away, a disordered rabble, thousands and thousands of them. Oh, they'd come together again in time – they were too many to be truly broken – but not today. Today he could let them go.

He turned his army to Andhun then, to the city the Scream-breaker had abandoned. The Marroc would keep their gates closed but he was ready for that. He would array his men outside, build his gibbets, hang Vathan after Vathan outside the walls to remind the Marroc who they were dealing with until they finally cracked and let him in. And then ...

And then? He wasn't sure. Burn the city down for trying to take the shield from him? Or let them live? What would the Screambreaker do? Both. Somehow he'd find a way to do both.

He'd barely even started, though, when the gates creaked open and a dozen Marroc soldiers carrying the shield of their puppet duke lined the entrance to honour him. A herald cried out from the walls, 'Duke Zardic of Andhun welcomes Prince Medrin, son of Yurlak, king of the Marroc!'

They weren't going to keep him out after all.

Fools.

Valaric stood in an alley, hidden in its shadows from the after-noon sun, watching the gates as they opened to let in the demon from over the sea. He wore his sword and his mail and carried a spear in his hand. His shield was propped against the wall beside him. The gates hung open, and for a while Medrin waited where he was, outside the walls, more and more men gathering around him.

Close the gates! Modris, let them see him for what he is! Don't let him in!

But the gates stayed as they were, and when Medrin at last advanced across the cobbles it was with a hundred men around him and more behind to keep the gateway clear. He entered the city slowly, the Crimson Shield carried close in his hand, tense, held high for all to see. No stones fell from above, no javelins, no arrows. Not yet.

Pity.

Valaric had thought about that. Thought about what one well aimed spear or arrow could do. But if a lone killer struck down the forkbeards' prince, the reprisals would be terrible. Andhun would burn.

Medrin stopped. He stood in the middle of the square. Marroc watched from the edges, from windows and alleys and side streets. Scores of them. Watching and waiting to see what would happen and doing nothing. *And what do I expect of them?* They were ordinary folk with no swords, no mail, no weapons to speak of. The only soldiers here were the ones who'd honoured Medrin's entrance and the duke's herald who stood on the walls above, head bowed. *So where are the rest of you? Kept in your barracks to keep the demon at his ease? Or waiting around the first corner?*

A murmur rose from the far side of the square. Valaric stepped out of his alley to see what it was, but it was only the arse-licker pretend-duke Zardic, come with a bare handful of men to fawn over Medrin and hand over his castle again. The demon-prince smirked and raised the Crimson Shield high over his head, turning it slowly so that every Marroc could see. 'The Shield of Modris the Protector!' he cried. 'Returned to you! I, Medrin, have brought it back to the land where it belongs! I, Medrin, have carried it into battle to face your enemies and I, Medrin, have defeated them! The Vathen! Tens of thousands of them! An army so great their numbers would have filled every street in this great city and still spilled through the gates and into the fields beyond! I, Medrin, son of Yurlak, have defeated them and I have done this for you.' Medrin cast his eyes around the square looking for the challenge, for anyone who would meet his gaze, but no, they all looked away. Even Valaric. *Not yet. Not while there's still a flicker of hope.*

The prince laughed. 'See,' he said to the man beside him, quite loud enough for even Valaric to hear. 'They really are sheep.'

The forkbeards laughed. The pretend-duke walked slowly towards the demon-prince, head bowed. The square fell silent. 'Prince Medrin, son of Yurlak, king of the Marroc, the people of Andhun greet and welc—'

Medrin cut him off. 'When I came to this city two days ago, the people of Andhun set upon me. A goodly number of bodies attest to this. Marroc mostly, but not all. I'm not interested in your welcome.' The duke opened his mouth but Twelvefingers waved him away. He pointed into the crowd and singled out two men. 'Bring those two to me, Duke of Andhun.'

Why are we such cowards? Valaric looked away. He knew what came next. The men would be dragged from the crowd by Marroc soldiers. They'd be flogged, and it would be Marroc hands holding the whips. Marroc arms and Marroc tools would build gibbets and these two men would be torn open and staked to wheels like the Vathen outside the city, hung beside the gates as a lesson to others and not a single forkbeard would even have to raise a hand to do it.

All of a sudden Medrin was shouting into the face of the duke: ' … until their leaders are found, and I expect you and your soldiers to deal with them as I require! Those soldiers who should have been out on the battlefield, fighting the Vathen!' he thundered. 'Now bring those men to me!'

Valaric picked up his spear and shield and stepped out of the shadows. He pushed his way through the few Marroc who stood around the edges of the square. 'Oi! Prince Forkbeard. Twelvefingers. Demon-spawn.'

The closest forkbeards turned and readied their weapons. Valaric stopped. Medrin was still shouting.

'Medrin! Demon-beard! Prince *nioingr.*'

Now Medrin stopped.

'I'm the one you want, you pox-scarred prince of filth. Twelve-fingered son of the mother of monsters. I'm the one who stood before you on the beach and I stand before you now.

I, Valaric of Witterslet. I, Valaric of the Marroc. I'm the one you want and here I am. You wouldn't face me then; do you dare to face me now, or are you the coward that even your own men know you to be?'

Medrin turned. He faced Valaric with the Crimson Shield held high. 'A Marroc crippled me some fifteen years ago, Valaric of Witterslet. Men die from such wounds as I took that day, and so they should, for it left me as weak as a child and what place is there in this world for a weakling warrior? Yet I didn't die. I fought for my life and I clawed it back again. I've taken this shield and I defeated an army that would have swept across your land. I will face you, Valaric of the Marroc, but only if you will face me as I am.' His words changed for the duke, but his eyes stayed on Valaric. 'Have your soldiers take this man and run a spear through his chest. Close the wound with hot pitch. Then we'll duel. If he fights well, we'll say no more of this. If he fights poorly, I'll have one man in every twenty taken from your city and sent back across the sea to live as slaves.'

Valaric clenched his hand around his spear. 'I came here to die so others might live,' he hissed. 'I'll take your challenge, prince of oafs.'

He felt a movement in the Marroc behind him, and then a man come to stand at his side.

'You try to take this man, Medrin, you come through me first.'

Gallow.

42

DEFIANCE

Gallow raised the Sword of the Weeping God high. He'd come to the square behind Andhun's gates to see what Medrin would do. To stand against him, to fight and die if he had to. And seen that he wasn't alone.

'You're neither shoeing my horse nor blading my scythe,' muttered Valaric.

'Settle that later?'

Valaric nodded. 'It can wait.'

'Horsan!' Gallow called him out. Medrin's sword-hand. 'The servant of a man with no honour shares in his shame. The servant of a man with no courage shares in his cowardice. The servant of a man with no heart shares in his disgrace. You bring shame and dishonour to your kin. You're a coward.'

Horsan pushed his way out from among the Lhosir, shaking his head, face set hard. 'I'll rip you apart, *nioingr*.'

Gallow ran at him. Horsan met him head on. The two crashed into each other and careened sideways. The lunge of Horsan's spear pierced the air an inch from Gallow's ear while Solace skittered off Horsan's shield.

'I knew your family from before I crossed the sea,' said Gallow grimly. 'Your father always thought you were carrying a bit too much fat on you. Lazy, he said.'

Horsan snarled. He circled more cautiously this time, crouched behind his shield, spear held in one fist over the top, point remorselessly aimed at Gallow's eyes.

'I was on the same battlefield as him when he died.' Gallow circled the other way, careful not to get too close to Medrin's Lhosir.

'Spit him, Horsan!' The Lhosir were cheering and jeering.

Gallow glanced around the crowd. The Marroc hadn't moved but there was a change to them. They were restless. One bent down. When he stood up again he was holding a stone.

'I didn't see him fall. Barely knew him. But we recited the names of the dead that day and everyone who fell was spoken out, their words and their deeds offered up to the Maker-Devourer. I've heard a thousand men spoken out like that, Horsan. Spoken out a good few myself. Last man I spoke for was Jyrdas One-Eye. How many men have you spoken out, Horsan? Any at all?'

No. He could see that. They probably hadn't honoured the dead yet. Too busy with Andhun and whether the Vathen would return. Times like this the fallen just had to stay where they fell for a day or two before they could be properly burned and honoured, but it made the Lhosir uncomfortable to think about it, that was the thing. Made them wonder, for a moment, if they were right. What if they were all somehow struck down? What if the fallen were never spoken out? What if they were lost, abandoned, alone after all they'd done. Unthinkable. Horrible.

A grim smile set on Gallow's face. 'No matter. The Maker-Devourer himself will speak for the Screambreaker and those who stood with him, and there were men there for your father. Who's going to speak for you, Horsan? When you stand beside the Maker-Devourer's cauldron and he turns up his ear to listen, what's he going to hear? Nothing.'

'We spoke out the Screambreaker. Every one of us. The rest have to wait.' Horsan's mouth twitched; as it did, Gallow leaped. The red sword smashed down onto Horsan's shield and split it in two. Horsan jabbed his spear at Gallow's neck, but Gallow simply lifted his own shield and turned the spear over his head. He kicked at Horsan's knees and staggered him. The air hissed as he lunged with Solace. The sword caught Horsan neatly between his hauberk and his helm, driving through the naked flesh of his throat. A great spurt of blood sprayed across the cobbles. Horsan opened his mouth to say something more but all that came out was a river of red. He fell to his knees and toppled over. Gallow turned to face the rest of them.

'So that was the best of you, was it?' yelled Valaric. 'You've forgotten who you are. Go back where you came from, fork-beards. Go back across the sea and stay there!'

One or two Marroc among the crowd shouted as well. 'Go home!'

'So who fights for Medrin now?' Gallow lowered Solace and pointed its bloody blade at the Lhosir one by one. They each met his eye but none of them moved.

Medrin's lips pursed as though he tasted something sour. He cocked his head and turned to the Marroc duke. 'You're shelter-ing a *nioingr* and a traitor. Hang him.'

'He's from across the sea, my lord.' The duke didn't move. Neither did any of the Marroc soldiers. 'My men can't touch him. A Marroc who lifts a hand against a Lhosir shall have that hand cut off, as you have commanded.'

'Gallow? He might have come from across the sea but he stayed and he took one of your women. He's a Marroc now. Hang him.'

The duke still didn't move.

'Hang him, or I will hang you.'

'No, my lord, I will not.'

Medrin took a spear from the Lhosir beside him, drove it into the duke's belly and kicked him over. He looked around the crowd and at the Marroc soldiers. 'So who else wants to be duke, then? I'll give it to whichever one of you brings me the head of that man there.' He pointed at Gallow.

None of the Marroc moved. Gallow felt the tension in the air, unbearable. They were on the brink of turning.

'Marroc! Be free!' Valaric hurled his spear at Medrin. The prince lifted the Crimson Shield, instinct saving him. Valaric's spear struck the wood hard, but when Medrin lowered the shield, it wasn't even scratched.

A Marroc raised his arm and threw a stone. Then another and another did the same. Medrin howled and the Lhosir burst out of their circle around him. Valaric and Gallow launched themselves forward. The Marroc soldiers lifted their shields and their spears to face the Lhosir, the men and women around the square throwing stones and whatever else they could find. The first Lhosir hit Valaric head on, shield on shield, spear points lunging. Everything narrowed to sharpened points of steel. And over it all he heard Medrin roaring, 'Kill them all! Burn their city! Leave nothing standing but bare stone walls!'

43

OUTSIDE

Lhosir poured through the gates of Andhun. The Marroc who'd thrown stones lay dead now, broken dolls, limp and ragged, trampled underfoot when Medrin's men let loose their charge. The rest had fled after the initial surge, and now Gallow and Valaric were side by side, pinned into an alley narrow enough for them to block with just the two of their shields, a dozen Lhosir pressing them.

'What happened to ...' Valaric twisted as the Lhosir in front of him hooked his shield with an axe while the next one back jabbed with his spear. ' ... going to Varyxhun?' He ducked another swing. The man in front of him howled as Valaric stamped on his foot.

Gallow barely heard. He could see Arda's face. She was smiling but she looked sad. *Pig-headed forkbeard.* In his hand Solace felt as light as a feather and the air hummed as the sword cut through it. In Marroc stories the red sword cut through shield and mail like an axe through cheese. The Lhosir still standing in front of him proved the lie of that, but it still moved with a life of its own, as though it was a part of him, and it had already split a couple of badly made shields. He lunged over a shield now, the sword biting at the neck of the Lhosir in front of him. It had a knack, it seemed, for finding the gaps in a man's armour. The Lhosir lurched away and then came back at him, forced by the press of men behind.

'You know what us forkbeards are like: can't resist a good fight.' Gallow stepped back. The Lhosir in front of him stumbled forward, lowered his shield for a moment to support himself and died as the red sword tore out his throat. 'I came to tell you to run away.' He lunged as the next Lhosir came, reached over the man's shield and stabbed, slicing his cheek.

Valaric ducked and stabbed beneath the next man's shield. He sheathed his own sword and snatched the dead man's spear as he fell. 'They'll get behind us soon.'

The next Lhosir didn't have a helm. Stupid, and Solace quickly split his skull. 'Then this will become a very bloody alleyway.'

'Hold them for a moment.' Valaric lunged and then leaped back and ran down the alley, leaving Gallow facing two at once. They pressed in on him hard then, swords stabbing around his shield while the men behind lunged with spears. A Lhosir learned to fight as soon as he was old enough to stand and hold a weapon. They learned to guard one another, how one man could hook away a shield and make an opening for another to lunge at unguarded skin, sometimes the man beside them with a sword or an axe, but more often the man pressed up close behind with a short spear. They learned how three or four together, if they worked as one, could kill almost any number of enemies until they tired, and now they turned that knowledge against Gallow. His own childhood had been the same: after the hook came the lunge, after the jab the thrust and then the swing. He knew where the spear thrusts and sword cuts would come, had honed all these in five years of war with the Marroc, but against four Lhosir, even ones who'd never faced a real enemy before the Vathen, he could barely keep them at bay. He retreated back down the alley, one step at a time, one lunge after another.

'Valaric!'

No answer and he couldn't look back. Didn't dare.

'Valaric?' A spear point sliced the skin of his neck. 'Valaric!'

Then he heard a roar behind him. For a moment the Lhosir faltered and then Valaric barged into the back of Gallow and splashes of something hot spattered his arms. 'You bastards like what comes out of the Grey Man's kitchens so much?' yelled Valaric. 'Have some!' He hurled a cauldron past Gallow's head. The Lhosir bellowed and recoiled and the air filled with steam and the smell of boiled cabbage. For a moment Gallow was free.

'Run!' Valaric pulled his arm. Gallow bolted down the alley on Valaric's heels as he raced for an open door. Valaric's spear was propped beside it; Valaric snatched it up, turned and hurled it. The first Lhosir dived sideways and the spear hit the one behind him, clattering off the side of the man's helm, the shaft spinning through the air. The last two Lhosir batted it aside but by then Gallow was through the door and Valaric was closing it behind them.

'The table!' Valaric rammed his shoulder to the door. They were in a kitchen. Gallow dragged the table from the middle of the room. The door shuddered as the first Lhosir outside kicked at it. Valaric let them force it open a hand's width and then stabbed his sword through the gap. The Lhosir backed away a moment, long enough for the two of them to push the table against the door and wedge it against a wall. 'Come on!' Valaric ran for a different door.

'What were you doing out there?' They ran out into an empty tavern hall.

'What do you mean?' Valaric stopped and shouted, 'Hoy! Any Marroc still here hiding away! Now's the time, lads! The forkbeards are here and they're burning our homes. Take up your arms!' The tavern remained empty and still. Valaric shrugged and ran to the far door. 'Good enough. The docks, Gallow. That's where we'll be. That's where we make our stand. We knew this was coming. We're as ready as we could ever be.' He pushed open the door and ran almost straight into another band of Lhosir.

'Maker-Devourer!' roared Gallow, raising his shield. The Lhosir ran at them, but as Valaric and Gallow turned their backs and fled, the Lhosir stopped, laughed and turned into the Grey Man instead.

'They'll regret that later when we rip their drunken bellies open,' snarled Valaric.

'What were you doing at the gates? Did you think Medrin was going to fight you?'

'No.' Valaric darted into an alley that ran steep down the hill towards the Isset, so narrow they had to squeeze along it with their armour and their shields scraping the walls. The buildings either side blotted out the sun, casting them into gloomy shadow.

'Well? Then what?'

'I thought I was going to die.' Valaric's words came out through clenched teeth. 'If your prince was the sort of man to stand up and fight for himself when another man called him out ... But he isn't and he never was, and I knew that. I went there to give myself up to him. Take as many of you with me as I could but let him have the nasty Marroc who'd stood up to him on the beach. You were right, what you said there. I thought if he had me then he might not burn the whole city. So much for that.' The alley opened into another street. It was empty: no Marroc, no Lhosir. Shouting came from further down the hill, the sounds of men fighting. The tang of smoke tainted the air.

'I fought the Vathen at the Screambreaker's side. I saw him fight their champion. I saw him take the Sword of the Weeping God.' He held the blade up so Valaric could see it clearly. 'I was beside him when the Vathen broke our line and he fell. Medrin let it happen. He turned the tide of the battle with his men but he waited for the Screambreaker to fall before he did.'

Valaric stared. 'The red sword? *That* is the Comforter?' His face went tight, almost as though he was afraid of it. 'Modris preserve us!'

'Solace. The Peacebringer.'

Valaric took a step away. 'Oh, I know its names. The Edge of Sorrows. The Unholy Comforter. The blade of the Weeping God that struck at Diaran the Lifegiver and would have killed all men had not Modris the Protector taken the blow on his shield.' He shook his head and backed further away. 'That's a cursed blade, Gallow, and it brings death wherever it goes. You should never have brought it into my city!'

'It's just a sword, Valaric.' Gallow frowned but Valaric was still shaking his head, fists clenched.

'No. You know the tale of the Weeping God. You know how he became what he is but it comes from that sword. It's a pitiless thing. It serves no one, or perhaps everyone with an even-handed faithlessness. Blood follows that blade, Gallow. And now you've brought it here, and look around you.'

'The Vathen brought it here, Valaric, not me.'

Valaric seized Gallow by the shoulders. 'But *you* brought it into Andhun. Take it *away*! Ah. Modris preserve us! Forkbeards again!' He let go of Gallow and ran down the street towards the harbour. The Lhosir who'd gone into the Grey Man were coming out again. Gallow ran after Valaric for a few paces and then stopped and turned another way. He didn't believe in cursed swords just as he didn't believe in Modris and Diaran and the Weeping God and the rest of them. Stories, that's all they were. Some swords were better than others, no more. The skill of the smith and the quality of the metal he worked saw to that, but in the end they were all made from the Maker-Devourer's cauldron just like everything else.

But Valaric was right – there was a better place for this sword to be.

He turned his back on the docks where Valaric's men were waiting, and headed towards the keep on the top of the cliffs.

Medrin.

44

THE SCREAMBREAKER'S MEN

By the time Tolvis and the Screambreaker's men reached Andhun's gates, whatever had kicked off the fighting was done and over. Lhosir still trickled into the city, chasing with eager feet and hungry eyes after the scent of plunder and blood. A few of them loitered sulking around the gates, ordered to keep them open.

'And where are the Vathen?' Tolvis asked them but they only shrugged.

'Fled in the night,' they said. 'It's the Marroc against whom we hold the gates.' They weren't happy about it either, denied their share of plunder. Men who'd done something to earn Twelvefingers' disfavour. Tolvis passed on into the city. The cobbles were littered with bodies. Marroc mostly, from the looks of them, but there were Lhosir here too. A few of the bodies were soldiers, freshly dead in their mail, even with their swords and spears still lying beside them. Most of the Marroc wore simple clothes, the ordinary folk of the city in the wrong place at the wrong time. Many had been cut down from behind, stabbed in the back. Only a few had found the courage to die facing their fate.

He found the Marroc duke. When he turned over the bodies of the dead Lhosir to see their faces, he found Horsan. He laughed. *So much for you.*

Smoke wafted in wisps from the streets that led down towards the harbour. The Lhosir who came in after Tolvis and the Screambreaker's men headed that way. A few stopped among the dead, taking a spear if they didn't have one, or a sword or a helm. A couple were crouched down, stripping bodies of their mail. The stragglers weren't Medrin's men or anyone else's so

Tolvis paid them no mind. They could head off down the hill towards the harbour – so much the better if they did – but *he* was aiming for the castle. Twelvefingers wasn't stupid. You couldn't come into Andhun and murder their duke and burn the place down without making sure you had the castle first, not if you were planning to stay. The plunder would be down in the harbour, but Medrin would be up there.

There were going to be some problems later, when it came to explaining to King Yurlak why he'd taken it on himself to hunt down the king's only son and stick his head on a spike. *The Screambreaker told me to* probably wasn't going to be good enough. Ah well. He could think of an excuse later.

Valaric ran through the streets to the first barricade. The Lhosir thought the Marroc were sheep and maybe they were; maybe they didn't have the madness in their blood that the men from over the sea called courage and bravery and honour. Didn't make them stupid, though.

'Valaric!' Sarvic was there keeping watch, ready for the fork-beards to sweep down the street.

'You heard then.' Valaric stopped in front of the barricade. Sarvic nodded. 'How many men have we got down here?'

'Hard to say. We had two hundred this morning before you left. When word came of what you did and how it went with the forkbeards ...' Sarvic shook his head. 'It's gone through the docks like fire. Most people are running for the sea. There's boats already leaving.'

Valaric winced. 'I'd hoped ...' But what had he hoped? That thousands of men and women who'd never raised a hand to another soul in their life would suddenly take up arms against an army of rampaging armoured monsters? Of course they were running for the boats.

'A few are staying. Hard to know how many.'

'You told them what they have to do?' Sarvic nodded. Valaric looked around. Enough men to hold the barricade for a few minutes. He looked at Sarvic long and hard, remembering Lostring Hill and the scared man he'd seen there. He nodded. 'Go to the harbour.' He pointed to three more of them, men he didn't know, but all soldiers in mail with shields and axes. 'Go to the boats. If there are men down there who think they can take everything a family has to let them onto a ship, show them your steel and explain to them why they're wrong. Give them a choice: They can keep their weapons and use them on the forkbeards or they can give them to someone else who will. I'll not have Marroc turning against Marroc.'

The other three turned and left without hesitation, glad to be let go and not to face the forkbeards. Sarvic didn't move.

'Well, go on then.'

'No.' Sarvic shook his head. 'I don't want to run.'

'Everyone who stays is going to die. Our lives buy time for the others, that's all.'

'I said I don't want to run.' When Sarvic's eyes didn't falter, Valaric clapped him on the shoulder.

'You want to kill forkbeards? Then come with me. Not long now.'

Tolvis looked over the litter of bodies in Castle Square. Marroc mostly. They'd put up some sort of fight in the end. Too little too late though, because there were hardly any Lhosir among the dead and the men at the castle gates had forked beards and waved at Tolvis as he came forward. Half a dozen of them. They looked tense, stamping their feet, eyes constantly roving. Tolvis grinned at them. He recognised this lot. Medrin's men, every one of them.

'A fine morning for sacking a city!' He waved back as he got up close. 'Wish you were down there, eh?'

The gate guards snorted. Who wouldn't really? Nothing to do up here. They'd had a great big fight yesterday and they'd won, but they'd all lost friends and half of them had lost family, some cousin or other at the very least, and what came after a big fight was a couple of days plundering to make up for it. And here they were, missing it. Tolvis nodded. He understood perfectly.

'The Maker-Devourer sends you some luck then.' He nodded back at the men he had behind him. Fifty or so Lhosir. The Screambreaker's men, what was left of them. Men who'd fought a dozen battles and lived through them all. 'We're here to relieve you. Go and have some fun. Kill some Marroc and get drunk.'

He had their attention now. He could see the thoughts running through their minds. *That would be nice, but Twelvefingers told us to guard the gate.* 'Prince Medrin ordered us to stay,' said the first man doubtfully.

Tolvis shrugged. 'Stay then. When the other guards on the inside come out to go off a-looting don't take it too personal if they laugh at you.'

The man shook his head. 'That won't happen. You can't go inside.'

Tolvis took his time over his next words. 'Thing is, you see, that *is* where we're going. Sure you don't want us to take over at the gate here? It was the Screambreaker himself said we should. *You've seen enough over the years. Let the young ones have their share of the plunder.* Or something a bit like that anyway.' Tolvis laughed. 'Me? I'm so old and bashed around the head, I can't remember *exactly* what he said. I probably couldn't remember how to plunder a Marroc city either. Best you lot get on and do it. Make a proper job of it.'

Medrin's men shuffled their feet. 'And you'd give us your word over the Maker-Devourer's cauldron that you'd all just stand here and not let anyone into the castle, eh? You included. You'd have to share blood with us about that.'

Tolvis shrugged. 'Not sure I could do *that.*'

The man let out a great sigh. 'Thought not.' He drew his sword and shook his head. 'Can't let you in, Loudmouth.'

Tolvis raised his shield and his spear. 'Ah well. Pity. I salute you. I'll speak you out to the Maker-Devourer myself when the time comes. Anything you want me to mention?'

'How about you just shut up and we get on with it?'

Tolvis took a deep breath. 'Fine, fine. I'm just trying to make it a bit easier for everyone.' He lunged with his spear, quick as a snake. The man caught the point on his shield and stepped back. In half a blink the six of them were in a circle, shields locked together. Tolvis left a dozen of the Screambreaker's Men to deal with them and moved on into the castle yard. Another handful of Medrin's men were lounging there, bored and not sure what to do with themselves. They found an answer to that quickly enough. After the gate guards, Tolvis didn't bother trying to talk his way past the rest.

They fought well. He'd give them that as he stepped over the bodies. They even managed to take a few of his men with them. Not many, but what did you expect when you put boys against men? Still, he'd speak out their names if he had the chance when all this was done. Brave men, all of them. Foolish, perhaps, but then the Maker-Devourer had never cared about *that*. Just as well really.

On a hill not far from the battlefield where the Screambreaker had killed the Weeping Giant and set his fellow Vathen to flight, Gulsukh Ardshan watched from the back of his horse.

'Bashar,' he said without taking his eyes from the city.

'Ardshan?' Behind him, hidden by the bulk of the hill from the Lhosir who'd stayed outside Andhun's walls, two thousand Vathen were waiting for his order. A pitiful fraction of the army that had marched to sweep the Marroc aside, but here and now it would do.

'Now, Bashar.'

45

DARE TO DARE

Gallow ran up an alley, turned into a yard, found himself in a dead end and turned back. He tried to remember how Tolvis had led him to the castle from the river on the night they'd sold his Vathan horses, but they'd been deeper inside the city that night. There were the roads he used to follow when he'd been in Andhun before, but Lhosir in Andhun then had known better than to stray into dark and narrow alleys, especially after the Screambreaker crossed back over the sea. They'd walked in groups in the wider streets, always watchful and wary, and Gallow couldn't use these now.

He saw Lhosir here and there, groups of them, mostly running toward the sounds of fighting or screaming or the smell of burning. They too kept out of the alleys. The Marroc didn't, but they were all just desperate to get away. Whenever they saw Gallow coming, they fled.

But all he had to do was keep going uphill and so he did, keeping away from the main streets and the gangs of Medrin's Lhosir until he reached the Castle Square. The gates hung open. No one stood guard but there were bodies outside, a lot of them. Gallow picked his way through, casting his eyes around for anyone who was still alive. The bodies were Marroc at first. A few ordinary folk and a few dozen Marroc soldiers who'd made a stand and been overwhelmed with a handful of Lhosir around them. Inside in the castle yard there were plenty more dead, now all Lhosir. He found two locked together. One had his axe stuck through the other's collarbone, half into his neck, wedged fast. The second man's sword had been driven right through the first man's face, pinning him to the stones.

Fighting among themselves? He ran past them, across the castle yard and into the open doors of the keep.

The forkbeards came down the street at a slow run, shouting throat-cutting threats and battle whoops. Valaric watched from a window overlooking the barricade. They slowed as they reached it, forming a shield wall and levelling their spears as they advanced. He waited. The Marroc behind the barricade threw stones and pieces of wood and burning torches. The fork-beards batted them away, laughing. The Marroc were ordinary men from the harbour – fishermen and boatmen and oarsmen and sailors – not soldiers. They had no mail, few of them even had helms, and their weapons were boathooks and clubs and axes, whatever they'd been able to find. The barricade was a cart on its side and piles of crates. But they didn't run. Valaric felt a warmth course through him. Pride, that's what that was. *We don't have to be sheep. We don't.*

The forkbeards reached the barricade and started stabbing over the top of it with their spears, round the sides of it, anywhere there was a gap. At the edges they started to pull at the crates and boxes, tearing them down. Valaric's men shouted back, swinging their clubs and hooks, but the forkbeards were clearly going to pull the barricade down and sweep them away.

Or so they thought. Valaric lifted the first crossbow and cocked it. He looked at the handful of men around him and then through the window at the Marroc up on the other side of the street. He nodded, then leaned out and fired the crossbow down into the forkbeards. Picked his shot carefully, straight into the back of the neck of one at the front. He watched the man go down.

'Next.' He backed away from the window letting someone he didn't know, a fisherman, take the next shot. They had five weapons, three windows, seven men. On the other side of the street he had much the same. He left them to it, ran down the stairs and into the alley round the back where a dozen Marroc waited for him. These were soldiers, the few that he had, and Sarvic was with them. He nodded grimly and with a roar they ran out into the street, plunging into the rear of the forkbeards, who were trapped by the barricade and just waking up to the death coming down on them from above. From behind the barricade, bottles of burning fish oil began to fly and suddenly the forkbeards were the ones dying.

His spear sang in his hand. *Three years in the forests, hunting you down. Picking you off one by one. Taking you as I could. You trained me well, you bastards.*

Gulsukh Ardshan and his horsemen came over the hill, a solid wall of horse and men and steel. The ground trembled under the pounding of thousands of galloping hooves. He felt a terrible elation as the Lhosir still outside the city looked up and saw what was coming and snatched up their shields and spears and formed into circles but the Vathen didn't bother with them – they were too few to be any trouble later. Instead, the Vathen swept through the Lhosir camp like a storm. Spears struck men down, javelots arced out from the riders, a steel rain that scythed down those who stood to fight and those who turned and fled alike. The camp was trampled into mud and ruin, the wounded and the stricken crushed underhoof. In a blink the Lhosir were scattered – as easy as that – and as they passed on towards the gates of Andhun, Gulsukh was gritting his teeth. *Why couldn't it have been that easy before?*

The open doors to Andhun keep beckoned Gallow inside. He ran up the steps and into the huge gloomy hall where the Screambreaker had once held his feasts. He paused for a moment there, uncertain which way to go. There were no dead men here – the fighting had been out in the yard. Whoever had come this way must have swept on inside. Somewhere.

He listened, hoping to hear sounds of a fight or cries of victory. *Medrin, where would you go? Where would you hide?*

A scream, long and thin, echoed down the far stairs. *Good enough.* Gallow ran through the hall, past the high table with its finery and its silver and leaped up the stairs behind it.

They killed perhaps half the Lhosir before the forkbeards pushed their way through the barricade. The Marroc behind it emptied the last of their oil over the wagon, set it alight and ran. The ones at the windows with their crossbows melted away. Valaric and Sarvic and the other soldiers turned and fled, not up the street but away into the maze of alleys. More forkbeards were coming down from the castle anyway. Time to go. Valaric made sure he was the last, backing down an alley too narrow for the forkbeards to get past him without killing him first. They howled and swore and yelled, but he kept his shield high and backed quickly away, and with his spear jabbing out they couldn't touch him. He stopped a few feet from the next street.

And now I have you trapped again. 'Burn, demon-beards!' he screamed, and shutters opened above and oil and fire rained on the forkbeards.

Tolvis found Medrin where he knew the prince would be. Hiding up in the rooms of the dead duke. He had a good few men with him too, a couple of dozen maybe. A few were faces Tolvis remembered from the monastery and old One-Eye's ship. They were waiting for him at the top of the spiralling stairs in the doorway, clustered around it so that he couldn't get through without killing them. Which was fine and fair enough – they couldn't get down the stairs and go anywhere else after all, not unless they fought their way through every man Tolvis had with him. Still he stopped. Gave them a chance, that was only fair.

'Fine men of the sea.' He held his ground carefully out of reach of a spear thrust. Maybe they had a bow of some sort and some arrows up here and maybe they didn't, but even men like these wouldn't stoop that low. 'May I offer you a parley?'

'Dog's piss on your parley, *nioingr!*' Ah. Durlak.

'Did I hear they're calling you Durlak Trueshaft now? Horsan was your brother, wasn't he? Fought well too, what I saw of him. Strong like an ox and he knew how to use a spear and a blade as well as any. So who laid him out? Wasn't me or any of mine but I'd like to know.'

'The Foxbeard.' When Tolvis cocked his head, Durlak added, 'Gallow.'

'Ah.' Tolvis smiled. So Gallow was still in Andhun, was he?

That would make one of the many things the Screambreaker had asked of him a little easier.

'The *nioingr* turned on our prince as you've done. There's a blood feud between us now.'

'Really?' Tolvis raised an eyebrow. 'You might want to be careful with that if he killed Horsan. Still.' He opened his shield a fraction, exposing himself momentarily. A small gesture of peace perhaps, or one to invite a speculative thrust. 'If it's a feud you want, don't let me spoil it. I'm sure he's not far away. Go and fight him if you like. I'll not stop you. I've no grievance with any man here save one.' He frowned. 'No, actually, two. Which one of you was it struck Jyrdas in the back when we were fighting in that dingy little monastery?'

'Giedac. And Jyrdas killed him right there and then.'

'Did he? Good for One-Eye. Well that only leaves the coward who told him to do it then. So if you don't mind letting us pass, we'll deal with him as is right and proper and leave you to your looting. Must be plenty to be had from a place like this. If you were *permitted*, of course.'

A flash of greed crossed Durlak's face but his jaw tightened. 'No, Loudmouth. I already know you killed Latti. How you tried to kill Dvag.'

'Latti made his own choice. Was a fair fight that. Dvag played me false. *He* was a liar. Did I kill him? He was alive when I left him.'

'The Vathen found him. And then Horsan and I found the Vathen. And you'll not pass this door, Loudmouth.'

There didn't seem to be much to be said after that. Tolvis rolled his eyes. 'Bloody forkbeards eh?' he said. 'All the same. Never know when to give up.'

For a moment Durlak grinned. 'Secret of who are, Loudmouth.'

Tolvis nodded. He eased up the last few steps and the two of them set about killing one another.

46

DARK ENTREATIES

Gallow ran up the stairs and stopped halfway. A Lhosir faced him, ugly and angry, shield close and spear held out. He kept his distance though, unsure of whom he faced.

'Who goes there?'

Valaric sprinted down the next street, on towards the harbour. Three forkbeards from the alley were chasing him. They were actually on fire but they were still coming. *Modris!* Were they simply too stupid? He rounded a corner and there was the next barricade waiting for them. And Sarvic.

'Get down, get down!' Grumpy Jonnic too. Valaric threw himself to the cobbles, skittering across them, his mail throwing up a shower of sparks. From behind the barricade a dozen men rose and fired a ragged volley of crossbow bolts. The men he'd had beside him overlooking the first barricade. Two of the three burning forkbeards fell and stayed still. The third jerked but stayed on his feet, even with two bolts sticking out of him. Valaric jumped up and stuck him with his spear.

'You people *really* don't know when to stop!' he screamed. He looked back up the street. More forkbeards were coming, dozens of them. Further up the Isset smoke rose over the water and drifted down towards the sea. They were burning things again. He jumped over the barricade and readied his spear for the next fight. Marroc ran screaming through the streets behind him, heading for the sea. A few picked up sticks or knives and joined the barricade. Valaric watched them from the corner of his eye as the forkbeards stormed towards them. Saw their courage fade to fear and watched them melt away. A handful stayed. He admired them, and he pitied them too. They weren't soldiers and the forkbeards would slaughter them. He shouted at them, waving them away.

'Go! Go to the ships. Help others get away from here. Live!' They stared at him, holding their ground. He took a step forward, waving his shield. 'Go, you stupid Marroc!' This was the last barricade before the docks. There weren't any more. He'd stand and fight here until there weren't any forkbeards left or until they killed him. Or until they found some other way round through the alleys and came at him from behind.

The Marroc, with their leather aprons and padded jackets for armour, with their clubs and knives for weapons, simply stared back at him. A few shook their heads. Stupid fools were going to die.

'Valaric!' Jonnic. The forkbeards howled and whooped as they ran down the street towards the barricade, spears high, shields tight. Valaric bared his teeth. There were no bowmen waiting to shoot down from above this time, no men waiting to stab them from behind. He'd make his stand here with whatever men were left who would fight beside him. Behind their barricade they'd hold this street as long as they could. And that was that.

'Crossbows!' The Marroc with crossbows rose again from behind the barricade and let loose. Most of the bolts hit the forkbeards' shields but a couple went down, and then the forkbeards were on the barricade, howling and swinging their axes. Valaric snarled something even he didn't understand and met them shield to shield, blade to blade, whispering prayers to Modris and Diaran as he did that the fight would be long and hard and he'd at least take a few of the enemy with him before he fell.

Tolvis was breathing heavily and bleeding from where one of Durlak's lunges had ripped open his face before Tolvis's sword had skewered him. A flap of skin hung off his cheek. The hole went right through; he could touch his tongue with his finger. If he'd had any looks before, they were gone now. The whole side of his head felt as if it was on fire.

He stepped over Durlak's body and the handful of Medrin's men who'd stayed to hold the doorway. In the small space of the spiral stairs and the tiny room beyond, spears and axes had no space to move. It came down to thrusting swords. They didn't like that. Tolvis didn't like it either and he was glad when Medrin's last few guards retreated into the space of the old duke's chamber. He stopped for a moment, turned back and rolled Durlak over. The dead man's eyes were still open. Sign of a good spirit. Tolvis dragged him away. 'I want to speak this one out,' he said to the Lhosir coming up from the stairs. 'They fought well. Brave. I owe it to him. Go and find Medrin.'

The Screambreaker's men nodded grimly. Most of them had blood on their swords and on their mail now. Lhosir blood. Medrin might rail at them for killing their own kin, but these were men who remembered how it was when Yurlak had first taken the throne, before the Screambreaker and the Marroc and crossing the sea. *How we used to fight and feud among ourselves. Like it was. The old way.* Maybe they'd wait or maybe they'd just kill Medrin without him. Most of them had known the Screambreaker better than he had. Some of them had been in the wood with him but there were some too who had fought beside the Screambreaker against the Vathen and watched him fall. Men who hadn't died while Twelvefingers had stayed on the top of his hill, watching and doing nothing – they had a grudge of their own to feed. Maybe they had spirited the Screambreaker's body away. It felt right that someone had done that. A dozen men had seen him fall and no one ever said he wasn't dead, but this way it was the Maker-Devourer himself who'd come away from his cauldron for the old Nightmare of the North. Made for a good story. A legend, even.

When he had Durlak in a corner out of the way, he crouched beside the dead man. 'Durlak. Don't know his father, don't know his family, don't have their roll of deeds to lay out beside him. I don't know what else he did in his life, fair or foul, but I was the one who fought him and I was the one who killed him, and I'll say to any who'll listen that he faced me without fear, that he fought fiercely and that he died bravely. Maker-Devourer, I offer you this man for your cauldron for he will enrich it with his spirit.' He screwed up his eyes, growling at the pain from his cheek.

'Tolvis?'

He looked up. A last pair of soldiers had come up the stairs. Stragglers from the fighting outside in the yard or at the gates perhaps. For a moment his eyes wouldn't focus in the gloom. He recognised the voice, though.

'Gallow?'

Gallow looked down at Tolvis crouching over a dead Lhosir wearing a bracer that marked him as one of Medrin's men. Loudmouth had blood all down the side of his face and over his neck and shoulder. 'You look a mess.'

Tolvis snorted then winced in pain. He stood. 'Nothing that won't heal, Truesword.'

'What are you doing?'

'And it's good to see you too. And how was the battle for you and so on and so on? Finishing Medrin, that's what.'

'Where is he?'

Tolvis nodded towards the door that led to the duke's chamber. 'Hear all that ruckus? Take a guess. He's got nowhere left to run.'

Gallow frowned, struggling to understand the mangled words that came out of Tolvis's mouth. 'I'd see someone about that mess of a face,' he said and turned towards the sounds of fighting.

'Nothing like a good scar to add to my fine looks, eh?'

Tolvis stayed where he was. Gallow couldn't make himself look any more. Wound like that didn't kill you straight away, but more often than not it went bad and green and oozed pus and rotted and then there was nothing to do but cut out whatever had gone bad. Not much to be done when it was a man's face. *Maker-Devourer spare him that. Let it heal clean or give him a good death first.*

The old Marroc duke's room wasn't anything more than a big open space with a bed and a few hangings, a place for dressing, a hole in the corner for shitting and pissing, a table by the window with a quill and ink, a chest and a few piles of furs on the floor. Medrin and the last of his Lhosir were backed into a corner. Three of them and the prince himself, though they were far from finished. Medrin still had the Crimson Shield strapped to his arm, a short stabbing blade held high and ready over the top of it. A dozen or more Lhosir penned him in, holding him at bay. They shouted at him while Medrin and his three bared their teeth and hurled back taunts and insults, challenging the Screambreaker's men to come forward and finish what they'd started.

'Turn on your king? You're outcasts already! *Nioingr*, all of you.'

'Yield, traitor!'

'You'll be hunted to the end of the world. Kill me and my father will do it. Let me live and I'll hunt you myself!'

'You betrayed the Screambreaker!'

'He fell in battle! He got what he wanted!'

Gallow pushed past them. As he did, he drew Solace from its sheath. 'Yield, Medrin. End this. Go back across the sea and stay there. Say what you like about what happened here, just don't come back.'

'Never, Foxbeard!'

'Then go back in pieces.' Gallow shrugged. 'It's all the same to me.'

He closed on the prince and Medrin backed away behind his men. Gallow smiled. 'See. In the end you always were a coward.'

'*Nioingr!*' With sudden fury, Medrin leaped forward again, slamming the Crimson Shield into Gallow and lunging with his blade. The shock staggered Gallow, knocking him back as though the shield had a strength of its own beyond Medrin's arm. The prince's blade eased past his guard and skimmed off his mail. 'Die!' Twelvefingers lunged again, high this time at Gallow's collar, their shields still pressed together. Gallow barely dodged aside while Medrin kept pushing forward. 'You always had poison in your blood for me, you sheep-loving clean-skin no-beard! Now I'll let that poison out!'

With their shields locked together Medrin's short thrusting blade had the advantage over the long edge of the red sword. Gallow raised Solace over his head and brought it down but Medrin parried the blow with his own steel, keeping so close that Gallow could smell his breath. 'Yes,' said Gallow, 'I have.' With a mighty heave he threw Medrin back and for a moment

they stood apart, circling each other. 'You led us to the Temple
of Fates, Medrin, and you left us to the Fateguard.'

'And were you any better?' snarled Medrin. 'You let Beyard
die!'

'*You* let us both die, you snivelling shit! "Hold them! I cannot
be found here!" Do you remember those words as you ran?
And we did hold them, Beyard and I, and at the last he threw
himself into them and screamed at me to run too and there was
nothing else I could do! But I held your words in my heart and
I've carried them with me for fourteen years, and you haven't
changed at all.'

'*Nioingr!*' Medrin charged again. Gallow brought the red
sword down. Medrin caught it on the Crimson Shield, and a
shock ran through Gallow as though he'd been stung by a spark
from his father's forge. His arm fell limp and the red sword hung
from his fingers. For a moment his grip on his shield loosened.

Medrin's blade lunged past, catching him on the shoulder,
digging into the mail with enough force to split open its links.
Gallow felt its point bite into him, scraping against bone. He
jerked away, stumbling back. The pain was staggering. Medrin
bared his teeth and came at him again, slamming the Crimson
Shield into him and lunging at Gallow's face this time. Gallow
could barely hold his sword. His shield arm felt as weak as a
child's. He jumped back as Medrin's edge sliced past his nose.

'You wanted to fight me, clean-skin? You always did. So fight
me!' Gallow tried to grip Solace but his fingers were still numb. It
was all he could do not to drop the sword. Medrin slammed into
him again and again, a lunge each time, pushing him back and
back while Gallow's shield arm grew weaker with every blow.

They parted for a moment. Medrin wore a vicious smile.
'Now you know better than to strike this shield, but I'll take that
Vathan sword too. Yield, clean-skin. Yield and give me the Edge
of Sorrows and I'll put it to fine use. Beyard was your friend? He
was mine too and I've not forgotten his fate. Give me that sword
and I'll have revenge for both of us.' He took another step back.
'We'll do it together. I'll even spare the rest of these men. They'll
be outcasts but I'll let them run a few days before I hang them as
ravens over their own houses. Yield, clean-skin!'

Gallow shook his head. He let go of his shield and let it slip off his arm and crash to the floor. 'No.' When he tried to lift the red sword, his arm twitched and refused.

Medrin shrugged. 'Look at you. Raise your blade at least before I finish you!'

'Take me if you can, demon-prince.'

'So be it. And then the rest of you will follow, and then I will take that sword you carry and settle what we started all those years ago.' He launched himself again, as he had before, each time always the same, the shield to batter his enemy down and the stabbing lunge over the top. Gallow pulled the red sword out of his one hand and into the other, threw himself sideways and swung as Medrin passed. The prince screamed. Something clattered on the floor. When Gallow staggered back to look at what he'd done, Medrin was hugging his arm to his side. Blood ran down his mail. His sword lay on the floor and the hand that had held it still gripped its hilt.

'No! No!' he screamed at Gallow. 'No! What have you done to me?'

Gallow turned to face him. He held the Sword of the Weeping God out straight before him. 'The sword against the shield, Medrin? Or do you yield?'

'Kill him,' shouted Loudmouth from behind the rest of his men. 'Finish him properly. Let him end well at least.'

Medrin lowered the Crimson Shield. His face was filled with murder and hate. 'Yes, Foxbeard. Give me that at least. Let me die as a Lhosir should die. It's what your precious Screambreaker would have done.' He had his own blood all over him. He was already pale.

Gallow nodded. He lowered Solace. 'He would. But I'm wondering, Prince Sixfingers, what *you* would have done.'

47

JUSTICE FOR ALL

The Vathen reached Andhun and attacked. The Lhosir saw them coming and tried to close the gates but they were too late and Gulsukh and his horsemen were too quick. A hundred were inside before the Lhosir could form a wall of shields. It hung in the balance for a minute but that was all, and then Gulsukh and his riders broke the Lhosir. He called his bashars to him as they came through the gates and gave them their orders. Two hundred to stay here, to hold the gates and tear them down so they couldn't be closed again. Another hundred to ride back out after the Vathan clans retreating across the countryside, to tell them they didn't need the Weeping Giant and his god-touched sword, that Gulsukh had broken the Lhosir without either and that Andhun lay helpless and waiting for them. Others he sent down towards the Isset to take the bridge and hold it against any who would try to destroy it, and to the docks and to the harbour to find the Lhosir soldiers and the Marroc and kill them, but above all to stop them from leaving in their ships.

Some he took himself, up the hill from the gate towards the castle, where surely whoever commanded this city would be waiting for him.

Valaric's spear point rammed into a Lhosir collarbone and stuck tight. The forkbeard snatched at it and roared, pulling it with such force that Valaric had to let go or be pulled off the barricade. He switched to his axe until that stuck in a shield and was wrenched out of his hand. He drew his sword and fought on, kept hitting them but achieving nothing much, while all around him the Marroc were dying. *Damn them – why did they all wear armour? Where did they get such mail, so many swords?* But he knew the answer to that. They'd taken it from all the Marroc they'd killed for the last fifteen years. Iron and steel were cheap to the forkbeards, they had so much.

A Marroc fell at the far end of the barricade, blood gushing from an arm severed at the elbow. A forkbeard pulled himself up before anyone could take the dead man's place. Valaric swore and shouted and then realised there wasn't anyone left. The forkbeard swung his axe and caved in the skull of another Marroc and then jumped down, howling and chopping left and right. Valaric swung down behind him and stabbed him in the back of the head. He tried to climb back up before another forkbeard could get over the barricade but his legs failed him. There was no strength there any more. His arms could barely hold his sword and shield. He gritted his teeth and hauled himself back up anyway. Most of the Marroc he'd led here were dead. Sarvic was still up, Jonnic too. And the rest ... the rest were ordinary men who just didn't want to see their homes go up in flames.

'Enough!' he shouted. He looked at Sarvic and Jonnic. *We're the ones with mail. We hold them long enough for the others to get away.* He simply didn't have the energy to say that but he didn't need to. A look was enough.

Jonnic nodded. Sarvic looked at him too but his was a different look. His was *Look, Valaric, look!*

Behind the forkbeards at the end of the street, men on horseback were coming. Soldiers. A mass of them. Valaric had no idea who they were but they didn't look like forkbeards and they weren't dismounting as Marroc soldiers would. The forkbeards had noticed too and had started to turn.

Vathen!

The Vathen drew back their arms. Javelots rained on Lhosir and Marroc alike.

'What would you have done?' Gallow said again.

'Put an end to it,' slurred Tolvis. He sounded as though he was talking with his mouth stuffed full of food.

'No.' As Medrin slumped against a wall and the Crimson Shield fell from his other arm, Gallow stood over him. He closed his eyes for a moment at another wave of pain from his shoulder.

The feeling in his sword arm was coming back and it was like being stabbed by a thousand needles. He sat Medrin up, lifted his arm, wrapped a belt around his severed wrist and squeezed it tighter and tighter until the bleeding stopped. 'Pitch?' he asked. 'Is there any?'

The last three of Medrin's men looked uneasily from one to the other. The others shook their heads.

'Fire? Torches?'

The prince was breathing too quickly. He was pale as death now, his eyes barely open. Tolvis stood watching. 'First you try to kill him, now you're trying to save him. Why, Truesword? So you can hang him beside the gates for the Marroc to see, the way he used to do to them? I'll not have that. I might turn my back if anyone speaks him out but I'll not have a prince of the sea strung up like that. Yurlak's son? No. Put an axe in his hand and kill him properly.' Behind him Medrin's men were surrendering their swords.

Gallow stood. 'It's not for me to decide, nor for you either. I mean to give him to the Marroc. Let them choose what to do with him.'

Tolvis shook his head. He tried to smile but the ruined side of his face was too swollen. 'Truesword, you know perfectly well what the Marroc will do. Hanging him won't be enough. They'll rip him to pieces and feed his parts to their dogs, and when word of that comes back across the sea to Yurlak, he'll shout for every man who can so much as hold a stick. He'll rouse them out of their homes and into a ship within a week. They'll sweep across this land in a tide of blood and slaughter that'll make the Screambreaker's campaigns look like a wedding feast. It won't be conquest and plunder this time. He'll be coming to wipe away the stain of the Marroc who'd killed his son. Is that what you want?'

Gallow shrugged. 'We stand on Marroc stone. They should be the ones to choose.'

Loudmouth turned away. A Lhosir came with a torch. 'Put his sword in his lap, Gallow. Finish it here. He died in battle after his first great victory against the Vathen. Give that to Yurlak. The Maker-Devourer will know the truth. Let that be enough.'

Gallow ignored his words but took the torch and held the blade of the red sword in the flame. Fire from burning wood should never have been enough to make a piece of iron even start to change its colour, but the sword seemed to glow with an an inner light in the flames.

'You might kill him doing that,' said Tolvis.

'I might. Hold him down and put some leather in his mouth.'

The Lhosir held Medrin down. Gallow gripped the prince's arm between his knees and pressed the hot steel into the wound. Blood sizzled and flesh cooked. Medrin's eyes flew wide open, his back arched. He screamed and bucked but the Lhosir held him fast, and after a moment he fell still again. His eyes rolled back into his head. Gallow took the sword away and loosened the belt around Medrin's arm. The bleeding had stopped.

'Is he alive?'

Gallow pressed his ear against Medrin's chest. 'His heart is faint but it still beats.'

'You'll not give him to the Marroc, Gallow,' said Tolvis.

'Do I have to fight you too?'

'No.' Tolvis pulled his axe from his belt – Gallow's axe – and handed it back, haft first. 'Not if you just let it go. Best you have this back, I think.'

Gallow took the axe. He looked at the Lhosir around him, a dozen and then some. They were with Tolvis, all of them, and he couldn't fight that many even if he hadn't been stabbed in the shoulder. And he didn't want to.

'Do what you want.' He turned his back on them and walked away.

'Run! Run for the ships!' Valaric waved the rest of the Marroc away from the barricade. 'You too, Sarvic.' He stood and jabbed his sword at the forkbeards climbing the barricade. 'No reason to stay now. Let them fight among themselves. Leave them to it.'

Still alive. Well that's a surprise. He ran down the street, left into an alley and across to the Riverway. People streamed past him, running, screaming, heading helter-skelter for the docks. He looked up the river towards the bridge. There had been another barricade there but it was smashed now, bodies littered around it. His eyes hunted for forkbeards to kill, but he didn't see any.

Why are you all screaming?

A Vathan jumped his horse over the disintegrating barricade and hurled a javelot into the back of a fleeing Marroc. A dozen more followed him.

Oh. That's why. Modris! He gripped his shield and stepped out into the street.

Gulsukh Ardshan slowed as he reached the square outside the castle. *No one to greet us?* Just a lot of bodies and open gates with no one guarding them. He urged his horsemen on, riding with them, seizing this second set of gates before anyone could close them. There were more bodies in the yard beyond. And in the middle of it two handfuls of forkbeards, standing and staring at him as though he was the Weeping Giant himself risen back from the dead.

One carried the Crimson Shield of the Marroc. Another had the red sword, Solace.

Mine!

He pointed his spear at them and screamed.

48

HOLDING THE DOORS

Valaric took the first Vathan rider down, rising out of the crowd of fleeing Marroc with his sword and sticking it straight through the rider's leather jerkin and between the ribs underneath. The rider tipped back. First thing Valaric did was grab his spear. Against a man on a horse a spear did a lot better than a sword.

He snatched it in time to turn it round and skewer the next Vathan. The spear flew up out of his hands, gone as quickly as it had come. The next rider slashed with a sword. Valaric leaped out of the way then turned the tip of a spear with his shield. The riders were simply hacking at him as they passed, moving straight on through the screaming Marroc beyond. There were more and more of them, a trickle turning to a flood. And here he was, standing around waiting to be trampled. Useless. He darted into an alley. At least the horsemen wouldn't trouble him there – wouldn't even fit.

'Why are there so many of them by the river?' he hissed into the air.

'The bridge, Marroc,' said the shadows behind him. Valaric almost jumped out of his mail. He spun round, lunging with his sword, and the steel skittered off a shield. He'd had a forkbeard standing right there, still and quiet in the shadows of a doorway, and he hadn't even seen him.

'We can fight if you want, Marroc,' said the forkbeard.

'Do I know you?' Valaric peered. Behind their helms it was hard to tell one forkbeard from another. This one's beard was grey. He looked a bit like the Widowmaker, except Gallow had said the Widowmaker was dead.

'Not that I know, Marroc. So is it to be fighting or not?'

'Five fingers of the sun ago I'd have said yes.'

'I know you would. So would I. But the Vathen have the day now. Andhun will be theirs by sunset.'

The forkbeard had no sword. Slowly Valaric put his own back in his belt. 'Who are you?'

'The bridge, Marroc. Take down the bridge and the Vathen can't cross the Isset. Nowhere else for a hundred miles and then you're at the Crackmarsh. I'm told they could cross the Crackmarsh if someone showed them the way, but then again a clever man might make a whole army vanish in that swamp. Take down that bridge and by the time the Vathen have built it again, Yurlak himself will be here with the whole horde of the sea.'

Or I'll have time to raise an army of Marroc to fight both of you. Valaric looked the forkbeard up and down. 'And how would you take down the bridge, old man?'

The forkbeard laughed. 'Was always a chance it would come to this.'

'I can't trust you.' Valaric shook his head.

'And I can't trust *you*, Marroc.' The forkbeard pulled a knife from his belt and made a shallow cut on the flesh of his forearm. 'May the Maker-Devourer spit me into the Marches if I raise a hand against you while that bridge still stands. And take a look, Marroc. I have no sword. No spear. No axe.'

Valaric looked him over. He was old and battered. His mail was ripped in places and there was dried blood all over it. Some of it, he was sure, was the forkbeard's own.

'Well?' The forkbeard offered Valaric his knife.

'While that bridge still stands.' Valaric took the knife and cut himself. They clasped arms, blood to blood, and it felt the strangest thing in the world to Valaric in the burning ruin of a town that this forkbeard's kinsmen had set out to destroy.

Tolvis gave Medrin to the three Lhosir who'd stood with their prince. Let him be carried by his own soldiers. Gallow picked up one of their shields. He looked at it and his lip curled. Medrin's men. The Legion of the Crimson Shield. They'd had them painted so they all looked the same, like Medrin's god-borne shield itself.

'And what are *you* going to do with him?' he asked Tolvis, since Loudmouth hadn't yet stuck a sword in Medrin's hand and then finished him as he'd said.

'Wait for him to wake up, if he does. If he doesn't I'll build him a pyre and one of these three can speak him out and Yurlak can at least know that his son died well enough, even if he didn't live as he should.'

'And if he lives?'

Tolvis shrugged. 'Go home, Gallow. Go back to that Marroc woman of yours.' They trailed down the spiral stairs and into the Marroc duke's hall. Gallow's fingers felt for the locket under his mail. *Go home.* He could do that now. He'd only stayed to try and save the Marroc of Andhun from Medrin, and he'd largely failed at that.

'What *are* you going to do with Medrin?'

Tolvis shrugged. He opened the doors to the castle yard and strode out towards the open gates. 'I don't know, Truesword, I simply don't. Lost at sea, perhaps. We'll have to talk, all of us.' In the middle of the yard he stopped and turned. 'Truesword, before you and I part, the Screambreaker gave—'

A column of riders trotted through the castle gates. Vathen. Dozens of them. They paused, as surprised as the Lhosir, and then one of them lowered his spear and pointed it straight at Gallow and howled.

'Feyrk's balls! Back to the keep!' Tolvis bolted back the way they'd come and the other Lhosir scrambled after him. Didn't matter how fierce a man was; caught in the open and surrounded by horsemen he died and died quickly. The last of the Lhosir fell across the threshold with a javelot in his back.

'Go!' shouted Tolvis. 'Take the cave path. I'll hold the door.'

'No, you won't.' Gallow helped him close it and then shoved his shoulder against it. 'You go. *I'll* hold them.'

Tolvis snorted. 'You can hardly hold your own shield.' They pressed themselves against the door.

'Half your face is missing.'

'Don't need a face to fight!'

The door jerked ajar as the Vathen threw themselves against

it. Gallow shoved back, forcing it closed. 'You'd think there'd be a bar or something.'

The door shuddered again. Tolvis hissed. 'Well then, Truesword, shall we stand and face them like men?'

Gallow tossed him his axe – the one he'd given to Tolvis on the road away from Andhun and Tolvis had just returned. 'You'll be needing this.'

The door shuddered again. 'Is that it?' Tolvis yelled. 'My dead grandmother could push harder.'

Gallow blinked. Looked at him hard. Even with both of them putting their whole weight against it, the Vathen were coming through the door at any moment. 'One stays, one runs.' Gallow gritted his teeth. 'They're your men. You go.' When Tolvis didn't move, Gallow laughed. 'If you like, Loudmouth, I'll fight you for it. Besides, it's my turn.'

'What?' Loudmouth stared at him as though he was mad but he must have seen the certainty in Gallow's face, the simple resolve not to move.

'In the Temple of Fates. We had the ironskins on us, on the other side of a door just like this. One of us could run but not both. Almost came to blows about who got to hold them. That time it was Beyard. This time it's me. Now take the bloody axe and run before I hit you with it!'

As the door shook again Tolvis turned and looked at Gallow one last time. 'A hundred men will speak you out, Truesword,' he cried, and was gone.

No, Gallow thought, *they probably won't*. For a moment as he held fast, he touched a finger to the amulet around his neck. 'Sorry, but that's a debt I carried before you ever knew me.'

Tolvis sprinted after his men and caught them down in the kitchens, wrestling their way into the pantries, hurling kegs and crates out of the way. He tipped a huge barrel of pickles on its side, spilling salted water all over the floor. The trapdoor was still there, same door as had been there years ago when the Screambreaker had made this castle his and they'd all been waiting for Yurlak to die. He pulled it open.

'Come on then!' He sent two of his own men first and then

the three of Medrin's, still carrying their prince. With a bit of luck they'd get to the bottom and find Twelvefingers was dead. Would save a lot of trouble.

'You two!' He picked men with good legs. 'You stay up here. You hold the path for Truesword if he gets this far! You understand?'

The door flew open. Gallow bolted across the hall as the first Vathen tumbled in behind him, stumbling over one another. Voices sang in his head, calling him, telling him to turn and face them and cut them down, as many as he could. Telling him to die in the middle of a mound of Vathan corpses as the Screambreaker had done, to be sent on his way to the Maker-Devourer covered in the blood of his enemies, cup filled with glory. But there were other voices now, ones that hadn't been born in those long years of war at the Screambreaker's side. Arda. His sons and his daughter calling him to come home. And so he raced after Loudmouth and his Lhosir, across the hall and down the stairs behind it which would take him to the kitchens and the secret pathway through the caves and the tunnels to the beach. To run across the stones and the debris fallen from the cliffs and to the harbour and to the Marroc and Valaric and be rid of the red sword. Give it to some Marroc hero and jump into a boat and sail away up the coast and finally go home.

The stairs spat him out into a hall lined with doors, with an iron gate at the end through which streamed light. Sunlight. He'd gone the wrong way.

Back in the day he'd been in this castle long enough not to make that sort of stupid mistake, and so he wondered how he could have been so cursed until he realised that the old Lhosir songs were still singing in his head while those of the Marroc he'd come to love had fallen quiet. And for some daft reason he could hear the Screambreaker talking to him too: *So, Truesword. Does that answer your question? Do you know who you are now?*

Tolvis ran as best he could through the tunnels and passages to the shore, hustling Medrin's men as fast as they could go. The tide was high, waves breaking into the throat of the caves, and the beach path was drowned so they'd have to make their way over the rocks with the sea crashing around their knees, but it was that or stay and fight the Vathen, and the Vathen were far too many for that. Find a way back to the rest of the army, that was the thing.

'Go!' Tolvis shouted. 'Go ahead!'

He waited for a few minutes but Truesword didn't come and neither did the two men he'd left. He waited longer than he should have. By then he knew they wouldn't be coming.

The gate opened onto the cliffs. Gallow knew this piece of the castle. A narrow strip of grass between the keep and the sea where the Marroc dukes once flew their sea eagles for sport. There was just the one gate, some walls, a strip of land a dozen yards wide and then the cliffs and the sea. He ran to the edge and looked down. Fifty feet below him the waves crashed against the bottom of the cliff.

A strong man, skilled and daring, might have climbed it, and he was all of those things and yet he paused.

Boats were flooding out of the harbour, big and small: Marroc fleeing the Lhosir and now the Vathen. There was a small one at the bottom of the cliff almost beneath him, barely past the breaking surf. Behind him the Vathen poured out into the sunlight. They fanned out around him, suddenly cautious. Gallow looked from them to the sea. And then he looked back again.

Gulsukh held up his hand, commanding his men to stop. One Lhosir. Wounded by the way he held his shield, but he had Solace the Comforter in his hand, and he'd turned to face them all. Gulsukh stepped forward. He took a deep breath and bowed his head. This beardless Lhosir would give him the sword in front of all his men. *Give* it, not have it taken, and then they'd all see that Gulsukh was the heir to the Weeping Giant and everything would change. They could go back to their homes or they could continue their conquest, one or the other, but it would be his to decide and even the priests of the Weeping God would have to bow to that.

He paused a little longer, letting the Lhosir see how hopeless his situation was. Gulsukh kept his head bowed. The Lhosir seemed to understand: he took off his helm and placed it on the grass by his feet. Then he sheathed the sword.

'I honour your courage,' said the ardshan as quietly as the rush of the wind and the hiss of the waves below would allow. 'Your skill. Few men could do what you have done.'

'Why?' The ardshan's eyes twitched as the Lhosir unbuckled his belt but held on to the Comforter, still in its scabbard. 'Why? What have I done?'

'You're the warrior who killed the Weeping Giant.' Gulsukh frowned at the expression on the man's face. 'Are you not?'

'No. That man was the Screambreaker.' The Lhosir shook off his gauntlets. 'He fell beside me. I'm just a man who took up his sword.'

The ardshan raised his head and looked this *just-a-man* in the eye. He felt a quiver in his heart as the Lhosir met his gaze.

49

THE SEA

The old forkbeard knew his way around the city, no doubt about that. Knew it better than Valaric did, as though it was his home. He led Valaric through the maze of alleys down by the river to a place where a boat lay tied to a post and together they rowed across. There were Vathen already on the other bank but they weren't rampaging through the streets, not yet.

'Keeping the bridge,' said the forkbeard. He rowed them to the massive tree-trunk piles that rose from the base of the cliff on the western bank of the Isset and supported that end of the bridge, monstrous pines from far away in the Varyxhun valley, floated down the river. No one lived down at the foot of these cliffs. There were no houses, no roads, no paths. Just sheer rock.

'What's your plan, old man? Cut it down with an axe?'

'Something like that.'

'But I don't have an axe and nor do you.'

The old forkbeard drew the boat up against the cliff and tied it fast to an outcrop of stone. He hauled himself onto a narrow ledge and sat down beside one of the great trunks. The air stank of fish. The forkbeard produced an axe from among the stones and tossed it to Valaric. 'Now you do, Marroc.'

Valaric stared at him. He was hurt. You could see that. The way he moved gave him away. Either that or he was even older than he looked. Every movement was pain to him. And yet ...

'Who are you?'

'Care to cast your eyes upward, Marroc?' asked the old man. Now he had a flint and tinder. Underneath the western edge of the bridge a dozen kegs had been tied to the piles. Slick wet stains spread over the wood beneath them, all the way down to the sea. Fish oil. 'Never could make a keg that sealed properly in this town, you lot.' The old forkbeard shook his head, idly striking the flint until the tinder caught and he had a small smouldering pile of grass. Next thing he pulled out from behind the piles was a small stick wrapped in cloth. The stick stank of fish too. He offered it to Valaric. 'Yours if you want it.'

'What?'

'Seems to me it should be a Marroc who sets the bridge ablaze.' He tossed the stick to Valaric, who caught it without thinking. 'Come on, quick now, before this goes out.'

Valaric scrambled out of the boat. He shuffled past the old man to sit on the ledge. The forkbeard carefully lit the torch.

'Set it as you like. I'd watch out for bits of blazing wood and oil falling on your head though, so don't stay to admire your handiwork too long.'

The old forkbeard jumped into the boat. The next thing Valaric knew he'd cast off and was drifting away on the current and Valaric was stuck there on the ledge alone. He looked up. Yes, a man could climb the cliff easily enough. Maybe not if it was on fire though. 'Hey! What are you doing?'

'I have somewhere else to be. You can swim can't you, Valaric of Witterslet? Don't wait too long before you use that. It won't burn for ever.'

'Who are you? What's your name?'

The old forkbeard waved. 'Don't think I want any of those any more. Take care of your city, Marroc. Look after it. What we've left of it.'

Valaric watched him go then yelped and almost dropped the torch as it burned his fingers. He touched the torch to the stream of oil dripping down from above. It lit very nicely, as if it had been mixed with something else. He stayed for bit and watched the flame climb steadily towards the leaking kegs under the upper beams of the bridge. As it reached the top, the fire began to burn more brightly.

It occurred to him then that maybe he *should* start swimming.

The Vathan with the crested helm held out his hand. 'The sword, Lhosir. The Sword of the Weeping God. Give it to me. No need for more to die. Give it to me and go in peace. This battle is lost to you.'

Gallow levelled the sword at the Vathan. 'Come and take it.'

The Vathan took a pace towards him. For one long moment Gallow thought he might even do it, that he might just hand this cursed sword over if the Vathan had the courage to lower his weapons and come close enough to simply take it from his hand. Maybe that was the sign of someone who'd earned it. What had *he* done, after all? Taken it from a dead man.

The Vathan took his step but then stopped. 'I am the ardshan of my people. Give me the sword!'

'Not if you can't take it. If you can't take it then you haven't earned it.'

The ardshan turned his back. 'Kill him. But do *not* touch the sword.'

The other Vathen hesitated. Gallow had seen it enough times before. The mustering of courage to charge enemy shields, knowing that some of you must die but that if you don't then death would come for all. The red sword held them at bay but they'd find their courage in a moment.

'*Arda!*'

He turned and flung the sword over the cliff, as far out to sea as he could. The ardshan watched the Sword of the Weeping God arc out into the sky, eyes wide in horror. Before he could speak, Gallow was already running along the edge of the cliff – one step, two, three – and then the Vathen launched themselves towards him. Before they could reach him, he turned and leaped as mightily as he could, following the sword out over the cliffs and past the breaking waves to the sea.

'Arda!' Tolvis heard the shout above the crash of the waves. From the top of the cliff men were suddenly peering down at him. Vathen, and the way they looked and pointed was quite enough. By the time they were firing their arrows and throwing their javelots he was already running.

'This way. There's a ship.' Medrin's ship. The one he'd used to sail out of Andhun, assuming it hadn't been washed away or found and burned, or taken already by some other band of fleeing

Lhosir. But a couple of miles of running along beaches and climbing cliffs and racing through woods and climbing down to the sea again later, the ship was still there. There were even a few dozen Lhosir standing around it. Keeping guard for some reason. Tolvis couldn't imagine what they were doing there but now wasn't the time to be thinking about that. As he and the others approached they waved and shouted and he waved and shouted back, 'Get the ship in the sea! Get the ship in the sea! The Vathen are coming!'

By the time he got to the bottom of the cliff the ship was already out in the surf, the sail rising. That was when he realised these Lhosir were more of Medrin's men, quite sharp enough to see what was coming towards them. Next thing Tolvis knew there were a dozen men on his side and twice that on the other, all with swords drawn and facing each other, with the Vathen coming over the hill in about one minute and the barely living body of Medrin Twelvefingers on the beach between them.

The Lhosir glared at each other. Tolvis closed his eyes. 'Really? Do we have to? I mean, right here and right now?' Medrin Twelvefingers? He'd be Medrin Sixfingers now.

No one moved.

'Well I don't know about you lot, but I've got an errand to run before we all kill each other. Let me know how it ends.' He turned his back on the lot of them and walked away. Then he remembered the Vathen and ran instead. He didn't look back.

EPILOGUE

VARYXHUN

A rda's hand still smarted from where she'd slapped Fenaric. She'd slapped him two days ago. Quite a slap then.

She sighed. More of a punch really.

He wasn't going to come back. Not this time. He'd still got half the money she'd made from selling the horses. *Her* money but she couldn't quite make herself get worked up about it the way she ought to. *Scheming little thief.* But Fenaric was only trying to do what he thought was right for her. Just couldn't get it into his thick head that she didn't want what anyone else thought was right for her. She wanted ...

She wanted *him*. Stupid pig-headed bloody-minded selfish forkbeard Gallow. She wanted him. And she was slowly realising that she wasn't going to get him.

Word of the battle of Andhun made its way up the river in bits and fragments: the Lhosir had been wiped out. They'd beaten the Vathen. Sometimes both, sometimes neither, and all said with gleeful joy. Andhun had fallen and then it hadn't. Stories were like that. Rubbish mostly, but if she was putting all the stories together right, whatever had happened had been bloody.

Stupid man hadn't been supposed to do anything except take his stupid vicious bastard Widowmaker half-friend or whatever he was back to his own kind. Half-friend? Hadn't even looked like *that* most of the time.

Stupid man. Stupid.

She had to stop for a moment to wipe her eyes. Stupid smoke from the stupid forge that Nadric could barely use any more making her eyes water all the time. At least he had that set up now. Maybe they had some chance of making a little money again and not starving when it came to winter.

Stupid men. Both of them. Leaving her with their children to look after and not coming back again. Something in the air up here near the mountains. Must be. Eyes seemed to water a lot since they'd come here.

'Arda Smithswife?'

She jumped and looked up at the ugliest forkbeard she'd ever seen. One side of his face was a mass of scarring, red and fresh.

'Who wants her?' He wasn't the first to have made his way this far south.

The forkbeard held out a purse. 'My name is Tolvis.'

The name meant nothing but the purse had her eyes. 'And what do you want, Tolvis from across the sea?'

He tossed the purse to her. 'I came here to give you this. A debt owed to Gallow Truesword.' He might have turned and gone after that and she might have let him too, since if Gallow had been alive he'd have delivered the purse himself; and then she could have beaten him around the head and cursed him roundly for taking so long and leaving her in the hands of that miserable carter who'd turned out to be far less of a man than she'd thought. But there was a hesitation to him, and to her too, as if there was more to this story than a bag of silver.

So she brought him inside and offered him goat's milk and cheese, both of which he took with unusual grace for a forkbeard. In his turn he gave her an axe. Gallow's axe, and she knew for sure then that Gallow wasn't coming back.

'You were a friend, were you?' she asked. 'Or did you loot his body?' But not that, or why come all this way to hand her a bag of silver? Yes, and she could see she'd insulted him. 'I'm sorry,' she said. Probably the first time she'd ever said sorry to a forkbeard.

He told her about Gallow and how it was his fault that Gallow hadn't come home, and of the crossing of the sea and the Crimson Shield and the fight with the Vathen and then in Andhun and what he'd done and how he'd finally come to his end.

'You were in his thoughts.' Tolvis had a distant look in his eyes. 'Always. That was always what he wanted just as soon as he'd made everything right. To come back to you.'

'Bloody idiot didn't though, did he?' Stupid eyes watering again. Stupid mountain air. 'So he died thinking it was me then, did he? Who gave him away to the Vathen?' Almost more than anything else, that was what she couldn't bear.

'The Screambreaker told him otherwise.' Tolvis smiled. Or tried to, as best his ruined face would let him. 'And Gallow believed him. And I'll not ask.'

She couldn't stop the tears. Had to look away. 'Bloody idiot,' she said again.

'Not the only idiot either.' Tolvis laughed and shook his head. 'Well I didn't have anything better to do, what with Medrin's men taking the only ship we had and leaving us on the beach and the Vathen hunting all over for us. So I went back. Last place they'd look. They were all a bit mad, mind you, on account of some crazy Marroc managing to fire the bridge across the Isset. The air stank of fish oil for days, but I think it was the bridge collapsing into the river that upset them rather than the smell.' He sighed and a perplexed look furrowed his face. 'They searched the beach for Gallow's body, you know, and for the sword too. I watched while they waited for the tide to go right out. They searched and searched, then and every low tide since, and for all I know they're searching still.' He grinned. 'Man jumps off a fifty-foot cliff into the sea in mail, he generally sinks right quick to the bottom by my reckoning. Same goes for swords. But they never found him and they never found Solace. The sea took them. Took him away and maybe washed him up somewhere and maybe didn't.'

He got up and she let him go, but when he was at the door and the wretched mountain air had stopped blurring everything for a moment she told him he could stay if he wanted. It was a long journey he'd come, and Varyxhun was a bit full of Marroc running from the Vathen just now, and he'd pay far more than he ought for a place to sleep, if a forkbeard could find a place at all, and that was hardly fair considering why he'd come. And the Lhosir Tolvis, he said well maybe, because he could do with a couple of days without there being Vathen in the morning and Marroc in the afternoon and brigands in between and all of them trying to kill him.

'Forkbeard wants it easy?' she mocked.

'Yes,' said Tolvis without any bitterness but maybe a touch of the wistful. 'Sometimes a forkbeard does.'

Pug-ugly scar though she thought to herself when he went to get his horse. But she was smiling as she thought it, and that was good, because there hadn't been any smiles for a while.

And Tolvis Loudmouth stayed, for a while at least. After all, the Vathen still hadn't crossed the Isset and likely wouldn't for a while now, so he was hardly going to miss anything. But mostly he stayed because he could have sworn that the very last time he'd looked back as he'd run from the hail of Vathan spears and arrows, he'd caught a glimpse of a boat amid the waves and some old Lhosir soldier hauling something big and heavy out of the water.

Or maybe that had just been wishful thinking, because the next time he looked the boat had been gone. But yes, he stayed a while in Varyxhun just in case, because if Gallow Truesword wasn't drowned after all then sooner or later this was where he'd show his face.

PROLOGUE
THE RAKSHASA

The gods had sent Oribas away from his home, out to the edge of this ocean of sand where it met the sea at the far fringes of what the Aulians had once called their own. They were mocking him for the audacity of asking for their help but he'd come anyway because he had nowhere else to go. He'd not expected to find anything except perhaps a snake with a novel poison or else a slow death from thirst and hunger.

He stared along the beach. An hour ago he could have looked either way for miles along the flat sands and the barely restless waters and seen nothing, not a single thing. It had been like that for days.

But now it wasn't. He quickened his pace. Something was on the sand. Something large. A chest, perhaps, washed up by the sea and wrapped in seaweed. *Filled with the treasure of the gods?* He laughed at himself. More likely it was the half-eaten corpse of some giant sea creature or a piece of a wrecked galley.

But it wasn't either of these things. When he came closer it was a man. Two arms, two legs. Surely dead so not much use, but wrapped in armour of metal rings. Maybe he had a use for that? The man was clinging to the remains of a mast or tree trunk, his arms still wrapped tight around it. He was lying on a shield and his hand was clenched tight around something that hung from his neck.

Oribas rolled the man over and his eyes grew wide. As well as his shield the man was clutching a sword. A strange dark reddish steel, unusual but a fine weapon. Oribas reached down to take it.

Under the bright desert sun the man's eyes flicked open.

THE FATEGUARD

The door shuddered again. '*Open!*'

Beyard turned. 'Shall we take our punishment like men then?' But Medrin was already at the window. He vanished down the rope and that was that. Gone. *Craven bastard.*

'*Open this door!*' The roar from outside was furious this time. The other Lhosir, the blacksmith's lad Gallow, pushed an empty chest across the threshold and sat on it. Beyard sat beside him, wedging the door shut. '*Open up! Beardless cowards!*'

Beyard spat. He cast a grin at Gallow. 'Shall we cast the runes together while we give our noble lord a minute to make good his escape? I dare say we can hold them here for hours if needs be, but another minute or so should do it.' He glanced over his shoulder as the door shook again. '*My dead grandmother could push harder,*' he yelled. '*Go away and find some friends with some strength in their arms. I can give you my word we'll wait if that helps!*'

A roar of rage answered. The door groaned as whoever was on the other side threw themselves at it. '*Whoever you are in there, I know there's more than one of you. I'll strangle you with each other's guts!*'

'*Only after I take out yours so I can teach you how to tie proper knots!*' When everything fell quiet, Beyard pressed his ear to the door. There were footsteps and then more voices and he leaned away just in time before the the door shook hard. Two men now, and this time they forced it open a crack. An arm reached around. Beyard bit it and it withdrew with a howl. The shouts from outside gathered force, but then they fell silent. A low gravelly voice spoke instead. 'Give me your axe.'

Fateguard, and for all his bravado, Beyard felt a chill. He

gritted his teeth against the fear. 'I reckon we've given him long enough now, don't you?'

Gallow nodded. 'You go first. I'll hold them.'

Beyard looked at him. Not that either of them could see much in the dark, but they'd been friends for long enough that they didn't really need to see each others' faces any more. 'Truth is, my friend, whoever goes last gets caught. You know this.'

'They won't catch me.' But they probably would. And if it came to a fight, well then they could both handle themselves well enough but that was hardly much use when you were challenged by an ironskin. He glared viciously at the window. Most likely whoever stayed would lose his hand for being a thief and spend the rest of his life wishing he'd been hanged.

'Yes they will.' The door shuddered and the axe struck its first blow. 'My father will pay blood money if that's what it comes to. Yours can't. Go.'

Gallow hesitated. 'Piss poor gang of thieves we turned out to be.'

Beyard chuckled. 'Piss poor.'

Gallow nodded. He clasped Beyard's shoulder and squeezed and then pushed off from the door and bolted for the window, throwing himself through the space between them as fast as he could. He almost fell out head first and then he had the rope, catching himself, and that was the last Beyard saw of him.

'I will not forget,' he whispered to the moon and then he lunged for window himself as the door burst open. Men sprawled in, lit by torches from behind, tumbling over the chest and all falling to the floor and he was half out of the window and so very close to being free when a hand clamped onto his ankle. His first kick didn't break him loose. Another hand grabbed him, and after that he stopped struggling. Maybe the other two would get away, maybe not.

They did. He slowly realised it when the Fateguard and the priests kept asking him over and over who else had come to steal their precious Crimson Shield. They didn't even know how many had been in Beyard's gang, but nothing he could say would make them believe that he and the others had only come for a look, merely to see the forbidden shield that even Corvin the Crow couldn't be allowed to carry. No, they'd come to steal it, the priests were certain and wouldn't be swayed because they'd seen the signs in the sky and omens in the entrails of dead pigs. There was a thief coming, and here he was, and so there would be consequences, and if Beyard's father ever offered to pay blood money to save his son then Beyard never heard of it.

The frost-wind of the frozen north howled over black stone crags draped and spattered with snow. It moaned and screamed like the ghosts of the ever-hungry dead and wailed like the widows they left behind. Birthed by ice-wraiths and abandoned it was a cruel wind, heartless and without mercy, a wind that flayed any thought of kindness. The sun hung low on the horizon, weak and pale and muted. Here at the far end of the world even a midsummer morning offered only ice and storms. Mountains as old as time grew in this place. Pitiless cliffs forged at the very beginning, hard as iron and bitter as juniper. No place for men, no place for life, no place for light, and yet etched somehow into this shattered landscape wound a road, steep and hostile and paved with ice. It wound among them, picking its way from the ice-choked sea as though stalking some unseen prey, hidden as best it could from that hate-filled wind; but here and there it had no choice but to break its cover to rise towards its destination. To their delight the snow and the wind found it, winkled it out of its hiding and lashed it without remorse. The air filled with their frenzy to bury it, this intruder made by men.

Along its whole length, one thing alone travelled this road. A heavy wagon of old weathered wood and fat sausage-fingers of rust pulled by creatures that might once have carried the idea of a unicorn at their heart, but had been birthed by a vision burned and blackened and twisted. They were not alive and their hoof-beats rang on the icy road like cold black iron, four horned nightmares driving ever onward, ever upward, eager now as the end approached. They threw their burden against the howling wind, rocking from side to side, groaning wood and creaking metal hurled against the tireless icy teeth of the storm. They devoured the remorseless road and defied the savage wind until they came to a place where the mountains had been sheered by some great hand and nothing remained but a cavernous void and falling snow; and there they stopped beside an iron gate that might have swallowed a ship, and waited. They stamped their feet but no steamy breath came with their snorts for they were dead things, and even the snow and the stone shivered at their cold. In this landscape, life stopped at the edge of the sea, at the ship that even now nudged its way away from the ice floes to the shore – stopped but for the single soul inside the wagon, a chained man, huddled and freezing, his life flickering and sputtering and close to its end.

A shadow shifted from the great iron gate to the wagon and crept inside. It spoke a word, and its whisper was like a snake across parched desert sand. It held out a crown of black iron. You didn't escape from monsters who could reach through time and space. Not once they knew who you were.

'Beyard,' it said, and put the iron crown forever over his head.

'I will not forget.' He clung to it and held it in his heart and spoke it out, over and over. 'I will not forget.'

There were consequences for the others as well, not that Beyard heard of them until long years had passed. A lost coif – *we were playing at fighting the Marroc, father, and it fell down the well* – cost the smith's son an extra year of working in the forge before his father let him cross the sea to join the Screambreaker's war band conquering the Marroc. Medrin crossed sooner and almost died in his first battle, and when he came back half a year later, he was as weak as a newborn and it was years before he was strong again. The Crimson Shield itself left on the same ship that carried Beyard. It rested a while on the Fortress of the Fates on the island of Brek, but other thieves came before it had even had time to gather dust, the real thieves of all the priests' omens.

And slowly both it and Beyard were forgotten.

THE END OF FARRI MOONTONGUE

PART ONE

The night was moonless and the stars were hidden behind a heavy bank of cloud. It was almost impossible to tell where the black sea ended and the black cliffs began. A soft steady rain hissed into the restless sea. Choppy waves pawed at the Lhosir ship's prow as she slowly turned into the wind and slid quietly to a stop. Even in the rain, orders were given in whispers and the ship carried no lights. On each side of the bow, sailors lowered anchors gently into the water. When they were done with that, they lowered a rowing boat and threw a net over the side and four men climbed down. Two were sailors in rough linen clothes. The other two wore mail and all four were wrapped in heavy thick furs against the biting cold. This was the Ice Mountain Sea, and another few days north towards the Frost Wraiths the water would already be turning to ice. Once the four men were in the boat, a tightly wrapped bundle followed them down. Swords and axes, helms and shields for the warriors, two poles as long as the boat itself and a dozen much shorter ones. The sailors lowered their muffled oars into the waves and started to row while the two men in mail watched their ship fade into the night and then turned ahead, looking out for the crash of waves on the shore, the phosphorescence of the surf breaking at the foot of the cliffs. Farri Moontongue had chosen the night for this with care and patience, the darkest and most dismal hour, but he'd been past here in daylight too, and often enough that he could find his way around these shores with his eyes closed.

They heard the surf before either man saw it. The Moontongue crouched in the bows with a short pole, watching for rocks to fend away, but the oarsmen had steered true and the boat ground to a halt in a tiny cove of soft pale sand. No one said a word – there was no need. The sailors took to dragging the boat out of the water while the Moontongue and the second warrior strapped their shields to their backs and the poles too, their axes to their belts, and walked slowly up the beach to the foot of the cliff and started to climb. It was slow laborious work in the dark on the black rain-slick stone. When they reached the top the Moontongue crouched down and waited, silent, listening to the rain. There was no cover here – nothing grew on these cold and windswept islands except long tough grass that clustered in hummocks and tufts. After a few long seconds, the Moontongue wiped the rain from his eyes.

'Follow.'

He crept away, moving lightly through the wet grass but slow and careful. The moors up on the cliff here were riddled with cracks and crevices and holes beneath a thin skin of grass and earth; indeed, the very stone of the islands themselves was honeycombed with fractures, some of them too narrow for a man's hand, others wide enough for a ship to sail right through. The Moontongue led the way, steady and methodical. After an hour, maybe a little less, they crested a low rise and there it was, another half mile in front of them on top of the cliffs where a part of them fell away and the island had its only harbour: The Temple of Fates. From this far away there wasn't much to see except a few dim specks of light through the drizzle, but as they got closer, the lights became clearer, bonfires burning under sheltered tower-top roofs like beacons. The darkness was too thick to make out much more. When they reached the wall, they followed it around until the Moontongue abruptly stopped.

'Here.' There both took their shields off their backs and then the poles. Neither could really see what they were doing, but they'd practised it together with their eyes shut, night after night until they were perfect. The poles became a ladder. The Moontongue scaled it to the roof of the temple kitchen while the second warrior held it fast; then, once he was up, the second warrior climbed too and pulled the ladder onto the roof beside them. The Moontongue tied a thin piece of dark cord to the bottom step. He lowered the cord over the far edge beside a moss-stained pillar and then dropped to the ground with barely a sound. The second Lhosir followed. The ladder stayed where it was on the kitchen roof, but with the cord they'd easily pull it down.

They ran across the open yard. The doors to the Hall of Fates were closed but not locked and the Moontongue quickly eased one open and slipped inside. As he did, light spilled the other way from dozens of burning candles.

'There.' The Hall of Fates was shaped like an arrow, a wide triangular space pointing into the heart of the temple and a long narrow low passage that led from the main gates. It was, the Moontongue supposed, meant to be the arrow of time, of fate itself, claustrophobic and constricting at first until at last a man arrived at the wide open space of his destiny. The Moontongue had come in through the inner doors and thus emerged already at his own destiny and heading backwards. He wondered for a moment if he should read any meaning into that. Then the other warrior pointed. High on the wall straight ahead hung what they'd come here to steal. The Crimson Shield of Modris the Protector. Legend said that whoever carried the Crimson Shield was invincible in battle, but the last person to carry it had been Prince Yarric, son and heir to King Tane of the Marroc. Prince Yarric lay dead now on some battlefield, surrounded by the crow-pecked corpses of his Marroc guard. The Moontongue's own brother Corvin had killed him, Crimson Shield and all, which only showed what little use legends were. Afterwards the Fateguard had crossed the sea to claim it for their own. It was a unheard of that they should do such a thing.

There were so many reasons the Moontongue could give for being here to steal it back again, but none of them were true ...

He shook his musings aside – losing himself in wondering wouldn't do, not here. He walked briskly across the temple and took the shield down off the wall. It was heavy but not unwieldy. Then he hung his own shield in its place so no one could have any doubt who the thief had been. The second warrior picked up a stout iron-bound strongbox. In the candlelight he grinned. Farri Moontongue nodded back.

'Moontongue.' The whisper came from somewhere in the

deep shadows down the passage to the temple's front gate. Then suddenly the clank and grind of iron on iron.

'Go!' Farri Moontongue drew his axe and watched the shadows a moment longer while the second warrior turned and bolted back the way they'd come. The sounds of the iron devil from the shadows changed from slow strides to fast ones and then to a run, and there it was: a black shape, candlelight gleaming off the dark iron of its armour, faceless beneath its mask and crown. The Moontongue stood in its path with his axe and stolen shield ready. The ironskin had no shield of its own, nor, perhaps, had much need of one. It lashed out with its sword but the Moontongue caught the blow easily on the Crimson Shield and his axe was already swinging its reply. The first cut severed the iron devil's hand and then the backswing buried its blade into the ironskin's temple, so hard and vicious that the side of the iron mask split right open and the blade must have gone a full inch into the iron devil's skull. It stuck there fast. For an instant they stood, the Moontongue tugging on his axe, the iron devil swaying and surely about to fall dead, except it didn't; and when it didn't then even Farri Moontongue, perhaps the most fearless and terrible Lhosir alive, let his axe go and turned and ran.

The second Lhosir already had the ladder down and was halfway up it as the Moontongue came racing out. The iron devil came after them, Farri's axe still sticking from the side of its head. As the Moontongue reached the bottom of the ladder and started to climb, human shouts began from among the dormitories. As he pulled the ladder up behind him, he caught glimpses of two more iron devils glinting in the darkness, running after them. Well they could run, those ironskins, but they couldn't climb.

The two Lhosir dropped down the other side of the kitchens and the darkness quickly swallowed them. By the time the first of the Fateguard reached their abandoned ladder, the Moontongue was long gone. The Fateguard stooped to the ladder and picked it up and sniffed it and set off towards the cliff, stopping now and then to crawl in the grass and sniff at the dirt, but the Moontongue never saw how close his pursuers came, for by the time the first of the Fateguard reached the cliff's top, the Lhosir were already pushing their boat back out into the waves; and by the time the first glimmers of feeble dawn broke through the dull stifling carpet of cloud, Farri Moontongue and his ship were nowhere to be found.

VALARIC THE WOLF

Falgir Longarm raised a hand and stopped walking. Behind him thirty Lhosir warriors grumbled to a halt and stood around, groaning and stretching their legs. They were, as far as Falgir could tell, in the middle of nowhere with nothing but this stupid old road stretching ahead of them – probably all the way to the end of the world if anyone could be bothered with walking far enough to find out – and only ever deep dark forest on either side. Hardly anyone lived out here south and east of Tarkhun and frankly Falgir could see why. The trees didn't want to be disturbed. They resented him for even being there. They were even trying to take the road back, though the Marroc still used it enough to keep it passable.

'Tane took a thousand men into the Shadowwood. If the Marroc are to be believed, the road leads through the forest to the mountains and a hidden valley with an old fortress and a route across the Isset. Go ahead and see how the land lies.' The Screambreaker's orders. Falgir had been half drunk at the time and it was pretty clear the Screambreaker was punishing him for what he and his men had done outside Tarkhun and in that Marroc hamlet whose name he couldn't even remember any more. It hadn't seemed fair then and it didn't seem fair now. His men had fought hard and were hungry for the spoils of war and so was he and so he'd let them all have what they wanted. Why not? What was the point of all the fighting if not for the plunder that came after?

Why not? Because now here he was, that's why. He let out a long heavy breath and glared at the trees. They'd been walking all day, they were tired and surly and hungry and whether the Screambreaker liked it or not, Falgir had had enough for one day. They'd make their camp here and speed be damned. At least it was warm. Be even warmer if the trees ever deigned to let the sun touch the ground.

Behind him several of the others had thrown off their helms and dropped their shields and were sitting on edge of the road, sucking at skins of water from the Isset. Falgir dropped his own shield and was about to do the same when Hardis Hardhand suddenly pitched over and fell flat on his back. Falgir stared, bemused, and the forest was so quiet and still that it took him a couple of seconds to see the arrow sticking out of Hardhand's eye, and in that time Henris Redface toppled over with another arrow in the back of his neck; then a moment later Erki Blackfinger was staggering about with one sticking out of his throat and Jassi Dogface was bellowing and hopping from one foot to the other with a shaft right through his hand. Something hit Falgir in the ribs hard enough to make him stagger and double over but not hard enough to punch through his mail. He snatched up his shield and dropped to a crouch. 'Arrows! Marroc!' Not that any of the rest of them needed telling by now – they all had eyes as good as his, after all. For a few seconds everyone was moving and shouting at each other and then they were all crouched in a circle, shields locked together, eyes peering over the rims with their helms firmly back over their heads.

The arrows stopped. The forest returned to its silence as though nothing had happened. He had four men down dead on the ground – he hadn't even seen what happened to Yurk Flamebeard but he wasn't moving – and Dogface with his hand and Jeski One-Thumb was limping about with an arrow in his thigh just above the knee. He stared at the darkness between the trees. The arrows had come from the north side of the road, a little to the east. 'Longshanks, bring yours with me. Silverborn, start back. I think we've found enough.' He waited a little longer, a few hundred heartbeats now since the first arrows flew. When no more came he took Longshanks and his brothers and cousins off into the woods. They crept carefully in a line, shields up high. The Marroc had to be out there. He'd find their spoor or else spook them into running so he could chase them.

Two hours later they hadn't found a thing. They must have

been almost a mile into the trees when they heard a scream and then a shouting in the distance behind them. He led his men running back but they were far too late and by the time he got to the road the Marroc had vanished again. Silverborn and the rest of the men he'd left behind were scattered around and every single one of them was dead, some of them hacked up so bad that he couldn't even tell how they'd died. Or rather, which wound had killed them. They looked as though they'd been savaged by a pack of bears.

He stared up at the sky. They had another two or three hours before the sun set and then maybe another half an hour of twilight if they were lucky before it got so dark that none of them would be able to see their own hands in front of their faces underneath these trees. Then he took a long hard look at the bodies.

'Back to Tarkhun,' he said sharply. 'Now.' He set off at a brisk walk. Wasn't right, leaving the dead out in the open like this, not speaking them out to honour the deeds they'd be remembered for. Wasn't right and his men felt it, but staying here and building a pyre would take up the rest of the day and then they'd be stuck out here through the night and …

The others weren't following him. That shit-stain Longshanks was ignoring him as though he hadn't heard or seen and was busy telling his men to go back out into the woods in twos and threes and gather wood.

'Back to Tarkhun now is a long walk,' said Longshanks as Falgir came back. 'That what you were going to say?' He was nodding as though he was quite sure that was what Falgir had been meaning, though they both certainly knew better. 'Best we stay and see these men on to the Maker-Devourer's cauldron.'

'Likely as not we'll follow them if we do,' grunted Falgir.

'Man can't turn his back on his fate.' Longshanks could turn his back on Falgir, though, and he did, and that right there and then was the end of Falgir being a leader of any men except himself.

Whoever it was that killed Silverborn and the rest, they didn't come back that afternoon, nor in the evening either. Longshanks had his pyre and they tossed one corpse after the next onto the flames and spoke them out, told the uncaring skies and the hostile trees everything that mattered of each man who'd died: who they were and how they'd taken their name and who'd given it to them; of the battles they'd fought and the sons they'd sired. It all came out, the good and the bad. That Hardis Hardhand had murdered his own brother by clubbing him from behind when they were both drunk and all over some woman who didn't want either of them, they spoke that out as loudly as they spoke of his courage at Selleuk's Bridge beside the mighty Lanjis Halfborn. The truth of a man's life, that was all that mattered, bare and raw and unadorned. They'd almost lost the light before they even started and by the time they threw the last man onto the flames – Silverborn himself – and spoke him out, the night was half gone. Afterwards they sat in twos and threes, backs to the pyre, letting it warm them and light up the forest, dozing and talking softly to one another while they waited for the dawn. Even so, Falgir must have closed his eyes and slept an hour or two before the sun rose.

He opened them, groggy-headed. The air stank of burned flesh and wood smoke. There was someone prodding him, and when he stared at the face looking down at him, it took him a moment to understand why it had no beard.

Marroc.

He started to scramble to his feet and then stopped at once. Someone had lifted up his mail coat and there was a spear point pressed hard between his legs.

'Ah go on, Jonnic, you can geld that one if you want.' He didn't see who spoke. Before he could move again the spear jabbed sharply into his crotch with a hideous pain that made him scream and curl up into a ball, hands pressed between his legs. He lay there, howling, waiting for the Marroc to finish him but they didn't. They walked away and left him there.

Eventually he managed to get up. His hands were covered in his own blood and every step was burning agony. The rest of the Lhosir, Longshanks and his men, lay scattered around the pyre. They were covered in blood and their beards had been cut off their faces and the skin from their chins too. They'd died without a sound. In their sleep, most of them, their throats cut. A few had been shot in the face by an arrow from a man standing right over them, the shaft driven through so hard that it had gone right through the skull and into the earth beneath. Dead, every single one, and their swords and axes and spears and shields taken.

He thought the Marroc had gone and so he took his time, but in the end there wasn't anything to do except head back to Tarkhun and hope he didn't bleed to death on the way and that he got there before the wolves out hunting found him helpless and smelling of fresh blood. But as he limped away, a single Marroc came out of the trees again. Falgir growled and started to run as best he could, bent half over in pain, but the Marroc just watched and laughed and called out after him: 'Run, you gelded dog, run. Go back to the Widowmaker and tell him what happened here. Tell him to come on through the Shadowwood whenever he wants. Tell him that Valaric the Wolf waits for him.'

COLD
REDEMPTION

And each man stands with his face in the light of his own drawn sword. Ready to do what a hero can.

Elizabeth Browning

BEYARD

1

THE AULIAN WAY

Addic stopped. He blew on his hands and rubbed them together and took a moment to look at the mountains behind him. Hard to decide which he liked better: the ice-bitter clear skies of today or the blizzards that had come before. Wind and snow kept a man holed up in his hut with little to do but hope he could dig himself out again when it stopped. A clear day like this meant working, a chance to gather wood and maybe even hunt, but Modris it was cold! He stamped his feet and blew on his fingers again. It wasn't helping. They'd gone numb a while back. His feet would follow before much longer. Cursed cold. He looked back the way he'd come, and it felt as though he'd been walking for hours but he could still see the little jagged spur that overlooked the hut where he'd been hiding these last few days.

Up on the shoulder of the mountain beyond the spur a bright flash caught his eye, a momentary glimmer in the sun. He squinted and peered but it vanished as quickly as it had come and he couldn't make anything out. The snow, most likely, not that snow glinted like that; but what else could it be so deep in the pass?

Snow. Yes. Still, he kept looking now and then as he walked, until a wisp of cloud crossed the mountain and hid the shoulder where the old Aulian Way once ran from Varyxhun through the mountains and out the other side. The Aulians had fallen long before Addic was born, but that didn't mean that nothing ever came over the mountains any more. The winter cold was a killer, but shadewalkers were already dead and so they came anyway.

He quickened his pace. The high road was carved into the mountainside over the knife-cut gorge of the Isset. It was hardly used at the best of times, even in summer when the snow briefly melted. No one had come through since the blizzards, and so he was left to wade thigh-deep through the snow on a narrow road he couldn't see along a slope that would happily pitch him over a cliff if he took a wrong step. It was hard work, deadly tiring, but he didn't have much choice now and at least the effort was keeping him warm. If he stopped to rest, he'd freeze. And it probably *hadn't* been another shadewalker high up in the mountains, but if it was then he certainly didn't want to be the first living thing it found.

By the time he ran into the forkbeards, hours later, he'd forgotten the shadewalker. By then he was so tired that his mind was wandering freely. He kept thinking how, somewhere ahead of him, one of the black lifeless trees that clung tenaciously to the gentler slopes above would have come down and blocked the road completely and he'd have to turn back, and he simply didn't have the strength to go all the way back to his safe little hole where the forkbeards would never find him.

And there they were: four of them, forkbeards armed to the elbows and riding hardy mountain ponies along the Aulian Way where they had no possible reason to be unless they'd finally caught wind of where he was hiding; and the first thing he felt was an overwhelming relief that someone else had come this far and ploughed a path through the snow so that he wouldn't have to, and how that was going to make his walking so much quicker and easier for the rest of the way. Took a few moments more for some sense to kick in, to realise that this far out from Varyxhun the forkbeards had come to hunt him down, winkle him out of wherever he was hiding and kill him. He might even have been flattered if he'd been carrying anything sharper than a big pile of animal pelts over his shoulder.

The crushing weight of failure hit him then, the futility of even trying to escape; and then a backhand of despair for good measure, since if the forkbeards had learned where he was hiding then someone must have told them, and there weren't too many people that could be. Jonnic, perhaps. Brawlic, although it was hard to imagine. Achista? Little sister Achista?

His shoulders sagged. He tried to tell himself that no, she

was too careful to be caught by any forkbeard, but the thought settled on him like a skin of heavy stone. He set the pelts carefully down and bowed in the snow. The forkbeards seemed bored and irritable, looking for trouble. 'My lords!' They were about as far from lords as Addic could imagine, but he called them that anyway in case it made a difference. Maybe they were out here on some other errand. He tried to imagine what that might be.

'Addic.' The forkbeard at the front beamed with pleasure, neatly murdering that little glimmer of hope. 'Very kind of you to save us some bother.' He swung himself down from his pony, keeping a cautious distance. It crossed Addic's mind then that although the forkbeards had horses, they were hardly going to take the High Road at a gallop in the middle of winter when it was covered in snow, nor even at a fast trot unless they were unusually desperate to go over the edge and into the freezing Isset a hundred feet below. And if they knew him, then there *was* only one reason for them to be out here. He turned and ran, or tried his best to, floundering away through the snow, not straight back down the road because that would make it too easy for them but angling up among the trees. The snow shifted and slid under his feet, deep and soft. As he tried to catch his breath a spear whispered past his face.

'Back here, Marroc. Take it like a man,' bawled one of the forkbeards. Addic had no idea who they were. Just another band of Cithjan's thugs out from Varyxhun. They probably looked pretty stupid, all of them and him too, not that that was much comfort. Struggling and hauling themselves up through the steep slopes and the drifted snow, slipping and sliding and almost falling with every other step, catching themselves now and then on the odd stunted tree that had somehow found a way to grow in this forsaken waste. The forkbeards were right behind him. Every lurch forward was a gamble, a test of balance and luck, waiting to see what lay under the snow, whether it would hold or shift. Sooner or later one of them would fall and wouldn't catch himself, and then he'd be off straight down the slope, a quick bounce as he reached the road maybe and then over the edge, tumbling away among the rock and ice to the foaming waters of the Isset. Which for Addic was no worse than being caught, but for the forkbeards it was probably a worse fate than letting him get away. Perhaps desperation gave him an advantage?

But no, of course it was *him* that slipped and felt his legs go out from under him. He rolled onto his back, sliding faster and faster through the snow, trying to dig in his feet and achieving nothing. He could see the road below – with two more forkbeards standing on it right in his path – and then the great yawning abyss of the gorge. He threw out his arms and clawed at the slope but the snow only laughed at him, coming away in great chunks to tumble around him, past him. He caught a glimpse of the forkbeards on the road looking up. Laughing, probably, or maybe they were disappointed that the Isset and the mountainside were going to do their work for them. Maybe he could steer himself to hit them and they could all go over the edge together?

Two forkbeards on the road? He wondered for a moment where they'd come from, but then he caught a rock which sent him spinning and flipped him onto his front so he couldn't see where he was going any more. A tree flew past, bashing him on the hip; he snatched and got half a hand to it but his fingers wouldn't hold. Then he hit the road. One foot plunged deep into the snow and wrenched loose again with an ugly pain. His flailing hand caught hold of something and tried to cling on. *The forkbeards, maybe?* Again a moment of wonder, because he could have sworn he'd only seen four forkbeards with their ponies and they'd all been chasing him, so these had to have come the other way, but that couldn't be right ...

A hand grabbed him, and then another. He spun round, tipped over onto his back again, felt his legs go over the edge of the gorge and into the nothing, but the rest of him stopped. The forkbeards had caught him, and for one fleeting second he felt a surge of relief, though it quickly died: the forkbeards would have something far worse in mind than a quick death in the freezing waters of the Isset.

A cloud of snow blew over him. When it passed he brushed his face clear so he could see. He was right on the edge of the gorge, the Isset grinning back up at him from far below. Two men stood over him. They'd let go and they weren't hitting him yet and so his first instinct was to get up and run, but getting back to his feet and avoiding slipping over the edge took long enough for his eyes to see who'd saved him. He had no idea who they were or what they were doing out here on the Aulian Way in the middle of winter, but they weren't forkbeards after all.

The bigger of the two men held out a hand to steady him. They weren't Marroc either. The big one, well, if you looked past the poorly shaven chin, everything about him said that he *was* a forkbeard. Big strong arms, wide shoulders, tall and muscular with those pitiless glacier eyes. The other one though ... Holy Modris, was he an Aulian, a real live one? He was short and wiry, wasted and thin and utterly exhausted, but his skin was darker than any Marroc and his eyes were such a deep brown they were almost black. He was also bald. Their clothes didn't say much at all except that they were dressed for the mountains.

The four forkbeards were picking their way down from the slopes above, slow and cautious now. The two men who'd saved his life looked at him blankly. They were half dead. The Aulian's eyes were glassy, his hands limp and his breathing ragged. The big one wasn't much better, swaying from side to side. Addic thought of the flash he'd seen from the mountain shoulder hours ago and for a moment wonder got the better of fear. 'You crossed the Aulian Way? In winter?'

The forkbeards were almost down now and they had their shields off their backs. The first one slid onto the road in a pile of snow about ten paces from where Addic was standing. He pulled out his axe but didn't come forward, not yet. He watched warily. 'Hand over the Marroc.'

The big man stood a little straighter. 'Why? What's he done?' He was breathing hard and his shoulders quickly slumped again. He looked ready to collapse. *An ally, maybe? But against four forkbeards?* Addic glanced down the road, back the way he'd come.

'Pissed me off,' said the forkbeard with the axe. 'Like you're doing now.'

The stranger growled. The Aulian put a hand on his arm but

the big man shook it off. 'Three years,' he snarled. 'Three years I'm away and I come back to this.' The other forkbeards were on the road now, the four of them grouping together, ready to advance. The stranger drew his sword and for a moment Addic forgot about running and stared at the blade. It was long, too long to be a Marroc edge – or a forkbeard one either – and in the winter sun it was tinged a deep red like dried blood. 'Three years.' The big man bared his teeth and advanced. 'Now tell me how far it is to Varyxhun and get out of my way!'

'Three days,' said Addic weakly, bemused by the idea of anyone telling four angry forkbeards to *get out of my way*. 'Maybe four.' The forkbeards were peering at the stranger's shield, an old battered round thing, painted red once before half the paint flaked off. It had seen a lot of use, that was obvious.

'Move!' The stranger walked straight at them.

'Piss off!'

Addic didn't see quite what happened next. One of the forkbeards must have tried something, or else the stranger just liked picking fights when he was outnumbered and exhausted. There was a shout, a red blur and a scream and then one of the forkbeards dropped his shield and bright blood sprayed across the snow. It took Addic a moment to realise that the shield lying on the road still had a hand and half an arm holding it.

'*Nioingr!*' The other three piled into the stranger. Addic wished he had a blade of his own, and if he had might have stayed. But he didn't, and there wasn't anything he could do, and so he turned to flee and ran straight into the Aulian.

'Hey!'

'Out the way.' He pushed past. The darkskin had a knife out but obviously didn't know what to do with it. 'If I were you, I'd run!'

The Aulian ignored him and took a step toward the fight. 'Gallow!'

Addic heard the name as he fled. It stuck with him as he ran. He'd heard it somewhere before.

2

ORIBAS

'Gallow!' The knife Oribas had was for stripping bark and carving wood, not for stabbing mad armoured men with forked beards, and even if it had been, he wouldn't have known how to use it.

The man Gallow had saved ran off down the road, back the way he'd come. Oribas watched him go. He ought to do the same – that would be sensible – but he didn't. It would be nice to think his decision had something to do with honour or loyalty or friendship but the truth was crueller: he simply didn't have the strength. He could barely even stand, and that was after Gallow had half carried him for the last two days through blizzards and snowfields deep enough to bury a man. Oribas couldn't understand how Gallow was still on his feet, never mind spoiling for a fight.

One of the forkbeards slammed Gallow with his shield and he stumbled. Oribas wanted to shout at them that it was hardly fair, taking on a man who'd just walked the Aulian Way in winter, but instead he put his knife back where it belonged and sat in the middle of the road and closed his eyes. His legs had had enough. Besides, the forkbeards probably didn't care about what was fair, not after Gallow had chopped off their friend's arm – he was lying in the snow, clutching his stump.

They were both as weak as children from crossing the pass but it still surprised Oribas when Gallow went down. A second forkbeard was out of the fight by then, sitting in the road rocking back and forth, holding his guts. But then Oribas saw the red sword fall from Gallow's hand and disappear into the soft snow at the big man's feet. He saw Gallow stumble, one of the forkbeards jab the butt of his axe into his face before he could find his balance again, and that was that. The forkbeard who'd knocked him down went to look at his comrade who was now lying still in the road. He wrinkled his nose and prodded the body with his boot. 'Fahred's gone. Bled out.'

The other one still on his feet stamped through the snow to Oribas and picked him up by his shirt. 'The Marroc! Where'd he go?'

Oribas pointed down the road.

'And you didn't stop him?' The forkbeard snorted with contempt. 'To the Isset with you then!'

He didn't so much throw Oribas over the cliff as simply let go and push. Oribas stepped back to catch himself, screamed when his foot found only air and kept on going, and down he went, spinning as he fell. The rest happened with blurring speed. For a moment he was looking towards the river far below, seeing that the cliff was actually more of a steep and jagged mess of stumps and skeletal branches and sharp prongs of stone waiting to smash him to pieces. There was a dead tree sticking out below him that probably wouldn't take his weight but he reached out a hand for it anyway. His satchel slipped off his arm as he hit a boulder, flew down ahead of him and snagged on the tree, and then his fingers closed around the wood and his other arm was swinging around to grasp the bark as well, and his shoulders felt like they were being torn out of their sockets ...

The wood let out a horrible crack, shifted and shook him loose. Now he wasn't falling as much as sliding, and a hundred fists punched him in the chest and the thighs as he spread-eagled over the stones and scrabbled for purchase. His foot hit something solid, twisted him sideways and drove his knee up into his ribs, almost pitching him out into the void again. His fingers were like the talons of an eagle, grabbing hold of whatever was there. And then he was still. By some miracle, he wasn't falling any more.

For a time he stayed exactly there, gasping, arms and legs ablaze with the effort of it but not daring to let his grip go even a fraction. His lungs were burning. Waves of pain washed over him. He tipped his head back and rolled his eyes as far as they'd go, looking up, half expecting to see the forkbeard who'd pushed him staring down, ready to drop rocks on him. But there was nothing, only sky. He shifted, trying to get himself more comfortable, then levered himself up onto the ledge that had caught him. The road was about twenty feet above. The boulder that he'd hit was half that. The dead tree would be a mere handspan beyond him if he got to his feet and stretched for it, but a handspan was still a handspan. His satchel hung off the end. It was all so close but all desperately beyond him.

He hugged the ledge, listening, waiting for the forkbeards to see him when they finally threw Gallow's corpse off the edge too, but they never did. He heard snatches of their talk for a few minutes, taut and angry, but neither came to the side of the road, and then he heard them mount their ponies and move away. He supposed they must have gone, but he waited a while longer to be certain. He had a good long look at the cliff above him. Gallow would have scaled it without a thought, like he was bounding up a flight of steps. Oribas summoned his courage and called out but got no answer. Gallow was dead or unconscious or the forkbeards had taken him then. In his mind he saw the big man lying helpless in the snow, slowly bleeding out. He'd have to climb up by himself. Ought to. Ought to right now. Get up onto the road and see what had happened but his arms and hands didn't have the strength, his legs weren't long enough.

He sat and wondered what to do, and after a time he felt the cold creeping in through his furs, making him dopey. He'd fall sooner or later. Even if he kept awake through to nightfall, the cold would kill him before the next morning.

'Hedge-born forkbeards!' The shout came from close by on the road, probably loud enough to reach right through the valley. '*Nioingr!* All of you!'

If there was more, Oribas didn't hear. By then he'd taken a lungful of cold air and was yelling as loud as he could, and he kept on until a face peered over the edge and stared at him in wonder. It was the Marroc the forkbeards had been chasing.

'You're alive! What happened to your friend?' The Marroc's face was screwed up in confusion. 'Do you need help?'

'Yes.'

The man disappeared and came back a moment later.

'Forkbeard whelps took all my furs,' he said. He looked at Oribas expectantly.

'Have you got any rope?'

The Marroc shook his head. 'No.'

Gallow had been carrying both their packs, had been for days. 'My friend had some,' he said. 'Is he still up there? They didn't throw his body over the edge. If he is, he has some.' He closed his eyes and bit his lip.

The face disappeared and then came back for a second time. 'No, no body up here. Plenty of blood over the snow, but that's all. Someone got hurt bad. You sure they didn't throw him over?'

'Yes.'

'Then they must have taken him with them.' The Marroc frowned. 'Why would they do that?'

'I don't know.'

'Why do they do anything? Because they're forkbeards. Why'd you help me?'

'*I* didn't.' Oribas looked miserably away. 'I just stood and watched. As for Gallow? I don't know. It's what he does but I never understood why.'

The Marroc peered closer. 'Gallow? That his name?'

'Yes.'

'Funny. They were looking for a Gallow in these parts a few years back. Is he one of them? A forkbeard?'

'A Lhosir. Yes.' Oribas felt his heart sinking. Neither of them had any rope. This man was going to leave him here because there was nothing else he could do. The cold was chilling him deep now. His fingers and his feet were numb. He could feel himself slowly shutting down.

Another pause. 'Are you an Aulian?'

'I suppose, if that means anything any more. Look, there are some trees on the slope above the road. You could cut some strips of bark and make a rope with those if you haven't got any.' His hands were turning stiff even stuffed down inside his furs. His legs were going too, not from the cold but just from having nothing left to give after the bitterness of the mountains.

'I don't know about that. Actually, I reckon you can just climb up from there unless your arms and legs are broken.'

'No, I can't.'

'Yes, you can. It's not even that hard.'

Oribas shook his head and turned away. 'I barely have the strength to stand, my friend.'

The next thing he knew, snow was falling around him and the Marroc was climbing down. He made it look easy. A moment later he stood beside Oribas on the ledge. 'See. Stand up.'

'I don't think I can.'

'Then how were you going to climb a rope?'

Oribas shrugged forlornly. The Marroc shoved him sideways, almost tipping him off into the river. Oribas swore. 'Are you mad?'

But for a moment he'd forgotten how tired he was. The Marroc nodded. 'Better. Now how about you either stand up or I push you off this ledge and into the river. Either your legs get you up there or I do you a mercy.'

It was the sort of thing Gallow would have done and it made Oribas feel pathetic and stupid. The Marroc coaxed and cajoled and threatened him until he wrapped his arms around the Marroc's neck and his legs around the man's waist, and then the Marroc climbed the slope for both of them as though he was half mountain goat. He swore a lot and called Oribas all sorts of things that Oribas didn't understand and a good few that he did, and it took what felt like most of the rest of the day; but he did it, and when they got to the top they both fell onto the snow-covered road and lay there panting and sweating.

'Thank you.' Oribas had lost count of how many times he'd already said that.

'Your friend saved my life. Modris put him there. He wouldn't look very kindly on me leaving you after that. You all right now?'

Oribas sat up. Standing was too difficult. 'I will be. I just need a moment.'

'Lhosir turd-beards.' The Marroc wandered around the churned and bloodstained snow where Gallow and the Lhosir had fought. He chuckled to himself and shook his head. 'You and your friend were heading for Varyxhun, were you?'

Oribas nodded.

'That's another three or four days on foot. Those forkbeards came all this way looking for me and then they let me go and took your friend instead. What happened?'

Oribas told him as best he could remember it. By the end the Marroc was grinning. 'Took two of them down, did he? Good for him. But what were you doing out here?'

'Gallow was on his way home. He never said much about it.' Which was a long stretching of the truth but he didn't know this Marroc who'd saved his life, not yet.

The Marroc was poking around in the snow. 'There's a few farms between here and there. You should get to Brawlic's place before it's dark. Knock on his door and give him a penny and tell him that Addic pulled you off a cliff and sent you to him. He'll put you up in the warm for the night and feed you a bowl of something. You look like you could do with it.' The Marroc paused and began digging in the snow. 'Hello, hello? What have we here?'

Oribas felt himself rocking back and forth. He didn't mean to; it was just … happening. And though he tried to look up, his head kept dropping towards his chest. The Marroc was burrowing into the bloodstained snow where Gallow had fallen. 'O sweet Modris!' He lifted out something long and dark that looked a lot like a sword, but now Oribas couldn't lift his eyes to see properly. 'Your friend. Gallow, was it? He ever call himself anything else?'

Oribas nodded. His eyes slowly closed. Then the Marroc was shaking him, hauling him up, propping him under one shoulder. 'No no no, Aulian, you don't go and stop working on me now.' He slapped Oribas with a handful of snow. 'Fine. I'll take you to Brawlic's farm myself. Good a place as any to go. This sword, is it what I think it is?' There were a lot of names for the sword he had in his hand. The red sword. Solace. The Comforter. The Edge of Sorrows. Oribas might have added a few of his own but he only shrugged and started to slip to the ground. The Marroc lifted him up again. 'What *were* you doing out here anyway, Aulian? What were you *really* doing here?'

'Oribas,' said Oribas. 'My name is Oribas. It's a very long story.'

'I want to hear it, Aulian. All of it.'

3

THE LORD OF VARYXHUN

Cithjan of Varyxhun rose late. He dressed himself in Marroc finery and stroked the two braids of his forked beard and drank a bowl of warm honeyed milk that a Marroc serving girl brought to him. She had a frightened face, but so did all the Marroc in Varyxhun these days. He paid no attention as she took out the chamberpot from beneath his bed. When he was good and ready to face the day, he left his room and walked out into the dark passages of the castle. As he left, the iron-masked Fateguard that King Medrin Sixfingers had sent to watch over him fell in behind. The Fateguard made everyone nervous, even Cithjan. The ironskin almost never said a word but you always heard him coming, clanking in all that iron he wore. And then he'd stop and become utterly silent, and that was when you knew he was right behind you. Cithjan shivered.

He broke his fast with warm bread and cold meat and more honey, too much of all of them which was why he'd been getting steadily fatter ever since he'd crossed the sea to serve his new king after old Yurlak had finally died. The Fateguard stood behind him, silent, watching. You couldn't argue with him as a bodyguard, but Cithjan quietly wondered whether the ironskin needed to be there *all* the time. It meant no one ever wanted to talk to him, and that wasn't particularly useful when he was supposed to be the governor of a province permanently on the brink of revolt. The ironskin was almost certainly a spy, too. King Sixfingers was always watching. The ironskins had stayed in their temples before Yurlak had died. Then Sixfingers had gone and struck his bargain with the witch of the north and now, for whatever unholy reason, they were his.

Once Cithjan was done eating, he took his time walking to

the Hall of Thrones where old King Tane had held his court for a few weeks, back when the Screambreaker had been whipping his Marroc arse all the way from the sea to the mountains. Varyxhun was as impregnable a place as Cithjan had seen, layered up the side of a mountain in tier after tier of walls and gatehouses over a single winding road, and that was before you got to the castle proper. If the old Marroc king had held fast, Cithjan reckoned the Screambreaker would still be outside, trying to winkle him out. But Tane had headed off down the Aulian Way looking for Maker-Devourer-knew-what. He'd cut himself and the wound had gone bad and he'd died.

The Hall of Thrones was a big room, gloomy and foreboding. The way it picked up and echoed every noise had everyone walking around on tiptoe and talking in whispers as though someone had died. It was like that all the time, every bloody day.

'Well?'

The Marroc they'd given him to deal with all the other Marroc slid up to the throne and fell to his knees. Cithjan had given up telling him not to do that.

Clank clank. The Fateguard standing at his shoulder shifted slightly. The Marroc seemed to shrink into himself. Grisic. He was a weasel. You never knew with any Marroc quite where their loyalties were, and Cithjan had dark suspicions about this one and so he set little tests now and then. Grisic hadn't given himself away yet, but maybe that accounted for his nervousness.

'There are two farmers from Pottislet, your highness ...'

Cithjan rolled his eyes. *Highness.* Another habit the Marroc refused to break. 'Governor.'

'Yes, sir. Governor, sir.' *Fawning creep.* 'Two farmers from Pottislet come to beg for your aid your high— Governor. They say that ice wolves have come out of the mountains and are ravaging their herds.'

Ice wolves? Had anyone ever *seen* an ice wolf? 'Really? Another feeble effort to lure Lhosir soldiers out into the wilderness where they can quietly disappear?' Maker-Devourer knew they'd had enough of that.

'They beg you—'

'Send them away, Grisic.' They were under siege here in

Varyxhun. Men vanished every few days, just disappeared without a trace, but everyone knew exactly what happened to them. If they were Lhosir they had their throats cut and vanished down the Isset into the Crackmarsh. If they were Marroc the options were more varied: some simply vanished down the Isset like his own men did; others turned out to be alive and well and living out in the wilds where they happily murdered Lhosir if the chance came their way; a few of them had been hauled off to the villages deep in the hills where no one gave a stuff about threats and reprisals and had been ripped to pieces by horses for being collaborators – or, as Cithjan looked at it, for having gone on with their lives as best they could without murdering anyone. A few, the really lucky ones, got to be strung up in Varyxhun Square itself in the middle of the night. Each morning they were waiting for him. If his eyes hadn't started to go a bit dim, Cithjan might have been able to see them from the castle walls. It took time to erect a gibbet and hang a man and cut his belly for all his entrails to dangle out, and yet no one ever saw or heard a thing. They'd done it to a Lhosir once last summer. Cithjan had seen to it that they never did it again. *Do what you like to each other. Touch one of us and you all pay dear.* It was a simple message.

Clank clank behind him. He shuddered. Grisic flinched as he rattled on through other irritations that should never have come to Cithjan. More ice wolves. A shadewalker seen in the forests around Haradslet. An irate plea from Tevvig Stonefists at Boyrhun for more arrows, since his previous messages had been ignored and now he didn't have any left and there were Marroc rebels openly shooting at his men. Yes, of course, three thousand arrows, and by the way what previous messages? But no need to ask Tevvig about that since it happened all the bloody time. A Lhosir messenger alone on the road? By the sound of things, this one had ended up disguising himself as a Marroc woman to get through to the Aulian Bridge and cross to this side of the Isset. Now there was a thing – a Lhosir disguising himself because he was afraid – Sixfingers would have his head if he ever heard about *that*. So yes, three thousand arrows and fifty armed men from Varyxhun and half the garrison out of Witches' Reach to make sure the arrows arrived safely, and Stonefists was welcome to keep the men as long as he made sure the Marroc around Boyrhun learned a lesson or two. A hundred of them hung along the roadside should do the trick. Rebels for preference, but any would do because the rebels got their food and shelter from somewhere, right? Grisic did a good job of keeping a straight face at that. He barely winced at all.

Boyrhun was thirty miles away as the crow flew, but since it was across the other side of the Isset gorge, it might almost have been in another country. The whole west bank of the river was virtually in open revolt and there was no pretending that Varyxhun would stay quiet if he left to sort it out. If he marched down the valley, crossed the Aulian Bridge, marched up the other side and set about murdering enough Marroc to make them get the message, then yes, he'd get all that done right enough, and then he'd have a fine view across the river as Varyxhun went up in flames. Sixfingers might put up with a little unrest, but he wouldn't put up with that.

Clank clank. Did the Fateguard ever get tired? He'd never seen this one rest, or eat, or do anything other than what he was doing right now, standing like an angry statue, putting the shits up everyone.

'There's one other thing.' Grisic's smile was ashen. 'You put a bounty on the Marroc bandit Addic Snakefeet.' Cithjan frowned and then nodded as though he remembered. He put bounties on so many Marroc these days that he'd long ago lost track of who and why. 'Fahred and three of his men went out to bring you his head. They've come back.'

Four Lhosir out on the road? And they'd come back at all?

'They were set upon and—'

Cithjan rolled his eyes. 'How many of them are dead?'

'Just Fahred himself. They say they were set upon by an Aulian and –' he hesitated '– a Lhosir with no beard.'

Clank clank. 'A Lhosir?'

Grisic was bobbing up and down like a frightened hare. 'They killed the Aulian. They brought the Lhosir here. They said ...' He frowned. 'They thought you might want to see him. He was carrying a shield of the Crimson Legion.'

Now there was a thing. 'One of Medrin's men? Stolen, most likely.'

Grisic bowed. 'Yes. As you say.'

'Well we can't hang him with all the Marroc. Send him to the Devil's Caves.'

Clank clank. Cithjan turned, ready to snap at the ironskin fidgeting behind him, but the Fateguard had moved around beside him and was leaning over. Cithjan couldn't help himself from shrinking back. The black iron crown and mask would do that to anyone, wouldn't they? The ironskin hissed, 'I would like to question this Lhosir first.'

Cithjan stared at the Fateguard. After a moment he blinked a few times and nodded. 'Yes. Well. You can do that. If you want.'

Clank clank clank. The Fateguard stalked across the Hall of Thrones, the echoes of iron on stone freezing everyone in their tracks. No one moved. When he was gone, Cithjan let out a deep breath – for some reason he'd been holding it. He stared after the ironskin and then at Grisic. 'You'd better show him where to go then, hadn't you?'

The Fateguard in his iron mask strode through the doors of the Hall of Thrones. Eyes cast his way were full of dread. Marroc ran at the sight of him and even Lhosir tautened their faces and gritted their teeth and waited desperately for him to go away; and that was but the smallest of the curses on those who served the Eyes of Time.

The Marroc snake Grisic slithered out of the hall behind him and trotted on ahead, bowing and scraping and beckoning as though he wasn't quite sure whether he was leading a man or some sort of animal. He wore his mask of servility well, but the Fateguard had blessings to go with their curses, and one such blessing was to see the truth of a man's heart. Good or evil, kind or cruel, the men of iron cared little, but liars made the ice-cold blood burn in their veins, and this Marroc had a yellow streak of treachery to him.

He ignored Grisic. Varyxhun was an ancient castle, carved out of the mountainside by Aulian miners, comforting in its darkness and its age and its deep old roots tunnelled far into the stone. He crossed the courtyard, past gates that had never been sundered by any foe, not even the all-conquering Screambreaker. Below them, the gatehouse stairs wound down. There were tunnels here forgotten even by the Marroc, tunnels that reached all the way to the town of Varyxhun and perhaps further, as far as the old Aulian fortress at Witches' Reach or even the Aulian Bridge, the great span that crossed the gorge of the Isset before the river tumbled through cataracts and rapids into the swamp of the Crackmarsh.

The Fateguard embraced the gloom. He took a candle to light his way, but when the Marroc weasel took a torch for himself, the Fateguard gripped it in his iron-clad hand and crushed it out. Gloom and darkness were an ironskin's friends. They were where he belonged, in the shadows with the shadewalkers; but then he'd been to this place so often he could have done with no light at all. The place where prisoners came and were broken and made to talk, where he would listen and hammer a nail into a man's flesh for every lie that he heard.

He passed two cells without bothering to look. The smell was of old rot and filth. He stopped at the third. Here was the Lhosir. Beardless, weak and thin and pale and beaten, but here he was.

There's only one way into the valley of Varyxhun for a Lhosir, and that is to cross the Aulian Bridge. Yet not for you. The Fateguard stared hard at the man in the cell. He had an air to him. A meaning. A significance felt even in the Hall of Thrones, but there was something else, something the Fateguard had not expected. 'Gallow? Gallow Truesword. Gallow Foxbeard. Gallow the thief of the red sword.'

The Lhosir looked up and stared. He seemed neither frightened nor pleased, merely resigned. Slowly the Fateguard lifted off his mask and crown. Light burned in the beardless Lhosir's eyes and then at last a flash of recognition. 'Beyard?'

The Fateguard curled his lip. 'Hello, old friend.'

4

UPRISING

Oribas had little memory of his last few miles down the Aulian Way. The cold had reached inside him by then, the sunlight was fading and he was as close as he could be to dead without actually dying. He had some hazy notion of being dragged off the road and along a track between the black leafless bones of winter trees, of climbing and climbing, step after remorseless step up some steep winding path, of being hauled through a doorway, of light and heat and a delicious warm fire, and then he'd been asleep.

He thought he might have been asleep for a whole day, but only an hour or two passed before he woke again. Now there were half a dozen Marroc in a big open room that, as far as he could see, was their whole house. A young woman was waving a pot of something warm and delicious-smelling under his nose. Oribas stared at her. Maybe he was delirious with fatigue or with disbelief that he was somewhere warm, but she had the most beautiful elfin face and he couldn't stop looking at her.

She reddened and looked away. 'I know you want rest,' she said, 'but you need some food first to give you back your strength.'

Behind her, the other Marroc were looking at him. Addic smiled but the others were less friendly. They were passing the red sword between them, the Edge of Sorrows. His eyes strayed back to the woman. She looked small and young and determined. Her smile, when it came, was a shy fragile thing. 'Who are you?' he asked her.

She shook her head. 'Eat.'

'You have beautiful eyes. Full of sadness and steel and passion.'

She laughed at him, and he had to smile back at the way her face lit up. 'And you have a mind addled by the cold.' She fed him one spoonful at a time, and it very likely wasn't even remotely the best food he'd ever had, but that was how it seemed.

'My friend,' he asked when his eyes started to close again. 'What happened to Gallow?' But she only smiled and nodded some more and he wasn't sure she even heard him, and after that he must have fallen asleep again, because when he woke up it was the middle of the next morning and the house was empty and he felt deliciously wonderfully warm.

'Drink.' The woman was squatting beside him. She must have woken him again. His head felt clearer now, sharp and focused, not all blurry like the night before. He remembered what he'd said and cringed and felt stupid.

'I'm sorry.' He sat up and looked at her, properly this time. She was offering him a warm bowl of something brown and lumpy and full of grease, and even if it was the same as whatever she'd given him yesterday, a night over the warm embers of the fire hadn't done it any favours. He wrinkled his nose and tried not to gag; he *was* hungry, though, and he ached all over. And she *was* pretty, in a boyish sort of way.

'Addic says you were in the mountains.' She shook her head as though at an errant child. 'In the winter? You're lucky the cold didn't take you.'

'I know. But there were two of us. What happened to my friend?'

'Addic's outside.' She smiled. 'I'll tell him you're awake once you've eaten.'

'No. My other friend.' The food wasn't so bad when he managed not to think about it, not to look at it and not to let it linger in his mouth any longer than necessary. 'The one who came with me across the mountains.'

'Like you?' She touched his cheek and it took him a moment to realise why – she'd never seen someone like him before. 'Where do you come from?'

'Somewhere far away. I lived in a desert on the other side of what was once the Aulian Empire.'

'Then it must have been something very important to make

you come all this way and cross the mountains.' Somehow, without realising it, he'd emptied the bowl.

'I came because my friend asked me to.'

'I'll find Addic.' She rose and left him and he watched her go, eyes following her to the door with an unexpected longing until she was gone. Fate had carried Gallow all this way with her sweet false promises of family and friendship, and Oribas had followed; now he was trapped by the winter in this land with nothing and no one, and Gallow was surely dead. Cruel and unkind to bring a man so far and then cut him down so close to home.

Three Marroc came in. Two had knives in their hands. A broad brawny one with a straggly beard and a thin-faced clean-shaven one with a mean look in his eye. The third was Addic. The brawny one grabbed him by the arm. 'Aulian, I should cut your throat!'

Addic put a hand on the brawny one's arm. 'This one's not a sorcerer, Brawlic. He didn't summon the shadewalkers.'

'Three already in one winter and the forkbeards do nothing!' The thin-faced one tutted and shook his head. 'No wonder people are so restless. I'm sure they'd love nothing more than an Aulian they could call a sorcerer, just so they could hang him in Varyxhun square.' He walked slowly to the corner of the room and picked up the Edge of Sorrows from where it stood, propped against the wall. They had no scabbard for it – that was still hanging from Gallow's belt, or perhaps some other Lhosir now. The thin-faced one lifted the sword and swung it a few times. The air whistled and moaned as it parted before the rust-red steel. He looked at Oribas. 'So you came over the mountains with a Lhosir with no beard who fought some of his own on the Aulian Way and saved Addic's life. That right? Addic says you called him a name: Gallow. What was his deed name, Aulian?'

'His what?'

Addic stepped between them. 'Forkbeards give themselves names. What was the rest of his name?'

Oribas blinked, confused. 'He said he was Gallow Foxbeard among his own.'

The thin-faced Marroc turned to the other two. He brandished the sword and his face had a greedy gleam to it. 'The Foxbeard. Then you know what this is, Addic? You know ...'

Addic held up a hand but his eyes had a hungry glitter to them too. Yes, he knew all right. He crouched down beside Oribas. 'The forkbeards came here hunting one they called Gallow the Foxbeard three summers ago after Andhun fell to the Vathen. They were after a sword. Did he ever call this sword by a name?'

Oribas shook his head. He felt weak and stiff but his wits were back where they should be now and they were saying that they didn't much like the looks on any of these Marroc faces right now. They knew the red sword for what it was, or they thought they did. The Edge of Sorrows if you were Aulian. Other names to others.

Addic smiled but the glitter in his eyes was made of daggers, not of laughter. 'I'll tell you what I've heard of Gallow the Foxbeard, Aulian, and then you can tell me if this is the man who kept me from falling into the Isset and stood and fought four of Cithjan's bastards. He was a forkbeard who never went back across the sea after old Tane died. When the Vathen swept out of the east with the Sword of the Weeping God, he was there when the forkbeards met them outside Andhun and they slaughtered each other. The forkbeards say the Widowmaker slew the Weeping Giant and took his sword, and that Gallow was at his side when he fell and that he stole it for himself. They say it was because of him that Andhun fell to the Vathen and that he's why their king is Medrin Sixfingers where once he had twelve. Most tales say Gallow drowned in the seas below Andhun's cliffs, but others whisper he came this way, looking for the Marroc family he'd left behind. Either way, neither his body nor the sword were ever found.' Addic bared his teeth. 'Is this the Gallow who crossed the mountains with you, Aulian? Because if he is then we've all heard a great deal of his deeds, good and ill. And this sword is Solace, the red sword of the Vathen, taken by the Widowmaker and whose edge our fork-beard king greatly desires.'

Oribas licked his lips. 'I'll tell you of the Gallow I knew. Decide for yourself if he's the same Gallow Foxbeard of whom you speak, for I cannot say, and he never called his sword by any name that I recall. I come from a desert at the far edge of what was once the Aulian Empire—'

'You speak our tongue,' interrupted the thin-faced one.

'Where I came from I was a scholar. I learned many tongues. Many years ago a monster came to my town. It wore the guise of a man, though it was not, and we didn't know it for what it was, not for many weeks. It brought ruin and murder and much worse. You speak of the ghosts of the old empire, of the shadewalkers. This creature was a thousand times more terrible. Rakshasa, it was once named. When finally it was revealed, it left us all but destroyed. I followed its trail but I could never find it, nor find a way to destroy it. In my despair I prayed to the old gods in a place we call the Arroch Ilm Daddaq, the Tainted Well. They sent me a vision and I followed that vision to the shores at the end of the world, and there I found Gallow, washed up from some shipwreck with others of his crew. He told me he had come from a place the Aulians knew long ago as the Glass Isles, to which the gods sailed after Mouth Catht split asunder. I understood: now the gods had sent him back to me. They had listened to my prayer after all and here was their answer. Together we hunted the Rakshasa that destroyed my town. We hunted it for many months and in the end we found it and put an end to it. All these things you speak of?' He shrugged. 'The gods sent Gallow to me. All he ever asked of his fate was to be allowed to return to his home across these mountains. He told me he was once the Gallow Truesword who fought beside the Screambreaker, but that that man was long gone.'

'What about the sword, Aulian?'

'I have a name, Marroc. I am called Oribas.'

Addic nodded. 'And I'm Addic. My surly friend here is Brawlic and this is his farm. His wife Kortha has cooked the food you've eaten and my sister Achista has fed it to you. My other friend here is Second Jonnic.' He laughed. 'The last of six brothers, Second, and his poor father ran out of names. There are some who call him Vengeful Jonnic instead, though, and with good reason.'

Second Jonnic watched Oribas coldly. 'My brother who shared my name was killed by the forkbeards in Andhun.' He turned to Addic. 'He's only telling us half the truth. He knows more and I'll have it out of him.'

Addic raised a hand. 'Brawlic has given him food and shelter and the forkbeards would have thrown me into the Isset were it not for this man and his friend. He's no enemy.'

Oribas looked from one to the other. 'I thank you for your kindnesses. If there is a way to repay you, I will do what I can.'

Jonnic spat. 'If the forkbeards get hold of him, they'll find out about all of us now.'

'I've no wish to be a part of any of your troubles.' Oribas kept his voice calm and quiet. 'If you could tell me where the Lhosir will take Gallow ...'

'Your friend is certainly dead. And once they know who he is, the forkbeards will be back, looking for this sword.'

Addic shook his head. 'If they killed him then how will they know his name? And if they don't know his name, how will they know there's a sword to find?' He grinned.

Jonnic ground his teeth. 'All the more reason this one can't stay where the forkbeards might find him. We know perfectly well what the best thing would be.'

'I do, but he's clearly not fit to cross the pass again, not in this state.' Addic's eyes narrowed on Oribas. 'You hunted a monster worse than a shadewalker? And defeated it? How?'

Oribas struggled to his feet. His legs felt as though they were made of wool. For a moment his head spun. He looked around the room, searching for the woman Achista, Addic's sister, but she wasn't there. Then he searched for his satchel for a while before he remembered where it was – hanging from the dead stump of a tree dangling over the Isset. The thought of trying to get it back made him shudder. He fiddled at the pouches on his belt instead while the Marroc watched him suspiciously. 'The ruins of old Aulia were beset by shadewalkers after the empire fell. There were those who took it upon themselves to hunt them. Shadow-stalkers and sword-dancers. I am neither of those things but I have seen them work.' He walked stiffly to the fire and threw a pinch of powder from one of his pouches into the flames. The fire flared, leaping out of the hearth and high towards the roof for a moment. The Marroc gasped and recoiled. 'Creatures like those have their weaknesses. Salt. Iron. Pure ice-cold water. And fire.'

'He's a witch,' hissed Brawlic. 'Get him out of my house!'

Addic put a hand on the farmer's arm. 'He's not a witch. Are you, Aulian?'

'I'm a scholar. In my hunt for the monster that destroyed my home, I studied such things. I don't begin to understand the magic that brought them to be, but I understand how they may be sent back where they belong.'

Addic pulled Jonnic aside. The two whispered to one another while Brawlic stared with open hostility at Oribas. Whatever decision the other Marroc reached, Jonnic didn't like it. Addic held up his hands. 'Shadewalkers cross the mountains now and then. When they come, all we can do is step out of their path. Even the forkbeards fear them. Can you defeat one?'

Oribas shook his head. 'Not alone, for I'm no warrior. But I can show you how.'

Addic started to laugh. 'You see, Jonnic. And imagine what the people of Varyxhun and beyond will say when a Marroc comes among them carrying the sword Solace and slays a shadewalker. That's how we'll have our uprising.'

Jonnic snorted. 'I say we take it to Valaric the Mournful in the Crackmarsh. Or across it and back to the Vathen. Let *them* fight the forkbeards.' He stared at Oribas. 'You came over the mountains. Across the Aulian Way after the first winter snows. Why?'

Oribas shrugged. 'It was Gallow.' He smiled faintly. 'He wanted to go home.'

5

GALLOW

In the gloom under Varyxhun, in Gallow's cramped and dank stone cell, Beyard picked up the empty cess bucket. He turned it upside down and sat on it. Gallow squatted in a corner, watching.

'Seventeen winters,' said the ironskin. 'Eighteen soon.' His voice was like grating metal, not the voice that Gallow remembered, and his face was pale and hollow, his eyes rimmed red and steeped in shadows. But he was still unmistakably Beyard. 'I heard about you, but not for a long time. No one knew who you were until you stole King Medrin's sword.'

'It was never his sword,' whispered Gallow.

Beyard's lips drew back. His teeth were a perfect white. He made a noise that might have been a laugh but that came out more like a wet cough. 'We both have our reasons not to like our king. I never gave away your names, either of you. Look at me now, Gallow. My reward is a skin of iron punishment to atone. For what? For being the only one with the courage to stay and stand fast when we all three broke the old laws? Why did you come back?'

'I never meant to leave.' They stared at each other in silence. Gallow took in the man who'd once been his friend, back when they were both filled with boyish bravado. The armour of the Fateguard, the iron strips and plates, covered him from head to toe. The Fateguard were the holy fists who guarded the Temple of Fates and enforced the will of the Eyes of Time, both cursed and blessed. They were rarely seen outside a temple and Gallow had never heard of one taking off his mask. More often than not they were the worst *nioingr* who would never have any other chance to atone, but that wasn't Beyard. Beyard had never been a coward. 'Are you my executioner?'

That wet coughing sound again. Beyard shook his head. 'Not I. But there will be one, have no doubt. Who will you have to speak you out when you hang?'

'I doubt there's a single Lhosir who'd do that now.'

'Then I will do it.' Beyard shifted. Metal ground on metal.

'What happened to you?'

The iron man looked down at himself. 'To me? See it for yourself. After you ran—'

Gallow bared his teeth. 'I did not *run*, Beyard! I would have stood beside you. Willingly. Do you not remember how it was?'

For a moment a light flashed in the Fateguard's bloody eyes. 'I remember, Gallow. We each paid our own price for our foolishness. I saw Medrin cross the sea; but fate found him out and I saw him back again with a wound that should have killed him, that left him crippled and for many years but half a man. I saw him rise each day with barely the strength to walk. I saw him fight for every scrap of strength. He came to the temple daily for a time. Suddenly a very pious man when it looked like he might never again lift a sword. Sometimes I wonder how loud he screamed when you crippled him for a second time. Medrin Sixfingers. Perhaps his punishment is finished now. But you? I never told them your name, just as I never told them his. The Eyes of Time searched for you and found nothing. And when neither of you found the courage to step forward, the punishment fell on me alone. I was made as you see me because I wouldn't betray your names. And because of what we'd done.'

'We did *nothing*!'

'But we had intent. We should not have been where they found us.'

Gallow looked away. 'I shouldn't have let you face them alone.'

Beyard rattled and shook with grinding laughter. 'Then we would *both* be men of iron. What difference would it have made? Besides, fate has its ways. Fate found Medrin without my help. The Crimson Shield was at the bottom of the sea with the Moontongue by then and its other thieves long forgotten. What did fate find for you, Gallow the smith's son?'

'I crossed the sea,' said Gallow. 'I fought with the

Screambreaker and after a time he named me Truesword. When it was done and Yurlak looked as though he was going to die and Medrin would take his crown, I stayed behind. I meant to cross the mountains into Aulia to be as far away as I could be but I never even reached Varyxhun. Before I knew what had happened, another eight years passed and I was a husband with a Marroc wife and a father with two sons and a daughter.'

'Truesword. I heard that name but you're Foxbeard now. I know about the Vathen and how you fought them and how you found the Screambreaker half dead and carried him back to Andhun, how you sailed with Medrin to reclaim the Crimson Shield and how you and the Screambreaker stood side by side in his last battle against the Vathen. They say you killed him there and took Solace, the red sword of the Vathen, from his hand as he fell.'

'I took his sword when he fell but I didn't kill him.'

'No.' A baleful look settled on Beyard's face. 'You turned on your own kind and cut off Medrin's hand as the Vathen swept through Andhun. I know you threw yourself into the sea and I know it was the Screambreaker himself who hauled you out of it, so I know you didn't kill him and I know the Vathen didn't either.' Another wet hack of a laugh and Beyard cocked his head. 'You were meant to come to us, Gallow. You were owed to us, you and Medrin both. Fate granted the Screambreaker a year and a day beyond what should have been his death to bring you back to us. He'd earned it. He dragged you from the sea when you should have drowned and told you your fate, yet you refused it.'

Gallow shook his head. 'I remember his words, old friend: "It's the nature of men like us to fight our fates."'

A coldness filled Beyard's eyes. 'I'm not your friend, Gallow. Not any more and not for many years. And you are Lhosir. You should know better than to turn against your fate.'

'I wanted to go home, Beyard.' Gallow's shoulders sagged. 'To see my sons. To be with my wife. To make more. To work the fields and the forge. Simple honest things, building a home. That's all.'

'But it was not your fate, Gallow.'

'No.' This time Gallow spat out a bitter laugh. 'The Marroc fled Andhun in a hundred ships. It was a calm day, clear, a balmy sea. And then in the night a storm came and scattered us and when the sun rose we were alone and lost, and ever since, with every step I've taken towards my home, fate has carried me ten away. Three years, Beyard. Three years and I've crossed half the world.' He looked around the cell, overwhelmed by despair. 'And here I am. Three years. I don't even know if she's still alive. Or my children, and if they are then they must certainly think I'm dead. She probably has another man. I suppose I hope for her that it's so. And now I'll never know, will I?' He looked up and touched his shirt. Beneath it, against his skin, an old locket hung on a worn chain. A little piece of Arda he'd taken with him into battle when the Vathen had come. The one thing over all that time he'd never lost. That, his shield and the cursed red sword.

'You should know better than to fight fate.'

'Medrin is king now, is he?'

'Yes. King Medrin One-Hand. Medrin Sixfingers. Medrin Ironhand, or Silverhand if you prefer. Yurlak scoured the world before he died for any who could make his son whole again. An Aulian came, a dark one, but it was the Eyes of Time who gave Medrin the hand he has now, one of iron and silver. A poor substitute for flesh and bone. Yurlak lived long enough to see it and then he died.' Another wet laugh. 'Yurlak scoured the world for you as well, Gallow Foxbeard. I swear it was his fury that kept him alive so long. But Ironhand? He means to cross the mountains and rebuild Aulia itself. He sees himself an emperor.' Beyard shook his head, a savage snarl on his face. 'Medrin, eh? Fool he is, but he's not the man either of us knew. He's a leader as his father was before him. A king with an iron hand.' Beyard rose. He picked up his mask and crown. 'I'm glad, Gallow, to have set my eyes on you one more time. I'll not tell Cithjan who you are. He'd send you to Medrin in chains and Medrin would bring down every world of pain that he knows upon you. He'd find this wife and these sons of yours and make blood ravens of them while you watch. So no, I'll not tell Cithjan. You were a better man than that. You will be Gellef Sheepstealer and you will merely hang for the two men you killed.'

'Two?'

'The other will die in a few days. I am ironskin, so I know his fate.'

'What of the Aulian who was with me?'

Beyard put the mask and crown back over his head. 'You should know how it is with our kind. They threw him into the gorge of the Isset.'

Which left him with nothing. Gallow held his head in his hands. 'All this way. I brought him all this way. I told him he didn't have to follow.'

'A man can't escape his fate. I'd plead for you, for the sake of the friendship we once shared, but you turned on your kin, Gallow. You should not have done that.' Beyard stood in the door of the cell and turned, face hidden now behind bars of iron. 'Does the red sword swim beneath the waves below the cliffs of Andhun? Did you lose it on the other side of the world?'

Gallow froze, head bowed and eyes filled with tears for those he'd never see again. The sword. Solace, the Comforter, the Peacebringer, all those names the Marroc and the Vathen had given it, and it had done nothing but mock him from the moment he'd held it in his hand. Oribas called it by its Aulian name: the Edge of Sorrows, for the Aulians had always seen the truth of the curse it carried. 'I never lost it, Beyard,' he said, slowly looking up as he did. 'I carried it out of the sea of Andhun and I carried it across the world and back again. I carried it across the ruins of Aulia and along the length of the Aulian Way. The men I killed? It tasted their blood.'

Beyard stiffened. 'It's here? In Varyxhun?'

'If the men I fought didn't think to bring it back then it's lying beside the Aulian Way. In a place where only I will find it.'

The Fateguard stepped back inside and stood over Gallow, eyes boring down into him. 'Where, old friend? Where is it?'

Gallow shook his head. 'I'll not give it to Medrin. Not for nothing.'

Beyard's iron-gloved hands reached around Gallow's neck and tore the locket with the snip of Arda's hair away from him. 'I will find them. Whoever they are. I will punish them until you show me.'

Gallow met his eyes, unflinching. 'Will you? You were my friend once and a far better man than that. Has the iron skin of the Eyes of Time taken the Beyard I knew?'

'I am Fateguard,' Beyard hissed, but his eyes flicked away in a flash of shame.

'All I ask is to know whether my family lives.'

'And what use is that knowledge? If you find they're all dead, if your woman has another man, if your children are scattered and gone, will you go to the hangman more easily? For these are all likely things. Or if you find that they wait and still mourn after all this time and all is as it was and could be again, will you die at peace?'

'Let me see them and I'll show you where the sword is hidden.'

Beyard shook his head. 'Take me to the sword and you'll live until you have what you came here for.'

'For your blood oath, Beyard, I'll do that.'

Again Beyard shook his head. 'I'll swear to you on the Fates themselves. For my kind that is an oath cast in iron, but I cannot give you a blood oath. I am Fateguard, Gallow. I have no blood to offer.'

6

THE SHADEWALKER

The Marroc let Oribas rest for three days, eyeing him watchfully, talking among themselves in careful huddles while Oribas took care never to pry and spent his time staring into the fire and helping around the house as best he could – simple chores that needed little strength or skill. They fed him plenty of greasy stew and he held his nose and smiled and tried not think too much about the delicate care that his own kin put into the feasting tables of his homeland. The big Marroc Brawlic still made the sign of evil when he thought Oribas wasn't looking and the thin one still wanted to murder him. Sometimes Oribas caught Achista looking at him and then looking quickly away with a smile, but she was rarely in the house and it was the older woman who brought him his food now, Brawlic's wife Kortha. But on the third evening when Achista came into the house, she looked at him and didn't smile and instead pulled Addic and Jonnic away from the fire where they'd been whittling wood. The three of them talked in urgent whispers until Addic nodded and slipped his whittling knife back into its sheath. Then he came and sat beside Oribas. 'Aulian, there's a shadewalker.' He stared at Oribas hard. 'It's been seen again. Near Horkaslet. If you still say you can lay it to rest, then you and Jonnic and I can leave to hunt it in the morning.'

Oribas stretched out his hands. When the Marroc talked to him, they talked of little but shadewalkers and sometimes the Edge of Sorrows and what he knew about both. They'd been waiting for this. 'Salt? Iron? Water? Fire? You have these things?'

'You have the fire. Water is all around you. Iron and salt we have. Jonnic?'

Jonnic disappeared outside. When he came back, he was

holding a sword in a scabbard crusted with snow. He looked Oribas in the eye and leaned into him and drew out the blade. It was old but clean and meticulously oiled. 'Not a forkbeard sword, this. An old Marroc one. Hard iron.' He slammed it back into its scabbard and handed it to Addic.

They left not long after the next dawn on the back of three mules, ploughing a path through the fresh snow down the little valley from Brawlic's farm, following a small fast river until it turned to run between two peaks towards the valley of the Isset. Jonnic led them to a place where one of the great Varyxhun pines had fallen across the water. He dismounted and gingerly led his mule across the giant trunk. Oribas and Addic followed, and together they climbed a steep twisting trail that rose up the other side of the valley towards the next ridge. The Marroc didn't talk, and by the end of the day they were across a high snow-bound pass and into the next valley along. They spent the night in the barn of some farmer that both Addic and Jonnic knew, the Marroc leaving Oribas with the mules while they went into the house. Addic came back out with a bowl of stew despairingly similar to the ones Oribas had so happily left behind. They slept not long after sunset and rose again early in the morning, reaching a hamlet by the middle of the day that was little more than a dozen houses and barns. Addic talked to one of the Marroc, who nodded and pointed and made a sign against evil, and Oribas didn't need to hear a word to understand perfectly. *Shadewalker. That way.* So they set off across snow-covered fields, all of them more upright in their saddles now. Jonnic held his head craned forward, making little jerking movements from side to side. Addic's foot twitched. About a mile from the hamlet they stopped at the edge of a dense stand of pines, black against the mottled mountainside, and Addic pointed. 'It's in there.'

'I've never faced a shadewalker before,' Oribas told him. 'I know what they are and I know what will stop one but I've never faced one.' Shadewalkers preferred dark places. Places with no sun, which was why they rarely came to the desert.

'You should have told us that before we left, Oribas.' Addic slipped off the back of his mule.

Jonnic stayed where he was. He spat. 'If we were going to get rid of this Aulian, here would do. Far enough away from old Brawlic that the forkbeards would never suspect even if they found him.'

Addic snorted. 'And bring them down on Ronnelic and Jonna and Ylya and Massic and the rest? Why, have they done something to offend you?'

Oribas yawned with a careful precision. 'In Aulia it is considered impolite to discuss a man's murder while he's standing right in front of you. I would hate to inconvenience your friends with my death. Perhaps it would be more convenient for us all if I were to stay alive?'

Addic laughed. 'I'm sorry about Jonnic. He hasn't quite grasped the idea that there are people in the world who are neither his Marroc friends nor forkbeards out to hang him.'

'I've quite grasped the Vathen,' snapped Jonnic. He glared at Oribas. 'When I cut a man's throat, his body goes in the Isset. Won't be a trouble to anyone. No *inconvenience*.'

Oribas spared him a smile. 'Then I shall remain glad that it's Addic and not you who carries the iron sword.' He turned away from Jonnic with as much bad grace as his Aulian manners could muster. 'An iron sword driven through the shadewalker's heart will kill it. Steel will sometimes work but more usually the creature appears to have been slain only to rise again in the days or weeks that follow. I've heard of the same shadewalker being put to rest four times before it stayed at peace, but when you truly kill it, you will know. There will be no doubt.' Just saying the words made him think of the Edge of Sorrows and all the names that the Marroc and the Lhosir had for the red sword. Was *that* what it was for? Putting shadewalkers to rest? 'Shadewalkers were knights once, soldiers of the Aulian emperor. They remember little of who they were but they have not forgotten their skill. Most still carry their old swords and armour.'

'We know.' Addic's lips were pressed tight together. 'We've seen them. Too many of them.'

'The sword-dancers learn to fight with such skill that they can cut the armour from a shadewalker's skin and pierce its dead bones with one thrust. The shadow-stalkers learn ways to make a shadewalker so weak that it can barely move. We have neither here, but we will confront it as though we have both. Whoever takes the sword must make the final thrust, but you must also defend us while I weaken it. Where's the salt?'

Addic jerked his thumb at a sack strapped to the back of his saddle.

'Addic, if you carry the sword then your friend Jonnic will need a torch and some of the salt as well. The shadewalker cannot cross a line of salt. I'll trap it in a circle. Once that is done, the rest is much easier. I will throw furnace powders over the creature and Jonnic will set his torch to it. When it flares you must all stand back, but be ready, for it will only burn a moment. As the flames die we throw pure water and more salt. If we strike well, it will fall as though dead, but don't be fooled. The iron sword must finish the creature. Is your point good and sharp?'

'You know all this but you've never faced one of these creatures?' Jonnic looked ready to run.

'I've seen it done. Where I come from there were men who would hunt them and bring them to my school just so that we could be shown.'

They entered the trees on foot, the pines packed too closely for mules and so dark that they would quickly be lost. Addic took the lead, Jonnic came at the rear. They moved slowly and with care, squeezing between the branches.

'You'll need to lure the creature into open ground,' Oribas whispered. A circle of salt would be almost impossible amid these trees.

'And how will I do that?' hissed Addic.

'My understanding is that shadewalkers are very easily lured.'

'Lured how?'

Oribas tried to sound unconcerned, as though he was talking about trapping a badger or a hare. 'As with any hungry animal, one baits one's trap with food, Addic.' They all knew he meant them.

'Have you ever see a man taken by a shadewalker, Aulian?' whispered Jonnic behind him. 'Their faces are ...' His words faded. Oribas understood. The faces of their victims were the worst. They were unrecognisable. Thin and stretched as though they'd been sucked to nothing from the inside.

'Yes,' he said quietly. 'I have. I lost a friend once and I've seen other victims too.' The friend had been more Gallow's friend than his but they'd travelled for many miles and many days together. He'd died in the foothills along the Aulian Way and Oribas hadn't been there to tell Gallow and his sailors how to fight them. Too busy chasing a monster of his own.

The trees shivered and rustled ahead of them. Too much for a small forest creature and something as large as a deer wasn't likely to come into a wood like this. A bear? Oribas wasn't sure but the idea of a bear frightened him even more than a shadewalker. Salt wouldn't stop a bear. His fingers drifted to his belt, opening the pouches lined with waxed paper that held his saltpetre and the fierce-burning powdered grey metal that came from the alchemists near his old home. Would a flash of fire scare off a bear? He had no idea. Deserts didn't have bears. From the way Gallow had talked, probably not.

A branch cracked. A shape emerged from the gloom ahead, ragged clothes hanging over rusting mail, an old round wooden shield, scarred and stained, and a long notched sword almost trailing in the blanket of needles that covered the forest floor. Face as pale as the snow, eyes wide open, skin taut over the bones of its face, the shadewalker came towards them at a steady pace, without a sound save for its footsteps and the whip of a branch now and then as it brushed across its shield. In front of Oribas, Addic froze.

'Modris protect us,' he croaked.

'Diaran!' cried Jonnic behind them. He took a pace back and then another. As the shadewalker advanced, he turned and ran. Jonnic, who held the torch and so their fire. Oribas stumbled as Addic backed into him.

'What do I do?' the Marroc quavered.

Oribas backed away too, grabbing a fistful of salt from the bag over his shoulder. A man could always outrun a shadewalker if his legs were good. Why were these Marroc so afraid?

The shadewalker lifted its sword as it came closer, one of the old blades of the Aulian emperor's guard. Fine swords if you could find one in good repair and they reminded Oribas of the long-bladed Edge of Sorrows. The Marroc had left the red sword at home and he thought now they might wish they hadn't. Addic lifted his shield to defend himself, but he was still backing away and he was white with fear.

'It's just a man who forgot when to die,' hissed Oribas. He stepped around Addic and threw a handful of salt at the shadewalker's face. It rained down in a fine dust. The shadewalker stopped and hissed; for a moment its guard was down but Addic was too gripped by fear to strike at it. Oribas threw down a line of salt across the earth between them. 'It cannot cross!' He shifted around between the trees, laying down more salt, trying to encircle the shadewalker.

The creature cleared its eyes. It advanced on Addic again and then reached the salted earth and stopped. Its head whipped around to Oribas as though it understood exactly what the Aulian was doing.

'Get your friend Jonnic back here!'

'Jonnic!'

The shadewalker turned. It walked quickly now, straight at Oribas, swinging its sword in its hand. Oribas laid another line of salt. 'Can you make fire? Do you have what you need?' He watched Addic fumble in his bag and then shake his head. The shadewalker stopped abruptly again a few feet from Oribas, held by the salt a second time. Its eyes were white and a blue like water from a glacier. Oribas hadn't even known what a glacier was until Gallow had dragged him over the mountains, but he'd seen eyes like these before. Gallow had them. Ice-man eyes they called them in the desert, always had, even long ago, and now he wondered: where had these shadewalkers come from, these men who'd once guarded the old emperors of the world? Too tall and broad-shouldered to be Marroc, too pale-skinned to be Aulian. Or did the pale skin and those eyes simply come as a part of what made them?

They stared at one another. When Oribas walked toward the end of the arc of salt, the shadewalker moved with him. It kept moving, stepping gingerly along the line until it found its end and looked up. Its dead face didn't change but perhaps its eyes gleamed a little brighter as it sensed its victory. It advanced quickly. Addic cried out, turned and ran while Oribas simply stepped over the line of salt to be on the other side. The shadewalker came at him, stopped abruptly at the salt and began to walk along the line again, looking for a way past. Oribas tracked the arc of salt he'd laid out, slowly and carefully, trying not to look at the shadewalker stalking the edge of his barrier. He moved from one end to the other and laid down another line. The shadewalker ignored him until it found a way through, but Oribas stepped calmly over the salt a second time and then stood and waited. The arc was three quarters of a circle now. 'One more dance, restless one?'

As soon as the shadewalker started looking for a way past again, Oribas ran, dropping salt as he went. When he was done he stepped back and watched. For a time the shadewalker followed the line. After it had gone round the inside of the circle three times, it stopped and turned to stare at him.

Oribas bowed. 'Can we both agree that you will wait here while I find my friends?'

7

THE RAVINE

Beyard demanded Gallow's oath not to run away and so Gallow gave it to him. Now he was in his mail and with his shield and helm, sitting on the back of a borrowed horse with the ironskin and a dozen Lhosir around him. Two were the men he'd faced on the Aulian Way – Arithas and Hrothin – and they stared at him with open hatred and spat at his feet and growled *nioingr* to his face. Gallow wondered at the return of his mail and his shield and helm, but those were in case of Marroc archers hiding in the woods. It seemed that among the villages in the high hills the Marroc were almost in open revolt.

'We know about you, *nioingr*,' snarled Hrothin.

'That's twice, Hrothin. Call me that a third time and you'll have to give me a sword and let me kill you,' said Gallow coldly. Beyard snarled and the two Lhosir backed away, their surly glances raking over him.

'Those two will be your watchers.' Beyard watched them go. 'One of the men you killed was Hrothin's brother. He has a blood feud with you now.'

'You're going to hang me, old friend. Hrothin will be disappointed.'

Beyard dangled Gallow's locket in the air between them, the one with a snip of Arda's hair inside. 'A feud is settled between families, Gallow, not just the men who start it. I can give him yours if I choose.' There was little of Beyard's face to see through the iron mask and crown he wore. Certainly not his eyes. 'They're only Marroc.'

Gallow's voice dropped. 'The Beyard I once knew would never sully himself like that.'

'But I am of the Fateguard now. I serve other ends.' Was that a glimmer of resentment lingering in there for whatever the Eyes of Time did to make the servants of fate as they were? 'I know you didn't slay the Screambreaker, as so many say you did, but you still led Marroc men against their king, you struck Yurlak's son and took his hand and now you've killed two of your kinsmen without cause. What would your old friend say to that, Gallow?'

'He'd ask why I did each of those things and he'd listen as I told him. Perhaps he might even agree I was right.'

They spent three long days plodding up the Aulian Way through ice and trampled snow. The fourth took them up into the start of the mountain pass where Gallow had first met Addic. The snowfalls since had been light but it still took hours of searching to find where Gallow had killed Fahred, walking their horses slowly along the road, Hrothin and Arithas pointing to features of the landscape here and there – *No, it was further than this; I remember that stone on the way back; No, too far* – but it was the horse tracks that settled it, for the Lhosir had dismounted to fight and no one else had been foolhardy enough to take a horse up the narrow path of the pass in deep snow. They found the place where they'd run up the slope after the Marroc, the snow still pockmarked by their steps, and then the scar in the white where the Marroc had fallen and slid and almost gone over the edge. They found where Gallow had killed Hrothin's brother and, as they burrowed into the snow, the stains of his blood.

Gallow watched. There were other tracks here. Someone had come back after the fight. Hard to say whether it was one man or two, certainly not more, but the way the snow had been scattered about made it clear they'd been looking for something. The Lhosir poked about until Beyard pushed them all away.

'Back! Before you make it worse!' He turned to Gallow, face hidden behind his mask. 'Are you lying, Foxbeard? Was the sword never here?' But he knew better. Arithas and Hrothin hadn't paid it much thought at the time but they'd noticed the blade he'd drawn was longer than they were used to and remembered it falling into the snow. They'd been there and they'd seen it, even if they hadn't known the Edge of Sorrows for what it was.

The Lhosir untied him from his saddle and pulled him down and Gallow walked up the road, tracing the fight in his head. Arithas and Hrothin had beaten him down where Beyard was sniffing at the snow. One Lhosir had come further past, a few yards on to where Oribas had been. The snow there was churned and trampled, most of it pushed over the edge. A struggle, perhaps. The Marroc they'd saved must have run but Gallow couldn't see any other prints. He'd run through his old tracks then, which made sense because he'd have been quicker that way too.

Gallow looked over the edge. Trails of snow lay in broken lumps down the side of the ravine, but when he looked up the snow was pristine. It had fallen from the road then. Someone had gone over. Oribas, as Beyard had said; and then he saw the Aulian's satchel still hanging from the dead branch of a broken tree, a dozen feet below him.

When he turned, Arithas and Hrothin were right behind him. He looked them up and down. 'Which one of you threw him over?'

Arithas sneered. 'He didn't even—'

Beyard had tied Gallow's hands in front of him so he could knot them to his saddle. Gallow grabbed two fistfuls of Arithas's furs and dropped to his knees. He drove his head into the Lhosir's groin and pulled, hard. Arithas doubled up and pitched forward onto Gallow's back. Gallow straightened, pulled him off his feet and let go. By the time Arithas even knew what was happening, he was over the edge. He shrieked once and then Gallow heard the crack of him hitting a boulder and the rattle of falling stones over the echoing hiss of the Isset below.

Hrothin grabbed him. 'And over you go too, *nioingr!*'

Gallow's fingers closed on Hrothin. 'Third time. Shall we go together then, brother?' he hissed. They were face to face, nose to nose.

'Hrothin!'

Beyard was too far away, though, and Hrothin's blood was up. 'Filthy *nioingr!*'

'Fourth time.' Gallow spat in his face. 'You have to stand by those words with steel now.'

'I have to stand by nothing for you, Marroc!'

'Hrothin!' This time Beyard's shout was so loud and deep that it seemed to rumble through the ground itself and at the same time shake the air. Beyard was stamping through the snow towards them.

'You must get cold out here under all that iron,' Gallow said. 'Where's Arithas?'

Hrothin snarled. 'The *nioingr* threw him over the edge.'

The iron mask turned to Gallow. Beyard's voice shook with cold fury. 'You'll hang for what you are, Gallow. A *nioingr*. No one will speak you out. No one will say your name. You'll be spat upon and dogs will eat the scraps of you and you'll be forgotten. You'll not cheat that fate. I'd thought you a better man, but Ironhand was right to name you Foxbeard. Leave him, Hrothin. Arithas was an idiot.' He pushed the two Lhosir apart and then punched Gallow in the face, the iron gauntlet smashing his nose and jarring loose a tooth. Gallow hardly saw it coming. He staggered back. As he did, Beyard stooped and snatched one foot from under him, tipping him over onto the road. The Fateguard dragged him by his foot through the snow and dumped him by the other Lhosir riders.

'Two men came here after the fight. They've already taken what we're looking for. They walked down the road and now we've trampled their tracks. One of them was hurt. He was leaning on the other.' He drove a boot into Gallow's ribs. 'Put this one back on his horse and tie him to it. We're hunting for Marroc now. If he gives any more trouble, cut off a foot. Or a hand. Yes, a hand. The king would like that.'

Gallow spat blood into the snow. 'I gave no oath about not killing your men, my friend. And that one murdered Oribas.' But quietly he wondered. *Two* men walked away? One of them was surely the Marroc. But the other?

8

THE BURNING

Oribas took his time leaving the wood, partly to give his heart a chance to stop beating so fast, and in part because he managed to get lost on the way out and wander through a lot more trees than he had on the way in. The Marroc were waiting in the middle of the field, sitting on their mules, watching like a pair of scared starlings ready to take flight the moment anything came out. They looked at Oribas in amazement.

'I have it trapped,' he said as he reached them. 'I'll need your help to kill it. Fire and cold iron. I'll need your sword.' When neither of them moved he poked Addic in the leg. 'Well? Shall we put a shadewalker to rest or shall we wait for the next rain or snow to take away my salt and let it go?'

Addic dismounted. Jonnic stayed where he was at first, but when Oribas reached the edge of the trees, he got down and followed. They let Oribas lead the way this time and he heard them whispering, cautiously but not cautiously enough, in the stillness under the trees. *What if he's leading us to it? But that's exactly what he's doing! But what if it's a trap? Have you lost your head? I mean he's an Aulian too: what if he's in league with the shadewalkers? Idiot.* At least there was no talk of throwing him into a ravine this time.

The shadewalker was where Oribas had left it, standing as still as a statue as though it had grasped the futility of trying to break the circle of salt and was simply waiting for it to go away. Addic and Jonnic crowded behind Oribas, who still wondered at their fear: if his circle of salt had failed then the shadewalker wouldn't be here. The hard part came when one of them had to step inside to finish it.

'Now what?' asked Addic.

'Light a torch.'

Jonnic fumbled with a tinderbox, dropped it, picked it up, struck a few sparks and burned his hand. He couldn't take his eyes off the shadewalker.

'Give it to me.' Oribas reached out but Jonnic jumped away as though the Aulian was a snake. Eventually the Marroc got a flame going and lit a brand. Oribas took careful steps closer, looking for the line of the salt. Salt and snow. Belatedly he realised how lucky they were that the trees here were dense enough to keep most of the snow off the forest floor. Out in the fields under their blankets of white his circle of salt would never have worked.

The shadewalker stepped back as though daring him to cross. It was watching him. Oribas took a fistful each of saltpetre and powdered metal from his pouch and crossed the line. The shadewalker sprang at him at once but Oribas was ready. He threw the powders in its face and stepped smartly back, stumbling a little as its sword swung past him. 'Now burn it!'

Jonnic stood frozen. Addic snatched the torch and threw it, straight and true. It hit the shadewalker in the chest and a whoosh of flame shot up. It dropped its sword and staggered, stumbling this way and that, trying to get away from the fire. Oribas picked up a lump of snow and hurled it. 'Cold pure water.' The flames were dying already, the metal and the saltpetre enough to scorch it but never enough to set it alight. He'd heard of some people using oil to burn the creatures, and Gallow said the Marroc of Andhun made an oil from fish which ran like warm honey and burned as easily as dried grass, but so far he hadn't seen a drop of it among the Marroc of the mountains.

Addic gave him a bemused look and then he and Jonnic began to pelt the shadewalker with snow. Oribas filled his hands with salt again. As the shadewalker reeled he stepped back into the circle and threw both handfuls. The shadewalker hissed and crackled, its skin blackening. A terrible smell knotted Oribas's stomach. The creature's struggles stopped. It fell to its knees and pitched forward and lay still on its soft bed of fallen needles and sparse trampled snow. The Marroc stared at it.

'Is it dead?'

'It was already dead,' said Oribas. 'That wasn't as much flame or salt as there should have been. It must have been weak already. It'll be still for a while now. An iron sword through the heart will end it for ever.'

Neither Marroc moved. Oribas rolled his eyes. He crossed the line of salt and knelt beside the prone shadewalker and started pulling at its mail. The Marroc just stared and backed away, and it was hard work doing it on his own because the shadewalker was big and heavy and stank enough to make him gag, and there was always the nagging worry that maybe his books were wrong and everything he'd heard wasn't quite as he remembered it and the shadewalker wasn't in a torpor that would last for hours, and what, exactly, was he going to do if it started moving again before he was finished?

He rolled it over, tipped another handful of salt over its face and went back to struggling to haul its mail high enough over its chest for someone to stab it through the heart. Addic came to help him at last and then Jonnic, both of them ashen-faced and quivering like squirrels but at least they had an urgency to them. When it was done, Oribas stood up. The two Marroc scuttled back, scuffing his circle of salt to ruin, a carelessness that would have earned Oribas a week of cleaning chores back when he'd been learning his craft. The three of them stood together, looking. Underneath its mail, the shadewalker's clothes were rotten and ragged and stained.

'Where do they come from?' asked Jonnic. Oribas shook his head.

'Aulia. The end of days, but no one knows for sure how they came to rise. The armour, their swords, their clothes, all these say they were the emperor's guard at the fall. No one knows exactly what happened. Not the start of it. When the city of Aulia itself died, it was no surprise that the rest of the empire collapsed. But as to *how* Aulia died?' He shrugged. 'As the histories I learned tell it, a black mist fell over the city that lasted for three days, and when it lifted, every single creature was dead. The few who escaped before it engulfed them say the mist swept outward from the imperial palace, but as to its cause?' He crouched down beside the dead thing, screwed up his face, fingers pushing down into ragged clothes and the cold dead flesh, searching for the gap between the ribs. 'Aulia was built on the slopes of a volcano. The emperors were ever digging tunnels under their palaces, always deeper. It's said the last one was searching for an entrance to the underworld, looking for his wife and sons lost at sea ten years before, but the Aulians were always diggers, always tunnelling under the earth. My teacher thought perhaps they broke open a monstrous cave filled with poisonous gas, for such things do occur and there had been times before when the mountain leaked fire from its summit and belched poison from the many caves and tunnels that riddled its flanks.' He stared at the shade-walker. Fumes, his master had always insisted. Poisonous air from the mountain that found a way from deep inside the earth through the emperor's tunnels; but Oribas knew of no gas that would make a dead man rise and walk the earth and neither did anyone else. 'Some say the emperor's tunnels finally reached the underworld and that a part of the underworld spilled out as a result. A punishment from the gods.'

'Modris and Diaran protect us,' whispered Jonnic, and both the Marroc made little signs to ward away evil. Oribas had seen Gallow do the same. He'd always laughed at such superstition, but not now, not with a dead shadewalker right here in front of him.

No, not dead, not yet. 'You need to finish him.' Addic handed Oribas the iron sword without even looking at him. Oribas waved him away. 'I've never held a sword in my life save to carry it from one place to another and I do not intend to start. You can do it. A simple thrust.' He poked himself in the chest over his own heart and then poked the shadewalker. 'Here. Between the ribs. Drive it deep and hard.'

Addic offered the sword to Jonnic. Jonnic shook his head and backed hurriedly away as though Addic was mad. Oribas stayed where he was, kneeling beside the shadewalker with fingers held where the sword would need to go. His hands were shaking. Addic lifted the sword and held it, point down and *his* hands were shaking too. He let the tip rest on the shadewalker's chest.

'There.' Oribas backed away. Addic's knuckles were clenched white. The Marroc muttered a prayer and rammed the sword hard down into the dead thing's flesh. At first nothing happened. The shadewalker didn't move or make a sound save for a twitch as the sword drove into it.

'Is it dead?' Addic stayed where he was, staring. Oribas found he didn't know. All he'd learned on shadewalkers and how to bind them and confine them and put them to rest but no one had said what happened afterwards. Some sort of release of the energy that held them between life and death seemed expected.

'Look!' Jonnic pointed. The shadewalker's flesh was starting to darken, only a tinge at first but then spreading rapidly. Its belly swelled up and then collapsed in on itself. Addic reeled away at the smell, the spell broken. Oribas caught a lungful of it and threw up, staggering away, scuffing the circle of salt himself this time.

'Gods preserve us!' He threw a handful of snow in his face and drew in lungfuls of clean air well away from the shadewalker. It was the sort of smell he was sure he would carry with him for ever, just a whiff of it, always in his clothes and his hair and on his skin. They gathered themselves together and went back to look, hands held over their mouths. Where the shadewalker had lain was now no more than a collection of bones. A skeleton dressed in rotten cloth and rusted mail.

'I'd swear that was a forkbeard when it was alive,' muttered Jonnic, and Oribas wondered if he might be right.

'Best forkbeard I've seen for a while then,' said Addic. 'Wish they were all like that.' He turned and a smile broke over his face and he grabbed Jonnic by the arms and shook him. 'Look! Look at it! Look at what we did! We killed a shadewalker!'

'*You* killed it, you mean,' said Jonnic. He looked distant and thoughtful, then a smile settled on his face too. 'We did, didn't we? We really did.'

Addic grabbed Oribas. 'They can be killed! They can!'

'Put to rest,' said Oribas mildly.

'Aulian, don't you see what this means? We can send the shadewalkers away!'

'I'm hoping it means you're not going to throw me into a ravine now,' said Oribas, and then he smiled too, because the flowering of understanding in another man was always a joy to see, whoever they were. 'Also food and shelter for the rest of the winter would be nice. Until the snows clear and I can make my way back over the pass. Do you think you could do it again now you know that it can be done?'

They rode back to the half-dozen houses that made up the hamlet of Horkaslet. Since no one would believe what had happened until they saw the evidence with their own eyes, Jonnic dragged the Marroc out of their houses and their barns to come across the fields. And after that, when they'd seen it, they forgot what they'd been doing and broke out the best food they had and got roaring drunk on mead and ale, both drinks that Oribas had never met before and hoped very much to meet again. The Marroc ate until their bellies were swollen. They sang songs and talked the stupid talk of drunk men, about how Addic and Jonnic would ride and rid the mountain valleys of the shadewalkers and then rid them of the forkbeards too while they were at it, until they all passed out in a stupor.

The three stayed another day and spent that evening doing more of the same before Addic decided they ought to be going back. They took their time about leaving, and as their mules plodded down the valley, Addic asked all manner of questions. He asked where to get the powder that made them burn – which Oribas didn't know, this side of the mountains, but he described the fish oil, and Addic nodded – and about shadewalkers and what had made them and about Aulia and about what other magic Oribas knew, until Oribas had to tell him there was no magic to it at all, but if they could find a way to get back his satchel from where he'd left it hanging over the Isset then he'd be happy to show them a trick or two.

They sheltered for the night in another barn with another farmer who knew Addic and Jonnic well enough but laughed heartily at their stories of killing a shadewalker. He told them they should drink less and looked askance at Oribas and his strange skin. After they left him, Addic was sombre. 'Three, this winter. Three seen already and the real cold hasn't come yet,' and Oribas had no answer to that; but later another thought crossed his mind.

'There's one thing I would ask of you. I'd like to know what happened to my friend, the Lhosir who saved your life, Addic. I would like to know if Gallow is still alive. Is there a way, do you think, to find out?'

9

BRAWLIC'S FARM

Beyard led the Lhosir from Varyxhun back down the high mountain pass. He rode at the front and now and then stopped and got off his horse and knelt down in the snow and pushed his face towards it and sniffed. Men left traces. Not only the tread of their boots but a deeper mark. It was said among the Lhosir that no one could evade the Fateguard once they had the sight of the Eyes of Time upon them, and it was true. Beyard closed his eyes behind his mask and touched the iron to the snow and knew, without knowing how, that two men had passed this way days ago, the two men that he was following. The essence of their presence remained.

He did it over and over again until he lost count of how many times, but as the light was starting to fade he did it once more and found they were not there, and knew that they'd left the Varyxhun Road. He turned the grumbling Lhosir around and led them back until he found a winding twisting track where men had passed since the last heavy snows. He sniffed again. This was the way.

He knew where they were going now. The track wound back and forth over a ridge and down into one of the higher valleys. From the top he saw smoke a few miles away. Chimney smoke. He stopped and pointed. 'That's where we sleep tonight.'

The Lhosir moved with purpose now, hurrying down the ridge before the day ended and plunged them into the deep quick darkness that came after a mountain sunset. They wove between stands of towering Varyxhun pines, across the uneven ground and the thick drifts of snow. They lost sight of the smoke, and when the last rays of the sun sank below the horizon they started to mutter among themselves. All of them knew how cold the mountainsides became at night and how quickly any warmth faded. Beyard snarled at them. Cold? He felt nothing else. Out here in the snow and ice and the falling dark, or in a warm summer meadow with the sun blazing down, or standing in the flickering orange glare of a funeral pyre. Always the same. Always cold.

He whipped them with words and it wasn't quite full dark when they spied the farmhouse ahead of them again, large and welcoming with its warmth, firelight flickering between the cracks in the shutters and sparks rising into the night from the chimney. One house for one family of Marroc, a couple of barns for the animals. Beyard felt the mood around him change. An easy fight, a full belly, mead and a warm place to sleep – yes, the Lhosir weren't muttering now – they were eager, but the coldness inside Beyard only bit deeper. None of those pleasures were his any more. Pleasures were forgotten things among the Fateguard. Cold and iron and the weave of fate were all he'd know for the rest of time. The Beyard of long ago yearned for something else, but that Beyard was a distant voice now, all but lost in a blizzard of howls.

The Lhosir dismounted and left their horses far enough from the farm not to be heard. They argued about what to do with Gallow, whether to leave him with a couple of men to watch him or to take him with them; and in the end they took him because they couldn't agree on who'd stay behind to do the watching. Beyard undid his bonds and tied him again, this time with his hands behind his back. 'So you don't throw anyone into something that's not good for them, *nioingr*.'

'That's the second time you've called me that, old friend.' Gallow's voice was as cold as the snow. 'A third time and it's axes and shields.' Under his mask the old Beyard stirred at that. Might even have smiled. Axes and shields. The right way to settle matters, not some spiritless hanging.

He pushed the Foxbeard on, letting the other Lhosir lead the way. The deep twilight was perfect. The Marroc would be inside and huddled around their fire. They'd probably eaten and they'd be sleepy. Might be as many as a dozen living here but only a handful would be fighting men. If it came to that then it would be bloody and short and swift, and the women and children would answer his questions, not the men. The women always knew all the secrets; and they always talked when you held their children over a fire for long enough. And once they'd talked, Beyard let them go. Lhosir didn't make war on women and children.

They were almost at the house, creeping through the snow, voices dropped to whispers, swords already out of their scabbards. The Lhosir at the front were creeping around the wall towards the door, peeking in through the cracks in the shutters when Gallow turned. 'If the Aulian is here, he's done nothing wrong, Beyard.' He stopped.

Beyard pushed him on. 'There was an Aulian. Arithas threw him into the ravine.'

'Two men came down the Varyxhun Road. There was only one Marroc that day. Oribas knows Solace for what it is. He'd know to take it and hide it.' The Foxbeard didn't believe in his own words though. It was hope without conviction.

'Your Aulian is a witch, is he? A man who can fly?' But Beyard frowned under his mask as he spoke. No way to know who made the tracks he was following, but it *was* a long way to climb just to go back for a sword unless you knew exactly what it was you were looking for. And how would some Marroc know the Comforter when he saw it? 'Did you truly bring it back?' He didn't need to ask, not really. In the snow where Gallow had said to look, he'd felt the residue of something that wasn't a man. The remains of a strand of fate that belonged to something other.

'I did.'

'Why?'

The Foxbeard looked at him as though the question had never crossed his mind. 'What else would I do with it, old friend? Who else should carry its curse?'

The Lhosir were at the farmhouse doors now, waiting for his signal. 'Kneel.' Beyard pressed Gallow down into the snow. He took another piece of rope and bound Gallow's wrists to his ankles. 'I have your oath that you won't run.'

'You do.'

'What does your Aulian look like?'

'Like an Aulian. Short and dark to our eyes.'

Beyard looked up and down the valley. Even if Gallow broke his oath there was nowhere for him to go. Hobbled as he was he'd never get back to the horses, and out here at night a man would freeze to death and Gallow wasn't strong, not now, not after crossing the mountains. 'If I don't find you here when I come back then I will hunt out your family. If they're still alive, I'll give them to Hrothin.'

He left Gallow there and headed for the farmhouse, waving at the Lhosir to break in. Dressed in all his clanking iron, a Fateguard was never good for stealth. Being noticed was what they were for after all; and so he left the other Lhosir to smash in the door to the Marroc farm and start the shouting and the screaming and, even though he ran after them, by the time Beyard crashed in, they were almost done. Three Marroc men lay dead or dying. Women wailed. One of them ran for a window and hurled herself at it, bursting through the shutters. A big man with an axe threw himself at the Lhosir going after her and got himself skewered for his troubles. The last man went down a moment later and Beyard was left with a couple of Marroc women huddled quivering in a corner together and four children. The dead men scattered around the farmhouse floor were armed too well to be mere farmers.

'Bordas, Torjik, go and get the woman back. She can't have gone far. Niflas, go with them. Bring the Foxbeard in here before he freezes.' He turned to the cowering women and children and crouched in front of them, the iron mask of the Fateguard looming in their faces. They were terrified and they were right to be. 'Listen well, Marroc. Tell me what I want to know and I'll leave you be. Deny me and I will turn my back and let my soldiers do as they will. Two men came here some days ago. One of them may have been hurt.' He paused, watching their eyes, all of them. There was always one face to give the truth away; and yes, they knew the men he meant. His eyes settled on the one who gave away most. A boy a few years short of being a man. 'They had an unusual sword. Long and with a touch of red to its blade.' Yes. Solace had come here. 'And was one of them perhaps a stranger? A foreigner? A darkskin?' Yes to that too, but something was wrong. There were no glances towards the bodies as he asked his questions. The men and the sword had been here, that was clear, but now they were gone?

There was only so far they could answer with their faces. He walked to the fire and pulled out a burning branch. The flames licked over his iron gauntlet as he reached into the blaze but he never felt the heat, only ever cold. Between them the Marroc told him everything with an honesty born of fear. The bandit Addic had come with a half-dead Aulian he'd found on the road and, yes, the red sword too. They'd stayed a few days and then gone with another to hunt a shadewalker. Beyard took a while to believe that, but in the end he did. As for the sword, none of them knew. The men had taken it with them when they'd gone, or else they'd hidden it in the barns perhaps. The burning branch never left Beyard's hands. It never once touched their skin.

Fear gives birth to truth. He rose when he was done, oblivious until then to the other Lhosir moving around him, tearing the house apart, helping themselves to food and mead or else simply standing, watching.

'The men we're looking for will return,' Beyard told them. 'We wait for them. These ones are not to be touched.' The Lhosir didn't like that but they could live with it. The Fateguard were joyless souls. He looked about, missing something. 'Where's Gallow? Where's the other woman? Where's Niflas?'

But it was a while longer before Niflas came back and when he did he held up a handful of tangled rope and dropped it at Beyard's feet. 'Bordas and Torjik are still looking, Fateguard, but they're gone. Both of them. Gone and taken our horses too.'

10

ACHISTA

In the failing light Gallow struggled with the ropes around him. He tried to bunch his legs to pull his hands in front of him, to bring the bonds to where his teeth could work on them, but Beyard had tied them too tight, and so he lay in the snow, rolling helplessly back and forth. Shouts and screams echoed from the farmhouse and then one of the shutters slammed open with a crack of wood and firelight spilled out into the night. A figure struggled from the snowdrift beneath the window.

'Marroc!' he cried. 'Marroc, here!'

The figure glanced his way, turned a moment, hesitated and then turned back. 'Who's there?'

A woman's voice. Gallow answered, 'I can lead you to the forkbeard horses.'

The figure ran towards him, arms and legs flailing through the deep snow. Yes, a woman. She stopped when she saw him though. 'You're one of them!' She turned away and started to run.

'Have you seen an Aulian? His name is Oribas!'

He couldn't think of anything else to say but that was enough. She stopped again. 'What's *your* name?'

'Gallow.'

The woman came back. She had a knife in her hand. She looked him over, face filled with indecision while the rest of her twitched with the desire to run far and fast before the Lhosir came after her.

'I can take you to their horses!'

'You're the one who saved Addic?'

The Marroc on the road? Gallow shook his head. 'I never knew his name.' He rolled and turned his ropes towards her. 'Quickly!'

'Addic brought your Aulian friend here. He spoke of you.

Fine words.' The woman knelt beside him and took her knife to the ropes that hobbled him. *She'd seen Oribas!* Somehow he'd been thrown off a cliff and lived!

'We crossed the mountains together. Is he hurt?'

The rope snapped free. The Marroc woman shook her head. She kept glancing back at the farmhouse. The crashes and cries from inside had been muffled by the snow but now they'd fallen quiet. The Lhosir hadn't yet come out to chase her down but maybe that was because they didn't think she'd get far in the dark. The need to run filled her eyes as she sawed at the rope around his wrists. 'Gallow. I've heard of you. Everyone has. Gallow the Foxbeard, who turned on the forkbeard prince and cut off his hand and stole away with the Sword of the Weeping God. No wonder they have you all trussed up.' She gave him a hard look. 'How do I know you won't cut off mine?'

'You don't. But I won't.'

'Forkbeards were everywhere looking for you a few years back. Murderous mad they were about what you did. Still are, I expect.' The rope split and Gallow's hands flew apart.

'I had my reasons.'

She looked him up and down, the knife held between them, the point at his belly. 'You can keep them. Forkbeards murdering forkbeards is good enough for me.' She took a wary step away. 'Lead then, Gallow Foxbeard, and move fast. Don't you worry about me following. I'll be there, just not so close in case you lead me false.'

'Why would I do that?' Gallow picked himself out of the snow and set off at a run, following the Lhosir tracks back the way they'd come. The moon gave enough light; the woman would have seen them easily enough without him.

'Forkbeards are forkbeards, that's why.'

The horses were exactly where the Lhosir had left them, stamping their feet and snorting at the deepening cold. Gallow let them all loose and mounted one. He watched the Marroc woman throw herself at the back of another and scrabble and pull herself up until she was sitting upright. She didn't look like she'd ever been on a horse before. 'If you can't ride then you should come up with me.'

A derisive snort answered him. 'We go our separate ways now, forkbeard.'

Gallow shrugged. With a kick he urged his horse into the others, chasing them away and scattering them. Anything to make it harder for Beyard to follow. The Fateguard would, though. That was what they did. When he looked around, the Marroc woman was lying in the snow.

'*Nioingr!*' A shout from the farm pierced the night. 'Now we're going to kill you, Foxbeard.' The Lhosir had discovered his escape. They were coming. The woman looked at him, brushing the snow off her. Gallow reached out a hand.

'Get up behind me!' She was shivering already. The shouts from the farmhouse were getting closer and quickly. They weren't stupid. The horses were the first place to look.

The woman hissed at him. 'Go your own way, forkbeard!'

'Then I thank you for setting me free. Go back to your house, woman.' He turned his horse away from her. 'You won't escape these Lhosir on foot.'

'So sure?'

'They have a Fateguard with them. He'll find you.'

She ignored him, tried to mount her horse a second time and ended up flat on her back in the snow again. Gallow unwrapped his fur cloak and threw it at her. 'Take this at least! You'll not last the night out here without it.' And without it *he'd* likely freeze too. He'd have to kill the horse. Find a deep drift and dig in until the morning. Kill the horse and climb inside its carcass like Hostjir had done in the old sagas. Was that even possible?

The woman looked at the furs and then looked at him. 'Damn you, forkbeard.' She picked them up and threw them back at him and then stood beside his horse and held up her hand expectantly. 'Well, help me up then.'

As soon as she was pressed up behind him and Gallow had wrapped the furs around them both, he felt a jab in his ribs through his mail. 'I still have a knife, forkbeard. You might have saved my brother Addic and you might have helped me out but that doesn't make us friends. I'll fillet your liver if you even blink wrong.'

Gallow almost smiled but then a bitterness welled up inside

him. Arda might have said the same, the wife he'd left behind. She'd come from the mountains too. Did they make all Marroc women like that up here? He missed her. Three years spending every day trying to find a way back to her, and now he'd come so far and was so close to what had once been home, and …

But now wasn't the time. He pushed the horse on and drove it as hard as he dared through the night, following the trail the Lhosir had made back to the ridge and winding down the other side, back to the Aulian Way, the Varyxhun Road as the Marroc called it. The snow here was only a few inches thick. Older falls had been piled into embankments on either side and had half melted in the afternoons and then frozen like granite each night, over and over until there were ice walls on either side of the road half as tall as a man. He pushed on and on down the gorge of the Isset towards Varyxhun while the night grew ever colder. The woman stayed slumped against his back. He thought she was asleep until she suddenly shifted and poked him. 'Here! Stop! Go up that trail there.' In the dark he could hardly see it, but when she pointed, there it was, a break in the ice wall beside the road and a narrow path up through the trees. The horse was close to the end of its legs, breathing hard, fighting against the cold. His own hands and face were numb too.

'Where are we going?'

'Never you mind. It's not far and that's all you need to know.'

The last ten minutes were slow. The black branches of the trees blotted out the sky and the stars and the moon flickered between them. The track wound back and forth, climbing up the slope. It was hardly a track at all in places and Gallow had to stop more than once to see which way it led, but it ended at a tiny log hut, empty and with no door. The Marroc woman slipped out from under their furs and went inside. Gallow blew on his hands and rubbed them together, trying to find some feeling in them again. The horse snickered and butted him as he got off. He patted its neck. 'Sorry. No blankets.' Likely as not the cold would kill it before the morning and then they'd be on foot and Beyard wouldn't be far behind.

The Marroc woman was building a fire. 'Woodsman hut,' she said as he came in. 'No one comes here this time of year.'

'Except Marroc hiding from forkbeards?'

She gave him a sharp look. 'I still have my knife. Don't you try anything.'

Gallow looked at the door, at the roof. Too small to coax their horse inside. He went back out and tied it as close to the door as he could, then stripped the saddle off its back and tied his fur cloak around it instead.

'What are you doing?' The Marroc woman looked at him as though he was mad. 'We'll need that!'

'How far is it to Varyxhun on foot?'

She shrugged, striking sparks now at a little nest of tinder. 'Three days, give or take. Depends how fast you walk.'

'Beyard will catch us before then.'

'Never heard of him,' She cupped her hands over the first tiny flame and blew softly, fanning it.

'The Fateguard.' Which didn't mean anything to her, so he added, 'The one in the iron mask.' *That* did. She looked up sharply and made the sign of Modris the Protector. 'So we need the horse.'

She snorted. 'People see you riding a forkbeard horse in Varyxhun, they'll have you off the back of it and hanging from a gibbet before you can blink.'

'And why shouldn't I ride a forkbeard horse? I'm a forkbeard.'

She straightened and looked at him long and hard. 'Yes.' Her fingers tightened on the knife. 'Yes, you are.'

He helped her to build up the fire, careful to stay away from her as best he could in the cramped space of the hut. When it was done he curled up as close as he dared and let its warmth seep into him. The Marroc woman sat on the other side, watching. Her eyes drooped but never quite closed; and why would they, when all the Lhosir had done among the Marroc was a litany of rape and slaughter and carnage? No, he understood her wariness. In her place he'd feel the same.

He closed his own eyes and rubbed the feeling back into his face and fingers and listened to the silence of the woods, and then suddenly light was streaming in through the door and it was morning. He blinked and sat up. The Marroc woman was fast asleep, snoring gently. He stoked the embers and then went outside and there was their horse, still on its feet, pressed against the wall of the hut with his furs wrapped around it. It gave him a baleful look and nudged him as he searched the Lhosir saddlebags for anything to eat. Back inside he shook the Marroc woman; as soon as he touched her she jumped and scrambled away, one hand going into the fire in her haste, the other grabbing for her knife. Gallow backed off as far as the walls would let him. He sat down and tore bread from the Lhosir saddles in two and threw her half of it. She snatched it out of the air, then looked at her hand and winced. 'Forkbeards are full of lies!'

'Oribas would have something for that.'

'The Aulian.' The anger fell out of her face. 'What do you forkbeards want with him? What's he done?'

Gallow shrugged. 'It's not Oribas they're looking for, it's the sword I was carrying.'

She stared at him, and for a moment the mistrust vanished into wonder. 'Gallow Foxbeard and the Sword of the Weeping God. So it's all true, is it?'

'Was Oribas there? And the sword? Has Beyard got them both now?'

The old look of suspicion settled back over her face. 'There was a shadewalker. Your Aulian claimed he could put an end to it. Addic went off with him to see if he could.'

'Where did they go? How do I find him?'

The woman took a deep breath and then seemed to come to some decision. 'Horkaslet. They went across the ridge to Horkaslet.' Then her hand flew to her mouth. 'We have to stop them from going back to the farm! The forkbeards will be waiting for them!' She still held the knife and now she waved it in Gallow's face. 'You! You have to take us there. Quick! Before it's too late!'

11

A WARM WELCOME

The Marroc were cheerful as they rode the last miles towards home. Oribas tried to let the mood take him with it, but there were too many glooms weighing on his mind. Gallow, his strange and unexpected friend for the last year. Whatever he'd told the Marroc, whether or not the gods had sent Gallow as an answer to his prayers, he was still just a man returning to his family. Harsh of fate to let him come so close to what he so wanted and then take him. And then there was his own fate too, hanging loose in the great weave now the Rakshasa was gone, flapping in the wind. The monster had given him a purpose and a direction and now that was over.

He stopped and got off his horse while the Marroc wandered on. They were riding beside a stream, rustling its way down from the mountains, swathed in ice but not so frozen that the water didn't break through here and there. He cleared a patch of snow, plucked a blade of grass and tied a knot in it and set in the water. 'If you've killed him then you've done wrong. You should have let him have his last years among those he loved. If not, if you truly sent him to me to kill my monster, leave him be. Give him his peace.' They were words spoken to gods, though the only gods Oribas knew were the old gods of Aulia and they were far away. As an afterthought he set another knotted blade adrift. 'If you've killed him then I would like to go home now.'

Jonnic waited up the path. Addic walked slowly back. 'Have you found something, Aulian?'

Oribas shook his head. 'A little prayer, that's all. To wish us all to our homes in warmth and safety.' He pushed past Addic and mounted again. The desert where he'd been born was littered with temples to the Aulian gods, all empty and desolate now, abandoned just as the gods themselves had been after the empire fell. To the desert child in Oribas, water was the sacred goddess and always had been. Quiet and unassuming, asking little save that she be nurtured with love and care, fickle though, and deadly when she withdrew her blessings.

'Amen to that.' Addic followed him and together the three rode in silence over the rise to Brawlic's farm. Smoke rose from the chimney. There was no one about. Maybe that was to be expected late on a winter afternoon. Oribas's world had little to say about farms, nor about mountains or winter or all this cold and snow and how men set about living in the middle of it.

The Marroc left their horses in the barn and called out, and suddenly there were armed men everywhere, soldiers like the men in the road that Gallow had fought, big and tall, cloaked in thick heavy furs with mail underneath, with axes and shields and swords at their sides and helms that hid half their face but not the braids of their forked beards.

'Forkbeards!' Addic had his iron sword in his hand as the Lhosir reached him but they didn't stop to trade blows. The first charged into him, taking Addic's sword on his shield, and battered him back, and before he could find his balance, the next one crashed in and knocked him to the ground. Jonnic was already running with three more Lhosir chasing after. Oribas simply stood where he was, helpless and with no idea what to do.

'Alive!' A monster came out of the farm behind the soldiers, a terrible golem made of black iron, or so it seemed at first until Oribas understood that this was simply a man, huge and fierce perhaps, but a man clad in metal. He wore a crown on his head and a mask over his face. 'Alive, you dogs!' he cried again, and then he saw Oribas and came straight towards him. There were more Lhosir behind him, swords drawn, watching. Addic cried out, a scream of fury and fear, as the forkbeards pinned him to the ground. The metal man strode closer.

Oribas turned to flee but barely managed a handful of strides before an arm with fearsome strength caught his shoulder and spun him round and a palm smashed into his face and knocked him flat. He blinked, bewildered by the brightness of the sky, and then darkness fell as the shadow of the iron man loomed over him. The mask was a twisted visage, as though of a demonic man burned deep by fire. Between vertical slits in the metal, deathly pale skin hid among the shadows. Oribas squealed, 'Shadewalker!' It was the first thought that came into his head. His hand was at his side, resting on the shoulder bag where he kept his salt – he scrabbled back in terror and scraped out as much as his fingers could claw together and threw it at the iron mask. A moment later a boot stamped on his arm, hard enough to bruise bone, and pinned him there. A spear point came to rest against his throat. The Lhosir soldiers around him laughed.

'Not a move, Aulian,' the spearman growled.

The iron man tore off his gauntlets and the mask and crown and clawed at his face. His skin was sallow and greasy, his hair lank and ragged, but he was no shadewalker.

The spear point dug into his skin. 'What have you done, Aulian?'

'Salt,' gasped Oribas. 'Only salt. I thought he was a shade-walker!'

The Lhosir roared with laughter and the spear withdrew a little. 'Salt in the eyes of a Fateguard? Maker-Devourer, but that's a thing. You have a fierce heart in there, Aulian.' The Lhosir's eyes gleamed and the spear waved over his face again. 'Stay right where you are if you want to keep it beating.'

The iron-skinned man rubbed snow in his face. He took his time and then slowly replaced his mask and crown and his gauntlets. He turned to Oribas, who squirmed with fear again, not sure which looked worse, the iron man or the spear that would skewer him if he moved. The iron man growled. 'Let him up, Niflas. If he runs, catch him.'

Niflas lifted his spear and backed away, laughing. 'This one? He couldn't run from a flock of angry birds.'

'If he gets away from you I'll make a cloak out of your lungs.' The iron man came closer.

Oribas stared up as the Fateguard towered over him. 'What are you?'

The iron man ignored his question. 'Aulians don't come over the mountains any more. You're the first that isn't a shadewalker for twenty years. But you didn't come alone, did you?'

*

The Aulian didn't even blink but Beyard saw the answer in the sparkle of his eyes. He nodded, as much to himself as to anyone. 'No, I know who you are. You came across the mountains with Gallow the smith's son, Gallow Truesword, Gallow the Foxbeard.'

Foxbeard. The Aulian's eyes flinched and gave him away. So Gallow had called himself Foxbeard, the name King Medrin had given him.

Beyard looked over his shoulder. They had the second Marroc now. He'd take them inside and deal with them properly: show them their women and their sons and daughters, still alive and unharmed, and tell them exactly what they would have to do to keep them that way. There would be no mercy for the men and they'd know it. Pointless to pretend otherwise, but he'd send them back for Cithjan's judgment for the sake of things.

He turned to the Aulian again and held out Gallow's locket. 'The Foxbeard. He's still alive.' Strange, the flash of glee he felt at that, same as when Gallow had thrown Arithas into the ravine. 'Why did he come back. Because of this?' He waved the locket. Wide eyes said yes. Sixfingers would never believe it but Beyard did for he'd seen the same answer in Gallow's own eyes. All this way for a woman. For his sons, and so that was how Beyard would find him again. He looked at the Aulian, peering hard as if he could look inside the man. 'And you? Will he come for you?' The Aulian thought not. Beyard's eyes bored harder in, searching the twisted skeins of fate that ran though him and finding strangely little. 'What have you done, Aulian? What is your crime?'

The Aulian shook his head. 'None ... nothing.'

'Then why are you are afraid?'

'You ... I am afraid of you.'

Underneath his mask Beyard's face didn't change. *Of course you are, Aulian.* 'But there's more. What are you hiding?' The Aulian shook his head. 'But I smell a death on you, Aulian. You have killed.' A strange death, though. Not fresh but old as stone.

The Aulian closed his eyes. His head drooped as though he was announcing his own death. 'A shadewalker. I helped to lay a shadewalker to rest.'

Beyard sat back on his haunches. So it wasn't the red sword. Killing a shadewalker – that wasn't what he'd expected at all but the Aulian wasn't lying. The Fateguard cocked his head. 'You're a brave man to face one, Aulian, and a clever one to win. You should be proud, but all I see is fear. Why so afraid?'

He asked about the red sword but all he got was confusion. The Aulian knew exactly what it was but he had no idea of the where and so Beyard let him be, telling the Lhosir to treat him well. He'd go back to Cithjan with the others, but as far as Beyard could see he'd done no wrong. He might even take the Aulian back to Varyxhun himself and let him go; and then he wondered at that. Why? For the Foxbeard? Yes, but then still, why? Why did Gallow's return trouble him so?

No matter, not now. He would get to work on the Marroc. They knew where the sword was hidden and it wouldn't take long to convince them to share their knowledge. As for Gallow, there was only one place he was going. Fate whispered patience in Beyard's ear and so he took his time. He settled himself in front of what would have been a pleasantly warm fire for any but a Fateguard and stared at the two Marroc. He still had their women and their children, all well and unharmed, all with their fingers and hands still attached in all the right places and none of them scarred by burns, not yet. He showed the Marroc his mercy and explained with slow and careful patience how their womenfolk and their sons and daughters might stay the way they were, and though the Marroc refused to say a word, in the end they gave themselves away, eyes darting here and there, answering his questions without a sound, looking to the place where the sword was hidden. Beyard had his men rip up the floor, had them pull back the skins and furs and dig in the remains of an old firepit beneath. They didn't have to go far to find a wooden crate half-filled with bundles of arrows and a few old swords underneath. He looked at the Marroc askance when the Lhosir showed him what they'd found and gave a little nod. The Marroc men had sealed their fate and they knew it. Varyxhun would see two more gibbets.

The red sword wasn't in there with the rest, but all he had to do was look from the stash of arrows to the quivering women and children and they were telling him before he even said a word, confession flowing out like he'd broken a dam. Hidden under the hay in the barn, and five minutes later he had it in his hand. He swung it in arcs and listened to the air moan as the red steel cut it. The wailing of ruined souls, perhaps, or maybe simply the way the steel had been forged.

12

VARYXHUN

Her name was Achista. He got it out of her after the second night when they were sneaking into the barn of some Marroc farmer she didn't like. 'Forvic has a loud mouth when there are none of you forkbeards around but he's happy enough to take your coin when he thinks there's no one to notice. It'll be a pleasure to make some trouble for him.' Gallow simply nodded and told himself that he wanted no part in this, that it was none of his concern what Marroc did to forkbeards or forkbeards did to Marroc. All he wanted was to go home.

He touched a hand to his chest, to the locket he'd carried there for the last three years, only to remember that Beyard had it now.

'Praying to your uncaring god, forkbeard?' Achista settled into farmer Forvic's hay. Gallow kept carefully away from her. 'Or are you looking for your heart? Wasting your time there. You lot don't have any.'

She didn't want to hear his story, not at first, but for some reason he needed to tell her. He said little about the early years, fighting in the Screambreaker's army, killing Marroc left and right. He'd been the same as the rest of them then. They'd none of them seen any wrong in it – just the way of the world, the soldier's way, the strong taking from the weak – and he could say he was sorry as much as he liked; it changed nothing about what he'd done and she'd never believe him anyway. So he told her the truth and left it that, and then how after the war was done he'd turned his head towards Aulia; how he'd met Arda on the way and all the little things that sparked between them. How she'd shouted as he'd left her to fight the Vathen, how he'd sailed with Medrin to bring the Crimson Shield of Modris back to Andhun, the bargain he'd struck with Corvin Screambreaker and everything that had followed. Years adrift, and now all he wanted was to go home to Nadric's forge and make nails and wire and horseshoes.

He thought perhaps she'd fallen asleep long before he finished and perhaps she had, but in the morning when she looked at him he found her face was softer than it had been the night before and she put a hand on his arm instead of poking a knife at his ribs. He saw the fear in her eyes, the almost-knowledge that they were too late, and that was when she told him her name.

They reached Horkaslet late in the afternoon to find that the Marroc and their strange Aulian friend had left the morning before; and since there was only one trail to be followed for the last few hours to Horkaslet and they hadn't crossed paths, they both knew it was pointless to go in pursuit. They did anyway, Achista's face tight with grief amid the joyful Marroc of Horkaslet, still drunk at the slaying of their shadewalker. They rode on into the night and found the farm where Addic and Oribas had stayed only the night before, and in the morning they rose with the dawn and set off for the mountain trail over the ridge into the next valley and Brawlic's farm. Their Lhosir horse fell lame that afternoon and so they walked the last of the way along the mountain stream, back to the farmstead they'd fled together three nights before. Perhaps the walking was as well, for by the time they saw the gibbet they were both too tired to run. Achista stared while tears ran down her cheeks. Gallow's stomach clenched with an old anger. At least the hanged man hadn't been ripped open to have his lungs splayed like wings from his back. Then she ran and Gallow turned his head, not wanting to see any more. Beyard had done this. His oldest friend had hanged this man and Gallow couldn't bring himself to see what else he'd done inside. He wished he had a sword with which to follow her in case Beyard's Lhosir had lingered; but in time she came out again and there were others with her, Marroc women and children, and they stopped at the threshold and stared at him. They were too far away for him to read their faces but he felt their hate.

'Go!' Achista snatched the reins of the horse from his hand. 'Filthy forkbeard. Just go!'

Gallow stared at the hanged man. 'This is why I did what I did. This and far worse.'

Achista spat at him. 'That was Brawlic. This was his farm. Those are his sons and his daughters. Would you like to see them weep for him?'

'I'm sorry about your family.'

A useless thing to say but he couldn't think of anything else. Her stare was a hard one and he deserved all of it. She shook her head. 'They weren't my family, but Brawlic was a good man. Then again, he's not the first good man you forkbeards have murdered and he won't be the last either. The iron devil of Varyxhun has taken my brother Addic and your Aulian friend too and I *will* avenge them, and if you see him before you die, you tell him that.' She spat again, at his feet this time.

'Where?'

Achista turned away, leading the Lhosir horse towards the barn. Grief had made her older.

An animal growl built in Gallow's throat. He went after her, grabbed her by the shoulder and spun her around, and for a moment she was afraid of what she saw in him. '*Where*? Where did he take Oribas?'

She pulled herself free. 'You don't change, do you? Forkbeards for ever, whatever you say. Addic and your Aulian friend were here the night before last. The iron devil left for Varyxhun with a dozen forkbeards at first light this morning. Two days from now they'll be in Varyxhun castle. The day after that Cithjan will hang them. They're dead, Gallow. Your friend. My brother.'

Half her face cried out to him in pain. The other half saw just another forkbeard and looked at him full of furious murder. She walked away, and Gallow knew better than to follow.

'Varyxhun.' He nodded to himself. 'Very well, old friend. I was heading that way anyway.'

They'd left the Marroc women and children alive and untouched, and that, Beyard knew, was right and decent. The Lhosir didn't make war on women and children but the Marroc men were a different matter. He hanged the farmer and had the others bound and hooded. The Aulian he allowed to ride free. The Aulian, as best he could see, had done nothing wrong and the man made him curious.

'Gallow was a friend once,' he said, but the Aulian always had eyes full of terror and dread whenever Beyard looked at him and he soon gave up. No one ever had words for a Fateguard, only screams.

The road up to Varyxhun castle split from the Aulian Way a mile from the city gates and zigzagged back and forth up the mountainside, six tiers of it, through six impassable gates beneath six murderous walls. There Beyard handed over his prisoners for Cithjan to do as he wished, for they were his problem now. Gibbets for the Marroc at the very least, but the Aulian seemed valuable and, as far as Beyard could see, innocent; and so it came as a surprise some days later when he found the Aulian had been sent off to the Devil's Caves with all the rest. The waste troubled him but he had other business.

'So many years, old friend, but we are not ones to forget.' He took off his iron gauntlets, opened Gallow's locket and sniffed at the tiny snip of hair that lay inside. 'I will find them, old friend. I will be waiting.'

13

THE CRACKMARSH

Reddic ran fast through the cold muddy water meadows of the Crackmarsh. The sunlight was fading. His lungs burned and his legs too, but he ran anyway because no amount of pain was worse than stopping, not with what was following him. He'd come into the swamp with an axe on his hip and a shield on his arm and two other men he barely knew. All those were gone now. The ghuldogs were all that was left.

He reached a small island, a low hump of sodden earth rising out of the shallow water, a few sickly old trees clutching it tight among a withered web of roots. He stopped for a moment, had no choice any more, just couldn't go on without a moment to rest, leaning against hard wet bark before his legs gave way beneath him. Back through the haze of rain he couldn't see anything except dull grey water and the scattered ghost shapes of other tree-crowned hummocks like watching sentinels. The ghuldogs were there, though, not far. Following him, steady and patient. Waiting for the dark. Waiting for his strength to fail. Waiting with their cold clammy limbs and their heartless rending claws and biting fangs.

A splash whipped his head round, desperate eyes searching for the source of the sound and finding nothing. He whimpered and pushed away from the trees, back into the water to run again. The clouds grew darker. The sun behind them sank further. The rain grew heavier. He was soaked. Freezing water ran against his skin and down into his sodden boots.

'Modris!' The wail burst out of him as his legs failed. He stumbled and slip-sprawled into the water. They were behind him, close, and they'd eat him if they caught him, and so he forced himself onto his hands and knees and looked up. Somewhere there had to be strength left in him.

Shapes moved through the haze. Bent and hunched. Two, then three, then half a dozen. They came slowly, sniffing him out. They fanned around him and he knew this was the end. He had nothing left. When he tried to stand, he couldn't. On his hands and knees he watched them and wept his misery out. The ghuldogs sniffed closer. Cautious now that he wished they'd simply take him and be done with it. The closest of them stopped a stone's throw away, near enough to see it clearly through the rain. The relic of a man, sallow and gaunt, but with the head of a savage wolf, patches of mangy fur clinging to its skull, eyes burning red, fangs bared, saliva dripping from its jaws into the swamp. It took a pace closer and then another, each step slow and delicate and precise. Stalking him, though the time for stalking was long past.

Reddic closed his eyes. He fingered the sign of Modris the Protector hung on a loop of leather around his neck. Begged the god of the Marroc to save him though there was clearly no salvation to be had. A haunting hooting cry rang through the wind and the rain. Something between the howl of a wolf and an anguished cry of despair. He waited for the end.

A hand took his shoulder. He flinched and whimpered and screwed up his eyes, but the hand was just a hand – no talons, no fangs – and when he opened his eyes and looked up it was a man standing over him. A hard-faced Marroc man in mail with a spear, and when Reddic rose shaking to his feet, he saw that the man wasn't alone, that there were a dozen more in a cautious circle. The ghuldogs were still there as well, shapes in the rain-haze, watching.

The soldier helped him to his feet.

'I was looking to find Valaric's men.' Reddic couldn't keep the quaver out of his voice. 'I want to fight.'

There and then he didn't sound much like a man who'd picked up his axe and left his home to join the last free Marroc in their stand against the forkbeards but the soldier only nodded. There might even have been a hint of a grim smile. 'Well, you found us. Welcome to the Crackmarsh, Marroc.'

14

THE DEVIL'S CAVES

Oribas had told Gallow a lot of things when they'd crossed the desert together. More were forgotten than remembered but Gallow knew that the Aulians had come over the mountains once. Oribas said they'd never reached far into what were now the Marroc lands because the mountain valleys were too cold and wet for their liking, but they'd made their mark. Gallow had seen their work for himself: the fortress of Witches' Reach at the far mouth of the gorge, the impossible span of the Aulian Bridge across the Isset beneath it, the road that reached as far as Tarkhun, halfway to the coast, and of course the unconquerable stone of Varyxhun castle, etched into the bluffs that overlooked the city.

They'd built the first town of Varyxhun too but there wasn't much left to see of their handiwork now. It hadn't ever been much to the Aulians, but then the Marroc had come to the valley, drawn by the peace the Aulians had brought, and the town had grown. Gallow passed silently through the open gates. Aulians had stood here once, and later King Tane's huscarls, but now the soldiers who leaned on their spears and glowered at everyone who passed were Lhosir. They stared openly at Gallow's shaven chin and he heard their muted growls. *Nioingr.* One of them spat at his feet as they passed. He let it go. Had to. For Arda. For Oribas.

He stopped and looked past them. The main street of Varyxhun ran straight as an arrow from the gates to the market square in the middle of the town. It was a river of half-frozen mud and slush, piles of dirty snow pushed up against the walls of the wooden houses that lined it. He'd come through here once long ago with the Screambreaker and his army, chasing after the fleeing Marroc king. They'd stopped for a while to throw a few spears and arrows at the walls of Varyxhun castle, perched up on the crags of the mountainside overlooking them, but not for long. Assaulting the castle was impossible. They'd already fought their way across the Aulian Bridge and then past the fortress of Witches' Reach that defended the entrance to the valley. They'd been tired and battered and bloodied by the time they reached the city, and there had stood the castle as it did today, staring down at them from hundreds of feet of sheer rock, the single narrow road winding back and forth beneath a slaughter of walls, defended by gatehouse after gatehouse after gatehouse. They'd settled for helping themselves to the town, feasting on its food and its mead and its women. They hadn't burned much, but then the Screambreaker had grown more thoughtful towards the end of his campaign. It was Tane he wanted, not the castle, and that meant making Varyxhun his home. They bled it dry but they hadn't killed it, and then it turned out that Tane had slipped out right under their noses and died somewhere in the mountains, weeks earlier while he was looking to escape along the Aulian Way. The war was suddenly finished, and when the Screambreaker turned his eye to the castle once again, he'd found the gates hanging open, the huscarls who'd defended them dead by their own hands. And that had been enough. The Lhosir had quietly melted away. They'd gone to Andhun, the last Marroc stronghold, and after that most of them had gone home.

Now Lhosir in mail and helms walked through the mud of Varyxhun once more. Marroc hurried past them, eyes down. Gallow hadn't been keeping track of the days, but Midwinter was surely close. In Middislet they'd celebrated for days, burning effigies of the Weeping God on Midwinter night and drinking mead until dawn to toast the birth of the sun and the first sunrise of the year, all of them roaring drunk. There were no hanging effigies of the Weeping God in Varyxhun though. Perhaps they had little to celebrate this midwinter.

Gallow wrapped himself in his furs, covering his face as best he could. The last time he'd been here had been in summer and these fringes of the town had been a sea of mud. The cold had changed that into hard frozen dirt covered in an inch of treacherous slime made of mud and animal dung and melted snow. At least the smell wasn't as bad as he remembered. Along the street by the gates, hanged men dangled from gibbets, blackened and withered by time, skin pecked to shreds, twisting languorously back and forth in the wind. There were half a dozen of them, Medrin, or whoever ruled here in his name, always reminding the Marroc of their lords and of the price of dissent. There was a tavern by the gates. It had been the Horn of Plenty once, with some of the best Marroc ale in the valley, but it had changed its name now – to the King's Hand, with a crude wooden six-fingered hand painted black hanging over the door. Whether the Marroc meant that as homage to their king or as mockery Gallow couldn't guess. He looked further along the road towards the market square where traders and travellers congregated. If there was any word to be had of Nadric the smith or Fenaric the carter it would be there. But when he asked, the Marroc all saw his Lhosir face and shrugged or turned away. As far as he could tell, no one knew the names. If they did, they kept their knowledge to themselves.

He slept in a hen house and left Varyxhun the next morning, alone and on foot with nothing more than the clothes he wore – mail and a helm under thick furs. He stared up at Varyxhun castle, wondering if Oribas was there, if the Aulian was already dead or whether he was still alive and in a dungeon, waiting to hang. Stared and wondered what he could possibly do, alone against so many, then looked with his fingers for Arda's locket around his neck and remembered again that it was gone. He bowed his head. No. There was nothing to be done. Alone he could make no difference.

I'm sorry. But I came here to go home, not to die.

He didn't give much thought to where he'd sleep or what he'd eat. He'd come this far. Fate would provide, and if he had to chop wood every night for a barn to sleep in and a bowl of soup, that's what he'd do. Middislet was maybe a dozen days away, fewer if he crossed the Crackmarsh. If Nadric had left Varyxhun then Arda would have gone with him and that's where they'd be. After three years of trying to get home, a few more days didn't seem like it should be too much bother, but he felt her closeness now, an urgency that grew quietly inside him. Every time he touched the place where her locket had once sat warm against his skin and found it missing, its absence felt like a fresh wound.

He avoided the Lhosir he saw on the road. The Marroc in turn steered away from him as soon as they saw his face and his eyes and knew what he was. He spent the first night in a barn and chopped wood even though the Marroc farmer was clearly terrified and desperate for this strange beardless forkbeard to go away. While he had an axe to borrow, he cut himself a staff for walking. A new pair of boots would have been nice. The old ones had seen him across the Aulian Way and the desert before. They leaked and had holes in their soles and his feet were wet and freezing.

Every time he stopped, he looked back, thought of Oribas and almost turned around, then thought of Arda and made himself go on. It felt wrong though. Weak. When one day he stood before the Maker-Devourer's cauldron and faced the challenge *Did you live your life well?* what could he say? Yes, I did, except for the day when I turned my back on a friend.

But I have a wife who needs a husband. Children who need a father. And one man against a castle? Even the Screambreaker didn't try it and he had a whole army. Yet it still seemed wrong to simply leave. It was enough to make any man weep, a choice like that, but he knew he'd chosen what a Marroc would choose, not a Lhosir. He'd lessened himself.

On the third morning out of Varyxhun a pair of Lhosir warriors on horseback trotted by. They shouted as they came, warning him off the road, and a few minutes later he saw why. A heavy wagon appeared, a great creaking wooden cage of a thing pulled by six plodding oxen. Another Lhosir sat at the front, shouting and cursing at the beasts. In the back a dozen men were penned in the cage. Gallow stood off the road to watch them pass. The captives were mostly Marroc, shivering and freezing in nothing but rags despite the biting wind and huddled all together, but in their midst he saw another face, darker than the rest. Unmistakable. An Aulian.

'Oribas!' The Aulian looked up as the wagon drove on.

Another Lhosir rider came past, bringing up the rear. He stared at Gallow for a moment, eyes lingering on the furs obscuring Gallow's clean chin before shifting deeper into the trees and snow along the roadside. His head kept darting this way and that as though he was looking for something. Gallow ran after him, caught up and trotted alongside him. 'What chance for a brother from across the sea to take a ride on your wagon?'

'You're better off walking,' snapped the soldier. 'And if you have deeds yet undone, get off the road well before the sun sets.'

'Why's that then?'

The soldier looked at him as though he was mad. 'New to the valley, brother? Marroc, that's why.' That was what he was looking for. Marroc with bows, hiding in the trees.

'These prisoners – where are you taking them?'

'If you don't already know then it's none of your business.' The soldier stared hard at Gallow for a moment then curled his lip and went back to eyeing the trees. Gallow let him go, but as the wagon and its riders pulled away, he picked up his pace and kept it in sight. Oribas! It was as though the Maker-Devourer had heard him weep and had given him a second chance. No Lhosir could ignore a sign like that.

He tried to think. The Lhosir would want a place with stone walls and a good strong door. Witches' Reach was the obvious, yet in the middle of the afternoon the wagon turned off the Varyxhun Road and onto a track that was almost too narrow for it to pass, winding among the black bones of trees beside one of the thousand nameless freezing streams that ran off the mountains to join the Isset. Out of sight of the road, it stopped. The three Lhosir riders clustered with the wagon driver around the cage. The driver opened it, poking the prisoners out into the snow while the riders stayed mounted, eyes scanning the slopes for danger. They were nervous, all of them. The prisoners huddled together, backs against the wind until the riders waved their spears and herded them further up the track. The driver stayed where he was. He unharnessed his animals, whacking them with a stick to get them to move. Gallow watched a while longer as the soldiers hurried the shivering Marroc away up the track. The driver was turning his cart. Gallow racked his memory. There was nothing up here, nothing he could remember, only some caves, not even a village.

He stepped out of his hiding place and walked briskly along the track. The wagon driver was swearing at his animals so hard that he didn't even look up until Gallow spoke. 'Why not turn the wagon round on the road?'

The driver jumped almost a foot up into the air. He had a knife in his hand in a flash. Then he looked Gallow up and down and saw he was Lhosir and relaxed a little. 'Maker-Devourer! A brother should know better than to creep up on a man!' He frowned. 'What's a brother doing up here? This track doesn't go anywhere.' He didn't put his knife away.

Gallow shrugged. 'Hard place to turn a wagon this size. Want some help?'

The Lhosir stared. Gallow's furs were wrapped across his face, hiding his chin. Finally the driver put away his knife. 'That would be much appreciated.'

'But why not turn the wagon back on the road?'

The driver glanced up the track. The riders were almost out of sight. 'Last time we did that, three of the sheep collapsed before we even got this far. It's better if they can walk at least to the caves. I mean it's all the same in the end, but having to pick them up and drag them all that way ...' He shook his head as he finally got all but two of the oxen separated from the wagon. 'Let's get this turned then. If you want to help, push on that side there.'

'Where you taking them?' Gallow asked, careful not to let his fur slip.

'Devil's Caves.'

Yes, that was the name, remembered from more than a decade past. 'And what do all those filthy Marroc do up there that's better than hanging from a gibbet?'

The driver laughed. 'Well ...' He grinned and drew a thumb across his throat. 'Same thing, really. Just without ...' He frowned, sudden caution in his eye as though he'd seen a thundercloud slide across Gallow's face. 'Name's Fraggas. I don't recognise you, brother, and I know most of our kin who travel these roads.' His hand was slipping to his knife again.

'I think you've heard of me though.' Gallow let the fur slide off his chin. 'Gallow. Gallow Foxbeard.'

Fraggas the carter had just enough time for his grin to turn sour at the edges before the end of Gallow's staff hit him in the face and knocked him flat in the snow. 'You kill them, do you? Where no one sees. Is that it?' He didn't wait for whatever answer might bubble out of the carter's shattered nose along with all the blood but helped himself instead to the knife and the axe from Fraggas's belt. Then he ran up the path, following the trail in the snow. If the caves were close he needed to catch the other Lhosir quickly, before they started cutting throats. Somewhere a god was laughing at him. Fraggas had boots that looked fine and new and were just the right size, but Gallow had no time.

15

THE ICE CAGE

He ran hard, scrambling up past cascades and waterfalls until the track levelled again in a snowy ravine whose walls rose fast and grew quickly steep. The Lhosir soldiers saw him just as he caught sight of the caves where they were heading. The Devil's Caves, marked by piles of stones and bones. One of the riders turned and charged. Gallow lifted his walking staff as though it was a javelot, hurled it and threw himself into the snow, rolling under the rider's thrust. The staff caught the Lhosir in the face, knocking him backwards. Gallow didn't wait to see whether he fell. He ran on towards the other two who were already cutting down the scattering screaming Marroc. 'Oribas!' He could see the Aulian. Three Marroc were already dead, sprawled crimson streaks across pristine white. The rest were floundering through the snow, running as best they could with their hands tied behind their backs.

Oribas threw himself down beside one of the dead Marroc. The two remaining Lhosir riders split. One skewered the nearest Marroc while the other turned his spear at Gallow and charged. Gallow twisted away from the thrust. He grabbed the shaft of the spear and levered the point down into the snow and the earth beneath until it jammed against something solid and wrenched out of the rider's hand. As he passed, Gallow snapped around and hurled the spear with every ounce of his strength into the man's back. It caught the Lhosir between the shoulders. He arched and fell off his horse, howling. Gallow ran at him before he could get up, but now the first rider was coming back, his face smeared with blood from Gallow's staff and he still had his spear. The second was getting to his feet, swearing a storm and trying to shake the spear loose from his back where it was caught in his furs. He held himself crookedly. The spear might not have pierced his mail but it hadn't been wasted.

'*Nioingr!*' The first Lhosir spurred his horse at Gallow. Gallow watched the tip of his spear, looking to see which way to dive, but at the last minute the Lhosir's eyes flicked away from him to something further up the valley and he veered away. The second Lhosir had dislodged the spear and now lurched at Gallow, axe in hand. He held his shield awkwardly, his arm pressed in against his body as though he couldn't lift it any further. His face was strained with pain. With a shield of his own, Gallow would have laughed at him. As it was, he backed away.

The third rider hurtled past, cantering down the valley after the first. Something flickered through the air after them. He jerked in the saddle but kept riding.

'Give me your name,' hissed the Lhosir with the axe.

'Gallow,' said Gallow. 'Truesword to some, Foxbeard to others.'

'Truesword.' The Lhosir nodded. 'I heard the Screambreaker gave you that name. I was at Andhun when he fell. I saw you there. I know your deeds both of that day and the day that followed. Not so true to our king, were you? Nothing but a Marroc-loving *nioingr* now. Pity. It would have been a fine thing to die by the hand of the old Truesword. Why did you do it?'

Gallow backed further away. 'Give me your name, brother of the sea. I'll speak you out after I kill you.' But the Lhosir didn't get a chance. As he opened his mouth, an arrow took him in the throat. Gallow threw himself flat and looked towards the mouth of the cave. Two men with bows were coming slowly towards him, arrows nocked, strings partly drawn. If he ran they'd both get a shot before he could reach any cover. His mail and his furs would probably be enough to keep out an arrow, but then there was Oribas.

A third archer was moving among the Marroc prisoners, calling back the ones who were still running and cutting loose each man as they reached him. Gallow scrabbled up to the dying Lhosir. The Lhosir's mouth moved but the only sound to come out was a choking cough as blood poured out into the snow. Gallow pulled at the Lhosir's shield. 'Maker-Devourer, I don't know this man but he faced me in battle and he fought well and he did not run. There is bravery here. I offer him to you for your cauldron.' He took the Lhosir's hand and pressed the dying fingers tightly around his sword. The soldier's eyes held his. *Thank you*, they said, then rolled back and he was gone. Gallow gave the spirit a moment to separate from the flesh, then took the man's shield off his arm and the sword out of his hand and rose to a crouch to face the archers. They'd stopped, thirty paces short, arrows at the ready.

'I don't care who you are,' he said. Behind the shield all they could see of him was his face. 'The Aulian prisoner is my friend and I'll take him. The rest is none of my business.'

One of the archers lowered her bow, but it was only when she spoke that Gallow recognised her. Achista! He knew her voice. 'What were you doing to that forkbeard?'

'I was speaking him out, Achista. It's our custom. He was brave. He didn't run.'

'But you should. If you had any sense.'

The other Marroc swore. 'He knows your *name*?'

Achista laughed. 'This is the one who helped me escape the iron devil. The Foxbeard.'

Gallow turned back to the dead Lhosir and unbuckled the man's belt. He eased it out then rose and slipped it on under his furs. Next he started on the boots. They weren't as nice as the wagon driver's but they looked good enough and were certainly better than his own. 'I don't have any business with you, Marroc. I came for the Aulian and now we'll leave with no blood spilt between us. You can have this one's mail and his helm. I'll have his furs.' Oribas would need them. The Aulian hadn't even seen what snow was until they'd reached the edge of the mountains. 'You won't see us in Varyxhun again.'

'You're not going anywhere,' said the other archer.

Gallow finished stripping the boots off the dead man. They were tight but they'd do. He slipped the shield back onto his arm and picked the sword out of the snow and turned back to face the Marroc with their bows. 'If you were going to shoot me then you should have done it when I had my back to you. I have mail under these furs. Your aim had best be sharp, because if you don't take me down with the first arrow then you'll not get another.'

'Achista!'

One of the prisoners was running towards her, another trotting less happily in his wake. Achista turned and her voice changed, suddenly filled with delight. 'Addic! You're alive! Thank Diaran! You stupid clod! And Jonnic! How did you let them catch you?' Gallow squinted at them. The first was the Marroc from the Aulian Way.

The Marroc slowed and stared at Gallow and his eyes widened. 'You? Has Modris sent you to be my guardian?'

Achista's eyes flicked over to Oribas and lingered just a moment longer than they needed to. They moved back to Gallow. 'Addic, what do we do with him?'

The other Marroc, the one who'd come up behind Addic, snarled, 'He's a forkbeard!'

'Jonnic, I wasn't asking you!'

Gallow didn't move. 'Among my people I'm a traitor with no name or honour. I will go. Let that be enough.'

The Marroc Jonnic spat, shivering in his rags. 'Addic, Cithjan sent us both up here to be killed in the caves where he thinks no one will know. I say we put the forkbeard there.'

Addic was shivering too. No surprise, since the Marroc prisoners were wearing little more than shirts or tunics and half were barefoot in the snow. Gallow reached carefully back, never taking his eyes off the archer, and tossed him the furs from the dead soldier. 'No point saving your life just to let Father Winter have you.'

'No, Jonnic. Let him go.'

'He'll go and—'

Addic put a hand on the other Marroc's shoulder. 'It doesn't matter. A life for a life.' He let go, picked up the furs and nodded to Gallow. 'Debt paid, forkbeard. You can go.'

The archer behind Achista growled and bared his teeth as he lowered his bow. Gallow ignored all four of them. He strode and then ran towards Oribas, loosening his furs as he went. 'Aulian!'

Oribas was shivering like a leaf in the wind. Gallow threw him his furs and the Aulian dived into them. Gallow grabbed him by the shoulders and shook him. 'The Lhosir said they'd thrown you into the river! I saw your bag! How by the Maker-Devourer's beard did you end up here?'

Oribas's teeth were chattering. 'Well, they did throw me over the edge but not quite into the river. And after that, by way of the Marroc man whose life you saved and then a shadewalker and a devil in iron. Not to mention the coldest wind that has ever scoured this cursed earth. I tell you, Gallow, I might just be a simple man from the desert but I cannot see what woman in any land could be worth living in this when you could have the warmth of the sun on your skin.' He looked up at the sky, his eyes poking out from Gallow's furs. '*Is* that even the sun, or is it some feeble candle dropped by one of the gods as he passed in his chariot of clouds?'

'Cheer up, desert man. How many times have you been thirsty in my land, eh?'

'Do not speak too soon, Gallow – I might yet die of thirst because my jaw is frozen shut!' Oribas stepped back from Gallow and punched him on the shoulder. 'I thought you were dead, my friend.' His smiled faded. 'Like your friend in iron.'

'They were going to hang me but they found out about the sword. They took me with them to look for it and I escaped. I'm sorry, Oribas. I thought *you* were dead, and so I led them to you. Did they find it?' Oribas nodded. Not that it mattered to Gallow. Let Medrin have the Comforter.

He looked down the valley. The two Lhosir riders who'd fled were long out of sight. It would take more than a full day for them to get back to Varyxhun but Witches' Reach was closer. Behind him the Marroc were arguing among themselves. 'We can't stay here, Oribas.'

Oribas snorted. 'Gallow, I can't even feel my feet. I need a warm fire and some boots. And some clothes. And possibly to live in a different country. One that doesn't freeze my lungs with every breath.'

The Marroc were moving into the shelter of the caves now. Two of them walked off towards the trees, carrying axes. While Gallow watched, Addic came over. He was shivering and his face was blue with cold. 'I owed you my life, forkbeard, and now

I've paid it back. I'd like to let you go, but ...' He shook his head. 'You're a forkbeard. The others are afraid you'll lead your kin back here. We can't leave before the morning – the cold will kill us. Jonnic and Krasic will be back with what we need by then, and you go your way while we go ours. No blood. Will you share our fire in peace, forkbeard? Do I have your word?'

Gallow looked at Oribas. The Aulian was still weak from their crossing of the mountains, never mind everything since. He nodded. 'You have my word, Marroc.'

Addic turned to Oribas. 'Oribas of Aulia. We killed a shade-walker together. I won't easily forget that. You too are welcome to join our fire.' He looked back at Gallow. 'And you, forkbeard. I'll not call you an enemy but others might. I'd ask you leave your sword and axe aside.' A frown crossed his face. 'Why did you do it, forkbeard?'

'Do what?'

'On the road when the other forkbeards ...' He sighed and smiled. 'On the road. Why didn't you just let the Lhosir have me and walk on by?'

Gallow frowned as though the answer was obvious. 'Because when the strong do nothing, the wicked prevail.'

Addic nodded. 'Come on then. Even if they ride straight for Witches' Reach, no one's going to come looking for us until morning. We'll be long gone before anyone gets this far up the road.'

16

FRAGGAS THE CARTER

Fraggas didn't stay with his cart to see what happened after the *nioingr* smashed his face. He counted himself lucky to be alive and ran, leaving it turned half across the track and four of his animals wandering free. A Lhosir warrior wasn't supposed to run from anything but there were plenty enough Lhosir who did anyway, and even some who called themselves warriors. Maybe it was breathing all this Marroc air but, truth was, Fraggas had never been much of one for fighting.

It didn't help that he wasn't even back at the Varyxhun Road before two of the soldiers who'd been his escort came riding past, both at a gallop like the Maker-Devourer was nipping at their arses. They didn't stop, didn't even slow down, and so he ran as fast as he could until he reached the road and then wondered which way to go. He had maybe three hours of sun left before it got dark, three hours to get himself to some shelter, and it suddenly dawned on him that he was a Lhosir, alone, unarmed and on foot in country filled with hostile Marroc. The Marroc farms along the road were friendly enough places to their own kind, always ready to offer up a piece of floor and share their fire, but not to a forkbeard, and Fraggas was used to arriving at them with armed men at his back. The soldiers who'd come with him had been jumpy as rabbits from the moment they'd left Varyxhun. He'd heard their talk. It was getting worse. Marroc bandits on the roads, shooting Lhosir with their hunting bows and then vanishing into the woods. If you came away from Varyxhun then you came in numbers, with mail, helm and shield and preferably a horse, and Fraggas had none of those things.

He stood at the end of the track up to the Devil's Caves,

wondering which way to go. Back towards Varyxhun meant slipping into a farmer's barn for the night and hoping not to be seen, but maybe there was some chance of meeting Lhosir coming the other way. Heading on towards the Aulian Bridge meant walking on after nightfall. He wouldn't get to Witches' Reach until long after dark but there was a garrison there, a few dozen men who kept watch on the bridge for Marroc robbers and highwaymen, and for the Vathen too. The soldiers on their horses would have gone that way. Maybe they'd send men back for him?

So he hurried down the road towards Witches' Reach, walking as briskly as he could. His furs would keep him warm enough in the day, but not once the night started to bite. He'd seen too many men out here lose their fingers and even their feet. Marroc mostly – maybe half the prisoners he'd carried to the Devil's Caves were losing pieces to frost by the time he got them there – and he had no intention of following their example. Sign of the times it was, that Cithjan sent Marroc off to be killed in secret. They hadn't had any of this last winter. It had been gibbets then, lining the road outside Varyxhun, but instead of breaking the Marroc it only seemed to make things worse. The valley men had never taken well to being ruled by a forkbeard and more and more Marroc kept coming over the bridge from other places, every man with an axe to grind, men who'd lost a friend or a son – and that was if they didn't go into the Crackmarsh to pledge themselves to Valaric the Mournful, although Fraggas quietly thought the Marroc of the Crackmarsh had their hand in the troubles of the valley too.

Yes, Varyxhun had become a magnet for all the resentment of the Marroc. The whole valley simmered like an angry pot. When you travelled the road you saw these things. You saw who came and who went. You heard it in the taverns among the other carters, the snips of conversation from tables on the other side of the room, and you saw the glances and the murderous anger, more and more of it. He'd heard the soldiers talking. There were men dying on the road every other day. They were bewildered by the Marroc. Across the sea a man had something he wanted to say then he said it, and if that meant a fight then that's what there was. He didn't say it with an arrow shot from the shadows and then vanish into the mountains. More and more the older Lhosir were talking of home and going back to their farms. None of them much understood why Medrin Sixfingers wanted to be king over all the Marroc. Even Fraggas couldn't see the point to it.

He never would either, because as he was wondering that, a cart came struggling through the muddy snow the other way, a creaking farm cart with three Marroc men sitting on the back who saw a forkbeard walking in a hurry on his own and saw too that the road was empty. As Fraggas passed them, they jumped off and pulled him down and gave him the good stabbing they thought every forkbeard deserved. They took his furs and helped themselves to his unexpectedly nice boots and rolled him into the snow at the side of the road and drove on, pleased at what they'd done.

Later, the same farmers passed the track up to the Devil's Caves without much interest, although everyone from these parts knew what the forkbeards did up there. They stopped at another farm as twilight fell and exchanged greetings with the men who lived there. They all knew each other, at least a little, and as a payment for their food and shelter they gave the furs they'd taken from Fraggas. Good warm forkbeard furs, if a little bloody, but blood could be brushed out once it was dry. Their hosts wanted the boots too but the farmer's son who'd put them on was less than keen because they were good and warm, and so he kept them and left not long after the sun rose.

The same boots meant they were dead an hour later, skewered by twenty Lhosir horsemen coming the other way and led by the iron devil of the castle. Fate had it that one of Beyard's forkbeards knew Fraggas well enough to know his fancy boots. As the last Marroc slowly died, Beyard leaned over him and asked him where he'd found them, and then thought it strange that a carter who was supposed to be on his way back from the Devil's Caves should have been alone on the Varyxhun Road, on foot and hurrying to the Aulian Bridge instead of on his cart back to Varyxhun with his escort of soldiers riding beside him. He thought about this and then changed his plan and followed the track towards the caves. He had the red sword, Solace, the Comforter, hanging at his hip, and wondered if he might soon be using it.

17

SPIRES OF STONE

The Marroc looked at Gallow with grim dislike. He couldn't blame them. Many of their kin had died on the end of his spear and he saw in their eyes how these ones hated him for that. But he told them about the wars when they asked and he spared nothing, and then he talked of the coming of the Vathen and how he'd tried to save Andhun from Medrin Twelvefingers, how he'd fought him in the Marroc duke's own rooms and cut off his hand and made him into Medrin Sixfingers instead, and how afterwards he'd fled the city before the Vathan horde. Their faces changed at that. Gallow the Foxbeard, the *nioingr*, hated among the forkbeards, hunted for years. Several of them had heard of him, but nothing good. The forkbeards had turned Varyxhun on its head searching for him. They knew his family was somewhere hereabouts but they didn't know names and so they'd asked and searched and they hadn't much liked it when they hadn't found what they were looking for.

Gallow lapsed into silence as he listened to the Marroc talk. Beyard. The Fateguard had the snip of Arda's hair he'd carried all this time. He had her scent. The Edge of Sorrows alone wouldn't be enough for Medrin. He had to get to her first, before Sixfingers. Before Beyard, if he could.

He left the Marroc to their fire and wandered further into the caves, carrying a brand with him to light the way. The back of the cave, wide and flat-bottomed as though it had once been a river, rose into the mountainside. It wound steadily upwards for several minutes, a good wide passage, and then led him to a stone balcony over a vast amphitheatre, too large for the light of his brand to even touch the other side. Shadowy columns rose from the floor to the roof. Dim spikes of rock grew upward, and when he followed them he saw that more hung like icicles, dripping out of the darkness above, hundreds of them. When he held up his brand and peered across he still couldn't make out the other side but his flame flickered. He felt cold fresh air, just a wisp of it blowing over his face.

Then he looked down. A few feet below him lay a mound of bodies. He'd seen piles like this after battles when the dead were heaped together to be burned. There must have been a hundred of them. They hadn't rotted and there was no smell. They were frozen.

He went back, and there must have been something about the look on his face because the Marroc stopped their chattering and stared, and then Achista snatched a brand of her own and ran back to see, and Oribas and Addic too. Gallow kept his silence.

'Bastards.' Achista's face was pinched when she came back.

Addic looked at Gallow and shook his head. 'It was your kind that did this,' he said. 'Remember that.'

'Surely they were guilty of some crime?' said Oribas.

'The crime of being a Marroc!' snapped Addic.

'No, no!' Oribas raised his hands and shook his head the way he always did when he was about to explain to someone why they were wrong using arguments forged from unshakeable calm and rational logic, and which more often than not ended with him being dumped on his backside.

'Yes.' Gallow stopped him with a glance. There was no place here for a scholar's debate. 'Even Medrin never killed without a reason, but whatever that reason was makes no difference. When a man is put to death then his passing should be seen. It should be heard. Men might speak against him and others might speak for him. No matter the guilt, a death should carry a weight. A significance. My brothers of the sea would never treat one of their own like this, not even one they splayed apart and hung as the bloody raven of a *nioingr*. What they've done here is for animals, Oribas, not for men.' He glowered at the fire. 'Medrin. It wasn't like this before Medrin.'

No one spoke. Gradually the Marroc settled to sleep, but as Gallow closed his eyes, Achista crouched beside him. She hissed in his ear, 'It wasn't King Sixfingers, forkbeard. It was your precious Widowmaker. He was the one who started this.'

At dawn they rekindled the fire at the mouth of the cave and sat around it in glum silence, waiting for Jonnic and Krasic to come back with furs and boots and food for all of them. When two men leading a donkey came through the snow at the end of the ravine, the Marroc cried out and waved their hands. Two of the prisoners even ran out into the snow. Addic stood and stared and frowned. Achista too. The hairs on Gallow's neck prickled.

The first Marroc reached the newcomers and the men leading the donkey drew swords from under the furs and ran them through. Shields followed and then they charged. Addic snarled and took up the axe from the Lhosir Gallow had killed the day before. Achista strung her bow.

'Wait!' Gallow gripped his sword. 'There are more of them. There must be.' And a moment later they saw he was right. More Lhosir on horseback came over the rise, riding fast towards the caves, squashing into the mouth of the ravine. There must have been a score of them, more perhaps, all armed, and lumbering at the back on a great black horse came a man in iron. Beyard. And though for the Marroc to stand and fight was sure death, the sight gave Gallow a strange surge of hope, for if Beyard was here then he wasn't somewhere else and he hadn't gone hunting for Arda, not yet, and there was a chance to stop him or for Gallow to die and make his hunting pointless.

Achista let fly an arrow. It struck one of the Lhosir shields. Addic clenched his fists. 'I won't lie down and die! Every one of them we kill is a victory.'

He looked ready to charge out into the snow in his rags but Achista stilled him. 'There's a way through the caves, Addi.' Addic turned and stared at her as Gallow thought of the wisp of wind he'd felt back where the bodies of the murdered Marroc lay. 'Krasic led us though. That's how we were waiting for the forkbeards inside.'

'They'll follow us.'

There wasn't much to be done about that, but at least through the caves the Lhosir would be on foot and not on horseback. 'You lead,' said Gallow. 'I'll hold the rear.'

'You?' Jonnic snarled. 'And how do we know you won't turn your coat to save your skin?'

Gallow bared his teeth. 'Because I took King Medrin's hand off his arm, Marroc. What forgiveness do you imagine there could be for that? Besides, if I mean to turn against you, would you rather have me in your midst?' He pushed Oribas deeper into the cave. The Lhosir at the front were getting close and the Marroc were taking too long to get going. 'Go, Aulian. Get away.' He pushed Achista too. 'Dither and they'll be on us.'

He drew his sword and wished he had a spear, but at least he had a shield again and the Lhosir were in their winter furs, which would make them slow and clumsy. The Marroc ran into the depths of the caves, grabbing burning sticks from the fire to light their way. Gallow stamped out what they left – no reason for the Lhosir to see where they were going. And then the first two were at the mouth of the cave with the others on their horses only a moment behind. Gallow kicked the embers into their faces and ran at them. He brought his sword down on one man's helm, dazing him, and barged the other with his shield, staggering him so he tripped and fell and dropped his spear. Beyard and the rest of the Lhosir were almost on him now. No time to finish either of these then, but he took the dropped spear. If the caves grew narrow then a spear might serve better than a sword.

'Foxbeard! *Nioingr!*' Beyard dismounted outside the cave. The rest of the Lhosir paused as Gallow backed away.

'That's three, Beyard,' Gallow shouted back. 'You have to fight me now.'

'I know that, old friend. So let's be at it.' The Fateguard drew a long dark sword, too long to be either a Lhosir or a Marroc blade, and Gallow knew it at once. Solace. 'First blood drawn, shall we have? Or to the death? Make it easy for yourself. Face me here and be done with it. Sixfingers will have to settle for gloating over your head and I'll have no reason to go hunting for those who share your blood.'

Gallow almost threw the spear; but even if Beyard wasn't quick enough to dodge, the point would never pass through all that iron. 'Why don't you call me by name, Beyard? Have you forgotten it?

We'll have our reckoning but I'll be the one to choose the ground for it. That's my right and it'll not be here.' He turned and bolted into the cave, following his memory of the twists and turns of the tunnel until it spilled him out into the great underground cathedral again. He had no light to see by but across the darkness torches burned, bobbing up and down, the Marroc finding their way to the other side. The closest were a full spear's throw ahead of him. Maker-Devourer but the place was huge!

And dark, but he'd seen before that a ledge ran down from the balcony and that it was a twenty-foot drop to the floor below. And he'd seen where the Marroc bodies lay piled. He jumped into the blackness, landing on their frozen limbs and sliding down among them, then fumbled blindly towards the flickering of the torches, hands out in front of him feeling for the pillars and spires of stone, feet groping warily for pits and chasms. He couldn't see his hand in front of his face, nothing but the distant torches, and he hadn't gone far at all when the Marroc ahead started to climb some slope he couldn't see while the Lhosir reached the balcony behind him. He didn't see them but he heard, heard one of them pitch over the edge among the murdered Marroc and shout and curse his luck. The thought came to him then that a man could hide in this place. Simply slip to one side and let the Lhosir pass after the Marroc and none of them would ever know until they came out the other end. He could go back, take their horses and whatever else he fancied and vanish on his way to Middislet. Be there before Beyard could possibly catch him. He turned the thought over in his head without stopping, then tossed it aside. Oribas would probably tell him he should do it, and Arda surely would, but he'd given these Marroc his word. Besides, there was Beyard. He was Fateguard and not so easily fooled.

He felt the floor of the cathedral rise beneath his feet as he crept on. The Marroc lights were almost gone, all that was left of them a soft glow shining out of some passage high in the wall of the cave. The Lhosir behind him had torches of their own now. They were coming, jumping down from the balcony and running through the stone spires. They were gaining. With his own light to guide him, a man could run faster.

He slowed. Let Beyard keep his sword. Let the Lhosir and Marroc kill each other without him. Three years wasted. Three years and he hadn't seen his sons, and even a Fateguard's senses weren't perfect, and he'd still get back to their horses before Beyard knew for sure what he'd done.

'Gallow?' A hiss came from one of the spires as he passed.

'Oribas?'

An arm from the shadows grabbed his own, pulling him. 'The others wouldn't wait for you. I'm sorry.'

'I told you to run!' But now they could both stay! They could hide, the two of them, and yet he let the Aulian lead him on, not towards the fading orange glow further along the wall but in and out of spires of stone. There was some sort of path here, one that Gallow would never have found on his own in the dark. It twisted and turned and then they were at the brink of some depthless fissure, invisible in the blackness but Gallow could feel the space at his feet. Oribas led him on to where one of the stone columns had snapped and fallen. Tucked behind it was a narrow bridge, little more than a thick branch laid across the void. Oribas crawled across. 'It was easier with a torch.'

It would be a fine place to hold, a little voice said – one man against many for a time. He might kill a good few before they took him down. Or he still might hide as he'd planned and let Beyard and his Lhosir pass. But Oribas was leading him on, hurrying him, no thought of anything except to follow the Marroc, and so Gallow followed too, and the moment when outcomes might have been different was gone. He knew what drove Oribas on. When Achista had looked at the Aulian with that one lingering glance, it had landed like a perfect snowflake, and Oribas had caught it, impossible to resist, and of everything that the world took and gave, here was a thing that Gallow's heart understood without question.

Back across the cavern the dancing lights of Beyard's Lhosir were getting closer.

18

THE WIZARD OF THE MOUNTAINSIDE

A chista waited at the mouth of the passage. She had a bow. She could hold the forkbeards up and keep them at bay and maybe send one or two of them back to their uncaring god; and when she spoke her thinking aloud, she almost believed it, almost believed that she hadn't stayed simply because of the Aulian wizard.

He killed a shadewalker. Addic spoke of it with awe and it was nothing short of magic. The Aulian had caught her staring at him too, and he'd smiled and she'd scowled and looked away, but she couldn't pretend that her heart hadn't been beating faster, nor now as she waited watching the torches of the Lhosir dip and bob their way across the floor of the cavern. Her own light was guiding them, but it was also guiding the Aulian and his forkbeard friend.

She hurried them past when they finally reached her, pressing her torch into their hands while she waited on, alone and in the dark. She had her bow trained on the spot where the forkbeards would cross the fissure. As they reached it she let fly, her aim guided by the flame of their brands. The first arrow must have missed but she heard the forkbeards call out. The second drew a yell of pain and the third a flurry of shouts and movement. Some of the forkbeards dropped their torches. She'd slowed them, daring them to come onward in the face of a Marroc with a bow, and that, for now, was enough. She turned and crept away, fingers and toes feeling along the tunnel. Around the first bend she saw a glow of orange light. She'd asked him not to, but the Aulian had been waiting for her.

'It seemed only polite to return the favour.' He smiled and her heart jumped. The forkbeard Gallow muttered something

428

in his surly way and took off ahead, running over the stone with the torch held in front of him while she and Oribas followed, eyes down, careful not to look at the brightness of the flame but only at where each foot would fall; and after a time that felt like an age, with their torch burned almost down to a stub, the walls of the caves gleamed daylight white instead of fiery yellow and they were at the end, out among snow-covered crags and jagged lumps of black stone.

Below them the mountain sloped steeply down and disappeared over the edge of yet another ravine. The Marroc ahead had already cut a path across the pristine deep snow to where lumps of stone broke through the white once more. They'd gouged a great furrow, and now they were picking their way down among snow-drenched outcrops, descending with laborious care towards the edge of the precipice. Achista watched Oribas. She pointed and he nodded as he saw the bridge of three long ropes that spanned the ravine to another precarious path on the other side. As he started to follow she put a hand on his shoulder. 'Tread lightly, Aulian. The snow here is unstable.' She pointed to where a swathe had already come loose lower down the slope, sliding off the mountain to reveal ice and the rock beneath. Oribas took a step and almost fell as the snow swallowed him. He reached out to catch himself. His hand caught her arm and her hand caught his. She held it fast.

'Thank you.' He smiled again and she thought his smile might have been the kindest she'd ever seen. Simple and honest. None of the bitterness that festered among all the Marroc men she knew. 'I've seen this in sand,' he said. 'Sometimes it makes a crust. If you disturb it, it will give way beneath as you walk and the whole slope will slide.' He looked down thoughtfully. 'And in this case take you over the edge into that ravine. We should each follow the tracks of the others then.' He put a hand on the forkbeard's arm. 'Let Achista go first, Gallow. You, my friend, are far less delicate. You're more likely to upset the balance at work here.'

The forkbeard snorted. 'A desert man lecturing a Lhosir of the Ice Wraiths and a Marroc of the Varyxhun valley on the dangers of sliding snow?'

He let her go first though, and the Aulian was right, even if he *was* from the desert. She followed the trail left by the other Marroc, cutting high across the snowfield instead of down and straight for the bridge. She reached the rocks without the snow shifting under her feet and looked back for the forkbeard and the Aulian. The forkbeard was following, but Oribas had scrambled higher up where the slope was steeper still and the snowfield ended and black gnarls of mountain jutted out from the white. As she watched, he began digging in the snow under the stones as if he was looking for something.

Achista picked her way down to the edge of the ravine. When she reached the bridge Oribas was still up there and now Addic was already on the other side, shouting at them to get across before he cut the ropes. She waited for the forkbeard to catch up.

'What's he doing?'

Gallow stared back in bewilderment. 'Oribas!' The shout was loud enough to shake the snow off the mountain, but if the Aulian heard then he gave no sign of it. Even when the forkbeard bellowed his name louder, all Oribas did was raise and shake his head and turn back to his foraging. He moved from stone to stone, pushing at each and excavating until at last he found one that pleased him. He crouched and began rummaging through the pouches on his belt. The forkbeard shook his head. 'Go across! I'll wait for him. Tell the rest of them to go. I'll stay to cut the bridge.'

Achista tried not to look down at the tumble of boulders beneath her as she walked across the bridge, or at the sprinkling of snow that covered them. She could hear rushing water but she couldn't see it, lost as it was under the ice. Two dozen steps, give or take, to cross the ravine, and for that time everything else fled her thoughts. Just slow steady breaths and slow steady steps, each foot sure on the rope, one after the next. When she reached the other side and looked back the Aulian was on his way down. The forkbeard was still waiting but the others were already off and away along the path that climbed up the other side along the next ridge, all except Addic with his knife. Oribas picked his way through the stones and crossed as she did, slowly and carefully, muttering to himself as he came. He was halfway when the iron devil and the first of the forkbeards finally emerged from the caves. Achista waved at Gallow: 'Forkbeard! They're here.'

Gallow waited for Oribas to reach her and then crossed with sure quick strides, growling forkbeard prayers and oaths. As soon as he was across, Addic began sawing at the ropes. The forkbeard's eyes were wide as though he was about to go into battle and the bulk of him shook with each huge breath.

Oribas put a hand on Addic's arm. 'There's no need for that.' But Addic paid no attention and the forkbeard quickly set to helping too. Across the ravine the iron devil was following the path the Marroc had made. Oribas came to stand beside her. 'Do you see the stone where I stopped? The one I marked with the snow in the sign of your god Modris?'

Achista stared. Yes, she saw it now, the sign. She hadn't before.

'Where I dug out the snow underneath, do you think you could hit it with an arrow?'

She nodded. On the far side of the ravine the other forkbeards were coming out of the cave now. They must have realised they had no chance of reaching the bridge in time but they came anyway, some of them ignoring the Marroc path and cutting down the slope as fast as they dared. Achista watched while Addic and Gallow hacked at the last rope. 'Why?'

Oribas leaned and whispered in her ear. She almost jumped at how close he was. 'Another little Aulian trick, that's why.'

Addic let out a cry of triumph. The last rope snapped and whipped through the air as the end of the bridge fell. The fork-beards out on the snowfield stopped to watch but the iron devil kept on until he was standing on the far side, straight across from them. He saluted. 'Why cut those ropes, old friend? We could have fought in the middle of that bridge. Swaying from side to side over a pitiless drop. They would have written a song to us for that, Foxbeard, whatever the ending.'

Gallow laughed back at him. 'The ending would have been of two forkbeards plunging to their deaths as the Marroc cut the bridge and skipped away whooping in triumph. The Marroc would sing a song about that, right enough, but you'd not hear it across the sea.'

'Your Marroc not as friendly as you thought?'

'More friendly than my friends, old friend.'

Achista drew back her bow. The iron devil cocked his head at her. Oribas whispered in her ear. 'Wait! Wait until they're all close.'

The forkbeards were spreading across the slope now. They'd seen the place where the snow had sheared away and plunged over the edge and understood the danger now. Achista had to remind herself sometimes that the forkbeards came from a place of ice and cold too, that the Varyxhun valley was close to what they knew as home. It was easy to forget, but perhaps that was why so many of them came. She looked at the boulder Oribas had marked. 'What do you mean to do? Knock it over and then hope he doesn't see it before it bowls him into the ravine like an iron skittle?'

The Aulian smiled. 'That would do, wouldn't it? If you could get the iron-skinned one, that would be best. Although I admit I was hoping for somewhat more.'

'But he's not in its path.'

The iron devil drew his sword, the deep red sword that Addic and the Aulian had brought to the farmhouse. He pointed it at Gallow. 'The Marroc tell me it's cursed. I'm beginning to think they're right. Maybe you should keep it, Foxbeard.'

Gallow called back across the ravine, 'The Marroc are right, old friend. If Medrin wants it so badly, let him have it. No good comes of the red blade.'

'Now would be perfect,' murmured Oribas.

Achista took aim and let her arrow fly. The forkbeards out in the snow all cringed behind their shields. The arrow hit the underside of Oribas's boulder but nothing happened. The forkbeards turned to look. One or two started to laugh, but not the iron devil. His head whipped round. He looked up, looked across at the forkbeards all out in the open and roared, '*Get back!*'

'Again.'

She loosed a second arrow. This time there was a flash of light and a whoosh of flame and a loud crack where the arrow struck something Oribas had left behind. A stone the size of a small child tipped and slid and then tumbled, bringing a few others with it, rolling towards the forkbeards out in the open snow. They scattered, scrambling out of the way of the falling boulder, all except the iron devil who stayed absolutely still. Snow tumbled around the boulder's wake. Achista caught a glimpse of something very smug in the Aulian's face and then half of the slope across the ravine began to slip at once. The forkbeards wailed and screamed and down they went, caught in the sliding snow. The ones still close to the mouth of the Devil's Caves and outside the reach of the avalanche watched in helpless horror. For the others there was no hope, nothing anyone could do as a great cloud of powdery snow crashed over the edge of the ravine, enveloping everything in its path, rumbling and roaring, filled with cries that quickly faded as half the forkbeards were swept over the edge. Achista watched the iron devil stagger and fall and then he too was lost in the plume – a moment later a wall of fine ice and snow swept over her, stinging her face, buffeting her hard enough that she stumbled and fell onto her backside. As the cloud slowly sank into the ravine, she picked herself up. The forkbeards left by the cave mouth hurled dire curses. Two lucky ones lay in the jumble of broken snow at the edge of the slide, struggling to their feet, but the iron devil was gone and half a dozen others who'd been closest to him. Vanished. She looked into the ravine but all she could see was a cloud of settling snow. There were no cries or wails or screams. The forkbeards were dead and Oribas was smiling. She couldn't help but take a step away from him. Witchery. There wasn't anything else it could have been.

His smile faded. He frowned and peered into the ravine as though looking for something. Over on the other side of the slope one of the forkbeards was stringing a bow. A thing she could understand. She took aim at him before he could nock an arrow: he saw her and hid behind his shield; Achista shot her own arrow into it to make her point and grabbed Oribas by his arm. 'Come on!'

Gallow was shaking his head. He wasn't smiling at all, although he didn't seem surprised by what Oribas had done. 'The ironskin was my friend once,' he said. 'We were almost brothers.'

Achista pulled at Oribas. 'You had an iron devil for a friend, forkbeard? Well, now he's gone, and good riddance!' She ran after Addic and the other Marroc, dragging Oribas in her wake. The forkbeard with the bow was stringing it again so she stopped and took another shot at him and then at a couple of the others, sending them cowering behind their shields once more.

'Gallow, the ironskin stopped being your friend when they put the mask and crown on him,' said Oribas.

'And what would you know of the Fateguard, Oribas? They never crossed the mountains. What does an Aulian know of those who serve the Eyes of Time?'

'Little enough, my friend.' Oribas shrugged and shook his head and Achista saw the look in his eye. He knew something more, something painful, a burden he was keeping to himself.

'You never killed a man, Oribas.' The forkbeard looked grim. 'In the year we hunted your Rakshasa, you never once even lifted your hand to hurt another. There were times when you could have, times when perhaps you should have, but you never did, not once. The chase was ended, the bridge cut and gone. Why, Oribas? Why do that? Was there truly a need?'

The Aulian looked sombre as they trotted along the path in the snow in the wake of the others. His eyes didn't flicker and his face gave nothing away but Achista slowly realised that she knew the answer.

He'd done it for her.

19

THE BATTLE OF JODDERSLET

Addic sat beside a fire, warming his naked feet. It had taken the rest of the morning for them to reach Jodderslet, the nearest hamlet amid the isolated valleys nestled in the mountains around Varyxhun. He looked at the sky, hoping for clouds that might bring snow to cover their tracks, but the air was clear and the sun was bright and warm. The Aulian might have swept half a dozen of the forkbeards into the ravine but that still left near a dozen of them on the other side of the bridge. They'd find a way across. Half the little hamlets and farmsteads in the high valleys had never even seen a forkbeard before and it would surprise him if there was a single forkbeard who'd ever heard of Jodderslet, but that would change now. The forkbeards would follow. Forkbeards always did.

The other Marroc former prisoners were huddled around him, rubbing their icy skin, trying to get warm. They were hardly fighters. The farmers of Jodderslet milled around, bemused as much as anything else by the sudden arrival of so many strangers. *They* were hardly fighters either and they stared in bewilderment at Oribas. None of them had ever heard of Aulia, never mind seen a man from over the mountains. Half thought he was some sort of monster and made the sign of Modris every time they saw him. But they'd heard of forkbeards, and when Addic said that a band of them would be coming, they were none too happy. They collected whatever might pass for weapons: axes, a few forks, a spear or two and a couple of hunting bows, if you included Achista's. Addic looked around. Not a piece of armour among them. Not a single shield, not one helm, except on the forkbeard Gallow. Between the farmers and the prisoners there were two or three Marroc for every forkbeard they'd left on the mountainside but the forkbeards were soldiers, armed and armoured, while most of these Marroc were ordinary men who'd never fought with anything more than their fists.

'Maybe they won't come,' said one of the farmers, but Addic knew better. When did the forkbeards ever not give chase when a Marroc ran?

He left the farmers and the other Marroc to pick their weapons. Addic supposed they could keep running instead of fighting, but he and the others from the caves had no boots, only rags for clothes and there was nothing but snow out here. They were half frozen and exhausted already. Better to try and take a forkbeard or two with them. He crossed the barn to Gallow. 'And what about you? Will you fight your kinsmen a second time?'

'It's not my fight.' Gallow's face was pinched and bitter. He stood by the door to the barn, staring out into the snow, oblivious to the bustle behind him.

'No.' Addic turned away and then stopped. 'But it wasn't your fight back when you stopped me going over the edge of the Varyxhun Road and into the Isset either. You'd make a difference here.'

'By killing more men who were once my friends?'

'By saving those who might become new ones.'

Gallow stared at him with those ice-blue eyes that jabbed like spears. 'None of you will ever call me friend, Marroc, no matter what I do. There was only ever one of you who looked past where my forked beard should be. It's time I went to find her.'

Addic shook his head. 'When the strong do nothing, the wicked prevail. Your words, forkbeard, not mine.' He left Gallow to his gloom and sought out his sister instead, sitting in a corner of the barn with Oribas. The Aulian was drawing in the dirt with a stick and it took a moment for Addic to understand: he was drawing Jodderslet, a map of it. 'What are you doing?'

'I'm no warrior,' he said, 'but I studied all the great generals of the early empire – Kunessin, Loredan, Cronan and Allectus. I can't say it much interested me but we were obliged to study the history of war as much as we were obliged to study poetry and alchemy.' He poked at the dirt with his stick. 'The enemy will follow our trail. They'll emerge from the trees on the slopes above us. They'll have to cross this open space to reach us. The snow will slow them down. They'll be exposed.'

'And will you bring the mountain down on them again?' asked Addic sourly. The Aulian shook his head. Achista shot her brother a sharp look.

'No. But General Tullinus lost a thousand men crossing a swamp against savages armed with little more than knives and bows. While they're in the open ...'

'We have two bows; the forkbeards will advance behind their shields and we have no time to dig pits or built barricades.' Addic turned away and left them to it and went back to look for Gallow, to ask the forkbeard to at least leave them his sword, but the big man was gone and Addic couldn't find him. After that there didn't seem much to do except sharpen his axe, wait for the forkbeards and warm himself by a fire. Might as well be comfortable before he went out into the snow to die.

Achista watched him. Her brother, whom she loved more than any other man. He thought that by staying here they were all going to die, and he was probably right. She touched Oribas on the back of his hand. 'You should go with your forkbeard friend,' she said, 'before he leaves without you.'

Oribas shook his head. 'Gallow has a reason to go; I have a reason to stay.' Her hand was still touching his. He took it and squeezed it, and since Addic was likely right and they were going to die today, Achista leaned across the Aulian's maps and kissed him.

'For what you did at the ravine.'

Oribas turned away and let her hand go. He looked sad. Ashamed even. 'I feel no pride in that. Gallow is more right than he knows. Until today I'd never killed, neither man nor beast. I've slain monsters and showed others how, and I will show you, as best I can, how to fight the Lhosir when they come. But I'm no soldier and nor do I wish to become one. What I did at the ravine I did for my own reasons. Give me a spear and I'd probably hold the wrong end and stab myself in the foot.'

'You have no reason to be ashamed.' She spat. 'They were

forkbeards! Every forkbeard who died in that ravine is a fork-beard who won't be coming here to spill more Marroc blood.'

Oribas touched his fingertips to her face. 'Victories that last are not won by blood but by words and by forgiveness, Achista.'

'Then find your words, Aulian, and make the Foxbeard stay. Make him fight for us!'

Oribas shook his head. 'The gods sent him to me to defeat the terror that gripped my home. Perhaps they've sent him here to defeat yours now, or perhaps not. But either way we must all choose our own fates.' He leaned over and whispered something in her ear.

One of the farmers brought out a cask of ale. Addic and the other Marroc from the caves drank eagerly, lighting a little fire inside their bellies and talking among themselves of the tiny victories each had scored over the forkbeards before they'd been caught. A purse cut here, a horse stolen, a household made ill with rancid milk, a drunkard felled with a bottle and kicked in the street. None of them had ever killed. None of them had stood face to face with a forkbeard and taken up arms against him, nor even stared down the shaft of an arrow. Those were the men who hung from the gibbets in Varyxhun or lurked like angry shadows in the deep woods and the snow. These men were the ones who might have been branded or whipped or perhaps put to work as slaves back when the lord of Varyxhun had been a Marroc. Now the forkbeards simply got rid of them.

'Forkbeards! They're here!' Addic jumped up and looked for his sister, but she was gone and Oribas too. He ran outside. The forkbeards were coming out of the wood higher up the slope, just as the Aulian had said. The snow there was deep, up past their knees. Deep enough to make them wade and stop them from mounting a charge as they came in among the houses. Addic took a fork. That would do. Close enough to a spear. He stood. 'Face them!' he roared and farmers and prisoners alike came and stood beside him, near thirty men against about a dozen. They were going to die but they'd do it defending their homes and their families. 'Don't fear them!' he cried. 'They're just men! They die like any other. They have their armour and their shields but there's more of us, so grab them and take them down and be in at them with your knives. If you have the courage to stand then you can win!' He almost believed it himself. He looked around for Achista and the other Marroc who had a bow but they were nowhere to be seen. On a roof out of sight if they had any sense, waiting for the forkbeards to get close so they could pick their spots. Make each arrow count.

The forkbeards started down the slope. They walked quickly at first, shields loose by their sides. Then the one at the back pitched over into the snow and the one beside him cried out and turned and they all stopped and looked behind them. Addic counted. Thirteen of them. Twelve if you passed over the one who'd fallen. He didn't look like he was getting up again.

At the top of the slope, out of the trees, two figures emerged holding bows. Addic's heart skipped a beat. Achista! And the forkbeards were between them! Oribas appeared beside him. 'Out in the open, Addic. Exposed. Now they have to wonder how many more of you there might be waiting in the trees.'

'One dead forkbeard hardly makes a difference, Aulian.' The forkbeards were on the move again, coming down the slope more slowly now, their shields raised behind them against the two archers. They clustered together.

'Every battle must have its first man to fall. If only we had some fire.'

The forkbeards came on. Achista and the other archer followed them down, keeping their distance but still shooting arrows now and then, pinning them in their tight circle of shields and keeping their heads down. 'Work in twos and threes,' Addic told the others. 'Pick a forkbeard and pull him down. One of you takes his sword hand and holds it fast, one of you pulls away his shield, the third one goes in with the knife. Brothers together! Fathers and sons! It's like bleeding out a pig. Midwinter was just days ago. You do that?' There were was a murmur among the farmers he took to mean yes. 'Just the same! Best way to think of it.' And they could win, they could! If they held their nerve and didn't mind a few of them dying, the way the forkbeards never seemed to care.

At the bottom of the slope the forkbeards broke their circle and started to run. Another fell to an arrow and then they were close, and Addic felt the Marroc around him waver. 'Don't!' he cried, beginning to despair. 'Don't run! Stand!'

But beside him Oribas turned and fled. 'Don't listen to him. Run after me!' And the Marroc were only too eager as the fork-beards reached the edge of the deep snow and picked up speed. They turned and ran and Addic had no choice but to run with them, and they all fled together among the houses and barns of Jodderslet. The Aulian led the way. He kept glancing back as if to see whether the forkbeards were still there, as if something might have happened to make them change their minds. As if such a thing was possible.

They reached the space in the middle of the hamlet where the farmers let their pigs, their chicken and geese out during the summer. The Marroc scattered. Addic bolted past a house with a howling forkbeard right behind him, only to have a door open almost in his face. A stick holding a pot of steaming water swung out. The forkbeard ducked the stick but not the scalding water that poured over his head. He screamed and slowed, clutching his face. Addic turned. He didn't have much but he had his fork and now he swung it. The forkbeard lurched away, getting his shield up barely in time. A woman came out, still holding the stick with the pot on the end of it. She swung it at the half-blind forkbeard, cracking it across his helm and staggering him again. He stabbed at her wildly and this time Addic caught his arm and the three of them fell down into the snow together. They wrestled, and now the shield and the helm and the mail that were a soldier's friends in war became unwieldy weighty things that kept the forkbeard from rising. All three of them were howling and cursing and screaming in each others' faces. Addic had the forkbeard held down but now he couldn't move and the woman was bashing at the forkbeard with her stick and doing nothing more than making him even angrier than he was. Addic looked up for any other Marroc. Out in the open two forkbeards were fighting a third. It took him a moment to realise the one fighting alone was Gallow.

Another forkbeard ran towards him. Addic stared up help-lessly, but the man staggered and fell with an arrow in the back of his leg. Before he could get up, another Marroc appeared, one of the prisoners. His rags were bloody and he had a pitchfork in his hand. 'Need some help?'

Addic nodded, and grinned because he finally saw. The Aulian had drawn the forkbeards apart. He'd made them scatter and destroyed their invincible wall of shields before it was ever made. And the Marroc were going to win.

20

PARTING WAYS

Gallow watched as the Marroc broke and ran. He felt pity for them because that was what Marroc always did. The Lhosir charged without thought to how many they were and how many stood against them and the Marroc wavered and broke. It was the same every time.

He stood in the centre of the hamlet and watched it happen. The track out of the valley was marked with cairns of stones. If he followed it for long enough, it would take him to the little town of Hrodicslet. Three days in summer on a mule, the Marroc had told him, although they weren't so sure about in winter and on foot because none of them ever left their farms once the snows set in. Hrodicslet was on the far eastern fringe of the Crackmarsh, which meant it was a way out of the mountains without crossing the Aulian Bridge over the Isset. He knew Hrodicslet. Fenaric the carter had gone that way a few times. A week winding through the hills would take him home, but if he crossed the Crackmarsh he could be there in two days as long as the ghuldogs didn't get him.

Yet even though he knew the way, he didn't leave, not yet. He watched Oribas, perhaps his last friend in the world. The Aulian was here because he'd sworn an oath – sworn that if Gallow helped him to kill the Rakshasa then he'd take Gallow to the Aulian Way which crossed the mountains to Varyxhun. And after he kept his oath, he'd still stayed even though Gallow had tried to send him away. *Where shall I go? I have nowhere else to be.* Crossing the mountains had almost killed them both and yet now here he was, holding hands with a Marroc woman. So perhaps it was right that Oribas had come to this land. Perhaps it had always been his fate to find Achista and her people, as it had been Gallow's to wash up on that far southern shore where Oribas had found him; as it had been fate for Beyard to find him and for one friend to be the end of another.

Oribas wouldn't leave her. He'd fight for her in his own way, a thing Gallow understood above anything else. So he stayed as the Lhosir emerged from the wooded hill and smiled at the Marroc archers harrying them from behind, and then the smile faded as he watched the Marroc turn and run and an old bitter sadness welled up inside him. The weight of who he'd become. Always just one more battle before he could go home. He waited for the Lhosir to pour into the space in the middle of the hamlet; and as they did he stepped out from the open barn and roared out his challenge: 'I am Gallow Truesword! The Foxbeard! Fight me if you dare!'

The first Lhosir ran after Marroc prey but the next one slowed long enough to realise Gallow wasn't just another one of their own. Gallow put an end to the question by hurling his spear straight into the Lhosir's face. A spear was fine in a battle line, but up close and spread out like this he much preferred an axe or even his sword. Something short that struck from the side instead of a straight thrust.

'You!' Two more Lhosir were striding towards him. He charged them down, right in the middle of the farmhouses where everyone could see, and swung at the first, hard and fierce. 'All I wanted was to go home!' There was an anger inside him now, growing with every blow. Anger at the Marroc for needing him, for not standing on their own just one time. At the Lhosir for being here where they didn't belong. At Beyard for having once been his friend and at Oribas for killing him. At himself for not letting things be and leaving the Marroc on the Aulian Way to fall to his death. But most of all at fate. Fate had cursed him from the moment he'd picked up the Edge of Sorrows. Fate that had sent storms and pirates and demons and hurled him so far from his home. Fate that had taunted him year after year and pretended to relent only to spit in his eye. Beyard had known him. Other men had seen him. In time Medrin would learn that Gallow Foxbeard was back, the man who'd taken his hand, and then Medrin would turn the world on its head to find him and he wouldn't know one single moment of peace until one of them was dead. Fate.

His axe bit into a shield so hard that the Lhosir almost wrenched it out of his hand. Gallow snarled. Beneath the cliffs of Andhun the Screambreaker had fished him and the red sword out of the sea, and as he'd opened his eyes and coughed and spewed out the water that filled his lungs, the Screambreaker had offered him a choice. The Vathen had shouted and cursed and thrown their spears and shot their arrows, which splashed in the water around the Screambreaker's little boat but never struck true. The Screambreaker hadn't seemed to notice. He'd held out the red sword. 'No use to me. Not where I'm going.' And he'd looked at Gallow hard and then away to the Marroc ships fleeing from burning Andhun and then last to where a single Lhosir ship was setting sail from the shore. 'You didn't think you really got away all those years ago, did you?' His lips had curled and, for perhaps the first time, Gallow had seen the Screambreaker smile. 'But then it's the nature of men like us to fight our fates. I'll let you choose. After all these years I've earned that and so have you. Which way, Truesword? Which way will it be?'

And so Gallow had turned his back on fate, and fate had punished him ever since, for every single day, and now a rage broke inside him, for he could see that there would be no escape; and he screamed at these men in front of him, a cry of rage and anguish enough to make even two Lhosir warriors falter before him; and as they fell back, his axe kissed the face of one and cut the thread of his life; and the other, seeing a thing too terrible to defy, turned and ran; and Gallow stood there alone, quivering, murderous, eyes searching for any who dared stand in his path; and when no one did, he fell to his knees beside the man he'd killed and wept. He tore away the dead Lhosir's furs to be his own and put them on and walked through the bloody mayhem of Marroc falling on forkbeards and forkbeards slaying Marroc. Turned his back on them all and left.

The Marroc gathered slowly in the open space between the barns where Gallow had stood. It was done. The forkbeards were dead and none of the victors could quite believe it. Oribas darted around until he saw that Achista was still alive and her brother Addic too. He stared open-mouthed at the dead. Not that he hadn't seen dead men before – he'd seen far too many – but he'd never been death's architect. Not until today.

'How did you do it?' Addic fell in beside him. 'Because you did. It was you.' And it was.

'You always run. That's what Gallow said.' He saw Addic wince, though he hadn't meant it as anything more than a simple statement of the way things were. 'But I spent a year with him and what I learned was that your Marroc women can be every bit as fierce and terrible as a Lhosir. So I went to them and told them that their men would run, even though they could win this day if they wanted it, and I told them to make their own stand. These are their homes, their lives, their sons and daughters. Why shouldn't they fight? With ropes to trip, and sticks and yes, pots of scalding water, but most of all they shouldn't run and they shouldn't cower, and when their men saw this then they'd turn and stand and fight too. The Lhosir win because they aren't afraid to die, but there aren't so very many of them, and men are men wherever they are born, and all can be brave if they have the will put inside them. So that is what I did.'

'Truly, you're a wizard.' Addic shook his head, full of disbelief, and Oribas understood his wonder because he hadn't really thought it would work either. But the truth was all around them. The Lhosir were dead, and yes, a good few Marroc too, but far fewer than would have died if they'd simply run.

He wondered then whether he might have made a beginning of sorts, whether he might one day look at what he'd done here and know that he'd had a hand in making some consequence he'd never foreseen, and whether it would be for good or for ill. But he didn't have very much time to do anything with that thought before Achista threw her arms around him and hugged him and then hugged Addic too. 'Look,' she said. 'Look what we did! We won!'

Oribas was already looking. 'Yes,' he said, and felt a touch of dread at the joy in her voice.

She looked him in the eye and kissed him. 'Addic is right. You *are* a wizard, Aulian. A magician.'

'No. I …' He shook himself. A dozen Lhosir, that was all. They'd have killed the Marroc too and so he'd saved more lives than had been taken, hadn't he? He gently let Achista go, still uneasy. Gallow. Gallow would know. He'd never met a man with such a sure sense of what was right. But when he looked, Gallow had gone.

21

THE EYES OF TIME

U nder the snow Beyard stared at the past. The Screambreaker was across the sea, basking in his shattering of the Marroc King Tane outside Sithhun. The Crimson Shield of Modris the Protector had been carried to the Temple of Fates in Nardjas and three boys had slipped inside in the dark to steal a glimpse of it before it vanished far into the icy north. But the stealing had not gone well. He remembered the room where the Fateguard had cornered them, the air ripe with fear, shaking at the sharp crack of metal slammed into wood and a door pushed half open. And he was the one who'd turned to the others to ask if they'd stand and take their punishment like men.

Medrin was gone so quickly that Beyard had to blink to remember he'd even been there. Out through a narrow window covered in moon-shadows as sharp as a blade, friends betrayed to a fear that would one day cost him dear. Medrin Twelvefingers, defying his father in those years when that's what all boys did.

Which had left the two of them. Him and Gallow, parading their courage, shouting their defiance, holding their fear deep inside. Metal groaning, wood cracking, splinters flying. The iron-skinned men of the Fateguard were coming and they'd spat in fate's eye. 'My dead grandmother could push harder than that.' 'They'll never catch me!' 'You go!' 'No, you!' 'I'm too fast for them.' They were both wrong. He knew that now, now that his own skin was sheathed in iron too.

He'd been the oldest and so he'd stood his ground the hardest. He remembered Gallow's hesitation. The fear in his moon-caught face. They'd both known they'd never see each other again. Both been so sure of it.

How wrong.

'I will not forget.' They weren't Gallow's words in the end

but his own after Gallow was gone. For the brief moment he stood, before the ironskins smashed through the door and he tried to run and they caught him with ease and took him off to the frost winds of the north, winds birthed by ice wraiths, and abandoned him there. He remembered the wind most of all, a cruel gale that flayed any thought of kindness, that moaned and screamed like the ghosts of the ever-hungry dead and wailed like the widows they left behind as it tore at cliffs that were hard as iron and bitter as juniper.

'I will not forget.' He clung to it. In a wagon of old weathered wood and fat sausage-fingers of rust, pulled by unicorns born burned and blackened and twisted, he held it in his heart and spoke it out, over and over. 'I will not forget.' They weren't alive, those nightmare horses, and when at last they stopped and stamped their feet, no steamy breath came with their snorts and even the snow and the stone shivered at their cold.

The Eyes of Time had been waiting. And then, for a long time, nothing.

In the ravine littered with fallen snow and broken Lhosir, Beyard understood that fate was not done with him yet. His life belonged to it and always had. Inside his case of battered iron something stirred. The Eyes of Time had made him what he was. He'd sworn vows that couldn't be broken, even by death. The Fateguard were cursed men and he knew it, and fate didn't choose to let him go. Metal grated as he moved, the fingers of his sword hand opening and closing, reaching for a blade he no longer held. His eyes opened and saw nothing but darkness, buried in snow. His lungs, which had been still, took a new lurching breath. His muscles creaked and strained, his bones groaned and shifted and the snow heaved and crumbled as he rose. He stood unsteadily amid the wreckage and looked about him. Up and down the ravine at the dead men who had served him. To the bridge that had almost saved him, the tangle of ropes to which he'd clung as others fell around him. Pieces of it lay about him now, broken where they'd snapped under their unwonted burden and pitched him down to the snow and stones below. He stumbled and staggered among them, lost and wondering who he was and where and how he'd been the lucky one and clung to the severed ropes of the bridge and hadn't been smashed like all his kin. The Eyes of Time would know the answer, and perhaps the Aulian who did this, and even, deep down, a part of him knew it too. Knew it and feared it enough to know he never wished to hear it.

He shied away from the thought. The snow fell past him as he clung to the severed bridge and so was there to break his fall. Snow and his iron had saved him. Let it be so.

He began to dig, looking for the sword he'd held as he fell, the red sword of the Weeping God which must one day face the Crimson Shield again and repeat the old story of the Marroc, of Modris the Protector and Diaran the Lifegiver and the Weeping God who must bear so much pain. He pulled it from the snow and stared at its blade and then he sheathed it and stared at the thing held tight in his other iron hand, still safe. An amulet on a chain. A locket. He took off his iron gauntlets and held it in his cold white fingers, opened it and sniffed and then put it away and donned his crown once more and began to walk up the ravine, patiently looking for a way out.

'I will not forget.' His words were soft as the broken snow. They'd sealed their destiny by what they'd done, all of them. The others simply didn't yet know it.

ORIBAS

22

WITCHES' REACH

The tower of Witches' Reach was a crumbling old thing of stone built two hundred years before when the Holy Aulian Empire had been at the height of its power. Traders had found the way across the mountains. A legion of soldiers had crossed in their wake and for a time the Varyxhun valley had been a part of that empire, the furthest the Aulians had ever reached to the north. They brought engineers and architects and felled the mighty pines and built their bridge across the Isset, perhaps planning a great conquest of the plains to the north, but the invasion had never happened and fifty years later the last of them had withdrawn back across the Aulian Way to warmer climes. As well as their great bridge and the impregnable Varyxhun castle, they'd left behind them two watchtowers that looked down on the entrance to the valley from the heights over the bridge: Dragons' Reach on the far side of the river and Witches' Reach on the near. Dragons' Reach was a tumble of broken stone after the mountain beneath it had crumbled in the great Ice Winter sixty years later, but Witches' Reach remained, commanding the road to Varyxhun. The Aulians hadn't known the paths and trails of the high valleys and thought nothing could come into the valley without being seen by the garrison there. The forkbeards apparently thought the same. Cithjan had put a hundred men into the tower at the start of the winter, charged with keeping the Varyxhun Road and the bridge clear of Marroc outlaws, and so far the fifty of them that hadn't ridden off to Boyrhun to kill Marroc over on the other side of the valley instead were doing a fine job of it.

Which was why Oribas was crouched beside Addic halfway up a mountain, squinting at the fortress.

'I want to show you something.' Achista squatted next to him holding what looked like a scrunched-up bedsheet. She flapped it open to reveal a crude picture of a battle hammer daubed from corner to corner. 'The banner of King Tane. When this flies from the top of Witches' Reach, every Marroc crossing the Isset will see it! Varyxhun will rise and turn on the forkbeards!'

Oribas had no idea whether or not she might be right. He'd certainly met a lot of angry Marroc after Jodderslet. He'd also seen the insides of Varyxhun castle and knew that anger wasn't much substitute for mail and steel. 'If you took the tower, it would take two days for word to reach Varyxhun. Another two or three for the Lhosir to come. They'll surround you. I don't see how you can escape once they arrive. Your flag will not fly for long.'

Addic stood behind them. 'While it does, every Marroc and forkbeard leaving the valley will see it. Sixfingers himself will hear of it. We'll make Cithjan look a fool.'

'Men made to look fools can become mightily fierce.'

Achista rolled the flag into a bundle again. 'We can't run away when the forkbeards come! That's the point! We'll hold the tower as long as we can. Up and down the valley Marroc will rise to our standard and tear them down!'

'And if they don't?' Oribas raised an eyebrow.

'They will.' Addic put a hand on his shoulder. 'But if they don't then the forkbeards will kill us. You don't have to come with us when we seize it, Aulian. You'd be most welcome, but this isn't your war.'

Oribas looked to Achista. 'I will come.' He took her hand.

They walked down the mountainside into the saddle below the tower and then away from the gorge of the Isset and into a thick wood of Varyxhun pine. Deep among the colossal trees Addic led the way to a clearing carpeted with dark blue autumn flowers where a camp of some fifty Marroc men waited for them. The Marroc here were grim-faced. Some had mail and helms and shields stolen from the Lhosir. A few had swords. Most had axes and nearly all of them had bows.

'Here's my Marroc army, Aulian.' Addic smiled. 'The first part of it.'

'How will you convince the Lhosir to open their gates?'

'Don't I have a wizard, Aulian?'

'Most of what tricks I had fell into the ravine on the day we first met.'

Addic vanished later that day and he didn't return for several more, but the first part of his plan was soon clear enough. The Marroc in the forest made no effort to hide their presence. They lit fires to keep warm and the smoke climbed up above the trees for the Lhosir in the tower to see. With each day that passed more Marroc arrived. Perhaps only a few, and mostly farmers with nothing but axes or a spear or a fork, but they all had bows and Achista drilled them for hours every day, making them whittle their own arrows and fletch them and shoot them into bales of straw, and for every arrow that missed its target, each archer was forced to make another. It taught them to shoot with care and thought over haste, though Oribas wondered how well that teaching would survive when their targets changed from bales of straw to screaming Lhosir. An armoured man with a shield wasn't as easy to kill with arrows as many archers liked to think.

He'd been in the camp for less than a week when the Lhosir made a sortie out of the tower to see what was happening in the woods. He was on the edge of the treeline when the Marroc lookouts came scurrying down from where they kept their watch. A score of Lhosir soldiers were coming on foot. The Marroc spoke with fearful glee and then raced back to the camp deep inside the trees. Oribas stayed where he was, hunkered down among the shadows and the snow. A man who chose to hide in a place like this and kept still and quiet would never be found unless those searching for him almost trod on him. More Marroc came running by. Oribas watched them rushing back and forth, leaving a confusion of tracks and trails. A few ran back the way they'd come, leaving fresh furrows in the snow. But not all: others picked their way back through their own tracks and crouched down to hide with their bows and their arrows. As long as the Lhosir didn't look too hard, it would seem as though a dozen or so men had fled into the deeper woods.

As the Lhosir came into view, one last Marroc burst from

cover, full of shouted warnings and movement as he fled. Oribas watched the Lhosir break into a run. They were like hunting dogs. They had the scent of a fight and could hardly hold themselves back. They ran in among the trees and Oribas tensed, for the greatest danger was now, and it only took one of the hidden Marroc to lose his nerve and bolt and the trap would fail. None of them did. Oribas waited until the Lhosir were gone, lost to sight but not to sound, then rose and hurried after them. He was the signal. The rest of the Marroc emerged from where they'd lain hidden.

The other part of the ambush belonged to Achista – Oribas wasn't there to see it happen but he knew how it would go: the Lhosir would follow the trail until it stopped at a huge fallen tree that barred their path. Then Marroc would rise from the shadows beyond and throw their spears. Archers on either side would pepper the Lhosir with arrows, and after that it would fall to a confusion of fighting. In the thick forest the Lhosir wouldn't be able to make a shield wall and muster a charge. There would be three or four Marroc for every Lhosir. Achista would repeat the victory of Jodderslet.

That was how it would be, and so when he heard the first shouts go up, the Lhosir roars and battle cries and the Marroc screams, Oribas dropped out of sight into the snow beside the trail. The sounds of the fighting rose to a peak and then petered away into the shouts of wounded Marroc calling for aid and a few furious roars of the last battle-mad Lhosir as they scythed down as many Marroc as they could before they fell. And then finally what he was waiting for: the sound of men running, the last Lhosir following their own trail back, racing out of the trees. *Legs. Shoot them in the legs.* That's what he'd told the bowmen. They'd be soldiers in mail coats, with helms, carrying shields, armour too thick for an arrow to puncture, but they had nothing to protect them below the knees.

They came, two of them, running fast, still with their axes and their shields even in their rout. Oribas willed the Marroc arrows to fly true but the Lhosir were moving fast and were hard to hit. A flurry of shafts zipped across the trail. One of the Lhosir staggered but kept his feet as an arrow hit him in the side and stuck out of his furs. Oribas gripped a rope lying beside him in the snow. He watched the fleeing Lhosir and then jumped up and pulled with all his might and snapped it taut across the trail. It took the legs of the first Lhosir and he sprawled in a flurry of snow. The rope jerked out of Oribas's hands. He staggered forward. The second Lhosir lurched sideways, half tripped over the first and stumbled on. Without thinking Oribas hurled himself, crashing into the last Lhosir's side and knocking him down. They flailed at each other in the snow for a few seconds but the Lhosir had twice the strength and twice the weight of Oribas and threw him off with ease. For a moment Oribas lay floundering on his back like an upturned beetle. The Lhosir pulled himself up. His face was a rictus of fury. He lifted his sword and there was simply nothing Oribas could do about it, no words or clever plans that would make the slightest difference; but before the Lhosir could strike a Marroc arrow hit him in the back, knocking him off balance, and then another Marroc flew out of the trees and bore the Lhosir down, hacking at his face with a knife, and then another and another, and by the time Oribas found his feet, the Lhosir was dead, a crimson pond of blood dripping out of his savaged throat. Oribas stared. Most of the dead he'd seen before had been half ripped to pieces, stinking and rotting and savaged by vultures under the desert sun, so it wasn't the torn flesh and the blood that held him. It was that he'd never seen a man dead at his feet who'd been trying to kill him only a moment ago.

He was still looking at the Lhosir when Achista and the other Marroc came jogging up the trail. Some were dressed in freshly scavenged mail, others carrying new swords and shields. They stripped the man at Oribas's feet with the speed of jackals. Achista pressed a sword into his hand. She was dressed in mail now, a hauberk that was too long for her and far too wide and made her look ridiculous, but it also made him want to take her and hold her long and tight because she was going into battle now and the death he'd seen made him realise that it was all horribly real. Before the day was out, it wouldn't only be Lhosir who were dead.

23

THE DRAGON'S CAVES

The Marroc pushed quickly through the forest and onto the slopes beneath Witches' Reach. Achista didn't lead them towards the saddle between the two mountains; instead she took them across the craggy snowbound slopes, picking a way between them until she reached a crack in the mountainside, a slit of a cave only a few feet wide but as tall as a house. A trickle of water ran out the bottom. Oribas bent to sniff at it and recoiled. Achista laughed. 'Where do you think the cess from the tower ends up?'

Inside the cave, far enough to be out of sight, a handful of wooden brands wrapped in cloth lay beside coils of rope and two small kegs of fish oil. The Marroc broke the seals on one of the kegs and dipped their torches. One of them got a tiny fire going and lit the first, then they lit one from another until every other Marroc had a burning brand. Through the orange flicker of the flames Oribas saw a path worn in the floor of the cave.

'This cave leads up into the tower?' he asked with a wry smile. 'Surely the Lhosir will have barred any such tunnel?'

'You Aulians built this tower.' Her eyes gleamed in the firelight.

'We do like to dig.' That old fascination with reaching down into the earth, to the shades that dwelt there. The last emperor might have dug the furthest, but Aulians had been delving into the soil and rock since before the empire was anything more than a town with grand aspirations.

'When the Aulians left they barred the tunnel with two seals. One was opened a long time ago. No one ever found a way to open the other. The forkbeards think they're safe.'

'But you've found a way?' Her eyes bored into him and he

understood. He shook his head. 'I'm not a wizard, Achista.'

'Addic said you'd know how to open the seals.'

Oribas laughed. 'Even if I did, how long ago were these tunnels closed? How many hundreds of years? Metal rusts, Achista. Stone crumbles. I will try but I very much hope you have another way.'

The passage rose into the heart of the mountain, the crack in the stone petering out into a tunnel, roughly hewn and so narrow that even Oribas was forced to hunch his head into his shoulders. The Marroc shuffled along in the feeble near-dark of their torches, creeping like spiders in the night through puddles and rivulets of foul-smelling water. The walls glistened with damp slime and the stink got worse the deeper they went. After an hour of climbing into the mountain's heart, the Marroc stopped. The passage opened into a round shaft twenty paces across that rose towards the mountain's peak and delved to its root. Below where they stood, the shaft was filled with scummy water. A narrow ledge circled it.

'This part is slippery.'

Achista sent one Marroc around the walkway to the far side. Metal rungs bolted into the stone rose into the darkness of the shaft. Oribas stared at them in horror. 'And how old are those?'

'Addic and I climbed them months ago. We marked the loose ones.'

They brought more torches. Oribas looked up. The shaft disappeared into darkness. 'How far does it go?'

'As far as the tallest tree in the forest.'

Oribas shrugged. Some of the trees in the Varyxhun valley were as tall as fifty men. He followed her around the walkway and started to climb behind her. He wasn't sure why he was suddenly at the front of the Marroc, but it seemed natural to be at Achista's side. 'Where's your brother?' he asked. 'Shouldn't he be leading this?'

They were twenty feet above the water now. 'I found this, Oribas, not Addic. If anyone should be here to lead ahead of me then it's Rannic, but he's with Modris now, casting his shield over us.' She tapped the rung just above her feet. 'This one's loose. Make sure you tell whoever comes behind you.'

They climbed only another few feet when there was a howl from below. Oribas turned his head in time to see a Marroc splash into the water, fallen from the treacherous stone walkway. The Marroc cried out once more and then sank like a stone. A second man fell after him as he crouched to try and reach his friend. He scrabbled at the wall of the shaft and managed to grab another Marroc around the ankle, but his hands kept slipping and there was no way anyone standing on the walkway could bend down to help him without pitching themselves into the water as well. He fell back and then lunged again. His fingers clawed at the stone.

One man already drowned, just like that, out of nothing. The pointlessness of it made Oribas angry. 'You have ropes!' he shouted at them. 'Use them! Pull him out!'

It took three Marroc to haul the second man out. It was as though the foetid water in the shaft clung to him, trying to drag him down.

They climbed on. Oribas didn't know how far. He counted the rungs for a while when his arms started to tire and got up to somewhere close to a hundred before he lost count because it now took all the will he could muster just to keep going. He'd climbed ladders and stairs aplenty in his time but none like this; and when they finally reached the top, his arms and his shoulders felt like lead. Achista held her torch out over the edge and waved it so that those below could see the end was in sight, then, when there were a half-dozen of them safely up, she pulled Oribas to his feet and led him on. They were in another passage now, wider and made with more care, typical Aulian work lined with bricks and tiles, though the floor was still rough bare rock. Oribas looked for inscriptions or engravings or murals but everything was crusted in filth. When he stopped to scrape some off, Achista pulled him on again. She dragged him to a wall with a circular stone door in the centre. To the right of the door four bronze wheels dark with verdigris stuck out of the stone, each engraved with symbols that had almost disappeared over time. Oribas took her torch and inspected them. There were six signs on each wheel, animals, the totems for each of the six Ascendants who'd once stood guard over the empire. A chill ran over his skin right to his feet and back again and wouldn't leave him alone. He'd been to places like this before. He brushed a little of the dirt aside, nodded to himself and then walked away. 'And now we turn back,' he said to Achista as he passed her.

'You can't open it?' Her look was tragic.

'I probably can but I certainly shouldn't. I'll tell the others. No need for the ones still climbing to come up all this way for nothing.'

Achista darted in front of him, stopping him with a hand pressed to his chest. 'Please.' He opened his mouth, but before he could even begin to tell her why he shouldn't, why none of them should even go near a place like this, why the Lhosir in the tower were taking their lives to the edge of the abyss simply by being here, she put her other hand on his cheek and stared at him with such wide, hopeful eyes that she killed his words dead. He stood agape. 'Please,' she said again. 'It's the only way in. We have to! We have to try. If we don't try, what are we?'

Gallow would have said the same. And if Gallow had been here and told him to open it then he would have done so even while he was explaining exactly why no man alive should ever enter a place that had been closed with a seal of the Ascendants. 'This isn't a seal to keep us out, Achista. It's a seal to keep something in.'

'Whatever was inside has been dead and gone for hundreds of years now.'

'Yes,' said Oribas, turning back to the door. 'It has. And it should stay that way.'

She took his hand and held it tight. 'After the Aulians left, they say the Reach became the home of a Marroc prince. They say that beneath it he found an Aulian treasure vault. For twenty years he tried to open it until at last he solved its puzzle. They say he found the answer written on a nearby rock. The day after, he left with all his men and headed north and was never seen again. After that, no one lived in Witches' Reach until the forkbeards came.'

Oribas shook his head. 'I have another story for you. A long story for another time, of the Rakshasa that killed my home, my town, my people, my family and many others besides. I prayed and the gods sent Gallow Truesword and together we destroyed the creature.' He turned to face her and looked her hard in the eye. 'But before Gallow, I tracked the Rakshasa back to the place from which it came. I found a seal like this that had been opened. Thousands of lives, Achista.' He went back to the wheels beside the door and gave one an experimental tug, half hoping that it wouldn't move, that the mechanism inside had corroded solid. And the wheel didn't turn, but even as he shrugged his shoulders ready to walk away again, Achista had an unlit torch pushed through the wheel to make a lever and was pulling on it with all her weight, and with a jerk it shifted. The sound of grinding stone and metal echoed through the passage. She looked pleased with herself and started to push at the round stone door. Oribas pulled her away. 'The seals are held closed by a riddle, Achista.' He brushed dirt from the stonework on the other side of the door. 'There are four mechanisms inside the stone. Each wheel must be set to the sign of the correct Ascendant to move the bars that prevent the door from opening. When all four are set correctly, the stone can slide aside. They are not easily made and so are not made lightly. Something on the other side of this seal was not meant to be found. And to be sealed here, in a place so remote from the heart of the empire ...' He shook himself. 'If I open this for you, Achista, you must promise me: no one will touch anything on the other side unless I say it is safe.'

Achista set to work on the other wheels, loosening each until she could turn all four. Oribas finished clearing the dirt from the inscription beside the door. The words carved into the stone were old and worn but still deep enough to read: '*Here buried under the mountain lies the iron witch, drowned in the river and laid out in salt where the wind and the sun shall be guardians amid this place of snow and ice.*'

Achista squinted at the wheels. The other Marroc were crowding close now, drawn in by their curiosity. 'But these are just animals.'

'The six Ascendants are the Earth, the Sun, the Fire, the Sky, the River and the Night. Each has its totem.' Oribas frowned. 'Buried under the mountain. A statement of fact, but the mountain is also the Earth.' He skipped to the other side of the door and turned the top wheel to the sign of the bear, the totem animal of the Earth. Without a torch for a lever it took the two of them to make the wheel move, Achista's hands pressed onto his. 'The iron witch?' He shrugged. 'Laid out in salt? Not sure. Drowned in the river is obvious, and the wind and the sun are simple enough too. Guardians in this place of snow and ice. Cold could be the earth again but it's always four different Ascendants. Winter is the season of Night, so maybe that.'

'There are only four wheels, Oribas.'

'I don't think Night is right, not for a place like this. Earth, River, Sky, Sun. Those are the clearest. Bear, fish, bird, dragon. We'll try that first.'

They wrestled with the wheels. As the final one ground into place, the stone groaned and shifted. The wall shook and a deep rumble echoed through the passageway. Oribas backed away. 'If you can move it, I think the door will open now. Have a care, Achista. I have no idea what lies beyond.'

'I know.' She nodded at several of the Marroc, who started to lever the stone aside. Her smile was a weak one.

The Marroc pulled the stone back far enough for someone to squeeze through. They all looked at Oribas expectantly. He shook his head. 'Did any of you bring salt? No? Thought not. Well don't expect me to go ah—' But Achista was already worming her way through and so he didn't have any choice but to follow her. 'The old Aulian priests made these seals to keep the very worst of their demons locked away,' he hissed. 'Things worse than any shadewalker. Believe me when I say I know what sort of creatures they were. If there's a way into the tower, it may have another seal like this one, one that can't be opened at all from the inside.' Whatever they'd put here, there would be other wards though, surely. *Laid out in salt*, and salt was a ward to those creatures. Perhaps they could creep through and creep out the other side and …

'It's the only way to the forkbeards, Oribas.' She held up her torch. 'Besides, look!'

His skin was a-prickle from head to toe but at last he saw what Achista was trying to show him: the tomb wasn't a tomb at all. It was a Lhosir storeroom. They were in the cellars of the tower.

'I told you there was another door, one already opened,' said Achista. 'Some say the Marroc prince who lived here took the treasure he found and went north, and others that something terrible came out and everyone died. And there's some who say he wasn't a Marroc at all. But it was all hundreds of years ago, and whatever was here is long gone. Today there are only forkbeards.'

24

THE ROAD TO MIDDISLET

Gallow didn't look back. Not once. He walked away in stolen boots from the Marroc victory and from the last friend he had left to him after three years of searching for his home. He wore the furs of a dead kinsman and the mail and helm that the Screambreaker had given him outside Andhun. He carried a spear and a sword and an axe and a shield all scavenged from battlefields, and three years of longing in his heart.

The Marroc farmers' trail was marked by cairns of stones that rose from the snow so that even in the winter a traveller wouldn't lose his way. As the light fell he sought shelter where he could find it. A woodsman's hut the first night, the next at a farm among the animals where frightened Marroc stared wide-eyed at his steel, prayed to their gods that in the morning he'd be gone and then thanked them when he was. The only tracks he saw in the snow were of animals crossing from the shelter of one stand of trees to another. The path wound down a sharp-sided valley through stands of giant Varyxhun pine that towered over everything, around boulders strewn about a stream that danced through its heart. Twice he had to wade through snow as deep as a house, cutting a path through a great broken swathe of it that had tumbled down from the slopes above. He had nothing he could use to make any fire and so when twilight fell and there was no shelter to be found he simply walked on through the darkness, guided by the stars and the moon, the only way to keep warm. The cold nipped and bit at him like an angry puppy but it held no fear. He'd crossed the Aulian Way after all, higher and colder and longer than this.

The sides of the valley broke apart. The slopes became more gentle. The stands of pine became a great forest of lesser trees and the stream beside him swelled to a river as other waters joined it. The air grew warmer, the snow under his feet thinner and more broken. He reckoned on being a day away from Hrodicslet when he came to a camp beside the road where the embers of a fire were still warm under his fingers. He sat down beside it and rubbed his hands and blew at the ash but it was too old to glow and light into flames again. There was nothing else to see save for a few marks in the snow where men had sat not long ago and a simple shelter made of branches, a place for a man to sleep out of the wind and the snow. He felt eyes watching him but nothing more. He didn't go looking.

Cold and exhausted and hungry, he reached Hrodicslet. Now at every farm Marroc slammed their doors in his face. They were hospitable folk to their own kind, or so the carter Fenaric had once said, but no one had shelter for a forkbeard.

'I'll pay you! I'll work for you!' he shouted at their doors, but none of them opened again. When the sun began to set and yet another barrage of curses turned him away, he kicked the door open again before the Marroc inside could bar it. There were three of them, an old man and a younger one and another who was little more than a boy. 'What Marroc turns a starving freezing man from their door?' The words sounded hollow even as he spat them to the floor. Any Marroc, that was the answer, if the starving man was a forkbeard.

The men backed away from him. Animals milled around, pigs and goats and chickens all driven inside for warmth and shelter. The young one snatched up a lump of firewood. The old one yelled a curse through gritted teeth, never taking his eyes off Gallow. 'What do you want, forkbeard?'

A dog like a wolf padded out from between the hanging furs that separated the night room from the rest of the house, sending the chickens squawking and flapping away. It bared its teeth and growled at Gallow.

'Make your dog be still or I'll kill it!' But the Marroc didn't move. The dog snarled and drew back to its haunches and still the Marroc did nothing, and then the dog sprang. Gallow lifted his shield. The dog scrabbled for purchase, bit at the wood and then fell. It crouched, glowering and snarling, and then launched itself again, this time at Gallow's arm. Gallow raised his axe out of the dog's reach and twisted to let it fly past. It snapped at him, seizing his furs in its jaws and almost spinning him around.

He brought the axe down on the back of its head and the dog fell dead. The Marroc boy screamed and threw himself at Gallow, swinging his lump of wood. Gallow bashed him away with his shield and there was his hatchet again, singing through the air straight at the boy's head. He pulled the blow at the last but for a moment he'd meant it. For a moment he'd happily have killed the lot of them.

He shoved the boy away. They all stared at him in hatred.

'Damn you, Marroc!'

'Damn you too, forkbeard,' hissed the old man. 'Take what you want and be gone.'

'I'll do that. Where are the women and children?'

The old man glanced at the night room. The younger one clenched his fists and shook his head. *So that's what they thought of forkbeards, was it?* And then he thought of the way it had been with the Screambreaker's army and wondered how he could possibly blame them. 'Make sure they stay there. You two go and be with them.' He pointed his axe at the old man. 'Not you. You stay.'

'What do you want, forkbeard?'

Gallow growled and raised his fist and they did as he asked. He made the old man show him where they kept their food. He took as much as he could carry and a leather bag with a strap to carry it. Everywhere he went would be like this until he was home. There'd be no shelter, no charity, nothing for the hated forkbeard. Fate again, laughing at him. 'I didn't want to kill your dog, old Marroc. I have nothing against dogs.' The old man's face stayed as it was, a mask of hidden fear and sullen hate. 'I'll take my rest in your house tonight. You'll stay in your night room, all of you. If you do as I say then I'll be on my way in the morning and you'll not see me again. If you come out, if you seek help, if any one of you raises a single hand or word against me, I'll kill every person here. I'll burn your farm. I'll go back to my kin and they'll burn your neighbours. We'll hunt you until every single Marroc here lies bloody in the snow. Do you understand me, old man?'

The words hissed out of him. 'I understand you, forkbeard.'

'Then go to your night room and keep your kin there with you, close.'

He pushed the corpse of the dog outside and closed the door behind it. After nights in the mountain snow the house was deliciously warm. In the morning he left with a clutch of fresh eggs. The Marroc had seen just another forkbeard and so that's what he'd become. The realisation haunted him. This was how it was for the Lhosir here; and what if some forkbeard happened upon Nadric's forge, hungry and desperate? Would Arda have the sense to keep her peace?

He skirted around Hrodicslet to the edge of the Crackmarsh, the quickest way home. The fringes of the marsh were boggy but not waterlogged, not like the water meadows they became each spring. The ghuldogs were mostly quiet in the winter, hiding in their burrows. Nothing much came out into this dead open landscape with its stands of twisted trees, not at this time of year. He crossed it without trouble, walking on through the night to keep warm, dozing in the warmest hours of the day, surviving on the food he'd stolen.

Stolen. He'd never been a thief before. At least, he'd never seen himself like that. The Screambreaker's army had plundered the Marroc lands, taking what pleased them, burning whatever caught their eye to burn. The spoils of war though, not thieving, although from where he stood now it was hard to see the difference.

The edge of the Crackmarsh took him to the caves and the woods where the villagers of Middislet had hidden when they'd thought the Vathen were coming, all of them except Arda, who'd stayed alone to defend Nadric's forge because she was fed up with soldiers coming and taking everything that was hers. He remembered that day well, as clear as he remembered the day he'd first seen her, and the memories made a longing that drove him onward, heedless of the pain in his feet and his legs, the weariness in his bones. He couldn't be sure that she was there, whether any of them were even still alive, but each time he closed his eyes he saw her, waiting all this time.

One way or another, he was coming home.

25

WHAT HAPPENED TO
TOLVIS LOUDMOUTH

'There's something else I want from you, Loudmouth.'
Three years ago Tolvis Loudmouth had stood beside the
Screambreaker. It was the morning before the battle that would
see the Screambreaker take the red sword from the dead hands
of the Weeping Giant and then fall in his turn. Tolvis was
hardly ready to be asked for any other favours, given what the
Screambreaker had just told him about keeping Twelvefingers
from burning Andhun, but you didn't say no to the old man so
he'd kept his mouth shut for once. 'If I die tomorrow, take my
body and speak me out in secret. I'll have no great celebration
for all the things I've done. Then take this where it belongs.'
He'd handed over a fat purse of silver. Tolvis knew exactly what
it was because it was the same fat purse he'd given to Gallow
Truesword a couple of weeks earlier when he'd traded it for
Truesword's plundered Vathan horses.

A hundred men saw the Screambreaker die later that same
day, moments before the Lhosir broke the Vathan army.
Afterwards, when they couldn't find his body, they built a pyre
to him anyway and spoke him out. And then Twelvefingers
turned on Andhun and the Marroc there, and Tolvis had led
a band of the Screambreaker's men to stop him, and Gallow
had chopped off Medrin's hand and turned him into Sixfingers
instead of Twelve; and then the Vathen had turned out not to
be as broken as everyone thought and by the next sunrise half
of Andhun belonged to the horsemen, someone burning the
bridge across the Isset was the only thing keeping them out of
the other half, and Sixfingers was on a ship back across the sea,
hovering somewhere between life and death. Tolvis had watched
Gallow fall from the cliffs into the sea and thought maybe he'd

seen a man with a boat trying to haul someone out of the water or maybe not, but either way it was hard to be sure because the air over his head had been full of Vathan arrows and javelots at the time and mostly he'd been trying not to die.

He hadn't gone home nor sought the remnants of the Lhosir army. By then he'd had enough of it all, and so he'd gone inland instead, all on his own, because Gallow had been a friend, and being a friend had to be worth something. He'd gone to Varyxhun and poked his nose around for Arda Smithswife and eventually found her and gave her the purse full of silver that Gallow had always meant her to have, and she'd taken it with thanks. And maybe it came from living with a Lhosir for eight years or maybe it was simply the way she was, but it didn't seem to trouble her much that he was a forkbeard. He'd stayed a while because he wasn't quite sure whether Gallow was dead or alive, but if he was alive then he'd certainly find a way back home from Andhun and it seemed only right that he should keep an eye on his friend's family until then. A week grew into a month and then two. Varyxhun filled with Lhosir looking for Gallow Foxbeard, the traitor, the *nioingr*. Tolvis kept away. They'd have been happy enough to hang Loudmouth too.

Two months turned into three. By then they all knew that Gallow wouldn't be coming back, though none of them said it; and he still stayed, and Arda never minded about that as long as he made himself useful, and none of them said anything about the Lhosir looking for the Foxbeard. When the Fateguard came, they left, quietly, going back to Nadric's old forge in Middislet, and the months turned into a year without any of them quite noticing. Nadric was getting too old to earn his living at his forge but Tolvis knew how to work a farm and he had a strong arm and a quick enough wit to learn the simple things. As that first winter came, Arda took to being away for days at a time. Tolvis never asked, not then, and she never said, but she came back with food, and more than they needed. There were Marroc in the Crackmarsh, bandits and renegades sworn to fight the forkbeards. He knew that was where she went, but it wasn't his business and so he left her to it. The villagers in Middislet weren't that keen on forkbeards just like all the other Marroc, but Middislet wasn't Varyxhun or Andhun and they'd never had blood ravens lining the roads. Mostly everyone got quietly on with their lives, and if Arda had swapped one forkbeard for another, so what? Loudmouth had a quiet suspicion that half the Marroc thought he was Gallow just come back from the fighting with a big mess made of his face. Besides, that first winter was a hard one and there were plenty of people grateful for the food Arda brought out of the Crackmarsh.

A year turned into two and Arda came to him one day and told him that if he was staying he might want to cut off his beard, and it hadn't surprised him greatly either when, after he did it, she'd taken him to the night room alone. There wasn't any ceremony about it, but she was lying with him and laying Gallow to rest both at once, and he'd been happy enough with that. Some of the Marroc said things behind her back and others said them to her face, but she only shrugged and pointed out that people had always said things behind her back even before she'd married Gallow, and that she had no truck with anyone whose life was so joyless they had nothing better to do than make misery for others, nor did she care in the least as long as there was food for her family. Gallow's silver made her rich in the village, she still vanished off among the Crackmarsh men for whole weeks at a time, and it wasn't as if there were baskets full of spare men going at the market who'd look after her and her half-forkbeard children. She made Tolvis laugh, and he made her laugh too, and when Sixfingers came back across the sea with a new hand made of witch's iron and set about raising armies to fight the Vathen, Tolvis kept to himself, not wanting anything to do with it.

'Loudmouth!'

He looked up from where he was supposed to be cutting nails for Nadric. There weren't too many Marroc who bothered to talk to him in Middislet. They were used to him, tolerated him with grudging reluctance, but no one said they had to like it. But now and then Fenaric the carter came by, and Fenaric didn't seem to care who Tolvis was, even though Arda made it plain that she couldn't stand the carter and wouldn't spare him a word.

'I've got news, forkbeard. You might want to hear it.' He

looked from side to side as though there might be someone lurking in the shadows of the forge.

'What's that then?' Tolvis was careful to be civil with the carter. Varyxhun was turning bad. Tolvis quietly thought that if there wasn't an uprising in the spring then he'd eat Nadric's forge, and if there *was*, well he wanted to be far away from it. And then there was Sixfingers. He hadn't forgotten Gallow, that was for sure. Probably thought of him every time he looked at the stump where his hand used to be. Probably hadn't forgotten that Gallow had had a family. So yes, he gave Fenaric the time of day, careful to keep an ear to the ground.

Fenaric sat himself on a log beside the forge fire. 'Could do with new tyres for the wagon,' he said.

So he was short of money. Tolvis nodded. 'I'll talk to Nadric and see what's to be done.' That's how it went. Little favours for snippets of the world outside the village.

'Was up at Issetbridge.' He sniffed and looked about as though he was bored. 'Heard a story that a dozen forkbeards got killed up in the high valleys. Not the only story like that, either.'

'Glad that's not near here then.' Cithjan had a fondness for hangings from what he'd heard. Thought if you hanged enough Marroc everything would be sorted out. Maybe if he hanged every last one of them, it would.

'Reckon it's going to get bloody, forkbeard.'

'Reckon so, carter.' Tolvis went back to cutting nails. If that was all Fenaric had then he could pay for his tyres.

The carter stayed where he was though, so there was clearly more. Funny thing about the trouble in Varyxhun – it made the Marroc in Middislet more unsure about Tolvis. Reminded them how much they were supposed to hate all forkbeards; but at the same time Tolvis knew it set them thinking about how it might not be such a bad thing to have one living among them if the trouble spilled over the Aulian Bridge. 'There was one other thing I heard. Something about a sword. That sword the Vathen were supposed to have with them at Andhun, the one you forkbeards took off them.'

Tolvis stopped cutting. 'Oh yes?'

'Well I don't know for sure what's true and what's not, but

what I heard was it went missing when the Vathen kicked you lot out of Andhun.' He cocked his head. 'You know different?'

'No, that's about the right of it.' Tolvis tried not to look interested.

'There's a rumour going around Issetbridge that the iron devil of Varyxhun has found it again.'

Tolvis almost choked. 'Anyone say how?'

Fenaric stuck out his bottom lip and grunted, and Tolvis knew him well enough to know this wasn't just the carter trying to get some tyres hammered for nothing. After a bit Fenaric stood up. 'That's about it.'

'That was news worth having, carter. I'll see about those tyres.'

'No hurry. I'll be good for another month. If they're ready for the next time I roll through, that would be fine.' He walked away.

Tolvis Loudmouth sat and stared at the forge for a very long time and hardly cut any nails at all after Fenaric left. The carter had earned his tyres but Tolvis wasn't sure what to make of it, because if the red sword hadn't drowned off the cliffs of Andhun then maybe Gallow hadn't drowned there either, and a pang of something came with that thought. Not fear, exactly. Sadness, and that was when he realised how content he'd become here, doing nothing very much and being in no way important.

He didn't tell Arda. The return of the red sword wouldn't mean anything to her, but he took to sleeping with his own blade kept in the corner of the night room, which she noticed and gave him all sorts of grief for until he made up some story after Fenaric had gone about outlaws roaming the Fedderhun Road. And then the day after that Vennic came screaming through the village with some wild tale about a man made of iron riding the fringes of the Crackmarsh. Vennic hadn't seen it himself but he'd heard from another shepherd out in the hills and now he had it in his head that a shadewalker was coming. The rest of the village laughed in his face. Shadewalkers never rode horses and they didn't wear iron or venture out in the middle of the day, and anyway this was Vennic, who saw ghosts in the moon and devils in the shadows and thought Modris talked to him through his sheep.

Tolvis kept his mouth shut. He'd seen enough to know it was a Fateguard that Vennic's friend had seen, the iron devil of Varyxhun. After that he took to sleeping with his shield in the night room too, and with one eye open, and that was probably why he sat up in the small hours of the morning a few nights later, wide awake and quite sure there was someone outside. He slipped his sword out of its scabbard and slid his shield onto his arm and crept to the door to the yard and opened it a crack, and right there in front of him was the shadow of a man swathed in metal and with a shield of his own on his arm. Tolvis let out a cry and jumped back, ready for a fight, but the iron devil in the yard didn't move.

'Tolvis Loudmouth?' Iron grated on iron. 'Well I certainly wasn't expecting to find *you*. Still, Sixfingers keeps a special place in his heart for both of you.'

26

THE IRON MAN

Middislet was still miles away when the sun set but Gallow kept walking. Perhaps there was shelter to be found in the hills that edged the Crackmarsh but he wasn't looking for it, not now. He knew how close he was and he knew this land, and besides there were Marroc in the woods and caves here. He'd seen them. Bandits or thieves, he didn't know which, but it didn't matter. He was a forkbeard alone and so he kept on going. He could almost have walked these last miles blindfold and still found his way home.

Snow started to fall, muffling the darkness and silencing the wind. The night was black as ink when he reached the forge and the house was still. Everyone inside would be sleeping. He listened at the door and heard nothing, no snores, no snuffles, no wheezes. But this was home, still the way he remembered it, and his heart was beating fast. Three years. Anything could have happened. He didn't know whether to knock or simply open the door and creep inside.

He was still standing there when he heard movement, the scrape of wood across the floor and then the chink of metal and a footstep and the door opened, and in the night Gallow stared. There was a man. He was holding a candle. Not Nadric, not Arda, but ...

'Tolvis Loudmouth?' Gallow stared. The side of Loudmouth's face was a mass of scars from that last fight in Andhun. He looked fatter and his forked beard was gone. But most of all Gallow simply couldn't understand what he was doing here. Here in Middislet at Nadric's forge. It made no sense. Words started and then faltered.

'Gallow?' Tolvis couldn't find anything to say either.

Gallow couldn't think, couldn't think of anything at all except that Tolvis had been a friend, one he'd never thought to see again. He offered his arm and Tolvis took it and they clasped each other. 'Loudmouth?' He shook his head in disbelief again. 'Your beard ...'

Tolvis was laughing, almost weeping with joy and surprise and dismay. 'The silver I got you for those horses in Andhun. The Screambreaker.' He shook his head. 'There didn't seem to be a particularly good moment for giving it back, what with the whole chopping Medrin's hand off and being chased through the castle by a Vathan horde. And then you didn't come ... You held the Vathen long enough that we got away. I couldn't keep all that silver if it wasn't mine and so I went to Varyxhun after Andhun fell and I found her, and then I stayed in case you came back and weren't dead after all, and then I never quite ... left ...'

'Loudmouth.' Gallow shook his head. Now he looked closer there were bruises and a bloody gash on Loudmouth's face. Fresh, no more than a day old. 'What's wrong?'

Tolvis looked over his shoulder. He glanced at the night room. 'Maker-Devourer, Gallow, I'm so sorry.'

Gallow's heart beat even faster. 'What, Loudmouth? What is it?'

He had tears in his eyes. His hands grasped Gallow's arms. 'I looked after your family, Gallow. I've done what I could but Sixfingers never stopped looking.'

'My sons?'

Tolvis looked away. Gallow grabbed his shirt and shook him. 'Arda? What, Loudmouth? *What?*'

And then the furs around the night room shifted and a shadow moved out of them and a rasp cut the night. 'This was always where you'd come, Foxbeard. I've been waiting for you.'

The scrape of metal on metal and then a shape unfolded itself from the darkness behind Tolvis, a man cased in iron, and Gallow knew, though he couldn't see the face that lay beneath the mask in the moonlight, that this was Beyard. Who else? Gallow hissed, 'You're dead!'

'Did you weep for me, old friend? Did you build a pyre for me and speak me out?' Between them Tolvis hung his head. Beyard held out the amulet with the lock of Arda's hair and threw it at Gallow's feet. 'You were quick, Truesword, but I was quicker. Across the Crackmarsh and the bandits and the ghuldogs knew enough to leave well alone. I watched her. Your children too. I know why you came home.' He pushed Tolvis aside and offered out his hand. 'Come, old friend. No need for Sixfingers to know. You understand what he'd do if he did.'

Snap their ribs from their spines and pull their lungs through their skin and fly them like wings, suspended from gibbets and wheels. Blood ravens. Gallow's hand gripped his sword. He shook his head. 'Where are they, Beyard? What have you done?'

'They're in the cellar. Unhurt. Aren't they, Loudmouth?'

Tolvis bowed his head. He nodded, eyes closed.

'I have no interest in them, Truesword. Medrin need never know. You can't escape your fate but no one else has to share it.' His face turned a fraction to Tolvis. 'Even this one. We'll leave, you and I, quietly in the night. Loudmouth here will lie with your woman and raise your sons as his own. We both know he'll raise them as he should.' Beyard made a wet rasping sound that might have been laughter and tipped his head to Tolvis. 'After all, I didn't make you stay, Loudmouth. You could have left me alone with them if you'd wished. But you couldn't do that, could you?'

Tolvis seemed to fold in on himself. He shrank back into the darkness of the house. 'I looked after them, Gallow. We thought you were dead. I kept them safe.'

Gallow hesitated. He looked from Tolvis to Beyard and back again. 'I'll kill you, old friend, if I have to.'

Beyard nodded. 'As I will you, old friend. I will kill who I must.' His sword was already in his hand. The red sword, Solace, and now he levelled it at Tolvis. 'This one tried already. He fought well, but I am Fateguard now and my skin is iron.'

'Swear on your blood, Beyard. No harm to my wife and my family. Swear you won't come back for them. Swear you won't come back for Loudmouth.'

'I told you in Varyxhun, Gallow: I can't swear on what I don't have.' Beyard dropped to one knee, though the sword remained pointed at Loudmouth's throat. 'They think you dead,

Truesword. The family you left, they belong to another now. I've watched. Your sons call Loudmouth father. Your wife calls him husband. Your fate lies elsewhere and always did. Leave them be, Truesword. Let us go into the night, the two of us alone. I've not forgotten that Sixfingers fled and left us once long ago. I've no love for him, only duty.'

Tolvis hissed, 'Then don't serve him!'

'I must.'

Gallow slowly slid his sword back into its scabbard. He looked at Loudmouth and sniffed the air and looked at Beyard again, standing once more with the red sword still in his hand. Three years of searching and now the last gift he could give them was to leave? Let them go? 'I'd see them one more time. I'll not wake them. Then I'll come with you.'

'It's best they don't know, Truesword.'

'I know.'

Tolvis turned and gripped Gallow's arm. 'They're strong and filled with life. That much I did well.'

Gallow walked inside, treading lightly. The smells were such an old familiar comfort that they almost made him weep. He crept down the steps into the stale warmth of the cellar and crouched down beside each of the sleeping figures there. His sons: Pursic, who'd grown into a boy in the years he'd been gone, and Tathic. His daughters: Feya, who was losing the baby looks he remembered, and Jelira, the daughter who wasn't his but whom he'd taken to be his own, almost a woman now. And Arda. He crouched beside her for the longest time of all, drawn by the temptation to wake her. She looked exactly as he remembered. No one who glanced at her in the street would have said she was beautiful but to Gallow she was perfect. He swallowed hard and forced himself to rise. Beyard was right: what good did it do for her to see him now? She'd shout and scream at him for not coming home and she'd wake everyone else, and then she'd probably go up and start throwing pans at the ironskin.

Three years across half the world to be here though. Tears blurred his eyes. They were alive. Well. Safe. Perhaps if he went with Beyard then they might stay that way. Loudmouth would take care of them and Tathic and Pursic would grow to be fine young men who didn't remember too much of their real father. Perhaps that was for the best. What did he have to offer them now? A life of being hunted, that's what. And Arda, in her cold harsh practical way, would tell him the same, no matter how much she was screaming inside, and no one would ever see her weep except maybe Loudmouth now and then.

He climbed quietly back up the steps. 'Thank you, Beyard. Thank you for that.'

'You were my friend once.' The iron man beckoned, eyes on Loudmouth. 'Come, Truesword.'

Gallow followed Beyard outside. Every step felt as though he was walking through stone, as though he was wading up the steep slope of one of the great dunes from the desert that Oribas called home. It seemed such a long way to come only to end like this.

'It is your fate, Truesword. Set for the three of us all those years ago.'

Gallow thought about that for a bit. 'I turned my back on that fate once.'

'And look what it brought you.'

'You two talk too much.' Tolvis hurled himself at Beyard. A sword flashed in the moonlight, cutting at Beyard's face. The Fateguard stepped back. Neither of them carried a shield but Beyard was in his iron, covered head to toe in it, while Tolvis had a thick sheepskin night shirt and nothing else.

'Must we do this again?' Beyard lashed out, fast as lightning, but Tolvis danced away, quicker still and too quick for Beyard to catch. The air moaned. The Fateguard still carried the red sword.

Tolvis howled like a wolf. 'Come on Gallow! There's two of us now!'

There was no reading Beyard's face under his mask but his voice was low and cold. 'I was kind to you last time, Tolvis Loudmouth. I won't be kind again.'

'That's the sword that cut off Medrin's hand, is it?' Loudmouth jumped away as Beyard swung again. 'As good as any to take my head.' He flicked a glance at Gallow. 'Help me, Gallow. I can't fight him on my own. Tried that already. If he kills me, who looks after the others?'

Beyard glared. 'Stand your ground, Truesword. I'll keep my word if you keep yours.'

'And I've always wanted to kill a Fateguard,' shouted Tolvis. 'Everyone says you can't. Everyone says the Fateguard don't ever die but that can't be right. You're just men under there.'

'Stop, Tolvis!' Gallow lunged to pull Loudmouth away but he was too quick.

'And what, Truesword? Stay here and hide while you go meekly to Medrin? Damn you! I told you to make an end of him there and then.' He shook his head. 'I came here to give your woman your silver and watch over your sons as a true friend might do, but I've broken that friendship.' His sword clattered off Beyard's iron arm. 'I stayed too long. I've lain with your woman and called your sons my own.' The air screamed as Solace sliced an inch in front of Loudmouth's face. 'You were the one who stayed to hold the Vathen. If one of us must die today then let it be me, Truesword, not you, not this time.' He caught Beyard another ringing blow, this time on the hip. The Fateguard lunged, untroubled. The tip of the Edge of Sorrows stabbed into Loudmouth's side as he danced away.

'Stop!' Gallow had his axe in his hand. Beyard swung the red sword's tip towards him at once.

'Stand your ground, Gallow Truesword!'

Through the open door into the house the cellar swung open with a crash. Arda. Gallow turned away, hiding his face. He roared at Tolvis again but neither of them would listen. Tolvis slipped inside Beyard's guard. His sword skittered sparks from the Fateguard's iron crown. Beyard cuffed him away.

'You! Forkbeard pig-poker!' Arda ran out behind Gallow. He knew what was coming and stepped away and had to turn. She had a half-full chamber pot, ready to crack him over the head with it, and then she saw his face and froze and the chamber pot fell from her fingers and crashed between them, spilling itself over their feet. 'You!' Her mouth fell open. He'd never seen her eyes so wide. 'Gallow?'

'Arda!' He wanted to reach for her but his arms wouldn't move and he had an axe in one hand and a shield in the other. She didn't move either. Just stared and stared as though she was seeing a ghost; and perhaps to her that's what he was.

Loudmouth whooped as his sword clattered on Beyard's armour again. 'Sooner or later, Fateguard, I'm going to find a hole and slide this into you.' He jumped into the shadows of Nadric's forge. Beyard moved slowly after him.

Now it was Nadric at the top of the cellar steps, squinting. 'Gallow?'

Tolvis kicked a plume of ash from the forge's firepit into Beyard's face. The Fateguard stepped back and Tolvis lunged, stabbing at the iron man's eyes, but Beyard caught his blade with the Edge of Sorrows and for a moment they were pressed together. Beyard's knee slammed up. Tolvis squealed and doubled over, threw himself back, slipped and fell.

'Dada?' More faces were peering up from the cellar, squeezing past Nadric and running to the open door, staring out into the yard. Pursic, the smallest of them staring at Tolvis, not at Gallow. 'Dada!' Nadric tried to push the children back inside but they wriggled through his hands.

Beyard took a quick stride and stood over Tolvis. 'Brave, Loudmouth, but stupid.' He lifted the Edge of Sorrows ready to drive it down.

Gallow threw his axe as hard as he could, straight into Beyard's side. It bit into the Fateguard's iron and staggered him sideways. Beyard roared. His head snapped to Gallow and his face lowered. 'You've sealed all our fates now, old friend. None will be spared.' He kicked Tolvis and came at Gallow, the scattered embers of the forge fire crunching under his iron boots. Gallow drew his sword and lifted his shield and braced himself ready for the Edge of Sorrows to come.

27

A SIMPLE VICTORY

The Marroc gathered in the cellars of Witches' Reach, waiting until they were all up the shaft. Oribas looked at what the Lhosir had stored in the cellar-tomb. Kegs of ale and mead. Sacks and sacks of flour and dried peas and beans, strings of onions. A few baskets of nuts. Certainly enough to keep a hundred Marroc fed for a few weeks. He looked at the stone door, rolled right back now. They could close it behind them but there was no way to seal it from the inside; nor was there a way to open it again once the four seals had been locked. Oribas found a second door like the first, the way out into the rest of the tower, wide open and half smashed apart. Whatever the Aulians had buried here was long gone. Still, he checked through the sacks and the crates and baskets until he found some salt and filled the bag over his shoulder.

Achista beckoned the Marroc on. Beyond the second seal a staircase spiralled up into the bottom of the tower. They went up. Oribas recognised the room at once. It was hexagonal, with the stairs in the centre and six stone benches set one into each wall. They would have been altars once, one for each of the Ascendants, but now the Lhosir used them for tables and the whole room was piled with more crates and sacks.

Voices echoed down the staircase. Lhosir. Achista crept forward, finger to her lips and her bow in her other hand. She nocked an arrow and began up the steps. Other Marroc crowded around her, the ones with mail and helms; when Oribas tried to follow she pushed him gently away and shook her head and so he watched anxiously as the Marroc silently inched their way up until the first alarmed Lhosir shout came ringing down. The Marroc all started yelling and running and the men around him let out whoops and charged up the steps. Oribas found himself joining them, carried away in the rush. They burst out into a kitchen where three Lhosir already lay dead, riddled with arrows. The Marroc rushed on, most pouring out of a door into the yard between the tower and the wall that surrounded it, some pushing on up a flight of steep wooden steps. Sounds of fighting came from both. Oribas took the door. It was easier. He had no idea which way Achista had gone but he wanted to be near her. It didn't make any sense since there wasn't anything he could do except get in the way, but he wanted it anyway.

The curtain wall of Witches' Reach encircled the summit of the mountain with the tower built into it on the very peak. Half a dozen wooden huts and outhouses had been propped up against the stonework: stables and a small forge and storehouses, perhaps, or hanging sheds, or maybe the Lhosir slept out here. Oribas had no idea. The gates to the road down the mountainside and the Aulian Bridge hung open. A dozen Lhosir – some in mail, some not – were fighting twice that many Marroc. Most of the Lhosir had formed themselves into a circle of shields and the Marroc were keeping them occupied while they brought down the ones who'd been cut off from their fellows. A wide flight of steps rose to another door, the main door into the tower. Aulian steps. Indeed, everything about the tower was jarringly familiar. It looked like the towers Oribas knew from the desert, with their finely jointed walls in which every stone was different and no join ran straight for long, fitted together like a jigsaw with hardly room to slip a knife blade in between them. The outer wall was more recent and a much cruder thing, stones piled haphazardly together and thick with crumbling mortar.

The door at the top of the stairs burst open. Four Lhosir in mail hurtled out, smashing through the Marroc in the yard, cutting two men down as they went. Another dozen Marroc came after them, shouting and screaming and waving axes. The Lhosir punched through the Marroc surrounding the circle of shields and joined it and Oribas watched in admiration: the circle opened to receive them and closed again around them and then grew a little as the new Lhosir joined the wall. It was seamless.

'Take them!' screamed Achista. She stood at the top of the

steps and loosed an arrow at the Lhosir. It stuck into a shield and quivered there.

The Lhosir held their ground and the yard fell still for a moment, some Marroc finishing off the men they'd caught alone, the others standing back from the Lhosir shield wall. The Marroc outnumbered the Lhosir three or four to one but they were the ones afraid, and now that fear was turning against them. They started to back away. Oribas saw one or two Lhosir glance at the open gates and then back at the Marroc in front of them. 'Let them go!' he shouted. 'Let them run.' That's what Achista wanted, wasn't it? For word to spread of their defeat?

And then, gods preserve him, there she was, shouldering her bow and snatching an axe from the Marroc beside her and walking towards the Lhosir shields. She looked so small in her outsize mail shirt against the men in their furs with their forked beards. They'd kill her in a blink and he couldn't do anything, not a thing! He didn't have a weapon, and even if he had, he wouldn't have had the first idea what to do with it.

One of the Lhosir pointed at her and laughed; and then all the Lhosir were shouting, taunting the Marroc around them that they were afraid and had to send a woman to do their fighting, and Achista had pushed her way to the front of the Marroc and stood there for a moment, holding her axe, staring them down. Any moment now she'd charge them, he knew it, and then ...

He couldn't think what else to do. He snatched up a fistful of snow and scrunched it into a ball, let out a high-pitched cry – it probably didn't sound frightening at all but it was meant for his own courage – ran through the Marroc to stand beside Achista and hurled his snowball at the Lhosir. It was a good throw. It clipped a shield and broke apart into the face of the Lhosir holding it. A few of the Marroc laughed. He grabbed another handful and hurled that too, and then another and another, and now some of the Marroc joined in, pelting the Lhosir with snow as they stood behind their shields; and then in the midst of that someone fired an arrow and the Lhosir didn't see it coming. It hit one in the face and he staggered back, and then other arrows came; and perhaps one of them came from a Marroc who'd been with Oribas in the woods, for it flew low beneath the shields and struck a Lhosir in the leg. The wounded Lhosir howled and broke from the wall, charging as best he could, flailing his axe; and again the Marroc might have lost their courage if it hadn't been for Achista, who ran straight back at him. He batted her away with his shield and ignored her, but now two of the Marroc in mail ran at him. The three crashed together. The Lhosir took one of the Marroc down with a huge swing of his axe and then fell a moment later to the other. Achista picked herself up, and at that rest of the Lhosir charged. Oribas had no idea whether they were charging for the gates and escape or still thought they could win the day, but the Marroc split and let them through, and the Lhosir must have taken that as a sign that these Marroc had no stomach to fight, for the shield wall broke apart and they fell upon the Marroc as though they were a broken enemy, but the Marroc weren't broken at all. They surrounded each Lhosir as they'd learned in Jodderslet. They took them down one by one, pulling them into the snow and finishing them off with their knives; and every time a Lhosir cut one Marroc down, two more surged into him, leaping on his back, grabbing his shield, stabbing and hacking and slashing.

The Lhosir fought to the bitter end. The last two stood back to back behind their shields and whirling axes and killed three men before the Marroc withdrew and peppered them with arrows until they fell. Carnage filled the snow-covered yard. To Oribas it was a vision of horror but Achista was jubilant. She ran among the dazed Marroc from one to the next, grabbing them, shaking them, showing them what they'd done. The invincible fork-beards! Beaten! Again! She went to every single one of them, to the ones who crouched beside friends or brothers whose blood now stained the snow, touching them all. Then to the wounded, doing nothing useful except telling them how Modris would protect them and reward them for their courage. Oribas shook his head. Wounds from Lhosir spears and swords were savage things but here were Marroc men laughing and talking through their pain, covered in their own blood, men who wouldn't last the night.

He picked himself up and busied himself among them – treating wounds was one of the first things he'd learned. There wasn't much he could do for some and for others he lacked the medicines that might have saved them. But the cold of this place was his ally now. He pressed snow into wounds to staunch the blood and sent those Marroc who seemed to have nothing better to do into the tower to look for needles and thread and to get a fire going. The axe cuts were the easiest, ragged and bloody and horrible to look at but rarely deep. He set them aside to be stitched and cauterised. The men wounded by stabs from spears and swords were probably going to die but he did what he could for them. The Marroc watched with a mix of awe and horror when he packed wounds with snow then stitched them half closed but still open enough to drain. A few muttered under their breath about witchcraft, but they let him be. He was the Aulian wizard, after all, who'd laid a shadewalker to rest and opened the seal between the caves and the tower; and he was, they whispered to each other, sworn to serve the Huntress Achista who'd led them to victory at Jodderslet and now twice more. Oribas didn't remember swearing anything to anyone but he wasn't going to argue. Besides, if Achista had asked him there and then for an oath he might just have given it.

They let him work, and by the time he was finished with the easier wounds the sun had set and the Marroc had raised their banner from the top of the tower just as Achista said they would, had lit a great fire and were feasting on Lhosir food. Achista kept them busy carrying the bodies of their own dead away, deep into the woods where the Lhosir would never find them, and coming back with bundle after bundle of firewood. They'd have until the morning, she said, before the forkbeards knew what they'd done, and after that the gates would be closed and they'd hold the forkbeards at bay for as long as it took the Marroc to rise across the valley and throw them out.

That night she was alive with energy. She set watches and then picked two dozen men to creep down to the Varyxhun Road. They dragged out the bodies of the dead Lhosir, already stripped naked and scavenged for anything the Marroc could use. Oribas stayed in the tower so he didn't see, but he heard in the morning that they'd beheaded every one of them, scattered the bodies along the trail that led from the Varyxhun Road up the mountainside to Witches' Reach and left the heads piled on the Aulian Bridge. The Lhosir would know what they'd done. Everyone would know, and the edge of the Crackmarsh wasn't far away, where the outlaw Valaric had his hideaway with five hundred Marroc soldiers, all of whom had taken a blood oath of vengeance against Medrin Sixfingers for what he'd done in Andhun.

Oribas was glad to have no part of such dealings – instead he took a torch down to the old Aulian tomb. Not that he thought there was anything left to fear if the Lhosir had lived here for so long, but he wanted to be sure and he was curious to know what was so terrible that the Aulians had built a tomb so far from their homes. There were histories of all sorts of creatures, sorcerers and monsters hunted down and sealed inside these tombs. He knew of at least a dozen but he'd never heard of anything so terrible that it had been carried across the mountains to be so far away from the empire.

He moved through the crates and sacks, searching for the old Aulian crypt that was surely there. He found it eventually, a narrow crawlway that he could only get through by lying down and wriggling forward, holding the torch right out in front of him. There were strange scorings in the stone, deep grooves with no particular pattern to them. The crawlway was unpleasantly tight, as if deliberately too narrow for a large man to escape. It went on for a few feet and then opened into a small round chamber. In the centre stood a flat stone block large enough for a man to lie flat on top. Rising out of the block were six iron rods as thick as his thumb. They were stained and brittle with rust and all of them had snapped, but the rods had clearly once reached from the slab to the ceiling. Broken pieces of them lay on the floor, and there were deep holes in the stone of the roof matching the stumps below. The floor was covered in a pale grit. Oribas touched a few grains of it to his tongue. Salt.

He crawled around the chamber and found something else: two pieces of iron armour, a chest plate and a back plate. Each had three holes punched through them, sized and spaced to match the iron rods. He tested them against the width of the crawlway. They wouldn't fit, no matter which way round he tried them, but there were scratches on the inside of the chamber as though someone else had tried the same and had been much more persistent in their efforts.

He sat and stared for a while, wondering. It looked for all the world as though a suit of iron armour had once been pinned to the stone slab by six iron rods. An inscription even read *the iron witch*. What was it they'd had here?

There were no bones. That bothered him. After the tomb was opened someone might have come in and taken the armour for its iron, but why take their bones? Another thing bothered him too: the breastplate looked familiar. It looked like the armour of the iron devil who'd taken the Edge of Sorrows from Brawlic's farm. The Lhosir Fateguard.

He scraped around the edges of the stone slab for more inscriptions. Aulian priests liked to bind their prisoners with words and symbols as well as stone and metal and salt, but he found nothing, and that was strange too. There were places where inscriptions might have been, places where they ought to have been, but they looked as though they'd been scraped clean, the walls rubbed and scratched until no trace of words remained, only gouges in the stone.

He must have been there a long time but he didn't really notice. He dug more fistfuls of salt out of the bag on his belt because it never hurt to sprinkle salt over a place like this. He spilled half of it over the pieces of armour and spread the rest over the slab. Nothing happened, which was something of a relief. Afterwards, when he'd crawled back out of the crypt, he felt a little foolish and in need of some rest.

On his way up the stairs he found Achista coming the other way. She looked surprised to see him.

'I was looking for you,' she said, but he knew she wasn't. He smiled anyway.

'You found me.'

'What were you doing?'

'I was looking at the tomb. Just curiosity.'

'I wanted to thank you for what you did with the wounded men.'

Oribas wasn't sure that all the Marroc felt the same, and

they'd thank him even less when some of the wounds turned bad, when he started to drain fluids from the deeper ones, when the ones he'd known right from the start he'd never save began to die. That would be in the morning. Two of them, if he was right. He forced the smile back onto his face. 'And what were you really doing coming down here, Achista? After something from the Lhosir stores?' But the way her eyes suddenly wouldn't meet his forced him to think elsewhere. 'The seal?'

She nodded. 'We should close it. What if the forkbeards find it when they come?'

'If it's closed then it can't be opened again from this side. You'd trap us here. You know that, don't you?'

She couldn't look at him. He understood – this was what she and Addic had planned from the start. They'd hold for as long as it took. Either the Marroc of Varyxhun would rise or the Marroc of Witches' Reach would die to the last man. There'd be no running away because there was nowhere to go. 'Someone could always slip out and open the seal again from the outside. If the forkbeards hadn't found the cave and it was time for us to go.'

'Someone who understood how to make it work.' She meant him.

'Yes. I thought ... I thought perhaps you could wait somewhere nearby. And watch for our signal to come.' A signal that would never happen, or would be a column of flame as the tower burned with Achista and the last of the Marroc trapped inside, set on martyrdom. Oribas took her hands.

'As you wish.' He had to blink the tears from his eyes. 'But not today, Achista. Not today. When the Lhosir find the cave then we'll close the seal. But until then there's no hurry, is there?'

Her eyes shone in the torchlight, brim-full with sadness and joy. She leaned into him and rested her head on his shoulder. 'No, Aulian. I suppose a few more days can't hurt.'

28

THE FORGE

Deep under Witches' Reach Oribas poured his salt. Far away in the icy north the Eyes of Time shrieked in white burning agony. In the Temple of Fates in Nardjas and in Sithhun at King Medrin's side the iron-skinned men of the Fateguard staggered and howled. And in Middislet Gallow held his sword high, ready for the Edge of Sorrows to come down, but the blow never fell. Beyard clutched his head, fell to his knees and screamed at a pain he didn't understand. The Edge of Sorrows slipped from limp iron fingers into the snow.

Tolvis pulled himself to his feet and lifted his sword but Gallow stilled him. He stooped and took the Edge of Sorrows. Beyard knelt, breathing hard. He slowly raised his head and looked up. Gallow held the point of the red sword to his face.

'Go on,' whispered Beyard. 'Do it. I will not stop you.'

Loudmouth laughed. 'Don't you dare let him—'

Gallow cut him off. 'Get Nadric and the children back inside! Keep them away and leave this to me.' He tapped Beyard several times on the crown with the Edge of Sorrows and felt a tingle in his arm with each touch, a tiny shock with every tap. 'In the forge, old friend. In the shadows and out of the snow. Get up.'

'No!' Loudmouth was clutching an axe now. For a moment Gallow almost turned the red sword on him. It would be easy. Simple. One cut, and didn't he deserve it for what he'd done, stealing another man's wife and sons?

But that was the sword up to its old tricks and Gallow was wise to them. 'He was a friend for far longer than you were, Loudmouth. Just keep away. And you, old friend, take off that crown and that mask. I'd see your face one last time to remember you as we both once were. Young and stupid.'

Beyard lifted the iron helm from his shoulders. He stared at Gallow with pale dead eyes. 'How did you do it, Truesword?'

'Fate.' Gallow shrugged. Even with the mask gone he couldn't read Beyard's face. Sadness. Nothing more. Flakes of snow drifted down between them. Where they landed on Beyard's hair, Gallow saw, they didn't melt.

'Do it here, Gallow. Under the sky.'

Gallow hesitated. As he shifted, the candlelight from the house caught Beyard's face again. He looked as pale as a dead man.

'I swore I would not forget, old friend. I did not. I am Fateguard now but I gave no one your name then and nor have I now. Sixfingers will look for the sword but not for Gallow Foxbeard, nor for his wife and sons, not from me.' For a moment Beyard smiled. 'Piss-poor gang of thieves we turned out to be.'

'Piss-poor.'

'You saw the shield in the end. As did I, in time. Hardly worth it, was it?'

'It wasn't seeing it that mattered. It was the getting that close.'

Beyard rasped, or maybe laughed. He nodded. 'Yes.' Gallow tried to lift the red sword to finish it but his hand wouldn't move.

Arda strode out of the house in her winter furs and her boots. She hit Beyard in the face with a pan and he sprawled back into the snow. 'Three years, you pig!' she snapped, turning to Gallow. 'Three years and then you come back and you bring *this* with you!' She stamped on Beyard's iron-skinned fingers. 'Trees think better than you do! Now either finish this pasty-faced forkbeard or give me that sword so I can do it.' She snorted. 'Or you can give it to Loudmouth, not that he'd be any better.'

Gallow didn't know whether to laugh or cry. The first time he'd heard her voice in three years and it was exactly how he remembered it. He shook his head at Beyard. 'Sorry, old friend.'

'So am I.' Beyard rolled in the snow and kicked Arda's feet from under her. He caught her as she fell, staggered up and away from Gallow, and Gallow didn't dare strike because now Beyard had Arda held between them, one iron-gloved hand wrapped around her throat. 'Stay where you are, Truesword or I will break her neck.' Arda hammered furiously at Beyard but he was a man cased in iron. Her fists and feet rattled against him and did nothing. Beyard's fingers squeezed. 'Put the sword down in the snow. The others can still go.' His fingers tightened. 'You can't win, Truesword. There are men coming. Around the Crackmarsh instead of through it but they'll be here by the morning. Fight me and she dies. If somehow you win you'll still have twenty men hunting you by sunset.'

Gallow took a step away. 'Then I'll run, and you'll get neither me nor the sword and you can kill her if you wish. Just another Marroc, after all.'

Arda stopped struggling and stared. Beyard shook his head. 'No, Truesword. That's not who you are.'

'She's taken another man.'

'You were dead!' snapped Arda.

Gallow ignored her. Beyard was still shaking his head. He was smiling. 'That's still not who you are, Truesword.' He squeezed tighter, so tight that Arda couldn't breathe. He was strangling her, his eyes fixed on Gallow. 'Her corpse will be my shield if you fight me, Truesword.'

'Gallow!' Loudmouth. 'Ironskin, if you hurt her, I will cut you to pieces and feed them to pigs. I will piss on your corpse.'

'Wait!' Gallow let Solace fall by his side. 'Beyard, this is not who you are either. Let her go.'

The iron man's fingers loosened. 'You for her, Gallow?'

Arda pulled herself out of Beyard's grip. She hissed at Gallow, 'Just run when you have the chance, you stupid forkbeard.'

Beyard laughed. 'I can see why you chose her, Gallow. I'll keep her safe.' He caught Arda's hand before she could get away. 'You and Solace for all the other Marroc here. Her to keep you to your word.' He dragged Arda slowly back into the darkness of the forge. Gallow stared after her, eyes full of sorrow while her own thoughts were kept so tightly pressed inside that she was the same mystery to him as she'd been from the moment he'd met her. 'I will be here, waiting for you, old friend.'

In the house Loudmouth and Nadric were packing bags. Loudmouth gripped Gallow's shoulder. 'Nadric can take the children to the Crackmarsh as soon as it's light. Between us we'll kill the Fateguard. We'll wait here, and if he's not lying and more brothers of the sea come tomorrow, we'll fight them too. The two of us.'

Gallow shook his head. 'Beyard's not a liar. Take them now.'

'It's freezing cold and dark as soot!'

'By sunrise you'll reach the Crackmarsh. They'll be safe there.'

Tolvis shook his head. 'Feya's too little. She'll freeze. And Nadric's too old to—'

'Carry her.'

'But I'm not—'

Gallow had Loudmouth by his shirt, pulling him up close and almost lifting him off the ground. 'You want to stay here at my side and fight Beyard? I've seen you fight him once already. In the morning Medrin's men will come. My family will be long gone. You will see to that. What's between me and Beyard is none of your trouble. Get them ready. When you're gone, Beyard and I will settle this between us. I'll follow when it's done or else I'll be dead.'

'It should be me,' gasped Tolvis.

'But it's not you he wants, Loudmouth.' He let go. 'You cared for my family when you thought I was dead. Care for them now.' He turned and walked back outside, not wanting to meet the stares of his children. They hadn't seen him for years. What good did it do for them to see him now?

Back in the forge Beyard had Arda sat on the floor, tied and with a sack thrown over her head. He squatted beside her, still and silent, and for a long time Gallow stood there too, watching them both, remembering the days before he'd crossed the sea, and afterwards, roaming the Marroc lands with the Screambreaker's band, fighting, burning, killing, every unkindness that came with war.

'Did you miss it, Beyard? Not crossing the sea and going to war with the rest?'

Beyard took so long to answer that Gallow wondered if the Fateguard was asleep, but eventually he stirred and turned his head. 'No. And that seems strange even to me. Those of us chosen by the Eyes of Time, we serve ...' He seemed to struggle. 'We serve a different purpose now.'

'You serve Medrin.'

'That is a passing thing.'

They stood and watched without words. From the house Loudmouth's angry shouts crept out through the falling snow. Arda bawled insults at Beyard and Gallow alike from under the sack and told Gallow how much he was a fool and how much she hated him and how much Tolvis was a better man until Beyard gently laid an iron hand on her and told her she could say what she liked, there was nothing that would drive Gallow away because he wasn't here for her. He spoke quietly, telling her how Gallow had been brought to him in Varyxhun and what had passed between them, and the locket Gallow carried and how he'd used it to find her. When he was done she still swore and told Gallow he was useless, but her words had an edge to them, a touch of despair, and when she stopped, Gallow saw that she was shaking. Sobbing.

They heard Tolvis and Nadric and the children leave. For a time after that Gallow stared at the roof of Nadric's forge, listening to the darkness. Beyard remained silent. He didn't move, didn't creak or shift, and Gallow couldn't even hear him breathe, until suddenly he twisted and his arm flashed out. He threw one of Nadric's hammers so fast and so out of the blue that Gallow didn't even move. It hit him in the head, and the next thing he knew he was lying on his back in the snow outside the forge and Beyard was standing over him. The iron man was holding the red sword again, and there was a black horse in the forge yard with Arda struggling and yelling blue murder slung across its back.

A cold hand of iron touched his shoulder. 'It is true, True-sword. We do not sleep.' Beyard stood up and backed away. 'Get up.' As Gallow sat up, Beyard tossed him his helm, scored now by Nadric's hammer, and climbed onto the back of his horse. 'For a time there I thought I'd killed you. You were out like the dead.' He shook his head. 'Perhaps that would have been better. Damn you, Truesword. I'll give you a day. I won't hurt her. I swear that by the Eyes of Time. But I'll keep her so I know you'll come. I'll let Medrin have his sword, but we're not done, you and I. Find me when you're ready.'

Gallow struggled to his feet. 'Just take me. Let her go and take me.'

'No.'

They stood and faced one another, eye to eye. 'Why? Let her go!'

'No.'

'Curse you, Beyard, why? It's me you want!'

'Why? Fate. Memories. Who we once were. Because if I take you meekly back in chains then I'll have to give you to Sixfingers. Does it matter? All this way and here I am letting you go, but it was hardly fair throwing that hammer. Don't hide from me too well, Truesword. Come for me when you're ready.'

Gallow shook his head. 'I'll come for you. I'll come for both of you.'

Beyard smiled. He stepped back and raised the red sword in salute. 'I know you will.' Then he shook his head and glanced at the sky where the first light before dawn was beginning to grey the night. 'Medrin's men will come soon. I'll keep them away from your precious Marroc. When the time comes, fight well, Truesword.'

For a long time Gallow stayed where he was. Tolvis and the others were gone but he knew exactly where they'd be. Nadric would lead them to the edge of the Crackmarsh and the caves in the woods, to the place where the villagers of Middislet had always hidden when war swept towards them. He knew the way.

The sun began to rise. Cocks crowed. The people of Middislet would be waking and Beyard was gone. Gallow bowed his head and turned to the south, towards the Crackmarsh. He walked and ran as fast as he could, determined to find Loudmouth and the Marroc he'd seen in the hills and take them back with him, his own little army, and slay every one of Medrin's men if that was what it took.

But perhaps the years had made him careless, or perhaps his mind was too much on Arda or on seeing his children again after so long and what he might say to them. And so he didn't see the Marroc slip out from among the trees in the darkness behind him with a bowstring in his hand, nor hear him until the string looped over his head and pulled tight around his neck and he started to choke. He threw himself down, but two more slipped from the night and pinned him while the bowstring drew tighter and tighter.

'Well well. Another stinking beardless forkbeard,' hissed one. 'Take him with the other one. Valaric's going to want to see this.'

Valaric?

Gallow's eyes dimmed. But there were probably lots of Marroc called Valaric.

29

WHAT HAPPENED TO
VALARIC THE MOURNFUL

After he'd set fire to Teenar's Bridge and scrambled up the cliffs into the western half of Andhun, Valaric had sat and stared over the Isset and watched the eastern half burn. There was no way to know whether the Vathen had done it or whether it was the forkbeards or whether it was no one in particular and just one of those things that happen when two armies rampage through someone else's city at the same time. He watched the last of the Marroc boats sail out of the harbour and tried to remind himself that he'd made sure at least *some* people had had enough time to get away from the slaughter. He'd seen that coming, the vengeful forkbeards. The Vathen, though, he hadn't seen *that*. Not that it made a difference. Forkbeards and horsemen fighting each other was just fine. If they could have found somewhere else to do it then it would have been perfect.

He waited until nightfall to see who would win, but it wasn't until the next morning that he saw the Vathen moving at the other end of the ruined bridge. Knowing that the forkbeards had probably been killed to the last man didn't make him nearly as happy as it should have. He didn't know the Vathen but they weren't likely to be much better. He made up for the disappointment by turning on the forkbeards who'd been in the western half when the bridge burned. There were only a handful, and by the time the fires had died in the harbour, the western half belonged to the Marroc again. The Vathen wouldn't be crossing the Isset at Andhun, nor anywhere else on its lower reaches without a lot of boats, but anyone could simply ride and march across the Crackmarsh, so that was where he went, and quickly, gathering men around him as he did. They became a grim band, Valaric's Crackmarsh men, fighting the bestial ghuldog half-men night after night until they learned to leave them be; and then when the Vathen did finally come their way, Valaric murdered them in every way he could imagine. His men were never far from the Vathan camps. Sentries vanished. Scouting parties sank into the marsh under hails of arrows. His Marroc crept among them at night and spoiled their food and poisoned their water. They crippled horses as often as men. They learned to communicate with the ghuldogs in the most basic way and used them, drawing the ghuldogs to the Vathen, showing the half-men that the Vathen and their horses were easier prey, seeing to it that the Vathen had no doubt the stories were true and the Crackmarsh was full of monsters. It was an ugly bloody summer of murder and knives and honour had no part in it, but the Vathen never crossed the Crackmarsh.

Months passed. Summer turned to autumn. The Isset fell to its lowest and the Vathen tried one last time. They lashed together a fleet of rafts into a giant floating bridge, but by then the forkbeards had come back. Even in the Crackmarsh they knew that Yurlak himself had crossed the sea. Marroc fought alongside the forkbeards now, but not Valaric. He sat in his marsh and watched, waiting to pick off the winner.

The battle, when it came, made the slaughter outside Andhun look like a skirmish. Valaric didn't see it but he heard soon enough: the Vathen had beaten Yurlak. Then they beat him again and this time they killed him for good measure, but by then the winter was setting in and the Crackmarsh men had turned the ghuldogs into their own horde. There were thousands of the feral creatures, half dog and half man. Valaric led them out of the marsh one late autumn night and they swept in secret along the banks of the river, the ghuldogs sinking into the Isset in the daylight, the Marroc vanishing among the trees. They caught a new Vathan horde crossing the river, so many it would take them days. On the first night Valaric sent the ghuldogs into the camp of the Vathen who'd crossed while he and his Crackmarsh men cut loose the rafts that made the bridge and set them adrift and then melted away back to their swamp. Stories trickled to them of how the Vathan camp had been turned into a bloody horror. Ghuldogs took a man down, they ripped him apart and usually partly ate him, and even the men who got away with only a bite generally died or even worse. They were only stories, especially that last part, but living in the Crackmarsh Valaric came to know the truth.

The ghuldogs didn't come back – they stayed along the Isset, preying on whatever came their way – but the Crackmarsh was huge and there were always more.

The Vathen fared badly that winter. When they came again in the spring, Medrin Sixfingers was waiting for them, and Valaric wished he hadn't crushed the Vathen after all, for Medrin loved his blood ravens and hated every Marroc ever born. He came with more forkbeards and this time he came to stay. He hanged every Marroc who said a word out of place and drafted the men he didn't murder into his army. He wasn't like the other forkbeards. Valaric heard that much. He only cared about the winning of a fight, not the way of the winning, and he won that year against the Vathen on the back of his Marroc archers.

Some said it was the year after that the horror began – after Sixfingers broke the Vathen and drove them back across the Isset at last and set his mind to ruling his new kingdom – but Valaric knew better. The Crackmarsh began not far from where the Isset tumbled out of the Varyxhun valley gorge, close to the Aulian Bridge and Issetbridge. He knew that Medrin had sent the very worst of his forkbeards into the valley looking for the Sword of the Weeping God and for Gallow the Foxbeard. He knew about what they'd done there, the blood ravens. Varyxhun became as Andhun had been, as the rest of the old kingdom of the Marroc would become once Medrin finished taking out his hate on the Vathen. Sixfingers never forgot that a Marroc had nearly killed him once. It was a while before Valaric learned that it was Truesword who'd taken his hand and a while longer still before he heard the stories of how Medrin had had a new one made of iron crafted by the cold spirit of the Ice Wraiths, gifted to him along with the iron-gloved servants the forkbeards called their Fateguard but the Marroc knew by other, crueller names. The forkbeards called him Medrin Ironhand to his face, other things behind his back. Valaric called him worse and quietly carved Medrin's name into an arrowhead and kept it on a thong around his neck.

He was fingering it when Sarvic came and stood nearby in that lurking way he had where he never quite got around to saying anything, just stood closer and closer to wherever Valaric was sitting until eventually Valaric just wanted to stick a knife in his leg to make him spit it out. He never did, though. Sarvic had been at Andhun, and Andhun had turned him cold and hard. And he could shoot an arrow into a man's eye at fifty paces.

'Well?'

'Messenger from Fat Jonnic. A couple of forkbeards just wandered in from Middislet.'

'Well now they can just wander to the bottom of the swamp then, can't they? Feed them to the ghuldogs. They'll be hungry this time of year.' He frowned and looked at Sarvic hard. 'Why's Fat Jonnic bothering to tell me this?'

Sarvic shuffled his feet. 'One came with a handful of Marroc. They say the iron devil that crossed the Crackmarsh went to Middislet.'

Valaric stopped fiddling with his arrowhead. 'Middislet?' A smile spread slowly over his face. 'Nice and close. We might have to do something about that after all. Did they say how many men he's got?'

'None.'

Valaric frowned. He'd let the devil cross his swamp without trouble because none of them quite knew how to kill one, but what was he doing in in Middislet? 'Fat Jonnic did right. We'll go and see these forkbeards and ask them a question or two before we chop off their beards. And maybe pay a visit to Middislet. There's Vathen about this side of the river again. Forkbeards could get into all kinds of trouble in a place like this.' He raised an eyebrow, then saw that Sarvic wasn't rushing off to grab a fistful of swords and axes like he ought to but was doing his shuffling thing again. Valaric sighed. 'Yes?'

'Fat Jonnic got names out of the forkbeards, Valaric.'

'I hope he doesn't imagine I care. Unless one of them happens to be called Forkbeard Ghuldog-food, which I suppose would be funny.'

'No.' Shuffle shuffle.

'Oh what, Sarvic, *what*?'

'One of them said his name was Gallow. Gallow Truesword.'

Valaric shook his head. 'That Gallow's gone. Died in Andhun. But we can have some extra fun with whoever this forkbeard really is for that.'

'Thing is, Mournful, Fat Jonnic says the Marroc family say the same. They say they're *his* family. From Middislet.'

A numbness crept out from the inside of Valaric's head and crawled across his face. He nodded. 'Then, Sarvic, I think you'd better come too.' He watched Sarvic go and slowly shook his head. *Gallow Truesword? Back from the dead?*

30

OIL AND WATER

The first Lhosir to come to Witches' Reach didn't come up the track from the Varyxhun Road the next morning, but the one after. There were twenty of them from the garrison at Issetbridge below the mouth of the valley. Oribas and Achista watched together as the Lhosir crossed the bridge and rode up the Varyxhun Road, long before they turned onto the track up to the Reach. Achista smiled and took his hand. 'They're coming for us. They're coming to see.'

'How do you know?'

'I just know.'

The Marroc moved quickly. By the time the Lhosir reached the fort the gates hung open, the fire pits were stamped out and the Marroc were hidden away, the tower seemingly abandoned, all to lure the Lhosir inside. And they came, but they walked into the trap with their eyes wide open, with two men on horses outside the gates and two more further down the trail, and when the Marroc surged out of their hiding places and cut the Lhosir down with their arrows and their axes, the riders on the trail both got away. Oribas found himself busy again, stitching up more holes in the Marroc who'd been hurt. That night he heard the gates open and he knew that Achista was taking Lhosir bodies down to the bridge again to leave them where they couldn't be missed.

'Perhaps we'll have a day or two more before they come again,' she said, but they didn't.

By the middle of the next day, Addic had joined them from wherever he'd been with news that the forkbeards of Varyxhun were on the move. He'd watched them as long as he dared and then he'd ridden like the wind. They'd be at Witches' Reach the next morning, some fifty or sixty of them and perhaps more coming on behind. More still once Cithjan heard what had happened to the forkbeards from Issetbridge. Addic wandered the fortress with Achista, along the walls and in and out of the sheds and the forge and the halls inside the tower to the kitchens and the cellars and the old Aulian tomb below. Oribas left them to it. He stared at the mountains, up the Isset gorge to the snow-covered peaks around Varyxhun and beyond to the old Aulian Way. It didn't seem all that long ago that he'd thought Gallow dead and all he could think about was the spring and crossing back the way he'd come, away from all this cursed cold. Now? Now the thought simply wasn't there any more. When he looked for it, he found it didn't even make sense. There wasn't anything waiting for him back in old Aulia. No family, no friends, no people. The Rakshasa had taken those years ago. He could name three people on the other side of the mountains that he might have called friends in a pinch, the other survivors of the great hunt; and when he'd left them behind to cross the mountains with Gallow it had seemed impossible that he wouldn't come back, that they wouldn't be a band together for ever, fearless and unstoppable, hunting down shadewalkers and things far worse and sending them to their rest. Now he saw all that for the illusion it was. He couldn't imagine going back. He couldn't even imagine seeing the spring. He'd bound himself to these Marroc without seeing it happen, and now all of them were doomed. Perhaps it was as much an illusion as the one he'd left behind but that didn't matter. From where he was, it felt the most real thing in the world.

'I think my sister is in love with you,' said Addic quietly. The words were so in tune with his own thoughts that the Marroc's silent arrival didn't even make him flinch.

'And I think I am in love with her,' Oribas replied.

'She's not had eyes for a man for a while. There was a farmhand a couple of years back. A good man, I thought. They might have been married but the forkbeards killed him. After that I think she wedded her bow instead.' Addic shook his head and then pulled a satchel off his shoulder. 'I have something for you, Aulian.' Oribas stared and then smiled. His satchel. *His* satchel.

The one he thought he'd lost when the Lhosir had thrown him over the edge of the gorge back on the snowbound Aulian Way. 'One of Brawlic's men went and got it before the forkbeards killed him. I don't know how he knew it was there. He must have overheard some talk, I suppose. He was probably in Varyxhun to sell it but I got to him first.' He handed the satchel to Oribas, who looked inside. Someone had been through it, that was obvious, but everything that mattered was still there.

'Thank you.'

Addic leaned over the tower walls and stared out at the gorge. 'My sister wants to close the Aulian door so the forkbeards can't come in as we did. She'd seal us in here.'

'With me on the outside to open the door when she asks.'

'But she won't ask. And nor will I. You know that, don't you?'

'Yes, I do.'

'What I mean to say, Aulian, is that we should make the very most of the days we have left, all of us. Make her happy. Make both of you happy. You have my blessing.' He put an awkward hand on Oribas's shoulder and walked away.

'I had a thought. About the shaft and the way in through the caves ...' Oribas began, but Addic was already gone and his own thoughts were in too much turmoil. It was slowly dawning on him what Addic had meant. He stood and looked out over the river a while longer. The steep craggy sides of the gorge struck him as stern and majestic now instead of forbidding. The Aulian Bridge gleamed and the water sparkled in the bright winter sun. The Isset falls were a mile away and out of sight, but from the walls of Witches' Reach Oribas could see beyond the sudden end of the mountains to the flat brownish haze that the Marroc said was the Crackmarsh, and to the shapes of the dales beyond and around it. He tried to imagine the hills and the mountains covered in lavish green and dappled with the colours of spring flowers. Strip away all this snow and he could see that the Varyxhun valley would be beautiful. Still too cold, though. He climbed down from the walls. The Marroc were none too keen on opening the gates to let him out and made no promises about letting him back in again, but there was always the cave and the old Aulian tomb for that.

It took him a while to walk down to the forest and the old forest camp and find what he was looking for. By the time he got back to Witches' Reach, the sun was sinking. He found Achista among the wounded, bright-eyed as ever and listening to their stories, bringing them water and soup from the kitchen below. He watched her a while, marvelling at how she seemed to lift each one of them. It seemed a shame to ask her to stop and so he waited, simply looking at her until the sun kissed the hills outside. Then he touched her on the shoulder. 'I have something important to show you,' he said, and when she turned to smile at him, he led her away to the very top of the tower and its open roof. He pointed to the orange sun as it straddled the western mountains across the gorge.

'I'm a stranger from a strange land.' He took her hands in his. 'It makes me sad that I know so little of the customs of your people. Where I come from there is a proper way to this. I have no doubt there is a proper way among your people too, one that's different. I hope you understand. This is the Aulian way. One day you'll teach me the Marroc way. I have three gifts for you.' He let her hands go and forced himself to look at the sun and not at her. 'The first is this sunset and the memory of it, for the sun is always the most radiant thing bar one in any life, and that one thing that eclipses it in mine is you. When the sun sinks beneath the horizon, I will remain bathed in the light of knowing you, of being beside you, of remembering you and of the possibilities you bring.' He swallowed hard, knowing those possibilities were likely few and short, and knowing too that it no longer mattered. He reached into his satchel and drew out three of the blue flowers from the forest. 'The second are these flowers.' With delicate fingers he lifted off her helm and slipped one stalk over each ear and twined the last into her hair. 'The left is for the past we shared. The right is for the future. The third is for what matters most of all, for the now.' Last of all he offered her his gloves. He smiled and laughed. 'In my own land I would have offered you the most exquisite silk, woven with patterns of gold and silver thread. All I have here are these, which I have worn for months and are old and battered. They have served me well. They're a part of me. I offer them now to be a part of you. As I offer myself.'

He held out the gloves. Achista stared at them and then at him. Her eyes shone in the sunset. 'I don't understand, Oribas.' She cocked her head.

'I'm telling you, Achista of the Marroc, that I belong with you. And I'm asking whether you will belong with me, for the rest of our lives, however long or short they may be, whatever the dawn may bring. I'm asking you to become one with me, that we may both be the wings that the other may fly, that we might do together what neither of us could do alone, that, gods willing, we shall live long and bring great happiness to one another, that we shall raise sons and daughters together and watch them make us proud, that we shall herd our animals and grow our crops and work hard, side by side under the burning sun, and that we shall sleep softly in the same tent and hold one another in the cool hours of dark until we are old and grey and the gods call us away.'

Tears marked her cheeks. She looked away. 'Oribas, no. Whatever the dawn may bring? You know the answer to that. Forkbeards. You're not Marroc. I can't ask you to stay. I don't want you to stay.' She looked back at him. 'I want you to go. You have to close the seal and wait for—'

Oribas put a finger to her lips. 'For the signal you'll never give.' He smiled and nodded. 'I know. And I've thought about this long and hard today. I've watched you move among your kin. You bring a spark of hope to each and every one. I could never do that. Except for you. I'm not a fool, Achista. I know what awaits us. I've looked at the future. I'm a wizard, after all!' He laughed but not for long. 'If I leave, perhaps I will have a long life or perhaps not, but it will be one that is forever tarnished with regret. If my choice is between long dull empty years or one more day here with you then I will stay, and so I *will* stay, however you answer, and you cannot stop me. I will find means to make this tower impossible to enter, no matter how many forkbeards come, if that is what I must do to keep you. I would call down gods and raise up demons and fling fire from the sky if only I could find a way.'

He offered her the gloves a second time. 'I have felt this fire once before. A demon destroyed my world. I gave my life to bringing about its end. The gods sent to me what I needed, and now they have sent me to you. My fire then was vengeance but now I have another that burns with a kinder flame. My heart is yours, Achista of the Marroc, and you cannot change that, for my heart belongs always to me and so is always mine to give as I choose.'

She closed her eyes and bowed her head. Her voice broke to a whisper. 'I cannot ask you to stay, Oribas. I cannot.'

'You can ask me to stay or you can ask me to leave or you can say nothing at all, but it will make no difference. I will stand with you to the end either way.'

'You can't even hold a sword!' She shook her head, sobbing and laughing, smiling in a ring of tears.

Oribas reached a hand and lifted her chin so she was looking at him again. 'But I can hold you.'

She fell into his arms and crushed him and he held her back, long and tight. He lifted her head and kissed her, and for a long time the sunset and the glory of the Isset gorge and the mountains around them faded into nothing. Oribas thought he saw Addic poke his head up onto the roof, but he vanished again, and suddenly it was dark and cold and the sun was long gone and stars speckled the sky, and Addic really was there this time.

'Brother. I ...' Oribas watched her smile, and he was right: it was every bit as warm as the sun itself.

'Diaran and Modris watch over both of you.' Addic smiled back and beckoned them away, out of the cold, down through the belly of the tower, past the kitchens and the cellars to the old Aulian tomb where a brazier now burned beside a huge pile of furs that hadn't been there before. 'There's little enough joy for us Marroc,' he said, and he hugged Achista and then Oribas as well. 'No one will trouble you here before sunrise.'

And no one did, though neither of them got much sleep that night, and it was well into the next morning before they were finally awoken after they fell asleep in each other's arms amid a cocoon of fur. When Addic came down to them again, this time there was no sign of a smile on his face.

'The forkbeards have come,' he said.

31

THE CRACKMARSH

Gallow opened his eyes. He was in a cave. Three Marroc stood looking at him. 'Well,' said the one who'd given him the worst of the kicking. The other two stared. The torchlight behind them made them into silhouettes. They were soldiers and that was all he could see.

'That's him.' He didn't know the second voice but he knew the one that came after it.

'Gallow.'

Valaric. Gallow hauled himself up to his hands and knees. 'Need your horse shod or a new blade for your scythe, do you?'

'I thought you were dead.' Gallow twisted until he was sitting up. 'Might have been better if things had stayed that way too. Better for a lot of people.' For a long time Valaric didn't move. Then he let out a great sigh and turned away. 'Go on then, Jonnic, let him loose. Then he can tell us all about the iron devil of Varyxhun being in Middislet. You're not going to tell me you have nothing to do with that, are you, Gallow?'

'He's left Middislet by now.'

Outside in the sunlight the Marroc fed him and gave him water and returned what they'd taken from him. They were none too happy about it but they did what Valaric told them. He let Loudmouth loose as well after Gallow told him what they'd done in Andhun.

'Turning into a right forkbeard-lover, aren't I?' Valaric spat, then listened as Gallow told his story. 'They turned Varyxhun upside down looking for you,' he said when Gallow was done. 'Blood ravens lining the road. Dozens of them. All because of you.'

'If you put it that way, how many Marroc in Andhun died because of *you*, then?' snapped Tolvis.

'Was Sixfingers who turned on the city.' Valaric's eyes narrowed.

'Was Sixfingers who turned on Varyxhun.'

The two of them stared at each other, neither one giving any ground until a Marroc ran and whispered in Valaric's ear. He nodded. 'Forkbeards came past Middislet yesterday. One, maybe two dozen. They had the iron devil of Varyxhun and a Marroc woman with them.' He cocked his head, still staring at Tolvis. 'Didn't burn it down, didn't hang anyone, just passed through. Why are you here, Gallow?'

Gallow shrugged. He'd been asking himself the same thing ever since Beyard had sent him off into the night. Why? Why would a Fateguard do something like that? Because they'd once been friends? But that had been long ago and Beyard was an ironskin now, and so didn't the past and friendship count for nothing? Why all the trouble to hunt him down only to let him go? And if it was only the sword he wanted then he had that already. Why take Arda? It made no sense. No sense at all.

'Spying,' said Fat Jonnic. 'Why else?'

Valaric finally let his eyes move from Tolvis to Gallow. 'And what say you, Gallow the Foxbeard? Are you a spy?'

'I cut off Medrin's hand, Valaric.'

'So *you* say.' He leaned forward. 'But you know the Crackmarsh well enough to find these caves. Everyone in Middislet knows them. What about your friend?' His eyes flicked back to Tolvis. 'He a spy?'

Tolvis growled. 'Ask me to my face, Marroc.'

Gallow put a hand on Loudmouth's arm. 'I'd vouch for Tolvis with my life, Valaric.'

'A forkbeard vouching for a forkbeard?' Valaric sneered. 'What's a Marroc to make of that?'

'When Twelvefingers and his army stood inside the gates of Andhun, how many Marroc stood with you?' Gallow let that sink in a bit. 'I don't want anything from you, Valaric. Beyard has my wife.'

'Arda Smithswife?' Valaric chuckled and even Fat Jonnic laughed too. 'Good luck to him!'

Gallow flared. 'Mind yourself, Valaric!'

'Oh calm now, Gallow. We know Arda well enough. She'd come through the Crackmarsh now and then with a mule, heading to Issetbridge and back. She was a friend of the Crackmarsh men and did us favours now and then, and in return we kept the ghuldogs off her.' He snorted and grinned at Jonnic. 'Not that she needed much help with that, mind, not with that tongue of hers.' Then his face became serious again. 'The iron devil has a score of men with him. If he crosses the Crackmarsh again then we'll take him down this time. He might not die, but all that iron will rust if it's held under the water for long enough.'

Gallow shook his head. Beyard wouldn't be going through the Crackmarsh. 'Hrodicslet,' he said. 'There's a way into the Varyxhun valley without crossing the Aulian Bridge.' And he told Valaric and the Marroc about the trail from Hrodicslet into the high valleys and Jodderslet and the Devil's Caves while Valaric scratched his chin and began to pace. By the time he was done, Valaric was smiling.

'Show me this road and I'll take you to Hrodicslet.' He cocked his head. 'What do you say, forkbeard?'

'What about my family?'

'They can stay here with Fat Jonnic until they're ready to go home again. Safe as anywhere. Shall we go?'

Gallow nodded.

'Good.' Valaric rubbed his hands. 'Cithjan's iron devil has had it coming for a while now.' He nudged Gallow. 'You've got a forge. We'll melt him down if that's what it takes.'

32

SNOW AND FIRE

Addic might have seen fifty or sixty forkbeards riding out of Varyxhun castle but there were closer to a hundred of them around the fortress. They took their time, picking their way around the slopes below Witches' Reach, carefully outside the range of the Marroc archers on the walls. They ringed the fort with watchers and then withdrew and set about cutting wood for their fires and got a few of them going. The smell of roasting fat wafted up the mountain. Hours after they arrived two of them finally walked toward the gates with their shields raised, holding high a spear with a white rag tied to the shaft. Oribas watched them come.

'Oribas should talk to them,' Achista said.

Addic snorted. 'What's to talk about? Do you imagine they'll let us go? Either the valley will rise to our banner or the fork-beards will kill us, and I'd rather die on the end of their spears than be hung as one of their ravens.'

Achista shook her head. 'Nevertheless, Oribas will talk to them.'

Achista led them now, and however much Addic rolled his eyes, this was a thing Oribas had asked to do. He went to the gates, the Marroc opened them and he walked out onto the road, hands held high where all could see them. Fifty paces away the Lhosir stopped and waited. They looked at him in puzzlement as he drew closer.

'I am Oribas of what was once Aulia.' He stopped before them, hands still raised. 'In my own land a herbalist and a healer but now a prisoner of these Marroc. They've sent me out to hear your words and receive your spears. There are many arrows pointed at my back.'

The Lhosir carrying the spear frowned and peered at him. 'Didn't we send you to the Devil's Caves once already?'

'Yes, you did. There were Marroc waiting in ambush and so I became their prisoner instead of yours. They won't let me leave because I fled with them and I have seen their secret paths between the valleys.'

The Lhosir's eyes narrowed. 'So how is it they send you to do their talking?'

'Forgive me. I've given you my name; may I have yours?'

The Lhosir glanced past Oribas to the walls of the Reach. 'Skilljan, known as Spearhoof. Tell your Marroc friends my name. Some of them will know it.'

Oribas bobbed his head. 'I am here because the Marroc have nothing to say and nor do you. If I take one step past you on this road, Skilljan Spearhoof, I will fall with a dozen Marroc arrows in my back. I have no friends among either of you. If you turn your spears on me, you save them a few arrowheads. If you take me, there is little I can reveal save how to reach from here to the Devil's Caves without walking the Varyxhun Road. The Marroc don't believe you have anything to say that could possibly matter. If I'm honest with you, Skilljan Spearhoof, nor do I. I'll take them your name. Is there anything else?'

'Who leads them here?' asked Skilljan.

'A woman. Her name is Ylista but they call her Shieldborn.'

'Never heard of her. A woman leads this Marroc rabble, eh?' The Lhosir glanced at one another. 'Here's what I have to say, Oribas of Aulia: there will be no quarter or mercy for any Marroc here. I will grant the remainder of the day for you all to make your peace with your gods. On the morrow we come. For every day that the gates of Witches' Reach remain closed to us, one Marroc farm somewhere in the valley will burn with every Marroc who lives there still within it. To those who surrender before we come, death will be quick and merciful. Those we take in battle will be raised on poles as blood ravens to keep watch over the Aulian Way and greet the shadewalkers. I will find the names of those who die on our swords from those we take alive. We will hunt down their fathers and their sons and their brothers. Sisters and wives and mothers and daughters will weep and curse and throw salt over the cairns of their sons. Tell them that, Aulian.' The Lhosir cocked his head. 'Shall we speak again? Shall we say sunrise to hear their answer?'

Oribas shrugged. 'I doubt they will open the gates for parley a second time.'

'Nor will I have aught else to say. But I'll offer you the chance nonetheless. I'll bring some shields. Maybe you'd like to run away from those arrows and speak a little more about these secret Marroc paths, Oribas of Aulia.' The Lhosir bowed and turned away. Oribas returned to the tower and told Addic and Achista what the Lhosir had said.

'I'd like to speak with them again,' he said when he was done. 'The seeds are sown. I have an idea how you might win this battle.'

'How many of them are there?' asked Achista.

Oribas shrugged but Addic answered. 'Not yet enough to take this tower by force but too many for us to face in the open. And there will be more.' He shook his head. 'I say we fight on a few days until they're ready to overwhelm us, then we leave. We slink away through the caves and strike again elsewhere. It'll gall them that we've slipped through their grasp.'

Achista shook her head. 'Every day we stay, Marroc turn their heads as they walk along the Varyxhun Road. They see our banner. They whisper our deeds where the forkbeards can't hear. If we run the whispers will be nothing more, but every day we defy the forkbeards they grow louder. We'll stay until they're shouts hurled from every rooftop in Varyxhun!'

'These are simple men,' snapped Addic. 'They have farms and families and sons and daughters. Let them make their stand and go. Half of them are only here because they know there's an escape waiting for them.'

Achista glanced at Oribas. Oribas shook his head. 'Make ladders,' he said. 'Rope and wood. Things that can be thrown over the walls. Do that first. They will seem another means to escape. Keep them in the tomb where they can be watched with care. Perhaps some of these brave men here should be allowed to slip away once the end is in sight to spread the word far and wide of what you have done at Witches' Reach?' He didn't wait for an answer but left them and went back into the tower, down the stairs to the old tomb and the Lhosir stores. There were kegs there with the smell of fish oil to them. He opened them one by one and tested them to see which would most easily burn. When he'd found the ones that suited him best, he put them aside and returned to the Marroc above. Fire was a fine weapon in any siege. Let the Lhosir learn that when they came, if they didn't know it already. For the rest of the day he walked the walls and stood on the roof of the tower, watching the Lhosir camp. The Lhosir were busy in the woods, felling trees and building. They were careful to keep out of sight but there weren't too many things they could be making. Ladders or a ram or most probably both. Oribas watched their scouting parties circle the walls, looking for places where they might climb up the slopes under cover and bring up a ladder without being seen. There weren't any, but he thought he knew where they might try. And they had their own watchers too, climbing up the side of the neighbouring mountain where Achista had shown him her banner and told him what she meant to do. They'd be able to see down into the yard between the walls and the tower, and so Oribas had the Marroc build a few things that might look from a distance like Aulian bolt-throwers and carry them up around the gates. He waited with the oil until after dark, rolling out half a dozen kegs while the Marroc lit fires and sang and drank.

'Be sparing,' he warned Achista. 'As soon as it's gone, that's when you'll wish you had it the most.' He took her back into the tomb with a few other Marroc and as many buckets and all the rope they could find to lift water from the bottom of the shaft, as much as they could carry. 'You have enough water in the snow here for days but there's no call to waste it. The water down here is foul. Tip scalding pots of it over the forkbeards when they try to climb their ladders. If the time comes when you must drink it, heat it over a fire until it steams. Keep it there for one finger of the sun and then let it cool.

'It seems a lot of work when there's snow lying everywhere underfoot.' They barely had enough rope.

'Pile the snow outside into a mound against the gates in the night and pack it tight. It will strengthen them and be your source of water. Make other mounds elsewhere, against the wall of the tower. That too will be your water. Who knows what will come over the walls when the Lhosir attack. Animal dung and their own faeces, perhaps. Although perhaps not.' He frowned. 'In the desert heat it is effective. Here perhaps less so.' He climbed down the rungs of the shaft and called to the Marroc to lower the first bucket. As each one came down, he filled it five or six times and threw the water down the tunnel that led out to the mountainside. It would freeze into ice in the night, he thought. He did that and then filled each bucket one last time and tugged on the rope for the Marroc to haul it back up. The buckets banged and clattered against the wall as they rose and most of the water spilled, but Oribas kept them at it. When they were done, he tested the level of the water in the shaft. It was a handspan down from the level of the passage now. Good enough.

'What was the point of that?' Achista asked him when he finally reached the top again. 'The buckets were almost empty by the time we got them up.'

'Fill them with snow.'

She threw up her hands in exasperation and fatigue. 'If we're going to do that, why did we waste half the night with this?'

'Do your Marroc have something better to do?'

He thought he had her there, since although the Marroc should be resting before the fight began in the morning, they both knew that most of them wouldn't be able to sleep. But when she wrapped her arms around his neck, he realised he was wrong. '*I* do,' she whispered.

They didn't get much sleep that night either, and this time Oribas was up before dawn. He showed Achista the oil he'd kept aside and told her exactly what he meant to do. Then, before he went out to parley with the Lhosir again, he opened his satchel and set to work.

33

HRODICSLET

Two days of hard walking on the heels of Valaric and his men brought them across the Crackmarsh and to Hrodicslet, where little wooden jetties stuck up out of the snow and all the houses were built on stilts for when the Isset flooded in the spring and the swamps and bogs of the marsh turned into miles and miles of water meadows and a thousand creeks and channels. Some years Hrodicslet didn't flood but more often than not it did. Boats lay scattered everywhere, resting askew in the snow, half buried, tethered to the houses and walkways, waiting for the thaw and for the rising waters that would follow. Valaric sent Sarvic ahead into the town to find where Beyard and his men were staying.

'They've helped themselves to Elder Hall,' Sarvic said when he came back. 'Can't see where else they'd go.'

'No. Don't suppose you can.'

Gallow looked over Valaric's Crackmarsh men. They were surly seasoned soldiers who'd face up to a Lhosir, but Beyard was a Fateguard armed with Solace, and every Marroc knew that the Comforter was a wicked blade.

'You can look as doubtful as you like,' Valaric growled. 'Do you think I'm going to stand outside and shout at them until they come out in their mail so we can have a fair fight? It'll be creeping in at midnight with knives. It'll be cutting throats, and the ones who wake up won't be dressed for battle. You know how much a forkbeard in a nightshirt troubles me? Not much at all.'

'I'll not be a part of murdering men while they sleep.'

'Fine.' Valaric picked up a stick and began to strip the bark off it with his teeth. 'You two go in there and ask them nicely to give your woman back, and then later after we've done with cutting throats, we'll all stand around your corpse and think what bloody idiots you forkbeards are. Or stay here and pick your noses and wait for me to bring her back to you. Your choice.'

The sun set. Winter darkness came quickly in the mountains but in the marsh the twilight seemed to linger. Valaric and his Marroc sat in a circle around a small fire, swigging beer and playing dice to while away the time. Gallow and Tolvis sat together apart from the Marroc. Gallow wasn't sure what to make of Loudmouth now he knew the truth. He should be grateful. Most of him believed that. Grateful to a man who'd walked across a hostile land to hand a purse of silver to another man's wife and not kept it for himself. Grateful to a man who'd protected his family and hidden them away from Medrin when he could so easily have sold them. Grateful to a man who'd seen to it that his children had food and grew strong, who'd taught them right and wrong as a Lhosir should know it and how to hunt and forage and the beginnings of how to fight. Grateful to a man who'd lost his own family years ago and was content to take on the duties of another. Grateful, and yet Tolvis had done more than merely care for Arda and his children as though he was a dutiful brother, and even if all of them had thought he was dead, a part of Gallow seethed at that. Tolvis had taken what was not his to take. Among the Lhosir such things were only ever settled with blood.

'I'll leave,' Tolvis said. 'As soon as she's free, I'll leave. I'll return across the sea and never come back.'

'You'll never survive. Too many people know you. Medrin will hear. He'll have you hanged.'

'I have plenty of friends.'

'You have plenty of enemies.'

Tolvis hesitated. 'And which should I call you?'

'Friend. I'll tell you if it must be otherwise.'

'Don't blame Arda.' Tolvis held his head in his hands. 'I was the one who—'

'Stop!' Again and again he remembered standing over Tolvis on the road out of Andhun, axe in hand after Medrin had sent Tolvis to bring Gallow back to join him in his hunt for the

Crimson Shield. He'd looked at the soldier lying on the road scrabbling for his feet and had made up his mind that yes, he *would* go back and he *would* join Medrin and he *would* finally set his eyes on the mystic shield that had created the rift between them in the first place. He'd thought it might change something. And it did, but nothing good. He'd have given much to go back to that moment, to leave Tolvis lying there and ride on home. Leave the Marroc and the Lhosir and the Vathen to fight and fight until only one remained while he lived quietly in peace, far away from anything, drawing wire and hammering nails and hoes and ploughs and scythes.

'Stop,' he said again, more gently. He pressed his hands to his face. It made no difference now. There was nothing he could do to make those years come back and nothing he could do to make things as they'd been before he'd left. Loudmouth might go home but so what? Did Arda even still want Gallow? Did his children remember him? And even if they did, Beyard knew who he was and perhaps so did the Lhosir who rode with him. They'd seen where he lived and they knew his family, and nowhere would ever be safe again. 'I don't want to know, Loudmouth. This is how it will be. When I'm with you, I'll blame Arda and be grateful for the care you took of my sons. When I'm with Arda, everything will be my fault, since Arda certainly won't allow for anything else.'

'She has a tongue to her, that's for sure. I wondered sometimes how you survived for all those years.' Tolvis chuckled and for a moment Gallow smiled too. Arda with her sharp tongue and Loudmouth together? Surprising they were both still alive.

'She put a spell on me, my friend,' said Gallow. 'The same one she put on you. One that never went away.'

Tolvis thought about that for a bit. 'There's more than one Marroc in Middislet who calls her a witch when they think no one will hear.'

'I remember three. Shilla, because everyone knew her brother was an idiot but Arda couldn't stop telling everyone anyway in case they'd somehow forgotten. Jassic because he was sweet on Shilla.'

'And then there's old woman Katta in her hut, who comes

into the village once a week and makes the sign of Modris every time she walks past the forge.' Tolvis smiled.

'Still alive, is she?'

'I think she'll live for ever, that one. Didn't know about Jassic though. He died two winters back. Vanished. Didn't find his body for weeks. No one knows what happened.' Tolvis shrugged. 'Got hurt, couldn't get home and froze, I suppose. Shilla married Boric the spring after.'

'She was always playing those two off against each other.'

They sat in silence after that, neither of them finding anything to say until Valaric finally got up from the fire and the rest of his Marroc rose to follow him. 'You forkbeards coming or are you leaving it to Marroc to do your fighting for you?'

'I'll not murder men in their sleep.'

Beside Gallow, Tolvis shook his head. 'Nor I.' He stood up anyway. 'But you'll need someone to face the ironskin for you.' He followed as Valaric led his men into the darkness and the distant fires of Hrodicslet, and so Gallow rose too, because Arda would expect it. She'd expect him to cut throats if that's what it took to keep his family safe, but some things he couldn't do, not even for her.

Valaric knew Hrodicslet well enough to find his way around its outskirts in the starlight. With his men he crept towards the centre through the deep snow among the raised walkways until the Marroc found their way to the Elder Hall at the town's heart. Valaric led them to the small door at the back, hidden in shadows under the overhanging eaves of a house that was more like a barn. He took the stick he'd been whittling earlier and wriggled it between the door and its frame and then made a face and crouched down and wriggled it some more, trying to lift the bar that held it closed on the inside. He peered through the crack and whispered, 'Quick as you can, lads. No need for quiet. They're a-snoring on the floor in there.' Then he threw the door open and the Marroc ran inside, swords drawn, yelling and screaming, stabbing into the thick bundles of fur on the floor. Valaric grabbed Gallow's hand and pulled him, dragging him inside. 'You don't have to do the killing if it troubles you, forkbeard, but by the gods you'll be here to see it happen.'

He stopped, the two of them barely inside the door. The first Marroc were halfway across the hall, their cries dying on their lips. The Lhosir bundles of fur were thrown over not men but sacks filled with straw. And then all around the hall, the doors to the little rooms around the sides where animals were kept indoors for the winter nights were thrown open and there they were, the Lhosir, axes drawn and ready for battle. They howled and fell on the Marroc and the Marroc ran. Valaric seized Gallow by his furs. 'Forkbeard piss pot! You led us into a trap!'

A Marroc bolted through the door. Gallow pushed Valaric outside and then stood to bar the way to Beyard and the advancing Lhosir. The Marroc who'd led the way were already dead, cut down in the first charge. Two Lhosir ran at him; he blocked them both with his shield and swung his axe at their faces, forcing them back. Behind him Loudmouth tugged at his coat. 'The Marroc are running, Truesword, and we should run too.'

'No!' Beyard had seen him now. Most of the Lhosir were pouring out of the big door at the other end of the hall into the streets of Hrodicslet. 'Arda!'

'Will not be helped by our deaths! Maker-Devourer, Truesword, I'd die for her too; I'd die for both of you if it would help, but it won't, not this time. This time we must run!'

Run. A Lhosir never ran. That was what they all told themselves but the truth was that they did, more often than any of them would ever admit. He remembered old Jyrdas One-Eye, most terrible of the Screambreaker's men: he'd been happy to admit that he'd turned and run plenty of times when the odds didn't suit him. Hadn't been afraid to die when he thought it would make a difference but had no interest in it when it changed nothing. Even the Screambreaker had run once. They'd all run at Selleuk's Bridge, the one and only time the Marroc had got the better of them. He and Tolvis had run from the Vathen in Andhun. So yes, a Lhosir ran when it suited him, but Arda was in there, the woman whose memory had kept him alive for three hard years.

Tolvis pulled so hard that Gallow staggered back out of the doorway, and then Loudmouth was standing in front of him with his axe and his shield and no mail at all, facing three Lhosir who saw how easy he was going to be and grinned. 'Stay if you like, Gallow, but if you do then I won't budge from in front of you.'

So he ran, and Tolvis ran after him, and the Lhosir gave chase but Beyard called them back. 'Find the Marroc! Don't worry about them. They'll be back. I have something they want.' As the Lhosir stopped, Gallow slowed and looked over his shoulder. He could just about make out Beyard in his iron crown, striding out into the night. 'I kept my word, Truesword! I gave you a day and I've not hurt her!'

Gallow rounded on the cry with one of his own: 'Why did you let me go, Beyard? Why keep her but let me go?' But he got no answer.

They followed their own tracks back into the edges of the Crackmarsh, to where the surviving Marroc were gathering. Valaric stared at the two of them in disbelief while the other Marroc circled around, weapons drawn and faces tight with fury.

'I lost seven men tonight, forkbeards. Another man might think you knew all along that this was a trap. Another man might think you led us to Hrodicslet knowing they'd be waiting.'

'Kill them, Valaric! Feed them to the ghuldogs!'

Tolvis snarled, 'Who's first?'

Gallow pushed in front of him. 'I led you to some forkbeards, that's all. You were going to kill them in their sleep. I told you not to. You did this to yourself, Valaric. You knew a Fateguard led them.'

Valaric turned away. 'Go, Truesword. You're not welcome here any more.'

'Valaric!' Two of the Marroc almost jumped at him. 'They're forkbeards! You can't just let them go!'

Valaric stilled them with a wave of his hand. He didn't look round as Gallow and Tolvis left.

34

BETRAYER

The Lhosir were waiting for him as they'd promised. The same two but now they had the rest of their men only a hundred paces further down the road. They stood in a solid rank across the track, ready for battle, a wooden ram behind them. It couldn't be anything else. They'd been thoughtful enough to put a roof over the top of it.

Behind Oribas, the gates to Witches' Reach were closed. They'd be closed for the rest of winter now – the mound of crushed snow and ice behind them would see to that. Oribas had come down the wall on a ladder.

'They've heard of you, Skilljan Spearhoof. They don't strike me as particularly afraid. Shall I give you the message I have for you? The gates tell you all that matters. Their message is the same except in words more calculated to enrage.'

Skilljan Spearhoof nodded. 'Will you stay then, Oribas of Aulia? Tell me of these secret Marroc paths and I'll give you a kind death when the time comes. Kinder than the one you'll receive when we breach the walls.'

'I'd prefer no death at all, Lhosir.'

'My eyes tell me that the Marroc have been building Aulian spear-throwers in the night. Since they're farmers, I must suppose you were their architect.'

Oribas shook his head. 'There are no spear-throwers. The Marroc have neither the tools nor the skills nor the materials to make one. What your eyes have seen are a few pieces of wood thrown together to deceive you.' He looked up sharply, catching Skilljan's eye. 'I *could* show a man how, though, given time.'

Skilljan shook his head. 'Not enough to earn you your life,

Aulian. Cithjan himself gave the order to send you to the Devil's Caves. I cannot ignore my lord.'

'Would *you* send men to the Devil's Caves, Skilljan Spearhoof?'

The Lhosir started to shake his head and then caught himself and smiled. 'You're a clever one, Oribas of Aulia. No, I would not, but nor am I the lord of Varyxhun.'

Oribas turned back towards the tower. 'Do you have any words for me to take back?'

'None that any Marroc will heed.'

'There is one thing, Skilljan Spearhoof. Consider, as I leave you, whose people it was who first built this tower.'

'Oh, I know they were yours, Aulian. We all know that.'

'Our people liked to dig, Skilljan Spearhoof.'

'And what am I to take from that?'

'That I am one of my kind.'

Skilljan laughed. 'Are you offering to dig our cesspits, Aulian?'

'You may scorn me but I value my life, Lhosir.' Oribas left them in the road. The Lhosir waited for him to reach the walls and climb the Marroc ladder before they came on. They took their time and assembled on the slope below the gates, out of range of the Marroc arrows. A hundred of them perhaps, and they had their ram with its sharply sloping hide-covered roof on top and a dozen ladders. Around the back of the mountain three more groups of Lhosir picked their way through the tumbled stones. They didn't go to much trouble to hide themselves, nor would it have made any difference if they had.

With a howl the Lhosir raised their shields and ran at the wall, a tightly packed mass of them. The Marroc loosed a hail of arrows and a few of the Lhosir fell, but most of the arrows found only shields and mail. The Lhosir reached the wall and hurled their ram at the gates while the ladders came up from among them and tipped against the walls. Now on the tower roof, Oribas tensed. The first minutes mattered more than anything. The Lhosir were what they were and it would take a very bloody nose indeed for them to lose the will to fight, but the Marroc were flighty. They weren't soldiers seasoned in the blood and fire of battle, these men. If the Lhosir gained a foothold on any part of the wall then the Marroc would break and it would all be over. He closed his eyes and said a prayer to the gods. He wasn't sure which gods he should talk to on this side of the mountains, whether Marroc gods would even listen to an Aulian, but he prayed to them anyway. *Let the ice behind the gates hold. Let the Marroc trust in it and turn away the ladders. Let them win!* He might have added, *Let them keep back the burning oil until it would make the most difference and use their pots of boiling water instead*, but that seemed a strangely cruel prayer to any god, save perhaps the Weeping God of the Vathen.

Oribas couldn't see the gates themselves, only the Marroc on the walls over the top of them hurling spears and shooting arrows at the Lhosir trying to work the ram. He saw one ladder crest the wall only to be thrown back, and another and another, and then in one place further around a Marroc tumbled into the yard with a spear through him and then a second, and a moment later a Lhosir helm and shield appeared over the battlements. But then Addic was there. He drove his sword at the Lhosir and kicked him back down, and the ladder was quickly gone.

On the other side of the mountain the three groups of Lhosir were approaching the wall. Oribas shouted down to the handful of Marroc keeping back from the fight around the gates. They ran up to where he pointed and peppered the Lhosir with arrows. Among the rocks, the Lhosir were having a hard time holding their shields up as well as climbing and carrying ladders. The first group gave up after two of them were stuck with arrows fifty paces short of the walls. The second group got a little closer. The third, Oribas saw, tried a good deal harder: they almost reached the wall before they dropped their ladder, turned and fled, three arrow-pierced corpses littered among the boulders and the snow.

Around the gates the Lhosir pulled back, but then a rock the size of a man's head flew over the wall and smashed into the yard. Oribas squinted down the trail at the trees beside the road from where the stone had come. He couldn't make out what the Lhosir had there until it jerked and fired again. A simple onager and not a particularly big one, not even quite out of range of the Marroc archers, but that didn't seem to bother the Lhosir. The second stone was low, thudding into the slope beneath the wall. The third and the fourth hit the wall, and then suddenly three ladders came up at once at the same place, arrows showered the wall and half a dozen Marroc fell at once. Lhosir with bows! They almost never used them, but now they'd taken the Marroc by surprise and Lhosir were cresting the wall with no one in their way. Two of them reached the battlements and turned to face the Marroc running along the walkway. Three more scrambled up the ladders, lowered themselves to dangle off the walkway and jumped down into the yard. They ran for the gates to throw them open while arrows flashed past them, but then saw the ice and snow and stopped, unsure what do to. The Marroc on the battlements pushed back the Lhosir and threw down their ladders. The three trapped inside were scythed down, a few Marroc running across the stained snow to finish them off. Three more heads for Achista to mount on the Aulian Bridge.

The Lhosir withdrew not long after that. Oribas came down from the tower to tend to the wounded but there were few. Eight Marroc were dead and six injured, three with simple cuts that would mend easily enough if they didn't turn bad, one with an arrow though an arm that would probably mend, and two for whom the best Oribas could do was make them comfortable and hold their hands together while they prayed. As well as the three Lhosir in the yard Achista said she counted thirty dead outside. Oribas, when he looked for himself, thought it more like twenty, but he kept quiet. It didn't matter. The Marroc had beaten the hated forkbeards again, and whether there were fifty or sixty or seventy of them left outside on the ridge, it made no difference.

She caught him at twilight and pulled him down to the Aulian tomb and they made love for an hour as the sun set. 'Tonight,' she told him as they lay together afterwards. 'You go tonight.'

Oribas said nothing. The Lhosir would grow stronger and stronger. It made sense, before going was no longer possible. 'I wish you would come with me.'

'You know I must be here.' She kissed his ear and stroked his hair. 'I'll send the men who are too wounded to fight but who can still walk out through the passage. They'll hang our three forkbeard heads over the bridge and seek Valaric the Mournful in the Crackmarsh. Then the doorway must be sealed. If they're caught, the forkbeards will find it.'

He held her tight for a long time. They both knew it would be the last night they had. 'I will not die first,' he whispered in her ear as they rose and dressed.

'I'll hold you to that.' They both knew it would be her.

'The Lhosir will come in the night.' Oribas was thinking of the three groups that had attacked the wall at the back of the tower earlier in the day, particularly of the band that had pressed harder than the rest. 'The south-west corner. They left a ladder there.'

Later they stood at the top of the shaft and watched the wounded Marroc climb down, three of them, each with a Lhosir head slung over his shoulder. They kissed and held one another and then Achista stepped back through the round stone door and together, one either on side of it, they rolled it back into place until it lay between them.

'Goodbye, Oribas. Fare well,' he heard her call on the other side of the door, then heard her walk away. He turned the four seals, stood and looked at what he'd done and almost opened them again. It felt as though this was *her* tomb, that he'd sealed her in to die.

She'd left a torch burning at the edge of the shaft to give him some light. He moved it carefully away and waited until the other Marroc had gone ahead and then threw a few things down into the water. Easier that way than carrying them. By the time he reached the bottom, the faint flicker of orange light from the top was dim and fading. He worked quickly, doing what needed to be done, and then waited for the fire to go out. In the darkness he left, picking and sliding his way through the caves to the mountainside. The other Marroc were already long gone. They'd each choose their own path lest the Lhosir catch them and none of them would know that he'd followed. Achista's last try at keeping him safe.

But he didn't follow. Instead he turned the other way and trudged as quietly as he could around the edge of the mountain, towards the Lhosir camp.

35

THE AULIAN WAY

Skilljan Spearhoof had a few hours of bad and uncomfortable sleep. He'd started the day with some hundred fighting men and now he was down to more like seventy if you included the ones with wounds trivial enough to keep going. Bloody bastard Marroc with their bows. They were supposed to be farmers and beggars but half of them were in stolen Lhosir mail with shields and helms and swords and they didn't seem to have any shortage of those cursed arrows. Worse, the gates were stronger than he'd thought, which left scaling the walls and he'd already seen how badly *that* was going to go. He'd sent a rider back towards Varyxhun to say he was going to need more men – a lot more men – and that left him seething. Yes, there goes Skilljan Spearhoof who couldn't deal with a few angry Marroc farmers even with a hundred hardened Lhosir warriors at his back. And if it was true that the Marroc were led by a woman ... He held his head and shuddered.

He led the night-time sortie himself, creeping up the mountain round the back of the tower in the dark to get to the ladder than Foddis Longbeard had left for him and lost three men doing it. And it seemed as though the Marroc had crept into his thoughts and read his mind. They let him climb all the way up the blasted crags and set the ladder against the wall before a dozen of them popped up over the top and threw a hail of arrows at them and he was lucky to get away with no worse than his tail between his legs and two more men sent to the Maker-Devourer's cauldron. In the middle of the night he finally he got to his tent and tried to sleep, and tossed and turned and set his plans as best he could. The Marroc hadn't left him with much of a choice. In the morning he'd build his pyres for the men he'd lost and lick his wounds, and then he'd wait and pen the Marroc inside Witches' Reach until he had another two hundred men. After that he'd go for the walls again. It would be a bloody business scaling them, but with that many men he'd do it and then the Marroc could see what it meant to defy him.

'Oi! Spearhoof!'

Skilljan felt as though he'd only closed his eyes a minute ago. When he looked it was still dark, so maybe he had. He recognised the voice. Hardal Daggereyes. 'This had better be very important.'

'Oh, you'll like this.' Hardal didn't sound like *he* liked it. Skilljan sat up and rubbed his face and then wished he hadn't. His skin still stung like the lash of a whip from when he'd been working the ram and the Marroc had poured scalding water over them all. The hide roof had kept the worst of it off, but by then it had had its fair share of rents and tears from all the arrows and spears the Marroc kept throwing at it. There weren't many who'd worked the ram who'd come away unscathed.

'Well, what then?'

'Best you come out.'

His legs didn't like it much, nor the rest of him either, but Skilljan hauled himself out of his nice warm tent. The furs he'd worn all day still kept him warm but on bare skin the cold at this time of night was like being flayed. Hardal had two of the night sentries with him and three others. Two battered-looking Marroc down on their knees and whimpering and – Skilljan blinked – the Aulian.

'These two we found near the Varyxhun Road.'

'Runners.' Skilljan nodded. He'd expected a few, which was why Hardal had been out there in the first place. He'd hoped for more than two though.

Hardal shook his head. 'No. Look what this one had on him.' He held up a severed head. It took Skilljan a moment to realise he was looking at Geryk Frostbeard. Or what was left of him.

Skilljan growled and drew his sword, then stilled himself. He bent down and grabbed the Marroc's face instead, twisting it to look at him. 'We'll make a raven of this one in the morning.' That would make him feel better. It would make the others feel better too.

'On his way to cross the bridge, he was. Taking messages to the outlaws in the Crackmarsh. So was the other one. Apparently there were three, so we missed one.'

Skilljan clenched his teeth. So be it. He'd have more men before any band of outlaws could come crawling out of the swamp and maybe that would be just the thing to lure them. He frowned. 'I count three, not two, so how did you miss one?'

Hardal shoved the Aulian forward. 'We found this one on the way back, creeping into the camp. He says he wants to bargain with you.'

'I wasn't creeping, Skilljan Spearhoof. I was walking as any man would in the dead of night across moonlit snow.'

The Aulian looked scared, though, despite the defiance in his words. After the day Skilljan had had, anyone within range of his spear had a right to look scared. He laughed. 'There's no bargaining now, Aulian. We're long past that. Your Marroc are all dead men.'

'I wish to bargain for myself. For my own life. The Marroc inside Witches' Reach may all be dead men but I'm not Marroc, Skilljan Spearhoof.'

Scared, but he wasn't quivering and he stood still and spoke for himself, which in Skilljan's eyes spoke of at least *some* courage. 'I have to suppose that Cithjan sent you to the Devil's Caves for a reason, Aulian, even if I don't know what it was. For myself, I have no grudge against you.'

'I'll tell you why your ram failed if you like. The Marroc have piled up all the snow from the Reach against the gates. They packed it down hard and poured water over it through the night. The gates are frozen shut with a block of ice behind them as large as a shed.'

Skilljan looked at the Aulian and then turned back to his tent. Ice! Clever little *nioingrs*. So much for making a bigger ram. Maybe the Maker-Devourer knew how to smash a way through, but Skilljan didn't. 'Make those Marroc as uncomfortable as you like, Hardal, but don't let them die. I want their screams to reach the river when we gut them in the morning. The Aulian can have a clean death. Feed him.'

'Don't you wish to hear what I have to offer, Skilljan Spearhoof?' asked the Aulian.

'Not unless you have a way to get me into Witches' Reach.'

There was a long silence before the Aulian replied. 'And what, Lhosir, if I do?'

Oribas sat bound beside a fire in the Lhosir camp. Fear didn't stop him from sizing up their numbers and it didn't stop him listening either. They were angry, simmering with rage and impatient to avenge their fallen. In the morning they walked to the walls and waved a flag of parley to ask for their dead but the Marroc had already crept out in the night and hauled the bodies closest to the walls back inside. Skilljan's face turned thunderous. They all knew what that meant.

They tried a second time, easing into reach of the walls behind a line of shields and with one of their Marroc prisoners held in front of them. The Marroc asked for their man to be set free and then the Lhosir could have their bodies. When Skilljan refused, the archers in the fort killed the Marroc and drove the Lhosir away. Oribas's face went white when Skilljan told him that. 'They're madmen,' he whispered.

The Lhosir built their pyres and dragged away all the bodies they could reach. When they'd done that, they started on the last Marroc, and Oribas realised then why Achista had killed the first prisoner when she'd had the chance. For most of his life Oribas had been proud of his knowledge of the human frame. He'd worked with skeletons of men and cadavers. He'd been taught what organs were what and where they were to be found and what their importance was and what would happen if they were to fail. Now he tried to close his eyes and forget. The Lhosir stripped the last Marroc and laid him on his belly in the mud, close enough to one of the fires that the snow had all melted away. They held his arms and his legs while one of them took a knife and opened the skin on his back, one long deep cut on each side of the spine. They opened the cuts up wide and deep until bone showed beneath, and the screams were a thing Oribas knew he'd never forget. Then one of the Lhosir brought a strange-looking tool like a pair of long-handled tongs with cutting blades instead of metal fingers. One by one they pushed it into the screaming Marroc's wounds and pulled the handles apart, and each time they did, bone cracked and splintered. They were separating the Marroc's ribs from his spine. Oribas shut his eyes then and clamped his hands over his ears but he couldn't stop the sounds, couldn't stop that awful screaming. Worst of all though, he couldn't stop himself counting, to see if the Lhosir snapped every rib or only some, and he couldn't stop himself from wondering how many they'd cut before the Marroc could no longer breathe and so died.

The screams slowly faded. When it had been quiet for a while he opened his eyes and wished he hadn't. The Marroc was lying where he'd been before, only now he was lying on a wooden wheel with two fat stakes driven right through him and sticking out of the gaping wounds on his back near the shoulder. The dead man's lungs had been drawn out through the wounds and the Lhosir were draping them from strands of wire to make them look like wings. The blood raven. He'd heard Gallow talk of them.

When they were done they ran ropes around the two stakes and hung the dead Marroc from a pole. Three Lhosir carried him up towards Witches' Reach. Oribas didn't see what they did with him. Dangled him from a gibbet like the Marroc he'd seen in Varyxhun, perhaps.

They burned their own dead after that, standing beside each pyre to speak the deeds that each man had done in life and offering their souls to the cauldron of the Maker-Devourer. Skilljan Spearhoof had ignored Oribas until now, but as the dead burned and the Lhosir settled to an afternoon of feasting and remembering and watching the walls of Witches' Reach, he came at last. An old Lhosir came with him.

'Well then, Oribas of Aulia. Speak.'

'Witches' Reach was built by my people. There is an old Aulian tomb beneath it.'

Spearhoof looked to the old Lhosir. 'Sharpear here has been inside the tower. Tell us what you know.'

So Oribas described the parts of the tomb the Lhosir had turned into a storeroom and the round stone door they'd never been able to open. He told them of the caves on the other side, how the Marroc had made him open the door for them and entered the tower and taken it. How these men that Skilljan had caught and killed had sealed it shut again.

'So you're the one who let them in?' Skilljan bared his teeth. 'I should make a raven out of you too, Aulian.'

'I will open a door to anyone who has a knife at my throat and offers to remove it. The Marroc were good to their word. They meant to leave it to you to kill me.'

'Careless of them to let you go, then.'

Oribas shook his head. 'They didn't let me go, Lhosir. They were careless with the ladders they were using to go over the walls and rope up all your dead so they could cut off their heads and scatter them on the Varyxhun Road. Tonight I dare say they'll slip over the walls again and deliver their presents to you.'

Skilljan's eyes narrowed. 'Why did you come here, Aulian, when you could have run away?'

'And go where?' Oribas shrugged. 'I have nothing to do with this fight and no wish to be a part of it, but between you and the Marroc I have no choice but to choose a side. So I choose the side that will win. I will show you the way into Witches' Reach and open the door for you if you will swear in blood two things. You will let me live. I did nothing wrong but befriend a *nioingr* without knowing who he was, and for that I was sent to the Devil's Caves. You will become my kinsman and speak for me. You will swear in blood and I will lead you into Witches' Reach. Afterwards, while you bask in your victory, I will help you as best I can and you will shelter me until the snows melt in the spring and the Aulian Way is clear. Then I will go home.'

Skilljan Spearhoof laughed. 'I'll do all those things, will I? I have a different offer. You show me the way into Witches' Reach and I won't kill you as I killed that Marroc.' He crouched in front of Oribas and glared.

Oribas met his eye. 'I spent a year with a Lhosir, Skilljan Spearhoof. He was brave and strong and good to his word, and he taught me your ways well. I'll take you to the door. We will make a blood oath in front of your men. I'll open it and you'll lead your soldiers into the Reach and you won't look like a fool beaten by a few Marroc farmers.' Skilljan ground his teeth. Oribas smiled at him. 'When you see what I have to offer, you'll agree it was a small price, and so I'll have one more thing too. You'll give me one of the Marroc to do with as I see fit. Whichever one I choose.'

36

THE CHIMNEY

As the sun set, Oribas led Skilljan and three of his men around the mountain to the crack in the crags that led to the tomb beneath Witches' Reach. They crouched inside and Oribas fiddled with the flint and steel in his satchel until he had a tiny lamp burning. The Lhosir wrinkled their noses. 'What's that smell?'

Oribas began up the passage as far as the shaft. 'The cess of Witches' Reach makes its way down here.'

One of the Lhosir slipped and fell. 'Cursed greasy ice! I can't see a thing.' He made a retching sound. 'Stinks of fish.'

'Bring torches down the mountainside and the Marroc will know your purpose.' They pressed on all the way to the shaft, guided by the Aulian's tiny flame until Oribas stood in the mouth of the passage and pointed up. 'There are rungs set into the far wall. It was a long climb and slippery. One of the Marroc fell.'

'Show us.'

Oribas pursed his lips. 'At the top of the shaft is a door made by Aulian priests. I can open it. Go and look if you like. It's a long way and I'm not sure I have the strength to climb it twice in one night.'

'Twice, Aulian? The three of us will be enough to open the gates.'

Oribas laughed. 'You won't open any gates, Skilljan Spear-hoof. I told you: the Marroc have sealed themselves in with ice and only the goddess of spring will open those gates now. That is unless you mean to light a fire beside them and hold off fifty Marroc archers for as long as it takes for that ice to melt.' Skilljan growled at him. The problem took him longer to mull over than Oribas liked. 'The Marroc came in this way, all of them. A cautious man like me would wait until he had more swords to follow him.'

'You're not as cautious as you'd like me to think.' Skilljan shook his head and stared up at the shaft.

Oribas withdrew a little way down the passage. 'The door is closed,' he whispered, 'but the Marroc aren't stupid. They may still have an ear to it. They'll know by now that I am gone.'

'But not that you came to me.' The Lhosir whispered among themselves and then Skilljan and one of his men crept away, leaving Oribas behind with the others. While he was away, Oribas and the two Lhosir sat in the pale light of his Aulian lamp. The Lhosir barred his way out, but it didn't seem to trouble them when he left the lamp beside them and moved back to the shaft, and so they didn't see as he circled the stone walkway, sprinkling powder from his satchel into the oily water. Oribas was half minded to climb the shaft without them, but would they follow? So he waited, and from their numbers when Skilljan returned, Oribas guessed he must have brought very nearly his entire band, what was left of them.

'You first, Aulian,' hissed Skilljan. 'I'll follow.'

Oribas gave Skilljan his lamp. 'No sound. No light. I'll take you to the door. You can stand there and see it in front of all your men, and then you can murder me and grind your teeth in frustration or you can whisper your blood oath and I will open it.'

'We'll see, Aulian.'

It was a long slow climb, every bit as hard as Oribas remembered. Worse for thinking of what waited at the top. He'd never done a thing like this. A horrible, terrible thing by any reckoning. There would be no forgiveness, not from those he crossed. And it was strange, because the Oribas who'd left the desert would never have done what he was about to do now, would never have considered it, would have thrown up his hands in horror at such a betrayal, and yet he felt no doubt. He would die for Achista, he'd known that for a while, but then he would have died for other things too – for Gallow, for the shadow-stalker and the sword-dancer he'd left behind who'd stood with him against the Rakshasa, for many others too. But for this Marroc woman he would do things far worse. For her and only for her.

Below him, Skilljan Spearhoof snarled and snapped at him to climb faster. Oribas kept his pace measured, though he was as eager as the Lhosir to reach the top and be done with this evil. The damp walls of the shaft glittered dimly in the lamplight, the only light any of them had until they reached the top and Skilljan climbed over the ledge and gripped Oribas and shook him. 'If you've brought us all this way for nothing ...'

Oribas pulled himself free. 'Light a torch, Lhosir. We will need one.' Quickly, before too many of the Lhosir could follow Skilljan over the edge, he snatched his lamp and ran to the door. When Skilljan had his brand burning, he followed. 'Your oath,' hissed Oribas. 'And quickly, lest they hear us.' He started to turn the wheels.

'You have it.' Which only made it worse.

Skilljan lit a second torch and held them both so Oribas could see. The wheels moved more easily this time and it was done in seconds. Oribas bowed his head and took back the torch. 'Then the way is yours.' He stared at the look of glee on the Lhosir's face as Skilljan put his shoulder to the stone door and felt it begin to slide, then quietly walked away. There were six Lhosir up, then seven, and each one ran to the door with sword at the ready to race into the tower and fall upon the sleeping Marroc. None of them paid any attention to Oribas, their eyes focused on the slowly moving door, not even when he knelt down by the ledge to help one of them up and accidentally knocked over a bucket of foul-smelling oil that happened to be sitting by where he'd left it the day before. Nor as he stumbled back, holding his hands up in apology, and a piece of paper fell from his fingers and into the oil he'd spilled. Nor as he took his torch and lowered its flame to the ground. They only really noticed him again when the cavern lit up in a flash of light.

The oil he'd spilled over the edge caught alight and the fire began to spread across the floor. A Lhosir looked down to find his boots burning and tried to stamp them out. But it wasn't the Lhosir who'd already climbed the shaft that Oribas was looking at. He was crouching, making himself as small as he could, looking into the shaft.

The fire ran down the wall. It was slow, not as quick as Oribas had hoped, but the Lhosir clinging to the rungs had nowhere to go as the flames trickled towards them and the stones around their hands and in front of their faces burned. A gobbet of flaming oil dripped down the shaft, a bright falling star vanishing into the darkness. But only so far. For waiting for it was the rest of the trap Oribas had laid. The drop of oil hit the surface of what had once been water but was now oil laced with saltpetre. Oribas looked away as the whole shaft bloomed into bright burning light and the Lhosir began to scream.

In the old tomb Achista heard the stone move and the Lhosir's whispers grow louder. Through the cracks at the edge of the stone she saw the first flash of light, the signal Oribas had promised her. Thirty Marroc men gripped their spears and swords while a couple helped the Lhosir pull the stone door aside.

Skilljan Spearhoof froze at the first flash of light. He knew at once he'd been betrayed but he didn't yet know how. The hairs on his back prickled like a creeping spider. He let go of the door and turned to see the fire. The flames didn't seem like very much.

He turned back. The door kept moving even though no Lhosir was pushing it any more. He caught a glimpse of a face coming at him from the other side. What he didn't see was the spear point that came at him too, and so he died as steel pierced his eye and deep into his skull, the first forkbeard to fall but not the last.

The Marroc burst out from the tomb. Oribas stayed very still, face turned away from the flames, crouched in his corner, losing himself in the flickering shadows. The Lhosir could have found him if they'd chosen to look but most of them had no idea what has happening. It was over in a dozen heartbeats. The Marroc slammed into them and cut them down or pushed them back. Two ended up thrown over the edge. The Lhosir below were still climbing as fast as they could, roaring and swearing and howling as flames licked at their hands and reached for their faces and burned their forked beards. The Marroc waiting for them at the top were merciless. The Lhosir who fell vanished into the inferno at the bottom of the shaft. The last few started to climb back down but all they had waiting for them were flames and a thickening fish-stench of choking smoke.

Oribas turned away and then forced himself to turn back. There was nothing here he wanted to see but he needed to. He had to. Had to be sure he would remember what he'd done. He felt a presence at his shoulder. 'Come away.' He knew it would be her.

'I can't.'

'Yes, you can.' She leaned into him, wrapped her arms around his neck and nuzzled his ear.

'I will not forget that I have done this.'

'All they ever had to do was go. You've spared so many of us who never had that choice.'

Oribas followed her away, certain that he hadn't saved anyone at all, that these Marroc would stay here until the Lhosir starved them out, or burned them, or laid them low with axe and sword. But it was easier to listen to Achista's whispers than to the lost ghosts of the men who'd taught him how to do these things.

A few of the Marroc stayed in the tomb, watching. The rest crept up onto the walls of Witches' Reach and threw down ladders and slipped away into the night. They encircled the Lhosir camp and tore through it, pulling down the men that Skilljan Spearhoof had left to stand watch over his wounded and slaughtering the Lhosir to the last man. They took the heads of the men they'd killed and carried them down to the Varyxhun Road and the Aulian Bridge and once again left them there, another Marroc message of triumph.

Through it all, Achista held Oribas tight. Sometimes he hardly felt her. He sat in the tower, rocking back and forth. Every breath carried the smell of burning fish and burning fur and hair aflame. Between her soothing words he heard the Lhosir scream, howling with rage and fury and pain and, at the very last, a deep and horrible fear.

He didn't close his eyes to sleep that night. He was far too afraid of what he might see.

SOLACE

37

THE VARYXHUN ROAD

Beyard paused and stared at the Marroc woman Arda and wondered what he was doing. Only the Fateguard themselves could understand what it meant to be made into an ironskin, a man who served the Eyes of Time. Much was lost, many things that other men took for granted and would never willingly have forgone, and almost all those the Eyes of Time chose were given no say in becoming a Fateguard. Yet it was not all loss. With the iron and the sleepless eyes and the ever-present chill and the little need for food and rest there came an instinct for what was proper and what was wrong, what was fated and what was chance, what was a man's destiny and what was not. This was the instinct that had made Beyard let Gallow go in Middislet, the same instinct again in Hrodicslet. Something lay between them. Their fates had been entwined for a full score years and would not unravel so easily.

So he told himself, and he told himself too that it couldn't simply be that Gallow had once been his friend or that he was a better man than Sixfingers and always had been. The Fateguard had no friends, and fate cared nothing for right and wrong.

He followed the trail from Hrodicslet up into the mountains, tracing the path Gallow had made coming down. Snow began to fall, and for two nights and one day they were forced to wait in a Marroc farm while a blizzard wiped away every trace of every track that had existed before. When it was gone and the last snowflakes had settled, Beyard looked up at the sky, at the parting clouds, and smiled and followed anyway. Gallow had walked this road. He'd carried Solace for three long years and he left traces of his fate like a wounded man dripped blood.

He wasn't sure what it meant, this thing that lay between him and Gallow now. He passed through Jodderslet and didn't have all the Marroc there killed, even though he knew he probably should. His thoughts were distracted, and the more he sought for meaning, the more it seemed to elude him. He crossed into the Varyxhun valley through the Devil's Caves with every intention of returning to the castle. Gallow would come. He would come for his Marroc wife as surely as the sun would rise each dawn but the walls of Varyxhun would make him pause.

In sight of the city he stopped. Between him and the castle stood a host of Lhosir warriors. There must have been almost a thousand of them, and that, by Beyard's reckoning, accounted for nearly every Lhosir man in Varyxhun and almost half in the entire valley.

He stopped and watched. He was still watching when two riders broke away and galloped straight to him. 'Ironskin,' they called, breathless. 'Cithjan summons you!' And when Beyard stood before the man he was supposed to serve, Cithjan looked like he didn't even begin to understand why everything had turned out the way it had. Beyard pitied him for him for that.

'My Fateguard vanishes and now the whole valley is on the brink of revolt! Where in the Maker-Devourer's cauldron have you been?'

'Hunting Gallow Foxbeard.' Beyard gave that a moment to sink in. He drew Solace from its scabbard and held it up for Cithjan to see.

'Is that ...?'

'Yes.' Beyard put the sword away. 'I will leave the valley and take it to King Medrin when I can take the Foxbeard to him as well.'

'The Foxbeard is *here*?'

Beyard bowed his head a fraction. 'I have something he wants and so he will come to me. As I no longer need to hunt him, I am at your disposal until he does. Is there a war? Have the Vathen entered the Crackmarsh again? Has Valaric the Mournful called us to the field at last?'

Words tumbled out of Cithjan's mouth as he spoke of the Marroc of Witches' Reach – how they'd taken the tower and slaughtered two Lhosir attacks almost to the man. How they'd held the Reach for twenty days and sent messengers across the bridge to the outlaw Valaric to call for his aid. How Varyxhun simmered with discontent.

'Let Valaric come. I have a prisoner to be taken on to Varyxhun ...' He hesitated. Was that best? Foolish not to send her, but Gallow would go to her, not to him. 'No. I will keep her close.' He felt the uncertainty drain away. This was the right thing. 'I will lead your army, Cithjan.' Beneath his iron mask Beyard almost smiled.

The Marroc had wiped out the Lhosir in the shaft under Witches' Reach without losing a single man. When it was finished, Achista sent the last of the walking wounded with the severed heads of the Lhosir to the Aulian Bridge and on across the river, past Issetbridge, which guarded the mountain road to the Varyxhun valley, searching again for the men of the Crackmarsh. Addic went up the valley, murmuring and whispering in every tavern and inn where there were no forkbeards watching. The other Marroc Achista released were never meant to come back, but Addic wouldn't allow himself to be sent away and so Oribas went with him, and everyone knew that Achista had sent them both so they wouldn't be in the tower when the end came – all except Oribas and Addic, who had every intention of defying her.

They passed a few small bands of Lhosir heading for the tower but not enough to take it. They watched a party walking down from the Devil's Caves with a Marroc woman and the iron devil at their head and kept well away. They passed along the valley in secret, spreading their word until they found the Lhosir army from Varyxhun and then they watched it. In the valley Marroc came and went without being seen. In the winter chill, wrapped up in furs, even an Aulian passed unnoticed.

Addic watched the forkbeards trudging the Varyxhun Road. 'They're scared,' he said.

Oribas thought the Lhosir looked more angry than scared, but he kept this to himself. For the next three days the army moved slowly, swamping every village it reached. Most of the Lhosir slept in tents, which it seemed none of them liked. They crept along, stripping the valley of food and firewood as they went, almost deliberately slow. Addic and Oribas kept behind them, riding stolen Lhosir horses and covering five times as much ground, sweeping from side to side, heading into the high valleys the army left untouched. The Marroc were scared, everywhere scared, but angry too, and Oribas felt that more and more as they drew close to Witches' Reach again. People had seen the forkbeard heads strewn across the road, had heard the tales of bodies left out on the bridge night after night. Everywhere they went Addic spread the call: *Rise and throw the forkbeards down!* He burned with a barely held hunger. 'They're ready, Oribas. Just one more spark to light their fire, just one.'

Oribas wasn't so sure that a mere spark would be enough, but he kept that to himself too.

'Do you have any tricks to defeat this army?' Addic asked when the Lhosir were only a day away from Witches' Reach.

'I might suggest ways to defeat a few dozen here, a handful there, but this many?' Oribas shook his head. 'Melt away. Burn the tower for all to see and leave them with nothing. Take your secret paths and ways through the high valleys and strike at them somewhere else. They've made this army now and so they must use it. Strike them again and again, always out of reach. You have the speed, they have the strength. Take their city, take their castle, any town you wish. Draw them hither and yon and never face them. Make them look like fools.'

After the sun had set and they were left to stare down the mountain at the Lhosir fires, Addic chuckled and shook his head. 'You're right, Aulian, but you also haven't been here very long. Do you know what they'd do? Everywhere we went, they'd burn it flat. They'd burn Varyxhun. If they had to, they'd burn every Marroc out of this valley and simply leave.' He bared his teeth. 'What use am I inside the walls now? You go back to her, Aulian. You'll be her strength. You'll show her ways to kill forkbeards that I'd never see.' He stood up.

'This many of them?' Oribas shook his head. 'It'll be over in the first day. They'll swarm over the walls in a hundred places at once.'

'Then I'm glad I won't be there to see it.' He stood up. 'If every Marroc kills a forkbeard before he dies then the valley will be free of them quickly enough. Cithjan is here. I mean to take him. Another spark struck at the waiting fire. Tell my sister I love her. Get her out of there if you can. Drag her if you have to. Farewell, Oribas. It was good to know a proper wizard.'

He walked away down the mountain towards the Lhosir and Oribas watched him go. He felt lost. Bereft. They'd have no chances to flee after this. He'd go back to the tomb, back to Witches' Reach; he'd stand by Achista and they'd either die together or the miracle she hoped for would come and the Marroc would rise before the Reach fell, but Oribas didn't believe in miracles.

Or he could walk away. Not like Addic, but the other way. Turn his back on Witches' Reach and the Lhosir who surrounded it. It deserved a thought, at least, and yet if it did, he couldn't come up with one. The idea of not going back was inconceivable. Perhaps that was the most frightening thing of all. He'd rather die under a storm of Lhosir swords even though those swords terrified him.

He reached into his satchel without really knowing why and pulled out a tiny leather pouch closed tight with twine and sealed with wax. He only understood when he stared at it. A soporific. He started to laugh. The most preposterous idea of them all, that he might slip a poison into Achista's drink and put her to sleep and then carry her away past Marroc and Lhosir alike. Absurd, and even if he managed it then she'd hate him. Besides, he couldn't possibly get her down the Aulian shaft. He shook his head, put the pouch back into his satchel and looked around for anything else that might magic away a thousand Lhosir soldiers. Nothing. Yes, he might poison a few of them, make a few dozen too ill to fight. He might conjure fire a few more times before his powders were gone, but to what end? He couldn't save her, not this time.

He held his head in his hands. Addic had gone to his death in the Lhosir camp because he couldn't bear to see his sister at the end. That was one thing Oribas could do. He could make a poison so that when the end did come the Lhosir wouldn't have her. After a while he rose and left, traversing the mountainside.

A part of him said he should go after Addic, as if that would somehow do some good, and he was too busy wondering about that to notice when he crossed tracks in the snow where two other men had come down the mountain a little earlier in the twilight.

Addic slunk down the mountain and stopped a hundred paces short of where the Lhosir sentries should be. He couldn't see them though, which troubled him. He could see the forkbeards' fires and the edge of their camp and knew their sentries should be out in the darkness beyond. So he *ought* to be able to see them.

He was in the middle of frowning about that when he saw a subtle movement on the slope ahead.

He wasn't alone.

38

THE LHOSIR CAMP

'She talked about you all the time.' Tolvis Loudmouth knelt at the fringe of the Lhosir camp beside one of the sentries he'd killed and beckoned Gallow forward. Loudmouth was dressed in mail under his furs now, with a helm and a shield and a spear all stolen from the sentry. 'Always, Gallow did this, Gallow did that.' He put the other sentry's helm on Gallow's head and wrapped his furs around Gallow's face.

'Did she talk about Merethin?'

They looked each other over to be sure their faces were hidden. 'Never.' In the darkness no one would know them, but a beardless Lhosir wouldn't pass unchallenged. Beardless *nioingr* had no place among real men.

Gallow stood up and walked brazenly towards the edge of the camp. 'I heard about him all the time. Jelira's father. You'd think he was both a prince and a priest from the way she'd talk about him. He was Nadric's son, but Nadric told me once, when he was drunk, that she despised him. That's just the way she is.'

Tolvis didn't reply and Gallow supposed that was for the best. Better not to talk about Arda, not now. Was she pleased that he'd finally returned? He thought not. He'd been away too long. She'd given up on him and moved on. He was an inconvenience now, but however she really felt, she'd never let any of them see it – not him, not Tolvis, no one. She'd do what was best for her children, for her family.

They walked among the fires, heads bowed, moving quickly, two Lhosir soldiers on some irksome errand. They talked to one another about nothing very much: Gallow's boys and little things they'd done and how they'd grown while he'd been away. Jelira, and how she was the one who'd never let Tolvis touch her, who never let go even though Gallow hadn't been her real father either. Middislet and the tiny changes the village had seen. Things that didn't matter. Things to keep their minds away from Arda and from the thousand Lhosir soldiers around them.

Tolvis stopped beside a fire where six men were passing around a keg of Marroc ale. He crouched down beside them, back a little, face kept in shadow. 'What's that Marroc woman doing here, brothers?'

The Lhosir stopped their talk to look round at him, and when Tolvis asked again, Gallow watched where their faces turned. They laughed and shrugged and offered to share their fire and their drink – Tolvis and Gallow were brothers from across the sea after all, and even if their faces were hidden by the furs they wore against the cold, it was in their voices, in their words, in the way they spoke and moved. They were Lhosir and so they were friends, and the world was that simple. Tolvis shook his head and thanked them. The two moved on, easing closer to the centre of the camp. 'Your Fateguard friend has kept her close. We find him, we find her.'

Gallow hissed, 'He's drawing us to him. He knows we're coming.'

'He's an ironskin, Truesword, not a witch.' Tolvis clucked, shook his head and stopped another Lhosir to ask which way to the iron man. The Lhosir pointed and Tolvis thanked him. 'Is it true the Fateguard never sleep?' he asked. The Lhosir shook his head. To Gallow's surprise he made the sign of Modris to ward away evil as they parted. Modris, the Marroc god.

'How long did you wait?' The question hung in the air between them. It wasn't the sort of question that ever had a good answer.

'Before I gave up hoping you were still alive? A few months. Before I did anything about it? A year. Does it matter, Truesword? I watched over your wife and your sons when I thought you were alive and I watched over them when I thought you were dead.'

'You did more than watch over them.' Couldn't let it go. Here of all places, in the middle of the Lhosir camp.

Tolvis grabbed Gallow by his furs. 'You were *dead*. What would you have preferred? That I abandon them?'

A soldier glanced their way. Tolvis let go. Gallow clenched his teeth. 'I knew Beyard once. He'll have her in one of the tents close to a fire to keep her warm. He'll look after her as though she was a lady and he'll watch her every second. And yes, it's true that the Fateguard never sleep.'

'They must get very bored at nights then.' Tolvis stopped and nudged Gallow, pointing through the darkness to a larger fire in the middle of the camp and a big tent beside it where a banner flew. 'Cithjan. What did the Marroc do to drag even him out of his hole?'

'Beyard will be close.'

Tolvis changed course, skirting the Lhosir sentries around Cithjan's tent. 'Now there's a Lhosir I could do without. I came to thinking for a bit that when the Maker-Devourer made Sixfingers he must have spilled a bit, and that when he scooped it up, something else got in. Maybe he picked up one of the old hungry spirits from the Marches that he'd turned away long ago – maybe that's why Sixfingers has such a bitter streak inside him. Whatever he did with Medrin, he did it with Cithjan too. More and more of us from what I saw after you ... after you left.'

'It's not the Maker-Devourer's brew, Loudmouth. It's a disease. A disease of the memory. We're forgetting who we are.' Gallow fell silent as Tolvis pulled him behind a tent.

'Fateguard.' Gallow peered past Tolvis's shoulder. It took a while for his eyes to pick Beyard out, but there he was, sat still in the shadows. 'Don't they feel the cold either?'

'Beyard said he always felt cold. That nothing made any difference.'

Tolvis shivered. 'They're not natural.'

'No.'

They watched for a while but Beyard didn't move. After a time Gallow took a deep breath and made to walk towards him. Tolvis caught him before he could take more than a step. 'So.' His voice was urgent, as though he'd guessed what Gallow meant to do. 'I'll create a distraction. You slip inside and bring her out while they're all looking the other way. Right?'

Gallow laughed. He slapped Tolvis Loudmouth on the

shoulder. 'She's yours now. I saw how she looked at me and I saw how she looked at you.'

Tolvis shook his head. 'She will choose you, Gallow Truesword. Always.'

'I'm going to challenge Beyard. I have to. If he wins, he has me and Arda goes free. If he loses, he lets us go, all of us. For ever.'

'What makes you think he'll agree?'

'Because a part of him remembers that he was my friend once. Because of what happened in Middislet.'

Loudmouth shook his head but Gallow moved too quickly. Before Tolvis could stop him he was out in the open, lit up by the fire at the heart of the Lhosir camp. He threw back his hood. 'Beyard of the Fateguard! I challenge you! Gallow Truesword is here. You have called me *nioingr* three times and I will take what I am owed from you for that. My life or hers, Beyard. Kill me if you can, ironskin!'

Tolvis slunk off into the shadows. It wasn't the distraction he'd had in mind, but it *was* still a distraction.

Oribas circled half the camp before his legs finally agreed with what the rest of him had realised far sooner – that he could never poison Achista no matter now much it was the right thing to do and that he had to go back for Addic after all. They were shaking by then. All of him was shaking and it wasn't only the cold. He'd had enough courage, barely, for the burning of the Lhosir in the shaft under Witches' Reach and now, it seemed, he'd used it up. Or maybe the shaft had been different because it had been a trap laid with thought and care, a plan he could see even before he started, step by step from start to finish. Here … Here there was nothing but madness and the conjured thought of Achista's face when she heard that her brother was dead. The light going out of her. The hardness coming down like an armour he'd never pierce.

He had no idea how to stop Addic when he turned towards the camp. All he knew was that if he didn't turn now then he never would. He had no idea how he'd even find the Marroc, nor how to slip past the Lhosir pickets. The last, though, wasn't a bother. He didn't try. He walked straight at the camp until someone challenged him and then turned towards the Lhosir, hands held up to show he meant no harm.

'I have knowledge of a secret entrance into Witches' Reach.'

The Lhosir didn't seem to hear. He grunted at Oribas, 'What are you?'

'I'm an Aulian.' Oribas bowed. 'I know the secrets of Witches' Reach,' he said again. He had to try two more times before the Lhosir understood what Oribas was telling him and that it wasn't some trick or a joke. Once they got that far, Oribas didn't have to worry about slipping through the rest of the camp. They walked together straight to the heart of it, Oribas in front, the Lhosir behind, poking with his spear.

'Kill me if you can, iron man!'

The challenge came, welcome and wanted. Beyard looked up and then slowly, as though it pained him, he rose. Metal ground against metal as he stepped out of the shadows beside Cithjan's tent. Gallow was on the other side of the fire, spear thrust into the air. A dozen Lhosir were staring at the Foxbeard, faces in the shadows of the night lit up by the dancing flames of the fire. Most of them looked bemused. Beyard looked past them, looking for Tolvis Loudmouth but seeing only darkness. But Loudmouth was there. Beyard knew it.

Cithjan stumbled out of his tent rubbing his eyes. Beyard moved quickly before anyone could say something stupid and insulting. He strode out into the open, drew Solace and raised the cursed sword into the air, slashing at the stars. He roared and felt the watching Lhosir flinch. The Fateguard rarely spoke, and when they did their voices were low grinding whispers. Not one of them had heard a Fateguard roar, but this was Gallow and Gallow deserved it. 'Gallow Foxbeard! Here I am!' And the Lhosir flinched at that too, not at Beyard's voice this time but at his words. At the name, for there wasn't a single Lhosir here who hadn't heard of Gallow the Foxbeard.

An old anger swept through Beyard. *Foxbeard?* He lowered his sword and swept it across the watching men. 'Called True-sword by the Screambreaker himself. Braver than any of you.

Stronger than any of you. More a Lhosir than any of you. He chose the wrong side but did no worse than that.' He roared again and strode around the fire watching Cithjan's Lhosir step hurriedly back to give him space. The warriors he remembered from before the Eyes of Time took him would never have moved. Yurlak and the Screambreaker. Lanjis Halfborn and Jyrdas One-Eye. Thanni Thunderhammer and yes, even Farri Moontongue before he went stupid and tried to defy not only his king but the very will of the world. *Especially* Farri Moontongue. True Lhosir. Names and stories burned into his memory too deep for even the iron witch of the Ice Wraiths to wipe away.

'Gallow Truesword!' he cried again and saw him, the only Lhosir not to back away. Beyard saluted. No mercy this time. Quick and brutal. Solace would cut through wood and steel and flesh and bone and be done with it, and Beyard wouldn't feel a jot of joy at what he'd done.

Gallow levelled his spear and crouched behind his shield. 'If I beat you, I take the Marroc woman with me and I leave. If I don't, I'll be dead and you can let her go because you'll have no use for her.' The Foxbeard bared his teeth.

Beneath his mask Beyard grinned back. 'Someone get the Marroc woman!' He looked around, pointed his sword at a Lhosir who happened to be close and waved him on his way. His eyes flicked to Cithjan, who was starting to think. Beyard could see it happening and nothing good was going to come of it. He levelled Solace at Cithjan's face. 'This one belongs to the witch of the north. He's belonged to her for seventeen years. Keep your mind on crushing the Marroc, Cithjan. Truesword is mine and I will do with him as I please and answer to Medrin when I'm done, not to you.'

Cithjan's face darkened but he kept his mouth shut and that was all that mattered. Beyard turned back to Gallow and then knelt in the mud beside the fire. He was so close that the flames sometimes licked the iron of his armour but he felt as cold as ever. Always cold. 'I called you *nioingr*, Gallow Truesword, but you are not. Let all here witness my words. I spoke falsely of you.' Behind him they were dragging the Marroc woman out into the night.

'Then you owe me a boon.' Gallow still aimed his spear at the spot between Beyard's eyes.

'Speak it.' Beyard stayed as he was. On his knees, head bowed.

'Let her go.'

Beyard rose and turned and she was there, wrapped in furs, held between two Lhosir guards. To Beyard she seemed small and unremarkable. Nothing about her stood out at all. He walked to Arda, took her arm and, shooing the other Lhosir away, dragged her towards Gallow, Solace still in his other hand. He felt for the weave of her fate and even then found nothing. For a moment he pressed the point of the cursed sword up against her throat. Gallow didn't flinch.

'As you wish, old friend.' Beyard let her go, lifted his hands away from her and turned to the watching Lhosir. 'Let her walk free. Do not follow her. She is not to be touched by anyone here.' When she didn't move he pushed her, hard, away out of the space between him and Gallow. She stopped at the edge of the circle surrounded by uncertain Lhosir but they let her be, and Gallow and Beyard locked eyes at last. Gallow's spear point twitched, a flicker of a hair's breath.

'I thank you for that kindness, old friend.'

'And you're welcome to it.' Beyard swept an arm around at the Lhosir crowded around them. 'This time I will kill you, old friend, and you know it's for the best. But you will be remembered.'

39

FIRE AND LIGHT

The Lhosir shoved Oribas towards the heart of the camp. The blaze of fire cast everything else into mercurial shadow. Outside its light he couldn't see what was happening. Something, though. Over the crack and snap of burning wood he heard shouting. One voice and then another. A pause and then the second voice came again and Oribas's heart jumped. *The iron man.* Beyard. Gallow's friend. Was he too late, then?

He stumbled on, eyes glued to the ground for each footstep, stealing glances where he could but there was little to see. He heard another exchange of words and then a shout and a battle cry he knew well: *Gallow!*

Three more Lhosir stepped out from among the tents, faces taut, spears lowered, barring his way. They spoke in murmurs, all of them pressed close around Oribas as though he wasn't there.

' ... claims he's Gallow the Foxbeard.'

'He's called out the Fateguard.'

'It can't really be him.'

'The ironskin thinks so.' There was fear there, but disdain too when it came to the iron man.

'Cithjan's in a foul mood.' The Lhosir sentry prodded Oribas with a spear. 'I don't fancy your chances, Aulian.'

Another shout and then a gasp came from among the watching crowd and a chorus of jeers. The Lhosir pushed Oribas on towards the central fire and then stopped, and at last Oribas could see what was happening. Gallow was on his hands and knees, struggling to get to his feet. His shield was split in two. The ironskin was waiting for him to rise while the Edge of Sorrows in his hand gleamed like fresh blood in the firelight.

Oribas steeled himself. All this way to stop Addic from getting himself killed and now it was Gallow about to die instead. He held up his hands again, the universal gesture among Aulians, Marroc, Lhosir, Vathen and probably every other people under the sun. Showing he meant no harm, that he held no weapons. But although he held no steel, neither hand was empty and he still had the pouches at his belt.

'Gallow!' he cried. His voice sounded thin and weak amid the hooting and jeering of the Lhosir. One hand tossed a swan's egg emptied and refilled and then sealed with wax. He threw it up high into the fire and followed it with the pebble-like thing in his other hand, straight into the flames. 'Beware the sun!'

Oribas turned away. He closed his eyes, waiting for one of the Lhosir to cut him down.

The fire exploded.

Tolvis stopped listening to whatever the Fateguard had to say. They were living monsters, tolerated because they served fate and because the Lhosir believed in that sort of thing. As long as they stayed in their temple on Nardjas and watched over their mysterious artefacts and didn't interfere with the way of the world, Tolvis supposed they were harmless enough, but ever since Sixfingers had taken Yurlak's crown they'd come out to serve him. He probably wasn't the only Lhosir who didn't much like it, but three years hiding among the Marroc made it hard to be sure.

He skirted the centre of the camp. Beyard and Gallow were making it easy, drawing the eyes of every Lhosir who could be bothered to come out of his tent. He moved among them and no one looked at him twice, even as he sidled up to where the Fateguard had been sitting.

He watched two Lhosir march in and drag Arda out and watched Beyard let her go, and he wondered what he was supposed to do now. *Slip back and leave the camp with her? Yes. Get her out of here.* That's what, otherwise why were they here? He paused, looking at her and then at Gallow. He saw her eyes linger on the Foxbeard and felt a sharp pang of guilt. Gallow was putting himself out of the way – letting the two of them be free together – but that wasn't right. It should be him in there facing the Fateguard. He moved back behind Cithjan's tent and past it. And froze. Someone was creeping among the shadows, easing himself towards the circle of firelight. The man moved oddly, not strutting like a Lhosir but shifting furtively. Tolvis crept closer, shuffling sideways through the snow until he reached the tracks that the other man had left behind and then planting his feet in them, step for step so the sound of snow crunching under his boots wouldn't give him away. He came soundlessly up behind the man and put a knife to his throat. No braids in his beard.

'Hello, Marroc.' He pulled back the man's hood with his teeth. Warily he loosened his grip. 'Say something, Marroc, but say it quiet.'

'Kill me quickly, forkbeard.'

The voice was full of bitter hate. Tolvis withdrew his hand but his knife stayed at the Marroc's throat. 'How many of you?'

'Would I tell you if it wasn't only me? But either way that's what it is.'

Tolvis lowered his knife. 'That's a bit disappointing. I was hoping there might be hundreds of you slipping in for a good fight. I'm going to leave you be now. I'd been thinking of opening a vein or two on Cithjan while I was here but I'll leave you to it. You can nod your head now if you like.'

The Marroc didn't move. Tolvis was about to let him go when he heard another cry over the commotion of the fight: 'Beware the sun!'

An instant passed and then a light as bright as midday bathed the Lhosir camp.

Gallow came at Beyard low and fast. They smashed into each other, shield against shield, so hard that Gallow reeled, almost dazed. He stabbed down at Beyard's feet and felt his spear point scrape and slide off the Fateguard's iron skin. As they separated he stabbed again, this time straight at Beyard's face. Beyard saw it coming. He brought Solace down on the spear as it thrust forward and the red blade snapped the shaft in two. Gallow barely had time to draw his sword before Beyard shield-slammed him again. The air moaned as Solace licked at his face. He staggered under another blow. When he stabbed back, Beyard's shield was already there, but instead of rushing him the Fateguard paused. 'You cannot win this fight, Gallow.' He sounded almost regretful. 'Not even you. But I know you must try. I will make it worthy of you.' Gallow slashed at him. Beyard stepped back and caught Gallow's sword on his shield again. 'Why, Gallow, if all you ever wanted was to be left alone? Was that what you were thinking when you took Medrin's hand?'

Gallow lunged. Beyard blocked easily and hammered Solace into Gallow's shield. 'He had become a monster!'

'But he is your king.'

Gallow rushed in behind his shield once again and they crashed together. Bones jarred; but Gallow dropped at the last moment and hooked one foot behind Beyard's leg and shoved. The Fateguard staggered and went down. Gallow jumped at him, swinging his sword. Beyard took it on his shield. The blade skittered up and across it, scoring a deep mark in the wood. It threw sparks as it struck Beyard's iron mask. 'Yield, ironskin!'

'I cannot.' Beyard kicked at Gallow's legs and rolled onto all fours as Gallow jumped away. For a moment he was defenceless. Gallow leaped, dropping his sword and pulling out his axe as he landed, hammering the blade down into the iron on Beyard's back. It bit deep, splitting the Fateguard's armour, and stuck fast. Beyard grunted but he didn't fall. Gallow scooped up his sword.

'You see, Truesword.' Beyard was on his feet now. He took his time, the axe still sticking out of him. 'You cannot win, but when men speak your name in times to come, they will remember you for this. I'm sorry, old friend. I have nothing else to offer.' He ran at Gallow again and this time there was no holding back. They smashed together, shield on shield, once, twice, a third time, each blow knocking Gallow back. After the third, Solace came down like a hammer. Gallow threw up his shield and the red sword split it in two. Beyard kicked him, knocking him down, then waited for Gallow to rise again. An honourable fight to the bitter end. Gallow spat blood. 'When it comes, make it sure and quick, old friend.'

Beyard lifted off his crown and mask and threw them to the ground. For a moment they met each other, eye to eye. 'I'll do that much for you, Gallow Truesword.'

Someone was shouting his name over the ringing in his ears. A voice he knew. *Beware the sun!* Oribas! And he'd heard that cry before.

He drew himself to his feet and closed his eyes.

The first flash was the pebble, a crumbly cake of saltpetre wrapped in dried sheep's intestine. It flared strongly enough to dazzle the Lhosir already looking at the fire and to draw the eyes of the ones who weren't. It was bright in the night, but not as bright as what followed. The swan's egg was filled with desert oil, and when it broke it turned the fire into a tower of flame, a searing flare of light and heat that scorched the back of Oribas's neck. The Lhosir in front of him reeled, blinking to try and regain their sight as Oribas ducked between them. The fire roared, stretching for the sky. Oribas kept his eyes averted. The flames would die in a few seconds but the Lhosir didn't know that. They backed away. Oribas sneaked a glance towards Gallow. The big man was on his feet and had grabbed hold of the Marroc woman's arm. He buffeted and barged through the dazed Lhosir and they vanished into the shadows. The only one who didn't seem to be blinded was the iron man himself. Oribas dashed straight across the open circle beside the fire, taking a handful of salt out of his satchel, and as the flare of the fire died back he reached the Fateguard. Running past him, Oribas threw the salt straight into the ironskin's face and this time the iron-skin had no mask to cover him. Beyard howled and clutched at himself with his iron-gloved hands and staggered to his knees. Oribas didn't know whether to be glad that salt had brought the iron man down or whether to be terrified.

The flames died and the camp fell into darkness once more, no deeper than a minute before, but to those who'd looked at the fire it seemed an inky black. Oribas caught up with Gallow. He was running, pulling the woman after him. She was slowing him. 'Gallow!'

'Oribas.' He didn't look round. 'I heard your warning. How did you know?'

'How did I know what?'

'Where to find me?'

Oribas didn't answer. He tugged on Gallow's shoulder, pulling him until he stopped, and they crouched down together in the shadow between two tents. He put a finger to his lips. 'They'll be getting back their eyes now,' he whispered. 'No more running. Now we slip away in the shadows and in the quiet.' He looked from Gallow's face to the Marroc woman and back again. Gallow nodded. The woman looked bewildered and frightened, wide-eyed like a deer about to bolt. Oribas put a hand on her arm, and when she looked at him, put his finger to his lips again.

But she wasn't looking at *him*; she was looking past him, and when Oribas turned there were two Lhosir looking back. For a moment no one moved, all as surprised as each other. Then the Lhosir went for their axes.

Addic froze at the first flash. The forkbeard froze too so Addic jabbed an elbow hard into his chest and jumped away. The flash faded. He was about to run out from behind Cithjan's tent when the fire flared up a second time. The forkbeards around it reeled and the one who'd grabbed him staggered back, eyes squeezed shut against the light. Addic saw that his chin was ragged stubble, no forked beard at all.

He ignored Tolvis then and instead drew a knife and stabbed it into Cithjan's tent. He ripped a savage hole in the fabric and slipped through, and there was Cithjan himself, standing outside the front, silhouetted against the flaring flames, forkbeards all around him shielding their eyes and yet staring at the fire, and all with their backs to Addic. Addic rose out of Cithjan's tent, stepped up and slid a blade across Cithjan's forkbeard throat and then stepped away again, and it was over and done and Addic was back in the shadows before anyone even knew.

When he scrambled out the back of the tent again, the other forkbeard was gone. He saw a shape on the far side of the fire fling something at the iron devil, something that brought the devil screaming to his knees. His heart pounded, filled with fear and elation at what the wizard had done and with the thought that he might not die here tonight after all. As the flames subsided, he slipped away, circling the fire, following in Oribas's wake.

40

ONE MUST FALL

Tolvis blinked, trying to get the sparks out of his eyes as the fire died away. He looked for Gallow but the big man was gone and Arda with him. Outside Cithjan's tent another commotion broke out. Beside the fire a small figure raced past the Fateguard and the ironskin was suddenly staggering and howling as though someone had set him on fire. Tolvis started to move and then stopped as he saw the Marroc again, hurrying out from a hole in Cithjan's tent that hadn't been there a few moments ago. The Marroc took one glance over at the fire and hurried away. Cithjan was on the ground with two Lhosir crouched beside him and the fire was still bright enough for Tolvis to see the fury on their faces as they turned to look for his murderer.

The Marroc was circling the camp in the direction Gallow had gone. Tolvis set off after him.

Oribas looked up in horror. He scrambled to his feet as the Lhosir roared and swung but Gallow was up first. The Marroc woman screamed curses. Then a shape appeared behind the two Lhosir and one of them fell and warm sticky blood sprayed into Oribas's face. An axe bit into what was left of Gallow's shield, knocking it sharply sideways. As Oribas rose, the iron rim smashed into his temple.

Addic raced after Oribas and never mind the shouts from the bewildered forkbeards. They'd been blinded, dazzled, they'd seen their iron devil fall and then their leader and Addic planned on making the most of it. The Aulian was running too, though he was taking more care not to be seen. There were two others with him. They suddenly ducked down and vanished into the gloom amid the forkbeard tents and Addic lost them there, but not for long before a pair of forkbeards found them and shouted and a fight started. A woman's voice swore. In the gloom it was impossible to see much but he knew forkbeards when he saw them. There were two, with more coming from the other direction, but the first two had their backs to him. Addic ran up behind them, wrapped a hand under one forkbeard's chin, pulled it up and rammed his knife into the man's neck. Blood fountained across them all. The other forkbeard stepped back as a shape emerged from the shadows to face him. He slammed his axe into the other man's shield hard enough to stagger them both. Addic blinked as the man in the shadows rose. The forkbeard from the Aulian Way! Another figure started to his feet beside Gallow, caught Gallow's shield in the face and dropped down. Gallow slammed into the last forkbeard, shield against shield, knocking him back. Addic dropped to one knee and stabbed his knife into the forkbeard's calf. Enough to stop him. The forkbeard howled. More were coming the other way but suddenly they fell to fighting among themselves. For a moment Addic's path was clear and Gallow and Oribas were behind him, ready to run.

So he ran.

Tolvis rushed through the snow. Gallow and Arda and the Marroc already had one pair of Lhosir on them. He saw one fall and heard the other scream but now three more were running at them from behind. Tolvis threw himself after them, hauling two of them down. He twisted so his weight landed on one, knocking the breath from his lungs. As the other started to rise, Tolvis punched him in the face, knocking him back again. He didn't wait for any more but rolled to his feet and ran on. The third Lhosir was still ahead of him, chasing Gallow and the others. He'd catch them too. Arda couldn't run like a Lhosir soldier. No Marroc could.

'Marroc!' he shouted. 'Cithjan is dead! The Marroc attack! To arms! The Marroc have come up the mountain! The Marroc of the Crackmarsh!' Anything to add to the confusion. The Lhosir were stirring anyway, woken by the sounds of fighting and the shouts and now the horns blowing from the centre of the camp.

The more they milled around the better. With a spurt of speed he caught the last Lhosir and pulled alongside. 'Hello!' he said.

The Lhosir glanced at him, face set and determined. A flicker of confusion crossed his eyes before Tolvis elbowed him hard in the ribs and, as the Lhosir stumbled, stuck out his leg and sent him sprawling in the snow. The Marroc was at the front now, running with purpose up the slope through the fringe of the Lhosir camp and towards the silhouette of Witches' Reach. Tolvis caught up with Gallow and Arda and took her other hand. 'Truesword, when I said I'd create a distraction, what I meant ... Oh, never mind.' He kept his breath for running.

Gallow pulled Arda after him. For all Loudmouth's shouts about the Marroc and Cithjan being dead, the Lhosir weren't stupid. Some of them would give chase if only to see what the chase was for. And he and Tolvis might outrun Lhosir soldiers freshly roused from their beds but neither Arda nor Oribas had legs for the long chase. Although at least whoever was running ahead – and who else could it be if it wasn't the Aulian? – looked as though he knew where he was going, fast and full of purpose.

'Truesword, when I said I'd create a distraction ...' Tolvis took Arda's other hand and for a moment the three of them were running abreast, Gallow and Tolvis almost pulling Arda through the air. Behind them more Lhosir gave chase. Gallow had no idea why they were heading for Witches' Reach but it was maybe half a mile away and up a steady slope from the camp. The Lhosir would catch them first.

'Tolvis, look after Arda!' he said. He let go of her hand and fell back. He wouldn't have to slow the Lhosir too long for Arda to make it to the tower. What Oribas meant to do when he got there Gallow had no idea, but he was Oribas and he always had a plan, and Gallow trusted him for that.

As the first Lhosir caught up, he slowed, coming at Gallow cautiously, peering past at the fleeing figures.

'And who are you?' Gallow asked.

The Lhosir's eye snapped back. He saw where Gallow's beard was missing and his stare hardened. '*Nioingr.*' He nodded. 'Hrek Sharpfoot. And I mean to kill you, Foxbeard.'

'I don't doubt it.' Gallow charged and Hrek Sharpfoot charged him back, but Gallow had the slope in his favour and he was the heavier. They smashed into one another and Gallow kept on going, bull-rushing Sharpfoot back down the slope until he stumbled and fell and almost took Gallow with him. The next two Lhosir were on them now, slowing. Gallow bellowed a battle cry and waved his axe and then turned and ran again. A few dozen heartbeats, that was all he'd given Tolvis and Arda. It wasn't enough, not this time, but he'd do it again and again until it was. Until Arda was safe.

Tolvis ran in the wake of the Marroc, who didn't seem interested in waiting for anyone. Arda pulled her hand away. When he glanced sideways at her, she was looking back at him. 'Don't let him die,' she gasped. 'Not now. Not again.'

Tolvis nodded. He turned at once, mostly so she wouldn't see the pain her words caused him. That answered that then.

'Go, Gallow,' he cried as Gallow reached him. 'Be with her.' But Gallow only slowed. Tolvis swore at him. 'I said be with her, you wooden-skull!' But Gallow shook his head.

'There's no door to hold shut, Loudmouth. This time we face our enemies together.'

Arda glanced back once and only once and her heart beat hard and fast because they were both as stupid as each other and yet she loved them both in their own very different ways, one as the father of her children and the most fierce and unexpected soulmate, the other as a kind and tender friend and sometimes more, and now they were both going to get killed because a part of each of them was the same stubborn pig-headed idiot. She might have cried, but life was a hard thing and she'd seen her share of horror, and so she'd save her tears for later when she was somewhere she could spare some time for them. She ran after the stranger in front of her, abandoned to him by the men she knew, but she'd seen him kill forkbeards and so she took him for a friend. Shouts reached her from behind. The clash of swords. She didn't dare look back. Didn't dare because she owed it to them to run as hard and fast as she could. They were buying her seconds. Buying them with their lives.

'Achista!' screamed the Marroc in front. He was a good way ahead of her now, racing for the tower of Witches' Reach. She remembered seeing that tower for the first time, looking over the Varyxhun Road not far past the heights of the Aulian Bridge over the Isset. Fenaric the carter had brought her here. She tried not to think about that too much. Maybe she'd never know whether what she'd done had been stupid or right, taking the blame for Nadric's moment of madness. It had probably saved Nadric's life and maybe Fenaric's too, but it had driven Gallow away and in time she'd regretted that more than anything. 'Achista! Marroc! Lower the ladders!' Last she'd heard, Witches' Reach had been full of forkbeards.

Torches appeared on the walls. She was tiring. The Lhosir behind her were getting closer despite Gallow and Tolvis. She heard their shouts, both of them. They felt sharp inside her.

The gates to the Reach didn't open but a ladder came over the wall. The Marroc in front of her reached it and started to climb. Arda couldn't help herself: she let out a low wail. A ladder! Someone would have to stand at the bottom and hold the forkbeards off while the others climbed. Whoever did that would have no chance to climb it themselves. *No. No no.* Not Gallow, not after he'd come back after so many years, yet she couldn't bring herself to want it to be Tolvis either. *Do I have to choose?* But no, she didn't. She didn't ever get to choose. The men would do the choosing. And most likely, since they were cut from the same idiot cloth, they'd choose to stand together and she'd lose them both.

She reached the ladder and started up. The Marroc was standing at the top. As he reached to haul her up, he stared at her in horror. 'Who are you? You're not Oribas!' He looked aghast.

Arda grabbed his shirt and pointed at Tolvis and Gallow running towards the wall with a dozen Lhosir behind them. 'Help them!'

Another Marroc woman pushed along the wall. 'Addic! Where's Oribas?' A look went between the two. The woman's face turned ashen and then a tight mask of fury settled on it. 'Archers! Kill the forkbeards.'

A rain of arrows flew from the wall at the Lhosir, at Gallow and Tolvis and the forkbeards chasing them alike. Arda screamed at the archers, 'Not the two at the front! Not the two at the front!' The forkbeards kept on coming though, all of them, right up to the walls. Gallow was first. He dropped his broken shield and threw himself at the ladder, pulling with his arms. The Marroc on the walls kept loosing arrows, mostly at the chasing forkbeards but not all. One arrow hit Gallow on the head, bouncing off his helm and almost knocking him off the ladder. Two or three flashed past Tolvis.

Gallow screamed up at them, 'Friend! Friend!' and the Marroc who'd led them here roared at the archers to let him climb. More arrows flew into the onrushing forkbeards below. One fell and then another and the rest slowed, crouching behind their shields. Gallow reached the top. Arda wanted to rush to him but Tolvis was at the ladder now and Gallow was leaning over, urging him on.

Another forkbeard fell. The edge of panic had gone from the Marroc on the wall and now they took their time, picking their targets carefully. As the first forkbeards ran at Tolvis to haul him off the ladder, a dozen shafts hit them, cutting down two and staggering the rest, making them cower behind their shields again; and then Tolvis was out of their reach and Gallow was pulling him over the wall and they were grinning at each other and grinning at Arda and she wanted to run over to embrace them both and bash their stupid heads together but she just couldn't.

Instead she walked up to Gallow and brought her fist like a hammer down on his chest. 'Where were you?' There was a catch in her voice. She hit him again. 'Where were you? Where? What were you thinking! That you could leave us for year after year and then just come back again?' She had tears in her eyes and there was nothing she wanted more than to hold him and cry and laugh and perhaps hit him a few more times, but there was a wall inside her that wouldn't let her, a wall that had never let her show him how she really felt. She stepped away and looked at Tolvis instead. Did what she always did when she was angry, turned away to someone else.

Tolvis had an arrow sticking out of his side. A Marroc arrow. His face was pale and gleamed with sweat in the starlight. Arda jumped. 'Modris and Diaran!'

Loudmouth grimaced. 'It's going to hurt,' he said, 'but it's not going to kill me.' He turned her around and pushed her at Gallow. He took her hands and put them on Gallow's shoulders. Panic started to burn inside her and she didn't know what to do. Then Tolvis cracked his hand sharply across her buttocks and walked away, laughing. The shock paralysed her and for a moment the wall had a crack in it. Gallow wrapped his arms around her and she reached for him and they held each other close for a very long time, not saying a word.

'Where's Oribas?' he asked as they finally pulled apart.

41

AN AULIAN INTERROGATION

For most of the first hour after Gallow fled, Beyard stayed where he was, crouched beside the Lhosir campfire. He had no idea what it was that had burned him, nor who had thrown it in his face, but he wasn't surprised when three Lhosir showed up dragging the Aulian between them. He had Cithjan's men tie Oribas up and put him in a tent and watch him, constantly. He also had them empty his pockets and take away anything they didn't understand and lock it up in Cithjan's strongbox. For most of the morning that followed he contented himself dealing with Cithjan's murder.

A message would go to King Medrin Sixfingers to say Cithjan had been killed while putting down a Marroc insurrection and that he, Beyard, had assumed command. He thought long and hard about what to say about how it had happened and what had led up to it but there was no pretending now. He'd been protecting Gallow ever since his old friend had returned. Not in any useful, meaningful way, but little things. Not telling Cithjan about Gallow when he'd taken Solace. Not calling him by his name outside the Devil's Caves. Going alone to Middislet. Most of all, letting him go. A life for a life had seemed fair and due and fated to be, but Sixfingers would never see it that way and nor would Cithjan if he'd lived to hear of it. Even in Hrodicslet, not giving chase: time after time he'd held his hand but last night he'd meant it. A good fight, a fair fight, a fight to be remembered. A better end than Sixfingers would have given him. Last night he would have killed Gallow, and Gallow had understood and so he'd named himself in front of a thousand Lhosir.

And despite the pain that still burned his face, he was smiling because Truesword had escaped anyway and there was a part of him that was glad. Truesword. Now there was a thing. In Beyard's thoughts Gallow had changed from being Gallow the Foxbeard to being Gallow Truesword again. He tried to remember where and how it had happened. In the bottom of the ravine. *I will not forget ...*

He looked at the messenger he meant to send to Sixfingers. 'Ask him on my behalf for a new governor. Tell him ...' Even now he hesitated. 'Tell him that Gallow Truesword has returned with the red sword the Aulians call the Edge of Sorrows and the Marroc call Solace and the Comforter. I will send both to him together.' Not that Gallow would be taken alive. He'd see to that.

After the messenger there was the matter of command. Beyard dealt with that by telling the Lhosir that he would be in charge until the Marroc of Witches' Reach were crushed and responding to all objections with a malevolent silence. Cithjan had already sent half his force down to the Aulian Bridge to guard it against the outlaws and rebels in the Crackmarsh. He'd hoped the pleas from Witches' Reach might lure them out to where he could slaughter them. Beyard supposed it was a good enough plan to follow, and it left him with five or six hundred Lhosir against a few score Marroc. Good enough. He told everyone to go and make ladders and a ram and whatever else they usually made when they were attacking a walled fortress, and then at last he went back to the Aulian. He'd put it off because it was the part of the day he was most looking forward to and also the part that made him afraid. He couldn't remember being afraid since the Eyes of Time had given him his iron skin.

The Aulian was awake. Droopy-eyed and with a great lump on his temple, bruised and bloodied but awake.

'Again, Aulian.' Beyard sent the other Lhosir away, and when he and the Aulian were alone he took off his mask and his crown. He saw the Aulian's eyes widen for a moment. 'You were never meant to be sent to the Devil's Caves.' His voice was as dry as desert sand. 'Cithjan should have let you go. Or kept you in the castle as his guest until the pass opened in the spring. I dare say there's a great deal we could have learned from a man like you. How many Marroc are there in Witches' Reach, Aulian?'

'Sixty. Seventy. I didn't count them exactly.' The Aulian was terrified and was right to be. A Fateguard stood before him, an iron-made man, and the Lhosir were not known for kindness to their prisoners.

'Food? Water?'

'Whatever you Lhosir once stored there. I saw enough to know they have food for two or three months. Water? They have the snow. You won't starve them out in a hurry.'

'I never thought I would, Aulian. But I have to ask. What have they done to the gates?'

'Piled up snow behind them and packed it tight. It is as good as placing a block of stone behind the doors.'

Beyard nodded. He tried to smile, a thing he was never very good at since the Eyes of Time had made him into what he was. 'I would have let you go still, even after the Devil's Caves. I suppose it was your doing to bring an avalanche down on us.' The Aulian lowered his head, which was enough of an answer. 'Cithjan underestimated how many Marroc were in the Reach. He sent a smaller force first. Not all of them died but I would like you to tell me, in your own words, how most of them did. I know you were there.'

The Aulian bowed his head. 'You must give me a day, shade-walker. That is the Aulian way of these things. One day, and then we will imagine that your torturers have plied their trade and done terrible things and that I screamed and bled and begged for it all to end, and at the end of that one day I was broken. We shall both imagine this thing and then I shall tell you without the pain, and you will hear it without the unpleasantness and the expense. That is the Aulian way.'

Oribas was quaking where he sat but his voice was strong and resolved. Beyard lifted his mask back over his head. 'But we are not in Aulia and that is not the Lhosir way, and there is no expense, nor is there unpleasantness.' He sighed. 'I would like to send you back to Varyxhun to hang. But I can hand you over to the Lhosir here to take their time over you if you like. You're a foreigner, as good as a *nioingr*, so there's nothing they won't do if it amuses them. We are not a civilised people. Not in your way. So tell me about the other way into Witches' Reach you claim to know, or all those things you wish only to imagine will be visited upon you, one after the other. Or ...' he paused and leaned in closer '... worse.'

'Bird, fish, bear, dragon,' said the Aulian. 'There. I've told you the piece that matters. The thing you want to know. But they will be watching. The shaft is death to you now.'

Beyard lifted the red sword and grated the edge of it against his iron-gloved hand. The Aulian whimpered. His words tripped over one another in their eagerness. The cave in the mountainside, the passageway, the shaft and the old Aulian tomb. The sealed door – bird, fish, bear, dragon – and how it led into the cellars of Witches' Reach. How Oribas had opened it for the Marroc and how he'd lured fifty or more Lhosir into that same shaft and then burned them alive. The Aulian almost wept when he spoke of it, and there was more to his tears than fear: he was ashamed. Beyard understood. He almost reached out a hand, but they were cased in iron and were hardly things of comfort. So he let the Aulian speak on until he was done, and when at last Oribas fell to silence, Beyard let it hang between them for a long time.

'I know what it is to have shamed yourself,' he said at last. When the Aulian didn't reply he got up and looked outside the tent. The day was fading, the sun already low over the mountains.

'I was taught to battle monsters,' whispered Oribas. 'Not men.'

Beyard kept staring out at the orange sun hanging in a deep blue sky. The mountains before it were in shadow, a deep purple, almost black. He felt a terrible truth coalescing inside him, as yet unheard but demanding at last to be told. 'Why did you call me shadewalker?'

The Aulian didn't answer.

'What did you throw in my face, Oribas of Aulia?'

'Salt.' The word was a whisper, so quiet that Beyard barely heard.

'Salt. Again?'

'Yes.'

'*Just* salt?'

'Yes.'

Beyard let that linger a while. 'Why, Aulian? Why would you

throw salt in a man's face? Why did your salt burn so?'

The Aulian didn't answer but by then he didn't need to. The iron skin, the ever-present sense of cold, the ambivalence to food and even water, the sleepless nights and salt that burned. He'd been what he was for seventeen years and had never understood, and yet this Aulian had seen through it in days. If he'd still been able to cry, Beyard might have shed a tear for himself.

'No need, Aulian. No need.' His voice was like the grinding of stones. 'I am like them, am I?'

'Yes.'

'I am no longer alive.'

'No.'

The Eyes of Time had done this to him. He'd stolen into the Temple of Fates, for which the price was always death, and thought he'd escaped his punishment, but he hadn't escaped at all.

He slipped the crown and mask over his face once more. 'They will hang you in Varyxhun. It will be clean.' He strode out into the sunset, leaving the Aulian behind.

42

A SPEAKING OUT

The Lhosir took their time. They stayed in their camp on the first day of the siege and Achista stood on the walls watching, wondering whether Oribas was a prisoner among them or whether he'd found his own path to slip away. She couldn't bring herself to think of him held by the forkbeards, but nor could she bring herself to think of him simply walking away.

'We have to suppose the forkbeards have him,' whispered Addic. He stood beside her, looking down the slope of the mountain saddle to the Lhosir camp. 'We have to suppose they know about the tomb.'

'He wouldn't tell them!'

'But perhaps they knew already. Is it sealed?'

'If you sealed it when you left.' Achista couldn't remember what they'd agreed. Whether they'd even spoken of it. 'How many forkbeards this time?'

'More than enough.' Addic put a hand on her shoulder and squeezed.

'The Wolf will come out of the Crackmarsh.' She tried to sound as though she believed it. Not a word had come back, not one of the messengers they'd sent. She didn't know if any of them had even reached Valaric. The Crackmarsh was a hostile place, filled with monsters that only he and his men had learned to master.

Her brother stroked her hair. 'Cithjan sent as many men again to the bridge to guard against that. If Valaric comes, he'll have a hard fight to even get here.'

'Then there's no rescue and no escape.'

'Win or lose this day, sister, we've already won this war before a sword was drawn. I've ridden across the valley, back and forth.

Men will see what we've done. They'll rise as we did, not a few score as we are but in their hundreds and their thousands, from here to Andhun, in Sithhun itself. I've seen it with my own eyes and heard it with my own ears. The Marroc of Varyxhun are ready for you, Achista.'

'If they're ready then let them come.' She turned away.

Gallow and Arda spent the rest of that night together. Neither said much. 'I don't want to hear,' Arda told him when he started to speak. 'I don't want a word. You can tell me why it took three years to walk from Andhun to home when there's no forkbeards out there and I can get properly angry with you again. I don't want to be angry with you now.' And there were tears in her eyes, and Gallow didn't understand but he held her in silence as she'd asked, and it was beautiful because it was a closeness that had always been unacknowledged. Eventually they fell asleep holding one another, and in the morning light the Marroc looked at him askance, trying to work him out, this man who looked like a forkbeard but wasn't.

Some time later Gallow sat with Tolvis. Loudmouth's pain ran deeper than the Marroc arrow in his side and for once there was nothing Gallow could do. Late in the afternoon as he crossed the yard with a bucket of water, he found Addic coming the other way. They glanced uncertainly at each other. Each had been in the Lhosir camp that night for something different. Both had got what they went for and both now had a hole in them where Oribas used to be.

'I thought you were him,' said Gallow. All the way from the Lhosir camp to the walls of Witches' Reach he'd thought they were following Oribas. He'd never seen the skinny little Aulian run so fast, but then he'd never had a dozen Lhosir chasing him. In the dark he simply hadn't noticed. And Addic had thought that the Aulian was Arda.

Addic looked at his feet, at the ground, all around, anywhere but at Gallow's face. 'Oribas married my sister.'

'Oribas?' Gallow struggled to imagine Oribas even interested in a woman. Before they'd crossed the mountains every drop of his life and passion had gone on hunting the Rakshasa. After they'd defeated it he'd just seemed empty. Then Gallow started to laugh. Oribas, looking for something to fill the place where the Rakshasa had been, had found a fiery Marroc woman had he? Achista. The Marroc called her Huntress now. She was their voice and their fire, and who was he, Gallow, to say anything to that but *Well done*?

'Why are you laughing?' Addic looked stricken. 'I thought he was your friend.'

'The only one I had for a long time.'

'And now he's gone and you're laughing?'

'Because he came from another land and fell in love with a Marroc, just as I did.'

Then Addic smiled too as he understood. 'We make good women. Will you talk to her? Tell her something about him? They had so little time.'

'He might not even be taken, Addic, and taken is not the same as dead.'

'Cithjan sent Oribas to the Devil's Caves simply for knowing you.'

'But Cithjan is dead. You killed him. If the Lhosir have him then Beyard will decide his fate, and Beyard isn't Cithjan.' Perhaps they should leave the Fateguard as master of Varyxhun castle. Beneath the iron he was still the man he used to be, and that was why Medrin Sixfingers would never have it. Gallow passed the bucket to Addic. 'Here. Take this to Tolvis. Arda will be there. Perhaps she should talk to your sister. I was lost to her for years so I suppose she has some wisdom when it comes to waiting.'

Addic chuckled. He took the water. 'Don't say that to Achista.'

Gallow climbed the steps to the wall. He passed along the walkway over the gates where the mound of ice still lay pressed up against them. If the Lhosir brought up a ram and it was anything short of a whole tree, they'd be wasting their time. But if they knew how many Marroc were inside, they'd bring ladders. One between three. One man to climb, one man to hold the ladder steady and one to hold a shield and throw the occasional spear.

He stopped beside Achista. She seemed too small and young to lead these Marroc, and yet she did. He told her about the ladders, how the Lhosir would overwhelm the wall with sheer numbers by coming at it from everywhere at once. 'You can't hold it,' he said. 'You don't have enough men.'

She replied to the wind in a whisper barely heard. 'Oribas would have found a way.'

'No. Not even Oribas.'

'He was a wizard.'

'He still is.'

She shook her head and started telling Gallow of all the things Oribas had done, of all the miracles he'd worked. Laying a shadewalker to rest, the avalanche outside the Devil's Caves and the victory at Jodderslet even though Gallow had seen both for himself; then in the woods below Witches' Reach and opening the Aulian seal, luring Skilljan Spearhoof's Lhosir into the shaft and burning them there. Gallow understood. She didn't know it, but she was speaking him out, letting him go in the Lhosir way and reminding the gods of his deeds. When she paused, Gallow took over. He told her of the scared twitchy desperate man who'd found him washed up on a sandy beach a thousand miles to the south of the Aulian mountains. Of the determination that had kept him going after the monstrous Rakshasa, relentless and remorseless and unstoppable as the old Screambreaker himself. How he'd hunted the Rakshasa for year after year and never stopped until even the gods themselves had seen the strength of his heart and answered his prayers. 'He wasn't the one who laid it to rest, not at the end,' he told her, 'but Oribas was the one who laid the traps, who followed its trail, who saw through its tricks and disguises and in the end fooled it into its doom. I've never met a man who was so driven to his end, and the end he's chosen now is you. He will find a way, Achista of the Marroc. There's no man in the world who'll try harder and few better equipped to succeed.' He could feel the lightening around her, the shedding of her burden. She would still grieve, but it wouldn't crush her now.

'It was even his idea to mound up the snow behind the gates.'

'If he was here now, what he'd tell you to do was take as much snow as you can up to the roof of the tower and as many stones as you can carry.'

'Why?'

'Beyard will take the walls tomorrow, and quickly. Ladders won't help him get into the tower, though. He'll need to force the door. He'll have a ram but since the doors are a full man's height above the ground with steps that come at them from sideways, he'll have to build a ramp to use it. In time he will, and he'll get in – don't be mistaken about that. But the Lhosir with him, they'll be impatient and looking for a quicker way. They'll go at the tower door with axes and fire. The snow is for the fires, the stones for the Lhosir who try to light them or bring their axes.'

'Once they have us penned in the tower, we'll all die.'

'You set that to be your fate long before today, Marroc. Oribas may yet outlive us all.'

She laughed, a harsh broken sound. 'Oribas will arrive on the back of a dragon that he's awoken with some ancient Aulian spell to burn the forkbeards? Perhaps the dragon buried under Varyxhun!' She shook her head. 'No. It's done. We'll fight and shed our blood and die, all of us, and it will be the telling of our courage that will live on. We won't win, but our story will eat you forkbeards one by one, until none of you are left.' She twisted suddenly to meet his gaze. 'Why are *you* here, forkbeard? How is this your fight?'

Gallow stared down at her. So fierce. 'I had a dozen angry brothers of the sea chasing me and you lowered a ladder for me to climb and so here I am. When they come, I'll hold your wall for you as best I can. If the chance comes, I'll seek out Beyard and we'll finish what we started. I don't expect to live either, but perhaps he'll spare my Arda. Would you believe me if I told you he's a good man? Brave and honourable.'

Achista laughed and turned away. 'The iron devil of Varyxhun? He's a monster.'

'Can he not be both? He'll be fair, Achista. If he offers you mercy, at least listen. He'll be good to his word. Better than most.'

'There'll be no mercy.' Her eyes settled back on the Lhosir camp. They'd been busy with their axes today. They'd built a pyre for Cithjan and burned him, but Gallow was sure they'd built other things too. She was probably right. Beyard might give them quick clean deaths to honour their courage, but not mercy. That wasn't what the Fateguard were for.

'Tomorrow you'll need small groups of men around you, Addic, Tolvis and me. Four to each of us, the best swordsmen or axemen you have. Station the rest of your men evenly around the walls. We'll go to wherever the fighting is most fierce, wherever the Lhosir get a foothold on the battlements. It will come to us to try and drive them back. Someone must take charge of calling a retreat to the tower. These same four groups of men will keep the Lhosir at bay. Tell your Marroc that when the call comes to abandon the walls they must do it at once. They must turn and run as fast as they can with their bows to the tower and then stand at the doors. The Lhosir will take the walls faster than you can imagine. Those with swords will keep them back long enough for the men with bows to get to the tower but they'll not hold for long. Then the bowmen must hold the Lhosir in turn while the men with swords withdraw. Many will die when the walls fall, but if your Marroc don't understand that they must run like the wind when the signal is given, the Lhosir will take the tower too and it will all be done and gone in a day. You need to last. To be seen.'

'As long as we can. Will they really take these walls so quickly?'

Gallow looked out over the encamped Lhosir. 'Yes. There's only one thing you have in your favour.'

'One thing?' she asked.

'Beyard.'

'The iron devil?' She turned to glance up at him as though he was mad.

'He'll do his best to break you and he *will* win. But I think he'd be pleased if you somehow beat him.'

The Marroc woman shook her head. Definitely crazy. And maybe he was, and Beyard too, and all the old Lhosir who thought that way. Gallow raised a hand to slap her shoulder, one soldier to another. Paused, as he remembered she was a woman, then did it anyway.

'Rest well tonight,' he said. 'Tomorrow they come.'

43

THE WOLF

Valaric rolled his eyes. The Marroc was the third messenger from the idiots in Witches' Reach to get to him. There might have been more, but if there were then they'd fallen to the forkbeards watching the Aulian Bridge or the ones who patrolled the fringes of the Crackmarsh near Issetbridge or, most likely of all, to the ghuldogs. Valaric had no idea how many ghuldogs lived in the Crackmarsh but it was probably thousands and he only had a few of the packs tamed. The wild ones suited him. They all had their territories, loosely marked and understood, and Valaric's was more or less in the middle. If the forkbeards got ideas about coming in after him they'd have to pass a night amid the wild ghuldogs first. So far that had been enough to keep them away.

Eventually the messenger finished. In a grudging way Valaric admired the man. A Marroc who'd stood up to the forkbeards, who'd fought them and won and more than once. From what the man said, whoever was leading at Witches' Reach was a true Marroc hero, even if he was doomed. Valaric forced back a laugh. Trapping the forkbeards in a cave and then burning them? No wonder they were like angry hornets.

'I admire what you've done,' he said. 'But a horde of forkbeards is about to fall on your stronghold. You ask for my help yet at the same time the forkbeards are strengthening their garrisons all along the Isset valley, from the Crackmarsh to Andhun. The Vathen are mustering. In the spring they'll come again and the forkbeards know it. They might leave me alone in my swamp but they're all around it. They'll know if I come out.'

'Then what's the point of you?'

Valaric stiffened. The messenger limped from a cut on his

leg that was slowly going bad. Likely as not he faced a slow and miserable death. Maybe that was what gave him courage. 'The same point as you, you daft bugger, except I'll still be here a month from now and you won't.' He heard Sarvic mutter behind him and wasn't sure whether it was a murmur of disapproval or of agreement. 'How loud do you suppose the forkbeards would cheer if they can get rid of all of us before the Vathen sweep across the Isset again?' He sighed and beckoned the Marroc closer. 'Do you think I want to sit idly by and do nothing? No, but between me and Witches' Reach lies the garrison of Issetbridge and then the river itself. I have spies of my own, and what they tell me is the forkbeards have been watching the bridge like eagles ever since you started leaving their severed heads littered about the place. There's no other way to enter the Varyxhun valley. The forkbeards know this. I'd have to fight past whatever men they put on the bridge and with the Issetbridge garrison at my back. I'd be out in the open. They could slaughter us all. Not one of us would reach you, and then what?' He shook his head. 'Do you have a way to take word back to your friends in the tower?' The Marroc nodded. 'Then I'll do this much for you. I'll take the fight to Issetbridge. That might draw some of them away. If I find the bridge clear, I'll consider crossing it.' Not that there was any chance of that.

The messenger didn't like what he was hearing but it was all he was going to get. Valaric sent him away to be fed and watered and to have one of the Marroc who knew about herbs and things see whether his leg could be saved. The next morning they guided him to the edge of the Crackmarsh, which was as far as Valaric's men went. The leg, it turned out, was beyond help. In a way that made Valaric feel a little better about what he'd just done.

'Issetbridge then,' growled Sarvic eagerly after the Marroc had limped away.

'Don't be an idiot. They'll know we're coming and they'd shred us.' Sarvic looked confused. Valaric sighed. Sometimes Sarvic could be a little slow. Brave and deadly these days but still not so bright. 'Sarvic, how's he going to get across the Isset, if he even gets that far?'

Sarvic sounded surprised. 'Across the bridge of course!'

'Yes. The bridge. The one the forkbeards are watching like eagles. That bridge, and he can't even run. Maybe he'll get back to Witches' Reach but more likely the forkbeards will get him. Not that we're going to Issetbridge anyway.'

'But you said we—'

'Yes, I lied.' Valaric smiled at Sarvic. Such a lot still to learn, but he'd come a long way in the three years since they'd fought the Vathen at Lostring Hill and then the forkbeards in Andhun. 'I'll send a dozen or so men with a pack of ghuldogs to make a nuisance of themselves. See if we can't provoke the wild packs to come out after us and stir something up. Maybe that'll draw away as many of the forkbeards as they think they can spare.'

'And then we're going to sit here and do nothing?'

'No. Go back to Fat Jonnic and tell him to muster his men. I'll be waiting for him at Hrodicslet. I'll tell Stannic and Modric the same. No, we're not going to do nothing.'

'But?' Sarvic screwed up his face. 'I thought you said ... So we *are* crossing the bridge then. Are we?'

'No, Sarvic, because that way into the Varyxhun valley will just get us all killed, fun as it might be to have a good old spat with the forkbeards out in the open. But we don't have to go that way any more, do we? Because Gallow said there was another way: out from Hrodicslet and up into the high valleys and across and through some caves.'

Sarvic just stood there looking stupid. Valaric sighed again and shook his head. 'Just go and tell Fat Jonnic to get his men to Hrodicslet, will you?'

'Oh!' Understanding lit up Sarvic's face. 'So Gallow came down a different way from the mountains?'

'Yes.' Valaric shooed him away. Gallow had come down a different way and had gone back again, and he hadn't been the only one either. That had probably slipped Sarvic's mind, but then a lot of things did.

44

THE BLOODY WALLS

The Lhosir came at first light with their ladders. They didn't try to hide. They spread out, picking their way across the steeper slopes to the northern and western faces until they'd made a ring around Witches' Reach out of range of the Marroc bows. It took them almost until midday and they arranged themselves slowly and carefully as though they were in no hurry at all. Little fires sprang up here and there. The smell of cooking meat wafted in on the breeze. An old trick, although not much use when the Marroc had such a storehouse beneath their feet. As the sun reached its zenith, Beyard walked out from among the Lhosir barring the road and strode clanking to the gates.

'Marroc!' he cried. 'I promise you one thing. There will be no ravens. You have been brave and I will honour you for that. Your deaths will be quick and sure. Make peace with your gods, Marroc of Witches' Reach. I know of your tunnels and your caves and I am not interested in your surrender.' He turned to go and then turned back. 'Are you in there, Gallow? If you are, we weren't finished two nights back. Face me as you did then and I'll let your woman live. I'd do the same for your Aulian friend but he has Lhosir blood on his hands now and so he must hang.'

As he walked away, Achista sprang up behind the battlements over the gates. 'May you wander the Marches for ever, iron devil!'

Beyard didn't look back. He raised a hand as he went, and when he dropped it again a horn sounded over the valley. A great roar went up from the Lhosir, and on the western and the northern slopes they began to move, clambering through the rocks with their ladders and shields. The advance swept around the tower like a slow wave. On the steeper slopes they came with caution, taking cover behind the stones and boulders there from the archers on the walls, shields held over their heads. On the flat ground to the east and the south they yelled their battle cries and charged.

Arrows flew from the walls to meet them, but these were warriors in mail, with iron helms and broad round shields, and only a handful fell. The Lhosir reached the walls and the ladders came up. The Marroc pushed them back, but every Marroc pushing at a ladder was a Marroc not shooting a bow and the rain of arrows eased to a drizzle. The Lhosir put more of their men to holding the ladders and fewer to holding shields. They started to climb. As the first man crested the battlements, Gallow howled and raised his axe. The Lhosir lifted his shield to catch the blow and Gallow kicked out instead, blooding the warrior's face and sending him sprawling down the ladder into the men below. A few feet further on he knelt and heaved with two Marroc at another ladder. A spear stabbed up at him. Its point hit the stone beside his face and struck sparks across his eyes and then the ladder fell back into the sea of men around the walls. Another Lhosir screamed at him and then Gallow had that ladder falling back too, the Lhosir still clinging to it as he fell into the snow. He floundered and the Marroc archers saw an easy target. An arrow hit his head and creased his skin in a flurry of blood. A second hit the snow an inch from his face but then a wall of shields closed around him.

A hand reached up and grabbed a Marroc by the belt, pulled and hurled him over the wall. He screamed pitifully as he fell; a moment later a Lhosir warrior was scrambling onto the battlements. A Marroc swung an axe. The Lhosir caught the man's arm, twisted and tipped him off the wall. Gallow roared and charged, shield up, axe over his head. The Lhosir saw him coming and the two of them crashed together. Gallow twisted and tried to swing his axe round the Lhosir's shield. The blade caught the Lhosir on the shoulder, digging into his mail, and Gallow felt him flinch, and then a Marroc came from behind and rammed a spear into the Lhosir's back, shoving him into Gallow. If he wasn't already dead, Gallow's axe smashed into his helm and made sure. The man's eyes rolled back, his knees buckled, and he tipped sideways off the wall into the yard below.

The air stank of hot pitch. On the far side of the gates the Marroc were scattering. Lhosir carrying bladders on ropes crested the battlements. They hurled the bladders at the nearest Marroc and splattered them with steaming tar. On the western wall soldiers had topped the battlements and were holding Addic and his men at bay while more climbed up. More pitch-throwers climbed over the parapet, threw, and then and barged into the Marroc with their shields, drawing their swords. Gallow yelled at his band to follow and raced to stop them. He spared a glance for the tower steps, where Achista and three Marroc archers were watching for any Lhosir who reached the yard, all the time shooting at the Lhosir on the walls.

'The horn!' Gallow cried. 'Sound the horn!' The walls were lost. There were so many Lhosir on them now that hardly any Marroc could use their bows any more, and without arrows to keep them under their shields, Beyard's men were swarming over.

The last Marroc in front of him spun and fell into Gallow with half his face smashed in by a Lhosir axe. The Lhosir shoved him out of the way and swung an overhead cut. Gallow stepped back and levelled a backhand slash of his own but the soldier saw it coming. He was too unbalanced to get out of the way, but he turned his shield enough to catch it and staggered against the parapet. Behind him three ladders were against the wall and more Lhosir were already hauling themselves up. One fell almost before he could stand, an arrow through his neck from Achista's archers. Gallow slammed into the soldier in front of him and sliced a low cut at the man's ankles, shattering bone. The Lhosir screamed and swung back, a wild blow, then fell forward. Gallow shouldered him aside, tipping him off the battlements into the yard below, and moved to meet the next who was already lunging with a spear. On the eastern wall Tolvis was holding the Lhosir back, racing up and down the battlements even with the arrow wound in his side, hacking and slashing and shouting at the Marroc.

'For the love of Modris sound the horn!'

The Lhosir held the wall in two places now. More were on the battlements in front of Gallow, forcing him back with spears and shields, content to block him while others climbed up behind them. Further round they were sweeping the Marroc aside. Some of Achista's men had already turned to run. Arrows lashed the Lhosir on the battlements and some fell, but not as many as climbed. One Lhosir vaulted over the ramparts and dropped to the yard below. A spear lashed at Gallow's face and another stabbed at his feet. He hooked one of the shields facing him with his axe and pulled it back, and if there had been another Lhosir beside him with a spear, a lunge would have gone through the gap and struck home. But Gallow's men were Marroc farmers and hunters, unskilled in war. Another Lhosir jumped down to the yard and then another, and at last Achista blew the horn and everywhere the Marroc turned and fled, even the swordsmen who were supposed to hold the Lhosir back while the others escaped. The Lhosir howled and pressed forward. Terrified Marroc jumped down to the yard, taking their chances with the drop instead of running for the steps. Battle-mad Lhosir leaped after them. Men screamed as legs twisted and ankles snapped. Gallow stepped back and stumbled over the body of a dead Lhosir. One of the spearmen lunged at his face. He lifted his shield, pure instinct. He knew at once that he'd been drawn into leaving an opening, but before he could do more, he felt a second spear point slam into his ribs and something crack. His mail held. He stepped back again. The dead Lhosir slowed the spearmen too. It gave him a moment. He took it and ran.

The yard was a horror. Achista had waited too long. Marroc were reaching the tower but more were still leaping from the walls and there must have been a dozen Lhosir already in the yard now, screaming and swinging their blades. Men of both sides limped and hobbled and tore each other down. For now the Lhosir were too consumed by killing to make a wall of shields and charge the steps to the tower. The moment they did that, the battle was lost. Gallow glanced over the side of the walkway but the drop was the height of two men and he didn't dare, not in mail. He ran for the steps, the last man, half a second ahead of the Lhosir behind him. He turned in the air as he vaulted down, swinging his axe, taking out the soldier's feet, tipping him over so that the surging men behind tripped and they all tumbled together. An arrow flew past his head – Achista's archers at the tower door. As he looked back he saw a Lhosir slide to his knees with an arrow in his face and fall dead with a spear still clutched in his hand. Marroc cut off from the tower were being slaughtered but there was nothing anyone could do for them now. A hundred Lhosir were inside the walls, more coming every moment. Gallow reached the steps and found only Tolvis and three Marroc in a wall of shields and spears, holding the way. The wall opened to let him through.

'Here.' Tolvis passed him a spear so he could stab past their shields. A wild-eyed Marroc ran into them and then another, and then suddenly there were no more and they were facing Lhosir instead. Through the open doors at the top of the steps Marroc archers still fired into the yard.

Gallow shook his head. He ran up the steps, grabbed Achista and almost snatched the bow out of her hands. 'Get inside and close the doors!' He threw her in and glared at the other archers until they turned and then he ran back down the steps. He yanked Tolvis. 'Just run!'

They ran. The Lhosir bellowed and charged after them. The last defenders skittered into the tower through the closing doors and hurled themselves down to slide across the stone floor to the feet of a dozen Marroc archers with bows drawn. As the Lhosir threw themselves after the Marroc the archers let fly and the Lhosir fell back. Everyone inside raced to the doors, stabbing at the Lhosir, pushing them back or pulling them in and dragging them down, and then at last the doors were shut and the bars were dropped. They shook as the first Lhosir threw themselves against them.

'Up!' bawled Gallow. 'Up to the roof!' He led the way, a dozen and more weary Marroc following in his wake until they'd climbed to the open roof of the tower where Achista had had snow and stones piled as he'd asked. 'Bows! Shoot them now! While they're in their frenzy.' It wouldn't take the Lhosir in the yard long to gather themselves and hide behind their shields but every one the Marroc killed now was one fewer for later. Not that it would make any difference to the end.

He left the Marroc to their arrows, ran to the stones and picked a decent-sized one, peered over the edge and dropped it on the head of one of the axemen hacking at the door. They stopped after he felled a second; and then suddenly all across the yard the Lhosir were falling back to the wall, raising their shields. Achista yelled at the archers to save their arrows. The Reach fell still, the air quiet enough for Gallow to clearly hear the last screams and wails of the men left dying in the bloody snow. There were dozens of fallen in the yard and most of them were Marroc. He had no idea how many Lhosir they'd taken with them out of sight beyond the walls. He saw a few scattered in the snow below, but however many Lhosir were dead, half the Marroc defenders were dead too, the walls were lost and they hadn't even reached their first sunset.

Down in the yard a dull glint of iron caught Gallow's eye. Beyard. He walked among the fallen Marroc, lifting each one as he reached them. One moved as he approached, hauling himself away on his arms and leaving a wide smear of blood in the snow. Beyard reached down and picked him up. He looked at the tower roof – straight, it seemed, at Gallow – and drove a knife into the dying Marroc's neck. 'Quick and merciful,' he cried. 'I promised you that.'

He moved on to the next.

45

CAGED

Just as they did before the attack, the Lhosir took their time. A dozen of them made a wall of shields while others took it in turns to hack away the ice behind the outer gates. Once they had the gates open they left, and all Gallow and the Marroc saw of them for the rest of that day were a few scouts and sentries, watchers left on the walls behind barricades of shields and out on the trail down the mountain. That night they heard scrapings beyond the Aulian tomb door in the cellars and the steady strike of pickaxes on stone. None of them slept much.

The Lhosir were quiet the next day too except for the pickaxes in the tomb. When Gallow asked how thick the stone door was, none of the Marroc seemed to know. Addic thought about a handspan and it was hard stone too, but the Lhosir would be through it in another day. Outside the tomb, the Lhosir were busy in the woods, felling trees and cutting planks.

They broke through the Aulian stone that night and Gallow and most of the Marroc were waiting for them. As the first crack came and the stone began to crumble, the Marroc archers drew their bows. A large piece of the door fell away and a dozen arrows flew through it. Then Addic and others threw pots of oil through the hole. The next volley of arrows were flaming ones, and the space beyond the door where the Lhosir were at work lit up. The Marroc shot more arrows and poured in more oil and the Lhosir withdrew. When they were gone, Addic took a pick of his own and hammered at the door until the hole was large enough for the smallest of the Marroc to climb through and keep watch. When the Lhosir came again a few hours later, the Marroc set the last of their oil alight and poured it on the men climbing up the shaft. Beyard didn't try a third time.

*

'I still don't want to know.' Gallow wanted to tell Arda about the years he was away but she wouldn't listen. Something had changed inside her, something that had stood between them that was now gone. She slept curled up beside him, and when they found a place to be alone they made love the way they always had. She sat for long hours with Tolvis too, nursing him, and Gallow found no jealousy there any more, no envy, only pity for his friend, whose wound had been worse than any of them had known and who seemed to have lost the will to fight it.

The Lhosir brought up wooden shields and started work on a platform for the ram that would smash in the tower door. The Marroc sniped at them with arrows and stones, but they were short on both and the last oil had gone on burning the Lhosir in the shaft. The Lhosir were still down there too, the light of their torches and the sounds of their voices floating up now and then. For two more days Beyard's men worked on their ram and on the ramp that would let them drive it at the raised tower door. Now and then a few of them came with axes or tried to set a fire, and the Marroc on the tower roof threw rocks and snow and the last of their arrows until the Lhosir withdrew or Beyard came and ordered them back with his iron voice.

'Do you feel the death in the air?' Addic stood on the roof beside Gallow as the two of them stared at the Lhosir below. Beyard's shields kept the Marroc arrows at bay but they could see well enough what he was doing. Once the ram was in place it would smash the tower door to splinters and crush anyone caught behind. Beyard worked as though he had all the time in the world. The Marroc of Varyxhun hadn't risen after all.

Gallow nodded. They were going to die here, in vain, and everything would return to the way it was. Despair was a disease spreading among them, sapping their will. If Beyard hadn't gripped them so tightly, most of the Marroc would have run by now. He could hardly blame them.

'Is this what you came back for, Gallow the Foxbeard?' Addic laughed bitterly.

'No.' He'd come back for Arda, and now he had her that made every second worth living.

'I envy you.' Addic smiled as though he'd read Gallow's mind. 'This is how you forkbeards want to go, isn't it? Down fighting.'

'I'd prefer to grow fat and old watching my children, hammering ploughs and horseshoes.'

'I wish the Aulian was here with us. He'd find a way to win. Or a way to slip out at the last.' Addic laughed. 'Let the Lhosir smash their way into an empty tower.'

Gallow looked at the enemy below. 'Even Oribas couldn't find a way where there is none.'

'He would. He'd show us how to fly.'

'I wish he was here for your sister. But not for him. He'd weep, knowing there was no trick to escape this cage. Beyard will finish his ram tomorrow or the next day and then he'll smash our door. All that's left is to give a good account of ourselves before we fall.'

Addic spat over the edge of the tower. 'Doesn't it make you angry?'

'It's fate, Addic. Rail against fate if you will, but in the end it makes no difference. I spat at fate once, and all it did was tear me away and torment me for years in the wilderness and then throw me back right where I would have been anyway. Perhaps if our deaths are bright enough you'll light a fire in the hearts of your Marroc at last.'

'Perhaps.' Addic didn't turn away from the Lhosir below. 'But who will know, Gallow? Who will know?'

All told there were some five hundred Marroc hiding in the Crackmarsh. A surly bitter lot, Valaric's kind of Marroc, the sort of men who'd spit in a forkbeard's eye as soon as they saw him. Men who'd lost a little, men who'd lost a lot, all of them with nothing left but a hunger for forkbeard blood. Valaric waited for them in Hrodicslet and made the little town his, and then he marched them up the old track into the mountain valleys. They stopped at farms and the Marroc there gave what little they had. Not much food to spare, not with winter setting in, but a little, and most of all they pointed out the trail. At Jodderslet there weren't any forkbeards waiting for them, but Valaric was a cautious man and so he left the others to wait and took a handful of his best along the track up into the ravine and out again, across the mountain slope and into the back of the Devil's Caves. Still no forkbeards, so he sent a runner for the rest of his men. The caves made a good place to hide.

The messenger from Witches' Reach had had the right of it. What use was he sitting in the Crackmarsh, a whispered name and nothing else?

Addic left Gallow on the roof of the tower and went back inside. He crept down to the Aulian tomb and looked at what was left of the Lhosir supplies. He searched for anything that might burn the forkbeard ram and the ramp they'd built but they'd used all the oil driving them out of the shaft. He found rope, though, still a lot of that, plenty enough to climb down from the top of the tower and out to the mountain slopes if the forkbeards hadn't been keeping such a tight watch on them.

After that he walked among the Marroc. When the forkbeards smashed in the door, the Marroc were going to die. They knew it. He picked two men he trusted and made them each an offer: still a way to die but a different one, one that served a bit more of a purpose. He waited until dark and climbed up to the roof to join the watchmen there, made sure his rope was carefully tied and lowered it over the edge and watched the others go, one and then the other, climbing barefoot. He'd be last down, the one most likely to be seen, but as he reached for the rope a shadow came across the roof. At first he thought it was Gallow but it turned out it was the other forkbeard instead. Tolvis put his hand on Addic's shoulder.

'I can shout for your sister to come and scream at you,' he said, 'or I can go in your place. You choose.' And for a long moment the two of them stared at each other, and then Addic let go of the rope because here was a forkbeard who looked like he was wanting to die.

The wound in his side was a constant pain now but Tolvis Loudmouth ignored it as best he could. The two Marroc were almost down. He followed quickly. No mail because mail made noise. No swords or axes to scrape against the stone as they climbed down. No boots, even. They went barefoot, muffled in furs, each with a knife between his teeth. They didn't go over the north side of the tower because the Lhosir kept watch out there on the mountain slopes. Not the south side either, because that was where the gates were. Over the east side, where the tower cast a shadow in the moonlight, and when he reached the walkway of the wall below with no cries of alarm, Tolvis knew they'd almost done it. He slipped like a shadow down from the wall to the yard and crept behind Beyard's wooden shields. The two Marroc had already set to work, knives sawing at the ropes that held together the struts and beams that the Lhosir had built. Tolvis cut a rope and felt a piece of wood shift. He went to another.

'Who's there?'

He ignored the challenge and kept on cutting. The light of a torch flickered nearby. He shifted. Stopped for a moment, crouching in the shadows, gasping at the pain in his side. 'Oi! What are you doing?' The sentry had seen one of the Marroc. Tolvis darted from his hiding place, knife ready, but he was too late. 'Marroc! Marroc under the ramp! To arms!'

Tolvis silenced him anyway, taking him from the side and opening his throat. The Lhosir sentries around the Reach were already coming, calling out, rousing others. Tolvis took the dead man's axe for himself. No need for subtlety now. He swung the axe into the wooden pillars of the ramp.

A Lhosir ran at him. He let the man come, dodged aside and swung his axe again, still hacking at the wood, then ducked around it. 'I was Tolvis Loudmouth!' he bellowed. Ducked and swung again. The wood was starting to split. More Lhosir were coming. He saw one of the Marroc up and fighting, saw the other one fall. 'The Screambreaker named me. I fought at his side for five long years. I've done many things, some that were good and some that were bad, and all that time I've stood by—'

A spear plunged through him from behind, deep between his ribs, and ripped out again. He spun round. Blood flowed out of him like a river and the axe fell from his fingers. The Lhosir who'd killed him was hidden behind an owl helm. Not a man Tolvis knew. For a moment they stared at one another, then the

Lhosir drove the spear into Tolvis again, into his belly, twisting hard. Tolvis staggered. His hands reached out and grabbed the man who'd killed him.

'By what was right,' he gasped. With his last strength he dragged the Lhosir over, throwing them both against the wooden beams beside the ram. As his eyes closed for the last time, he heard the crack of splitting wood, and then a great and sudden weight pressed down and he heard nothing more.

46

FLAMES AT TWILIGHT

A corner of the platform in front of the tower doors sagged, then cracked and fell. The sounds woke Gallow, but when he climbed to the roof to look he felt no joy, only a heaviness. The Lhosir were swarming like ants around their ramp and everyone knew that the Marroc who had gone down there wouldn't be coming back. He heard the last one scream, 'For King Tane!' He'd walked this valley years ago with Screambreaker, chasing that old Marroc king. In the years since then he'd come to think that it was the Lhosir who'd changed, that they'd somehow lost what had once made them noble, and perhaps there *was* some truth to that, but mostly what he thought now was that they'd never been all that noble in the first place. Savages who fought better than the rest, that's all they were.

He never heard Tolvis fall. What did his life buy? Another day?

In the morning Beyard came to the tower doors, waving a flag of parley. 'Gallow Truesword! I would speak with you.' In the yard the Lhosir were cutting away the broken wood of the ramp. New beams already lay in wait outside the gates. When the Lhosir tried to make their repairs, the Marroc would use the last of their arrows and stones. When those were spent, they'd wait because there wasn't anything else they could do. The Screambreaker had finally got into Varyxhun castle because the last of King Tane's huscarls had killed themselves rather than be taken. Would that be what happened here? 'Gallow Truesword!'

Gallow looked down from the tower roof. 'Up here, Beyard!'

'Tolvis Loudmouth lies dead. At dusk I send him to the Maker-Devourer as befits the warrior that he was. He died well. Will you come to speak him out, Gallow Truesword?'

'What of the Marroc?'

Beyard put his hands on his hips. 'What of them, Truesword? I honour a Lhosir.'

Gallow paused. What did he know of Marroc burials? Almost nothing. Eight years living among them and he hadn't much idea how the Marroc made peace with their dead. 'Bury them!' That was all he knew.

Beyard shook his head. 'No one will bury anyone here, Truesword, not until spring, not unless you want to have at the ground with a pick.' He turned away. The Lhosir started rebuilding their ramp and raising their ram, and the Marroc went back to throwing stones and shooting arrows made from the crates and barrels in the cellars of the Reach. As the sun dipped towards the horizon, the Lhosir withdrew and Beyard returned. The ram was ready and Beyard stood beside it. 'Gallow! I mean to burn the dead tonight before I smash in your doors.'

Achista stopped him. 'It's a trap, forkbeard. The iron devil means to snare you.'

'Whatever you think of him, Beyard will honour his word.'

'I will not open the doors for you to do this.'

Gallow sighed. 'Yes, you will, because he has Oribas and I will ask for the Aulian's life.' He saw her face as she crumbled inside. It was a terrible thing.

The Lhosir left the yard until Beyard remained alone. 'Let us understand one another, Marroc,' he called. 'I withdraw my men so you may open your doors. This is no truce. When Gallow crosses the Witches' Reach, we will be as we were. Die well, Marroc. You've earned your places in the Maker-Devourer's cauldron.' Beyard turned and walked away.

Achista's eyes were red. Tears and not enough sleep. Gallow looked for Arda. She was staring at him from across the hall, but when he caught her eye she folded her arms and turned away. The same look he'd seen when he'd left her to fight the Vathen, years ago. *Give me a man who has enough of the coward in him to stay at home and keep his family safe.* Gallow took Achista's hands. 'If I don't come back, find a place for her to hide and make her stay there. I'll trade my life for hers and for Oribas if I can.' He bowed his head. Beyard might give him Arda, but not Oribas, not after what the Aulian had done.

Two Marroc pulled back the bars, Achista opened the tower doors and Gallow stepped outside. He'd barely taken a step when he heard it slam behind him and the bars grind back into place. It felt strange to be on the outside – as though he'd been set free of something.

Across the yard at the outer gates Beyard was waiting. The pyre was a little way beyond him, and there they stopped. Tolvis lay atop the wood, arms folded across his chest, eyes closed. His furs were dark and matted with blood. 'He bought you this day,' Beyard said. 'If it wasn't for him I'd have smashed my way in this morning. So honour him. Tolvis Loudmouth. I never knew him, though I heard his name after what he did in Andhun. Reviled below only yours. Why was he even here, Truesword? Why did you come back, either of you?'

'For Arda.'

'Both of you?'

'Both of us.'

Beyard shook his head. 'I'm told my heart stopped beating seventeen winters back. Sometimes in the dead of night when the silence is so thick it's suffocating, I close my eyes and listen for it. I hear nothing, so forgive me if I don't understand how a heart works any more. Your Aulian friend showed me a mirror that I should have seen a very long time ago.' He took off his mask and crown and Gallow saw that his face was burned and scarred as if by fire. 'You and Tolvis Loudmouth. Two fine brothers of the sea. Speak him out then, old friend, and let us all be back to killing each other.' He sounded sad, like the Beyard that Gallow remembered.

Gallow spoke of Tolvis then, of the life he'd led, of the battles he'd seen and the deeds he'd done. Of his years when he'd fought in the Screambreaker's war. He'd been there at every turn as the Marroc were crushed, and now he was dead so that a handful could live another day. As Gallow spoke, Beyard took a torch to the pyre and lit it. A few other Lhosir paused and stood, listening sombrely. Maybe they were old warriors who'd known Tolvis once, or maybe they simply respected the old way of speaking out an enemy who'd died well in battle. 'We're lessened by his passing,' breathed Beyard when Gallow was done. They were the old words for bidding farewell to a fallen friend but Beyard gave them a weight as though he truly meant them. 'Tonight we will be lessened by yours. I will speak you out myself.'

'I have a favour to ask, old friend,' said Gallow. 'Oribas.'

'The Aulian.' Beyard shook his head. 'He killed, Gallow. Many men and in bad ways. I've sent him back to Varyxhun to be hanged.'

But by now Gallow was looking at the mountainside beyond the pyre. In the twilight it seemed that it was moving.

A dozen Crackmarsh men hung back, armed with bows to take down any forkbeards travelling the Varyxhun Road from higher in the valley – messengers, perhaps, from the castle. The Marroc would shoot the horses out from under the forkbeards to stop them, whether one came or a hundred. Valaric took a handful of men ahead in case any came the other way. The bulk of the Marroc travelled in between, moving down the valley in secret. Surprise was a weapon Valaric couldn't afford to lose. An hour up the Varyxhun Road from Witches' Reach he stopped and left the vanguard with Sarvic and led his main force up the mountainside instead. It was slow going through the snow. The air was bitter, a harsh biting cold far worse than wintering in the Crackmarsh. He hadn't meant to, but Valaric saw now that he'd brought his men to a choice between victory or death. They'd either overrun the forkbeards and their camp and relieve the Reach or they'd die in the night, frozen in their boots. He called a halt on the side of the mountain as the sun began to set and they caught their first sight of the Lhosir camp. The Marroc couldn't light any fires of their own but the sight of so many enemies was enough to keep them warm. They strung their bows and sharpened their swords and their spears and their axes; they tightened the straps on their shields and their helms and rubbed their hands and paced back and forth. There were no fine words, not from Valaric. They all knew what they'd come for, why they'd gone to the Crackmarsh in the first place, and here it was.

The mountain darkness came quickly. A pyre burst into flame

up by the gates of Witches' Reach. It was a sign, Valaric decided: Modris telling him that now was the time. There was no great shout, no wild charge, but as one the grim-faced Marroc of the Crackmarsh poured down the mountain towards the Lhosir below.

Beyard faced Witches' Reach. He had his back to the mountain where the shadows had come alive. Gallow slowly drew his sword. 'Can we not settle this between us, old friend? One against another?'

Beyard looked sad. 'But I will win.'

'Perhaps.'

'What do you ask, Gallow? Beat me and I will let these Marroc go? I cannot. And what do you offer? If I bring you to your knees, will they meekly open their gates? No. Those days are gone.'

Gallow shook his head. 'They're not gone for as long as we remember them, old friend. For as long as we live.'

Beyard laughed, bitter as poison. 'Did your Aulian not tell you what I am?' He looked at Gallow's confusion and shook his head. 'I am dead, Gallow. The Eyes of Time took me in the Temple of Fate. The Fateguard sent me to the Ice Wraiths and the Eyes of Time gave me this.' He beat his fist against the iron he wore and looked up at the mountains around the Reach. 'I have liked these mountains ever since I saw them. Their cold unforgiving majesty reminds me of the last journey I took as a man, with blood that ran warm and a heart to beat and a soul that burned.' Venom filled his words. He took off one iron gauntlet and drew out the red sword, but instead of coming at Gallow with it he slid the edge across his palm. The flesh beneath his pale skin was dark but no blood dripped into the snow melting around Tolvis's pyre. He sheathed Solace and stared at his hand. 'I feel no heat from these flames, nor do I have warmth inside me.'

Abruptly he picked up his mask and crown and put them on his head. He paced back and forth and then drew Solace again. 'There's no happy outcome here, but an outcome there must be. Let's be at it, old friend.'

*

From the roof of the tower Achista peered towards the pyre. She watched Gallow and the iron devil stand beside it. She saw Gallow, lit up by the flames, draw his sword, and the iron devil too, and watched them begin to circle. The forkbeard wouldn't be coming back. Nor would Oribas. Most of the Lhosir were further down the ridge, sitting around their fires, warming themselves for the fight to come. She ran down the stairs that circled the inside of the tower, shouting to the Marroc to rise. Thirty men perhaps, no more, against five hundred forkbeards, but when she called them to arms they followed her gladly, the weight of waiting lifted from their shoulders, a burden pulled away. They threw down the bars and hurled open the doors and spilled into the night onto the Lhosir ramp, voices strong and clear, swords and helms gleaming in the light of the torches that lit up the walls of Witches' Reach. They would die but they would not be meek.

47

MEN OF FATE

Gallow and Beyard circled each other. Neither carried a shield and so there were no rushing charges to knock the other man down. For once they were wary. Gallow's eyes stayed on the edge of the red sword. So many names among the different people of the world – Solace, the Comforter, the Peacebringer – but the Aulians had the right of it: the Edge of Sorrows. For all the sharpness of its terrible blade, it carried a curse.

He put his back to the pyre and sprang, arms wide, sword out to swing at Beyard's head, and then changed into a chop to the hip where Beyard's armour seemed weakest, but the iron man held out the red sword like a spear, pointed at Gallow's chest. He stepped aside and Gallow had no choice but to cut at the sword or else impale himself on its tip. He'd seen it shear through mail in a way no sword should ever do.

Beyard whipped Solace at Gallow's legs. Gallow jumped away and turned, and now it was Beyard who was looking down the slope of the mountain saddle towards his camp. Shouts echoed up the ridge. Beyard took a step back. For a moment his head craned forward as if he was trying to see what was happening. Gallow flung himself at the iron man and brought his sword down as hard as he could. Beyard, half off guard, brought up Solace, but too slowly, and Gallow's blade cracked into the iron armour around his collar, into the space between shoulder and neck. Gallow felt it strike, felt the edge of his steel bite into metal, felt it stick and wrenched it free before the sword was torn out of his hand. He jumped away. Beyard swayed. Where Gallow had struck, his armour was cracked and misshapen, a large dark scar cut into it that ought to have cracked bones and drip with seeping blood. For a moment the two of them stared at one another. Then Beyard bowed his head.

'A well made blow, old friend.' He looked past Gallow towards the camp, towards the sounds of fighting. 'I wish I'd known you for longer.'

He took one step closer and then another, an iron-gloved hand held out before him, the red sword raised and poised. He snarled and the steps turned to a charge.

The Crackmarsh men slammed through the forkbeard camp like a herd of charging bulls. Valaric screamed at them to keep running, to smash down the forkbeards as they rose from their fires. Some stopped anyway, pausing to finish a forkbeard they'd dazed and left helpless, and Valaric was happy enough with that. Others stopped to fight other forkbeards who hadn't been knocked down and got themselves caught in duels, one against one, two against one, two against three. Keep moving, that was the thing. Tear through the forkbeard camp. Scatter them. Fight them in ones and twos, and whatever you did, don't let them gather together. He had no illusions about his men. They were hard and bitter fighters but they weren't forkbeards. If the Lhosir formed ranks behind their shields then the battle would be over.

He scooped up a burning branch from one of the fires and hurled it at three forkbeards standing together, then charged into them, battering one man down, veering away before the other two could stab him with their spears. He wheeled and ran straight into a forkbeard fighting toe to toe with one of his Marroc. Valaric rammed his spear into the back of the fork-beard's thigh and ran on. A pair of Lhosir with axes were racing across the camp, coming his way. He dropped into the shadows of a tent, stuck out his foot and tripped one and then surged up and brought his spear down with all his strength, splitting the mail that protected the back of the forkbeard's neck. He yanked his point free, blade dark with forkbeard blood. The second axeman skidded to a stop and spun to face him. Valaric bared his teeth. *Modris, but it feels good to be doing something at last!*

*

Gallow stepped aside as the iron man hurled himself forward. He struck Beyard in the side with all the strength his arm could muster. Beyard turned and stood for a moment, lit by Tolvis's pyre, armour gleaming, shoulders rising and falling with each heavy breath. He came more slowly now, with the patient purpose of a Fateguard, driving Gallow back towards the heat of the fire. The red sword arced and swung and the air moaned under its blade. Gallow raised his own sword to defend himself. Sparks flashed as steel touched steel. Beyard lunged, driving for Gallow's heart. Gallow leaped sideways, almost falling into the pyre in his desperation. He hurled another swing at Beyard but the Edge of Sorrows caught it easily and almost wrenched his sword out of his hand. Beyard swung and lunged again. This time Gallow stepped inside the blow and barged Beyard with his shoulder, staggering him back. He lifted his sword to drive it between the bars of the iron man's mask, but Beyard smashed the blade aside. The ring as the two swords struck sounded oddly dull. The red sword slashed at Gallow's face. Gallow stumbled again, and this time when the red sword came down and he blocked it with his own, his blade shattered. Gallow rolled away, snatched a brand out of the pyre and jumped to his feet, waving it at Beyard's face. The iron man caught it in his fist and held it. For an instant their eyes met, the fire burning between them, then Beyard punched Gallow with the hand that still held Solace. As he reeled, Beyard pushed him to the ground. A moment later the tip of the red sword rested on the back of Gallow's neck.

'Yield!' rasped Beyard.

The Marroc raced out of the tower, howling and screaming, hacking at the ramp the forkbeards had built, drawing them from where they stood watch. They came slowly, distracted by the fight at the pyre, but they came, and Achista and the Marroc fought them as hard as they could. But there were dozens of them, soldiers born and bred, and slowly they drove the Marroc back into a tight circle of shields and spears just outside the gates, pressing in, killing them one by one with no way out.

*

Valaric took the forkbeard's axe on his shield and rammed his spear point into the man's belly – maybe not hard enough to pierce mail but hard enough to wind him. As the Lhosir doubled over, Valaric lifted his shield and smashed its rim into the back of the forkbeard's head. He went down.

'Next!' In the darkness, amid the litter of campfires and the scurrying of men here and there, it was impossible to tell who was who and who was winning. It was everything Valaric had wanted though – a wild swirling melee with every man for himself. The forkbeards hadn't formed their wall of shields because he hadn't let them. He crouched down in the shadows. A Lhosir ran out in front of him. He sprang and brought him down, banging the forkbeard's head into the frozen ground and holding it there until his struggles eased enough for Valaric to get out a knife and open his throat. Not ten feet away a Marroc was fighting another forkbeard, the two of them locked together, grunting and swearing, the forkbeard slowly bearing the Marroc down. The forkbeard wasn't wearing his mail though, so Valaric ran to them and knifed him in the liver.

'Look!' The Marroc pointed up the slope towards the Reach. In the dim light around the gates Valaric saw fighting. 'They've come out for us,' said the Marroc.

'Crazy fools.' They were surrounded. He could see that even from here. He could see the pyre as well and two men fighting around it, and as he watched, one of the men fell. A savage growl prowled inside him, looking for an escape. 'Round up some others,' he snarled. 'Not too many. But we came here for Witches' Reach.'

'Yield.' Gallow was kneeling now. 'Yield and I'll give you a clean death.'

'Let the Marroc go. Let Oribas go. Let all of them go. End it all, old friend.'

'Look around you. It's ended already.'

'Yet still I will not yield.' Gallow started to rise.

The tip of the red sword pressed into his neck. 'Your Marroc are beaten, old friend.'

Gallow kept rising though the sword's edge cut into his skin.

He could feel the blood trickling down his back. Beyard could kill him with a flick of his wrist yet he didn't. 'No, Beyard. Lost is not beaten. You're Lhosir. You of all of us understand the difference.' He walked away and picked up the jagged stump of his broken sword. 'I'll fight you until you kill me, old friend.'

Beyard kept the red sword held out before him. Gallow walked calmly towards it. He swatted the Edge of Sorrows aside with his half-sword. Beyard stepped away. 'Stop,' he hissed. He sounded hoarse. 'Just go, Gallow.'

'I will not.'

'I don't want to kill you, old friend.'

Gallow flicked the red sword aside again. 'Then take your Lhosir and walk away.'

'I cannot.'

'Then I have no other choice to give you.' Gallow lunged and Beyard only moved at the very last moment. The jagged edge of Gallow's steel slid off the side of the Fateguard mask. The iron man stayed where he was. He didn't raise the red sword. Instead he lifted the mask and crown off his face and looked Gallow in the eye.

'There would be tears in my eyes if I could still weep.'

'Yield, old friend.'

'I cannot. No more than you.'

They looked at one another a moment longer. Beneath the pale scarred skin and the hollow cheeks and the red-rimmed eyes, Gallow saw the Beyard who'd stood beside him in the Temple of the Fates, holding closed a door, young and strong and fierce, the best of the three of them by far.

'Don't let him lessen us,' Beyard whispered and put back his mask and crown, and Gallow knew he meant Medrin. Medrin, who'd been with them that day and had run away.

The iron man lowered the Edge of Sorrows and was still. Gallow drove the spike of his broken sword through the bars of the iron mask. Beyard spasmed. The red sword fell from his hand. His weight sagged forward and Gallow eased him to his knees. 'Farewell, old friend.'

Beyard still had some strange strength to him. He knelt, head bowed, a spike of iron through his skull, and yet for a moment he didn't die. He gripped Gallow's leg.

'Peace.' Gallow pulled away. He picked the red sword out of the snow and brought it down with all his strength on the back of Beyard's neck. Solace. The Comforter. The Peacebringer.

Achista knew she'd die. The last dozen of the Marroc from the tower were pressed together. She'd never even fought a man with a sword and half the other Marroc were the same – pathetic, desperate – while the forkbeards were forkbeards. Even as she dodged and ducked and lunged, inside she cringed, waiting for the end. And then suddenly the forkbeards were drawing back. A score of them and they were pulling away, all of them staring down the trail from the gates of Witches' Reach to the pyre where one man stood holding the sword of the Weeping God. Gallow.

Slowly, with their shields still high and their spears still raised, the forkbeards drew away and melted into the night. They were Lhosir, after all, men of fate, and fate had spoken. Achista stared long after they'd vanished into the darkness. Stared as a horn sounded in the distance, deep and mournful. Stared at Gallow as he stood there doing nothing but looking down at the fallen iron devil. Then figures appeared out of the shadows heading up from the forkbeard camp – Marroc, led by a man with wild mad eyes, scarred and spattered with blood. He looked at her and at the others and then back again and held out his arm. 'Valaric,' he said. 'They call me Mournful.'

It was a miracle. She clasped his arm. 'Achista. They call me the Huntress.'

'Why did the forkbeards run? They never run.'

She pointed at Gallow. There was the answer, somehow. "But they didn't *run*. They just … left.'

Valaric nodded. 'Well get your men together, Achista whom they call the Huntress. We've work to do. There's plenty more forkbeards left where they came from.'

He ran back yelling orders and Achista watched him, too dazed by fate's sudden turn to take it in. The forkbeards would come again. Another army, bigger. But this time there would be enough Marroc to hold the walls for months.

She left the gate and walked to the pyre. Gallow was dragging the body of the iron devil towards the flames but it was too heavy and awkward for one man to lift alone. She took the iron devil's feet. Burning it felt right. Burning it into ash. Together they heaved it into the flames. 'You won,' she said. 'I don't know how, but you won.'

Gallow picked up the iron devil's head, still with the spike of his broken sword driven through its mask. He threw it into the flames and whispered words amid the crackling heat. Achista stared into the pyre, lost. It was like watching all the forkbeards she'd ever known burn, all the things they'd done and all the bitterness they'd wrought.

When she turned back to Gallow to ask him what he would do, he was gone.

48

READY TO DO WHAT A HERO CAN

Gallow stared at Beyard, wreathed in fire, his head still merci-fully cased in iron, the crown and mask of the Fateguard pinned in place by the spike of his broken sword. He'd been a man once. Even at the end neither of them had forgotten. The right thing now was to speak out his deeds, shout them to the sky loud and clear so the wind would carry his words across the world and through the Herenian Marches to the Maker-Devourer and his cauldron, but what was there to say? 'Beyard. A Lhosir of the old way. The best of us all. Maker-Devourer, take him to your cauldron. A friend once.' That was what mattered the most.

Achista was staring, mesmerised by the flames and their ever-fickle meanings. Her eyes were black and wide. Words grew in his throat and then died on his lips. He almost reached out to touch her, to bring her back from wherever she was, and then stopped. He was a forkbeard and she was a Marroc, and that would never change. Only Arda ever saw past to the man inside. Arda, who'd kept his heart alive for three long years, and now he had to leave her again.

The heat of the pyre burned his face. He stepped back, and then turned away and slammed the Edge of Sorrows down. Its point bit deep into the frozen earth, ever hungry for the piercing of things. He left it there and walked through snow pounded flat by a thousand fleeing footfalls. The Marroc from the keep were out by the gates now, the few that were left, dancing and singing and whooping. Addic was there and somehow Valaric too, Addic drunk with delight that he was still alive, Valaric yelling orders at his men who'd come from Maker-Devourer-knew-where on this night to save them. A miracle? A sign from the gods? Luck?

Fate? Gallow passed them by and felt none of it, no joy, no pride, no glory, just the weight of a lot of dead men whose blood had spilled for no great cause one way or the other. He walked up the steps to the keep, and there she was in the shadows beyond the doorway, looking out. Watching. Arda. He opened his arms to her and she walked to him and let him hold her tight. In his mail and his furs he felt like a bear and she so fragile.

'Arda.' He nuzzled her hair and held her, and for a long time that was enough.

'I know that look.'

'I killed a friend tonight.'

She didn't say a word.

'You are ...' He shook his head. Oribas would have found words of magic power, drawn patterns in the air with them, made them dance and sing to the tune of his heart, but that was Oribas, whose art was knowledge. Gallow had no idea how to tell Arda what was in his heart. Neither of them had ever been good at that.

Oribas, whom Beyard had sent away to be hanged, whom Gallow had walked away from once back in Varyxhun.

'Clod-head. I know. Come.'

She led him away to the cellars, to a quiet place where the Marroc left them alone and kept him there until the creeping grey of dawn spread across the mountain sky to the east. And when he thought she was sleeping and turned back the furs to slip silently away, she looked him right in the eye. She'd known all along that it would come to this.

'You're going to go again, aren't you?' She tried to sound like it didn't matter but she couldn't. Her voice was flat and dead.

'Yes.'

The Arda he'd left behind three years ago would have sworn and shouted and thrown things, screaming about family and loyalty, but now she only looked at him. 'Why, Gallow? Why?'

'Oribas.' And that was all. As if that should be enough. She stiffened, the old anger and resentment and all those other things still burning away inside her, hard to push away.

'Pursic doesn't even remember you.' She knew he'd seen

back in Middislet: Pursic at the top of the cellar stairs staring at Tolvis. *Dada!*

Gallow closed his eyes. His voice broke to a whisper. 'I know.'

She snorted, and for a moment she was herself again, the old Arda who was used to being around mud-brained forkbeards. 'Well, if you're going then you'll be not much use if you freeze to death.' She picked up a handful of furs and threw them at him. 'At least keep yourself warm.' She waited while he put on his mail and buckled his belt and arranged his furs, and then when he was dressed he led him by the hand to the gates of Witches' Reach and handed him his spear. 'I won't be here when you come back. Three years was enough. I'll not do that again.'

'They're going to hang him. He was my friend. I have to go.'

Her lips were dry. 'I know. And so do I.'

'If you ask me to I'll stay.'

She didn't doubt he meant it but it was such a stupid thing to say. She pushed him on and then stepped back. 'You stole my heart with all your forkbeard pride and your courage and your strength. I love you for what you are, Gallow, but what I need is a man who'll feed my children and protect them. Someone who's there. War clouds are coming. I need a man who'll stay at home and that's not you. So yes, Gallow Truesword, Gallow the Foxbeard, I want you to stay, I want that more than anything, but I'll not ask it. Only you can say which matters to you more. And if you ask me to wait, I won't. Not again.' She stepped back into the shadows of Witches' Reach.

'There's no peace for us, Arda.' Gallow shook his head. 'No peace. Not while Medrin lives.'

Arda nodded and turned her back and walked away because hell would freeze over before she'd let a forkbeard see her cry. Gallow called after her one last time but she didn't dare look back, and then he was gone. She climbed to the top of the tower and looked out over the dawn and saw him again, standing by the pyre of Tolvis Loudmouth, and she watched him pull a sword out of the ground where he'd left it the night before and turn and go. Watched until she couldn't see him any more, until she saw that he didn't look back, not once.

When he was gone, she dried her eyes and went looking for

Valaric the Mournful, the Marroc whose men had her children back in his hideout. There were things to be said about that and in no uncertain manner.

More Lhosir came later that day, the half-an-army that had been waiting by the Aulian Bridge to fall on Valaric's Crackmarsh men. They were righteously furious, and from all the stories told afterwards it was a vicious and bloody little siege until the fork-beards finally took the walls and built the iron devil's ram again and smashed down the gates and stormed inside. But at the end, the stories said, all they found was an empty tower. And Arda heard those stories too, but she couldn't have said if they were true because before the first of the forkbeards came up from the bridge, she was already gone.

No one had taken the red sword. A hundred upon a hundred Marroc plundering and looting the dead, and not one of them had touched it. Gallow pulled it free and sheathed it at his side. The cursed blade. His and his alone, stained by the blood of his oldest friend. He turned to face south, the road to Varyxhun, and when the Lhosir came later that day he was long gone too.

EPILOGUE

There were riots in the city. Oribas couldn't see but he could hear them and he could smell the smoke. The Marroc had been restless for days. Something had happened but no one would tell him what. Down in his cell he picked up rumours now and then and saw the odd Marroc being dragged off to the torturer and then later he heard their screams and sobs. He heard everything they cried, not that it added up to much, but there were more every day.

His cell was underground, but on the day they hanged him they hauled him up to the castle yard and he could hear and smell the turmoil clearly at last. He could see it too, written on the Lhosir around the castle, on their faces and in the way they held themselves. He looked up at the gallows and he could see it even there. They were going to hang him but he wouldn't be the only one. There were some Marroc to die too. Out here in the yard, pressed together with the other prisoners, he'd heard what it was that had the streets of Varyxhun filled with revolt. The forkbeards were beaten. The iron devil was dead and Witches' Reach still held.

Witches' Reach still held.

He stared up at the waiting gallows and knew that Achista was still alive. He would hang a happy man.

THE END OF FARRI MOONTONGUE

PART TWO

'*But by the end of my looking it was the Moontongue I came to understand. They say the Moontongue stole the Crimson Shield as a gift to Neveric the Black of the Marroc, that he meant to betray his brother and his king and that Neveric betrayed him in turn, but Moontongue had a sea more ambition to him than that. When I understood, Aulian, for a moment I was in such awe of him that I forgot to breathe. The Moontongue stole the Crimson Shield for himself, not for some Marroc. He believed he would see the future, know all things before they came to pass, and with that knowledge he would crush Yurlak and grind his brother to dust and lead a conquest the like of which the world hasn't seen since the glorious days of Aulia. He wasn't killed by some renegade Marroc.*'

The Marroc ship of Neveric the Black trailed in the wake of the Lhosir for two days before Farri Moontongue changed his course to meet them. There was a storm coming and he thought it best to get this over with before it arrived. The two ships eased up close to one another and the crew threw ropes and hauled on them until they were lashed tight together. The Moontongue kept his warriors away from their axes and their shields, not wanting to give away his intent. There was a wariness to the Marroc crew too, an uneasiness that said they weren't here for the peaceful bargain they claimed. When they were done tying fast the ships, the Moontongue stood on the middle of his deck, waiting for the shout that would kick off the fight, but it didn't come. Instead Neveric the Black came out and stood by his mast as the Moontongue stood by his own. The Marroc looked this way and that, almost anywhere but at the Moontongue and his men, as though he really didn't want to be here. As though he'd already lost.

'Well then Neveric, what is it?' shouted the Moontongue.

'We had a bargain,' called the Marroc, looking back at the Moontongue and meeting his eye at last. 'I promised you King Tane's gold for the shield. I'll honour that promise if you will honour yours.'

The Moontongue laughed back at him. 'I made no such promise. Two days on our tail, though. Persistent, I'll give you that.'

The Marroc looked away and then looked back. 'It'll go easier on you, forkbeard. I've not come for a fight but I'll give you one if I must.'

The Moontongue still laughed. 'Will you now? So here's what I think: since you're trying so very very hard to give it to me, I'll have your gold then, but I'll be keeping your precious shield.' His hand fell to the axe on his belt and everywhere on both ships men saw and tensed and reached for their own; but before he could draw it, more figures came out onto the decks of the Marroc ship – but these were no Marroc. The dark iron of their armour was almost black under the grey skies. Their iron boots clanked against the hard wooden deck and the Marroc kept well away from them, nervous and fearful. The grin stayed fixed on the Moontongue's face but the laughter died. Fateguard. Twelve iron devils to go with the thirty Marroc fighters. Changed things a bit, that did.

The iron devil who took the lead was missing a hand. The iron mask he wore was bent and misshapen and split along one side, exactly as though someone had buried an axe its side. So there couldn't be any doubt, the ironskin took something from his belt and threw it from one ship to the other so it landed at the Moontongue's feet. His axe. The one he'd left in the Hall of Fates.

'Yours, Moontongue,' grated a voice from whatever mouth lay hidden behind the mask. 'Now return what you took.'

The Moontongue picked up the axe and looked at it and yes, three nights earlier he'd left it buried in the side of this iron devil's head. He stared at it a little more and then nodded and picked up the Crimson Shield of Modris from where it sat propped against the mast. He strapped it onto his arm. 'This?' He held it up so everyone would see. 'You want this? Then you'll have to come and take it.' He walked steadily to where the two ships ground against one another and raised his axe and brought it down on the nearest of the ropes that held them together. 'Cut the ropes!' he cried.

Both ships erupted into sound and movement. The Lhosir warriors around him snatched up their shields and drew out their axes and ran for the ropes. The iron devils launched themselves at the rails, leaping across the narrow gap of sea between the two ships as thought they were acrobats, not men carrying their own weight in metal. They crashed among the Lhosir, swinging their swords left and right. The Lhosir met the blows with their shields and their axes.

Baldi Heronhand slipped away as soon as the fighting started. He stood in the Moontongue's cabin, looking at the iron-bound chest that Svarn Bloodaxe had taken from the Temple of Fates. None of them had seen how to open it and the Moontongue hadn't allowed Svarn to take his axe to it, but now it seemed to Baldi that the Moontongue's orders were less important than they'd been a few hours ago. So he took his axe to the hinges and shattered the first in two blows and the second in one. The box fell off the Moontongue's table and landed on the floor. The lid came half off and a pale brown grainy sand spilled out – no, not sand, salt. He picked up the box and put it back on the table and finished ripping the lid away. Salt? Was that all? But then he saw the glint of something golden.

The Moontongue caught the blows from the Fateguard easily. The Crimson Shield moved with a will of its own, anticipating each strike before it came. He faced the one-handed iron devil and parried blow after blow, turning each one and every time his own axe bit back at the iron armour. He struck the devil in the thigh and the hip and the arm, each time scoring a deep mark in the Fateguard's iron skin, but nothing seemed to slow it. Around him his men were falling, one by one, and though the Fateguard lost a hand here and there and maybe a foot and Moontongue saw one with his iron masked caved in and one missing half his arm, still they kept coming. The Marroc, he saw, had stayed on their ship and they were cutting the ropes as fast as they could. They just wanted to get away.

Heronhand pulled out the golden thing from within the box. It was a tube, an exquisite map tube, but small – hardly even the length of his forearm. Each end was stoppered with an ornate golden cap that slid reluctantly off when he tugged. The fitting was perfect. He took it in his shield hand, picked up his axe and ran back to the fight. One of the iron devils had its back to him. He took out its knee with one massive swing and dodged past as it buckled and toppled backwards. He looked over to the Marroc ship, already starting to move away, and at the Lhosir he'd known and fought with for a dozen years who now lay dead scattered around the fury of the Moontongue. Two of the iron devils were too crippled to stand but even those were still moving. The rest fought on, relentless. He saw one Lhosir warrior drop his shield and pick up a massive axe as long as his leg and use it to cut one of the iron devil's arms clean off and probably shatter half his ribs too, and the devil kept on. The last of the Lhosir were mostly in a circle now, shields locked together, fighting as best they could against an enemy that refused to die. At the far end of the ship, one man cut off from the others ran and leaped over the side, launching himself at the Marroc ship. He fell short and landed in the sea and vanished at once, sucked down by waves and the weight of his mail.

Someone fired an arrow from the Marroc ship into the melee. Then another, and then Heronhand saw they were bringing up a brazier, ready to set their arrows aflame. They were still close though, very close. Close enough. He ran and jumped onto the rail of the Moontongue's ship and hurled himself across the churning water between the two ships and almost made it. He hit the side of the Marroc ship and grabbed at it, slid, dropped his axe and caught hold of the rail with one hand. He swung his other arm, still with his shield strapped to it and still holding the golden case, and hooked his arm over the rail. He started to haul himself over when he found himself staring up at a Marroc with a spear aimed at his face. The spear jabbed him right under the nose, hard enough to break two of his teeth and rip half his upper lip.

'Stay on your own ship, forkbeard.' The spear drew back and then paused as the Marroc saw what he had in his hand. He dropped the spear and picked up an axe instead. 'Give it, forkbeard. Give it and I'll let you live.'

The Lhosir shook his head. The Marroc grinned and brought the axe down on Heronhand's arm, breaking it through the mail. Baldi Heronhand screamed. As he fell, he felt the golden case torn out from his fingers; and then the freezing water of the Ice Mountain Sea swallowed him and he sank like a stone.

No one saw the Moontongue fall and lived to tell of it. Maybe he never did. The Marroc set fire to his ship and sailed away and left it adrift and maybe the fire took him before the Fateguard could bring him down, or maybe they were still fighting when the storm broke some hours later and sent them all to the bottom. But either way, that was where it ended, out in the Ice Mountain Sea, with Farri Moontongue, the Crimson Shield of Modris and twelve of the Fateguard all sent to the bottom of the sea together. And some years later, if one of the Fateguard was seen to come to the temple in Nardjas with a misshapen mask split open at the side by a fierce blow from an axe and smelling faintly of the sea, there was no one left from that day who might have noticed and started to wonder.

WITCHES' REACH

The wagon drove slowly over the new road the Aulians had built. It ran from where they were still constructing their mountain castle to where a freshly raised tower looked out over the rush of the Isset gorge and beyond. Another few miles along the river past the tower, where the gorge was narrowest, they'd already erected an immense scaffold that stretched right across the river. They were building a bridge, or so they said. Missa had gone to look at it last week and taken a right earful and almost a beating for wandering so far, but it had been worth it. She'd never seen a thing like it. Men hanging from ropes a hundred feet up in the air over the roaring water, and stones the size of houses being slowly levered and rolled down the road and lined up along the bank. They were building a stone arch and they'd nearly finished it, but when she'd asked one of the Aulians if that was the bridge, they'd only laughed at her and said no, the arch was only the beginning, and something about it being there to support a second arch, and that second arch itself only being built to support the construction of a last and much greater arch that would support the bridge itself. It left her wondering if she'd be old before it was done, but the laughing stonemasons said no, it might take another year or a bit more depending on the winter, but then it would be done and they could all go home.

She crept from her perch looking down on the road and ran after the wagon as far as the tower. It was full of what looked like sand, except it was clumpy and course and an odd pale colour, a sort of off-white brown. Every time the wagon took a bump or a rut in the road, it shook and some of the sand fell off. She picked up a handful of it and took a closer look and found it stuck to her damp fingers; and when she sucked at them a few minutes later, they tasted of salt. She put some in her mouth to see and that's what it was. Salt. A wagon full of priceless salt. After that, she made sure to scoop up whatever fell out.

A dozen workmen were waiting outside the tower. They already had shovels and as soon as the wagon stopped they started scooping the salt out into sacks. Missa watched them a while until she was bored. She was about to leave when she saw that there was something hidden under the salt, slowly being uncovered.

It took them another hour to clear it out. What was left was a body – at least, it had two arms and two legs and a head. Missa supposed it was some sort of soldier since it was dressed from head to foot in armour made out of plates of dark metal. The workmen put down their shovels and set about dragging the body out of the wagon and into the tower. It took all twelve of them to carry it, resting on a sturdy plank of wood that in turn rested on their shoulders. When they were inside, Missa slipped in after them. No one paid her much attention. There weren't many children out here in the valley and the few there were tended to get treated well by the soldiers and the stone-masons. Reminded the Aulians of home, they said, where they all fervently wished they could be.

The procession moved through the tower's open hall and down a set of spiral steps. It took a good long time to manage that, with a great deal of swearing and cursing, and then there was another one, a lot longer than the first. It ended in an odd room, hexagonal, with the stairs through the centre and six stone benches set one into each wall, one for each of the Ascendants and each with an altar except for one, where instead of a wall there was a wide circular opening. The men were already carry-ing the body inside, and when Missa moved to follow them, one turned back and shot her a warning glance. 'No, Missa. Wait out there. This isn't for you.'

There were more men inside and so Missa hung in the doorway and craned her head to see what they were up to, but when the workmen put down the body and came back out, they shooed her away. They went back up and carried their sacks of salt down into the tomb and then came out again. Missa waited until they were back to whatever else it was they were supposed to be doing and then crept in to look again, but by now the men inside the tomb were done and were coming out. They frowned at her when they saw her but they didn't send her away like the others and so she stayed, pressed against the back wall, watching. As the soon as the last man came out they all started to work on dragging a stone across the opening to block it, and she saw that the stone was a door, rolling sideways across the gap between two walls as thick as she was. To the right of the rolling door, four burnished bronze wheels stuck out of the wall, each engraved with symbols. There were six signs on each wheel, animals, the totems for each of the six Ascendants who stood guard over the empire. She stared at the way the wheels were set while the men wrestled with the stone. Snake, dragon, bear, fish.

The men finished moving the stone and stepped away, catching their breath with an air of relief and satisfaction as though they'd finished some great work they'd never quite been sure wouldn't go terribly wrong. One of them, the oldest, went to the bronze wheels and turned them all a few careless turns. It puzzled Missa when the men all went back to trying to move the stone to open the door again, puzzled her even more when it didn't budge and more still when the men stopped and grinned and laughed as though that was exactly the way things were supposed to be. They filed off up the stairs, carrying their lanterns with them, and Missa hurried after, not wanting to be left alone in the dark. She didn't know what she'd seen, but no one had minded her seeing it so at least she wouldn't be in any trouble. The door and the bronze wheels were interesting though, and she found herself thinking about them as she left.

Later that day she decided she'd play a game and pretend she had her own special door with its odd lock. She scratched a circle on a wall of rock to pretend to be the door and four more circles to be her bronze wheels, and then scratched a little symbol by each one, the way they'd been when she'd first seen them before the men had closed the tomb. Snake, dragon, bear, fish.

'There,' she said to the rock. 'And now you're open and I can go in,' and she danced off, imagining what might be on the other side.

She forgot about her pretend door soon enough and the real one too and moved on to other things as children do, but the rock never forgot the marks she'd scratched into it. It held them patiently and bore them on its skin long after Missa was gone, long after the last Aulian followed, long after every man in the valley had forgotten what was buried so carefully under Witches' Reach. Held them, waiting.

THE LAST BASTION

In the end it is our defiance that redeems us

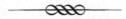

WITCHES' REACH

'So where's the Foxbeard then?'

Outside Witches' Reach, Sarvic stared at the pyre for a good long time after Valaric had finished his tale. Valaric shook his head. The Marroc from the fort didn't know either. They were exhausted, bleak-faced and grim even in their triumph. There were a dozen left and the first messages to reach the Crackmarsh had spoken of five or six times that number. Proud men, all of them, or they would be once it sunk in what they'd done. Names to be remembered.

'Varyxhun probably,' said a short needle-faced Marroc who stood in their midst, and it was only when she spoke that Sarvic realised she was a woman. 'He'll have gone to Varyxhun. And I'll be following him. The fortress is yours, Valaric the Wolf. Be sure you have a good look at the Aulian door in your cellar. Could be there aren't any forkbeards about know the secret of where it goes, but most likely there are. Still – could be a way out for a man clever enough to use it.'

Everything was black outside the circle of light from the pyre. Valaric stared at the flames a long time, Sarvic beside him. 'Strangest thing,' Valaric whispered, eyes fixed on the corpse of the iron devil still wreathed in fire. 'Couldn't have been that many forkbeards who saw him fall, but the ones who did, they just stopped. It was like they'd seen the sun go out and it went through them like fire through a hay barn. I saw forkbeards truly afraid tonight, Sarvic, though I dare say they'll get over it.'

They talked some more then about how mightily upset the forkbeards waiting by the Aulian Bridge were going to be to find that Valaric had slipped around behind them. They'd know by morning and they were only a few miles down the Varyxhun

Road. Valaric reckoned that gave the Crackmarsh men until maybe a couple of hours after sunrise. A busy night for most of them then.

When they were done with their own wounded and finishing off any forkbeards too hurt to get away, they collected their dead and dragged them to be buried in the snow of the deep woods below the ridge where the Lhosir wouldn't find them. After that they returned to the dead forkbeards, cutting the heads from the bodies. Valaric sent Angry Jonnic and a few others off to the Varyxhun Road with them, a trail of grisly little presents for the lot by the bridge to find when they came.

Sarvic had gone long before dawn but it was easy enough to imagine how that went. Brought a smile to his face every time, but by then he was slipping away to Varyxhun, up the valley with the needle-faced Marroc woman Achista and half a hundred others. Achista was off to rescue some Aulian wizard from the hangman, so she said, but Sarvic reckoned they might as well rescue a few Marroc while they were at it, and the two Jonnics figured that if they were going to be doing that, well then they might as well be 'rescuing' the whole of Varyxhun castle, and it was only afterwards that Sarvic realised this had been Valaric's plan all along – to keep the forkbeard army out at Witches' Reach while half his Crackmarsh men quietly crept off and did just that.

Gallow caught up with them that first day, set on the same thing as Achista. She asked him something about his family and his face went blank. The look Sarvic saw on him was a horror, like he really didn't give a shit about anything any more. Like he just wanted to die with as many forkbeard corpses around him as he could possibly manage. It made him shiver, that look.

VARYXHUN

1

THE HANGED

There were riots in Varyxhun. Oribas couldn't see what was going on but he could hear the screams and he could smell the smoke. No one told him what had happened, but on the day they decided to hang him and hauled him up to the castle yard he could hear and smell the turmoil. He could see it written on the Lhosir around the castle, on their faces and in the way they held themselves. He looked up at the gallows. They were going to hang him but he wasn't going to be the only one. There were Marroc too. Pressed together with the other prisoners, he heard what had filled the streets of Varyxhun with revolt: the forkbeards were beaten. The iron devil was dead and Witches' Reach still held.

Witches' Reach still held.

He knew then that Achista was still alive and so he'd hang with a smile on his face.

There was an angry crowd somewhere outside the castle. Oribas could hear them shouting, calling out the names of the Marroc who were to die beside him. The snow was thick on the stones and the walls wherever it hadn't been trampled into ice. A heavy fall had come in the night but now the sky was clear, the sun cold and bright, the frozen air as sharp as broken glass. There were a few Lhosir in the castle yard, come up from Varyxhun to watch, but not many. The last time he'd been here Varyxhun had been thick with Lhosir fighting men, each sporting the forked braided beard from which they got their name. Today the castle felt empty. Maybe the cold was keeping them away or maybe they'd gone to Witches' Reach and now half of them were dead. The thought brought a flash of glee, quickly turning to shame. The death of a child, the death of a woman, the death of a man, he'd been taught there was never a place for joy in any of these things.

Then again... In the deserts of old Aulia people had robbed him, tricked him, lied to him, but no one had ever tried to kill him. Since he'd crossed the mountains with Gallow, it never seemed to stop.

An old Lhosir marched him up the steps onto the scaffold. At least the castle walls and the mountainside into which it was built kept them sheltered from the wind that scoured the valley; even so his hands were already numb in the cold. From the scaffold he could see a few Marroc among the Lhosir in the yard. Not many, but he could see the gates now too, the last of the six gates that rose in a single solid line up the mountain slope and barred the switchback road from Varyxhun to the castle. A line of mailed Lhosir soldiers with spears and shields stood across the entrance to the yard, barring the way to a crowd of hostile Marroc. Behind them lay the Dragon's Maw, a gaping hole in the mountainside barred so tight with thick rusting iron that even a child couldn't slip through. The dragon of Varyxhun lived in that cave, the castle's guardian, waiting to devour any army that breached the last gate. The dragon was only a story but the crowd was real enough. The air was taut with their anger.

He looked at the Marroc men beside him. He had no idea who they were or what they'd done but he'd heard their wails and their screams for mercy in the darkness over the last few days and it seemed to Oribas that they were mostly ordinary men from Varyxhun. He heard his own name called from the crowd now and then, or more often 'The Aulian'. He wasn't sure how the Marroc even knew who he was, never mind what he'd done, but they did. It was a terrible thing, shameful, not something to shout about, but the Marroc shouted anyway.

The Lhosir hangman positioned Oribas on the scaffold, hands tied behind his back, facing away from the crowd with the rope right in front of his eyes. *The iron devil is dead.* He had to wonder about that, had to wonder how anyone had managed to kill the ironskin and who else knew how a creature like that could be laid to rest; and then wonder who had made it and what for, and why the iron devils of the Lhosir seemed so akin to whatever had once been entombed beneath Witches' Reach; but he couldn't find any answers and there was a limit to how much wondering even Oribas could manage, staring at his own noose.

The hangman turned him round to face the crowd as the last of the Marroc were poked and prodded to the scaffold. The fork-beards inside the castle were mostly old or crippled; the ones who were fit to fight had gone with Cithjan to Witches' Reach. Now Cithjan was dead and half his army with him, but the other half was still out there, and while it was, the peace in Varyxhun remained fragile as a winter morning.

He hadn't taken everyone. The Lhosir who held back the Marroc at the gates weren't old or wounded. They were arrogant, these forkbeards, but not stupid.

A bull-like voice called out his name and began to proclaim his crimes. A few of them were true, the worst ones, although the Lhosir seemed to have added a few more for good measure. Oribas couldn't imagine why. Burning fifty men alive was enough, wasn't it? Certainly enough to hang a man but he'd have done it again in a flash if it was the only way to keep his Achista safe. At the edge of the crowd a Lhosir soldier with furs wrapped across his face against the cold was heading for the gatehouse dragging a Marroc woman in his wake, pulled along by a rope tied around her hands. A weight of sadness pinched Oribas's lips. Keep Achista safe? She was still in Witches' Reach and he was certain she wouldn't leave. Sooner or later the Lhosir would get in and then they'd kill her. The ironskin had promised them all clean deaths, but now the devil was gone. And Oribas was here and about to hang, and he'd promised her he wouldn't die first, and now there was nothing he could do. Nothing.

The reading of his crimes finished with the promise that Oribas would die here and now in front of these witnesses, and with a reminder that the Lhosir god – the Maker-Devourer – didn't give two hoots what a man did with his life or how terrible his deeds might have been as long as he was honest. Oribas didn't have too much of a problem with that. Here and now he envied the Lhosir for the simplicity of their belief. His own gods were more fickle.

Hands pulled Oribas towards the noose. They were

surprisingly gentle. The Lhosir with the Marroc woman had dragged her to the gates and now he was arguing with the guards holding back the crowd. It was an odd thing to be watching when he was about to die, but it *was* strange. The Lhosir was mad. If the guards let him through, the Marroc outside would surely rip him to pieces!

There was something about the Lhosir though, something familiar. There was something about the Marroc woman too, but then the world went dark as the hangman slipped a hood over his head. Oribas yipped and shouted for it to come off, that he wanted to see – wouldn't any man want to see for every last second he lived? But the hood stayed. He felt the Lhosir step away to reach for the noose, and then a great roar went up from the Marroc outside the gate. A murmur rumbled around the scaffold and then sharp cries of 'To arms.' Hands grabbed him, not so gentle this time, holding him, pulling the rope over his head. Oribas let himself fall limp, slumping in the hangman's grasp before the noose could go round his neck. The Lhosir swore. For a moment he hauled Oribas right off his feet, then he grunted and let go, and Oribas fell hard to the wooden scaffold. He lay there, winded for a moment. The sounds around him now were of a battle.

A hand grabbed him by the foot and pulled him across the wood, then jerked. Something heavy – a body by the feel of it – fell across his back. Oribas pulled himself free and wriggled until he was on his knees, head so low that it almost touched his feet. He shook himself as hard as he could until the hood fell off and the first thing he saw was a dead Lhosir sprawled across the scaffold with two arrows sticking out of him. There was mayhem at the gates. The Lhosir with his Marroc woman was gone. The Marroc had surged forward and the ...

Gallow?

He stared. In the middle of the forkbeards at the gate, breaking their wall of shields from behind, was Gallow. And the Marroc crowd were pushing forward, and the ones at the front suddenly had swords and spears and shields, passed up from the men behind, and ...

The Lhosir with the Marroc woman – *that* had been Gallow.

Oribas scanned the gates, looking for the woman and not finding her; then he saw a figure running up to the battlements where a single Lhosir stood watch. She'd thrown off her cloak and was carrying a bow. *Achista!* She was too far away for Oribas to make out her face but he knew her from the way she ran and how she nocked an arrow to her bow and drew back the string and hesitated a tiny moment before she shot. He knew her from the way she moved as surely as if she was standing right in front of him.

The Marroc on the scaffold had fled, taking their chances with the forkbeards below. Bodies lay around it, more Marroc than Lhosir. The forkbeards from the yard were mostly at the gates now. They might have been old or crippled but they were still Lhosir, and there wasn't a man among them who wasn't armed and ready to fight. But they weren't enough. From his perch Oribas watched their shield wall buckle and break and the Marroc force their way through. This was no mob – these were soldiers pouring into the yard, followed by the ordinary men and women of Varyxhun. People like the Marroc who'd been waiting to die with Oribas.

A Lhosir climbed the steps to the scaffold with a bloody sword in his hand. He snarled at Oribas and lifted it high. Oribas squealed and dropped to his haunches, ready to hurl himself into the snow below, but an arrow caught the man in the chest before he could move. The forkbeard sank to his knees, blood bubbling out of his mouth. Achista. Other Marroc were on the battlements now, some of them shooting at the forkbeards; still others hammered on doors with their axes, forcing their way into the gatehouse and the towers that overlooked the road below the castle. Oribas looked for Gallow again but the Foxbeard was lost in the seething melee. There must have been a hundred Marroc in the yard now and the Lhosir were falling fast. A last handful ran back to the inner gates, to the windows and halls and buttresses and towers and balconies built into the mountainside that passed for the castle's keep, but the Marroc were hard on their heels.

The yard quietened as most of the fighting moved inside to the old Aulian halls and galleries. Some Marroc rushed in, hungry for blood and plunder, others remained outside, surrounding the Lhosir who hadn't yet been killed, finishing them off and looting the corpses. Marroc soldiers moved through the castle towers, dragging out any Lhosir they found inside, dead or alive. It probably hadn't taken ten minutes from start to finish and the castle of Varyxhun had fallen. Varyxhun, which had once held at bay ten thousand forkbeards led by the Screambreaker himself, lost to a rabble of angry Marroc.

'Oribas!' Achista had her bow across her back and a knife in one hand. She ran straight at him and almost knocked him flat as she crushed him in her arms. Then she was behind him, cutting at the ropes around his wrists. 'Stupid Aulian! Do you understand what you did to me when I heard you were taken? Do you?'

He tried to laugh. 'It was quite deliberate. You should have seen the precision with which I threw my head against the edge of a Lhosir's shield. It was exquisite.' He tapped the lump on his head and the scar, still raw. 'I saw Gallow. Where's Addic? Did your brother escape too?'

'He did and he's here. Inside now, I expect.'

Oribas stretched his arms and rubbed his wrists. He looked at the noose behind him. 'It would have been worth it,' he said, almost in awe of his own words.

'What would?'

'To have died for you.'

Achista took a step away and slapped him. 'Don't ever say anything so stupid again!' And then before Oribas could think of what to say next, a gang of Marroc hauled a snarling Lhosir up onto the scaffold, all of them kicking and punching him. Down in the yard other Marroc turned to watch, shouting and cheering.

'Hang him! Hang him!'

More Marroc were trickling through the gates, the hungry-looking ones, the scared, the weak and the slow. The mob was after any Lhosir, alive or dead, and the Marroc soldiers who'd led the assault were letting it happen, turning away and heading inside the castle. The men on the scaffold hauled the Lhosir to his feet and slipped the noose around his neck. Oribas barged into them. 'What did he do?' They pushed him away. Even Achista had a hand on his arm, pulling him back. 'But what did he do?'

The Marroc who'd put the noose over the Lhosir's head shoved Oribas hard, knocking him down. 'He's a *forkbeard*!'

'But you can't ...'

The words died in his throat. Behind the scaffold someone pulled a rope. A trapdoor opened, the Lhosir dropped, the rope snapped taut around his neck, and that was that. Oribas thought he even heard the bones snap. The Marroc on the scaffold raised a fist and whooped and the crowd cheered. 'One less forkbeard! Got any more? Yes? Which one next?'

The soldiers on the walls watched and joined in with the cheers. Those Lhosir still alive were beaten down, a few simply murdered, others dragged toward the scaffold. Oribas pulled himself angrily to his feet. 'This isn't justice and this isn't right!' He made for the Marroc hangman again but this time Achista blocked him.

'This is war, Oribas.'

'No, this is murder.' Though was it any worse than fifty men burned alive under the ground? Hard to say, and maybe it was the guilt that drove him now. 'You're better than this!'

There was pain in her eyes, and Oribas realised with a sickening feeling that it wasn't guilt or shame, but sadness that he didn't understand why this killing had to be done. He faltered, and then another Marroc grabbed hold of him and was shoving him out of the way. 'They were going to kill you, darkskin.'

'For what I did, Marroc, not for what I am! It may seem small to you but on that difference the Aulian Empire was forged!'

'And now it's gone.' The rest of the Marroc ignored him.

'At least the forkbeards had a reason.' Although they hadn't had any real reason when they'd set out to kill him for the first time, when they'd carted him off to the Devil's Caves with a gang of ragged Marroc simply for knowing the name of Gallow Foxbeard. And, really, what was he doing here, defending the men who'd been about to kill him?

One by one the Lhosir were pulled and pushed and dragged and shoved to the scaffold. They were hauled up the steps, manhandled to their feet and nooses were shoved around their necks, and they were hanged. Five at a time because that was how many gallows the Lhosir had built, with the mob baying for the blood of every single one of them. Oribas turned away.

2

SARVIC

Before the fighting kicked off, Sarvic was with the mob, right at the front of it. Valaric was either on his way from Witches' Reach by now or else he was still there, taunting the forkbeard army that had meant to stop him and his Crackmarsh men from crossing the Aulian Bridge. Without Valaric, that left Sarvic and Fat Jonnic in charge. Jonnic was somewhere in the middle of the mob doing what he did best – shouting at people what to do. Sarvic was at the front, and that was just fine. He'd come a long way since he'd turned and run from the Vathen at Lostring Hill and been saved by a forkbeard. The same forkbeard he could see now, arguing with one of the soldiers at the gate.

The Marroc around him all wore thick heavy furs. This being the Varyxhun valley in winter, the forkbeards didn't think anything of it, but the nice thing about furs was what you could hide underneath. Mail, for example. An axe. A sword. Further back, other Marroc carried spears and helms and shields, things even a bear pelt couldn't hide. When Gallow appeared behind the forkbeards barring the gate, Sarvic quietly passed the word back. Fat Jonnic's shields crept forward through the mob.

Gallow shoved the forkbeard in charge of the gate into the spearmen facing the Marroc. One of the forkbeards in the wall of shields staggered and took a step forward. His spear dipped and that was all Sarvic needed. He lunged, grabbed the shaft just behind the point and pulled hard, pushing the tip down toward the road as he did. The forkbeard stumbled another step forward. The soldiers either side snapped back from the glances they'd been throwing behind them but by then it was too late. Sarvic had always been quick as an eel, and he was between their spears before they could run him through. He pressed up to the forkbeard who'd staggered out of the wall, getting in nice and close. He raised a long knife high where all the other Marroc could see, then he rammed it into the man's neck and pulled at him, yanking him out of the shield line while his blood spurted everywhere. Spears were fine weapons for keeping an angry crowd at bay but now the forkbeards had an armed man inside their points and it left them with an interesting choice: hold on to their spears and keep the mob back or drop them and take out an axe. So now was the time. Either the rest of the Marroc rushed the forkbeard line or Sarvic had about two breaths left in him before someone smashed his skull.

The Marroc surged forward. They didn't hesitate, and right there and then Sarvic knew they were going to win. Behind the forkbeards, Gallow had thrown back his hood and drawn out the red sword Solace and was shouting and roaring about who he was and what blade he carried and daring anyone to face him and all sorts of other nonsense. For a moment the forkbeards looked uncertain. It was enough. The crowd fell on them like a spring flood from a broken dam.

Sarvic barged on through, past the silence of the Dragon's Maw and into the yard. A few more forkbeards stood about, some of them still looking up at the scaffold, others frowning at the gate, the quickest-witted of them already starting to move. He let out a murderous roar. The more forkbeards he killed before they realised they were armed and should be doing something more useful than gawping, the easier it would be. He headed for the scaffold, intent on cutting down every forkbeard in his way. Up there was a man supposed to be an Aulian wizard, half the reason they were there, but at a quick glance Sarvic couldn't tell the prisoners apart. If he was honest, he wasn't all that bothered.

A forkbeard came at him swinging a hatchet. Sarvic raised the shield he didn't have, swore and threw himself sideways instead, rolling across the cobbled yard and crashing into the legs of another who bellowed a curse and lifted something big and heavy-looking. Sarvic knifed him in the foot and scrambled away from the scream that followed. He wasn't going to reach the scaffold after all, but back by the gates the wall of shields had stayed broken, and more Marroc soldiers were getting into the yard and throwing off their furs to show the mail they wore beneath. The men who'd been hiding deeper in the crowd rushed forward with shields and spears and more swords and axes. A good few carried bows. Sarvic snatched a shield off a Marroc he half-recognised from the Crackmarsh and shouted something he hoped sounded inspiring. Not that anyone needed much encouragement by the looks of things.

Beside him the needle-faced Marroc woman from Witches' Reach shot an arrow into a forkbeard stupid enough to make himself an easy target by standing up on the scaffold. Achista the Huntress, that's what the Marroc of Witches' Reach called her, and in reply she called them her Hundred Heroes, the dozen of them she had left. They deserved it after what they'd done. As far as Sarvic saw it, every one of them should be a lord or prince just as soon as the last forkbeard sailed back across the sea.

A hand on his hood yanked him back. He staggered and almost fell as an axe sliced the air past his eyes. 'Is it bedtime, Sarvic?' Angry Jonnic shoved him aside and drove the forkbeard back, battering him with his shield.

'Up yours!' Sarvic lunged low and fast with his knife, neatly hamstringing the man with the axe. He left Angry to finish him off and pushed on towards the castle keep. The forkbeards were scattered now. One climbed onto the scaffold. A last prisoner was still up there, shaking off his hood. The prisoner's skin was dark and Sarvic had heard enough about the Aulian wizard to pause for a moment to see what would happen. But the forkbeard didn't turn to ice or explode or burst into flames, he just took an arrow for his pains. Apart from his dark skin the wizard looked oddly ordinary to Sarvic – scared out of his wits and close to shitting himself, much as anyone else ought to be.

The forkbeards from the gate were retreating to the steps of the Aulian Hall of Thrones. Marroc swarmed around them, swamping them. The stream of men passing into the yard turned to a flood. Sarvic snatched up an abandoned spear and stormed to where a few more forkbeards were making a stand on the steps. Cithjan the Bloody had once held his council here but he was dead now. The iron devil had burned him and spoken him out and then Gallow had killed the devil. Which was all a snarling shame: they could have done with hanging Bloody Cithjan high over the gates for every Marroc in Varyxhun to see, him and his ironskin too.

The forkbeards on the steps faltered and broke before Sarvic could get to them. He saw Gallow's massive frame thunder inside with a dozen Marroc in his wake and followed as fast as he could. He'd been starting to get the hang of killing forkbeards that night outside the Reach when they'd turned and fled, and he might have cut down one or two as they ran, but forkbeards never ran and it had taken him by surprise when they did. He'd watched for a moment before the savage inside had called for blood and by then they were away. Now his luck was out again. He forced his way into the Hall of Thrones. Marroc were on the floor, the kin-traitors who'd worked and lived in the castle and served the forkbeards, cringing and cowering and begging for mercy now as they were beaten half to death. Sarvic spat on them as he passed. The hangings would start as fast as they could. Every Marroc who'd made this place their home would swing and they'd deserve it too. Valaric might have something to say about that, but the Wolf wasn't here, and by the time he was it would be done and too late to argue.

Sarvic skidded to a stop. The forkbeards were mostly gone, but not all of them. Two stood in front of Bloody Cithjan's throne. Old men whose strength had long faded from their arms, but they were armed and armoured and already three Marroc lay dead in front of them, pricked by forkbeard steel. Sarvic grinned and started towards them. Strange lot, forkbeards. Wicked bastards, evil and vicious and mean in a fight, but they had their superstitions. Like back at Witches' Reach when the Crackmarsh men fell on their camp in the middle of the night and Gallow killed the iron devil. Some of the forkbeards had turned and melted away like any sensible man should, but the ones up inside the fortress hadn't. They'd retreated in silence behind their wall of shields. Even when Sarvic had run up close and taunted them and thrown spears and stones, they hadn't answered. Right in the middle of the battle and they'd left. Just lost all interest in it, as though the fall of the ironskin mattered more than fighting a rabble of angry Marroc, and Sarvic hadn't thought there was a forkbeard alive who'd give up a good fight for anything less than a severed limb. After the first few jeers, Sarvic and the other Marroc had mostly stood and watched them go, uneasy at their own victory.

Now two of them were ready to die to defend a dead man's chair. Sarvic was happy to oblige them, but another stood in his way. Huge in all his furs, even from behind there was only one person it could be: Gallow the Foxbeard, who'd faced down the iron devil of Varyxhun. Sarvic remembered clear as the sun: the Foxbeard standing beside the pyre and on it the ironskin, and then Mournful telling him how it was, how Gallow and the iron devil had fought as the Crackmarsh men swept down the mountainside. How the iron devil's red blade Solace had shattered Gallow's sword and how the Foxbeard had killed him anyway, ramming the splintered remains of his blade through the devil's mask.

The rest of the Marroc scattered, looking for plunder or other forkbeards to kill or whatever drove them now. Sarvic looked the two old men up and down. Warriors once. Didn't take much of an eye to see that in the way they held themselves, in the way they gripped their spears.

'Nioingr,' hissed one of them. He was staring at the clean-shaven chin where Gallow's forked beard should have been.

Sarvic sidled up behind Gallow, too close for him to ignore but not so close he got in the way. 'Need a hand, forkbeard? You can leave them to me if you like. I'd take that as a favour.'

If Gallow heard, he didn't show it. His eyes didn't leave the men shielding the throne. When he spoke he sounded tired.

'Nioingr? The last man to call me that was Beyard Ironskin. He ate those words.' He drew out the sword Solace and let them see the red steel of it. Sarvic stepped back, hissing at the cursed blade. 'Beyard carried this. We fought by the pyre of Tolvis Loudmouth and I sent him to the Maker-Devourer by his own sword. I placed his body on the pyre and I spoke him out and I have no doubt that the Screambreaker himself will welcome him. A better man than any of us.' He looked at the red sword. 'The Marroc named this blade the Comforter and call it cursed. The Vathen named it Solace, the Peacebringer. The Aulians called it the Edge of Sorrows.' He pointed the sword at the two forkbeards. 'You're Garran, named Fleetfoot once. I remember what they said of you, that you could run faster than the wind. You were with the Screambreaker at Selleuk's Bridge. I was there too and I saw you. You didn't run like the wind that day. You didn't run at all. The Marroc broke us yet your brothers had to tear you away. Lay down your spear, Garran Fleetfoot. Even the Lhosir can't always win. The Marroc have the day here. Cithjan is dead. Sixfingers' Fateguard is gone.' He shrugged. 'Our brothers of the sea who fought for the walls of Witches' Reach are scattered and broken. What sense is there in dying for all these things that went before you? Set down your spear, Fleetfoot. Walk the Aulian Way to Tarkhun and beyond. Sail your ship home and live your twilight years in peace among the family you left behind. You've long done enough to enter the Maker-Devourer's cauldron.'

Sarvic tried not to snort. *Walk the Aulian Way?* Let Gallow explain to the mob outside why they should let a couple of forkbeards go when they could just as easily hang them.

But it wouldn't come to that. The old forkbeard shook his head. '*Nioingr,*' he hissed. '*Nioingr. Nioingr.*' Three times, after which Sarvic knew there could be no going back. He breathed a quiet sigh of relief. No one would have to explain anything to anyone then. Just two more dead forkbeards. So much the better.

Gallow lifted his shield as the second forkbeard lunged and then jumped back as Fleetfoot stabbed at his feet. The red sword swung sharp and hard and sheared the shaft of Fleetfoot's spear. Sarvic started forward but Gallow was faster, lunging at both of the forkbeards, barging into the other Lhosir, shield against shield with enough force and weight to send the old man sprawling. Sarvic darted in quickly to put the point of his spear to the fallen forkbeard's throat. 'Very happy to kill you, old man. *Very* happy.'

The forkbeard didn't move. Gallow battered Fleetfoot back, driving him with blow after blow until he was pressed against a wall. 'Eat your words, old man! Eat them!'

Garran Fleetfoot glared. He dropped his broken spear, lifted an axe from his belt and lowered his shield. 'I know you, Gallow Foxbeard, and I'll unsay nothing. You took the sword you hold from the dead hands of the Screambreaker on the battlefield outside Andhun and you cut off the hand of our king with it, and instead of facing your fate you fled in fear. No, Foxbeard, I will eat nothing. *Nioingr.*'

Marroc were gathering around Sarvic now. Not the Crack-marsh men, who'd already pressed on deeper into the castle's labyrinth, but the Varyxhun mob that followed. They had an evil about them, a hunger for vengeance. Before Sarvic could see it coming, one seized the spear in his hand and jerked it down, too quick for him to stop. The spear sliced into the old fork-beard's throat. He gasped. When Sarvic snatched back his spear the Marroc let go but it made no difference. The forkbeard's blood sprayed into his face as he gurgled a curse and grabbed at Sarvic's leg, and then he was still.

The Marroc who'd done it laughed. 'Filthy goatbeard.'

Sarvic turned on him and then changed his mind and backed away. He'd barely taken a step when the rest of the mob fell on the dead forkbeard. Knives and clubs rose and fell as they beat and hacked him to pieces. Sarvic watched to see if he felt anything but he didn't. No pride, no shame, no joy, no regret. Nothing. The forkbeards were all going to die anyway, and when he looked at the angry men around him, come with cudgels and murder and hate to revenge themselves for everything that had been done to them, how was he any different?

Gallow had the other forkbeard pinned to the wall now. Garran Fleetfoot swung his axe. Gallow caught it on his shield and pushed and twisted it away. For a moment the old man was exposed, his shield useless and on the wrong side. The red sword lunged and drove into his ribs, cracking a fistful of them. The forkbeard gasped and staggered but his mail was good enough to keep the red steel out of his skin. Sarvic smiled to himself. He'd remember that. He'd have that mail.

The old man wheezed. He pointed at the mob ripping the other forkbeard to pieces. 'See what they are, *nioingr*? We're better than them!'

He dropped his shield, switched his axe to his other hand and lifted it high, wide open, as good as asking Gallow to finish him, and Gallow obliged him. The red sword flashed, blood sprayed across the Aulian walls and Sarvic watched the forkbeard fall. Gallow stood over him. 'You fought well, old man. Like Beyard. He never stepped aside from the path. It's the path itself that strayed. It's Medrin.'

The look on Gallow's face was like he'd killed his own brother; and then it changed to something dark and harsh – so dark that when he turned and strode away Sarvic forgot about the dead man's mail and followed. He'd seen that same look before, that morning after Witches' Reach.

3

ONCE A FORKBEARD

Gallow turned away from the Hall of Thrones and left the Marroc to their looting. Servants would be hauled out of their hiding places. If they were lucky they'd get away with being beaten bloody, but he'd been among a victorious army after enough battles to know what happened next. Nothing that a decent man would care to remember, and it would be like that here too. Worse.

He hesitated a moment then shook his head and moved on. Not his business. Let the Marroc sort out their vengeance without him. He'd come across the mountains to be with his family, that was all, and now he'd come here to this castle for his last real friend, the Aulian, and if Oribas was alive and safe then only one other thing mattered and it wasn't in Varyxhun. So he chose not to look at what was happening around him and pushed his way past the Marroc still surging into the hall. They were throwing down the braziers now and tearing the hangings off the walls, hangings that had been there long before any Lhosir had come to the valley. Their own treasures, if only they knew it.

Their business. Not yours. That's what Arda would say. Three years away and then a few days and nights trapped in a fortress and expecting to die, and then Valaric had come, and the fork-beards had gone away, and all of a sudden everything he sought was right there in front of him, begging to be taken, and he'd turned his back and left her there because ... because Beyard had sent Oribas to be hanged and Oribas was his friend. Left her and lost everything, and he'd had to, because sooner or later Medrin would know he was back and the hunt would begin, and if he simply went home then one day he'd wake up to find Medrin standing over him with a thousand Lhosir and Medrin would kill them, all of them, slowly and with a great deal of lingering, because nothing would ever make up for the hand that Gallow had taken from him in Andhun. Medrin made the choice into no choice at all but Arda still wouldn't wait for him, not again, and he could hardly blame her for that. Better to blame fate.

He forced his way out into the yard. The mob was thinning, more and more Marroc crowding inside, pushing and shoving, climbing past each other, desperate for a share of the plunder. Around the scaffold he could see the bodies, Marroc and Lhosir both. Five Lhosir swung from the gallows. Small gangs of Marroc moved among the corpses, stripping them, shaking them. He saw the flash of a knife. Murdering them if they weren't quite dead then. The Crackmarsh men were up on the walls, but Valaric was back in Witches' Reach and the soldiers only stood and watched.

Not. His. Business.

Arda would be on her way home by now, back to the Crackmarsh to be with their children. *His* children. His sons and his daughter. He should have gone with her, wished he could, had always wanted to, but Sixfingers wouldn't let him. He turned away, sick of it all. 'Oribas? Oribas!'

The nearest gang of Marroc stopped what they were doing and stared at him. Their malevolence filled the air. There were four of them and their glances around the yard were already drawing in others. They dropped the Lhosir they were looting and closed in. Gallow took a step back. The Crackmarsh men had a hungry hate for forkbeards but they kept it to themselves around Gallow because Valaric had told them the story of the Foxbeard and what he'd done. The mob from the city beneath the castle, though, all they saw was another forkbeard even if he was shaven. They eyed him, and the longer they did, the more Marroc turned to look. Gallow had seen it before, a wolf pack setting itself to bring down a bear.

He'd seen how to stop it too. He stared right back at the four Marroc, picked out their leader, drew his sword and moved briskly forward. Marroc always turned and ran and this one would be no different. There'd be no need for blood; the threat would be—

A stone hit the side of his helm, hard even through the iron. He staggered sideways and suddenly a snarling Marroc was flying at him. He braced his shield and then there was another coming from the other side and another from behind and more of them all around. He raised the Edge of Sorrows but the first Marroc didn't flinch. The red sword sighed as it cut the air. Before Gallow could stop himself, he'd split the Marroc's face in two; and then the others came and the sword wanted more while he stared at what he'd done.

A second Marroc crashed into his side and tore at his shield. He battered the man away and tried to run but another tackled him from behind and staggered him; yet another grabbed his sword arm high around the shoulder and held on, trying to drag him down, and then another had his shield again, and however hard he forced his way onward, for every Marroc he shook off, another two came at him. He felt a knife stab at him, jabbing hard at his mail coat. Something hit his head, another stone or a stick, and then a hand had his leg and his foot, pulled hard, and he couldn't break free. He staggered, hopped, and finally fell with a half a dozen Marroc on his back.

'Hang him! Don't kill him down there; hang him for everyone to see! Hang the forkbeard!' He growled and snarled and twisted and writhed, trying to shake the Marroc off, but there were too many. One got his helm and someone hit him on the head with a stone. Light crashed through the back of his head and the sound of everything changed as though he was underwater again. Drowning as he'd been off the cliffs of Andhun after fleeing the Vathen. Should have sunk beneath the waves there, but somehow the Screambreaker had come in a little boat, sailing away from his own death towards the Herenian Marches, given one more day of life to do whatever needed to be done; but in the moments before, as the water had swallowed Gallow, the sounds of the world had fallen away like this. He felt another sharp pain in his back and then the weight came away and he was being carried, dragged, and his eyes were still open but there was only light, horrible flaming lances of light.

The Marroc dropped him. He lay still, fingers clawing at a ground that was softer and warmer than the crushed-snow cobbles of the castle yard. Wood. The noises were slowly changing again. The Marroc mob, shouting and screaming. He opened his eyes. Everything was blurred. Bright blue sky above, a swirling sea of movement below.

Hang him! Hang him!

He blinked as the world swam back into focus. He was on the scaffold looking out over the heads of a few dozen angry Marroc. When he tried to get up, someone stamped him back down. He felt as weak as a baby. A great weight pressed on him, men sitting on his shoulders and his legs. They had his arms, were tying his wrists behind his back. Then hands reached under his shoulders and hauled him up. His sword was gone, his shield and helm too. He tried to shrug the hands away but the Marroc were too strong and too many. They pushed and shoved him and hauled a rope over his head, scraping it across his face, settling it around his neck. Panic washed away the dizziness, but too late. He snarled and raged and almost fell.

'Hang the forkbeard!'

The noose tightened and a vicious voice hissed in his ear, 'Ready to meet your uncaring god, forkbeard?' The voice grew into a shout. 'Shall we hang us another one?' The crowd howled with gleeful joy.

Something hit the scaffold by Gallow's feet. When he turned his head to look, an arrow was quivering in the wood. He couldn't turn enough to see his executioner, but he felt his shiver of hesitation. Then another arrow hit the scaffold, and this time the mob saw it too. A cluster of soldiers was coming down the steps to the Hall of Thrones and forcing its way through. He saw Achista with her bow and an arrow nocked, Achista and Oribas. They shouldered their way onto the scaffold. 'Jonnic! What are you doing?'

The executioner barged past Gallow. 'Killing a forkbeard.'

'Let him go!'

'Do I answer to you now? No, I answer to Mournful, and he's not here.'

'Are you dim? I said let him go!'

'Or you'll shoot me?' The hangman pushed forward. The soldiers around Achista pressed forward until they were all almost nose to nose. 'Kill a Marroc to save a forkbeard, would you? You know what we do to women who give themselves to forkbeards.'

Oribas punched him, and for a moment Gallow was so surprised that he forgot he was standing with a noose around his neck. The Marroc lurched back and drew a hand across his face and then laughed as Oribas clutched his fist. Achista shoved past them all and stood beside Gallow, looking out over the crowd. 'This is Gallow Foxbeard. The man who slew the iron devil of Varyxhun. The forkbeard who cut off Sixfingers' hand.'

'Still a forkbeard!' yelled a voice from the crowd.

'Hang him!'

'Look what he did!'

'He's a killer!'

The mob parted around the Marroc man Gallow had killed, eager to show his crime. He barely remembered doing it. An instinct, lashing out before he fell, that was all. Achista stared at the body, the fire stolen from her mouth. Then she looked at him. 'You did this?'

Gallow nodded. 'He came at me.'

'And you killed him.'

'I had little choice.'

'Angry Jonnic! Get your smelly hands off that noose!' Another Marroc soldier was pushing through the crowd. Another face Gallow knew from a long time ago. He squinted, trying to remember where it had been.

'Piss off, Sarvic. I don't answer to you either.'

'But you do answer to Valaric and Mournful'll string you up by your toes. I'll vouch for this one. Years ago he fought among the Marroc against the Vathen at Lostring Hill. I stood beside him in the shield wall. He's a forkbeard, yes, but we lost that day, and in the rout that came after the second Vathan charge he saved my life. Angry, I see you up there all hungry to kill another forkbeard and I have that hunger too. But a life for a life, I say. We both saw what happened here.'

'What I saw was a Marroc killed by a forkbeard. Seen too much of that these last years.'

Achista turned her back. 'This forkbeard is *nioingr* to his own kind. Do you understand what that means?'

'Means they won't care what we do to him.'

'Means you're doing their work for them.'

Jonnic snorted and shouted at the crowd. 'Anyone else? Anyone else want to spare this forkbeard, or can we get on with it? Just one of you and I'll let him live. Can't say fairer than that.'

An eager murmur rolled through the crowd, but then another Marroc pushed through them and climbed onto the scaffold. 'When the devil Sixfingers was prince of Andhun, three forkbeards threw me into the Isset and left me for dead. Then another one pulled me out, this one, and if he hadn't, I'd have drowned. I'll spit at him in the street now just as I did then. But I'm with Sarvic: a life for a life. Let this one go to never come back.'

Achista pushed past Jonnic. 'Now take him down.' There was steel in her voice. She snatched the rope and pulled it roughly off Gallow's head and no one moved to stop her. When she was done, Angry Jonnic punched Gallow in the kidneys hard enough to stagger him even through his mail and forced Gallow down to his knees. Achista squatted beside him. 'You're not welcome, Gallow Foxbeard. Varyxhun belongs to the Marroc now. Leave this valley and never come back. If you do, you'll be what Jonnic says: just another forkbeard to be welcomed with spears and arrows. Do you understand?' Her voice softened. 'Go home, Gallow. Go to Arda. She'll open her arms quick enough, for all her blunt words.'

Oribas pushed forward. 'Achista!'

She turned to him. 'You'd better choose whether you follow him or stay, Oribas. I know he's your friend and I know he came here because of you, but I can't change what has to be. If you have to go, I won't begrudge it.'

Gallow hauled himself wearily to his feet and shook his head. 'No, old friend. I've nothing to offer you and I don't want your company. I came home for my family, and if Beyard hadn't sent you here to be hanged then that's where I'd be; and I'd be there without you.'

He clapped Oribas on the shoulder and picked his way down the steps from the scaffold and through the hissing crowd. He walked to the Marroc he'd killed, picked up his helm and put it on slowly and deliberately. He found his shield and a spear and, last of all, the red sword. Then he turned to face the crowd, a Lhosir warrior dressed for battle. The mob glared back, full of hate but with fear now too, and when he walked towards them again, they parted easily. He stopped by the scaffold. 'I wish you a long and happy life, Achista of the Marroc, and your brother too.' He glanced toward the Marroc who claimed they'd fought together at Lostring Hill. He remembered it, a distant thing: fleeing at full tilt down a grassy slope, a Marroc ahead of him, Vathan horse cutting at them as they ran, throwing the Marroc to the ground, catching a Vathan javelot on his shield. Angry Jonnic had called him Sarvic. Yes, that was him, but he'd changed, a frightened goat become another wolf. 'My greetings to Valaric when he comes. Tell him he'll be more than welcome to have his plough fixed or to buy some nails once Sixfingers is dead.' He almost laughed. Sarvic stood there looking confused, but Valaric would understand.

He looked at the other one, the Marroc he'd hauled out of the Isset three years back. He remembered doing it, but he hadn't ever seen the man's face until now, not properly. Then at his one last friend, the Aulian. He raised his spear in salute. 'Oribas. You were always a better man. Remember that. Remember what you told me.' He turned away from the Marroc and from Oribas and this new beginning they had before them, and rubbed his neck where the noose had touched his skin. His heart felt strangely empty. *Go home?* But he couldn't. Not until they'd be safe and forgotten, and that would never happen, not while Medrin was alive.

Inside the gates he stopped by the Dragon's Maw. The Marroc soldiers there looked uncertain, and when Gallow drew out the red sword they stepped back in alarm and drew their own. But Gallow reversed his grip and drove the sword into the hard-packed dirt between the cracked stones of the yard.

'Yours,' he whispered to the sky. 'For whoever is foolish enough to take it.'

Achista stood beside Oribas. They held hands as they watched Gallow go. 'What was it you told him?' she asked.

Oribas didn't answer for a very long time. When he turned to look at her, his face was pale and he looked as if he'd seen a ghost.

'What was it?'

'A long time ago.' He shook himself. Shivered as if trying to free himself of something. 'A long time ago I told him that every heart is wicked. That there are no good men in the world at all, just those who have the courage to look at their own deeds with honest eyes, and those who don't.'

A hundred fishing boats once sheltered in the sweep of Andhun Bay, protected by cliffs that swept the north-east winds from the Storm Coast up into the air and over the tops of their masts, but no more. The Marroc had taken to the sea when the Vathen came. Their ships had gone and the harbour had burned and the busiest port east of Kelfhun was gone in a single day. Few ships came now.

It was a sight then, when a white ship sailed across the mouth of the bay, driven by the freezing winds that blew down from the Ice Wraiths of the north. She didn't turn towards the harbour but men still stopped to look. Eyes followed her, wondering who might be coming; on both sides of the Isset they stared. In the eastern half of divided Andhun the ardshan of the Vathen paused at the window of his stolen castle and peered and then called for the Aulian tinker he'd taken to keeping around like a court fool. Across the waters of the Isset and the cliffs that kept the two halves of the city apart, the Lhosir looked with more knowing eyes, for she was a Lhosir ship and the white of her sails and her hull gave her away: she was a priest ship from the Temple of Fates on the edge of the frozen wastes, and that alone was reason to stare. White as though she carried the snow of the north through the waters with her, she passed Andhun Bay and sailed on a little way along the coast to the first cove where a party could put ashore. There she dropped her sail. Boats eased their way through the waves, and by the time they'd landed the first party and had returned to come back with the next, Lhosir riders from the city reached the cove. They came filled with questions from their lord of Andhun but their words died in their throats. The men on the stony beach were clad in iron. There were twelve of them.

The next boats brought men more familiar. Holy men, as far as the Lhosir had such things. Chanters of nonsense and rhyme who sent their words not to the Maker-Devourer but to the Fates themselves and to the frozen palace far to the north.

The boats went back a second time and headed for the shore once more. The holy men cried out for all to look away but the Lhosir were too curious and unafraid to do such a thing, and so their eyes burned as the last burden of the white ship came ashore. The ones who stared the longest remembered only white and light and a terrible brightness. The ones who looked away more quickly would say afterwards that what they had seen was another of the Fateguard, armoured in an iron skin but missing chest and back plates, and that what was there instead was the whiteness of ice and the brightness of the cold winter sun and patterns of both that wove with such a brilliance that for a while they thought they were blinded.

All understood at once what they saw: the Eyes of Time come down from the iron palace. A thing that had never happened in any remembered life.

The Fateguard commanded the Lhosir to get down from their horses and then took them, and the Lhosir – those who could still see anything at all – were left to watch the Eyes of Time and the iron-skinned men of fate as they vanished across the hills.

MIDDISLET

4

NADRIC'S SECRET

The wind roared and moaned and the rain beat on the roof of the forge and swirled inside, another winter storm come howling off the seas to the north. Arda stood, steadfastly ignoring it, drawing wire. The forge fire kept everything nearby comfortably warm and dry, even in the bitter tail of winter. Tathic and Pursic sat in the dirt nearby, keeping out of the rain, playing with the little wooden figures Nadric had carved for them while they'd been hiding in the Crackmarsh. Nadric wasn't much of a carver but they had at least the suggestion of legs and arms and a head, and that was enough. Pursic jumped his toy man onto Tathic's and the two boys started wrestling on the floor.

'I'm Valaric the Wolf! You're a forkbeard. Yaargh!'

Forkbeard. The word still made Arda stop. Made her look up too, eyes scanning the track to the big barn and the road beyond to Fedderhun, or else the other way, south to the Crackmarsh and then the long way round to Hrodicslet. A month ago she'd watched him leave Witches' Reach and head south for Varyxhun. An hour later she'd followed with a dozen Crackmarsh men, but they'd quickly turned from the Varyxhun Road and followed the secret trail through the Devil's Caves and Jodderslet. A mountain path had taken them to Hrodicslet and to the Crackmarsh, where the villagers of Middislet always hid in troubled times. To her children. To Nadric, who'd been father to the Marroc husband she'd had before the forkbeards had killed him. To Jelira, the oldest, the one who wasn't *his* but remembered him better than the rest. To her sons Tathic and little Pursic. To Feya, their daughter. She'd vowed she'd never let herself think of him ever again and she broke that vow every single day. Gallow. Gallow, the clay-brained, sheep-witted, onion-eyed, flap-eared clod.

The boys roughhousing on the floor thumped into her feet and stopped and looked up. Pursic and even Tathic and certainly Feya barely remembered him. They'd come to know Tolvis as their father, and Arda quietly wondered if they understood that Tolvis Loudmouth was dead and gone for ever now. At least you could mourn for the dead. Speak them out like the forkbeards did or bury them and know where their bones lay and now and then go and talk to them. Couldn't do that with Gallow. He'd chosen something else. Found a thing that mattered to him more than her and his own children. Lhosir thought differently and there was nothing any woman could do about that, so she was better off with him gone, or so she told herself. She'd been miserly with the silver he'd sent back from Andhun and still had enough to make her worth a look from a Marroc man looking for a home, even if he'd have mouths to feed that weren't his and even if she was tainted by two forkbeards now. Although it was *her* silver and she wasn't sure she wanted another man anyway. If it wasn't for Nadric losing his strength, she might have kept things quietly as they were and done without, thank you very much.

She sighed and turned back to drawing her wire. Men would be knocking on the door for Jelira soon, not for her. She was Marroc through and through and close on her fourteenth year, which certainly made her old enough for the village boys to be interested.

Made her old enough to help in the forge too. She could cut wire into lengths for nails. Or wind it and cut it for links for all the mail that Nadric was quietly making. Valaric the Mournful had done her a favour looking after her little ones and he hadn't forgotten who she was and where, and nor had his men still left in the Crackmarsh, and there were precious few forges where a man could make mail without the eyes of a forkbeard on his back.

She caught the thought. Snatched it out of the air and held it dangling, wriggling before her eyes, full of guilt. *Forkbeard.* She'd always called him that, right to his face, in good moods and bad. And he'd taken it. Never complained. And then she smiled and started to laugh, though the tears that came weren't of joy, because really what did it matter? She'd sent him away, and that had been the right thing, right for her and right for their children, though it hurt like a nail in the knuckle.

'Arda Smithswife?'

She almost dropped the draw plate. She spun round, hand reaching for the forging hammer that was never far away, but it was only Torvic, standing out in the wind and the lashing rain, leaning in around the corner of the workshop and flicking drips of water from his eyes. Torvic, who'd walked with her back to the Crackmarsh so she didn't get murdered by ghuldogs or the sentries Valaric had left behind.

'You're early,' she snapped. 'Wasn't expecting you for another two days.'

Torvic slid into the workshop. He cast an eye up and down the road. 'Sixfingers is on the move.'

She flinched. The name put her on edge every time. King Medrin and the doom looming over them all since he learned that Gallow was still alive.

'He's heading for Tarkhun.' Torvic snorted. 'The Vathen are getting restless again. When the weather breaks we'll be back to forkbeards and Vathen killing each other. And us Crackmarsh men, we'll be in the middle, happy as anything ...' He laughed and then caught himself and looked up sharply. 'No offence.'

Arda shrugged and shook her head. 'He's gone, Torvic. I don't know where and I try not to care. Say what you like.' She smiled. Forced it. Took some getting used to, being mistress of her own house again but knowing that Gallow was still alive after all.

A nasty grin spread across Torvic's face. 'Valaric let slip that he's got the Foxbeard in Varyxhun carrying the Comforter at his side. You ask me, Mournful can't wait to get Sixfingers across the Aulian Bridge so he can start picking and poking.'

'Is it true? Is Gallow with Valaric?'

Torvic's grin froze and then fell off his face piece by piece. He looked away. 'Best I know, your Gallow left the red sword in Varyxhun and headed out the valley. He hasn't been through the Crackmarsh. We'd know. Sixfingers holds Issetbridge and the forkbeards that were in Varyxhun have got Witches' Reach and no one crosses without their say-so. So I'd say he's still in the valley, but no one knows for sure.' The crooked grin grew back. 'Valaric's been putting it about that the Foxbeard had family in Hrodicslet and now they're in Varyxhun. Close enough to the truth, eh, but far enough to keep the forkbeards from coming across the Crackmarsh again.'

It was like the weight of a wet fur cloak coming off her, though she tried to sound as though she didn't care. 'As long as they're on the other side of the Isset, they're no bother to me.'

Torvic made a face. 'I'd keep my worries for the Vathen. Not often they come this far south but we see them now and then.' He hunched his shoulders and pushed out into the rain and came back again a moment later leading a bedraggled mule. 'Flour. Good for the rest of the winter.' He hauled a sheet of oiled leather off the animal's back and then threw down a couple of sacks and a pair of strong leather bags and emptied out a string of onions and a leg of cured ham. 'Keep your bellies full for a bit.' He went back to the mule. Arda picked up the onions and the ham and put them carefully to one side. She started to fill the leather bags with squares of mail. Making it up into a coat that sat well on a man was an armourer's job, but long hard hours went into drawing the wire, cutting the rings and riveting them together into lines and squares the size of a man's hand. Didn't take much skill, but it did take a forge and tools and a willingness for hard work. Nadric had the tools and the forge and everyone in Middislet knew how to work. Valaric paid in food and the winter had been a hard one. They were grateful, all of them.

She looked up when she was done. 'So. Are you all going to die up there when Sixfingers comes?' She spat out the forkbeard king's name. A ritual that was habit now.

'He could bring every forkbeard ever born, he still wouldn't get into Varyxhun castle. The Screambreaker had ten thousand men and even *he* couldn't do it. Anyway, you know the story. If the sixth gate ever falls, the Isset itself will wash the castle clean. Can't lose, can we?' He chuckled.

Arda snorted. 'The Screambreaker didn't bother trying, and his ten thousand were more like two by the time they got to Varyxhun. And they were knackered, worn to the end of their boots.' Little things she remembered. Gallow had never said much about the Screambreaker's war, all his years of killing good Marroc men. Hadn't been something either of them wanted to hear, but little things still came out now and then.

Torvic rummaged around in the mule's packs and threw a small leather bag at her, about the size of a hand. 'That's for Gallow,' he said when she caught it. 'If he comes by. From his Aulian friend.'

'What is it?' Arda opened the bag and sniffed. Some sort of pale crumbly grey stuff.

'Salt. In case.'

'Salt?' She laughed. 'Well *you* know how to keep a woman sweet!' Then she shivered and her smile died. Salt was for shadewalkers. And Fateguard too, as it had turned out, but the less said about *them* the better. One of the things you learned when you were stuck in a besieged fort with an Aulian wizard for company. Other things as well. Mostly things she didn't care to dwell on.

Torvic was looking at her like he had a bad taste in his mouth. 'Something else.' He stepped out and then came back in out of the rain with a second mule, even more bedraggled than the first. There were large pieces of metal tied across its back. He pulled one off, and it took a moment before Arda understood what it was. A mask and helm and crown made of iron, which could only mean it had once belonged to the iron devil of Varyxhun. The devil Gallow had said was once a friend, who'd taken her in a cage from her home. Some friend. She looked at the pieces of armour like they were a nest of snakes.

'Valaric said to give it to you. Maybe you can melt it down and make something. Or maybe if Gallow comes by there's some proper thing to do with it. Some forkb— some Lhosir thing.' He dragged the rest off the mule's back onto the floor. A whole set of iron plates. The iron skin of a Fateguard. She shuddered. The Aulian wizard had had things to say about the iron devils.

'Melt it down?' *If Gallow comes by.* Torvic had said that as if he was hoping for it but Arda wished he hadn't because a part of her was hoping for it too. A part hoping and another part praying that he didn't.

'Forge something with it.' Torvic shrugged. 'Whatever you want. Valaric wants it gone, that's all, and he doesn't want Sixfingers getting it back.' He nodded at the floor. 'It's good iron that. Worth a bit.'

He wasn't wrong either, and maybe it would feel good to turn those pieces of cursed metal into something of value. The other villagers would help. They'd be glad to. A little victory, but still, the very sight of it made her skin crawl. Valaric wanted it gone? She could understand that. 'You want me to hammer this out into wire and make it into mail for your men. Will they take kindly to wearing the skin of the iron devil of Varyxhun?'

Torvic shook his head. 'Not when you put it like that, no.' He shrugged. 'Do what you like with it. No one wants it back, not in any shape. Just get rid of it. Bury it if you want.'

Across the yard, the back door of the house opened. Nadric stood at the threshold. He stared at Torvic, scowled at the rain and then hunched his shoulders and hurried across to the forge. 'This your friend from the Crackmarsh?' He looked Torvic up and down. 'Rotten day to be living in a swamp when you could be under a roof with a nice warm fire.' He flashed a look at Arda. 'Getting ready to stick some forkbeards?'

'This is Torvic.' Arda stepped away from Nadric, distancing herself. They'd never quite got past what he'd done three years ago on the night that Gallow had left and never came back. Gallow's choice, but a part of her would always blame Nadric for doing something so stupid.

Nadric beckoned Torvic closer. 'Come over here then, Torvic of the Crackmarsh. I have something for you.' He pushed his way past Arda to the back of the workshop, to the corner full of dust and cobwebs where he kept the bits and pieces he couldn't bring himself to throw away. The scrap corner. Arda had never paid it much attention except to note that in the three years Gallow had been away all it had done was grow. Gallow had kept his armour there once, his sword and shield and helm. There was still a single Vathan javelot.

Nadric pulled away an armful of old tools and broken wood and then some sacking. Underneath was a wooden chest bound with iron and three thick leather straps. Torvic crowded closer as Nadric started to undo them and even Arda couldn't help peering over his shoulder. She'd had no idea the chest was even there. 'Pull it out where we can all see it, then!'

'Pull it out, she says.' Nadric chuckled. He finished with the straps and threw open the lid. Arda stared.

'Diaran preserve us.'

'Holy Modris, old man. Where did you get them?'

Nadric cackled. '*Get* them, young man? I *made* them. Me and that other forkbeard, the one who's dead now.' Tolvis. Arda winced. 'Been making them for the last three years. Still got *some* strength in these arms.'

Inside the chest were arrowheads. Thousands of them. Arda and Torvic and Nadric stood together, staring at the pile. Torvic couldn't keep his mouth closed and Nadric couldn't stop chuckling.

'How long?' asked Arda. 'How long were you making them?'

'Ever since Gallow left.'

'No.' Arda shook her head. 'You didn't make all of these. I'd have known.'

Nadric laughed. 'I made a lot of them. It started after the Vathen—'

He stopped abruptly. They'd both said everything they had to say about that night long ago, loud and furious, and they both thought they were right. Gallow had brought a wounded forkbeard back after Lostring Hill. The Widowmaker. When the Vathen came looking, Gallow had killed them and he and the Widowmaker had gone and never come back, and it had been Nadric's fault and Arda had never forgiven him.

'It wasn't so bad. Not like what the forkbeards did across the Isset.' Torvic coughed and Nadric turned to him, shuffling away from the anger in Arda's face. 'They killed the animals we couldn't take with us, you see. That was how it started, because they left all their arrows behind and that was money that was, if there was anyone who'd buy them, only no one wanted to be making the trip to Fedderhun to see if the Vathen would trade them for food, not when they were Vathan arrows in the first place.' Nadric shook his head. 'Was a hard winter after that summer with so many animals dead. We were back from

Varyxhun by then.' He peered sharply at Torvic. 'Was Arda who kept the village alive, not that she'll tell you. Her and that silver the forkbeard brought with him. They had food in Varyxhun and the Wolf was in the Crackmarsh.' He nodded at Torvic and the mule outside and then the sacks of flour and the onions on the floor. 'Was how that all started. Arda here and that other forkbeard. We did what we could. No one in the village had money or anything to give that winter. They had them arrows, though, and so they gave them to me.'

'And you never said a word?' Arda snapped. 'Money, that is!'

Nadric waved her away. 'Ach, you've enough to keep this house fed for a good long while.' He leered at Torvic. 'She hoards that silver like a squirrel hoards his winter nuts.'

'And for much the same reason!'

'Anyway.' Nadric shrugged her aside. 'People owed us and there was plenty of old pieces of metal about after all the fighting that summer. Broken bits of this and that. People took to keeping whatever they could find, and that winter it came to me. I thought a fair time about what I might do with it.' He kicked the box. 'There you have it. Broad heads mostly, the older ones, but later I took to making them like the Vathen do. Narrow points. Up close they'll put a hole in a forkbeard, those ones, even if he's wearing mail.'

Torvic bent down and tried to pick up the box. He heaved and huffed and his face went red.

Nadric laughed. 'Careful, friend. You'll do yourself an injury trying to lift that. Needs a wagon, that does. There's a few pieces of Vathan mail at the bottom too and some other bits and pieces. I been hoarding it for you, for when the need was right.'

'Can't take a wagon into the Crackmarsh.' Torvic winced. 'And I've only got two mules here and no spare bags.' He gave Nadric a long look. 'I'll come back, old man. I'll bring more mules and take them off your hands. What do you want for them?'

Nadric shook his head. 'Nothing. Was forkbeard silver that bought the metal when it comes down to it. Give it back to them, nice and hard. That'll do nicely.'

Arda stepped between them. 'I'll take six sacks of flour and two legs of pork, Torvic.'

'No, you won't.' Nadric glared. Wasn't like him to stand up for something but he had a fierce look on him now. 'Forkbeards killed Merethin. Your husband, woman, your first one, and my son in case you've forgotten. Forkbeards can have this lot back for nothing.'

Arda's face tightened but she kept her peace. Torvic looked from one to the other and then nodded to Nadric and backed away. 'Take me a few days. When I see Mournful I'll see what he says.'

5

HRODICSLET

The drunken forkbeard was going to be a problem. Mirrahj watched him, keeping a careful distance. He was sitting in the mud in the middle of Hrodicslet, not doing much except singing to himself, and that was fine until any of her riders got anywhere close, when he stumbled to his feet and lurched and started shouting and swinging his axe. No one wanted to go anywhere near him and Mirrahj Bashar could see why.

'Let me shoot him,' grumbled Josper. 'Put an arrow or two in his legs, that should shut him up.' Josper was sulking. The rains might have broken the day before but the Marroc town was soaking wet. The streets were rivers of mud and the houses were all built on stilts, as if mud was only the beginning. Josper liked to burn things, but around here he couldn't even find tinder to start a flame.

'No.' Mirrahj waved him off. 'Circle the place again. Find some Marroc and chase them into the marsh. See which way they go.' Josper rode away laughing. He'd enjoy himself with that until it got dark and the ghuldogs came out. He'd be back sharp enough then though, tail between his legs.

Which left her with the forkbeard. Other times she'd have let Josper have his way, but this one interested her. A forkbeard on the wrong side of the river. Just the one, not some raiding party, which begged the question: how did he get here? And that in turn begged the answer she was secretly looking for: a southern passage around the Crackmarsh and across the Isset. Because there had to be one, there simply *had* to, and if the forkbeard knew it then she wanted it out of him.

Mirrahj got off her horse. She checked the buckles on the little round shield strapped to her left arm and headed towards him.

Shrajal and two of his riders came out of a house dragging a pair of screaming Marroc children. 'Don't get too close!' He was laughing at her. 'That one bites.' He made a show of stringing up his captives but he was watching her all the time. Waiting for her to fail, just like Josper was waiting too.

The forkbeard stopped singing and started staring as Mirrahj came close. He tried to get up, fell over and then finally found his feet. Mirrahj drew the short curved sword at her side and stabbed it into the mud. Her helm followed. She shook her hair, letting the braids fall around her neck. Sometimes men didn't know what to do when they realised she was a woman. The forkbeard stumbled a step towards her, half drew the axe from his belt and then put it back. 'Men all too scared, are they? That's you horse buggerers. No pride.'

She smiled. He was a big one, even for a forkbeard, but it made no difference. The rest of the ride could have him once she'd got what she wanted. She turned to Shrajal. 'You hear that, Shrajal? Forkbeard says you're scared of him.'

'Forkbeard can come here and say that if he wants. I'm not going anywhere.'

They both laughed. Mirrahj turned back. 'They're not scared of you. They're waiting for me to tell them what to do with you. What are you doing here? There aren't any forkbeards on this side of the Isset.'

He seemed to forget she was there. He tipped back his head and howled. 'Medrin? Medrin! Waiting for you. Here I am! Come and get me!' His eyes dropped suddenly back to Mirrahj again. 'I'm the one who took his hand.'

'You took King Sixfingers' hand? I don't believe you.'

'Believe what you like, Vathan.'

'You were in Andhun when we stole it from you, then?' She took a slow step closer. 'I was there too.' Another step. 'How did you get across the Crackmarsh, forkbeard? Did you walk or did you ride? How did you get past the ghuldogs and the Marroc who live in there?'

The forkbeard sat down with a heavy *splat* in the mud. 'I didn't. I came through the caves and down the mountains like everyone else.' He rocked back and put a finger to his lips and a lazy smile moved over his face. 'But don't tell the other fork-beards.'

So he does know! A surge of anticipation sparked through her. Behind the forkbeard another handful of men spilled into the mud from the big hall at the heart of the town. They were whooping and cheering. A moment later a curl of smoke followed them out through the door. Mirrahj laughed. Someone had finally got a fire going and Josper had missed it. She took another step closer. 'Tell me about these caves and this path down the mountains.' When he didn't answer, she stifled a flash of irritation. 'You were in Andhun, were you? Does that make you a soldier?'

'Always a soldier.' The forkbeard laughed. 'Too much of one.' He started to rise, slipped in the mud and fell flat on his back and then finally stood up again. 'You look mighty fine for a Vathan.'

'And you're ugly even for a forkbeard. If you're a soldier, how many came with you? Where are they?' There were flames under the eaves of the burning hall now. A haze of smoke and steam hung over its thatched roof. More of her riders were coming, looking to light a brand and see if they could fire a few of the other houses too. They were watching her.

The forkbeard rubbed his misshapen nose. 'Soldier? I'm not anything. Nothing. *Nioingr.* That's what they call me. You can say it three times if you like. Then I have to kill you.'

Nioingr. A traitor and an outcast. In that case, maybe he'd tell her what she wanted freely. 'What's your name, outcast?'

'Gallow Foxbeard.' He grinned at her as though that was supposed to mean something.

'You're a long way from home, Gallow Foxbeard.'

'Home?' The forkbeard howled with bitter laughter. Mirrahj took another step closer. 'Careful, Vathan. I've killed plenty of your kind.'

'I'm unarmed, forkbeard.'

'Lhosir don't make war on women and children.' He spat. 'Didn't used to, anyway.'

'You're a strange one.' And not much use drunk. She'd have him alive and let him sober up in a cage and then she'd set about finding out whether he knew a way across the Isset or not. Or maybe Josper would find one for her after all, or one of the Marroc prisoners would know of one and the forkbeard wouldn't matter any more. Either way her ride would take some pleasure from a forkbeard's screams. Another scratch of vengeance for what they'd done outside Andhun.

She walked towards him with purpose now. He cocked his head and his face screwed up, trying to make sense of it. He waved his axe at her. 'Piss off, Vathan.'

'I don't think I will.' She stopped right in front of him, so close he could have swung at her, but he didn't. 'Well, forkbeard, whatever you think, you're going to fight a woman today. Look.' She threw aside her shield. 'I've made it easy for you. Fists. No steel.'

'Girl, I'm twice your size.'

But he was steaming drunk too. Mirrahj stood in front of him.

'Leave me alone. Go away.'

'Make me.'

Down the street behind him there were about a dozen of her men watching them now. Even the ones who'd lit brands were waiting. 'My men are watching us, forkbeard. I'm their bashar.' Which made it a matter of pride and face. He had to understand *that*, didn't he?

He closed his eyes. For a long time he stood like that, head tipped back to the clouds, and Mirrahj reckoned she could have just walked up behind him, wrapped an arm around his neck and choked him and he wouldn't even have noticed. But she waited. Eventually he looked at her again and groaned because she hadn't vanished like she was supposed to. He sighed and threw down his axe and his shield. 'Maker-Devourer, girl. Come on then. I'm going to pull those leathers down and spank your arse.'

She crept closer, one shuffle at a time until he lunged and she ducked and darted behind him, and it was even easier than she'd hoped. She jumped onto his back and wrapped her legs around his waist and one arm around his neck, gripped it with the other and squeezed as tight as she could. He staggered, turning round and round as though he didn't quite understand that she wasn't simply behind him. Damned forkbeard was built like a bull, with a neck so strong that she had a moment of doubt. Shrajal was watching her though, and the others who weren't out chasing Marroc. She'd staked her right to be their bashar on taking this forkbeard down, and that made it a bit late for doubts.

'I had a daughter like you,' slurred the forkbeard. 'Like a bloody limpet. Could never shake her off.' He didn't do any of the obvious things, like run backwards and smash her into the wall of a hut or throw himself down on his back and try to drown her in the mud. If he did, she wasn't sure she could hold on. Wasn't sure her ribs wouldn't snap, if it came to it, but then it had always been a gamble. He was stinking drunk and it made him stupid.

One hand tried to get a grip on her arm. The other pawed over his shoulder, trying to grab her face. 'I had brothers,' she said. 'Lots of brothers.' She grunted at the effort. The muscles in her arms were burning at the pressure she was putting on the forkbeard's neck, and he was still talking? She squeezed harder. 'Lots of brothers. All bigger than I was.'

'No brothers, me.' The forkbeard was losing his strength. 'Made my own. All brothers. Before ...' He stumbled and sank to his knees.

'Well I had lots.' Mirrahj forced herself to keep her arms tight. 'I had a man as well, and he was big like you, and I always beat him even so.'

'I had a wife.' The forkbeard's arms dropped to his sides. 'So where is he, your man?' Another few seconds and he finally went limp and toppled over into the mud.

'He died,' she said quietly. 'Fighting forkbeards like you.' She stayed on his back, squeezing until she'd counted to twenty in her head. Then, only then, she let go and stepped back. Her furs were covered in mud. It was oozing through the forkbeard's fingers. He was face down and so heavy that she almost couldn't roll him over onto his back to stop him from drowning. She did, though, and then put an ear to his chest. He was still breathing.

'Shrajal! Bind him and get him out of here.' She made a sharp gesture to the riders who'd stopped to watch. They turned and set about what they'd come to do: looting everything they could carry and burning whatever would burn in this godforsaken swamp. Mirrahj climbed back onto her horse and rode among them, watching, shouting encouragement here and there. Her arms were still burning.

They dragged the last few Marroc out of their homes. There wasn't much worth taking and only a little food this far towards the backside of winter. The sky was darkening, more rain on its way. As it started they rounded up the Marroc animals they'd taken. They'd slaughter themselves a feast before they moved on, sleep in the houses they didn't burn, warmed by the fires of the ones they had, and tomorrow they'd leave. Deeper into the mountains or further around the fringes of the Crackmarsh, one or the other, looking for the south passage across the Isset. They wouldn't stray far though, not for another day or two. Josper deserved his chance with the Marroc.

'Bashar!' It was almost dark when Shrajal caught up with her again. As he reined in his horse he was brandishing something that looked like a sword but wasn't. A scabbard.

'Shrajal.' Mirrahj let her face settle into an amused disdain. Shrajal was young and eager – a little too eager.

He thrust the scabbard at her. 'Look! Look!'

She looked, and at first there was nothing to see. A scabbard for a Vathan sword. An ornate one, and she wondered for a moment if he meant it as a courting gift, which made him more stupid than she'd thought. But the scabbard was too long for a Vathan blade, and then the designs in the metal around the top of the sheath caught her eye, and she knew she was wrong and Shrajal was sharper than he looked. 'Where did you get this?'

He answered with a grin. 'The forkbeard.' He probably hadn't ever even seen it before but he still knew what it was. Mirrahj, who *had* seen it, had no doubt at all. He was holding the scabbard they'd lost at Andhun. The Peacebringer's scabbard, and if the forkbeard carried that then maybe he knew the fate of the red sword itself and Shrajal had every right to look pleased with himself because nothing mattered to the Vathen more than the Sword of the Weeping God.

Mirrahj nudged her horse a step closer so her mount was

almost touching his and leaned over. 'Spread the word and then go after Josper and bring him back. After we're done here we head straight back for the ardshan in Andhun.' She smiled. 'Have some fun with Josper. Tell him what you found.'

6

ARROWS AND SALT

It was more than a week before Torvic returned, and when he did he came with three other grim-faced Crackmarsh men. Arda waved them into the house and they tied up their mules and came inside, pleased to be out of the gales blowing from the Storm Coast. While the other Marroc exchanged greetings with Nadric – because he was the man of the house – Torvic went back outside and Arda went with him. He had two enormous hams. 'No flour,' he said. 'But I've got this.' He passed her a bag of cured fish strips, tough and oily and salty and delicious. 'Valaric thanks you for your kindness. We'll take the arrowheads. After that ...' Torvic scratched his beard.

Arda hoisted one of the hams over her shoulder and turned to go, keen to be out of the wind, but Torvic put a hand to her arm and caught her. He leaned in close. 'There's a band of Vathen about. They sacked Hrodicslet. About a week ago. They burned what would burn and took a few slaves and chased off everyone else. Seems like they're looking for a way across the Crackmarsh. Could be they'll come here before long.' They were face to face now, close, Torvic looking at her intently. She felt her pulse quicken. Stupid really, but she hadn't had anyone stand so close to her since Witches' Reach and it made her think of Gallow in all the good ways she was trying to forget. She took a step back, giving herself a little space.

Torvic raised his voice over the wind. 'We followed them most of the way here. They were pushing a hundred. They turned north but that doesn't mean they won't be back.'

Back in the house the stale air was a relief. Jelira was staring at a soldier who couldn't have been much older than she was, and he was staring back, and they were both smiling and looking away and then looking back and smiling again, and Arda wasn't having any of *that*, not with a man from the Crackmarsh who'd vanish at the drop of a hat and probably be dead before the year was out. She slid the ham off her shoulder and thrust it at Jelira. 'You can take this out to the workshop and hang it round the back where the birds and the rats won't get at it.'

The young soldier began to get to his feet. Arda glared at him until he squatted down again.

'The Vathen must have passed only a few miles from here.' Torvic shook his head. 'Heading for Fedderhun, and in a hurry.' He was looking at Nadric now, a steady gaze full of some meaning that filled Arda with unease. 'Haven't seen the Vathen come so far south in a while. They're looking for something. Only a matter of time before they come back.'

Arda fixed Torvic with a hard stare. He was leading to something, if only he'd spit it out. Only he was gazing at Nadric, as though she didn't count, and she wasn't having *that* either. 'Well, if they do then we'll be sure to be nice to them.'

Torvic reached into the bag he'd given Arda and helped himself to a fish strip. He cocked his head. 'Valaric could make good use of anyone who knows their way around a forge. In Varyxhun.'

'How interesting.' Moving the forge then, that's what he wanted, and when she looked at the three men he'd brought with him, she wondered if that was why they'd come. 'Any travelling smiths come through, I'll be sure to mention it.' She glared at Torvic, trying to make sure he understood she wasn't moving anywhere for anyone, not now, and he'd said his piece and now could he please have the sense to let it go?

'We'll be here a few days,' he said. 'Going to head north and have a look around between here and Fedderhun. Keep an eye in case there's more Vathen on the move. You mind if we leave the mules here with you?'

'You do that.' Arda's voice had a finality to it. 'You're welcome to stay under my roof as long as you're here. Mules too.'

Torvic smiled. He had an easy smile, not forced. 'That's kind of you, Arda Smithswife. When we're back, we'll talk a bit more about what we've seen.' And the forge, she supposed. He'd talk about the forge and moving it and her and all of them up into the mountains again where Gallow had sent them three years back. She'd be buggered if she was going to let that happen a second time.

She nodded. 'You do that, Torvic. I'll be made of ears.'

Torvic took his Crackmarsh men and left the next morning, nice and early. The Vathen had had a beardless forkbeard among the slaves they'd taken but he hadn't seen any need to mention that. Might have been Gallow, might not. Either way he reckoned Arda didn't want to know and so he kept his peace and made sure the others did too. They all knew who Gallow was. They'd all followed the Wolf to Witches' Reach and seen what happened there.

He sent two of his men north-west, scouting the fringes of the marsh in case the Vathen were doing the same. He kept the young one, Reddic, close, with his eyes for Arda's daughter, and trudged up the north road towards Fedderhun until they picked up the trail of the Vathen from Hrodicslet. The Vathen were travelling too fast to catch on foot but Torvic followed them anyway until he was sure he knew where they were heading: north and west to the coast road and Andhun. Then he turned north and for another day they followed the winding waters of the Fedder. The winds off the Storm Coast fell away and the air grew still. A bitter cold drifted out from the Ice Mountain Sea and settled over the land.

By the time they slunk into Fedderhun, the ground was freezing at night and it was snowing again. They spoke to the Marroc there and kept their ears open but all they got was a name: Mirrahj Bashar, who'd taken her ride south to look for a passage around the far side of the Crackmarsh and had never come back. By the sound of things, no one had expected her to. Full of ghuldogs and Marroc bandits, the Crackmarsh. Torvic often wondered whether there might be some way to get the forkbeards and the Vathen into the Crackmarsh at the same time, have them kill each other in the swamps and water meadows and then let the ghuldogs finish them off while the Marroc just watched it all happen. Fat chance, but it was a nice dream.

The Vathen around Fedderhun helped themselves to whatever took their fancy and largely left the Marroc fishermen of the town alone. They didn't seem to be doing anything much except kicking their heels and as far as Torvic could tell most of them didn't want to be there at all. They wanted to be in their home pastures for the winter, curled up in their tents, not here in this godsforsaken outpost. They were here because someone had told them to be and so they were making the best of it until whoever that someone was allowed them home. Or so it seemed to Torvic.

They learned as much as they could, which seemed like it wasn't much at all, and left after a couple of days, and they were hardly out of the town when the snow started again. It fell steadily all through the day, thick and heavy, covering the land with white and then, as the light faded, the clouds cleared away to the south and Torvic was looking up at a deep blue sky. They'd need more than a fire and some warm furs out in the open tonight, but it wasn't much of a worry. Nice thing about moving through this part of the world: the farms were scattered and easily missed but they were there if you looked for them, and the Marroc who lived here were happy to share their fires and their shelter and even a little food to hear a few travellers' tales. And there weren't any forkbeards, but there *were* old friends here and there.

Torvic stopped at a house with a pair of small barns nestled beside it in a hollow, almost snow-bound already, and banged on the door. When a scar-faced Marroc opened it, Torvic grinned, and the scarred Marroc hugged him and dragged him inside.

'Stannic. Long time.'

'Torvic!' Stannic let him go and looked Reddic up and down. 'This lad yours?'

Torvic shook his head, chuckled to himself – no daughters here for Reddic to make eyes at, thank Diaran! – and sent Reddic back outside to settle the mules and strip their saddles; and by the time he came back Stannic's wife had fetched some cheese and milk and a few turnips, and Stannic had opened a jug of mead and his three young boys were peering from behind the curtain to the night room with eyes hungry for stories and the evening was looking very comfortable indeed.

'He ever tell you about Lostring Hill?' asked Stannic as soon as Reddic sat down, and then he told the story anyway, even though Reddic had heard it a dozen times by now, about how he and Torvic and Sarvic and the two Jonnics and a few others had fought the Vathen with Valaric the Wolf, and how they'd run away with a forkbeard who'd turned out to be Gallow Foxbeard. Reddic listened as though he'd never heard it before, which made Torvic smile even more. By the time he was done, the food was gone, the fire was dying and the eyes gazing out from the night room had long since closed.

'The Vathen came as far south as the Crackmarsh after,' said Stannic as they settled down for the night. 'Valaric ever tell you that story, Torvic?'

Torvic nodded, because yes, he knew all about it, and so did anyone who'd lived through Andhun and the months afterwards, but then he saw Reddic shake his head. Reddic was too young to have been at Lostring Hill or at Andhun after. The first forkbeards had probably come from across the sea before Reddic was even born. To him they were simply the way of the world. Hadn't stopped him running away to the Crackmarsh though.

Stannic belched. 'Lad, you've heard of the Widowmaker, curse his soul, the Nightmare of the North? That was who the forkbeards sent to hold the Vathen outside Fedderhun. Well he lost, didn't he, and it was Valaric who found him after the battle, out of his senses, and he let the Widowmaker go. Let Gallow take him away.' He jerked his head down the track towards Middislet and the Crackmarsh. 'That's why half of Middislet looks like it was only put up yesterday. Vathen tore a good piece of it down.' He poked the fire with a stick and watched the sparks rise with the smoke.

Reddic leaned sideways and let out a long fart. 'Did they find him?'

'The Widowmaker? He died fighting them outside Andhun the day before the city fell.'

'I knew *that*.'

'Well, how'd you think he got to be at Andhun a month later if the horse shaggers had found him Middislet?' Stannic laughed and shook his head.

'Could have escaped.'

'No. He got away.' Stannic stared into the flames, remembering, and Torvic stared too, remembering much the same, fleeing through the woods with Valaric and the Foxbeard and then the two Vathan horses and the rest and the aftermath of the battle, and then the days after, riding for Andhun. He looked suddenly up at Stannic.

'You ever face him? The Nightmare of the North?'

'Go against him?' Stannic shook his head and laughed. 'Never wanted to go and fight when I was younger. Scared, I suppose. I was about the age of your lad here when the Widowmaker came and I didn't have the balls to run away and be a Crackmarsh man even if there'd been such a thing. Forkbeards didn't come by these parts for years, and when they did they weren't as bad as everyone said they'd be, not back then. That was after Tane died and Varyxhun fell. Just wanted to go home, I think. Most of them did, too.'

Reddic looked awed. Torvic grinned. Lostring Hill wasn't something he talked about that much because everyone who hadn't been there made out that the Marroc who'd survived the battle were heroes, whereas Torvic knew perfectly well that most of them had been shitting themselves as much as everyone else and just kept their heads a little better and got lucky. He snorted. 'You remember the Foxbeard said he saw horses? And then he and Valaric went on their own to look, and Valaric came back and it was just him? How we all thought he'd done for the forkbeard?' He chuckled again and looked at Reddic. 'The Wolf only told us the truth later, and even then only because there were some Vathen who just wouldn't stop following us until Valaric skinned a few of them to find out why. That's when it came out. Ask Sarvic if you like – he was there too. Don't ask Valaric though. Valaric doesn't talk about it. He and the Foxbeard got a history ...'

He froze. A noise. Outside. The look on Reddic's face said he'd heard it too. Then it came again. A heavy broken shuffle, as though someone was dragging a load through the snow in long slow pulls with a good rest between each one. Reddic jumped up, startled, eyes darting from one door to the other and one hand already on his axe. 'Forkbeards?'

Torvic shook his head. 'Not out here.'

Stannic waved at them both to sit down. 'Wolf maybe. If it is then it's got something. Leave it be. Dead of night in that cold?'

He snorted but now Torvic got up too. 'Didn't sound like an animal to me.' He crept to the door and opened it. Cold air froze his face but at least the winds weren't the gales they'd been a week ago. The moon was full and high, its light bright on the snow except where long deep shadows spilled from the wood pile and the low barns. A soldier in mail and a helm stood not more than a dozen yards in front of him. Hard to make out much in the moonlight but he had a naked sword hanging loose and long from his hand and he was too big to be a Vathan. Torvic snatched his shield from beside the door and whipped out his axe. 'Reddic! Stannic!' The soldier was a forkbeard. Had to be, although only Modris knew what a forkbeard was doing all the way out here. He couldn't see the forkbeard's eyes but he felt them staring at him, and when the forkbeard moved, he lurched a stride closer, dragging one leg as though crippled. Crippled was good. Torvic tried to tell himself that one crippled forkbeard was more a gift than something to fear but he couldn't quite make himself believe it. One forkbeard out here all on his own? One?

Then again, the Vathen had taken a forkbeard from Hrodicslet. It made him pause a moment. He took a step closer and peered. 'Foxbeard?'

The forkbeard took another step and this time it wasn't so slow. His sword came up fast and lunged and Torvic barely got his shield in the way. The sword was odd. It wasn't a forkbeard sword. Too long, Torvic thought as he brought his axe down hard on the man's helm, not hard enough to split the iron but hard enough that the forkbeard would see stars long enough for a killing blow. But the forkbeard grabbed at his shield as though he hadn't felt anything, and Torvic stepped back, and that was when the moon caught the forkbeard's face and he saw it wasn't a man at all. The sight froze him stiff, and in that moment the shadewalker drove its long Aulian sword through Torvic's guts and then caught him as he crumpled. While one hand still held the sword, the other grabbed Torvic by the throat and pulled him close. The shadewalker stiffened; and as it squeezed Torvic's life out of him, its crippled leg twisted and straightened and its eyes gazed hard at the door.

And that was how Reddic found him, Torvic gasping and gurgling while his blood ran out of him over his belly and down his legs and dripped off his dangling feet to pool blackly in the snow, and the shadewalker on the other side of him, crushing his throat. For an instant Reddic was paralysed, and in that second the only sound was the snap of bones as the shadewalker finally crushed Torvic's throat. Reddic struggled for breath and backed away. The shadewalker dropped Torvic and looked at him. It stepped forward, almost into the doorway, and that was when Reddic remembered there were five more people in the house behind him and three of them were children.

'Shadewalker!' He slammed the door in its face and hurled himself against it. 'Shadewalker! Stannic! By Modris! Get up! Run!' He was screaming now, willing the others to get out of their beds and into their furs as fast as they possibly could. There wasn't anything to do when a shadewalker came except run, every Marroc knew that. Even the forkbeards didn't try to fight them because they couldn't be killed, and they couldn't be killed because they were already dead. They wandered aimlessly, served no purpose. No one knew what they were or why, save that they came across the mountains from Aulia now and then,

The door rattled. The shadewalker slammed into it hard enough to knock Reddic back a step. The Marroc were piling out of the night room, the children already wailing in fear. Stannic pulled on his boots and wrapped another fur around himself and picked up a hay fork. He threw open the other door and roared at everyone to get out. Against Reddic's shoulder the door rattled again. The shadewalker pushed it open another inch.

'I'll hold it here as long as I can.' Reddic wasn't sure why he'd said that except that he was the one holding the door closed and no one was helping him and so he was pretty much stuck with it and never mind how much he wanted to piss himself and sink to the floor. Stannic was still throwing cloaks and furs and blankets to his wife and his children. Reddic's feet slipped back. A gap opened wide enough for a finger to slip through and then for two and then three, and that was when he turned and let go, and Stannic was out the other door a step ahead, still carrying armfuls of furs. Stannic ran, glancing over his shoulder now and then, while Reddic shot past them all, legs pumping as hard as they'd go, flailing and floundering in the snow. After a minute he stopped to catch his breath. When Stannic's wife caught him, gasping with her children pecking at her heels, Stannic snapped at them all to wait. He stood and stared back at the farm and at the tracks they'd left behind them in the snow. The shadewalker was following, out in the open now, walking fast and steady, clear as anything.

Stannic stared at it as he handed out the furs, then met Reddic's eye. 'Not the first time I've had to run from a shade-walker and probably won't be the last. They're not so quick and they don't run but they don't give up easy neither, and they don't feel the cold. Follow us until sunrise, this one, most likely, and pick off whoever drops. So we go steady, quick as we can but slow enough we don't have to stop much, and we keep warm, and we don't leave anyone behind. I'll take the front, you take the back. Keep your eyes on it, lad, and if the cold bites too hard, you shout for help and I'll come.' He slapped Reddic on the shoulder. 'You did good, lad. Held it back long enough so we got what we need. Modris walks with us and we'll all live to see the sun again.' The shadewalker was getting closer. Stannic set off. 'Shout to me, lad, if it gets too close.'

Sometimes Reddic forgot he wasn't many years from being a boy. Others he felt it sharp as an Aulian knife.

7

MIRRAHJ

'Forkbeard king's on the move.' Gallow woke up slumped over the back of a horse. The ground was right in front of him, swaying from side to side, lurching up and down with the animal's gait. He flinched. His hands were tied behind his back, his ankles bound together and the whole of him lashed tight to the saddle beneath. His head throbbed. Bits and pieces of Vathan conversation drifted over him. 'Where?' 'Somewhere down south.' He tried to remember what had happened the night before. Trouble. Fighting. He'd been drunk. Marroc running and screaming and men on horses ... Vathen. And then the Vathan woman, and then ... And then he didn't remember.

A dozen Marroc trailed along behind the horsemen, hands bound, pulled by ropes tied to Vathan saddles. If anyone fell then the Vathen wouldn't stop. Gallow closed his eyes again. No point letting them know he was awake because then they'd only drag him like the others. He let himself drift, trying to doze away the throbbing between his eyes.

The sun was still high when the Vathen finally stopped and made a small camp. They threw together a fire and sat around it roasting haunches of meat while they left their animals to graze. The horses looked thin and hungry and the Vathen tucked into their feast like starving men. Some of them taunted the Marroc with strips of fat, dangling them and then whipping them away again, but they stopped when the woman from Hrodicslet came past and barked at them. Gallow's eyes followed her. The other Vathen deferred to her. She was their bashar then. And now he dimly remembered. Hadn't she told him that before ... before whatever had happened?

She saw him watching her, and while the other Vathen

stamped out the fire and rounded up their horses, she cut the ropes that held him and tipped him onto the ground and poked him with her toe.

'Come on, forkbeard, move. Else I'll think you're dead. You might think I'll leave you and you'll slip your ropes and escape, but there are some things I want from these Marroc, and I'm thinking that if I let them bleed a forkbeard it might loosen their tongues a little.'

Gallow rolled onto his back and looked up at her. 'Lhosir make poor slaves. What do you want from me, Vathan?'

'Right now for you to get to your feet.' She tied a rope to the horse's saddle. As Gallow struggled to rise she hauled him up and then strung the rope around his waist. When that was done she cut the ropes around his feet. She didn't touch the ones around his wrists.

'It's easier to walk with your hands at the front.'

She flashed him an unkind smile. 'So it is. You want to know what I want from you?' She walked a little way to her own horse and led it back and tapped at the scabbard tied across its saddle. *His* scabbard. 'I want to know where to find the sword that goes with this.'

Gallow shrugged, but she was laughing before he could even open his mouth. 'Of course, forkbeard, of course you don't know, haven't the first idea, can't even imagine what I'm talking about. Save your breath for the walk since I won't believe a word you say right now. When you're ready you can tell me how you came to have the scabbard, at least. Or do you propose to tell me that some Marroc hung it on you for a joke when you were drunk last night?'

Gallow twisted his neck from side to side, trying to ease out the knots in his muscles. He felt the joints and the bones crack. 'I'll tell you exactly, Vathan, for I see no secret to it. My name is Gallow. Some once called me Truesword. Most call me Foxbeard now. I fought beside the Screambreaker at Andhun. I was there when he defeated your giant and took the red sword and I was beside him when he fell. That's how I came to be carrying both that scabbard and the sword you're looking for. Is that what you wanted to hear?'

The Vathan cocked her head. 'Go on.'

Gallow closed his eyes. 'Let your Marroc slaves go.'

The woman howled with laughter. 'A forkbeard asking mercy for Marroc slaves? There's a thing. I'm sure *they* won't beg for *you.*'

'No.' Gallow bowed his head.

'Well, if ever you find a Marroc prepared to take your place, I'll let you go, forkbeard. But for now there are other things I want from these Marroc and so you'll have to tell me more about what happened to Solace as we walk. Do you think you can manage that?'

'You told me to save my breath.'

She smirked. 'Are you the forkbeard who threw Solace off the cliffs of Andhun into the sea?'

'Yes.'

'And you jumped right after it?'

'Yes.'

The woman looked at him askance. Behind her the rest of the Vathen were getting ready to leave. 'I've stood at the top of that cliff, forkbeard, so I'm quite sure I don't believe you. But suppose for a moment that I did: how are you still alive?'

Gallow wasn't sure he had much of an answer to that. When he didn't speak, the Vathan woman laughed and her eyes called him a liar. She turned away and vaulted onto her horse. She didn't free his wrists so he could walk more easily but as the Vathen rode off, she circled back to take the reins of his horse and led him to the front where everyone could see and had him trot along behind her. She didn't once look back at him.

The Vathen rode at a hard pace for walking. Gallow didn't see what happened to the Marroc at the back of the ride, but when they stopped again in the evening on a ridge looking down over a steep valley, most were still there. No one came to untie him so Gallow sat down and stretched his legs while the Vathen set out their camp and lit their fires. He looked down at the valley. He knew this place. At the bottom was the road that ran from Hrodicslet and round the hills to Fedderhun. On its way it passed Middislet only a few miles from Nadric's forge. *From home and from Arda.* As he gazed he walked deep among those memories, so deep he didn't notice the Vathan woman until she squatted beside him, drinking water from a deerskin bottle. 'I imagine you could keep up that pace for days.' She drank deeply.

'I imagine I could.' Gallow closed his eyes. The sun was setting and the air would get cold quickly even this far from the mountains.

'Yes. A forkbeard like you should manage well enough. I'm guessing three more days to Fedderhun and then we'll pick the pace up. Another five or six to Andhun.'

'I'd like some water, please. Walking makes me thirsty.'

'Polite too?' She laughed. 'But where's your beard, forkbeard? I feel stupid calling you that when you haven't got one.'

'I cut it off.'

'Why?'

'Talking makes me thirsty too.'

'Sit up then.' When Gallow managed to get himself sitting, the woman moved closer and tipped the bottle against his mouth. She was careful and he managed to drink more than she spilled.

'This is your ride. The others answer to you. You're the bashar here?'

'So I am. Where's the sword, forkbeard?'

'I left it behind.'

'Where?'

'A place I passed through.'

'Why?'

'Because it's cursed.'

She snorted. 'I hear the Marroc say so. I thought you forkbeards knew better.'

Gallow turned and smiled at her, though there was no friendliness there. 'I carried the red sword for long enough to know that the Marroc are right. If I had it, I'd give it to you.'

She laughed. 'I doubt that very much, forkbeard.'

'That doesn't make it any less true.'

'You're not going to tell me where it is. But you know. I can see that. That or it's all been lies right from the start and you just found the scabbard empty washed up on the shore somewhere. I think if I try to beat it out of you, I might kill you before you talk, and the ardshan would have my hide for that. So you can keep your secrets, forkbeard. I'll take you to Andhun and the ardshan can try. I'll be curious to see if it can be done.'

'It's a long way to Andhun, Vathan. A lot could happen.'

'It could.' She stood up and took the bottle away. 'Hungry yet?'

'I'll live.'

'I bet.' She chuckled. 'I've killed forkbeards. Two. Three years ago in Andhun. I hated your people once but not so much now. Don't think for a moment that'll help you if I have to hunt you down. I'm the bashar of this ride, as you say. Challenge me and I'll open your throat and damn whatever it is you might know.' She turned and started off, then stopped and looked back. 'One thing puzzles me, forkbeard. What were you doing in that Marroc town, just you and none of the rest of your kind?'

'Looking for a place to get drunk.'

'In a town full of Marroc?' She hooted with glee. 'You forkbeards are mad. I'm surprised they didn't slit your throat.'

'But they didn't.'

She went away then, back to the fires to be among her men, but later, when it was dark and the Vathen were settling to sleep for the night, she returned with a ragged half-eaten leg of fire-burned meat, cold again now, with the fat congealed among the flecks of charred flesh and skin. She poked Gallow with her foot until he stirred, and when he sat up she dropped the meat on his lap. He wriggled until he had it wedged between his knees. Doubled over he could reach it with his teeth. He tore at it carefully, wary of dislodging it. The woman watched him. 'You're a strange one, forkbeard. The Marroc all scream and cry and wail to be let go. They beg and wave their hands. The forkbeards I've met before were all full of curses and threats. They never gave an inch and they all came to bad ends. But you? You just sit here as though none of this really matters.' She snorted and laughed at the same time, an odd squeaking sound.

Gallow glanced up between mouthfuls. 'Your ropes are strong and your knots are good, Vathan. I told you already that Lhosir make poor slaves and I'll be no different, but why waste my strength fighting what cannot be fought?'

The Vathan shook her head as she got up. 'You intrigue me, forkbeard, but that was a dull answer. Do better.'

He slept as best he could in the lashing winds blowing off the Storm Coast to the north. In the morning the Vathan woman poked him in his shivering ribs until he was on his feet and they were away again. She ignored him for the rest of that day and for most of the next one too, until his throat was swollen with thirst and his legs ached and his belly knotted with hunger, but on the third night, as the Vathen camped amid a wind that howled like a fury and whipped the trees and the grass and staggered men whenever they took a careless step, she came back to him again. She held water and meat still warm and dripping from the fire in front of him, and shouted over the gale, 'Amuse me, forkbeard. Never mind the sword, if that somehow troubles your honour. Tell me the story of how a drunken forkbeard found himself in a Marroc town so far from his fellows and then simply didn't care when a Vathan bashar took him for her slave.'

Another day without water would be the end of him. He wasn't sure if the Vathan woman would let that happen but the smell of hot fat drove him wild. And in the end what did it matter? He laughed. 'Strange that you should ask that tonight.' The land around them had been familiar for hours. He remembered riding across it with the Screambreaker after Lostring Hill. Middislet was less than a dozen miles away, somewhere to the south and the west – Middislet and Nadric's forge and Arda and home – but he didn't dare breathe a word of any of that. So he told her instead how the ghost of the Screambreaker had been waiting for him after he'd thrown himself into the sea from the cliffs of Andhun, of the choices he'd been given there and of the choice he'd made. Of how storms and slavers had taken him ever further from his home. A year as a slave, an arena fighter, then a wanderer and a corsair, and finally on a ship again, looking for the way home and yet another storm that sank him and washed him up on a beach in a distant land to the very far south. And always he had the sword. He told her how he'd clung to it, gone back for it, always kept it somehow with him in each escape, the red sword and his old shield of Medrin's Crimson Legion. He watched her eyes as he told her and saw the hunger there, and so each night he told her more.

The Vathen reached Fedderhun and then the sea and the

coast road to Andhun. The gales blew themselves out and in their place a stillness settled in the air. A cold was coming, a bitter cold drifting down from the Ice Wraiths in the distant north. The Vathen stopped in Marroc villages, each one quietly getting on with its life until a hundred Vathan riders threw them out of their homes and hearths for a night and ate their food and moved on. In a Marroc house around a Marroc fire Gallow told the Vathan woman of Oribas – how the Aulian had found him washed up on the beach with the last of his crew and nursed them all back to life – and of the Rakshasa, the great monster they'd hunted together while Gallow always looked for roads north that would take him home. As snow fell outside, he spoke of how he found the pass through the mountains, the Aulian Way to the Varyxhun valley, and at the same time the secret that would kill the Rakshasa, how he'd gone back to the desert and to Oribas to finish their hunt and how he'd lost the red sword in that battle, the one and only lie in everything he said. She looked at him hard when he told her that and asked many questions, and he knew she didn't know whether to believe him but here and now he didn't care. In a way he was speaking himself out, since the Vathen in Andhun would surely kill him once they knew who he was. They'd ask him about the sword over and over, and either he'd break as they tortured him or he wouldn't but the end would be the same.

She came back, that was what mattered, and when the cold came as he knew it would and the snow lay thick and men shivered and died under their blankets at night, she made sure they kept him warm. He got her name out of her. Mirrahj Bashar. He couldn't think of much reason to lie about the rest and so he told her how it was: how a forkbeard had come across the mountains after three years of looking for the way home and found himself caught between the Marroc and his own people. How other forkbeards had been looking for the sword too and how they wouldn't let him be. How he'd found himself fighting his own brothers of the sea, killed the man who'd been his best friend in the world and found his family at last only to leave them again. How his wife had sent him away. How the Marroc had thrown him out and how he'd long ago burned all bridges with his own kin.

'So you see, Vathan, there's no peace for me and never has been, except for this. I'm done. Kill King Sixfingers and then perhaps I can go home. I'd like to see my sons grow into men, even if they want nothing to do with me. But if that's not to be then best I stay away. Far away. It's no hurt what you're doing, taking me from where I was.'

Mirrahj Bashar listened quietly to it all, and when he was done she didn't laugh or spit, only shook her head. 'I'm sorry, forkbeard, but I don't think that's your future. We'll see the walls of Andhun tomorrow.' She touched his face, a finger on his cheek. Gallow had lost count of the days they'd been on the move since Hrodicslet but it had been more than a week. Like it or not, he was growing a beard.

As she'd said, the middle of the next day brought them to Andhun. Gallow looked up at the gatehouse as they rode beneath it, thinking of the times he'd been this way before. With the Screambreaker more than a decade ago. With Tolvis Loudmouth on the day he'd decided not to go home just yet after all. Walking the other way with Valaric the morning after he'd burned Jyrdas on the beach, with a hundred Marroc howling for his blood. They crossed the square where he and Valaric had stood, side by side, alone against Medrin and his men. He'd never thought to see Andhun again.

Instead of the castle, the Vathen swarmed into the horse market. If they'd been Lhosir they would have kicked a few Marroc for the fun of it, and the Marroc would have shouted back and maybe thrown stones and fistfuls of dung, and then before you knew it there would have been blood and dead men all over the place. The Lhosir liked a fight, and once they started they weren't that keen on stopping. But the Vathen simply told the Marroc to go and then waited, and the Marroc went and no one killed anyone.

'Last chance, forkbeard.' Mirrahj came and sat beside him after she'd eaten with her ride. She offered him a piece of gristly meat and a skin of water. 'I'll give you to the ardshan tomorrow. If you're who you say you are, he'll remember your face and kill you slowly. I've been kind to you, forkbeard, kinder than others might have been. Tell me where the sword is. The ardshan will get it out of you in the end anyway.'

'In the desert of Aulia, far beyond the southern mountains.' Gallow smiled and drank the water. Mirrahj snatched the meat away from him.

'You're lying to me, Gallow Foxbeard of the Lhosir.'

'It's the only answer I have for you, Mirrahj Bashar of the Vathen.'

'If I let you go?'

'But you won't.'

'I might promise to kill you quickly and without pain.'

'I wouldn't believe you.'

'What if I told you that I meant to find the sword for myself and overthrow the ardshan and proclaim myself Daughter of the Weeping God and rule over all my people?'

'Then you're no different from any other.' He almost smiled. 'A dull answer. You can do better.'

Mirrahj Bashar laughed and threw the meat to him anyway. 'Enjoy it. It's the last you'll see.' She made as if to leave and then stopped and looked at him intently. 'You know what I think? I think you're telling me the truth when you say you left it behind. I think you're telling me the truth when you say it's cursed and when you say you want nothing more to do with it. All that happened to you, you choose to blame on Solace. Foolish, but then you *are* a forkbeard. There's a change in your face when you talk about things that matter, and so I believe you, all of what you say except the where.' She shuffled closer. 'You *did* leave it behind, but not in Aulia. That's the lie. So where is it, forkbeard? It's somewhere closer, isn't it?'

Gallow shook his head and looked away. Saying nothing, that was the best defence when the questions started. The whole truth or else say nothing at all.

'If you'd left it somewhere that was beyond grasping, you'd have told me, safe and sure that it didn't matter. So it's not in Aulia, but if you didn't lose it in Aulia then you brought it back.'

Gallow caught her smiling at the corners of her eyes. He shrugged.

'Nothing to say, forkbeard? You left the sword up in the mountains, didn't you? There's a road from Andhun that heads south on the other side of the Isset. Goes all the way up there. The Marroc call it the Aulian Way. Not too hard to guess where it goes.'

'It's on the other side of the river,' murmured Gallow. 'There's no place to cross. You know that.'

'Oh, but there is. Go far enough and there must be. Tell me, forkbeard. Tell me and take me to it and I'll let you live. I'll let you go. I know what it's like to want to go home.'

Gallow shook his head. Mirrahj got up and patted him on the shoulder. Later she came back and brought him the remains of a roasted goat's leg, one with some decent meat still on it, and Gallow knew it was a goodbye of sorts. Made him wonder if Medrin's Lhosir would have treated Mirrahj Bashar as kindly if they'd taken her. Probably not, all things considered. He ate his fill, rolled onto his side and let his thoughts drift. If they killed him, so be it. Tomorrow was another day.

8

KING SIXFINGERS

In the darkness of the new moon the Legion of the Crimson Shield slipped into the waters of the Isset in a hundred tiny boats and pushed away from the banks. Each had a muffled paddle, but for the most part there was no need for them for the river was already beginning to swell with the first meltwater from the mountains. In each boat a handful of soldiers hid under fur cloaks, eyes at the front to watch their way, tugging on strings to one man at the back trailing a paddle in the water to steer them. There were no words, no whispers. They floated in silence.

On the far side of the river Thanni Ironfoot and two dozen men had crossed the Isset at dusk, hours before the little boats left. Now they ran, trotting along the bank in ones and twos, watching for Vathen. It was a dangerous sport. There might not be any Vathan sentries on the river at all so far north of Tarkhun and the massing Lhosir army. Or there might be any number. If that was the case then Ironfoot and his hunters had to find them and kill them quickly and without alarm, and all the while they had to stay ahead of the little boats, and that meant they had to run through the night. Which was just as well, because the night was as cold as an ice witch's kiss.

Three miles short of Andhun they found their first watchers. Three Vathen, clustered up close to a fire. The cold was a blessing, Ironfoot reckoned. Man stood around for long away from a fire on a night like this, he froze and died. So the Vathen were beside their fire, two snoring like old drunks while the third sat on a log, head drooping and jerking back up again. Ironfoot got close enough to hear the Vathan's breathing. The Vathan's head jerked up one last time. Ironfoot came from behind and covered the space between them in three long strides, clamped a hand over the man's face and opened his throat with a long-edged knife. He held the Vathan good and tight well after the blood stopped spraying out towards the river. He'd done it quietly enough, but by then the other Vathen had stopped snoring. They'd stopped breathing too. The Lhosir cleaned their knives and ran on.

A mile out of Andhun they slowed. The banks of the river grew steeper as the Isset closed in on the sea, as though the land itself had risen to try and keep the water back and the river had simply cut deeper and deeper. A steep ridge rose in front of them and Ironfoot smelled smoke. He crept closer and saw a Vathan down by the bank, awake and alert. He threw a stone. The Vathan looked the other way and Ironfoot ran silently up behind him and split the back of his neck with an axe. Then he waved the men running behind him to a halt, made a circling motion and pointed to the ridge. He took a moment to catch his breath and then led them away from the river at a fast jog, following the bottom of the slope until they'd covered a good half a mile; then they climbed it, quiet as thieves. The men with the best legs went on over and down the other side to keep on to Andhun; the rest followed him, creeping back along the top of the ridge. He had no idea how far behind the little boats were by now, but no real distance.

Close to the river again he could finally see what he was dealing with – fifty or sixty men, so surely at least one other sentry watching the river and probably two. He waited for his Lhosir to get ready. They looked at one another and closed their eyes and muttered words to the Maker-Devourer, then went forward on their hands and knees, silent as owls. Close up he could hear the Vathen talking, the handful who were awake – away on the side of the camp looking down over the Isset. Half his men spread out behind him and got on with the business of slitting sleeping throats. He led the rest himself, just four, creeping silently through the night like shadows, closer and closer to where the Vathen sentries—

A shout broke the silence behind him. What or why made no difference and he didn't look back, just rose and rushed forward.

The Vathen turned. They saw him coming, but only so the surprise was still written on their faces when he ran his spear into the belly of the first and buried his axe in the face of the next. The other two sentries cried out before they died but it made no difference now. The Vathen were waking up faster than his Lhosir could kill them. Then again, his Lhosir were in mail and furs and had their spears already in their hands. Made for an interesting fight for a while. Short, maybe a hundred heartbeats before it was done, but tense as a drawn knife.

When they were finished, Ironfoot looked out over the river where the Vathan sentries had sat. He could see the first shapes in the water, silently drifting with the current towards Andhun. Hard to see what they were without a moon, but then he didn't need to see to know they were the boats.

When the first shouts woke him, Moonjal Bashar jerked upright to see the dark shape of a man standing over him. The man had a spear raised ready to run him through. In that moment Moonjal couldn't have said whether the man was a Lhosir or a Vathan or a Marroc but the sight was enough. He threw himself sideways, rolled as far and fast as he could and tipped himself off the side of the ridge. He tumbled and bounced down the slope and landed in a thicket beside the river, too winded to do more than lie still.

'Where are you, bandy-legs?' When he looked back he could make out the shape of a man coming cautiously down the slope after him. The words gave him away: a forkbeard. Moonjal stayed exactly where he was, still as a mouse. The Lhosir wouldn't see him unless Moonjal moved or the forkbeard trod on him. The man had a shield as well as his spear and he probably had a sword or an axe on his belt. Moonjal had all of these things too, only they were lying on the top of the rise next to the furs where he'd been sleeping.

He was shivering already. *That* was what was going to give him away. Or the mist of his breath. Cursed cold!

The forkbeard wasn't stupid. He was coming at a steady pace, not rushing, keeping his shield low to guard his legs, poking his spear into each clump of grass. He was heading the right way too. 'Come on, horse boy. Come and play.'

Moonjal's fingers touched the haft of the knife strapped to his calf. It was a nice knife, an old piece of Lhosir steel sheathed in Aulian gold and looted from Andhun. Strapping it to his calf had been to make sure no one stole it but he'd not say no to luck, however it came. He bent forward now, fingers closing around it, as slowly and gently as he could, trying to stay invisible.

A twig snapped beneath him as the knife came free. The forkbeard's head whipped round, looking right at him. The man growled under his breath. 'That you, horse boy?' He was coming straight at Moonjal now, crouched low, shield covering almost all of him, spear jabbing. Moonjal froze. If he moved a muscle, the forkbeard would see him now, or hear him. If he tried to get up and make a dash for it, the forkbeard would run him through with his spear. If he tried scrambling deeper into the thicket ... He had no idea how thick the undergrowth was. He might get away or he might not, but the forkbeard would still be after him and he'd still be on his hands and knees.

The Lhosir eased in closer. Moonjal stayed absolutely still, hoping the forkbeard didn't tread on him. A snapped twig. *Could* have been an animal. The forkbeard stopped with his feet so close they were practically touching Moonjal's arm. The Vathan heard him breathing, slow and harsh, the long deep breaths of a stalking hunter. He was whispering to the air, 'Where are you, Vathan?'

The bushes rustled and shifted above Moonjal as the forkbeard lunged with his spear. Moonjal held his breath. The spearman took another cautious step. His foot came down on Moonjal's leg and slid sideways. Moonjal jerked – couldn't help it – and for a moment the forkbeard lost his balance. He grunted in surprise. Moonjal rammed the knife into the forkbeard's thigh, nice and high under the skirts of his mail, and hacked hard. The forkbeard staggered back, tripped and fell. For a moment as he toppled over they were face to face in the blackness, but then the forkbeard was down and Moonjal was hauling himself to his feet and never mind the thorns that shredded his hands. He started to run but then realised the forkbeard wasn't moving.

When Moonjal went back to look, the forkbeard was dead. The grass around him was sticky and wet with blood.

Shouts rang out from the top of the ridge. He crouched beside the body for a moment and looked up. The slaughter was still going on but no one else was coming down. Good enough. He stayed with the forkbeard long enough to help himself to the man's shield, helm and spear, but by the time he'd armed himself, the sounds of fighting were dying down. He could hear voices, forkbeard voices, which meant his ride was destroyed or fled and the forkbeards had won, and that was when he realised he had no idea how many of them were here, just a short march from the walls of Andhun, in the middle of the night and on the wrong side of the river.

He dragged the dead forkbeard into the thicket and started to strip him. He was mostly done when the first of the boats began to drift by. At first he couldn't imagine what the large misshapen lumps were, then he saw one of them move, saw a forkbeard head poke out from under the furs at the front, and understood. But by then it was too late.

King Medrin Sixfingers, king of the Lhosir and the Marroc and bearer of the Crimson Shield of Modris the Protector, peered at the walls of Andhun rising ahead on either side of the river. The Vathen had spent three years making sure he couldn't simply build a fleet of boats and cross the Isset into the eastern half of the city and now only a fool would try an assault from the river. There were walls along the eastern bank and lookout towers and simply nowhere for boats to land short of the harbour. There were a dozen sentries, all carefully protected from arrows and archers in walled-in posts that could only be reached through long stone passages from as far away as the city gates, and each lookout had a bell and a small fire to light, both of which could raise the alarm. Three full rides of Vathan warriors had their barracks along the river defences, armed with thousands of javelots. The ardshan's Aulian tinker had shown the Vathen how to make little stone throwers and ballistae to fire their javelots harder. They had a good collection of Marroc fish oil too, for throwing into the river and setting the water alight. More to help their eyes than to burn Lhosir maybe, but to the Vathen watching the river either was as good as the other.

For three years Andhun had been split in two like this, and for three years Medrin had waited, but no more. He gave the word, and the little boat that carried him turned towards the shore still a full half-mile from the city walls. Behind him a hundred other boats did the same.

Only a fool would try an assault from the river.

At the edge of Andhun harbour, among the rocks and the breaking waves at the foot of the cliffs, a handful of men encased in iron rose out of the water and clawed their way to the shore. No one saw them come. There were caves at the bottom of the cliff and some of them led up into the castle. A few of the iron-skinned men clambered into them, but most crept and scraped along the foot of the cliffs. The passages under the castle were no secret any more. They'd be guarded and the ironskins had other duties tonight. They walked around the cliff paths, fourteen of them clinging to the shadows. Now and then they stopped, pausing as idle eyes awake in the middle of the night swept across them. They were no ordinary men, these warriors. They were the Fateguard, servants to the Eyes of Time, all Lhosir once but something else now, thieves and murderers and rapists and traitors, the worst *nioingr*, outcasts handed over in chains to the white ship that sailed now and then to the land of the Ice Wraiths. Now they had come back.

The Eyes of Time had not made them to be subtle tools but they had instincts beyond those of ordinary men. They slipped through the edges of the lower city, away from the castle, away from all the places where the Vathen might keep watch, sidling through the darkest narrowest alleys where the Marroc lived. Once they saw a Marroc thief coming the other way. The thief saw them too. He squealed and ran to cower in the darkest place he could find. They let him go – he'd not warn any Vathen, after all. They climbed steep and narrow alleys, closer and closer to Andhun's gates, past the door to the Grey Man inn and along the very same alley where Valaric and Gallow had once held half an army of Lhosir at bay long enough for the Marroc to flee to their ships and boats – or so the story was told among both the Marroc and the Lhosir in their very different ways.

There wasn't much to be done about the gatehouse itself. There were Vathan guards outside the doors, standing close to their braziers and rubbing their hands, and then there were the doors themselves, thick iron things held shut and barred from the inside. The Fateguard entered the square. They walked quickly now, keeping to the shadows for as long as there were shadows to be had, then brazenly out in the open.

'Stop! Who goes there?'

The Vathen were quick to pick up their spears and shout the first alarms. When one turned and ran, a Fateguard threw his spear and brought him down. The guards screamed and threw themselves forward. The Fateguard barely slowed their pace. They shattered spears and bodies and bones without a thought and then the Vathen were dead or fled and broken.

One of the Fateguard stood before each iron door and placed a palm against it. Fingers of brown rust spread across the iron like cracks in glass – across the door and across the skin of the Fateguard alike. The fingers spread in fast fits and starts, fattening as they went until both the doors and the skin of the Fateguard were crazed with brown cracks.

Alarms sounded up and down the city, then finally a bell from the castle itself. More Vathen came but they were too few and too late. The Fateguard ringed the gatehouse doors, their iron skins turning aside the Vathan spearheads, their swords striking with the deadly speed of snakes. A dozen Vathen died, their blood spreading in dark puddles across the stones. The last few backed away, fearful yet entranced. The iron doors were flaking and so too were the two Fateguard whose magic was eating them. Both were pitted and cracked. Dead leaves of corroded metal peeled away and snapped and fluttered to the ground. With a crack one of the rusting Fateguard snapped at the waist and toppled sideways. His hand remained pressed to the door, welded in place by the rust. The rest of his armour broke into pieces as it hit the cobbles. The armour was hollow now, nothing but dust left of the man who'd once been inside.

The other Fateguard kicked at the doors. Ruined iron buckled and twisted and then the hinges snapped and the bolts shattered. The gates fell, the iron turning to powder, doors and rusting Fateguard both. Inside the gatehouse the Vathan soldiers hurled their javelots and fired their crossbows. Bolts struck iron and did nothing. A well swung axe severed an iron hand at the wrist but the Fateguard barely seemed to notice. The axeman had enough time to see there wasn't any blood, to feel the horror rise inside him before a sword slammed into his belly, doubling him over, and then came again, point first down on the back of his neck and out through his mouth. He spewed his own blood over his feet as he died, and there on the floor right in front of him was the severed hand, still in its iron skin and not a drop of blood at all. Nothing but old dead meat.

Andhun's gates were already opening as the last of the Vathen died. Back outside the gatehouse, shadows began to move – Lhosir, running out of the darkness, their king leading the way. They poured through the gates and swept as fast as they could through the upper city, straight for the castle. The Fateguard retraced their steps toward the sea, down to the foot of the cliffs and along the shore.

This time they turned for the caves.

9

THUNDER AND LIGHT

A crash woke Gallow in the night. His eyes flicked open but the rest of him stayed perfectly still. The sky was dark, just starting to grey where the sun would rise in another hour, as shouts spread through the horse market: 'Arms! To arms! Forkbeards!'

A Vathan ran past him, throwing mail over his head. The riders who'd been his guard were scrambling to their feet, snatching up their javelots, casting their eyes around wildly in the dark, searching for the enemy. Gallow rolled into the far corner of the yard and curled up in the moonshadows, trying to make himself small. Trying to be unseen.

'Get up! Get up!' He recognised the voice. One of the men who wanted to be bashar in place of Mirrahj. Josper, was it? Something like that. 'Forkbeards inside the walls! Arm your-selves! To your horses!' Three Vathen ran past heading the other way, then more and more spilled out into the yard, and now Mirrahj was screaming at them to stay together, and right in the middle of the chaos a dozen Lhosir burst in through the market gates and launched themselves at the Vathen, who almost broke even though they had three times the numbers. He saw Mirrahj and Josper both hurl themselves at the Lhosir, stalling their charge as the men around them wavered; and then at last the Vathen rallied and the Lhosir pulled seamlessly back behind their wall of shields and spears and withdrew to leave a dozen Vathen dead in the yard. Josper screamed at the Vathen to charge after them and Mirrahj screamed at them to hold and for a moment the two of them stood nose to nose ready to fight, but by then the Lhosir were gone. Josper swore something and spat. The Vathen dragged their horses into the yard and threw themselves into their saddles, some of them barely dressed but all of them furious. They hurtled away in dribs and drabs, Mirrahj's last cries echoing back: 'The castle! The castle!'

Forgotten, hobbled and with his hands tied behind his back, Gallow was alone. A quiet settled over the yard. In the distance he heard shouting and screams. He waited a moment in case the Lhosir came back or any last Vathen came rushing through, but none did. The sounds of fighting were fading.

Among the fallen lay one dead Lhosir. Gallow rolled across the yard towards him. Vathan javelots – light things for throwing from the back of a horse – were useless for what he needed, but a Lhosir spear was heavy with a good sharp edge that sliced and slashed as well as stabbed. He fumbled with his fingers, sliding the haft behind him, easing the bladed head against the ropes around his wrists and then rocking back and forth, slicing them thread by thread. The spear kept slipping and he kept having to find it again and line it up right, but one by one he felt the strands of rope snap, more and more pieces of it tickling his fingers. He felt the rope give, a bigger jolt this time, and then the spear slipped again and the rope unravelled and fell apart and his hands were suddenly free. A few seconds more and he'd untied the other ropes. He scrambled over to the fallen Lhosir and took the soldier's belt and his boots and all his weapons bar one. The last was a knife. He wrapped the dead Lhosir's fingers around it. 'I don't know this man, Maker-Devourer, but I saw him fall. His death was brave and worthy of your cauldron.'

He picked up the Lhosir's shield and saw its design, painted like the Crimson Shield of Modris the Protector. The last time Gallow had been in Andhun, the Legion of the Crimson Shield had been Prince Medrin's personal soldiers. He stared at it and at the dead Lhosir on the worn stones. Did that mean that Sixfingers was here? Until now he'd had every intention of running, caught between Vathan and Lhosir armies, none of whom were friends. But if Sixfingers himself was here ...

A terrible purpose swept into him. He hurried through the horse market. His sword hand itched. *Medrin.* If Medrin was here they could end it between them. One of them would die, and either way Arda and his sons would be safe. A snarl curled his lip – best if it was Medrin who was the dead one. He crouched in the black shadows of a doorway. No one would hunt him if Medrin was dead. The two of them could finish it; and even if the war wasn't done and the fighting wasn't over, he could leave all this far behind and go back to who he was, throw away his sword and hammer his spear into something more useful. Arda would have him again if he could promise her that was how it would be. Forget the red sword. Leave it with the Marroc in Varyxhun or lead the Vathan woman to it. He didn't know, didn't care. But Medrin had to die first. Right here and now nothing else mattered.

He picked up his Lhosir spear and walked out of the horse market, turned the first corner and was almost ridden down by a dozen Vathen.

'Forkbeard!' One of them threw a javelot. Gallow lifted his shield to knock it aside and then dived into an alley too narrow for the horses to follow. Jeers came after him. 'Coward! *Nioingr*! Sheep lover!'

'Leave him!'

The voice that rose over the others was Mirrahj. Gallow ran back to the end of the alley. 'Mirrahj Bashar!' The horsemen were disappearing back into the market, half-lost in the shadows cast by the houses pressed tight around them; but as he stood and watched she came back. She kept her distance on the back of her horse, spear levelled at his face, while Gallow kept his back to the alley and his feet ready to run.

'My pet forkbeard! Fortune smiles on you.'

'I mean to look for King Sixfingers so that one of us might kill the other. These are his men here. Where might I find him?'

'The forkbeards are at the castle. I'm sorry to tell you that they're already inside, so you might find it hard.' She lifted her spear. 'I'm glad the ardshan won't be ripping you apart, forkbeard. I'll look for you on the battlefield so I might do it myself.'

'I mean to kill him, Mirrahj Bashar.' Gallow saluted and backed away. 'You were a fine enemy. Better than many a friend.'

He turned, letting the night swallow him, and ran uphill, always uphill towards the castle. The alleys of Andhun, all too narrow for a man on a horse, made it easy. Now and then he darted across open streets, and sometimes there were riders and sometimes they saw him and shouted and threw their javelots but they were always too slow and they never gave chase. Some of the streets were empty, others he had to wait while dozens of Vathen cantered past, but they never looked down or to the side, always up and towards the castle. In one small square he had to creep around fifty riders. He could hear the Lhosir by then, their battle shouts splitting the night, barked cries of men with weapons ready, and he heard the beating of swords and spears on shields and the bellows of men readying themselves to fight and then the clash of arms, the animal howls, the screams of horses and of the dying. Yet as he drew close to the castle square, the sounds of fighting dropped away. For a few minutes the city fell quiet, and in that stillness Gallow reached its heart.

In the grey gloom of almost dawn, dead Vathen littered the cobbles. A hundred Lhosir barricaded the castle gates, shields pressed tight together, spears arrayed over the tops. They had their own dead too, dragged back through the ranks by now, but Gallow could see them through the thin line of spears, the Lhosir who were too wounded to fight dragging the dying back into the castle yard, talking among themselves to see who knew each man to speak them out. Scores of Vathan horsemen rode back and forth in front of the shield wall, just out of reach, taunting with words and javelots. The Lhosir held their ground, howling insults of their own and throwing the Vathan javelots right back at them. Fists clenched, spears shook, horses snorted and men bellowed, each side firing itself up for the next crash of iron.

At the edge of the square Gallow watched them all, and then he stepped out from the shadows and strode between them. Spears and eyes swivelled to greet him as he ignored the Vathen, stopped a pace short of the Lhosir wall and lifted his spear over his head and let out a roar: 'Medrin! Medrin Sixfingers! King *Nioingr*! Gallow Truesword waits for you!'

The Lhosir looked at one another and cocked their heads and shook them. One of them started to laugh and soon they all were. 'You just stay there calling for him.'

Someone threw a stick. A stone pinged off his shield. Then the ground under his feet was trembling – he could feel it tickling his soles – and the Lhosir weren't looking at him any more, they were looking across the square to the wide road down to the harbour.

'Medrin!'

The rumble of hooves grew louder still, and with a great roar another hundred Vathan riders thundered into the square and hurled themselves towards the Lhosir line, veered away from the spears at the last second and hurled their javelots. Stranded between them, left to choose whether to run or to be trampled, Gallow ran, and as he did he cast a glance back. The reluctant sun was creeping over the horizon now and the tops of the castle towers lit up, suddenly bright. In the square the Lhosir bellowed and roared their taunts, the Vathen howled and hooted back, javelots flew into shields, spears reached out to stab at man and horse alike. Animals and soldiers screamed and the air reeked of blood. Back in the shadows Gallow looked wildly for another way through, a weakness in the Lhosir wall. Then he saw the rising dawn light the balcony over the castle gates. Men stood there, and Gallow stared at them until the sun touched the square and struck his eyes, dazzling him, pulling him out of its shadows.

'Forkbeard!' A Vathan horseman pointed a spear at him. In a flash, a group of riders had turned towards him. He was still dazed by the light and the figure on the balcony. He turned to run and a javelot hit him between the shoulders hard enough to hurl him forward and sprawl him across the cobbles. The horsemen came up behind him. He could barely move. For a first helpless moment he couldn't tell whether his mail had held and turned the point or whether the javelot had driven right through him and he was about to choke on his own blood. He'd been kicked by horses a few times and that had hurt far less less.

Spears prodded at him. And then they stopped. 'Where is it, forkbeard?'

He laughed. When his mouth didn't fill up with blood, he hauled himself to his hands and knees and Maker-Devourer damn the pain that came with that. 'You followed me here to ask me that?'

He could hardly move his sword arm at all. He pushed

himself up and rose shakily to his feet. There were half a dozen Vathen around him, all with their spear tips an inch from his mail. Mirrahj looked down at him. It was a cold look. 'Where is it? Tell me and walk away.'

His back was agony but he still looked up past the Vathen, back to the castle and the men standing on the balcony over the square. He squinted until he was sure, but he'd known it right from the start. Medrin. Medrin had taken the castle. The Lhosir had won Andhun. Which meant there was nothing to stop them from marching on Varyxhun.

The Vathen followed his eyes, even Mirrahj. 'The ardshan,' she whispered.

'It's in Varyxhun,' said Gallow quietly. 'I left it in Varyxhun. Did you hear me?' He looked from one Vathan to the next to the next. 'Your sword Solace. It's in Varyxhun.'

Mirrahj leaned down and hissed, 'And where is this Varyxhun, forkbeard? Tell me!' It hadn't even crossed his mind that she wouldn't know.

'I'll do better.' He offered the hand that still worked. 'Keep your word, Mirrahj Bashar, and I'll show you.'

She smiled and laughed again, though it was a bitter sort of laugh. Once he was on the back of her horse, she turned and rode for Andhun's gates.

10

SHADEWALKER

Come the morning, Reddic was still alive, barely. He was still scared too and there was no barely about *that*. None of them knew how long the shadewalker followed them. Certainly for a while after they left the farmhouse. Stannic had been happy enough to pace it for a while. 'To see how fast this one goes,' he said. Reddic had stayed at the back as he'd been told. Once he got over his terror he caught up with Stannic and his family. He could see by then that the shadewalker wasn't about to catch them and kill them and eat them and rip out their souls and turn them into more shadewalkers or whatever it was they did. So he went to the front with Stannic because he was supposed to be a soldier of Valaric's Crackmarsh men, hard as nails and ready to fight forkbeards, and so that's where he ought to be. Stannic hadn't been best pleased but he'd stopped moaning once he decided the shadewalker had given up on them. This was the third he'd met this winter and the fourth in his life, and yes, the first one had made him shit his pants too, thanks for asking. But they weren't too terrible once you knew they couldn't run, and any man with his wits and both his legs could escape. They'd follow a scent through the whole night sometimes, so a man had to pace himself, but they always stopped at sunrise and disappeared into the dark. Or the three he'd met so far had all done that. When Reddic asked whether this one might be different, both of them wished he hadn't.

Come morning they were exhausted, blue with cold and half frozen, but Stannic had had the cunning to lead them in a great circle and so they weren't that far from the farmhouse where they'd started. They all stopped for a bit and agreed that Stannic would stay where he was and keep watch for the shadewalker in case it was still following them, and that Reddic would go on to the farmhouse with everyone else because, well, because they were all blue with cold and half frozen but also because they were scared the shadewalker might have gone back to the farm, all of them except for Stannic, who said he knew better. So Reddic went with the others and felt stupid because he didn't know the land and could only follow while they scrambled through trees and crossed streams and floundered in drifts of snow, and then it turned out that the shadewalker *had* gone back to the farmhouse after all, some time in the middle of the night, and eaten Torvic's face. Or just possibly it had dragged Torvic from where it had killed him and left him hung up in a field and then gone away, and it was some wild animal that had come and eaten his face afterwards. Didn't seem likely, but after he'd found Torvic and finished with puking everywhere, Reddic thought he liked that idea somewhat better.

'What are they?' he asked when Stannic finally came back, but he only shrugged.

'Cursed men,' he said. He followed the tracks the shadewalker had left around the farm. It had come back and taken Torvic and done what it had done and then walked around the farmhouse three times before heading away again. 'South,' said Stannic, squinting in the bright morning light. 'Middislet way, I'd say. Walking pretty straight.' He chuckled and punched Reddic in the arm. 'Brave man could follow its trail in this snow. Find where it's hiding from the sun and put an end to it if he knew how.' Reddic shuddered and Stannic laughed. 'Braver man than me, that'd be.'

'There was a man in Varyxhun who did that,' Reddic said. 'An Aulian.'

They cut Torvic down. Wasn't much they could do for him now. Couldn't even bury him, not in this cold with the ground all frozen and covered by snow, so they took him out into the woods. Reddic said some words, though he didn't know much about Torvic or who he was or why he'd thrown in his lot with Valaric and the Crackmarsh. He took Torvic's mail and spear and his shield because Valaric would skin him for leaving good stuff like that out in the middle of nowhere. Not much else to do. Stannic seemed to know him better, so Reddic left the two of them alone with the winter trees and went back to the farm and tried to get some warmth into his skin again. When Stannic came back he gave Reddic some food and some kind words, and later that morning Reddic took his leave and headed south. Seemed like someone ought to warn the folk of Middislet there was a shadewalker coming. Didn't follow its trail though, not for long.

He spent the next night under the roof where he and Torvic had stayed on their way north with a surly old farmer Torvic had known, like he had seemed to know everyone between Fedderhun and the Crackmarsh. They barred and barricaded the door and took it in turns to keep watch. None of them got much sleep but the shadewalker never came, and by the end of the next day he was in Middislet again. He went to the forge first, thinking they could spread the word and thinking too that it might be as well to load up the mules Torvic had left there, ready to leave in the night if that was the way it went, but when he got there and banged on the door, it wasn't Arda or Nadric who answered but Jelira. Reddic stared at her, not sure what to say, and Jelira stared back and then turned bright red and looked away.

'Where's the smith?' he asked when he found his tongue again.

'In the big barn.' Jelira flashed him a glance. 'Mam's there too. With everyone.'

'Right.' So he ought to be there as well, to tell them about the shadewalker, but his feet weren't moving.

'You staying or heading off?' asked Jelira.

'Staying.'

She nodded. 'I'll make sure there's some more furs airing then. Cold as the Weeping God's tears these last few nights. Hard work for some keeping warm enough to sleep.'

She was smiling and Reddic wondered whether he was missing something, and then realised that yes, he was. He blushed furiously.

'Your friends here too?' Reddic shook his head, and she must have seen the death in his face because her smile vanished. 'You best go up to the barn if you've got news.'

When he reached it, most of the village was gathered inside. As he listened, Reddic realised they were already talking about the shadewalker, except they were talking about at least two – two seen last night, one the night before. He said his piece and told them how one had killed Torvic and eaten his face. Half of them left before he'd even finished, off back to their farms to hammer their doors closed or to take what they could and get away, although where they would go in the middle of nowhere with the nights cold enough to freeze a man's beard Reddic had no idea.

When they were done talking, Arda grabbed him and pinched his ear and marched him back to the forge. 'Don't know what you were thinking telling them about Torvic like that.'

'But that's what it did!'

'Doesn't mean people need to be hearing it. You saw them. They're afraid enough.'

'Aren't you?' She didn't look it and didn't sound it either, but when they got back to the forge she had him bring Torvic's mules into the house and keep their saddles on them, loose so they wouldn't trouble them but still on their backs, and while Reddic loaded them up with Nadric's arrowheads, Arda piled furs beside them. When they were done with that she put the children to sleep in the night room and then sat with him and Nadric. They both fell asleep, snoring curled up on the floor, but when Reddic closed his eyes he kept seeing the ruin of Torvic's face, which was no good for sleeping, and that was why he was awake when the scraping noises started in the yard between the house and the forge. He sat there listening, chills like ice running through his blood, and it struck him hard then that there wasn't any man in the house except old Nadric, who hardly counted, and that meant it was down to him to go and see what it was, and he was scared like he hadn't been since that first night in the Crackmarsh when the ghuldogs were all set to eat him. He prodded Arda awake. Might have been a rat after all, or a dog or a mule broken loose or a sheep wandered into the village. Could have been any of those things but he woke her anyway in case it wasn't.

'Heard something,' he hissed.

'Might be a pig. Roddic's keep getting loose lately.' But she sat up, sleep falling off her like he'd thrown snow in her face. He tried to believe it was a pig. Nothing had come knocking on the door after all, not like Stannic's place.

'Well, go and look then,' Arda said. Reddic looked at his mail and wondered if he should put it on, but then Stannic hadn't had any mail and it hadn't troubled him. He picked up his shield and opened the door a crack.

There were three of them crouched in a circle in the middle of Nadric's yard, scratching at the dirt as though they were searching for something. Like one of them had dropped a coin. They didn't look up. Reddic eased the door closed again, quietest thing he'd ever done. Then he nearly crapped himself. 'There's three of them.'

'Three what? Pigs?' She was poking Nadric.

'Three shadewalkers!'

There was something sharp on her tongue waiting to come out but it died before it was given sound. The colour drained from her face. 'Sure that's what they are, boy?' And he was, and she knew it too.

Boy? Damn but he was fed up with people calling him that. He drew himself up, trying to find some courage from somewhere. 'Yes, quite sure, old mother, may Modris protect us.' He liked the way her eyebrow shot up when he called her *old mother*. Took his mind off the death waiting outside.

'Go and see whether the way's clear outside the other door.' She scurried through the curtain to the night room and started shaking the children, whispering urgently in their ears. Reddic went to the front door and put his hand on it and then stopped. Something made his skin crawl. Instead of opening it he bent to peer around the cracks at the side. Couldn't see much but ...

It was right there. Standing in front of the door, waiting for him, still and silent as a statue. The one from Stannic's farm. He whimpered and pointed. 'Right. By. The door.'

In the night outside a scream broke the silence. It came again and again, a shrill cry of terror. After a bit another voice joined it, lower and deeper, shouting out the alarm. Arda was shushing the children, putting them into their furs, all urgent movement, leaving herself until last. She snatched up a bag of something from the corner of the house where she kept her pans and pressed it into Reddic's hands. 'Never mind swords and axes, the best weapon we've got against their sort's in there. They come smashing in, throw it in their faces and run. Don't you worry about us. Nothing wrong with our legs.'

He looked at the pouch. Opened it and sniffed.

'Salt,' she said. 'The Aulian wizard from Witches' Reach sent it to Gallow. For the shadewalkers. Suppose he knew they'd be coming. Don't know how, but that's wizards for you.'

Reddic flinched. Salt? What use was a bag of salt? He scurried to the back door and peered through the cracks. The shade-walkers were still there, crouched together. Three in one place, four if you counted the one standing by the front door – he'd never heard of such a thing. The three in the yard looked like they were looking for something. He'd never heard of that either.

As he watched, one of them stopped scratching and cocked its head. It began crawling on all fours from the middle of the yard towards the forge, scraping away the snow and sniffing at the dirt beneath as it went. 'What are they doing?'

'As long as they keep doing it outside.' There was a nervous edge to Arda's voice, and the only thing that stopped Reddic from falling to bits was the way Jelira kept looking at him. She looked terrified and so he kept his face straight. Couldn't show how scared he was in front of women and children and an old man.

The crawling shadewalker vanished into the forge. The other two followed. Reddic hissed at Arda, 'They're out of the yard. We can run now.'

Arda was already stuffing her feet into a pair of fur-lined boots. She hurried Nadric to the door, dragging the two oldest children after her. Reddic didn't even know their names, only that the boys had been fathered by Gallow the forkbeard. You could see it in the older one. He had forkbeard eyes, ice-blue and cold as a winter night. Arda took the smallest in her arms and pushed the younger girl at Reddic. 'You'll have to carry her. She can hardly walk all night.'

Nadric stood by the door. Arda opened it and ran, hauling

the mules out after her. She was carrying a pan, brandishing it as though it was an axe. Reddic pushed the two older children outside. From the shadows of the forge the shadewalkers re-emerged. Each carried a piece of the iron armour Torvic had brought from the Crackmarsh. They moved quickly, not quite running but walking fast. Arda was still struggling with the mules. Reddic ran out between them. 'Go! Quick!' He lifted his shield and waved his sword, and for some reason the shade-walkers stopped short. Arda got the mules going and hauled them away from the yard. Reddic stayed close, moving as fast as he could, while the shadewalkers simply watched them go. Around the corner another one was striding towards them, the one from the door. Arda started to run, but this shadewalker ignored them too and turned for the yard and the forge instead. When Reddic looked back into the village he could see there were others. A dozen maybe. He followed Arda and the mules out into the fields.

The shadewalkers were converging on the forge, all of them. When she saw this Arda stopped to catch her breath. 'What have you brought here?' she asked in horror. 'What have you done?'

A scream from the village spurred them on again. 'Nothing. I didn't bring anything.' But Torvic had brought the cursed armour of the ironskin, and that was what the shadewalkers were after. Last he saw of them they were all gathered around it, sniffing at it, pawing at it.

And then they were gone, lost in the darkness.

11

THE RIVER

Mirrahj kicked her horse and cantered through the chaos of Andhun to the gates and another heaving mass of horsemen milling in helpless anger. The gates were open but no one seemed to know what to do, whether the city was won or lost, how many forkbeards had come, whether to flee or to rally and fight. As they fought through the press of riders, a voice pierced the confusion. 'Mirrahj Bashar!' Mirrahj pushed towards a score of Vathen pressed tightly together. They were her ride, part of it. 'The forkbeards have destroyed the gates! They can't be closed.'

'We leave.' She had to shout over the cries of the other Vathen.

'No!' Josper's voice. Gallow had come to know it and now the Vathan was pointing a javelot at him. 'And what's that forkbeard doing here? You should kill him.'

Mirrahj raised her own javelot and levelled it back at him. 'We leave because I say we leave, Josper, and the forkbeard comes because I say he comes.'

Josper folded his arms and shook his head. 'You're no bashar, Mirrahj. We need to fight these forkbeards. We need to kill them.' He glared at Gallow. 'Starting with that one.'

'Then lead them, Josper. If you can.' Mirrahj looked past him. 'You all know me. I say we leave. I have good reason but I will not say what it is.'

Mirrahj's horse stumbled sideways as another barged into it. The shouting rose to almost deafening and then a river of horses surged into the square from deeper in the city, pushing and shoving their way to the gates and riding out into the fields beyond. Josper looked at them and sneered. 'Hakkha Bashar. You say we should turn our tails and flee like he does?' He turned to the other riders. 'I say we stand and fight! Look at our numbers! The battle is barely begun and this ... this *un-woman* would have us turn and run!'

Mirrahj spat. She didn't say a word, only turned her horse and joined the push for the gates. The walls and the towers either side were empty, held by no one. Gallow looked back. He saw Josper rise in his saddle and raise his javelot to hurl it – whether at Mirrahj or at him he couldn't tell – but the spear stayed in his hand and Gallow and Mirrahj were through the gates. The press of horses burst into the open space beyond. The other Vathen veered east, but Mirrahj turned south towards the river. She galloped away, full of eagerness to be gone from Andhun and everything it held, but her horse had barely found its stride before ahead of them, lit by the dawn light, Gallow spied a handful of figures walking towards the city.

Mirrahj hissed, 'Forkbeards,' and Gallow thought she'd turn and ride away since there were six or seven of them and only one of her, but instead she lowered her javelot and kicked her horse faster, heading straight for them. The Lhosir scattered as she came, jumping out of her path. Half of them were limping. 'Die!' she screamed at them as she turned her horse for another pass. 'What are you waiting for?'

Gallow pressed into her. 'No, Mirrahj of the Vathen. These are still my people.'

She reined in sharply, twisted and wrapped one arm around his back then heaved and tipped him sideways so he fell off. It was done with such fast grace that Gallow was on the ground before he knew it. 'Then get off my horse, forkbeard.'

The Lhosir had gathered again, protecting their wounded with a tight line of shields and spears. They watched but didn't come any closer. Gallow walked slowly towards them. The one in the middle had a face he knew. 'Thanni Ironfoot.'

Ironfoot laughed out loud. 'Well, well. And what should I call you, Gallow? I remember your name was Truesword once, but I've heard other names since. I heard you married a sheep. Doesn't look like a sheep to me.'

'Call me what you like, Ironfoot. Seems the Crimson Legion has taken Andhun castle. Don't know that they're going to hold it. There's a lot of angry Vathen inside those walls. Best you go and help where you can if that's what you're minded to do. Are my eyes still good, Ironfoot? Did I see Medrin in Andhun as the sun rose?'

Ironfoot laughed again. 'And why would I answer a man who rides with a Vathan?'

'Tell Medrin something for me, Ironfoot. Tell him, in case he doesn't already know, that Gallow Truesword came looking for him to finish what he started. Tell him I'll be waiting for him in Varyxhun if he has the stomach for it. Tell him the Comforter waits there too, if he has the strength to lift it in those crooked fingers of his.'

'If he's there, Gallow-who-rides-with-my-enemies.'

'He's there, Ironfoot, and you know it. But I'll not make you lie for him.'

Thanni Ironfoot dipped his spear in salute. 'The Scream-breaker loved you, Gallow. I wonder what he'd make of what you've become. Maybe it's as well he's gone.'

'I wonder what he'd make of us all, Ironfoot. What he'd make of a king who deals with the ironskins, who makes war on women and children. What he'd make of those who follow such a king. I wonder that all the time. I'd not head for the gates, if I were you. Not yet. More Vathen there than even you can bite.'

He turned his back on the Lhosir. Mirrahj was still where she'd dumped him off her horse and so he walked back to her. She didn't stop him from climbing behind her again, though it was hard with his shoulder so swollen and stiff from the blow he'd taken beneath the castle. Ironfoot and his Lhosir watched but they didn't move.

'What did you just do, forkbeard?'

'Told Medrin where to find the things he most desires. Called him to where I can kill him. And then I can go home.'

Mirrahj didn't reply. After a long pause she turned her horse and rode away leaving the Lhosir behind. She stopped again on the top of a ridge overlooking the river. Long shadows of morning sun streaked the ground now but there was no missing the bodies or the streaks of bright red blood in the whiteness of the snow. Mirrahj dismounted and poked at the dead with her foot. Caught by surprise, half of them murdered in their sleep, throats slashed, the others cut down before they could lift their shields or don a helm. Gallow counted a score of Vathen and there were clearly more. A couple of forkbeards too.

'They did this.' Mirrahj was looking down from the ridge towards Ironfoot and his Lhosir, limping on towards the city. In the morning light there was nowhere to hide. 'This was Moonjal Bashar's ride. The ardshan's son.' She sat heavily among the corpses and closed her eyes and then stood up again and walked among the dead, turning them over one by one and looking at their faces. Gallow left her to it; by the time she was done the sun had risen a hand higher and he'd lost sight of Ironfoot's men, still heading for the gates. Chances were they'd be dead soon.

'He's not here.' Mirrahj Bashar leaned on her javelot and held her head in her hand.

'Why didn't you stay and fight?' Gallow asked. 'Your riders were ready for it. Best I could see, Andhun could still go either way.'

'Because I'm sick of it, forkbeard, that's why.' She rounded on him. 'Did you count the size of my ride when we entered Andhun? There were eighty of us. I knew them all. More than just their names. I know the names of the children they left behind when they followed the Weeping Giant across the plains. I know the names of their wives who'll never see them again and of the brothers they once rode with who are nothing but bones now. We don't belong here, forkbeard. This isn't our land and none of us wants to be here, but we have no choice any more. We brought the Sword of the Weeping God here and then we lost it and now we can't go back. We just can't. Were you lying in Andhun or was that the truth at last?'

'The truth.' A pall of smoke was rising over the city now.

'Then take me to it and I'll take it back where it belongs and every Vathan for five hundred miles will follow me. We just want to go home, forkbeard.'

The words touched him deep enough to make his eyes swim. 'Three years I carried that burden.'

'Three years.' Mirrahj nodded. 'And more for those who followed the Weeping Giant and his dreams in the early days before he had all the clans drawn to his banner. The start wasn't so bad. Riding and riding and riding across lands almost bereft of anything but grass and wind. We smashed a small Marroc army at Fedderhun and we felt the calling in our blood. And then Andhun. Bloody Andhun, and yet we took everything this side of the river in the end, but what it cost us ... What you forkbeards did to us.' She shook her head and wiped her eyes. 'I was just a rider then. I had a man, a bashar himself, though I dare say I wouldn't have kept him long. But he was strong and wild, and you took him from me, you and yours, like you took the sword. After that nothing was right.'

Gallow watched her. He might have offered her the comfort of an arm but she was his enemy and he was hers, even if the pain they shared was deeper than any race or creed. He forced himself to look away. 'Many died at Andhun. Why did you come back looking for me?'

'Because without you I'd never find the sword.'

'But I'm a forkbeard.'

'But you know where the red sword rests.'

'And now I've told you, shall I be on my way?'

Mirrahj laughed. 'I took you, forkbeard, and you didn't care. There was no fear in you, no anger. All I ever saw was relief. And it took me a while, but by the time we reached Andhun I understood – I understood why it sang to my heart. Whatever it was you were fighting, it was over, and you were glad, because in the end there was no victory to be had, not really, and you've known that for a long long time. And I saw that in you and I saw that in myself, and the moment I did I was no longer fit to be the bashar of my ride. That's why I let Josper have his way. Are you done now, forkbeard, or shall I show you my other scars? I have plenty.'

He couldn't answer that. She was right. He'd never have seen it for himself, only ever felt the relief that nothing he did would matter any more, and yet this Vathan woman, a stranger to him, had put it into words. That was why he'd gone after Medrin instead of fleeing. To die. To make it all end. The knowledge made him shiver.

'Take me to it and I'll take my people home.'

Gallow shook his head. 'It's just a sword.'

'The Sword of the Weeping God, forkbeard! Older than the world.'

'I carried it for three years, Mirrahj Bashar. It's a sword with a strange colour to its steel and a very hard sharp edge, and that's all.' He sighed. *Home.* They all wanted the same, really. The Marroc of Varyxhun busy hanging forkbeards. The Vathen. Even the Lhosir, most of them. He'd seen it in Thanni Ironfoot's face clear as day, just as he'd seen it in the eyes of all the Screambreaker's men a dozen years ago before they'd finally sailed back across the sea. Home. Peace. To build their houses and farm their land and raise their sons and daughters. For a moment Gallow wasn't sure who was left who wanted anything else. Medrin? The red sword itself perhaps? Hard to see why they were all still fighting.

Mirrahj threw down her javelot with a snort and vaulted into her saddle. She rode away along the ridge, out of sight, and was away for so long that Gallow wondered if she was coming back. When she did she was leading another Vathan horse. 'Can you ride, forkbeard?'

Gallow nodded.

'I mean actually ride, not just sit there tight as a drum and hope you don't fall off like most of you forkbeards do.'

'I learned across the sea.'

'Then she is yours.' She handed him the reins. 'Treat her well. Which way to the sword?'

They made their way through the snow along the bank of the Isset. Gallow's thoughts wandered as they rode. He'd been lost when the Marroc threw him out of Varyxhun, but not any more. Medrin would come after him, and Medrin would come after the sword, sure as the sun rose each morning, and there'd be no peace until he was dead, and killing him wasn't going to be easy, even if it was what had to be done.

'I'll take you to the sword,' he told her when they stopped by the river to drink and rest. 'But I can't give it to you. You'll have to fight to make it yours and then you'll have to fight a deal harder to keep it. And then later you'll wish you hadn't.'

He turned away from the river when they mounted again,

heading to the south and east toward the distant Crackmarsh. He'd come this way once before.

12

THE CRACKMARSH CAVES

The Crackmarsh had been full of Marroc when the winter began. Most had left with Valaric. He'd taken about every man he could spare; but when he wasn't called Valaric the Mournful, he was Valaric the Wolf – so the old Marroc knew him – and he'd always known that one day the forkbeards might drive him back and so he'd prepared for that. A few men stayed behind then, left to watch the hideouts, keep the tame ghuldog packs in line and to watch what the forkbeards were up to nearby. The old men, the injured, the crippled, the ones who couldn't fight and a few that Reddic thought Valaric had left behind just to spite them.

The two old men left to keep watch over the Crackmarsh caves near Middislet might as well have been a pair of blind goats for all the good they did. Arda led the mules along the hill path and through the woods at the frozen edge of the water meadows and right inside the caves before either of them even knew she was there, and when Reddic woke them up from their snores, they were obviously both drunk as lords. He left them to it. They had half a night of darkness before them and the air was as cold as death's fingers.

'We'll be needing a fire.' Arda was bad from the cold. She'd been the last to dress and she hadn't put on enough. Her hands were blue and her head kept sagging. The children weren't much better, their sobs of exhaustion long since fallen silent. Only fear kept her going. Truth be told Reddic wasn't much better either, what with the nights he'd had after Stannic's farm, but he was the man among them now and so he made his shaking fingers rummage through the bags lying open beside the snoring watchmen. He found tinder and then their stash of dry cut wood and painstakingly blew on the embers of their old fire until he had a flame again and lovingly carried it to a new spot. Nadric was already asleep by the time he got it burning and Arda was fussing with the children, settling them around him, wrapping them all in the furs off her own back to keep them warm. 'Any more blankets here?' she asked after Reddic had been staring at the fire for a few minutes, rubbing the feeling back into his fingers, and he could have kicked himself for not thinking of that before. He ran off to look but came back empty-handed.

'Sorry.'

She'd found some straw from somewhere and piled it as close as she dared to the fire. Now she was sitting cross-legged on it, hands stretched out to the flames, shivering. Reddic took off his cloak and laid it over her and then took off his mail and sat beside the fire on the other side, watching her shudder and curl up tight and rub her hands and blow on her fingers. He'd spent the winter in the Crackmarsh, a good few nights in places with no fire at all. He'd seen men shiver like this and fall asleep and not wake up again, the life stolen out of them by the winter. Fire or no fire, without his furs he was already cold. Nadric had all four of the children wrapped around him, bundled up so tight that Reddic couldn't have said how many were in there. Arda had given them too much – or rather she hadn't left enough for herself.

He got up and came round the fire and lay down beside her, wrapping his fur tightly around both of them, pressing up against her, giving her his warmth. She was cold, just a thick woollen shift and a thin linen dress underneath the fur cloak she wore, and beneath it her skin was like ice. He wriggled closer and wrapped an arm around her. She never moved or said a word. Within minutes they were both asleep.

His dreams were strange that night in the cave. He was paralysed and there were shadewalkers everywhere. He was in the cave and they were shambling around him, talking. Then he was back in Middislet. He watched them tear open doors and drag women and children out into the snow and the air was full of screams. He never saw what they did, but he knew anyway because he kept seeing Torvic with his face bitten off, walking about the place. Then they were coming for him too, and he could run, only these shadewalkers could run too. They chased him for what felt like for ever until he reached the edge of a cliff and had to stop because there was nowhere left to go, and they were all around him and they closed in and dragged him down and tore off his helm. He was about to die but suddenly he was somewhere else, somewhere warm. Now he wasn't seeing a horde of hungry shadewalkers but Valissi, the girl he used to see in Tarkhun washing clothes by the river, only now she was leaning over him and she was naked and she had one hand pressed between his legs.

He woke with a start. There'd been enough nights when Reddic had been huddled up like this with others of Valaric's men trying to keep warm, and there was no accounting for dreams. There were no women in the Crackmarsh. He'd seen men disappear together now and then, and they all knew what happened, said nothing and looked the other way.

His hand was pressed into Arda's breast with her own hand clasping it. He could feel the nipple, hard as stone, and when he shifted his legs, trying to find a more comfortable way to lie, she followed him, her buttocks pressing into his crotch. He had no idea whether she was awake or asleep.

He twitched. Couldn't help himself. He tried closing his eyes, tried to think of other things, even made himself think of the shadewalkers and Torvic with his face ripped off, but it wouldn't go away. He kept seeing Arda's face and Jelira's too, seeing for the first time how alike they were. Without even realising he was doing it, his hand slid off her breast and slipped downward. Arda's hand stayed with him. As his fingers slipped between her legs she let out a little whimper and twisted slightly towards him. Her legs opened and his hand went on under the fur, feeling along her thigh until he found her skin and then reaching underneath the wool and linen and round to the inside of her leg and sliding back again; and then he shifted himself and pulled up his own shirt and pushed down his trousers and pressed his hands between her legs, pushing them apart from behind. She shifted now and then. Little movements but all to make it easier for him. He slid inside her and thrust hard. His hand ran up her skin, reaching for her breasts. He grunted with each push but Arda didn't make a sound, only perhaps breathed a little harder, and then came and was still. She shifted once or twice more as he twitched inside her, then a moment later he was asleep.

The morning woke him, late winter sunlight bright through the stunted trees at the mouth of the cave. He was still wrapped in his own fur but Arda was already up. She sat across the re-kindled fire, boiling a pot of water and chewing on a strip of black bread, and there was a bewilderment of people around him who hadn't been here the night before. He stared at them, wondering who they were and how they were here and why he didn't remember them. Most were still huddled under their furs but a few were shuffling about or squatting by the fire. When he grunted, Arda shot him a sharp look.

'If those two in that other cave are supposed to be your lookouts, I'd have a word with them if I were you. Still snoring fit to bring down mountains, they are. I dare say there's fork-beards standing right across the Crackmarsh with their ears tipped to the wind wondering what they're hearing. We had a look around, found where they kept their breakfast and helped ourselves. Hungry?'

'We?' Reddic was still staring at the other Marroc. It was as if they'd appeared by magic in the middle of the night while he'd slept.

'Did you think everyone else in Middislet was just going to stay there?' She snorted. 'These caves were ours to hide in long before your Valaric came along.'

Reddic nodded. He wrapped his fur around him and came closer to the fire. 'What if the shadewalkers come here too?' He leaned in, peering into Arda's pot, but before he could see what was cooking she smacked him across the knuckles with the stick she'd been using to poke the fire.

'Then we go somewhere else. Mother not teach you manners, boy?'

He stared at her. That was exactly the thing his mother had done before the forkbeards had killed her. 'She died last summer. And yes, old mother, she taught me some.'

Arda poked another stick into the pot and stirred it. 'Well I'm sorry to hear she's gone. Been a lot of people dying these last few years and not many of them for much of a good reason, if you ask me. Still no excuse for having no manners. Even little Pursic knows better and this is barely his fifth winter.'

'I'm sorry.' Reddic sat and looked at her and opened his mouth and closed it again. Fidgeted and opened his mouth a second time. 'About—'

'Manners, boy,' she said again. 'Manners.' Her voice softened very slightly. 'You did nothing wrong, if that's what you were wondering. And you did good with those shadewalkers.'

Reddic shook his head. 'No, I didn't. I practically shat myself, I was that scared.'

'No different from the rest of us then. Reckon my Gallow would have said the same too. Kept your head, that's what matters. Better than some would do.'

'You didn't look like you were scared at all.'

Nadric and the children were stirring now – the light or the smell of Arda's pot perhaps – and more of the villagers from Middislet were coming to sit around the fire, muttering to each other, whispering their stories. Arda picked up her pot and came and settled beside Reddic. 'I was scared right enough, lad. I've had one husband lost to the forkbeards and another lost to the sea only to show up again three years later. I've carried five children and lost one when it could barely lift its head. Jelira and Tathic I've seen sicken and nearly die and then fight their way to the living again. I had one forkbeard in my bed for eight years and another for nearly two. I had the Widowmaker himself in my house and stitched closed a hole in his head – though not until after I'd had a good long think about dashing his brains out, mind. Shadewalkers? I've met men who've hunted them. I was in Witches' Reach when the forkbeards were about to storm it. The Wolf hadn't crossed the bridge out of his swamp and we were all going to die, and badly too. I had the iron devil of Varyxhun in my yard once and his fingers around my throat. So I've seen a lot that's made me scared and would give me the shits again if it cared to, but I know how to deal with it. Put another few years on you and you will too.' She glanced behind Reddic to where Jelira and Feya and Tathic and Pursic were sitting in a row, all quietly watching her. 'Them.' She nodded, and for the first time Reddic had seen, a smile settled over her face, a real warm smile full of love. 'They're what keep me going. There's nothing in this world or any other that scares me like the thought of losing my little ones.'

'I'm not little any more,' grumbled the older boy. 'Pursic's little. I'm not.'

'You're all still little to me,' Arda snorted. 'Who wants to eat?'

She lifted the pot and passed it round, tipping some sort of runny white sludge onto old wooden plates she must have liberated from the same place she'd found the food. The children eyed it hungrily and Nadric already had his fingers in it when Arda raised a hand. 'Wait!' She took out the pouch she'd thrown at Reddic back in the house, the magic Aulian salt. He watched in amazement as she sprinkled a few flakes onto each plate. 'Just a little, mind.' She crouched in front of her children. 'Remember how I told you I met a wizard from Aulia last time we all had to run away, when the iron devil came?'

'Before da killed him and made you safe again,' said Jelira loudly.

'Which da?' the smaller of the two boys turned to look at the bigger one.

'Both of them, actually,' said Arda without even a blink. 'They did it together. And that was when I met a wizard from Aulia. He gave me this magic powder to keep us all safe. Just a pinch of it and those shadewalkers won't hurt us.'

'Is the wizard here?' Pursic's eyes were as wide as saucers.

Arda shook her head. 'He had to go somewhere else.'

'He was sent away to be hanged for helping our real da,' said Jelira. 'And then our real da went away to save him.'

'That's right.' Arda looked uneasy now. She put a hand to her mouth and heaved a long deep breath.

Tathic sniffed at the porridge and tasted it. His face lit up. 'Does that mean we can go home now?'

'I don't want to go home,' said Jelira. 'I want to find Gallow.' She turned to Reddic. 'He's still in the mountains near Varyxhun. He went to help Valaric the Wolf fight the forkbeards and send them away.'

'If he didn't get himself killed already,' whispered Arda.

Reddic leaned forward. He smiled at Jelira, taking her attention for a moment. 'Not many call him Valaric the Wolf these days. Mostly the Crackmarsh men call him Mournful. Wolf was his name in the war against the forkbeards.'

'So why do you call him Mournful?'

'Because he lost his family in the war, and even though that was more than a dozen years ago now, he still mourns for them.'

Jelira's eyes grew wide. She took a step closer. 'Did the forkbeards kill them?'

'No.' He almost told them how it had been cold and starvation and how a shadewalker had walked through their village one late autumn day and cursed them all, but then he looked at them, cold and hungry and with their village filled with shadewalkers, and thought better of it. Instead he dipped his fingers into Arda's porridge. He looked down at the children and made a happy face. 'Mmm! Good! I might have all of this!'

It might have been an accident that Arda kicked him right after he said that, but he could have sworn he saw just the tiniest flicker of a *thank you* on the corner of her mouth. They talked for a bit after that about what they should do, all of them together. Go back to Middislet maybe, since shadewalkers were wandering things who never stayed in one place for more than a night. In the end they agreed that Reddic and a couple of the men from the village would go and have a look and see whether it was safe. They didn't wait for Valaric's two guards to wake up, and Reddic spent half the walk imagining Arda giving them a good shaking and shouting-at until they were awake enough to realise their caves had been overrun by fifty-odd men and women and children and they hadn't even noticed.

It was an easy enough walk to Middislet and back and the air was a lot warmer that morning. Dull grey clouds filled the skies and a wind was blowing in from the north and the west, freshening with each hour they walked. They reached Middislet with the sun at its zenith and found the village half empty but not dead. The shadewalkers were gone. When Reddic looked, there were a few villagers already back in their homes, those who'd hidden in their cellars or walked or fled a different way

and come back in the morning, as Stannic had done. He talked
to them until he had a dozen different stories saying which way
the shadewalkers had gone or how many they'd been – five, fifty,
a hundred, and every possible way except north. Reddic settled
for there being maybe a dozen and they'd headed roughly
south. It amazed him that no one had been killed. It was the
forkbeard Gallow, he heard one of them say, who'd told them
about shadewalkers and what to do when they came. He'd
played games with the children, the ones whose parents would
let a forkbeard monster anywhere near them, and he'd pretend
to be the shadewalker and they had to see how close they could
get without him touching them.

Reddic even tracked the shadewalkers a little way, before a
fine drizzle made him think better of it. On the way back to
the Crackmarsh the rain fell steadily heavier, blurring the snow
and then washing it away, but the last tracks he'd seen had the
shadewalkers going south, close past the caves, and maybe it
would be better to get back to Middislet tonight after all. He
hurried and ran the last few miles, leaving the others to follow,
but when he got back to the caves, Arda came running out. She
grabbed him by the cloak and shook him, and this time there
was no hiding her fear.

'Jelira's gone.'

And all he could think of was that it was cold and it was
raining and it would be dark soon and then it wouldn't just be
the shadewalkers that came out. Here in the marsh it would be
the ghuldogs too.

13

CROSSING THE WATER

'I came this way before,' Gallow told her after he'd settled the argument about how to get to the Crackmarsh by simply riding off, and after she'd finished shouting at him and threatening to kill him when she'd had no choice but to follow. 'After Lostring Hill I went back home, close to the edge of the Crackmarsh. This is how I came to Andhun from there.'

They stopped beside a frozen pond. Mirrahj reversed her spear and smashed the ice around the edge so their horses could drink. Gallow drew a map in the snow with a stick. 'The Crackmarsh is here, the Ironwood here. We go around the top of the Ironwood and then cross the marsh to the Aulian Way. The road leads to the Varyxhun valley.'

Mirrahj pinched her lips. 'Crossing the Crackmarsh? So there *is* a way.'

'Probably about a dozen.' Gallow yawned.

'And you know them! Tell me!'

Gallow shook his head. 'You'll see soon enough. Until then it gives you another reason not to kill me in my sleep.'

'And why should I do that?' Mirrahj spat a laugh at the snow. 'We've both turned our backs on our people now.' When he took her hand she flinched and snapped it away, got up and went back to the horses. He understood her bitterness. 'Well, I have no secret to hold over you, forkbeard, yet I'll sleep easily enough. I don't think you're the throat-cutting sort.'

'No.'

They passed two nights together, huddled up in the best shelter they could find with the horses standing over them among a thick stand of trees on the first night, with a fire Mirrahj managed to light from the last handful of tinder she carried. The air was still bitter with a killing cold and snow still lay on the ground, but at least the winds hadn't come back to flay the skin from their hands and faces and strip the last of their warmth away. On the second night they found a crumbling shepherd's shelter. When morning came, Gallow's horse was dead. After that, a wind picked up. Heavy grey clouds scudded in from the north and the west and it began to rain, dreary, relentless and grey; but Gallow *had* been this way once before, and although years had passed since the Vathen had driven the Marroc from this part of the land, none had come back. When he finally found the farmhouse where he and the Screambreaker had fought a handful of Vathen together, it was still there, still with a roof and its torched barn, empty and abandoned for all those years. Mirrahj nodded and looked impressed. 'And I'd thought you were bringing us this way just to see whether a Vathan was tougher than a forkbeard or the other way around.'

There were benches. Blankets. Everything the way he remembered it. There were dead Vathen too, three of them out the back by the remnants of the burned-out barn, one out the front, the one the Screambreaker himself had killed, and one still in the house, all skeletons long since picked clean by whatever animals had found them. Gallow dragged the one in the farmhouse outside in bits and pieces, a reminder of the war that neither of them wanted to remember. Mirrahj coaxed her horse into the shelter of the house and tended to it while Gallow searched through the larder. Everything was long gone, eaten or dissolved into mould, but outside in the ruined barn he found a crate with a sack of grain in it that was dry and only tasted slightly bad. He took it back to the hearth and filled an old pot with rainwater that had collected among the ruins. There was even firewood in the house, cut and ready underneath thick cobwebs, sheltered from the rain. Farm tools too, and when he searched he found a handful of precious flints. By the time they'd scraped enough shavings of wood to make tinder and lit a fire, the sky was dark as pitch. Neither of them said a word. They listened to the hammering of the rain and the wild tearing of the wind and stared at the fire, warming themselves, always watching to make sure the flames kept alive. As the house shed its icy chill they stripped off their soaking furs. The grain, after Gallow had boiled it soft, tasted of mould, but after three days without warmth or food it was like seeing the sun again after weeks of storms. They ate in silence, and for the first time since they'd left Andhun, Gallow eased himself out of his mail and let the warmth of the flames bathe his skin. 'We'll be in the hills tomorrow. There's not much shelter. Then we cross the Crackmarsh, dawn to dusk. The ghuldogs won't trouble us as long as we're out by sunset. The water meadows will be growing now. Might have a skin of ice at sunrise if the rain stops but don't let it fool you – you'll go right through as soon as you put any weight on it.'

Mirrahj shrugged. 'We have warmth and shelter. We should wait a day here. Rest until the weather breaks.'

Gallow drew out a knife and sharpened it on a whetstone. When the edge was good enough, he tugged at the stubby beard he'd grown in the days since Hrodicslet and lifted the knife to it.

'You should leave that,' said Mirrahj.

He stopped and looked at her. 'To what end?'

'What are you, Gallow? Are you Marroc or are you Lhosir? Which is it?'

'Can't I be both?'

'No. You may live among both and worship the gods of both but you cannot *be* both. What were you born?'

'You know very well I was born a brother of the sea.'

'And in your heart which are you?'

'Both and neither.' Gallow lowered the knife and poked angrily at the fire.

'You left your family to fight Sixfingers. Is that what a Lhosir would do?'

'Yes.'

'Is it what a Marroc would do?'

Gallow hesitated, which was answer enough in itself. 'Some of them,' he said.

Mirrahj looked at him hard. 'You're a Lhosir, Gallow Foxbeard, not a Marroc. However much you want to be, deep inside you have a forkbeard soul. That's how you were made and it's a thing you can't change. Be what you are, forkbeard.' She bared her teeth at him and then nodded across the fire. 'In my saddlebags you'll find a piece of waxed paper wrapped around some cheese. It's more than a year old and it comes from my homeland. It has a flavour strong enough to kill children and it's the most delicious taste in the world. Get it and I'll share it with you.'

Gallow found what she wanted and unwrapped it. The stink climbed up his nose and stabbed him right behind the eyes. 'Maker-Devourer!' He almost dropped it, then tossed it to Mirrahj. She cut off a piece and tossed it back.

'Vathan horse cheese, aged to perfection.'

He sniffed and promptly sneezed. 'That stinks, and of strong stale piss.'

Mirrahj waved the knife at him. 'You found us this house, forkbeard, so I'll forgive you a lot, but not that. You eat or you fight now.' Her mouth was angry but her eyes were smiling. Gallow took a deep breath and bit a piece. For a moment he let it sit inside his mouth, trying hard not to taste anything at all. Then he felt it wriggle, made a face and spat it across the room. 'It moved!'

Mirrahj collapsed with laughter. 'Your face! O forkbeard, your face!' He glared as she cut a piece for herself and chewed it. 'I'm not trying to trick you, forkbeard. This is what we eat, but I've yet to find anyone other than a Vathan who has a taste for it.'

She turned the cheese and pinched at something and then delicately withdrew a slender reddish wriggling thing. A worm. Gallow screwed up his face. 'You can keep your cheese, Vathan.'

'Forkbeard, this is how we welcome one another when clans meet. I invite you into my shelter. We share milk and I promise to protect you as long as you remain in my house; and by accepting my food you promise to protect me too, and my family. We might be enemies the moment you cross the threshold, there might be blood as bitter as wormwood between us, but when you come into my home and drink my milk, you vow to be my brother until you leave. You forkbeards welcome your guests by breaking bread and sharing ale with them but we don't have bread and ale.' She cut another piece of cheese and picked out the worms. 'Here. It's not exactly milk either, but it was once.'

Gallow forced himself to swallow as quickly as he could and washed it down with a long gulp of water, trying not to be sick. His stomach rumbled. Mirrahj got up and walked into the shadows in the far corner of the house. She stripped off her mail and her woollen shift and wrapped herself in a blanket. She hung the rest of her clothes neatly around the fire. 'You should do the same. It'll be nice not to be sodden for a while.'

Gallow was already stripped to his woollen shirt. 'Aye, before I sleep I will.'

'It's customary, as a stranger who's shared my milk, that we should tell each other of our deeds.'

'You already know mine. I've told you everything that matters.'

Mirrahj shuffled closer and sat next to him beside the fire. 'But not the Vathan way.' She touched his face and ran a finger along the length of his nose, over the dent near the bridge and along the old white scar that ran beneath his eye. 'Some wounds tell their own stories, others speak in hints and whispers. Where did this one come from?'

'A Marroc.' Having her so close was unsettling. He felt on edge, tense, and was suddenly very aware that she was naked under her blanket.

'A Marroc? Just *a Marroc*?'

'It was my first proper fight under the Screambreaker. Not far from Kelfhun. The Marroc then weren't as they are now. They still knew how to be fierce. It was a hard battle.'

'A whisker closer and you wouldn't have seen the end of it.'

For a moment Gallow laughed, remembering the day. 'I knew he'd hit me. I felt it. I didn't feel the pain but I felt the blow and suddenly I couldn't see. I thought he'd taken my eye out.'

'He very nearly did.'

'I hit him and hit him and hit him until I knocked his shield down, but I didn't kill him. The man behind me did that. Quick fast lunge through the throat the instant that shield dropped. The man who held that spear was Thanni Ironfoot's cousin. He died a year later. Ironfoot spoke him out. I was there to make sure he remembered that thrust.'

She traced another line along his cheek, fresher and redder though still years old. 'This one?'

'A Vathan. Lostring Hill. I don't remember his face or anything about him. I didn't kill him either.'

Her finger moved across the side of his throat. 'This one?'

He froze. He forgot that one, now and then, and then he'd find himself running a finger over it. 'From a Marroc, but a different kind of battle.' That was the night he'd found Arda. She'd been on the road from Fedderhun to Middislet with little Jelira on her back and a basket on her head. And it was late and there was no one else about and he was lost and trying to find his way to Varyxhun and the Aulian Way and so he'd walked towards her, a forkbeard, and she'd stopped and put down the basket and little Jelira and come to him swinging her hips because she had a child to protect and everyone knew what forkbeards did to Marroc women. And he'd stopped to stare at her, wondering what she wanted and why, and when she'd come close he started to ask her the way to Varyxhun and she'd flung her arms around him and then slid behind him, and the next thing he knew she had a knife at his throat and was making a fine effort to cut it. It had been a close thing but he'd thrown her off, bleeding from the gash in his skin, and he might have killed her or done what she'd thought he wanted in the first place, but he'd seen five years of that with the Screambreaker. So he'd taken the knife and then helped her to her feet and carried her basket for her while she carried her little girl, and he'd asked her about Varyxhun and found that he'd gone completely the wrong way out of Andhun and would have to cross the Crackmarsh. And she'd brought him into her home and they'd broken bread together, and he might easily have gone away the next morning but it turned out that there was a forge in need of a smith, and he was a smith in need of a purpose, and so he'd stayed a few days to help with a few things, and somehow one thing had led to another and he'd never left.

He touched the scar again. She'd marked him on the day they'd met so that everyone else would know he was hers. He'd said that, years later, and she'd laughed and called him a clod, but the twinkle in her eyes had given her away.

And now she was gone and here was the Vathan woman

Mirrahj sitting beside him and suddenly Gallow found he wanted her very much. He turned.

'Deep, that one?' She didn't stop him as he unwrapped her blanket and pushed it away.

'Deep.'

14

GHULDOGS

Reddic rolled his eyes and stamped his feet. He was sodden to his boots from walking in the rain and he wanted the dry and the warmth of the caves and their fires. 'When?'

'Hours ago!' Arda's face was red and puffy and her fingers kept curling like claws. 'I tried to make those other two look for her but they're worse than mules. So I went myself but she's gone into the Crackmarsh and I don't have the first idea which way. And I couldn't leave the others. Nadric and Harvic and a few of the men went out looking but none of them know where to even start.' She put a hand on his chest. 'You do. You live here. Find her, Reddic. Please.'

The men who'd come with him to Middislet were moving among the villagers, telling them what they'd found. Men and women were already gathering up their furs, their children, whatever they'd brought with them when they fled. They wanted to be home before dark, behind doors and shutters they could bar before the shadewalkers came out from their hiding places. When Reddic talked to the two old Crackmarsh men Valaric had left to watch the caves, they only shrugged. 'No point looking now,' muttered one of them. 'She's long gone. Ghuldogs might get her tonight or they might not, but you won't.' And they were probably right, but Arda wasn't going to understand the cold logic to waiting. What she'd understand was that, between the rain and the wind and the ghuldogs and the night, there wasn't much chance they'd find her if they left their search to the morning. So he pressed the old men and they told him Jelira had asked the way to Varyxhun and the two daft buggers had as good as told her how to cross the Crackmarsh to Hrodicslet and that there was a trail up into the mountains from there. And after that she'd gone. Gone looking for Gallow.

Reddic went back to the mouth of the caves, looked at the sky and reckoned he had three hours before dark. And the rain didn't look like it had plans to stop any time soon. He sighed and dressed himself as warm as he could, taking a few more furs from the two old men – not that they much liked letting them go, but Arda was about ready to kill them – and left. Him and Arda, while Nadric stayed to look after Tathic and Pursic and Feya and Jelira if she came back. Arda promised to flay the two old men alive if they didn't help too. She hung on to Reddic's arm. 'Promise me! Promise me we'll find her!' And she wouldn't stop, and so he promised and then wished he hadn't. Valaric was always loud about that sort of thing. A man gave his word to something, he'd best see it through.

They set off together in the rain, wrapped up in as many furs as they could wear, partly to keep warm and partly to keep ghuldog teeth at bay. The old men had been certain about the trail to Hrodicslet, at least, so Reddic followed the path as they'd described it. They ran, keeping up a steady pace, but after an hour Arda had to stop.

'I can't keep going like this. I'm sorry.'

'Then you shouldn't have come.' Which sounded harsh but he was right. He probably ought to have run off again there and then and left her with not much choice but to follow or get left behind alone in the swamp in the dark or else go back to where she ought to have stayed in the first place. He couldn't though, and if she'd said he had to go more more slowly then he'd have done that too.

But she bowed her head and turned back alone, hiding her face so he wouldn't see the tears. Better this way, Reddic reckoned. Better she wasn't there if the ghuldogs came, because then there wasn't much to do except run or fight, and Reddic had been chased by ghuldogs before and had learned how to run a lot faster after that. Better too that she wasn't there if he reached Jelira after the ghuldogs did. He shuddered at that, and with the light slowly failing he ran on alone into the Crackmarsh. To a man who didn't know the place, the water meadows and the swamps were a maze, tricky at best and often deadly. You came here and you didn't know their ways, you vanished, and Reddic could have filled a day with the stories he'd heard of men who'd disappeared. But he was a Crackmarsh man now. He'd lived among them for months and he'd learned their fickleness. He slowed to a walk when the sun set and true darkness came, but he didn't stop. A few stars were enough light. Give it another few hours for the air to freeze and there'd be a scum of ice over the water meadows, if the rain ever stopped. The ghuldogs didn't like that. It cracked and snapped under their feet. You heard them coming, if you knew what to listen for.

He stopped and swore. Somewhere he'd taken a wrong turn and now the path was getting muddier and turning him east instead of south. Hummocks rose out of the marsh ahead, little mounds covered in tufts of thick grass that rustled in the breeze. He stared, reaching out with his ears for the distant howls of ghuldogs a-prowl, but all he got was the wind. He knew where he'd gone wrong. Ten minutes back where the path was dry it came to an old tree stump, dead a hundred years. There was a fork. He'd gone right. He should have gone left. He turned around and then stopped again. He knew he should have gone left because he'd walked the track from the Middislet caves to Hrodicslet before. But Jelira hadn't. If she didn't know the way, maybe she'd made the same mistake too. In the dark he'd walked straight past it. Too busy thinking about how he wanted to be back in the caves. Jelira would have come past in daylight, though. She'd have seen it, wouldn't she?

What if she didn't?

He didn't know. He ought to go back now and he knew it. Come out with others in the morning and all go separate ways, but he couldn't. He could see Arda's face, how she'd look if he came back alone. How his own mother had looked the day his sister hadn't come back. And he could see Jelira too, eyes filled with hope and promise – what if she *had* come this way without realising she'd gone wrong? She'd follow the path as best she could, wouldn't she?

He walked on. After another half an hour the path was gone, no trace of it left. The hummocks that rose out of the water were bigger now. The first stands of stunted trees weren't far ahead, where the hummocks grew into hillocks and the water meadows grew deeper and swallowed a man who wasn't careful with his feet. Where would he go, lost and alone and with the light failing? Back, surely, but if Jelira had gone back why hadn't he found her? What then? What had he done when it had been him? He'd gone for the trees, that's what. For the shelter they seemed to offer, even though they didn't.

He heard a howl far away, and then another. The ghuldogs, talking to each other. Too far to worry about but that didn't stop his heart racing. Stupid. Trees meant shadows and the ghuldogs liked shadows, and yet the trees called out nevertheless, offering him the haven of their branches, and he almost started running, and never mind that he knew perfectly well that any ghuldogs nearby would be waiting there. And that they could climb.

A distant scream ripped the night over the steady hiss of rain. Not a ghuldog scream this time but a girl scream. *Now* he ran. In the dark with the rain it was hard to know which way or how far but it had come from somewhere ahead. Almost at once another ghuldog howl went up, closer this time, the howl of scent found and of calling the pack. Reddic's heart pounded. He glimpsed movement to his left, something bounding through the water. Not towards him but alongside, slowly converging. He almost turned to chase it off but he didn't have the nerve. Made him wonder though – how was he going to face down a whole pack of them if that's what it was? – but he kept running anyway. The ghuldog pulled ahead of him. Reddic let it lead. Thing clearly knew where it was going.

'Jelira!' He felt suddenly stupid now. And guilty. Guilty for leaving her. 'They can climb the trees!' People who didn't know better thought ghuldogs were just big dogs but they weren't. They had dog-like heads but their limbs were the arms and legs of a man and they had no tails. Man was chased by wolves, man climbed a tree. Everyone knew that, and so men chased by ghuldogs climbed trees too, and then watched in horror as the ghuldogs climbed after them. Not that they were much good at it, but usually it was enough that they could. Truth was, there was wasn't much you could do about ghuldogs except turn and fight them. They weren't keen on fire but there wasn't much chance of that out here, not tonight.

The rain answered his thoughts, falling more heavily. Over the hiss of it he heard Jelira scream again. A scream for help. They hadn't got her, not yet, not quite.

The ghuldog he'd been following reached the edge of the trees and vanished into the shadows. There couldn't have been more than a dozen trunks but there could have been a dozen ghuldogs too for all Reddic knew. He saw one of the trees shake as the first started to climb.

'Help! O Modris! Help me!'

The ghuldogs would have seen him by now. And yes, as he looked hard into the shadows he saw at least four still on the ground, as well as the one easing its way up the tree. Those on the ground turned to look at him, one by one. It was Jelira's scent that had drawn them and so it was her they were after, but it wouldn't take much for them to change their minds. Reddic drew his shield up in front of him and lowered his spear. Against a Vathan or a forkbeard, a man crouched, hiding himself as best he could behind his shield. Against a ghuldog a man stood tall and broad and made himself as big as he could. 'You look big enough, they all just run away.' Although the man who'd told him that was Drogic, who was about as big as a horse. Even bears thought twice when they saw Drogic coming.

If you were lucky the first ghuldog came straight at your throat and all you had to do was lift your spear a little and watch it skewer itself. Trouble with ghuldogs was they learned. As Reddic came closer, two of them split away from the tree and circled him, one coming from each side. They stopped, letting him know that he wasn't welcome, that he should leave, that the prey in the tree was theirs and not for sharing. Changed things, that did. A ghuldog in close turned a spear into a useless lump of wood and then it was time for a stabbing knife. Or his hatchet would do. He lifted the spear high, took careful aim at the ghuldog climbing the tree, threw it as hard as he could and ran straight forward. The spear caught the ghuldog in the chest and it crashed out of the branches. Reddic roared at the top of his lungs. The two still by the tree shied away, startled. He turned sharply back. The other two had chased after him as soon as he'd run and the closer one was already leaping. He ducked behind his shield, gripped it with both hands and slammed it into the ghuldog as it came at his face. It bounced off and landed and rolled snarling back to its feet. The other one skittered round behind him and for a moment he couldn't see it. He slipped the hatchet off his belt and jumped at the first. Keep moving, that was the thing. Keep moving, because when you fought a ghuldog pack there was always *always* one of them creeping up behind you.

Modris smiled on him for a moment. The first ghuldog scampered warily back out of reach but the creature from the tree, dead with his spear stuck through it, was right in front of him. He slipped his hatchet into the hand holding the shield and snapped the spear out of the ground. The ghuldog in front of him growled and bared its teeth. Reddic held the spear high up the shaft, disguising its reach, then stabbed out with it, almost throwing the spear and then catching it again by its end. The ghuldog jumped away but the blade still raked its flank and left a long bloody cut. It whimpered and fled.

Always one from behind. He spun around. The creature was already in the air, so close he had no chance to put his shield between them. He raised his arm to protect his face, dropping the spear as he did. The ghuldog's fangs closed around his elbow and bit down hard. Reddic screamed. He had no mail there, only furs, and yes they were good and thick, but the ghuldog's bite was like nothing he'd ever known. Like the blow of a fork-beard's axe, maybe, only it didn't stop. He howled and snarled and shook his arm but it didn't let go. He changed his grip, let go of his shield and brought his hatchet down on the ghuldog's skull and cracked it in two. The bite loosened but Reddic was past caring and he brought the axe down over and over until the ghuldog fell off his arm. His elbow felt as though the bones had been crushed to powder. In the dark he couldn't see if there was blood. Blood was bad. Blood meant the ghuldog had broken his skin. He wasn't sure what happened then, only that the Crackmarsh men whispered that if the wound from a ghuldog's bite went bad – and they always did – then a quick clean death was for the best.

There were still two ghuldogs close by. One howled, no more than a dozen yards away, summoning more of the pack. He couldn't find either his spear or his shield and his sword arm was too hurt to be much use. He looked up.

'Jelira, where are you?' He heard a voice. His foot trod on something hard and he almost stumbled. His spear! 'Can you see me?'

'Yes.'

'Take this then.' When he looked up he could see her as she moved. She was good and high, well out of reach of the ghuldogs if they jumped. He waved the spear at her. 'You know how to use this?' He looked about for the other ghuldogs and then jumped at the tree, hauling himself up fast with his one good hand and scrabbling feet, driven by a surge of fear. 'You stab it at their faces. Brace well and use both hands and pull quickly back so they don't grab hold of it. Strike hard and fast and don't be afraid to hurt them.'

He was gasping for breath. Maybe a braver man would have got her down from the tree and walked them home in the night and seen the ghuldogs off, but Reddic wasn't that man and, besides, his sword arm flared in agony whenever he moved it. Now he was up in this tree, he was staying.

He sat in the crook of a branch with his axe in his lap, and when more ghuldogs came he slashed and kicked at their clambering muzzles and Jelira stabbed with his spear until they'd bloodied three and the rest gave up. It was hardly what anyone would call heroic, but when the sun rose they were both still alive, and that was what mattered.

15

SCARS

Gallow and Mirrahj lost themselves in each other's skin. The night passed and then another day. They fingered each other's scars and stroked each other's hair and touched one another's faces. Gallow's lovemaking was angry and insatiable; Mirrahj was hungry and fierce. In between, lying naked around the fire, Gallow licked the salt off her skin and she drew his eye to the longest scar of all, a slice low across her belly. She'd had a child once then, and they'd cut her to get it out. An Aulian birth.

'I had a son and I had a husband. I lost my son not long after he was born but I lost my husband on the day they cut me and he came out. They said I'd never carry another child, and what use is a woman who can no longer make sons? He left me to go and serve with the Weeping Giant, and I followed because I could fight as well as any man I knew, and we went with the ardshan to the disaster of Andhun and there he vanished. I suppose some forkbeard killed him but maybe he ran away. By then I could beat him at everything by which a man measures himself. I learned to wrestle among the warriors of his ride. I learned ways to beat men who were bigger and stronger than me. It was to humiliate him after what he did in leaving me behind. He tried to throw me away and I wasn't going to have that. I don't know why the ardshan raised me to become a bashar after Andhun but I was a good one. You've been wondering that since the day we met – how is it that a woman leads men into battle?'

'But I watched and I learned the answer.'

'As no man's wife I could never have another Vathan. If I gave myself to a man then I would have belonged to them. So I didn't, because I wanted my ride, and men laughed at me and eyed me askance but they did what I said. Several tried to take what they couldn't freely have. A rightful challenge of my strength, they said, and so it was equally rightful when I killed them with their own knives. Josper was the first one I let live. I beat him to within an inch of his life in front of the rest of the ride. When I was done with him he could barely move for days, but I was careful not to break him. It was a lesson to the others. Mostly it stopped after that.' She pulled Gallow closer and clutched his head. 'You'll take me to the sword, forkbeard. You will. And then I'll take my people home.'

'I'll take you to where I left it.'

'Why is it that a bashar who is a man can take as many women as will have him and be admired and envied by his ride, yet I could not take even one man to be mine? Where's the justice in that?'

'A woman's place is raising children.'

'And a man's place is in the fields, flapping his arms to scare away the crows.' Mirrahj bit his ear. 'I carried one child, Gallow of the forkbeards. I know that pain. I've had an arrow through my arm and I can tell you that hurt a good deal less. Remember that when you go back to your Marroc wife.' He tensed and she laughed. 'Oh you will, forkbeard, and she'll have you too. You'd be stupid not to and so would she. Stay alive, do what you need to do, go back to her and never leave her again.'

They knew each other a little better by the time they left the farmhouse. A day and two nights out of the wind and the rain lifted their spirits, as did warm food, even if it tasted of mould. Even their horse seemed to feel better. The storms had lessened to a breeze and drizzle now, and they made good time to the edge of the hills and through them to the fringes of the Crackmarsh. For a while Gallow turned south until the Ironwood closed in and forced them to choose between the trees and the water meadows. Mirrahj eyed the wood with uneasy suspicion. 'I never heard of a ride who ventured far into any forest. I forget, is it a giant spider the size of a horse or an enormous snake that lives in this one?'

She spoke with scorn, as if laughing at such foolish superstitions, but her words carried a nervous edge. Gallow raised an eyebrow. 'I'd heard it was shadows and trees that came alive. The shadows start to move and frighten their prey and herd them towards groves of Weirtrees in the forest's heart. The groves close around you and the roots and branches wrap you up and the trees themselves devour you. Then too I've heard there's a race of people who live there, as old as the world itself. Small like children and dark like an Aulian. They were here before any Marroc.' As Mirrahj's eyes darted nervously about, Gallow laughed. 'The Marroc have their stories, but that's all they are. One day I'll tell you some Lhosir ones about the mountains of the Ice Wraiths.'

They sheltered on the fringe of the forest for a night and lit a fire and slept warm and dry under the branches, and perhaps Mirrahj slept with one eye open but no trees or shadows came alive and no fey-folk tried to eat them, and the next day they rose early and moved with the dawn as Gallow guided them into the water meadows of the Crackmarsh. He walked ahead and Mirrahj rode behind, but before the sun reached its peak she stopped him and pointed back the way they'd come, and when he followed her finger with his eyes, he saw riders, six of them, some half a mile away. He squinted, trying to work out who they were.

'Forkbeards,' said Mirrahj with a touch of wonder. 'They've crossed the river.'

Gallow climbed up behind her. 'They did that back in Andhun. Let's get away from them.'

'They've been behind us a while and they're following us. But I'll try if you like.' Mirrahj set off at a canter. Gallow wondered how she could be so sure they were Lhosir but then a horn blew and he knew she was right. Gallow looked back now and then. The riders chasing them were gaining, slowly but surely.

'Cover.' Gallow pointed out an island of trees rising out of the marsh a mile ahead of them. Mirrahj rode for it, but as they came close she suddenly veered away; a moment later their horse stumbled and fell and threw them both into the water. The horse thrashed and then found its feet and bolted and Gallow saw an arrow sticking out of its rump. He caught a flash of movement in the trees and a second arrow hit him in the shoulder, biting through his mail far enough to draw blood. He roared as he yanked it out of his arm. The Lhosir were still after them, gaining quickly now. Another arrow zipped from the trees. Gallow lifted his shield to cover himself as best he could and Mirrahj ran close behind him as they raced for the land. Another arrow hit his shield and then another, and then they were out of the water and into the trees and Mirrahj had her sword drawn with her own shield in front of her. She pulled one of the arrows from Gallow's shield and waved it in his face. The tip was nothing more than a narrow metal spike, no barbs or blades. 'This isn't a Marroc arrow; this is a Vathan war arrow. From close up it'll go right through mail, deep enough to kill.' She bared her teeth. 'We make them for hunting forkbeards.'

'Why are there Vathen in the Crackmarsh?'

'I don't know!'

They pressed close together, covering each other with their shields, crouching low and moving fast, deeper into the trees. The Lhosir on their horses weren't far behind but now they too were being peppered with arrows. Then the swish of a branch made Gallow freeze. He spun round in time to lift his shield and catch an axe flying at his head with an angry Marroc on the end of it. He stepped back, ready to lash out with his spear.

'Gallow! There are more!' Mirrahj had her back against his in a flash, always lightly touching him so he'd know where she was, so he could feel her movement.

'How many?' He caught another blow and jabbed his spear, trying to keep the Marroc away. 'I don't want to kill you, you idiot! You must be one of Valaric's Crackmarsh men. Leave us be and let us pass.' He felt Mirrahj push hard against him as she caught a blow with her shield. 'I fought with the Wolf at Lostring Hill and at Andhun against Sixfingers. I fought with him at Witches' Reach when the iron devil had it under siege. I was in Varyxhun when the castle fell. I'm not your enemy!'

The Marroc paused. One of the men facing Mirrahj shouted over their heads, 'Don't listen! He's just another filthy forkbeard.'

'Do these names mean nothing to you? Sarvic? Achista the Huntress? Addic? Oribas of Aulia? We fought together, all of us.'

Another shout came from deeper in the trees and now the

Marroc facing Gallow backed away. 'You want to fight for Valaric, forkbeard? Now's your chance.' He circled them and then was away, bounding through the trees with his friends. The Lhosir riders had come. There were five of them now and Gallow wondered whether the sixth was dead but then caught sight of him cantering through the water meadows back the way they'd come. The horn sounded again. Mirrahj started as if to run but Gallow shook his head. He pushed her down, crept behind a tree and put a finger to his lips.

'Fan out and find the Foxbeard. Never mind the sheep.' The Lhosir began to move into the trees, slow and cautious. With luck the first pair would die quickly and then it would be three on two and he'd finally find out whether this Vathan woman could fight as well as she said.

Find the Foxbeard. So they knew who they were chasing. Had they followed him all the way from Andhun? He pressed himself against the bark, letting the trunk of the tree shield him from the Lhosir. They'd do what they always did, fan out until they were a dozen paces apart and walk in a line, scaring up everything in their path. In the dead of night you could still hide when a search line like that came past, but not in the middle of the day.

Only one way to find out how far they'd come. Cripple one instead of kill him and then ask.

He could hear them getting closer, each careful pace. The *swish* of a caught branch as a man tried to duck beneath it. The crack of a dead twig, the squelch of a boot in the soft earth, the *clink* of a careless shield on mail. He waited until a Lhosir was about to step past the tree where he hid, then struck low and fast and hard, spinning out from where he crouched and slashing with his axe. Legs and feet, they were the weakness he'd learned in his years in the battle lines. His axe hit the Lhosir below the knee, snapping his shin and slicing it in two. The Lhosir screamed and dropped like he'd been hit by a stone, but Gallow was already up and moving, racing at the next; and even as he did he heard a second scream from behind. Mirrahj, and it was a scream of bloody fury.

He had two Lhosir in front of him. He charged at the nearest but the man was quick and had his shield round fast. They smashed into each other and staggered apart, and then the other Lhosir was at the first one's side and Gallow was facing two, shields overlapped, closing on him with the length of their spears against his axe.

'Forkbeard!' He didn't dare look back but he heard the rush of footsteps. 'On your knees, forkbeard!' He dropped to a crouch and then fell forward as a weight crunched into his back and sprang over his head, and there was Mirrahj, in the air between him and the other Lhosir, and for a moment they were too surprised to raise their shields. She rammed her spear into one of them, straight into his face. 'Behind you, forkbeard!'

He picked himself up. The second Lhosir jabbed at Mirrahj as she levered herself away from the first. Gallow saw the metal blade of his spear flash past her knee but by then there was another warrior almost on him. He stayed low, flicked his axe in an arc and let it go to fly at the Lhosir's legs and then sprang at him. The man jumped, letting the axe spin past him, and lunged. Gallow caught the thrust on his shield and turned it, and then he was inside the man's guard with a sword in his hand and a moment later he had it jammed through the Lhosir's throat. He let his eyes linger on the face for a moment in case it was someone he knew, but no: a young face, barely old enough to have a proper beard.

When he turned back again, the fourth Lhosir was running. Gallow let him go. Mirrahj was limping but she still held her shield and her spear high. When he looked for the last of them, he found the body close to where she'd been hiding, a great bloody pool over his chest. She'd stayed exactly where she was and waited, and then rammed her spear up under his chin, straight into his skull. Another face he didn't know.

'Medrin sends children to kill us.' He spat and went back to the Lhosir whose leg he'd shattered. That one would talk. One thing was answered already, though: the Vathan woman could fight.

16

SOUTHWARD

Up in their tree neither of them got much rest. They were cold and sodden and miserable and sorry for themselves when the sun rose but at least they weren't dead. Reddic almost had to force his legs to move again when the light finally drove the ghuldogs away. They weren't happy about it but slunk off, often looking back, sniffing the earth around the trees as though remembering who he was. Reddic watched long after they were gone before he finally jumped down. He landed hard and fell, and the jolt sent such a shock of pain through his arm that he cried out and for a moment couldn't move. His elbow was so swollen he couldn't bend it at all without feeling like he was being stabbed by hot needles. Jelira was little better. She could hardly keep her eyes open, and when she let herself slide out of the branches, she fell more than jumped. He tried to catch her and they sprawled among the mud and the hard roots of the trees, knocking his arm again. He lay there curled up, cradling his elbow for a while. When the pain finally died down enough for him to think again, he eased himself out of his furs and looked. Half his arm from shoulder to wrist was bruised. His elbow was purple and swollen to almost twice its proper size. Even touching it burned. There wasn't any blood though. As far as he could see, the ghuldog's teeth hadn't punctured his skin.

He made himself a sling, then slowly and painstakingly pulled on his furs again and turned to Jelira. 'Can you walk?'

She nodded and so they set slowly off back the way they had come. Jelira leaned on his spear more and more but they were almost halfway back to the caves before she stumbled and fell and couldn't get up again and Reddic had to carry her the rest of the way. It was hard enough getting her over his shoulder with his damaged arm, but it was either carry her, leave her or stay out with her for another night with the ghuldogs. Besides, she was lighter than he'd thought, and carrying her did a strange thing to his heart, as though her very presence gave him strength.

'Why did you leave?' he asked as he carried her, and she murmured this and that and none of it made much sense, but it wasn't like they had much else to talk about and he got it out of her in the end. Yes, she'd gone looking for the forkbeard she'd called her father and yes, she'd been stupid, and yes, she was almost more afraid of the scolding she'd get when they got back to the caves than she'd been of the ghuldogs.

They stopped a lot. He made her drink water and fed her what food he had. Later she managed to walk again for a while, but never for long, and by the time they reached the caves it was almost dark. He staggered across a line of grey sand that some- one had laid inside the cave mouth and fell to his knees and dropped her. The other villagers from Middislet were gone, but Arda and Nadric and the children were still there, and the two old Crackmarsh men. They fussed over Jelira and barely noticed Reddic was even there, and it was Arda who finally brought him a bowl of warm water and a pot of beans and barley boiled soft and flavoured with slices of onion and a pinch of Aulian salt. It was the best food he'd had for a long time.

'You found her. I owe you a debt, boy.'

He laughed. What he should have been thinking about was that he'd saved Jelira's life, how scared he'd been, whether his elbow would ever heal or that there were ghuldogs not far away and more than one pack of them too – not to forget the shade- walkers either – but what he was actually thinking was that it wasn't right that she still called him *boy* now that they'd lain together.

Arda backed away with a snort. 'Funny, is it?'

Reddic shook his head. But it was.

'I'll give you something else to laugh about then. There were shadewalkers here in the night. Two of them. Came right into the cave.'

The smile dropped off his face like an apple off a tree. 'Where did you run?'

'Didn't.' She went back to the line of grey sand and started poking at where he'd scuffed it, and he suddenly knew that it wasn't sand but salt.

'Did it work? Your wizard's salt?'

Arda nodded. 'Won't say we weren't all shaking scared it wouldn't. They walked right up to it and looked right at us. Stayed there staring for half the night but they never crossed it. Then they just went.'

'It does have magic then.'

'It's salt, Reddic. Just salt. I put a bit in that stew you're eating. Nice. Used most of it up on the entrance though.' She finished with the line across the cave floor. 'Them two useless old men went out after you did, after I poked and kicked and hid all their spirit and made it plain they'd get no peace from me until they did something useful. Came back screaming their heads off. Shadewalkers. Dozens of them, they said. All heading straight south.'

She looked pleased with herself. Reddic sat straighter. 'They're going away from Middislet then. You can go home.'

'Maybe, but not tonight. We'd best take it in turns to keep awake in case they come back. Make sure they don't get past.'

Arda stamped away, deeper into the caves and back to Jelira, and when Reddic hauled himself to his feet and went looking for her, she barely seemed to notice him and he couldn't think of what to say. He found himself following her from place to place like a lost sheep. As the darkness drew in she turned on him and told him he should get some sleep. 'Long day tomorrow.'

There were no shadewalkers that night after all and Reddic slept until late in the morning, the first good night of sleep he'd had since Stannic's farm. He woke and found Jelira sitting beside him, watching, and as soon as he moved she pushed a bowl towards him. 'Marsh deer stew,' she said. 'Morric made it.' One of the old men, and Reddic wondered whether he'd told her what a 'marsh deer' actually was. Probably not. There were no deer in the Crackmarsh. Hardly any animals with any good eating on them at all. What there was was plenty of ghuldogs.

He tasted it. Nodded. 'Good.'

Jelira smiled at him. 'Thank you for coming after me.'

There was a part of him that wanted to tell her how stupid it was to run off like that. But even as he was thinking it, he was looking at her and he couldn't. She wasn't that much younger than him. A couple of years, that was all. As he watched her, she watched him back and he felt himself blush and looked away. 'I suppose everyone's already had a right good time telling you how you shouldn't have gone off like that.'

The smile wavered. 'But I want to find him. I know he's not my father, but he was my da.'

'It was only a few ghuldogs.' Which was probably the stupidest thing he'd ever said and Valaric, if he'd heard it, would have hit him. He shuffled across the stone floor of the cave and sat next to her, wanting to be closer. 'It was a brave thing you did.' And Valaric would have slapped him for saying that as well. A *stupid* thing, and idiotic and outright selfish perhaps. But brave?

Jelira shook her head. 'It was stupid.'

And yet here he was, taking her hand and holding it in his and squeezing. 'Well, maybe a bit of both, but no harm done in the end. We're all still alive.'

She touched his arm. 'How is it?'

'Not so bad.' By which he meant it still throbbed and ached and was more swollen than before and he certainly didn't dare move it, not unless he wanted to double up in agony. But not too bad if he simply let it be.

She hugged him and held on to him a while. 'Thank you.'

'Jelira! Girl!' Jelira jumped like she'd bitten by a snake. Arda was staring at them from the mouth of the cave. 'Finish your eating and bring your walking legs. You too, boy.'

Reddic bristled as Jelira hurried away and left him to finish his stew – and it *was* good, and if you were a Crackmarsh man and you knew what was in it, you soon learned not to let it trouble you when your belly was rumbling. When he finished they were waiting for him outside. Arda looked him over. No smile or anything. 'Well then,' she said. 'Lead the way.'

'Lead the way where?'

'Varyxhun. That's where you're taking these mules, isn't it?'

He nodded.

'Right then. You'll be getting some company.'

He wondered why but he didn't ask. Maybe it was the shade-walkers. When he looked at the two old men they shrugged and looked away as if to say they thought she was mad, that he was mad too and they'd be having nothing to do with it. He ought to be saying something, he knew that, something about how it was a bad idea to cross the Crackmarsh with an old man, a woman and four children, but there was Arda staring at him, waiting for him to get on and do something, and he found he couldn't move or talk.

'Or are we waiting for night again and the ghuldogs and the shadewalkers? I know there's both about but I know there's places that are safe too.' Her eyes narrowed. 'Must be, and I reckon you know them, even if these old dodderers say there's no such thing.'

There were places. Little shelters that the Crackmarsh men had built. He looked about. Glanced at Jelira. Didn't know why.

'Well?'

'What happens after? What happens in Varyxhun?'

'After?' Arda's eyes bored into him. 'Valaric will pay well for those arrowheads I'm bringing him, that's what happens in Varyxhun.'

He couldn't read her face. Couldn't read it at all.

The crippled Lhosir had a shield with the mark of the Crimson Legion on it – Medrin's men. He was pale and he'd lost a lot of blood but he was alive. Gallow picked him up off the ground and slammed him against a tree. 'Where's Medrin?'

'You're the Foxbeard?'

'Some call me that. Heard of me, have you?'

The Lhosir's eyes flickered and he glanced at Mirrahj and spat. 'The *nioingr* who lies with the sheep.'

'You have my name. What's yours?'

'Forris Silverborn. For now.'

Gallow smiled. The Lhosir was young like the rest and hadn't yet done anything worthy enough to earn a name of his own. Silverborn meant he had riches in his family, that was all. Plunder from the Marroc, most likely. 'Were you even born when the Screambreaker first crossed the sea, Forris Silverborn?'

'*Nioingr. Nioingr. Nioingr.*'

Said three times, which meant they had to fight, and Silverborn could barely hop, which made it nothing more than a rude demand to die. Gallow slapped him. 'You don't end that easily, Silverborn. And is that truly what you want? To bleed out in the middle of this swamp where no one will ever find you except maybe a Marroc who'll laugh and piss on your corpse? No one to speak you out?'

'I know what I've done, Foxbeard. I don't need a reminder.'

'Do you now? And what *have* you done, Forris Silverborn?' He let that hang between them. 'Where's Medrin? Still in Andhun? I bet he isn't. On his way to Varyxhun yet?' Silverborn shook his head but there was a look about him as though he'd seen the king not so long ago, as if Gallow was close to the mark. And then there was the shield. Gallow hit him. 'The Maker-Devourer has no place for lies, Silverborn.'

'He's looking for you, Foxbeard. If you want to find him, all you have to do is stand in one place for long enough.' Silverborn stopped and looked up, suddenly staring into the trees behind Gallow. Gallow craned his head around. Away among the shadows stood two Marroc with bows drawn back and arrows ready.

'Turn round and face me!' snapped the closer of the Marroc. 'Hands where I can see them, and keep still or I'll poke your liver with my iron.'

Gallow glanced at his shield, leaning against a tree. These were the Marroc who'd shot him once and made him bleed through his mail, the Marroc with the Vathan arrows, and they were closer now, much closer. Beside him Mirrahj gripped her spear. She was limping from the slash on her knee. Gallow gave a little shake of his head. The first Marroc took a few cautious steps closer and slowly lowered his bow. 'You were the forkbeard at Witches' Reach. You're the one who killed the iron devil.' He waved to the other and sniggered. 'Gallow Addlewits, that's what Valaric called you.' He looked at Mirrahj. 'Why is there a Vathan in the Crackmarsh?'

'We're after Sixfingers.'

The Marroc shook his head. 'No Vathan in the Crackmarsh.'

He lifted his bow again and Mirrahj moved like a pouncing cat. She threw herself sideways and rolled behind her shield just as the Marroc's arrow struck it, quivering in the wood. She crouched behind it with her javelot poised, hidden except for her helm, ready to spring. Gallow jumped between them. 'No!'

The Marroc both had their bows drawn back. 'No Vathan in the Crackmarsh. Valaric says.'

'He's just another forkbeard,' snarled the other archer. 'Shoot him and I'll do the woman.'

'Shut your hole, Remic! No one shoots anyone.' The first Marroc narrowed his eyes.

The second laughed, and as he did, Mirrahj sprang. The first let out a startled cry but all there was to see of Mirrahj was her shield. His arrow struck wood and then she landed on him, knocking him flat. Gallow leaped forward as the second loosed his shaft. Mirrahj's head jerked sideways and she stumbled a moment, then she had the tip of her javelot pressed to the throat of the archer on the ground. Gallow crouched behind his shield as the second Marroc trained yet another arrow on him. 'Forkbeard! I don't care what anyone says you did, you're all the same!'

'Move and your friend's blood feeds this swamp,' hissed Mirrahj.

Gallow kept his eyes on the Marroc with the bow. 'Remic, is it? Weren't you with Valaric at Witches' Reach? We mean to cross the Crackmarsh, nothing more.'

'No.'

There was a moment before he let the arrow go. Gallow saw it in his eyes, the slightest narrowing in the set of his face as a resolve and a belief settled there. Even as his fingers slipped off the bowstring, Gallow ducked and raised his shield. The arrow thudded into its rim exactly where his eyes had been a second ago. The Marroc on the ground let out a piercing cry of anguish, cut off as soon as it started into a lingering dying gurgle. The archer reached for another arrow. Gallow turned his head, caught in indecision, looking at Mirrahj, but the Marroc on the ground was already bleeding out from where her javelot had ripped his throat.

She had her arm drawn back to throw it.

'No!' He was far to slow, and if she had heard him, she didn't listen. Her javelot hit the archer in the chest, punching straight through him and hurling him back. By the time Gallow reached him he was already dead. He whirled and glared at Mirrahj. 'Why?'

She put a foot on the dead man's chest and pulled on the javelot with both hands, tearing it out of him, then flicked a glance to the arrows in Gallow's shield and her own. 'Why? You have to ask me that, forkbeard?'

'They were Marroc!'

'And Marroc have your permission to fire arrows at you as the mood takes them? Very generous of you, but they certainly don't have mine. Let's find the horses these forkbeards were riding and go.'

Gallow shook his head. 'We've spilled Marroc blood in the Crackmarsh now. There'll be others. They'll hunt us.'

Mirrahj snorted. 'No, they won't! Some forkbeards came upon some Marroc and most of them died. Five forkbeards, two Marroc. They'll be heroes if they're ever found at all, and who's left to say exactly how it played out?'

She turned away and vanished back among the trees. Gallow left Remic and knelt for a moment beside the other Marroc. 'I don't know you, but you followed Valaric to Witches' Reach and I know how many Marroc died there and how they fought.' He turned to look around at the trees. 'A brave man, Maker-Devourer. He belongs in your cauldron.'

He went to the Lhosir with the shattered leg to see if he wanted to die with a sword in his hand but when he got there, he found that Mirrahj had beaten him to it, and when he looked for her, she was already out among the water meadows, cooing and clucking at the horses the Lhosir had left behind.

It wasn't long before they rode off, each on their own Lhosir mare. They left the bodies as they lay. No point burying a man in the Crackmarsh, even if you wanted to. The Ghuldogs just dug them up again.

VARYXHUN

17

THE WITCH OF THE NORTH

A chista and Oribas lay hidden in snow halfway up the mountainside. Half a mile away around the mountain at the edge of the treeline waited a dozen Marroc soldiers. They were the last remnants of the Hundred Heroes, the Marroc who'd crept into Witches' Reach and taken it from the forkbeards and started the fire that now burned across the valley. They'd been more like seventy, even at the start, and now most of them were dead, and Oribas knew all that because he'd been with them from the start, because he'd opened the Aulian seal beneath the Reach that had let them into the forkbeard tower above. But a hundred sounded better and no one felt like arguing.

He'd stood in this very same place that day. Witches' Reach perched on a small stumpy peak overlooking the Aulian Bridge across a saddle in the mountain. The Reach was full of fork-beards again now, which was why Achista was here with her heroes, watching them, sending runners and riders every day back to Valaric in Varyxhun across the secret mountain paths with word of their movements. The forkbeards had taken much of the lower valley back. They owned the bridge and the road as far as the Devil's Caves, or at least Valaric allowed them to think they did. Oribas wasn't sure anyone owned the road or the land between Varyxhun and the Reach any more. Neither army made much move to venture out from its walls. The Lhosir rode out in packs of fifty or sixty now and then, but never further than a single day's ride. They raped, pillaged, murdered, looted, took whatever farmhouse they fancied as shelter for the night and then rode back the next day before the Marroc could muster. After a few weeks of this every house and barn within a day of the Reach was a burned-out shell and the forkbeards didn't have any shelter any more. At the same time Marroc archers roamed the mountains from tiny caves and hideaways, shooting at any forkbeard they saw. No, it was winter that owned the road, and if Oribas had been in Varyxhun then he might have told Valaric to do something about that before the spring thaw came. Or Valaric might have quietly led his army into the Devil's Caves and out of the mountains and across the Crackmarsh and maybe bloodied the garrison at Issetbridge instead. Might, but Valaric was set on making his stand, on the Vathen crossing the Isset again to take war to the forkbeards once more, and so Oribas was here with Achista because she needed a scribe and because Oribas was very glad indeed to be beside her. Love was a strange beast.

'There. Again.' He pointed.

The forkbeards of the Reach were little more than dark specks on the snow, but now and then Oribas caught a flash of light from among them. He might have put it down to lanterns in the dark, but he saw the flashes in the daylight too, and at night they were too bright. They came and went like tiny stars exposed and then quickly covered. In the last week Medrin Sixfingers had come to the Reach. They knew that from all the flags and the fuss the forkbeards had made – the forkbeards had stopped riding out to burn Marroc farms too – but something else had come, days before, and Oribas had no idea who or what, only that he'd felt a deep and abiding unease ever since.

'We need to get closer.'

Oribas shook his head. Achista's idea of getting closer was to slip away when he was asleep and creep down the slope as close to the walls as she could get without the forkbeards seeing her. She was good at that while he was almost useless, but every time she did it he always woke up almost as soon as she was gone and then spent the rest of the night pacing the woods and chewing his nails until she came back.

Later, as the sun sank, they went back to the camp in the woods and Achista told Oribas what to write for Valaric. When that was done she dragged him to their tent before it was even dark and they made love to the quiet amusement and occasional hoots of the Marroc outside. Another sign Oribas understood.

Amusing him, occupying his thoughts and leaving him dozy and happy as twilight fell and she quietly dressed and slipped away. He watched her through lidded eyes, pretending he was asleep. Watched her look back at him with a lingering glance full of love and with a sadness he understood perfectly. He didn't try to stop her, but when he was sure she was away from the camp, he rose and quietly followed.

The Marroc nightwatchman was ready as soon as Oribas crept out of his tent. 'She's gone,' he said.

'I know.'

'See if you can keep quiet tonight, Aulian. People need their rest.'

'I'll be off in the trees. I won't keep anyone from their pillow.'

The Marroc shook his head and snorted. 'Pillow? Keep close, Aulian. There might be wolves or forkbeards out there.'

'I won't be far. But I will be quiet.' He spoke lightly. It was only half a lie after all.

He walked away and then wandered aimlessly in the trees as Achista had shown him to make his trail a hard one to follow, then climbed back past the place where they'd spent the afternoon wrapped around each other while they watched the Reach. He carried on around and down the further slopes until he was in among the massive trees where he'd once seen twenty Lhosir massacred and where, a month later and not all that long ago, a hundred Marroc dead had been carefully hidden where the Lhosir would never find them. There had been flowers on that first day. Deep blue midwinter flowers, the first colours of the year, or the last depending on how you measured such things. He'd slipped out and brought back three and given them to Achista on the day he'd asked her to be his wife. Silly sentimentality perhaps, with death as close as it had been, but he'd never regretted it, not once. It was one thing he'd done since he'd crossed the mountains that made him proud however he looked at it. One thing among many that did not.

He walked quickly through the immense Varyxhun pines, guided by the starlight. Out to the north over the plains and the hills that led to the sea the sky was filled with grey cloud, but here in the mountains it was as clear as Aulian glass. The stars twinkled and sparkled and the half-moon glowed bright. They reminded him of home. Of the desert. Those night skies had been cold and clear too. Sometimes he wondered if he'd ever go home but mostly he thought not. He couldn't think of a single reason why he should.

He passed through the trees until he was around the back of the Reach and began to climb again, cautiously now because the cave that led into the mountain and to the shaft beneath the Reach likely wasn't a secret any more. He crept as close as he dared without crossing open snow and then lay in the cover of a boulder for a good hour, watching and waiting, feeling the bitter cold of the night slowly dig under his furs and into his skin and deeper. No one moved. No guard on the cave then, and so he ran across the open snow to the crack in the side of the mountain and slipped in. There were no lamps here and the starlight quickly vanished as he walked deeper. He carried a lantern but didn't light it, not yet, knowing how far it would gleam and shine off the wet walls of the cave. In the dark he felt his way along as quietly as he could. It took longer and seemed further than he remembered but finally he felt the air change. Space opened ahead of him. He dropped to his hands and knees and crawled the last few yards until he reached the shaft and touched the surface of the water there. A thin crust of ice broke beneath his fingers. No one had tipped more barrels of fish oil down here then. He smiled bitterly at the thought. His finest hour, as far the Marroc were concerned, and the most terrible thing he'd ever done.

The walkway around the shaft was too narrow for crawling. He took the bag off his shoulder and left it in the tunnel, and then his boots as well, and inched around on his feet, pressing his back against the wall and feeling his way with his toes. Far above him another tunnel led to an Aulian seal that the Marroc had smashed open. For all he knew there might be a Lhosir on watch up there now, picking his fingernails, half-crazy with boredom. It made more sense than standing a man out in the open by the mouth of the cave. If nothing else, the inside was warmer.

Rungs set into the wall led up. Oribas climbed them slowly

and with care. Here and there he found the loose ones and the ones that were missing. The Marroc hadn't needed to make the climb any more treacherous than it already was – age had done that well enough – but they'd given it a good go nonetheless. At the top he half expected to peek over the edge and find himself staring at the boots of a forkbeard but there was no one there, and no light coming from the half-smashed door into the tomb. He almost relaxed. Almost, but not quite. Something still set his teeth on edge. Maybe it was the thought of entering an Aulian crypt in the pitch dark, even if he knew perfectly well that whatever it had once entombed was long gone, turned to dust or vanished away centuries ago.

Yet still ...

He hadn't understood, from the moment he'd left the Marroc camp and even before, quite why he was doing this. If there was a way into the Reach to be scouted then he was the last person to be doing it, and yet he'd come and he'd come alone and only a part of it was because of Achista. There was a sense of something. A sense of something here and he'd had it for weeks, long before the Lhosir king had come. The sliver of bone that he carried with him in a silver rune-etched tube quivered the way it had once quivered whenever the Rakshasa was nearby. The coin he carried that bore no face now bore the face of death. Something had changed, something that wasn't about Lhosir and spears and swords and arrows but had to do with darker things, and so here he was. Alone.

He eased himself over the rim and onto his hands and feet. Everything was silent and still, yet he was suddenly certain that the tomb was no longer empty. He pulled himself up and took two steps forward, then walked to the wall and took out a handful of his precious salt and spread it in a line across the passage. Most of the things he wished he had with him right now were back at the bottom of the shaft but salt was the one thing he never left behind. A part of him felt stupid for being so nervous. He'd been through the tomb a dozen times, after all. He'd found what had been imprisoned there and it was long gone, a couple of pieces of old iron armour all that was left.

Iron. Iron like the ironskins of the Lhosir Fateguard. The

same design and style. He finished his line of salt and stepped over it and immediately there was a presence. It had felt him make his wall and now a noise came from the other side of the broken seal, the grinding of metal on metal. He crept to the door, feeling his way, half of him wishing he'd brought a lamp, the other half glad he hadn't. He held a fistful of salt in each hand. It was right there. He was sure of it. Right on the other side of the broken seal, silently waiting for him to step through. His heart was pounding so loudly that the Lhosir in the tower above must be wondering what was going on in their cellar.

On the threshold he paused and threw a handful of salt ahead of him. A soundless dazzling light bloomed inside the tomb. The air shook as though the mountain had fallen and a silent shock trembled the air, throwing him away from the seal and back the way he'd come. As he scrabbled to his feet, a figure came through the shattered door covered in a skin of iron armour save for a black cloth wrapped around its torso. It wore a mask and a crown and from under the mask glowed pale blue eyes like glacier ice. It stepped through and lifted its hands to its head. Iron armour. Like the Fateguard but missing a breastplate, and Oribas suddenly knew it was missing a back plate too because those were the pieces that had been left in the tomb. The pieces it had once been forced to leave behind.

His salt lay scattered across the floor of the tomb, each grain glowing white like a tiny star.

The abomination lifted the crown and mask off its head and the ice-blue light of its eyes burned brighter. 'An Aulian.' Its words were in the old tongue, the perfect high speech of the priests and the magi of the empire at its height a hundred years ago. 'Come, Aulian!'

Not a Fateguard. Worse. Far worse. Oribas took two quick steps toward the monster and threw his other handful of salt in its face, then turned and screwed up his eyes. The blast of light came again. He saw it red through his eyelids and then another shock of air caught him and threw him back. He stumbled, almost scuffed the line of salt he'd laid across the passage and landed heavily on the other side. The creature opened its arms wide and strode towards him and Oribas couldn't stop himself from stepping back until he was on the brink of the shaft. It reached the line of salt and stopped and hissed. Oribas had to pinch himself. *It worked!* Mere salt was actually holding it. He made himself look at it now. Take it in, good and long though his eyes squealed and squirmed to look away. The armour of a Fateguard, without question, but the face behind the mask was of a man much longer dead. A shadewalker, perhaps.

A wisp of wind started around the creature's feet. A crumb of salt flew up into the air and swirled around it, touched its metal leg and flared into light. The creature looked at Oribas and smiled.

18

GHOSTS

There was a part of him that wanted to turn and leap into the darkness to get away. There was water at the bottom of the shaft, it wheedled, and it would break his fall, wouldn't it? And it didn't matter that he hadn't the first idea how to swim, because if he took a deep breath he'd float once he threw off the furs, and then surely he could haul himself out into the tunnel, even if he'd once seen a Marroc man almost drown trying the same with three men to help him. He thought these things as he swung over the edge of the shaft and started climbing down the rungs as fast as he dared. But no, the water wouldn't cushion his fall, not from this height, and chances were good he'd hit the wall on the way down and maybe the walkway at the bottom, and even if he didn't, he'd break his bones and his clothes would drag him down, and he'd drown before he could shed them. If he was even still conscious.

Up above, the dim light of the *thing* – he had no idea what it was, some creature half dead and half like the Fateguard and the shadewalkers – lit up the shaft enough for him to see how far the water was below, black and glistening like a hungry mouth. He saw the air swirl around the entrance to the tomb. *It*, whatever it was, was making a wind to blow away his salt, and he could be thankful now that he hadn't done such a good job of keeping it dry out with the Marroc in all that snow – it was sticky and crumbly and not the nice fine powder he might have wanted it to be. He tried not to look up, only down, one foot after the next, hand over hand as fast as he could, and when he slipped on a loose rung, he simply let himself fall to the next and clung to it for dear life.

A whistling began. It filled the shaft and a low moan rose

behind it. And then it stopped and everything was silent, and Oribas did look up now because he still wasn't quite at the bottom of the shaft and the silence meant the wind had stopped and *that* meant ...

It was looking down at him. Its pale blue eyes gleamed and there was a white wind swirling around it. It seemed to smile. 'Aulian ...' whispered the white wind, and it whirled into the shaft overhead and dived towards him. Now he forgot about how hard the water might be. He threw off his cloak and let go of the rungs, all other thoughts and fears wiped away by the ghost-thing hurtling towards him. He fell straight as an arrow, arms stretched up, cringing inside. He didn't even know how deep the water was, and then it hit him like a mountain, shaking his bones. It tore at his arms, almost pulling them from his shoulders, and snapped at his neck like a hangman's noose. It gouged the air out of him.

The cold might have been what saved him, a deep killing ice-cold that forced itself into his nose and his mouth and the back of his throat and stabbed him awake as he felt the impact suck him away. It crushed into his ears, a deep hard pain, and all he could hear was a terrible roaring. The light was gone. He kicked, half expecting to find the bones in his knees and hips and spine shattered into fragments but to his amazement they seemed whole, and whatever pain they had waiting for him, the shock of the cold and the fear had killed it for now. He burst to the surface, floundered, grabbed at something that turned out to be his fur cloak floating beside him and began to sink again. He clawed at it, pulling himself some way or other. Caught a glimpse of the passage out of the mountain's heart as he looked wildly around, and of the walkway, and then of the ghost-thing above still arrowing down at him. Instinct made him duck under the surface, but as he began to sink again he knew his instinct was wrong. He needed salt for a ghost, not ice-water. That was for other things. Desert things.

The ghost plunged in beside him and for a moment they were face to face under the water, the empty sockets of its eyes boring into him. It seemed to speak, though it had no mouth. *I've never had an Aulian. Your skin is already on its way.* Oribas kicked away, frantic to escape. He surfaced again and the ghost floated beside him, mocking him, but he reached out of the water and clawed at the stone floor of the passage and hauled himself up into the tunnel, inch by freezing inch, dripping, already shivering, driven by terror. The ghost opened its mouth impossibly wide and swallowed him. He felt it run through him, a bone-shiver deeper than the shakes born of cold, a weight on his soul and on his consciousness, dragging him into a place far deeper and darker than the water of the shaft. His eyes began to close, so heavy that nothing would keep them open.

His bag! Right there beside him! His fingers reached it. Touched it as his eyes closed. Fumbled at the buckle as his mind began to drift. Reached inside and found what they were looking for. Salt. And then the weight was suddenly gone and he opened his eyes and the ghost was hovering above him, swirling and spitting. His fingers clenched tight, Oribas drew out another handful of salt and threw it and the ghost dissolved in a shower of light and sparks and was gone. From high up the shaft came a cry of fury. Oribas didn't wait to see what followed. He stuffed his feet into his boots and snatched up his bag and another fistful of salt in case he needed it and stumbled away, forgetting in his fear how icy cold he was, how bitter the night air would be outside the cave to a man already soaked in freezing water. Forgot until he felt the first gasps of wind like knives into his skin.

In sight of the cave mouth he stopped. A monster was behind him, a cold seeping death ahead. Despair almost took him then but that wasn't who he was, not who he'd been taught to be. He opened his bag and let his numb fingers feel at the pots and the parcels and the waxed paper wrappings and the glass vials, questing for something that would turn back the cold.

Saltpetre. He could set fire to himself. *That* would keep the cold back. He snorted bitterly and closed the bag and sat there for a moment in the dark, lost. Then uttered a tirade of Marroc curses that he'd been learning in the company of so many soldiers.

A spark of light flashed by the mouth of the cave. The spark of a man striking a flint. He started to laugh. That would do nicely, wouldn't it? If there *had* been a Lhosir guarding the cave mouth after all and somehow they'd missed each other, and now maybe he wouldn't die of the cold after all but something even worse. They'd wanted to hang him for what he'd done in this very tower, and sometimes in the dark at night, as he saw the flames again, he thought that a mere hanging would be a kindness. Then again he'd seen a Marroc made into a blood raven and that had been far less kind. On the whole, hanging sounded better then freezing, but freezing sounded better than having his ribs snapped off his spine and two metal spikes driven through his chest.

The spark flashed again. He could always go back and drown himself in the water. Not that drowning sounded all that pleasant either.

'Oribas?'

He froze. '*Achista?*'

'Oribas! What in the name of Modris are you doing?'

'Shivering.' He picked up his bag and ran. In the starlight he could see her standing inside the entrance. He threw himself at her, burrowing under her furs for her warmth.

'Modris and Diaran! You're freezing! And sodden! What were you doing here? What were you thinking?'

'I was thinking that something hasn't been right here for quite some time, even before the Lhosir king came. And now I know I was right.'

'How?'

He shivered, squirming closer. 'Ah, you're so warm!'

'And you're freezing. What do you mean something not right?'

'There's a monster here.'

He felt the growl in Achista before he heard it. 'I know. And we'll find a way to cut off his head as well as his hand!'

'No, not the Lhosir king. Something worse. The creature my ancestors imprisoned here has returned. And I know why, and the iron-skinned men are its children.'

She stepped away, or would have if he hadn't been clinging to her like a leech. 'Tell me later. You're freezing. We need to get you shelter.'

'We need to get back to the camp.' To a fire, except the

Marroc hiding up the mountain didn't ever dare to light one.

'No.' Achista started to drag him down the mountain. 'It's too far. You'll freeze.'

He ran after her, tumbling and slipping through the snow back to the trees. He was shaking uncontrollably, steadily freezing to death, but at the edge of the wood Achista stopped. Something was ahead of them, ploughing through the snow, and Oribas would have said it was a man from the steady sounds of its shuffling except what was any man doing out in the forest at the dead of night?

Achista reached for her bow. She pointed. In the starlight he saw something move. A shape shambling through the trees. They stood there, both of them frozen to the spot as the shadow moved through the wood and passed them by, and when it was gone Achista stared after it and Oribas had no idea what it was that they'd seen. Tall enough to be a man. A bear, perhaps? 'I can't feel my face,' he whispered. At least his boots were dry and warm. Otherwise he'd probably have lost his feet by now. Good chance he'd lose a finger or two.

Achista shook herself free of her wonder. She pulled him into the trees until she found a deep drift and made him dig a hole for them both. She took his wet furs off him and laid them out and then took off her own and squirmed into the burrow, and Oribas squirmed in after, pulling her furs too. They huddled there together, as close as could be, the two of them wrapped in a cocoon for the night, shivering.

And in the morning they rose, stiff and half frozen but alive, and saw three sets of footsteps ploughing through the trees towards Witches' Reach. When they got back to the rest of Achista's Marroc, the watchmen in the night said they'd seen shadewalkers and the iron devils of the Lhosir Fateguard too; and over the days that followed more of them came, and forkbeards crossed the Aulian Bridge until the Reach was full and their camp sprawled around it, and it was barely another week before Oribas wrote his last message from Achista the Huntress to Valaric the Wolf in Varyxhun: *The forkbeards are coming.*

19

THE DEVIL'S CAVES

The paths through the Crackmarsh were slow and winding. A month or two earlier and they might have simply walked straight over the frozen boggy ground. Another month, when the waters were at their highest, they might have poled their way on a flat-bottomed raft. But in these months of early spring while the waters were rising but still far from their peak, there were only so many ways to go. Reddic led the mules and the children took it in turns to ride them. Arda followed, then Jelira and Nadric. They stayed in the hideaways that riddled the water meadows and the swamps and Reddic took them to what was left of Hrodicslet; and when they were through it Arda led him along a trail that ran south and east into the hills among tiny clusters of farms tucked away in the valleys. The Vathen had never come this far, nor any forkbeards, but it was a path Reddic knew well. They all did, all the Crackmarsh men who'd marched with Valaric to Witches' Reach.

They crossed the ravine where Valaric's men had built a new bridge of ropes. On the other side lay the Devil's Caves which ran right through the mountain to the Varyxhun valley. Marroc soldiers waited inside, Crackmarsh men, and when they saw Reddic and Arda their faces broke into smiles of welcome, though the smiles faded quickly when Reddic told them of the shadewalkers he'd seen. In the warmth of the caves, in the cathedral-like chamber of spires and columns near the passage out to the valley, Valaric's soldiers of the Crackmarsh told him in return of everything that had passed, of Sixfingers himself at Witches' Reach only a half-day's hard march away, of the forkbeard army that was massing, bigger and bigger, and more iron devils too.

'You staying here?' Arda asked him that night as they settled down around stones warmed beside the fires lit outside the caves.

Reddic shrugged. It would be nice to be among friends and to stay in one place for a while. To have other men around him so that he wasn't the one to whom everything fell when difficult things needed to be done.

Arda cocked her head. 'Well, you can do as it pleases you. No need for you to follow if you don't want to. First thing in the morning we're off to Varyxhun.' In the dim flickering light of the few torches kept going under the ground Reddic saw a pair of eyes watching them from where Nadric and the children had lain down to sleep. Jelira. Arda saw them too. 'We all are,' she added sharply.

'You should go back to your forge. To your home. You'd be safer. There's a war coming here and people run away from wars.'

Arda stared as though she hadn't heard.

'He's not here, you know.'

She looked at him hard now, as if she was waiting for more, but Reddic had nothing left to say. They both knew who he meant. 'I know.' She looked away at last. 'I asked too.'

'He killed a Marroc.' Jelira was still watching them.

'I heard. We didn't come here for Gallow anyway. Middislet isn't safe any more.'

Reddic had to laugh. Did she really believe her own words? 'And Varyxhun is? Sixfingers is going to march an army on it any day now. He'll sweep every Marroc in the valley out of his path. They'll all go running to the castle and he'll sit outside and wait until we all starve, because after Varyxhun there's nowhere left to run.'

'Still, it's where I'm going. So you staying here, are you?' She looked him over, and now he was the one who had to look away, though he stole a glance at Jelira as he did.

'I don't know.'

Arda smiled. 'You should. You've done good for us. If you were my son, I'd be proud. At least here you've got a way out when the forkbeards come. Might not be much back the way we came but you'll have a chance.' She reached out a hand and touched his cheek, stroked his face. 'You're young, boy, and you have a good heart. Live.' She touched his sword arm, still in its sling. The pain wasn't quite as bad now, but only as long as he didn't move it.

He put his other hand over hers but Arda pulled away and shook her head. 'Live,' she said again, and rose and backed away and lay down with her family, with her children and the old man Nadric, and Reddic watched as they huddled together and slowly fell asleep, one by one. He felt a great longing wash through him. He'd had a family of his own once, not all that long ago, and he'd thought of the Crackmarsh men as his new one; and they were too, but it only went so far.

He turned away. Forced himself to look somewhere else. Despite everything they'd been through he didn't feel tired, not tonight. *Stay or go?* Varyxhun was a dead end. Sixfingers would have the Isset running red with Marroc blood. He wouldn't leave anyone alive, not a man, woman or child. He'd wipe the valley clean and behind him there'd be nothing but a legion of blood ravens to be picked to bones by the crows. There weren't many here who'd stay to fight that future, not those men who still had a way out through the caves.

Live?

He looked at Arda and her sleeping children. They'd need someone to look after them. Ought to go with them then. Except the more he thought of Arda, the more he thought that maybe they didn't need anyone at all, thanks very much. And besides, with his arm as it was, a fat lot of use he'd be when an army of forkbeards came sweeping up the valley.

Another hand touched his shoulder. 'Hey.' He turned quickly, thinking it was Arda again, but in the flickering light of the candles the face was much younger. Jelira. 'So you're not coming with us?'

Reddic tried to smile. 'I don't know. I sort of think I should actually, but what use am I?' He shrugged. 'And I don't know the way.'

'We stayed there for a while when I was younger. After … Gallow went away to fight and didn't come back.' A smile spread across her face. 'It was so big! So many houses and so many people.'

'He's not there, you know.'

Her face hardened. 'That's what ma says but he'll come. He will. He came back before.'

And left again. That's what Arda had said and her face had said a whole lot more – anger and despair and wanting and resentment, and even Reddic had thought better than to pry.

Jelira bit her lip and touched his injured arm, her fingers light as a falling feather. 'You fought off those ghuldogs. That's what use you are.' Reddic lifted a hand and then didn't know what to do with it. Before he dropped it again, Jelira took it and pressed his palm to her heart. He could feel it beating under her shift. 'I want you to stay. But not like the other forkbeard did.' Her eyes were huge in the candlelight. She put her other hand to Reddic's chest.

'Then I will.' He shuffled closer. His hand stayed pressed to her heart, his eyes snaking past her to where Arda and Nadric and the children lay. Jelira stepped closer. She tipped back her head until the tips of their noses touched together.

'If the forkbeards win, I don't want to die alone.'

'Nor do I.' He reached his injured arm around her and pulled her closer still.

'Forkbeards!' A sudden shout split the rumble of snores and echoed through the cave. Reddic and Jelira jumped apart, looking about in panic as the shout came again: 'Forkbeards! Forkbeards are coming!' It ran through the caves like fire and suddenly Marroc everywhere were scrambling for their shields and their spears, jamming their helms on their heads while the few who had mail struggled into their shirts or hauberks. Reddic stood frozen. He stared at Jelira and she stared back, and then an old Marroc grabbed him by the arm and Jelira nodded and turned away.

'Live!' she cried after him.

'This way, boy.' The old Marroc ran up a slope at the side of the cavern and into the passage that led outside to a tiny valley beside a stream. A dozen Marroc soldiers were already there, clustered together with their shields held up and their spears wavering towards the night. Out in the snow Reddic saw figures moving in the moonlight. He couldn't tell how many there were. As he watched, more Marroc came in ones and twos, running and out of breath.

'Marroc!' A forkbeard voice pierced the chill. 'Traitors and rebels! This is your king. I'd ask you to throw down your arms but we both know that you won't. Good enough. I don't want you to. I don't know how many of you are in there, but I haven't brought many men. Most of them simply couldn't be bothered with you. So I'm going to sit here and watch. Come and get me if you have the heart. If you have women and children with you, you may send them out. They'll not be harmed. They may go back to their homes.'

In the semi-darkness figures formed into a line, a dozen of them, maybe a few more, but still less than half the number of Marroc now at the mouth of the caves. They came on slowly.

'Those aren't forkbeards.' The old soldier who'd dragged him out frowned and let go of his arm. Reddic peered. 'No spears. No shields.'

The moonlight caught them for a moment. The old Marroc gasped and Reddic felt himself wilt inside. The men coming towards him were clad in iron from head to toe like the devil that had led the last assault on Witches' Reach. His mouth felt dry. He took a step back and the other Marroc around him did the same. He could taste the fear in the air. They began to back into the cave and it was all he could do not to turn and run. Iron devils. Men who couldn't be killed. Already dead, some said, but they said it in fright-filled whispers. Then shouts rang out from the passage behind him too, and screams, and a moment later a half-dressed Marroc bolted out of the tunnel. 'Shadewalkers!' Maybe he didn't see the iron devils or maybe he didn't care. He ran straight at them. 'Modris preserve us!'

The iron devils broke into a run, slow at first but building speed. The fleeing Marroc swerved from their path but one iron-skin veered from the rest and cut him to the ground. The others charged in silence, each with an axe in one hand and a sword in the other, straight at the mouth of the cave. Faster and faster they came, while the Marroc soldiers wavered, wilted and then broke and turned and ran back into the tunnel before a single blow was struck, and Reddic ran with them, clutching his arm to his chest, and they were screaming in terror, only now there were Marroc fleeing the other way too, getting in their way. Someone barged Reddic from behind. He stumbled and tripped and fell as the iron devils crashed into the fleeing Marroc and began to cut them down. A man fell beside him, the back of his head split open by an axe. Another Marroc came the other way, bellowing with rage and fear, battering the iron devils back for a moment before they cut him to pieces. Reddic pulled himself free. Between the pressing walls of the tunnel someone trod on his leg, then his head. He managed to stagger to his feet but he could hardly see a thing and all he could hear were shrieks of terror, and there were men all around him, thrashing to get past each other but with nowhere to go. He dropped his shield and pushed forward in the dark. Men kicked and cursed him, and he shouted at them to turn back because there was nothing waiting for them but the iron devils and at least a man could outpace a shadewalker, but no one heard. He pushed his way out of the passage at last to where the tunnel opened into the cathedral of stone and jumped down off the ledge, wincing as his ankle hit the cave floor below and as he jarred his damaged arm. Inside the caves he could hardly see a thing. The only light came from those few candles that hadn't been tipped over and trodden out, yet sounds echoed everywhere, the rattle of iron on stone, the hiss of the shadewalkers, the scratch of steel, the shrill screams of men trapped with nowhere to go. 'Arda! Jelira!' A candle lit up a cluster of spires near where they'd been resting and he stumbled towards it. A lurching shape loomed at him out of the darkness. He yelped and jumped away but it was only a Marroc soldier with his arm almost hacked off at the shoulder, staggering in blind agony. 'Arda!'

'Reddic!' He heard Jelira but he couldn't see her. Another shape moved across the darkness in front of him. A shadewalker this time. He didn't see it, didn't see the swing of the sword until the very last moment, too late to do much except twist and lean back. The point of the shadewalker's sword scraped down the front of his mail hard enough to spark, hard enough for his chest to feel as though he'd been ripped open. He tripped over a ridge in the stone floor and landed hard on his shoulder. His damaged arm exploded with pain and he screamed. The shadewalker came after him. He scrabbled back to his feet and stumbled away. Anywhere.

'Reddic!' A deeper voice. Arda this time. He almost walked into a stone column, and then an arm grabbed him and pulled him and suddenly he was in among a small huddle of Marroc pressed tight against a cluster of the stone spires. Arda. He recognised her smell. And Nadric and Jelira and the children. 'Stay still and be quiet, you daft bugger!'

'Stay still?' His arm was agony.

'Yes!'

'We have to leave! We have to run!'

Arda gripped his shoulder so hard it hurt. 'Run where, boy? Now be *still*.'

Jelira's hand took his. Squeezed tight and didn't let go.

20

THE WIZARD OF AULIA

Oribas ducked under the shadewalker's sword and threw a handful of salt at its face. It let out an unearthly scream and reeled back. He shoved a flaming torch at it, burning it some more. Salt and fire and ice, all those things together had once stilled a shadewalker long enough for a stab of cold iron through the heart to finish it. 'Addic!' He looked desperately for the other Marroc but all he could see was the flicker of torches in among the trees. A handful. Everyone else had fled.

A heavy stone fizzed past his head and hit the shadewalker in the face and suddenly the air was filled with the stench of fish, and Oribas understood it hadn't been a stone at all but a pot of oil. He rammed his torch at the reeling shadewalker again, held it there until the oil started to burn and then stumbled back as flames engulfed the monster's face and chest.

'Iron! Cold iron!' Oribas took another handful of salt from his bag for when the flames started to fade. 'Addic!'

'Oribas!' Footsteps crunched the snow behind him but it wasn't Addic. Achista had a shield in one hand and a sword in the other – not that she had much idea of what to do with a sword any more than he did but she held it anyway. 'Everyone else has run. You need to come.'

Oribas shook his head. 'We can put this one to rest.' The flames were dying now. The shadewalker had stopped struggling and stood swaying from side to side. It stank of burned flesh and scorched fish, and when Oribas threw his second handful of salt into its face, it collapsed like a puppet with its strings cut. Oribas jumped on it at once, pulling at the mail coat it wore. 'Help me with this!'

Achista recoiled and shook her head. He understood. There

was something about the touch of cold dead flesh on the skin. Oribas had cut up a dozen bodies in his youth, long ago when he'd been learning his arts, and yet it still made his skin crawl, the clammy touch of the dead. The shadewalkers felt the same only they weren't quite dead, which made it worse. He pulled the mail up around the shadewalker's hips and then rolled it over onto its back and pulled further. The dark was a blessing. The last time he'd done this had been in daylight. What he'd seen he still carried with him, clear as yesterday.

He had to push hard to get at the creature's ribs. He couldn't get the mail any further without taking the whole coat off. 'Can you finish it?' The last time he'd done this the shadewalker's mail hadn't been so long. Easier to pull back.

Achista shook her head. She backed away. 'No. I can't. Not one of *them*.'

'A knife. Please. Iron.' Oribas reached out a hand. Achista pressed a haft into his palm. He levered back the mail and tried to get the knife as straight as he could over the space between the ribs where the shadewalker's heart ought to be. He almost had it and then paused. 'You have the courage to stand this close – why not one step closer still? I need both my hands to hold back the mail and that leaves me with none for the knife.' A half-truth, but there was a better reason: here was Achista the Huntress, the woman who'd led the Hundred Heroes into Witches' Reach and held it for a month while forkbeard bodies piled up around its walls and she shouldn't be afraid of a thing like this. 'You once stood and faced a forkbeard army with a sword you could barely use, my love. This is a dead man. Nothing more.'

'A dead man that lives.'

'I have stilled him.'

She took a step closer. 'I remember the forkbeards. You started throwing lumps of snow at them.' She laughed, high and nervous, and Oribas chuckled too, even with a dead man under his fingers.

'I could not think of anything else.' He knelt down by the body again and put the knife in place as best he could. 'Help me.'

She knelt beside him, shaking badly, face screwed up in fear though she'd stood and faced death from the forkbeards more times than he could count and he'd never once seen her afraid. Sad, perhaps, and often angry, but never afraid like this. 'It isn't right. It's a thing spurned by the gods themselves. Touched by the Weeping God's tears.'

'In this land it is a monster, Achista, nothing more. And I have slain many monsters.' The gods of the Marroc weren't the same as the old gods of Aulia and the shadewalkers came from across the mountains, not from here. He took her hand and put it over his own on the hilt of her knife, took her other hand and put it there too and then pulled at the shadewalker's mail. 'Close your eyes if you wish. It will go in easily. I'll count to thr—'

But she pushed down before he even finished and the iron blade slid as easily as he'd said between the creature's ribs. Oribas let go of its mail, grabbed Achista and pulled her away. 'Open your eyes. Look! Look!' The shadewalker was disintegrating at their feet, all the years of death and decay that had been held at bay let loose at once. Achista gagged and doubled over and threw up. The stink from the corpse was terrible. Oribas took up her knife when it was done and handed it back. 'How many were there?' he asked, but Achista only shrugged.

Later, after the shadewalkers had gone, the Marroc slowly came together again, calling out to each other. Dozens of the creatures had passed through the wood. Not as many as a hundred but perhaps half that number, and they'd walked with a purpose, and it was only chance that had taken them close to the Marroc camp and the Marroc had come out to kill them, thinking that they were forkbeards.

It was only much later that Oribas realised where the shade-walkers were all going with such purpose. To the Devil's Caves, but by then it was too late to do anything but bury the dead.

Reddic cringed. A shadewalker was standing right in front of him. Not that he could see it because the caves were now black as pitch, the last of the candles burned out or crushed under iron boots. The shouts and screams and the clash of arms had long since died away, fallen to a dwindle of distant wails as the last men in the caves were winkled out of their hiding places.

The shadewalkers were searching and they had eyes that pierced the utter dark and saw some light that ordinary men did not. And now the shadewalker was there, in front of him, and if Reddic reached out with his sword, he was certain he could have touched it. When it stood still it was silent, no hoarse rasping breaths to give it away, but he'd heard its feet scraping on the stone as it came closer and closer. Heard it come up to the line of salt that Arda had lain across the stone floor around where they hid.

For a long time it didn't move. Then he heard a clink of mail and more scraping as it turned away. He started to breathe again. It was the fourth to have found them. They showed no sign of leaving. He went back to rocking slowly back and forth, holding his arm, biting back the tears.

Oribas and Achista and her Hundred Heroes were most of the way to the caves when the Lhosir caught them, galloping up the road in the dead of night, guided by the moon. The sounds gave their coming away before anyone saw them, but they came fast. The Marroc threw themselves off the road among the grass and stones at the edge of the Isset and lay flat, praying to Modris that the forkbeards wouldn't see, but Modris wasn't listening. The Lhosir stopped a little way up the road and dismounted and came back. A score of them, thereabouts, not that many more than the Marroc themselves and so the Marroc got to their feet and dusted themselves down and readied themselves for a fight. Yet only one of the Lhosir carried a shield and wore the dark bulk of forkbeard furs. The rest of them ... In the moonlight they gleamed. They wore metal. They were the Lhosir Fateguard, iron devils to the Marroc, but Oribas knew them better still. Shadewalkers that hadn't yet lost their minds. Children of the thing he'd seen in the crypt under Witches' Reach. He reached for his salt as the ironskins moved closer, steady and cautious while the forkbeard stayed in their midst with his shield held in front of him. 'Well, well. I was after your friends in the Devils' Caves tonight, but I'll thank the Maker-Devourer for giving you to me too. Throw down your swords, Marroc. Give yourselves to me and I'll show mercy.'

Beside Oribas, Achista tensed. She hissed. 'Sixfingers! It's Six-fingers himself!' She whipped an arrow out of her quiver and drew back her bow. 'Sixfingers!' she cried. 'The one with the shield! Kill him and the forkbeards are beaten right here!' The arrow flew straight and true at the forkbeard's face and Oribas didn't see how any man could move so quickly, yet the Lhosir king did. His shield jerked up and caught the arrow squarely in its centre. The other Marroc jumped up and howled and ran at him but the iron devils stepped into their path with a casual disdain. Spears and swords struck sparks off their armour but nothing more, and then their own swords and axes fell, hooking shields aside, striking hard into mail, searching out hands and arms and necks and faces and all those places where men who weren't clad in iron showed their skin. Oribas sprinkled salt in a wide circle. Achista let another arrow fly. It caught one of the iron devils in the face, went straight through the bars of the mask he wore over his eyes and struck deep into whatever skin and bone lay beneath. It barely flinched. Oribas scattered more salt.

The Marroc turned and ran now and the iron devils chased them, all but a few who stayed by their king. Achista loosed another arrow at Sixfingers and again his shield caught it. She turned to Oribas, held out a hand to pull him away and then froze. Addic was staggering, hobbling from a terrible slash across his calf and there was a Fateguard right behind him al-ready raising an axe. Achista let Oribas go, screamed and hurled herself at it, smashing the ironskin sideways so hard that the two of them crashed to the ground.

'Addic!' Oribas darted out of his circle, took Addic by the hand and pulled him inside.

And then stopped and stared, aghast. The Fateguard had Achista. The Lhosir king held up a hand, stopping one as he lifted a sword to kill her. 'Lhosir don't make war on women and children. Hold her still!'

Two of the ironskins held her arms and her shoulders. Sixfingers stood in front of her. 'How many Marroc women fight with their men? I've seen a few and I've heard of another one. They call her the Huntress. Is that who you are? I should wring your neck.' Ten figures now stood around Achista, nine clad in iron and armed with swords and axes, the tenth a king, and Oribas carried no sword or spear or shield, but he ran at the iron devils howling like a dervish. In each clenched fist he carried salt which he threw in their faces, and for a moment Achista was free and the Lhosir king was right in front of him.

'And her Aulian wizard. I should have known. I'm not like them, Aulian.' He drew back his sword. Achista barged Oribas out of the way. She whipped out a knife and lunged, but Sixfingers only laughed at her and slammed her with his shield, knocking her down again. Oribas threw one last handful of salt into the air and bolted back to Addic, dragging Achista with him. She tried to haul Addic to his feet so they might all run together but Addic couldn't move.

She set her jaw and turned to face the iron devils and their king.

'A fine gesture.' Addic shook his head. 'And now what? The river, Aulian. If you can make the river you might escape. Run, both of you! Run!'

Oribas stared at the iron-skinned men of the Fateguard. 'Did you see any bows on their horses?' Addic looked at Oribas as though he'd gone mad but Oribas started to laugh. He stood beside Achista and put a hand on her shoulder and faced the Lhosir king and his Fateguard. 'I won't run from you. None of us will.' He leaned closer to Achista and hissed in her ear, 'Stay close. He cannot touch us. Trust me.'

Sixfingers moved nearer, his iron devils around him, his shield held in front of him again. 'Salt, is it? It hurts my Fateguard like a hornet's sting but nothing more. And hornets who sting are crushed.' He closed his fist.

'Come closer if you dare, Lhosir king. I travelled with Gallow the Foxbeard for a year. I know how you lost your fingers of flesh and bone, and now it seems you have new ones. Did the creature you keep in the crypt beneath Witches' Reach give them to you? By all means bring them into my circle.'

'Is it true, Aulian, that you burned fifty of my soldiers in the shaft beneath Witches' Reach?'

Oribas looked down for a moment. The shame of that still ate at him. 'I did.'

'How did it feel, Aulian, to send so many to such a terrible death?'

'I hear you hung as many blood ravens along the streets of Andhun in your time, King Sixfingers.'

'Far more than fifty, Aulian. Have you even seen a blood raven?'

'More. I have stood and watched it done.'

Sixfingers came to the circle of salt. 'A blood raven is there to be seen by the gods. Those men who died in your fire will wander the Marches for ever. No one will send them to the Maker-Devourer, nor speak out their names.' His eyes flicked to Achista. 'Her Marroc did the same, beheading every corpse so no one could say which was which.' He shook his head. 'War is war, Aulian. A man who fights well and stands up for his word will be rewarded in what comes after, Marroc or Lhosir or Vathan. Yet you deny men their just reward for honest courage?'

Achista drew back another arrow. Sixfingers stared at her and laughed. 'You know what shield I carry, Marroc? The Crimson Shield of Modris the Protector, stolen from your King Tane years ago by the mighty Screambreaker, taken from him by the Fateguard, stolen and lost at sea and found again. Loose your arrow, Marroc, and see what happens.'

Achista let fly at his face but the shield seemed to move even before her fingers slipped from the bowstring. The arrow hit the wood of it, close to the rim this time. She readied another.

'I want them alive.' Sixfingers was still laughing at them from behind his shield.

And Oribas laughed right back, because as the ironskins reached his circle of salt they stopped as though they'd walked into a wall. 'My people caught that creature you keep in your crypt hundreds of years ago. They defeated it and brought it here. Your iron-skinned men are nothing more than shade-walkers who don't yet know they're dead. My salt does more than sting, King Sixfingers. They cannot pass.'

Sixfingers drew his sword. He pushed through his Fateguard and stepped into the circle. 'But I can, Aulian.'

Oribas nodded. He opened his hand and held out a flat palm

piled with salt. 'Yes. You can. If that is what you wish. You alone may pass.'

Addic hopped forward on his one good leg, swinging his sword at the king's head. The Crimson Shield flew up and caught the blow, but at the same moment Achista let fly again. The arrow hit Sixfingers in the ribs and stuck in his furs. He had good enough mail to turn the point but it still made him scream.

'Come, king forkbeard,' offered Oribas. 'Enter my circle.'

For a while, lit up by the moon and the stars, Medrin Iron-hand, King Sixfingers of the Lhosir, clutched his side and stared in disbelief. Oribas watched. Crimson Shield or no Crimson Shield, Medrin wasn't about to fight alone against three, even if one was wounded, another was a woman and the last was armed only with salt and words.

Medrin smiled, mocking his own hubris perhaps, for with even just one other man beside him, everything would have been different. 'I salute you, Aulian. I see I shall lose more men than I would like when I take Varyxhun. My soldiers will know not to kill you. But then the Vathan ardshan of Andhun had an Aulian and they all knew I wanted him too, and that still didn't save him.'

He bowed and turned, beckoned his ironskins, and Oribas and Achista and Addic watched them walk to their horses and ride away. When the last echoes of their hooves had long since died, Oribas breathed a huge sigh.

'You work magic.' Addic shook his head. 'I said so from that first day. You're a wizard.'

Oribas laughed. 'I'm a scholar. I know things, that is all. And we can all be thankful that the king of the forkbeards isn't as clever as he thinks.' He touched the circle of salt with his foot. Medrin could have broken it – kicked the salt aside and made a path for his Fateguard to step through – and he hadn't thought of it, or else he had but had been afraid, and that was the only difference between the three of them being alive and the three of them being dead.

'Now what?'

'Shadewalkers. Iron devils.' Addic shook his head. 'Where does it end?'

'Varyxhun.' Achista offered him her shoulder. 'Valaric.'

It was a while before the other Marroc returned, slinking through the darkness to reveal themselves. Their talk was muted. Another handful of men killed and no forkbeards slain. It had turned that way of late, ever since Sixfingers had come. There were only nine of them left. Some said that the forkbeards could never win as long as even one of the Hundred Heroes was alive but none of the Marroc there that night much liked the notion.

They took it in turns to carry Addic. Achista led them to a ridge overlooking the road and then over it and down and into a sharp valley on the other side and then along another ridge until Oribas hadn't the first idea where they were any more; and then suddenly, as the dawn broke, he found himself overlooking a sharp ravine and realised they were above the Devil's Caves; and they kept very still and very quiet as they watched the Lhosir king and his ironskins file down the road, finished with massacring the Marroc hiding in the caves, and turn back towards Witches' Reach. In the quiet of the early morning Oribas made Addic lie on his belly and stitched his gashed calf closed, bandaged it as best he could and told Addic that if he ever wanted to run again then he'd best rest in a nice comfortable bed with plenty of food and water. They both laughed at that until Achista snapped them out of their joking.

'Look.'

Down around the mouth of the caves a single figure was moving.

The shadewalkers stayed for hours. For a whole day, or that's how it felt to Reddic, but at last they left and didn't come back and everything fell silent and dark. And of course it fell to him to be the one who crossed the line of salt and crept away in the pitch black, feeling his way on his one good hand and his knees until he reached a wall and then along it until he saw the light from out-side. Dead men littered the cave. He couldn't see their faces but he felt them, felt his hand press on someone's cold dead fingers or his leg slide in something sticky and wet that he didn't want to think about yet couldn't not. The passage out was the worst. More than half the Marroc of the Devil's Caves – fifty men or thereabouts – had died caught between the shadewalkers and the iron devils. A little sunlight reached in but being able to see the bodies he had to step on to get outside didn't make it any better.

There was no sign of the shadewalkers outside, or of the iron devils except the footprints they'd left in the snow. He realised that he had no idea, in the end, whether the shadewalkers had gone back the way they'd come or followed Sixfingers. He took a good long look around and then went back to the cave and started pulling out the bodies. Took a while with one arm, but clambering over dead still wet with blood was no thing for children. When he was done, he went back along the passage and called out, guiding Arda and Nadric and Jelira and the children with his voice. He let them pass and sat there alone in the dark a little while, contemplating all that he'd seen, and then went looking for Torvic's mules, still with Nadric's arrowheads bagged over their backs. When he led them back out to join the others, he heard a shout, harsh and hostile, and he was still blinking the sun out of his eyes when he realised an archer was crouched over the top of the cave mouth. Just the one, but her arrow was pointed at his heart. 'And you! Name yourself!'

He sank to his knees, too tired to be afraid. 'Reddic of the Crackmarsh men.'

'Who's with you?'

Arda threw down the axe she'd been holding. 'Arda of Middislet, and for the love of Modris put your bow down, girl. I know your voice, Achista of Witches' Reach. We had a few days together if you remember it, and if you're so keen on having someone to shoot then you should have come here a little earlier in the night. Plenty of choice then.'

The archer lowered her bow and scrambled down and Reddic started to laugh. He stared as tears streamed down his face. *This* was Achista the Huntress? He'd expected someone … well, *bigger*. But she smiled at Arda as she came close, though her face was full of worry and sadness.

'Smithswife! What brings you to the Devil's Caves?'

'Middislet isn't safe, that's what. Seems like there's nowhere safe, from what I see. Beginning to wish I'd taken my chances where I was.'

Achista spat. 'Sixfingers is in the valley. He'll be marching on Varyxhun in days.'

'We have two thousand arrowheads for Valaric,' said Reddic, gathering himself together. He slapped the mules they'd brought all the way from the Crackmarsh. It hadn't been easy finding them, nor leading them out of the cave.

'Then Valaric will thank you. We'll have need of them soon enough.' The Huntress waved up the slopes and a few minutes later there were a half a dozen more Marroc around them and a dark-skinned man that she called Oribas, and Reddic knew that this was the great and terrible Aulian Wizard, though Arda glared at him as though he was a snake.

'So you got him back, then.'

Achista turned to Arda. 'Barely. They were about to hang him. He was on the scaffold when we took Varyxhun castle. Addic rescued him off the gallows.' She swung back to her men. 'Sixfingers turned back for Witches' Rea—'

'Oi.' Arda glared. 'Where's my husband?'

Achista ignored her. 'Hasavic, you know the paths best. Can we get mules to Varyx—'

Arda stepped around, planted herself in front of Achista and poked her in the chest. 'I asked you a question, woman.'

Everyone stopped. Hands went to swords and axes but then fell away. What were they going to do – draw steel on an unarmed Marroc woman in front of her children? Achista frowned. 'Gallow left Varyxhun, Smithswife. He killed a man. Angry Jonnic wanted to hang him. And others. People who didn't know him. We sent him away. Probably for the best, what with him being a forkbeard. So he didn't come back to you?'

All the anger fell out of Arda. Her shoulders slumped. 'No,' she said. 'He didn't.'

21

THE AULIAN BRIDGE

The Aulian Way ran from Tarkhun almost due east to Issetbridge, through the fringes and spurs of the Shadowwood and then the Crackmarsh, roughly following the Isset with a typical Aulian straightness of purpose. Issetbridge itself lay at the foot of a mountain a few miles short of the bridge from which it took its name, the great Aulian Bridge that crossed the Isset and led to Varyxhun. From the town the road wound up the slope like a coiled rope spilled down the mountainside.

The town and the Aulian Way were both thick with Lhosir who had marched from Tarkhun. Gallow and Mirrahj followed the edge of the Crackmarsh, slipping between the bands of soldiers that swept the water meadows. They travelled at night and in the day they hid close to the cascade of the Isset falls, the impassable cataracts that divided the river in two. They skirted Issetbridge the next night, picking their way along trails and paths that wound up into the mountains, and rejoined the Aulian Way on the other side. Now and then they rode past bands of Lhosir heading towards the bridge in their dozens and hundreds, but no one challenged them. Gallow carried a shield of the Crimson Legion, stolen from the Lhosir in the Crackmarsh, and his beard was long enough now to split into two stubby little forks. He was one of them, one of Medrin's Men with a Vathan prisoner, and all the old soldiers who'd once fought for the Screambreaker and might have known his face were dead or far away. Medrin didn't want them.

They reached the bridge not long after dawn. Gallow and Mirrahj stared at it open-mouthed. A single arch of grey stone reached across the river from the base of the gorge cliffs on one side to the base of the cliffs on the other. Its peak rose a hundred feet above the water rushing beneath it, and was level with the sides of the gorge and the two halves of the Aulian Way. Whole trunks of Varyxhun pine, split down the middle and laid side by side, reached from each edge of the gorge to the centre, the midpoint held up by that one stone arch. In the Screambreaker's day that was all there had been, but now someone had built a crude wooden watchtower over the middle of the bridge.

Gallow pointed. 'Guards.'

'I saw the bridge in Andhun the day the Marroc burned it down,' murmured Mirrahj. 'But that was nothing like this. Who built it?'

'Aulians.' No one could match the Aulian masons. It left him wondering whether Oribas had the knowledge to build such a thing if he had the craftsmen to work the wood and stone. Gallow reined in his horse. The bridge was visible from the road for miles and so the road was visible from the bridge. Judging by the smoke of their morning fires there were soldiers at each end and some in the watchtower. He was about to ask her if she'd be his prisoner for one more time as they crossed the bridge, hoping that no Lhosir would question his shield and his face, but he saw the look in her eyes and knew the answer before he spoke. A part of him was glad. They'd enter the valley together as they meant to leave it, one way or the other, with shields held high and spears levelled at the hearts of their enemies. He laughed. 'You would have made a good Lhosir, Mirrahj Bashar.'

She turned her horse in a circle, shook her head at him and set off at a canter along the road, calling over her shoulder, 'And you might even have passed as a Vathan, Gallow Smallbeard, though your riding is poor. Mind, since you're a forkbeard, it's a constant surprise that you don't fall off.'

Gallow galloped after her. The Vathen made better riders it was true, but the Lhosir knew perfectly well how to deal with soldiers on horseback. A hedgehog of spears and shields and some archers, and once the riders were all rolling around on the ground wondering what had happened to their horses and why they were stuck full of arrows, then you fell on them with axes. Men who wouldn't face you toe to toe deserved no better.

The Lhosir at the bridge saw Mirrahj and Gallow but did nothing until Mirrahj spurred her horse to a gallop and lowered her spear. Two of Medrin's men hastily raised their shields and ran out into the road, saw they were alone and hastily ran out of the way again. As he reached the bridge, Gallow kicked his horse faster and rode alongside Mirrahj, putting his shield between her and the Lhosir behind them. Mirrahj's eyes were already on the archers in the watchtower, her own shield raised to ward off their arrows. Medrin's Lhosir threw their spears. One flew over them; the other hit Gallow's shield, stuck for a moment and then fell out a few paces later. His eyes shifted and he brought his shield around in front of him. 'The horses!' he shouted. 'They'll shoot for the horses.'

'And that's why we Vathen hate you forkbeards so much!' Mirrahj leaned suddenly forward until she was almost lying flat on her horse's back, her shoulders across its neck and her head almost resting between its ears. She raised her shield over them both. One of the archers on the watchtower released a shaft but his arrow flew long. The second was aimed at Gallow, who sat up straighter and drew his axe from his belt.

'Do you know who I am?' he roared. 'Gallow Foxbeard, come to take your king's head because his hand wasn't enough!' He threw the axe. The archer hesitated and then let fly too, but the moment cost him his life. Gallow lowered his head and the arrow glanced off his helm while his axe took the archer square in the chest. The Lhosir fell back onto the platform, tumbled over the edge and fell to the hungry river below.

Mirrahj slowed to let Gallow pass. Now she was lying right back in her saddle with her head over her horse's arse and her shield covering both her and her horse from the one archer that was left. Gallow galloped past her. 'Crazy Vathan!'

The Lhosir soldiers at the far end of the bridge had seen it all. They blocked the road now, seven of them in a wall of shields, spears bristling. Gallow slowed. He looked for a way past but there wasn't one, not wide enough for two horses, not without one of them taking a spear in the flank, and so he stopped a dozen feet short of their spear points and dismounted. Mirrahj drew to a stop behind him. His shoulders itched from knowing there was an archer still in the tower, but only a *nioingr* would shoot a man in the back.

One of the Lhosir facing him stepped forward, bold with a strong clear voice. 'Name yourself, enemy.' He was young, too young to have fought with the Screambreaker unless it had been against the Vathen. Gallow grinned at him and twirled his spear.

'Gallow Foxbeard. And you?'

'Bedris One-Eye. I've heard your name, *nioingr*. We know who you are.'

Gallow twirled his spear again. 'Call me that two more times, Bedris One-Eye, and you'll be obliged to stand against me to prove your mettle.' He peered. 'Seems to me you have two good eyes, boy, so how did you earn that name?'

'I'll stand against any *nioingr*, Foxbeard. I call you *nioingr*. And again, *nioingr*. That good enough for you?' Bedris stepped out from his men and faced Gallow.

Gallow laughed at him. 'Your name, Bedris One-Eye. You didn't earn it for yourself, so you've taken it from someone. I knew a Jyrdas One-Eye once. Fierce he was. I wouldn't have wanted to cross my sword with his when he was in his prime, that's for sure.' He lifted his spear slowly as he spoke, sinking down behind his shield so there wasn't anything to be seen of him except his feet and his face.

Bedris hissed, 'Jyrdas One-Eye sired me.' He'd settled into a fighting crouch now too. The other soldiers eased back, their eyes following the fight.

'Old One-Eye sired a great many bastards, I'd say.' Gallow crept sideways. 'He was a fine brother of the sea. One of the best. Be proud to have his blood in your veins.'

'I'll have yours on the—' Gallow's spear flew straight at his face, so fast and hard that Bedris didn't see it coming. He screamed and staggered back. Gallow caught the spear by its butt and pulled it back. Bedris collapsed onto the roadway, hands clutching at his head, blood running between his fingers. Gallow turned to face the other Lhosir but Mirrahj was already moving. One-Eye's warriors had lowered their guard to watch the fight and her horse jumped straight into the middle of them. She stabbed down and a Lhosir screamed and she stabbed again.

Then she was past them and on the road the other side and two more Lhosir were on the ground. Blood dripped from the tip of her javelot. Gallow eyed the men left guarding the bridge. Four of them and they would still fight. He aimed his spear at them but when they drew no closer he lowered it and pinned Bedris to the road, his spear point at the Lhosir's neck. 'Do you know how Jyrdas died? It started when he was hacked in the back with an axe. He killed the man who did it. Then he took a Marroc arrow in the side but he still killed three more and he was standing when the rest of them fled. He would have faced the Screambreaker himself had there been a need, without a doubt or a moment of second thought. He called your king *nioingr* and died with Medrin's dagger through his one good eye. I built his pyre and I spoke him out and then I found Medrin and I took his hand. Now I've taken your eye, Bedris One-Eye, and so you've earned your name. I'll not kill you today but I might just come for you again.' He turned to the others. 'Stand and fight us if you want. Only two of us and four of you, though you might remember you were seven a moment ago. And you might wonder if a Lhosir might serve his king better by living, by telling him that Gallow Foxbeard has crossed the bridge and waits for him in Varyxhun. Or not. Either way, as you wish it, brothers of the sea.'

He started to move, creeping towards them, covering himself all the time with his shield and with his spear aimed at their faces. If they were going to fight then they'd split and come at him from all sides, and then he'd have to run and it would all depend on Mirrahj, still on her horse, and how she could fight four men when they were packed so close around him. But the Lhosir only turned their shields to face him as Gallow circled past and stood beside Mirrahj and clucked for his horse. Nor did they move as he climbed into the saddle; and when he turned and took the Aulian Way to Varyxhun, the Lhosir by the bridge were still standing there, watching him go.

22

VALARIC THE WOLF

Trouble always came in threes. The first trouble was the trouble Valaric had expected: Sixfingers had left Tarkhun and come to the valley with his army of forkbeards. Well, that was the way it was supposed to be and the Wolf had known this day would come ever since his Crackmarsh men had slipped away from the Reach and helped themselves to Varyxhun instead. That had been a slap in Sixfingers' face and a taunt too: *The Widowmaker never took this castle. Can you?* Valaric had been preparing for the siege since the day he'd arrived. If he was honest with himself, he was itching for it.

He sighed. There was always someone in the shrine to Modris up at the top of the castle – Sarvic or Angry Jonnic or one of the others quietly praying for the Vathen and the forkbeards to fight to a bloody stalemate. Valaric hadn't bothered. He'd been at war with the forkbeards for more years than he had fingers and that was never how it went. The Lhosir were charmed. Luck never sent a plague to make their armies vanish into smoke or made the rivers flood and wash them away. The best luck he'd ever had was a bit of mud that made a forkbeard shield wall back up a hill a bit more slowly for fear of slipping, and what the mud had given, the rain that made it had taken away with what it had done to the Marroc archers. It hadn't surprised him when he'd heard that Sixfingers was in Witches' Reach, that he'd turned his back on the Vathen and chosen to crack Varyxhun first. No surprise that his iron devils had come with him either. Could have done without the shadewalkers. Even the whisper of them put the shits up his men. The Aulian would deal with them though. His men needed to see that.

He stared at himself in the mirror – another Aulian treasure left behind when they'd abandoned the valley to the Marroc warlords who'd claimed the castle until the first kings of Sithhun had tamed them. It was gold and a finer silver than you ever saw in Andhun. Every time he looked at it, he felt a warmth inside him, a reminder of who he was and why he was here, for not long ago a Lhosir had sat where Valaric sat now. Braiding his forked beard, no doubt.

The Aulians had left other things too. Like a great big cave right behind the sixth and last gate to the castle with great big bars across its mouth and, if you believed the stories, a great big dragon inside which would drown anyone who broke those gates down if you could somehow find a way to wake it up.

He sighed. Stories like that kept his men happy but stories didn't kill forkbeards. The Aulians had left behind a library too – the biggest on this side of the mountains. Not that Valaric cared, but Oribas spent half his time there and the other half wandering the castle, looking and poking, although what he was looking and poking *for* only the gods knew. So far all he'd managed to do was find some underground pools and get soaking wet. Books. Books wouldn't save them from Sixfingers any more than stories. Was it too much to hope that Oribas would find some other treasure, something he could actually use?

An angry fist banged on the door. Valaric glanced out the window at the sun and yes, it was about time. His second trouble was more straightforward on account of being locked up in the castle prison, but doing that had made his third. He took a deep breath. Stared at himself in the mirror and sighed again and then turned to face the door. At least it had a latch on the inside so she couldn't just barge in. 'No!' he shouted. 'And still no, and I'll have some more no for you later. Now go away!'

'It's not right, Valaric, and you know it.'

'He killed a Marroc, Arda Smithswife.'

He waited to see if there'd be more today but after a pause he heard her walk away. Maybe she was giving up. And then he looked at himself in the mirror again and laughed. *Arda Smithswife? Give up?*

Five minutes later he was breaking his fast with the Marroc who'd lead the defence of the castle: Achista and Addic of

Witches' Reach, who spoke for the Marroc of the valley; Sarvic and the two Jonnics, who'd come with him from the Crackmarsh; and the Aulian, whom everyone said was a wizard, dragged away from his books. They'd all fought the forkbeards before but he always got the same feeling whenever he sat with them: they were too young. They were brave and they'd fight and they'd stand on the walls of Varyxhun until someone cut their legs from under them, but they barely even remembered the days when the Screambreaker had rampaged. Except for Sarvic and Angry Jonnic, who'd been with him at Lostring Hill, none of them even knew what a real battle looked like.

'Sixfingers is moving up the valley now,' said Achista. Her men were watching them come. 'He'll be in Varyxhun tomorrow with five hundred men.' She didn't say anything about the iron devils but all the Marroc except for Valaric made the sign of Modris anyway. Valaric didn't bother because Modris wasn't going to help them, not this time. He closed his eyes. No point banging the table.

'As many men as we can spare. Get them down into the city and sweep it one last time. Food, arrows, weapons, oils, anything that burns.' He glanced at Oribas. 'Salt. If there's anyone still left they can keep whatever they can carry but nothing else. Forkbeards will just take it anyway. Make sure they understand – the gates close when Sixfingers comes and they don't open again for anyone. Anyone.' Felt like he was plundering his own people. He knew he was right – whatever he left he was leaving for Sixfingers – but that didn't make it any easier to do. 'Might be shadewalkers in the city tonight.' He glanced at Oribas while the others all quietly made the sign of Modris again. 'Salt. Do you have enough?'

'Enough to fight them, yes. Enough to bar them from the whole city?' Oribas shook his head. 'It cannot be done.'

Valaric's foot twitched. Oribas had laid lines of crumbly brownish powder across every entrance to the inner castle but people kept forgetting. Kept treading in them and scuffing them and Valaric was no better than anyone else. He wouldn't even have considered it if Achista and Addic hadn't told him how

Oribas had faced down Sixfingers and all his ironskins armed with nothing else.

'There are more than a thousand forkbeards in the valley now.' Achista passed her hands over the table where a map lay spread out, another relic of the forkbeard Cithjan. Valaric had found it helpfully marked with all the places where forkbeards had been killed on the roads, and so the first thing he'd done was send his Crackmarsh men out looking for the Marroc who'd done it to see if they wanted to do it some more. Forkbeards had a thousand men in the valley? Fine. He had about half that, but most of them were proper fighting men with decent arms and he had an impregnable castle too and enough food for months. Sixfingers would have to do better.

'There's more crossing the Aulian Bridge all the time.' Sarvic had been the one to come up with the idea of putting watchers on the other side of the river. The western side of the valley was wild and rugged and hardly anyone lived there. The forkbeards had never bothered much with it except for Boyrhun. Sarvic's men lit torches each morning before dawn to say how many forkbeards had crossed the bridge the day before.

Addic's fists were getting tighter every minute. 'You can't just—'

His sister put her hand over his. *You can't just abandon the town.* That's what stuck in Addic's throat. Truth be told, it stuck in Valaric's as well, but if they tried to fight out in the open then the forkbeards would smash them to pieces and they all knew it. The road from the city to the castle, on the other hand, was a series of switchbacks with a gatehouse in the middle of each all stacked one on top of the next and walls overlooking every inch. 'Jonnic, lead the sweep of the town. Achista, go with him.' Maybe the sight of their Huntress would give the Marroc of the valley who hadn't already run some heart; he'd not say no to a few more fighting men. 'Addic, the salt. Sarvic, sort him out some men.' Addic might never walk properly again and he certainly couldn't fight, not yet, but he understood the Aulian wizard's protections and railed about them more than the wizard himself. 'Sarvic, go to the fourth gate and work your way up one more time. Make sure everyone understands when to close the gates and yes, yes, I know they'll be bored to tears hearing it by now but they can hear it again. I'll be at the lower gates doing the same. Oribas, you can come with me.' They'd both be standing watch with the men at the first gate tonight but he didn't need to say that just yet.

He left the others to it and walked through the castle, taking his time, stopping to talk to the men whose names he knew. There was a chance, after all, that he wouldn't see them again, and so wherever there was any problem he stayed until it had been resolved and it was past noon before he even got out of the sixth gate and onto the road. There he looked down.

The sixth gate was different. The first five barred the middle of each switchback and made a neat line up the mountainside, with ladders running up from the top of each gatehouse to the next. When the forkbeards started up the road and began their assault on the first gate, the men behind the second would be standing fifty feet over their heads, shooting arrows and dropping rocks and whatever else they could find. When the first gate fell, the men behind the second would fall back to the third and do the same again. As Oribas had shown him, the Aulians had designed their fortress so that each gatehouse could be left and allowed to fall, one after the next, while the attacking army would be bombarded all the way to the top, and even the men who manned the roof of each gatehouse could escape after it was overrun by climbing the ladders so their feet would never touch the road. The sixth gate was separate, built right at the end of the castle road, a notch of wall jutting out from the battlements with a small space behind it and then the Dragon's Maw, while the castle yard opened up to one side. The forkbeards, if they reached the sixth gate at all, would be exhausted, battered, bloodied, the road behind them littered with their dead, and not a single Marroc would have had to raise his shield to defend himself. And yet when Valaric looked at the piles of stones and firewood, at the pots of fish oil carefully lined up along the roadside, it left him with a hole in the pit of his stomach. Their defence was based on an assumption that none of them spoke but all quietly made. One by one the gates *would* fall; one by one the forkbeards would take them, and in the end the forkbeards would win because the forkbeards always did, and all Valaric was doing was making it as bloody as possible. The feeling stuck with him right down to the first gate, looking down the castle road to Varyxhun. A grubby muddy market town when you put it beside Andhun and Sithhun and Kelfhun, not even a big one; but to the valley folk Varyxhun was a city and it was hard to imagine anything greater. Now a steady stream of carts was heading up the Aulian Way to the higher valleys. He watched them, suddenly not having much else to do, while Oribas wandered the gatehouse for what must have been the tenth time. When he came back he still hadn't found whatever he was looking for.

'My people liked to dig,' he said. 'I thought there would be tunnels. We were always good with stone.' He brightened. 'Sometimes when my people built a defence like this, there would be a stone with a chain. A dozen strong men pulling on the chain would bring the stone down and without it the building would fall in on itself and block the road. A last defence, you see.'

'Not much fun for the men pulling the chain.'

'In those days they were usually slaves. Sometimes even the officers didn't know. Famously so, in the battle of Iri—'

Valaric cut him off. 'Will the Vathen be any better?'

Oribas stared, mouth still open at what Valaric had just said. He shrugged. 'I don't know the Vathen. The only one I've ever seen is the one you have in your cells.' He paused, and Valaric already knew what the Aulian was thinking before he spoke it. 'Gallow would fight for you. You should let them both—'

'Don't you start on me too, Aulian!' Oribas was right though, and Arda was right. They were all right. Gallow would stand and fight Sixfingers to his last breath, and maybe the Vathan woman would too. And he could use every sword he could get, especially ones that had seen their share of fighting. But to have this castle defended by the very enemies he was trying to kill? He struggled with that. 'I suppose you don't know whether there's any truth to what the Vathan says about the sword either.'

'I've looked through the histories my people left in your library, but …' Oribas only shrugged. 'There's a secret to this castle.' He nodded up the slope to the tarn lake above it and then tapped the sacks of salt by their feet. 'A secret to its stories, to why my people came here and what they brought and why they built this castle where they did.' Salt. The castle cellars had been full of it, a thousand sacks, a hundreds years old. Valaric saw no reason not to drop it on the forkbeards when they came. Sack of salt was as good as a rock, after all.

'When you find out, you let me know,' he said, after they'd both been quiet for a bit.

'I will.'

Together they settled down to wait. To see what the night would bring.

23

SHIEFTANE

Spring came late to the mountain valleys, but it came at last. The sun shone bright and the air was warm and scented with pollen. Under his mail Reddic was sweating. On the top of the first gate beside him Valaric the Wolf and Sarvic and the three Jonnics and a dozen other men were probably sweating too. He hoped so, because that would mean it was the sun and the heat and not fear. On the road beneath the gate, within easy range of an arrow, stood a single forkbeard. He carried a shield and a spear with a white streamer tied to its top and he was just standing there. Further down the road, outside Varyxhun and away from the castle walls, another thousand forkbeards lined the valley, a single solid mass of shields blocking it from the Isset to the mountainside. The forkbeard on the road had Reddic's attention though, all of it, because the forkbeard on the road was Medrin Sixfingers and the shield he carried was the Crimson Shield of Modris.

Nearly three weeks since the ghuldog had bitten him and his arm still hurt. Nowhere as bad as it been on the way to the Devil's Caves but still sore. He hid it as best he could.

'I could shoot him,' muttered Sarvic. 'It wouldn't be any bother.'

Valaric growled, 'He comes to parley.'

'Fine. I'll take that up with Modris when I see him.' But he didn't lift his bow and they all watched in silence a while longer, sweat dripping off them. Reddic wiped his eyes. He didn't understand why they were all just standing and looking at each other and no one was talking. Down on the road Sixfingers looked bored and was leaning on his spear.

'Oh, get on with it.' Fat Jonnic nudged Valaric. 'He might not have sweated enough but I have.'

Reddic winced, but instead of throwing Fat Jonnic off the top of the gate Valaric sighed and closed his eyes and lifted the spear that had been sitting beside him all this time with its dirty white shirt knotted beneath the blade. He took one step closer to the edge and looked down at King Sixfingers. Took a long drink of water and then spat on the road below. 'Well then, Sixfingers?'

Medrin squinted up at them. 'I've heard your voice before.'

'You have. In Andhun I stood against you on the beach and behind the city gates, and I stand against you now. Pox-scarred prince of filth! Twelve-fingered son of the Mother of Monsters. I'm Valaric of Witterslet. Valaric of the Marroc. Valaric the Wolf and I carry the red Sword of the Weeping God. Do you care to face me this time, Sixfingers, or are you the coward that even your own men know you to be?'

Sixfingers lifted his spear, stretched his arms and yawned. 'Three years in your swamp, Valaric of the Crackmarsh, and not a single new rebuke? Truly, the turgid waters have seeped into your head. Or perhaps the ghuldogs have taken a bite out of you? As for your challenge?' He shook his head. 'I'll fight you, Valaric of the Marroc, Valaric of Witterslet, you and I alone, but I'll fight you at the top of this road not the bottom, between sundered gates ringed by the burned corpses of those who follow your foolishness. It won't satisfy me just to kill you now; I mean to make an end of you that all Marroc will see.' His voice rose as though he addressed the mountain itself. 'For a year and a day this will be a castle of ghosts. Not one who hides behind these walls will I spare. Not one. Men will hang and women too. Children will burn. Gibbets will rise and blood ravens will fly. The curse of the red sword lies on you all, Marroc of Varyxhun.'

Sarvic strummed his bow and then put an arrow to it. 'I've had enough of this.' But Valaric knocked the arrow aside.

Sixfingers looked up to the gatehouse again and cocked his head. 'Marroc who serve their king with good hearts tell me that tomorrow is your festival of Shiefa. They tell me you celebrate with ale and mead and dancing and singing and beckon the blushing bride of summer to shed her last clothes of winter.

I'm told it's a time for bonfires and bedding maidens and that even the dead rise to watch. Make your festival a grand one, Valaric of Witterslet, wherever that is. I'll give you three days of kindness before I return with iron and fire.'

He turned and walked back down the road to Varyxhun. The army of waiting forkbeards lifted their shields and spears and roared and beat them one against the other in a slow steady rhythm. Sarvic drew out another arrow, and this time Valaric rounded on him and pushed him so hard he lost his balance. Sarvic threw out an arm to catch himself and almost barged Reddic off the battlement. 'Sixfingers, Valaric! Sixfingers the demon prince of Andhun! Have you forgotten?'

Valaric grabbed two great fistfuls of Sarvic's mail and pulled him close. 'Have I forgotten?' For a moment his face twisted into such a fury that even Angry Jonnic paled and took a step back. Valaric set Sarvic down. 'No, Sarvic, I haven't. But that doesn't make it right to shoot a man in the back when he comes to parley. Not even if that man's the devil.'

'Took a finger of courage, coming up here like that all on his own.' Fat Jonnic sniffed and scratched his chin.

'And don't you go and start admiring him, don't you dare. *You* didn't see Andhun.'

Reddic and Angry Jonnic stayed on the gate with a handful of the Marroc from Varyxhun while Valaric and the rest of the Crackmarsh men climbed back to the castle. They slept the night on the battlements, eight of them out in the open wrapped up in their winter furs – the warm spring days didn't change how cold the nights could be. They spent the next morning there too, and by the time Valaric sent his Crackmarsh men to relieve them, Angry Jonnic was ready to go and fight the forkbeards on his own. They climbed the ladders from gatehouse to gatehouse, all the way to the castle walls where Sarvic and a few others stood watch, looking down at Varyxhun and the forkbeard camp and the glittering rush of the Isset winding off to the north. Sarvic nodded as Reddic came past. 'You wait and see. Sixfingers says he'll come the dawn after next. But he won't; he'll come tonight when he thinks we're all in our cups, raising them to Shiefa. Faithless forkbeard.'

Reddic thought he might go and look for Jelira, but even before he'd come down off the walls and crossed the castle yard, Valaric was waving at Angry Jonnic and so Reddic went too, and Valaric had the Aulian with him and a barrel full of arrows. He clapped Reddic on the shoulder. 'Those iron heads you brought? Fletchers from Varyxhun have finished making them into arrows. There's three thousand, give or take. That's ...' He frowned.

The Aulian smiled. 'Make them into bundles, ten arrows in each. One bundle to every man with a bow. What's left to stay in the armoury.'

'Ten arrows in a bundle?' Jonnic picked up ten arrows and then looked at the barrel. 'That's all? That's—'

'Not enough arrows,' finished Valaric curtly. 'So they'd better count.'

'Going to take us all day is what I was *going* to say!'

Valaric shrugged and pointed to two more barrels tucked in the shadows against a wall. 'Needs to be done though, so best you get on with it.'

Jonnic took a deep breath but Reddic got in first and put a hand on Jonnic's arm. 'Go and find the children who came with the smith from Middislet. They can do it. I'll stay with them and make sure it's done right.'

Valaric smirked as Jonnic stamped off. 'Arda won't let you anywhere near her. You know that, don't you?'

He was about to say he hadn't any idea what Valaric was talking about but by then the Wolf and the Aulian had turned away. The Wolf was laughing. And he was wrong too, because when Jonnic came back he came with Nadric and Jelira and the three children and there was no sign of Arda at all, and for a while Tathic and Feya helped with counting the arrows into tens and tying twine around them, until they got bored and wandered off to where Nadric and Pursic were playing. Jelira and Reddic finished the rest on their own. They talked, hardly noticing the time, Reddic about the family he'd had once and his new family in the Crackmarsh, Jelira about the days she remembered back before the Vathen, before the forkbeards came again, the days when Gallow had been her father. They talked about happy things, times and places and people that made them smile and forgot for a while about the harshness that overshadowed them. By the time they were done with the arrows, the sun was setting and Angry Jonnic was coming across the yard. He clutched a jug of something, held it close like it was a lover, and for once he looked more merry than angry.

'Looks like Sarvic and Valaric are wrong and the forkbeards aren't coming tonight after all.'

Reddic reckoned that was the mead talking, given the night had barely begun, but kept the thought to himself. Jonnic beckoned Reddic forward, but when Jelira came too he shook his head and put an arm around Reddic's shoulder and walked him away, whispering loudly and stinking of drink. 'Got something for you.' He struggled for a bit while he tried to hold on to Reddic and the mead jug and get something off his belt all at once. Eventually he pressed a key into Reddic's hand. 'Valaric says to let him go. I don't like it, mind, but Mournful don't ever listen to me any more.'

'Let who go?'

'The Foxbeard.' He snorted and shrugged. 'Valaric says for you to do it. So go on then. Do it.' He staggered off.

Jelira looked at him, face filled with worry. Reddic smiled and showed her the key. 'Valaric says to let the Foxbeard g—' He shook his head at his own stupidity. 'I mean Gallow. Your d—'

And then he couldn't have said how she covered the ground between them except that one moment they were a good ten feet apart and the next she was wrapped around him, head pressed against his chest, arms squeezing him as though she was wringing water out of a blanket. She led him by the hand to the sixth gate, skipping past the Dragon's Maw and down the winding stairs to the dungeons beneath, past the cell where the strange-looking Vathan woman hissed at them and on to another. There was a guard on watch, sitting beside Gallow's cell, pressed up against the iron bars. Gallow was on the inside, pressed up against them too, and it seemed odd to Reddic that Valaric would waste a man to guard the forkbeard and stranger still that any guard would sit so close; and then he realised this wasn't a guard at all, this was Arda, and this was where she'd been when Angry Jonnic had gone looking and for the rest of the day too.

She stood up as she heard Reddic and Jelira and scowled. 'Whatever you two want on Shieftane, I doubt very much I'm going to like it.'

Jelira threw herself at Arda and hugged her the way she'd hugged Reddic. Reddic just slipped the key into the cell door, opened it and stood back. And then took another step away as the Foxbeard unfolded himself from where he'd been crouched beside the bars and eased to his feet. In the cramped space he looked huge, a head taller than Reddic and twice as wide, with arms to wrestle bears and fists strong enough to stun a boar. But then Jelira let go of Arda and ran into the cell and threw herself at him, and that and the bemused pain and joy on the Foxbeard's face took away his menace.

'Valaric the Wolf says you're free to fight beside us,' said Reddic, which wasn't quite what Jonnic had said but it would do. But they'd already forgotten him. He watched the three of them wrapped up together tight in each other's arms, and a pang of longing built up inside him and he had to turn away. He went up to the yard and stared at the moon for a bit and then found Angry Jonnic and stole his jug of mead. In the Hall of Thrones half the Crackmarsh men and most of the Marroc from Varyxhun were singing and dancing. Up on the walls Sarvic and a few others kept watch, those who wouldn't trust a forkbeard's word, not ever. Reddic let them all be. For now he wanted to be alone.

When the moon reached its zenith, Jelira came and found him and asked him if he'd seen Nadric and the little ones. He pointed her to the hall and she went away again, but after she'd found them she came back and nestled beside him, and later Reddic took her hand and led her up to the castle walls and they sat on the battlements together and got drunk on Angry Jonnic's mead. Noises wafted up from the valley below but Jelira and Reddic were both lost, drunk on mead and each other, staring out over the Isset, which was lit up like silver by the moon.

*

The sun rose on the morning after Shieftane and then rose on the next and Reddic stood atop the first gate once more. Low grey cloud hung over the valley. The forkbeards were massing. The abandoned houses and taverns and stables and barns of Varyxhun had become their camp, and on the morning after the festival, as the Marroc nursed their sore heads, the forkbeards had erected an avenue of wooden poles along the castle road. Reddic didn't understood what they were at first, and then when he did, he wished he hadn't. Gibbets. While he'd been sitting and dreaming in the moonlight with Jelira, the forkbeards had rounded up the Marroc of Varyxhun who were too stubborn or too stupid to leave. Now they lined the road, dangling.

A column of forkbeards was winding its way out of Varyxhun. He watched a while longer until he was sure and then he ran to the wall. 'They're coming! The forkbeards are coming!' And when he peered closer he saw what it was that had kept them in the city these last few days. It wasn't some simple gesture of kindness that had made Sixfingers leave them alone until the festival of Shiefa was past. They'd been building, and now four siege towers eased their way onto the road.

There wasn't much to do now but watch and wait and pray to Modris.

24

THE FIRST GATE

Standing beside Valaric on the second of the six tiers of walls that rose up to the castle of Varyxhun, Gallow watched them come. The Lhosir marched up the road in the cool morning air singing an old song of the sea that Gallow knew well, a mournful lament for drowned men. A hundred feet short of the first gate they stopped. A few dozen pushed a ram towards the gate but they stopped short too. Gallow waited for the surge forward and for the fury of the battle to begin but it didn't happen. The Lhosir stood below him, out of reach of the gatehouse but right below the feet of the men lining the second tier, shields locked together over their heads, looking up in anticipation. For a long minute an eerie quiet fell over the road. Then Valaric raised his hand and held it high for three long heartbeats and let it fall, and as he did, a storm of stones and arrows flew into the shields from right above them.

The Marroc yelled and howled and hooted. The Lhosir held firm and took their punishment. Arrows stuck out of their shields. Men screamed and howled curses as stones hit them. Here and there Gallow saw a Lhosir fall, crippled or dead, but there were few. The air had a touch of sweat to it now, forkbeard sweat, men already sweltering under their mail and helms though the road to the castle lay in the shade of the mountain. No burning skin yet though. Valaric was saving his fire for when he needed it. The Lhosir simply stood there. They didn't even try to raise any ladders.

Gallow caught Valaric's arm and shook his head. Arrows into a wall of shields was a waste, even if they did hit a Lhosir now and then. 'They're drawing you in, Valaric. They're making you spend your arrows while their shields are strongest. Wait for them to make their move.' He looked at the stones around him. The Marroc had already thrown most of what they'd brought and the battle had barely started. Three hundred archers with some dozen arrows each and the same again waiting in the castle thanks to Arda and Nadric. Enough to kill almost every Lhosir who'd ever crossed the sea, but only if they were used with care.

Valaric's eyes blazed, itching for the fight. 'Every arrow, you beef-witted clods! Every arrow has to count! Every arrow and every stone! Hold! Hold!'

The first of the siege towers was getting close. The Marroc bowmen fell silent, and now it was the turn of the Lhosir to hoot and taunt and howl, peering from behind their shields and sticking out their tongues. There was a rhythm to their shouting, as if they were at the oars of their ships. The towers weren't for the gates, Gallow saw that now. Medrin meant to scale the walls directly from one tier of the castle road to the next, bypassing both the first gatehouse and the second. And Valaric, who had seen this too, meant to stop him. Marroc scurried to and fro, readying every stone and missile they could find. Valaric raised his hand again as the first tower came higher, as its top came close to the level of his feet. Every Marroc eye turned to follow him. The Lhosir watched too, hunched behind their shields. They understood what would come when that hand fell.

'Now!' Valaric's hand dropped, and the Marroc along the walls cried out to Modris, to old King Tane, to Diaran, even to the Weeping God. Stones and rocks and boulders rained on the Lhosir once more, and now lighted pots of fish oil burst among their shields. The Lhosir wavered and Gallow felt a pang of sorrow for them, for deep down these were his people. Nothing wrong with most of them, just men on the wrong side of a wall as stones smashed down shields and broke bones and snapped sinews. Arrows flew. Men wrapped in flames tumbled over the edge to the Aulian Way and the Isset below. Others slipped and fell, rolled on their backs; burning shields were hurled away. Medrin's Lhosir had no answer, no arrows of their own, no javelins, no stone throwers. Yet the towers came on.

'More! More!'

The Lhosir were packing themselves tight, pushing their

shields closer. A jagged piece of stone as big as a man's torso went over the edge and smashed into a dozen of them clustered together. Half were crushed where they stood, the others sent sprawling. Gallow saw one man stagger to his feet with two arrows in his chest and vanish back under the wall of shields. How deep they were through his mail was anyone's guess. Smoke rose up the walls now, acrid, thick with the stench of burning men, of fish and hair and skin. Over the shouting he heard Valaric whoop as the Lhosir died.

Gallow closed his eyes. Medrin. Medrin had made this slaughter. Medrin and no one else and so Medrin would pay to make it right.

The first tower began to slide slowly back. For a moment Gallow's heart was in his mouth, begging and praying and willing for it to slip and roll and topple and fall and crush the others. The Lhosir were yelling to hold it steady. Yet now, when it mattered most, the stones and the arrows gradually wilted. The boulders became pebbles. The road fell quiet again as though both sides were holding their breath, waiting to see, all except Valaric who was screaming at his men for more. But when Gallow looked, he saw why Valaric's Marroc didn't respond. There was no more. They'd thrown everything they had.

The Lhosir shouts found a rhythm again. The tower stopped then ground back up the road once more until it slid to a halt in front of Gallow, right in front of him because he'd been watching it and was waiting for it. A ladder on wheels, that's all it was, draped with heavy furs to protect the men climbing inside. At the very top the forkbeards had built a ramp like a drawbridge to cover the gap between the tower and the wall. Gallow readied his spear and waited for it to fall.

Now the tower was actually here, Valaric wished he'd saved some of the oil or the boulders. There was a runner on the way to the third gate calling for both but they wouldn't come in time. This wasn't how it was supposed to go. The forkbeards were supposed to die battering their way through the gates. Now his men were in the wrong place. He needed his soldiers here, all of them, and he sent a second runner for reinforcements, but it was all too late to make a difference. Cursed Sixfingers had out-thought him, that was the truth of it, not that any man around him would ever say so.

A dozen archers stood ready for the ramp to come down. Valaric stood in the middle of a semicircle of twenty men with spears and shields, the best of his Crackmarsh men with Gallow in the middle beside him. In his hand he held Solace, the Comforter, the red sword of the Vathen. In Andhun he'd told Gallow that the sword was cursed and he'd believed it too, but now he had no choice. 'When that ramp comes down, sod the arrows.' The forkbeards would be ready for that. They'd have their shields up, but maybe that meant for a moment they wouldn't see what was coming. 'When it comes down, we charge them. We hit them like bulls and we take their tower and throw it down on their heads!'

The forkbeards below fell quiet. Valaric and his men gripped their spears, waiting for the ramp to fall.

'Are you ready for us, Valaric of Witterslet, Valaric of the Marroc, Valaric of the Swamp? Are you ready to die now?' Sixfingers was somewhere below and not far from the foot of the tower but Valaric couldn't see where.

Beside him, Gallow let out such a howl of hate that Valaric winced. 'Medrin!'

There was a long pause and then Sixfingers seemed to be closer. 'Is that you, Foxbeard?'

'My sword hungers for you!'

'They say you killed Beyard outside Witches' Reach. I hear he had the better of you and let you win.'

Valaric threw Gallow a glance then nudged him. 'Answer! You have to answer!'

'I'll not be as accommodating, Foxbeard.' Sixfingers was taunting them now. 'I'll be with you as soon as I can. While you wait, perhaps you might discuss with your Marroc friend which one of you I should kill first.'

Valaric shoved Gallow again. Idiot. 'Bring your worst, king of dogs,' he bellowed. 'My wolves hunger for you!'

'Then enjoy your feast!' There was a venomous glee to Sixfingers' voice but Valaric didn't have time to wonder about that because the tower shuddered and the ramp crashed down, and he was already moving and so were his Crackmarsh men because if there was one thing that got you killed in a battle more surely than a spear or an axe then it was doubt.

But the men waiting for them when the ramp came down were no forkbeards. They wore closed helms and ragged mail. They carried long Aulian swords and small round shields and their skin, where it showed, was chalky white. Shadewalkers. Sixfingers, somehow, had sent shadewalkers, and for a moment Valaric felt every part of him turn numb. The Marroc beside him thrust a spear through one porcelain throat. The shadewalker staggered but it didn't bleed and it didn't fall. Valaric heard a wail of fear and a cry of despair. He felt the air turn cold and sour and his men falter.

Gallow smashed a shadewalker with his shield. Another lost its hand, cut off at the wrist. It dropped its shield and grabbed a Marroc by the throat and throttled him while the Marroc stabbed it over and over, but Valaric had his own dead man to deal with, slamming its sword into him, battering him back with a strength that wasn't human. 'Stand!' he bellowed. 'Stand and hold them! Get the Aulian!' Salt, that was the trick wasn't it? But none of them had thought the forkbeards would send shadewalkers to do their fighting – who would have thought they could? And, besides, shadewalkers only came out at night, didn't they? How had Sixfingers done this?

His men were already breaking and running around him, the shadewalkers stumbling after them and then stopping, staggering in the daylight. Valaric screamed a roar of rage and frustration and hewed at the dead thing in front of him. He slammed two blows into its shield, and then it blocked a third with its long sword but the iron blade snapped. Solace carved a line across the shadewalker's face. The creature howled, its skin fell in on itself, and before Valaric's eyes it crumbled into dust and bones and a dizzying stench of death. Valaric reeled and swung at the shadewalker strangling one of his Marroc and half severed its head. It too crumbled before him.

'See! They die!' But he was too late. His men had left him, even Gallow. Fled, and now there were shadewalkers all around and he could feel the tower shake as the forkbeards climbed through its guts, and then suddenly there was one looking right at him with his shield over his shoulder as he climbed. Forkbeards he understood, and this one couldn't do a thing about it when Valaric lunged. The point of the red sword split the forkbeard's mail as though it was cloth and bit straight through to his heart. The forkbeard's eyes rolled back in surprise. He fell limp and dropped among the others behind him. Valaric bared his teeth and grinned: this, *this* was what he wanted! He was standing at the top of the ladder and the forkbeards had to get past him. He'd kill them all, every single one of them. Alone if he had to.

'Valaric!'

And he *wasn't* alone. On the road behind him the shade-walkers staggered and lurched. Not a single Marroc had stayed, but two men stood firm nevertheless. The Aulian wizard with his satchels of salt and Gallow, battering the shadewalkers away from him.

From atop the first gate Reddic saw the Marroc surge into the forkbeard tower and then fall back and scatter and break, screaming as though they'd walked into the gaping maw of the Maker-Devourer himself. They ran like they had the devil at their backs and Reddic could see at once that the creatures who stepped onto the road were no forkbeards. They stood in a daze as though they'd never seen the sun. He gasped. 'Shadewalkers!'

'Look sharp!' Angry Jonnic didn't want to know. On the road beneath them the forkbeards were coming, a hundred or more with the ram they'd left short of the gates. A second tower was coming up the road and the next two weren't far behind. Reddic squinted at where the forkbeards had driven his Crackmarsh brothers away. The walls of the second tier overlooking the ram were already all but abandoned: where there should have been a hundred men with arrows and stones, now there were none. At the start of the day he'd been scared but there'd been a part of him that had thought they might win. Not any more.

'Ladders!'

The stone quivered under Reddic's feet as the ram hit the gates. He looked for something to throw but Jonnic caught his arm and shook his head. 'Wait.' He pulled Reddic away from the edge and pushed him down behind a merlon then shouted at the others to abandon the gate and go up to the next and pull the ladder up behind them. When Reddic made to get up to join them, Jonnic pushed him down again. 'I said wait!' He grinned and his eyes were wild and mad. 'The six of us up here won't stop them breaking through. Let them think they've got an easy ride of it. Let them think we've all run away like the rest. Keep nice and quiet and still. Then we can rain rocks and oil on them when they're not expecting it. Hurt them where it counts.'

'And then?'

Jonnic patted Reddic on the shoulder. They both knew what *and then* looked like. Reddic closed his eyes and shook his head. 'Scared?' Jonnic chuckled. 'There's no shame in that.'

But Reddic found he wasn't really, not any more. He'd gone long past scared and it was something else. 'There's a girl up in the castle. We spent Shieftane watching the moon together. I wanted to tell her something but I never did.' He shrugged and whispered a prayer to Modris the Protector. Beside him Jonnic did the same.

Valaric killed the next forkbeard to show his head at the top of the ladder. Oribas was scattering lines of salt on the road and Gallow was smashing the shadewalkers away, keeping the Aulian free to do his work. One by one he penned them in, and it seemed to Valaric that these shadewalkers were slow and clumsy and not so frightening after all. Yet there were no other Marroc here now. Just him and Oribas and Gallow against Sixfingers and all his army.

'Come on up, Sixfingers!' he bellowed. 'We're both here. The Foxbeard says I get to have at you first!'

'The sun, Valaric,' Oribas shouted. 'The sun steals their strength. But I have no fire to burn them, nor iron to kill them.'

'Your sword, Valaric!' Gallow had one of them wrestled to the ground and was smashing it over and over but it still thrashed and its mail turned his blade. 'The red sword. End them! I'll keep Medrin's curs whimpering in their holes for you!'

Valaric ran out from the tower and across the ramp. He

smashed the red sword into the head of the one wrestling with Gallow and then watched as the Foxbeard ran to take his place. The red sword hacked down another shadewalker. Now that he was outside he could see the forkbeards were bringing their ram up to the first gate and the Marroc on top were already scaling the rope ladder to the roof of the second, fleeing without putting up a fight. Valaric raised his fists at them all, screaming at the top of his lungs, 'Cowards! You sheep! You're everything they say of us! If this is the best we are then we deserve everything they do! Mewling hedge-born clay-hearts, all of you!' Tears were running down his face. The Crackmarsh men he'd had with him, those surly old soldiers he'd quietly thought as good as any forkbeard, they were all gone, cowering along the zigzag road, past the next gate where they had stone and wood and iron to keep the shadewalkers at bay. Probably none of them could even hear him. No one except the Aulian wizard, who shouldn't even be here, and Gallow, a forkbeard. It made him want to fall on his own sword.

The second tower was close. Soon it would reach the road and fall open and there'd be no stopping them. He let out a furious howl, grabbed one of the shadewalkers from behind, picked it up and and threw it over the wall onto the throng of forkbeards below. He turned back. 'I have iron enough for these, Aulian!' He swung the red sword and listened to the air moan as the steel split the wind. A shadewalker fell with its head torn from its shoulders, the next with its face split in two, a third with the point driven through the back of its skull. They tried to defend themselves, but against the red sword, out in the sun and doused by Oribas's salt, they were as feeble as children.

Peacebringer. The red sword wanted them. One by one the shadewalkers crumbled to dust.

25

THE RAM

A movement from inside the tower caught Valaric's eye, another forkbeard shield creeping up. Gallow was there. He brought his axe down and the forkbeard beneath bellowed an oath. Valaric laughed. The last two shadewalkers were helpless quivering things, paralysed by Oribas's salt, and they didn't even try to stop him as he took their heads. He looked up the road to the third gate, praying to Modris that his Crackmarsh men had found their spines again, but no.

The second forkbeard tower reached the road and stopped, and even Valaric knew better than to stand alone against the dozen angry forkbeards who'd come howling out of it. He grabbed Oribas, turned and ran, shouting at Gallow as he did and didn't look back until he reached the elbow where the road turned from the siege towers and second gate behind him and doubled back on itself up towards the third. Past the elbow there were Marroc on the walls over his head again, more men with stones and arrows and fire. Forkbeards were coming out of both of the siege towers now, scores of them, and Gallow still stood alone to face them. Valaric could have murdered him for that. A forkbeard facing dozens of his own kin when a hundred Marroc had been too afraid? And for a heartbeat Valaric thought about running back to Gallow's side, facing them together, the two of them against the whole of Medrin's army just like it had been in Andhun. Utter madness, but when he held the red sword he felt immortal.

The forkbeards were advancing slowly behind a wall of shields, taking their time, content to walk the Foxbeard slowly back. As Valaric watched, an arrow from up on the fourth tier took one of them in the legs. Gallow threw back his head and roared out his challenge once more: 'Here I am, Medrin! Waiting for you!' The first gate was being smashed in without a single Marroc holding his ground to defend it. The second gate had the forkbeards from their towers behind it already. They'd just walk up to it and open it.

Valaric walked through the third gate with the red sword over his shoulder. He growled and looked at the faces around him, the men who'd broken and run at the first drawn sword. But as he prepared to bellow out his furious contempt, Oribas touched his arm. The Aulian took his hand and raised it high, the red sword still firm in Valaric's gasp. 'Men of the Varyxhun valley! For years you've feared those creatures. Shadewalkers that many of you thought could not be killed. Today one man alone with this sword has destroyed them.' He dropped Valaric's arm and lifted one of his satchels of salt. 'I have fought them too. You saw me. I didn't kill any and I had no sword, but I didn't run because I did not need a blade.' He sprinkled a line of salt across the road. 'Salt! Nothing more, yet it is like a wall of stone to them. They cannot pass. Throw it on their skin and it burns them like fire. Salt!' He threw the satchel down and pulled Valaric up the road, muttering under his breath, 'You'll have to give salt to every man now. I have no idea how many shadewalkers are in this valley but it's many more than you put to rest today. Tell them it works on the ironskins too. Men must know how to fight whatever enemy stands before them. You cannot blame them if they run when they do not.'

Valaric looked back through the open gate at Gallow, still alone, still facing the forkbeards. He didn't understand why the forkbeards didn't simply charge and overwhelm Gallow with their numbers. He stopped at the edge of the road and looked down. The ram was still at the first gate but the forkbeards must have smashed through already because he could see them clearing rubble on the other side and trading insults with the Marroc atop the second. Now and then an arrow flew down. One good charge and he still might sweep the forkbeards off the road and smash their towers. One good charge, but that was what the gates were for. So that he didn't have to. So that he didn't have to lose so many men, not yet.

Stuck in his throat though. He yelled down the road at Gallow, 'Foxbeard! Save it for the sixth gate, not the second.' He sighed and shook his head because walking away wasn't what forkbeards did when they could stand and fight instead, however stupid it might be. Yet after a moment Gallow backed away and the forkbeards didn't follow. Valaric took a deep breath and let it out between his teeth. The second gate wouldn't hold long, not with forkbeards on both sides. 'Two gates lost in a single day.'

Oribas touched his arm. 'They still have to open it. Then they have to clear the road and bring up their ram and you can drop rocks and arrows on them all the way. Your men have seen that shadewalkers can die now and the forkbeards cannot easily bring those towers any further; and if they do then I have an idea or two about how we might stop them.' His eyes were gleaming. 'Imagine many stones hitting the men behind that ramp as it opens. Hitting them very fast and hard.'

Valaric felt suddenly light-headed. 'What I want, Aulian, is to imagine the dragon coming out of that cave behind the sixth gate and eating them all. That would do nicely.'

Gallow was walking through the third gate while the Marroc there all looked away, pretending he didn't exist, closing the gate behind him. The Aulian was nodding to himself, lost in his own plans. 'I'll go back up to the castle now. You've got enough carpenters there and rope and wood. I could have one made by sunset. And the dragon of your stories will drown them, not eat them.'

Valaric unexpectedly sat down, because it was suddenly that or fall over. He felt dizzy and had no idea what the Aulian was talking about. He looked at his feet in front of him. One of his boots was light and one of them was dark. Which was odd because they'd both been light at the start of the day.

It was blood. 'Oh …'

Oribas was staring at him. The Aulian knelt down and pushed at the mail surcoat that Valaric wore down to his knees. He poked at something and a sharp pain shot right up Valaric's spine. 'One of the shadewalkers.'

'I don't even feel it.' Did he want to look? That was a lot of blood, but he'd run all the way up the road so it couldn't be too bad, could it? But Oribas wasn't even looking at him. The Aulian was waving his hands at the nearest Marroc and yelling for a mule, and at Gallow, and calling for his satchel, and all with an urgent panic in his eyes. Valaric sat humming to himself. Some old tune his mother had used to sing when he was a boy, one he'd forgotten for years.

Reddic listened to the forkbeards yell at each other and then tuned his ears for the scrape of wood on stone that would be a ladder but it never came. After another hour, when there still hadn't been any forkbeards climbing over the battlements, he needed a piss. Jonnic snarled at him. There were forkbeards all over the road below clearing stones so they could move their ram. They hardly weren't going to notice if some Marroc stood up on the gates and relieved himself over them.

Reddic turned his head. There were more forkbeards further up the road. The second gatehouse was surrounded. But more to the point, the forkbeards on the second tier could see him if they cared to look down. He couldn't even sit up. Didn't dare move at all. After another hour he just let it out. It was an odd feeling, lying down and pissing in his pants. Couldn't say he could remember ever doing that before. And there they stayed, the two of them alone, lying still as statues because that's what Jonnic said, while the forkbeards pushed their ram and then their army on up the road.

Oribas had barely got two Marroc to bring a mule when Valaric tipped over sideways, white as a sheet. Gallow caught him and eased him to the ground but the bleeding was worse than the Aulian had thought and so there wouldn't be any taking him up to the castle to patch him together. He'd do it here. They needed him. Without Valaric, the Crackmarsh men would simply break.

Oribas waved back the Marroc with the mule and beckoned Gallow closer instead. 'Hold him.' He eased Valaric onto his back. Blood still ran freely out of his leg, though it should have clotted by now. 'Pull back his mail.' He rummaged in his satchel wondering why the wound wasn't closing. If the shadewalker had hit an artery Valaric would have died back on the road so it wasn't that, but it just kept bleeding. There were desert animals that used the same trick on their prey. Bit them and then left them to bleed until they were too weak to run. He'd never understood how they did that. Spirits. Bad spirits, his masters had said, which was another way of saying that they didn't know either.

'I never thought I'd come back,' said Gallow out of nowhere. 'It was right that I did. I've made myself whole again.'

Gallow had Valaric's mail pulled back. 'Now get his trousers down.' Needle and thread and Firaxian powders to make the bleeding stop. Marroc clustered to see what he was doing. They stared at him and so Oribas stared back. 'Do you want to be the ones fighting the shadewalkers? No? Then give me space to work! Fetch some wine. Good strong dark wine. The best you can find.' It might help Valaric or it might not but it would certainly help an Aulian scholar who'd never been so close to a battle in all his life until Gallow had brought him over the mountains. He set to work with Gallow crouched beside him with his weight on Valaric's shoulders.

'I made an oath on Shiefa's night. It was three years to the day since I left Middislet with the Screambreaker. I made an oath in blood, Oribas, a promise to fight no wars once this one is done. And after that I dreamed of how it would be if Medrin Sixfingers simply ceased, if he changed his mind and went home, if there was more to our horizon than bloody war and starving siege and a slow and unwelcome death. Can you do that, Oribas, wizard of Aulia? Can you make Medrin simply disappear?'

'No.' Oribas snapped. His stitching was ragged and there was blood all over his hands and yes, he was staunching it at last, but far more slowly than he should have. He shouted at the Marroc, 'Water! Bring water!'

Gallow stood up. 'I'll see we're ready for Medrin when he comes. We've lost two gates already. Yes, I'll be seeing to what needs seeing to, whether these Marroc like it or not.'

Oribas muttered and kept to his sewing, and of course Valaric woke up when he was only half done and almost jumped straight into the air even though he was lying down, and Oribas had to persuade him back and never mind how much it hurt. At least the wine helped with that, when it came.

The forkbeards were moving on now, swinging their ram around the elbow in the road. Past the second gate they were already clearing the stones the Marroc had left there to bar the way. A few Marroc still held the top of the second gatehouse, shooting the odd arrow to keep the forkbeards on their toes. It was never going to amount to much, holding the roofs of the gates, but Angry Jonnic still just shook his head when Reddic said they should go and climb on up to the second tier before the forkbeards cut them off.

'Sooner or later Sixfingers is going to come up that road. He's going to think he's safe, right until we put a pair of arrows into him.' Jonnic grinned and drew a finger across his throat. The ram rounded the corner.

Valaric just about managed to wait for Oribas to finish before he jumped up again. 'Gently on it!' The Aulian snapped at him. 'There must have been something on the shadewalker's blade. A wound shouldn't bleed like that. You should rest.'

But Valaric laughed and waved him away. 'Rest? You still have eyes and ears to see and hear that army, right? Rest? Don't you worry Aulian, there was nothing on the blade that cut me. I bleed. It's just the way it is.' Stupid thing for a man who'd made his life fighting, but then that wasn't how he'd ever thought he'd spend his time. A farmer like his father, like his brothers, like his uncles, like everyone he knew, and that's how it had been until the forkbeards had come and set to their rampaging. After that, knowing every wound would bleed had made sure he'd learned how to fight, how to take the other man down first, fast and hard.

He made himself forget the pain. Sixfingers was down there somewhere. He took a long look at the forkbeards and their ram and then moved among his men. He knew every one of them. Knew their names and who they were and what had dragged them from their homes and into the Crackmarsh to fight the forkbeards. Some had lost their families or their wives or their sons or their daughters. Others had stood up for themselves. A few had killed. And of course they had men come to the Crackmarsh to get away from Marroc justice too, but the marsh always heard the truth of what a man was running from in the end and when it did, they made their own justice.

He moved among the men who hated the forkbeards most of all. The ones who'd lost everything. The ones who'd come here ready to die, wanting it even. Men like him. He knew who they were, for they were the ones who looked at Gallow with stony dead eyes. Whose lips stayed tightly shut while their knuckles clenched white as he passed them. They stood together and watched the forkbeards below, threw taunts at them while the Lhosir laughed back from behind their shields and shouted insults of their own. One of the forkbeards threw a spear. Valaric plucked it out of the air and threw it back and it hit a shield hard enough to sprawl the forkbeard beneath across the road. The man wrenched it free and shook his fist. The others around him laughed.

The ram moved up towards the second gate. Marroc archers still held the roof, sneering at the forkbeards on the road and loosing an arrow now and then. A few men dead but it didn't amount to much, not unless you were the one with the arrow sticking out of you. Valaric waited until the ram was right up to the gate, until the forkbeards were getting ready to swing it, then he smiled and nodded. This time his stones were in the right place.

The first fell squarely on the nose of the ram, shattering its frame and smashing the front wheels. It slithered off the wood and into a half-dozen forkbeards and dropped them over the edge to the tier below. Valaric didn't see them land but he heard the screams as they went. The next two stones landed short. Men were crushed flat and the ram smashed sideways, throwing another few forkbeards over the edge as it slewed. The last stone was perfect. It bounced off the cliff and landed on the front of the ram again, and this time the back end jerked into the air, scattering forkbeards, twisted and then rolled as it landed and slipped over the edge. In a great rumble of stone and cracking wood and howling men, the ram tumbled off the road and smashed itself to pieces behind the first gate below, crushing a few forkbeards more as it did. Valaric picked up a bow and let fly a couple of arrows while the forkbeards were still reeling. After that he told his men to hold their fire and watched to see what the enemy would do. He looked at the siege towers, still where the forkbeards had left them. They'd be back with those, he thought, and that made him start looking for Oribas. Maybe the Aulian could think of a way to bounce a stone straight on top of them from right up in the castle. Save them the bother of all that walking back and forth.

He winced. The wound *was* going to be a bother. He could tell that now.

26

THE THIRD GATE

They felt the gate shake as each stone hit the road above then shudder as the ram crashed beneath them. Jonnic was grinning like a snake. Reddic could hear the Marroc up above shouting and forkbeards shouting back, but from where he lay he couldn't see much of what was going on. Later Jonnic moved across the gatehouse roof until he was overlooking the road up from Varyxhun. By then the fighting had moved on. A while later still, he cackled. 'You know what I see? I see a banner coming up the road.'

The forkbeards from the siege towers opened the second gate from behind and then held their ground wherever they found shelter from the Marroc above them, yelling taunts and insults up the mountain. Gallow stood on the fourth tier now, looking down. The men around him threw rocks when they thought they saw something they could hit, but for the most part the battle had gone quiet. In places the two armies were only a few dozen paces apart, but as the sun came round the mountain, even the insults stopped. The Lhosir crouched behind their shields and the Marroc archers taught them the hard way where was safe and where was not. Gallow understood exactly what Medrin was doing. He could have drawn his men back to the first gate until they were ready but he was trying to make the Marroc waste what missiles they had before the charge came.

Down below, the forkbeards lifted something up to the road behind the second gate. 'Another ram,' said Oribas.

Gallow frowned. 'They'll not split one of these gates with something that size.' He squinted, trying to make out what it was for. There were a score of forkbeards pushing it, maybe half a dozen on the ram itself, the rest with huge shields to keep the Marroc arrows at bay. Then as it climbed the road, a figure stepped out from the huddled mass of shields behind, an iron-skin, and as the Fateguard rounded the corner of the road and passed the men with their ram, it suddenly broke into a run and raced for the third gate. A storm of stones and arrows flew at it until Valaric screamed at his men to stop. They were all wasted on an ironskin and besides one Fateguard could hardly take a castle gate. It wasn't even carrying an axe.

The Fateguard ran to the gates and slid to its knees. It spread its arms wide and pressed its hands against the wood and iron and didn't move.

'Salt!' shouted Oribas. 'Rain salt on him!' Gallow was puzzled. Just another way to make the Marroc waste their arrows? Around him the Marroc pointed and laughed. Then fracture lines of rust spread out over the Fateguard's iron skin like water freezing on glass. The lines of rust spread across the iron of the gate too, to its bars and bolts and hinges. Oribas was still shouting, hurling salt over the edge of the road, the Marroc still laughing and taunting the forkbeards. The ironskin stayed where it was, perfectly still, until it finally fell under a barrage of stones from above and broke into pieces as though its iron armour was all but empty. And then the forkbeards charged.

Sarvic had a little line of stones each the size of a man's head lined up on the top of the third gatehouse. He stood poised behind one, waiting for the ram. The forkbeards hadn't even bothered to build a roof over it and they were going to suffer for that. He had a torch and his buckets and pots of fish oil too, ready to set alight and drench the forkbeards and burn them back down the mountain. He felt a strange elation. The forkbeards were doomed. They had their shields against the rain of stones and arrows, but here and there he saw men fall, arrows finding their way through the gaps, and Valaric still had his stone slabs to smash the ram off the mountainside.

The first blow of the ram hit the gates under his feet. The Marroc threw their stones and their burning oil. Sarvic watched the pots burst on the shields below and rivers of fire flow over their sides and pool on the road. Men screamed and the smell of fish and burning hair rose around them. The smell of victory. And then he heard the cry behind the gate, and when he ran to look the Marroc there had already turned and were fleeing up the road, waving their arms and screaming, 'The gates! The gates!' And the gates hadn't simply been split; they'd been smashed right down, their hinges shattered. They lay on the road now, twisted and askew on the rubble the Marroc had piled behind them and forkbeards were already scrambling through. They left bodies, plenty of them, and their ram. A score and a half of dead maybe, but Sarvic's heart pounded and filled with dread as he saw how many were still alive.

Valaric watched the third set of gates shatter. The iron devil had done this. He glanced at Oribas, who looked aghast. More fork-beards were coming already, their shields raised high, hiding something in their midst. When Valaric looked hard, he saw what it was: two more of the iron devils. They ran past the abandoned ram as stones and arrows showered them. A rock the size of a man's head hit one of the forkbeard shields, flattening the warrior who carried it, breaking a dozen bones and knocking the man beside him down into a pool of burning oil. The flames embraced him. As he screamed and rolled, three arrows hit him and he lay still. Another forkbeard fell and then another, and then they were climbing through the rubble behind the gate and Sarvic was screaming at his men to stop them. Another head-sized rock hit one of the iron devils, knocking it down and crushing its shoulder and arm but it hauled itself back to its feet and carried on. Stones and arrows pinged off its armour. The men on the gate were throwing everything they had at this one handful of forkbeards, and Valaric wanted to scream at them to stop because they'd have nothing left when the rest of the army passed beneath them.

The forkbeards and their iron devils were through, onto the open road past the third gate, to the elbow where it turned back on itself and rose towards the fourth. Sarvic was already shouting up to Valaric for it to be closed. Fat lot of good that would do if the iron devils got to it, Valaric thought – might as well leave it open and fight them on the road. Around him his Crackmarsh men were milling about, not sure whether to stay and throw stones at the forkbeards below or to form up behind their shields and face the ones coming up the road or whether to simply flee back to the fifth gate now. For a moment Valaric didn't know what to do either, and then Gallow came and stood beside him like an unwelcome ghost. 'The red sword, Valaric. The Edge of Sorrows will put an end to your iron devils.'

Valaric pushed him away. He knew he couldn't fight that many, not when he was limping with a bleeding hole in his leg.

'I'll do it.' Gallow held out his hand. 'Give it to me.'

'And if you do and then Sixfingers' forkbeards take you down and take that sword, what then?' He barged past Gallow. 'Oribas? Aulian!' The Aulian was arguing with Sarvic, the two of them bawling up and down the mountain at each other. A shout went up from the forkbeards below and they started to move again, surging for the third gate. 'The ram!' Valaric bellowed. 'Smash that ram down there off the road for a start.' He looked up towards the fifth gate but the Marroc behind it couldn't hear, not from so far away. He'd just have to trust them to drop rocks on the forkbeards as they came. Not too much of a worry. Fat Jonnic was up there. He'd be good for that.

Oribas was yelling at him: 'Salt! Salt will stop the Fateguard. But it takes only one Lhosir to scrape it away.'

Cursed leg was hurting like buggery. Everywhere around him people were shouting, wondering what to do. 'Go to the fifth gate, Aulian. Put your salt there, everything you've got.' More and more forkbeards were coming up the road, hundreds and hundreds of them. Arrows flew, whether Valaric wanted them to or not, and stones too, and Sixfingers had to be in among them somewhere, didn't he? Yet Valaric was damned if he could see where. The Marroc of Varyxhun were starting to edge away, turning in dribs and drabs to run back to the fifth gate. His own Crackmarsh men were on the edge too.

He felt a door close inside him, and then another and another until only one option remained. He nodded quietly to himself, pleased with where it led him. 'Sarvic!' Oribas was halfway up a rope ladder to the top of the fourth gate, a sack of salt over his back. 'Sarvic! Sarvic! Come up from up down there and go up to the fifth gate! Close them and then put every piece of stone you can find behind them. Tell Fat Jonnic to smash any ram off the road the moment it turns the elbow. Then get as many arrows as you can find and bring them here.'

The fourth gates stood closed. The forkbeards were almost on them, one iron devil in their midst. Arrows and stones rained uselessly on their shields. Valaric closed his eyes and took one long deep breath and then another. Enough. And when he opened them again, his voice was changed. Calmer now, more certain. Sooner or later it had been coming anyway. He raised the red sword over his head and stood atop the rubble behind the fourth gate. 'Marroc of Varyxhun! Shields and spears!' Maybe some of them had heard the orders he'd given to Sarvic, maybe not. 'Marroc of Varyxhun! Sword and axe!' If they had maybe they'd know the fifth gate was about to be sealed and that they were on the wrong side of it, that there was no going back. 'Marroc of Varyxhun!' Now he had their attention, he jumped from the rubble. With the tip of his sword he drew a line in the dirt across the road. 'When that gate falls, this is where we stand. Sixfingers comes no further!' He stood in the middle of the line and turned to face the gate, crouched behind his shield, the red sword ready to spike the first forkbeard who dared come close. Two hundred Marroc fighting men in stolen mail and helms with forkbeard swords and shields and spears all of their own. Ten abreast they'd bar the road. The iron devils would break these gates as they broke the last, and when they fell, the forkbeards would come though, and these men would either turn them back or else they'd die.

The first man to stand beside him was Gallow.

Angry Jonnic moved suddenly. He looked at Reddic and nodded. 'Get your bow ready and some arrows. Nice sharp ones. Easy now. Don't let anyone see us. That banner's coming closer.'

Reddic risked a peek between the merlons. There were a dozen or so forkbeards on horseback and everyone on the road was getting out of their way. 'Sixfingers?'

'How many banners do you see in this army?'

'Just the one.'

'Well then, who else?'

It still took him a moment to get his head round it. The forkbeard king himself, and he and Angry Jonnic were going to kill him. He found himself a good sharp arrow as Jonnic had said. One of the ones they'd made from Nadric's arrowheads, the narrow Vathan ones for poking through mail.

The Fateguard was almost at the gates. Oribas watched it. Its head was tipped back as though it was looking right at him.

'Well, wizard?' Sarvic was up from the third gate, twitching like a mouse who'd seen a hawk and then suddenly lost track of it.

'Salt and fire and iron.' Salt and fire and iron killed shade-walkers. He was fairly sure they'd work on the ironskins as well. *Fairly* sure. 'Can you shoot well enough to put an arrow though that mask?'

Sarvic laughed. 'I can shoot as well as any man, but that? That's luck.'

'Make sure one of your archers is lucky then.' Oribas closed his eyes briefly and ducked back behind the battlements, letting the Fateguard come a few steps closer before he rose with a pouch of salt in his hand and emptied it straight down onto the Fateguard's upturned face. His old masters had never taught him to lift a sword but everyone learned to throw: salt, water, holy oil, a dozen potions and powders. The salt burst over the Fateguard and it froze and then staggered as if blind. Oribas picked up the sack he'd carried over his back and hacked it open with his knife. He hefted it over the battlements, shaking more salt over the Fateguard and where it stood. The Marroc around him lit pots of fish oil and poured them over the wall. A choking stinking smoke of burning flesh and fish wafted up amid the screams of pain and the howls of rage.

'Arrows!' Sarvic fired first, his arrow pinging off the Fate-guard's mask. The next arrow missed completely and the next bounced off its armour. Amid the cries of burning men, more Lhosir pressed up the road. The ram was coming.

Another arrow struck sparks from the Fateguard's mask. The

ironskin turned its head away. Oribas swore, but then an arrow came up from the roof of the third gate below. It struck the Fateguard in the face, straight through its mask. For a moment Oribas was transfixed, and then the iron devil toppled back, wreathed in salt and flames, and Oribas screamed with glee. It *could* be done! He ran to the edge of the gate and looked down to see who'd fired the arrow but a spear struck the stone beside him and he cowered instead. Another hit the Marroc next to him in the throat.

The forkbeards charging up the road. He'd almost forgotten them.

Achista watched the Fateguard fall. She drew out another arrow and nocked it to her bow and waited for another one of them to make a mistake. Sooner or later they always did.

Reddic risked another look over the edge. The riders were trotting up the road and there weren't as many as he'd thought. Seven. Six iron devils, four at the front and two at the back, and one man in the middle carrying a bright shield that could only be the Crimson Shield of Modris the Protector, the holy shield of the Marroc which had stood in King Tane's throne room until the forkbeards had pillaged it.

Sixfingers.

'You ready?' Angry Jonnic clenched his teeth and spat. 'Pity Sarvic's not here, but he's not. Quick and steady and take your time to aim. Chances are we won't get a second shot. And he'll have mail on, and good mail at that. If you can, shoot him in the face.'

Reddic glanced at the rope ladder up to the second gate. The forkbeards had the whole second tier now, and the third tier too by the look of things, but the ladder was still there and no one had come down from above or up from below to make sure there were no Marroc left on the roof of the gatehouse. Their mistake.

'Now!' Jonnic rolled into a crouch and then stood straight with his bow drawn back in one smooth motion, all far too perfect for Reddic, who tried to get to his feet and draw back his bow at the same time but stumbled and almost fell over. He saw Sixfingers on the back of his horse look up. He saw Jonnic shoot his arrow straight at the forkbeard king's face, just like he'd said, and he saw the Crimson Shield jerk up with an impossible speed to catch the arrow and turn it away. He didn't see his own arrow because as he let it fly he slipped sideways and he had to drop his bow to catch himself as he fell. He landed on his sore arm and howled.

Arrows and stones and fire poured into the press of Lhosir around the fourth gate. A part of Oribas recoiled in horror and another part clenched in fierce glee. The gates hadn't fallen and the Marroc at last had the Lhosir helpless. Overhead, behind the fifth gate, they were tipping down every piece of stone they could find, oblivious to Valaric's orders. Oribas watched a chunk as big as a man crush a handful of Lhosir warriors and sweep three more off the road. He tried to spot the second Fateguard in the melee but it was impossible with all the forkbeards lifting their shields overheard to keep the arrows and stones at bay. Now and then when he thought he caught a glimpse he threw salt, but it was lost in the chaos. The forkbeards were being crushed and burned with no way to fight back. It made his stomach churn and yet he'd seen what they did to the Marroc who defied them. He'd been there and watched as they'd sliced open a man's back and snapped his ribs off his spine and drawn out his lungs, and these Lhosir would do the same to all of them if they won. To his Achista and to her brother Addic, to him and to Gallow. To Gallow's children and to every single Marroc they found, man, woman or child.

A Marroc beside him lurched and fell with an arrow in him. Oribas peeked long enough to see a few dozen archers back at the elbow of the road. Marroc archers bought with silver that the forkbeards had stolen from their fathers, that's what Valaric would say. He ducked, but most of their arrows were going up to the fifth tier. A few more arced overhead.

'The gates!' Oribas barely heard the shout. 'The gates! It's happening.' He ripped open another sack of salt and pulled it to the edge of the battlements, heedless of the arrows now. All he could see were shields packed together. He threw the salt anyway in case some of it found its way somewhere useful, but even as he did, the forkbeards suddenly moved apart and Oribas saw broken and empty pieces of iron armour lying on the road. Now the ram rushed forward. It took a dozen blows this time. Small consolation; but before Oribas could get to the ladder and scamper up to the fifth tier, Sarvic was pulling him face down into the stone as the arrows began to fall again.

Gallow saw the iron of the fourth gate brown with rust and flake and peel and split. He saw the dust rise off it with each blow of the ram and the first hinge snap. The stones piled behind the gates held the ram a while longer; and the gates, when at last they cracked and fell, toppled awkwardly, and the Lhosir had to clamber through them, over them and around them, picking their way through the rubble. Not that it made much difference. It was tempting, when the gates gave way and the enemy came screaming through, to give in to the fury, to let out his own scream and charge right back at them. Yell to shake their very bones and eat their souls, as the Screambreaker had done on the day he'd shattered King Tane's Marroc outside Sithhun. He felt the urge, hot and fierce, and beside him Valaric felt it too, but the forkbeards had to climb over the rubble and there were Marroc archers who still had arrows to shoot them as they did, and it was better to hold the line, to keep their shield wall waiting for the Lhosir when they finally reached clear ground. They growled at each other then, he and Valaric, snarled at one another to hold fast come what may. The first forkbeards came screaming with their spears raised high and Gallow lifted his shield to meet them and turn their sharp iron aside as he stabbed back with his own, while beside him Valaric savaged them with the red steel of Solace. They were mad, these Lhosir, swept away by fury. They'd survived the press of the gates, the fire and stones and arrows. They were burned and battered and now they charged without any thought for themselves. They hurled their spears at the very last with such force that the men who took them in their shields reeled and staggered, and then they smashed into the ranks of the Marroc with their axes raised high and brought them down, splitting skulls, hooking away shields, stabbing with knives, and for a moment Gallow felt the Marroc line waver under the ferocity of that first rush; but then beside him Valaric's red sword lashed out left and right with a fury that even the forkbeards couldn't stand and Gallow felt the Marroc harden again. They would hold. They could. They believed, and for once Marroc would face Lhosir and win, toe to toe, shield to shield.

He lost his spear, torn out of his hand when he drove it into a Lhosir's foot. He hacked and slashed with his axe, battering at each man who stood in front of him, and it was strange fighting in a line of Marroc because the soldiers behind him didn't do what they should, and when his axe hooked a shield, no killing thrust came at once from behind.

A spear sliced him open along the back of his arm. He barely felt it. An axe hit his shoulder, turned by his mail and he might not even have noticed. He couldn't hear over the noise, and it was a long while before he realised that most of the screaming was his own.

Angry Jonnic dragged Reddic to his feet. 'You crazy Marroc!' He was yelping with joy. 'Did you see what you did?'

Reddic stumbled up. Down on the road only a few dozen yards away the iron devils had stopped. They were staring up at him and in their midst a man lay sprawled across the road, hauling himself sideways by one arm, screaming in pain. Reddic blinked. *That's King Sixfingers?*

'I did that?'

'I think you shot him in the foot.' Jonnic loosed another arrow at the forkbeard king but he twisted and lifted the Crimson Shield in the way even as he screamed bloody murder at the pain. 'His horse threw him too. Now let's finish it!' But the iron devils had already jumped down to shield Sixfingers with their own bodies, and other forkbeards on the road were pointing and shouting. Some were already running at the gate with a ladder. Jonnic let another arrow fly, swore, let off one at the forkbeards with the ladder instead and then threw his bow over his shoulder. 'No use us staying here now.' He pushed Reddic ahead, who climbed as fast as he could with Jonnic right on his heels. When he got to the top of the second gate and looked back, the forkbeards had raised their ladder and there were iron devils climbing after them.

Reddic lunged for the ladder up to the third gate. They were rope ladders, lowered from above and just as easily pulled up again. He shouted out in case any Marroc were still holding the roof up there. 'Iron devils! Help!'

There were. Hands reached over the edge to haul him up and out of the way. He heard a woman call for the Aulian wizard to come down from the tier above. He twisted, looked back down and reached for Jonnic right behind him. Their hands touched and then the first iron devil threw an axe from its belt. Angry Jonnic arched and spasmed. His hand slipped out of Reddic's and he crashed back to the gatehouse below and lay still.

'No!' Reddic screamed. He almost climbed back down, even though he knew in his heart that Angry Jonnic was already dead, but other hands pulled him away.

'No,' said another voice, and then the wizard was there, breathless and wild-eyed. He pressed something into Reddic's hand. A pot of oil. 'Wait for it to climb. When I throw my salt, you throw this in its face. You understand?' The wizard sounded angry and suddenly Reddic was angry too. Red-hot furious angry. He nodded as the sounds of iron scraping on stone came closer. The ladder ropes shook. An iron-gloved hand reached over the battlement and there it was, the face of the devil. Its mask and crown. Reddic had never seen one so close. He wasn't sure any of them had. He saw it for a moment, long enough to remember for ever, and then the wizard threw a cloud of brown salt into the iron devil's face. It hissed and froze and Reddic smashed the pot over its crown. The wizard jabbed a burning brand into its face and it burst into flames.

'Move! Back to the fourth gate now!' An arrow tore the air and buried itself in the iron devil's face, straight through the slats of its mask. It tipped back, toppled and crashed into the tower below, knocking another ironskin off the ladder as it went. Reddic stared over the side. They'd landed on Jonnic, both of them. The one with the arrow through its face was still burning. It didn't move.

'Get the ladder up.' The archer reached past him. A woman, and with a start he recognised Achista. Then the Aulian wizard was pushing him.

'Up! Up! Plenty more of those to kill if you have the stomach for it. Plenty more.'

As he climbed, he heard the wizard and the Huntress behind him, arguing about who should go last.

Valaric didn't understand how the forkbeards were doing it but they were slowly turning the tide and winning. Never mind that they had to run through the gatehouse with men firing arrows down on them. Never mind that they had to clamber through the stones strewn across the road to break their shield wall and stop their rams, never mind the ribbons of burning oil and the stones that still fell among them, slowly they were winning, and the Marroc around him were falling one by one – falling dead or falling back. The red sword danced in his hand, happy and filled with purpose, yet no matter how many forkbeards he killed there were always more.

A spear stabbed at his leg, reaching under his shield. The red sword split it in two and lashed at the forkbeard who held it, but Valaric felt the pain as the wound Oribas had stitched together ripped open again. And he could hear the sword humming, he really could, but the noise was in his head, not in the world outside, and it was getting louder and louder, drowning out everything else, and then for a moment it stopped and suddenly there were no forkbeards left in front of him any more because they were backing away, turning and running, and the Marroc had won after all, for once they'd really won.

Valaric's eyes rolled back. He pitched forward and smacked face first into the hard stone road.

27

THE RED SWORD

Back on the top of the fourth gate now, Oribas watched the Lhosir leave. Others might have routed and fled but the Lhosir didn't. They moved quickly enough when the Marroc were shooting and throwing rocks at them but this was no broken rabble, no matter what the cheering Marroc thought. They'd had enough, that was all. They'd taken the first two gates and smashed in the third and the fourth, and all in one day. Against a castle that was supposed to be invincible, they might well feel pleased with themselves.

'Oribas!' Gallow was crouched over a body, beckoning. Oribas rolled his eyes. There was going to be a lot of this. He could probably resign himself to spending every day of the rest of his short life stitching Marroc back together just so he could watch them go and get killed again, but then what else? Was he going to sit and do nothing and watch them die? No.

He climbed down to the road and turned his head from the bodies as he walked. Lhosir mostly, this close to the gates. The air and the stones stank of burned flesh and that wretched fish oil and the road was slick with blood and a greasy ash. He wondered if someone ought to organise a counter-attack but none of the Marroc seemed to have the heart. If anything they looked more battered than the Lhosir they'd driven back.

Gallow's waving grew frantic. Oribas trotted to him and saw that it was Valaric. He'd ripped himself open again and lost a whole lot more blood and this time he wasn't going to drink a few cups of water and get up again. Oribas swore and set to work, and when he was done Valaric was still alive and even had a chance to stay that way as long as someone could convince him to just lie down for a few days. He found some Marroc to carry the Wolf to his bed and had Gallow swear in blood to see Valaric up to the castle and to sit on him if that was what it took to make him lie still. Then he took the red sword and put it in Gallow's hand. The Foxbeard, when he took it, held it as though it was a snake.

Oribas waved Gallow away after that and forgot him almost at once. There were a dozen other Marroc who needed him, a few lives to save that would otherwise have bled out and a few he couldn't help at all except to make them more comfortable. There would be many more, he knew, as the fighting moved up the tiers and the Marroc couldn't simply drop things on the forkbeards any more. By the time he was done, the sun was setting, a blazing fiery glory sinking behind the mountains across the river. Achista came and sat beside him and gave him some water. He drank it without any thought and passed it among the injured, and it was only when she took his hand and pulled him away that he realised she'd come for more.

'Valaric has sent for you.'

'Is that stupid man up and walking again?' Oribas ground his teeth. 'He has only so much blood inside him, and when it comes out I can't simply put it back. I've told him myself but perhaps my accent confuses him. Please explain to him that the next time he tears himself open he might die whether I am there or not. Even if I am, I'm not sure I'll be minded to stop it.'

'You can tell him yourself.' Achista dragged him to his feet. He followed with a numb reluctance, exhausted, and they walked up the road between knots of Marroc soldiers who clearly felt the same. As they passed through the sixth gate he looked up at it and at the Dragon's Maw beyond, barred to keep its mythical dragon at bay. Oribas didn't believe in dragons. Valaric had said that the castle was unassailable and Gallow had said much the same, yet they'd lost four gates in a day.

'I'm missing something.' He shook his head. 'My people came and settled this forsaken place with its bitter winter cold. They built this castle and their bridge over the river and the forts that look over it. They built a road halfway to the sea. They traded with the Marroc but they didn't stay and after fifty years they left. And the story they left was of a flood that rose to the very gates of their castle and swept everything before it.'

He turned to look Achista in the eye and stopped. He'd thought she meant to drag him back to the hall where Valaric held his war council but the look on her was quite different, a look he'd come to know. And she did drag him to Valaric's hall in time, but only after she'd taken him somewhere more private first, and when they finally walked in, long after nightfall, and Valaric snarled at him and demanded to know where he'd been for so long, Oribas only smiled. He felt calmer now.

'The tomb under Witches' Reach,' he said. 'The Aulians came here to bury something. All this way, and now King Medrin has brought it back. I've seen it.' He stopped to look at Valaric. The old Marroc looked white as a shadewalker himself, droopy-eyed, holding himself up by clutching on to the table. 'And you need to rest, Valaric the Wolf.'

Valaric smashed a fist into the table. 'And how long can I rest before the forkbeards are smashing in my doors? At this rate they'll be here by tomorrow! How do we stop them, Aulian? Your people made this place – how do we stop them?'

'Shadewalkers and Fateguard, Valaric the Wolf. We must put an end to their monsters. You still have walls enough to deal with the rest.'

Gallow sat in the castle yard, his back against the wall among the Marroc soldiers, exhausted and rocking back and forth, picking at the dead skin on his fingers and yet quietly smiling. Arda sat beside him and held his hand while the little ones played tag in between the Marroc. Jelira was somewhere else with the young soldier Reddic. A little storm crossed Arda's face whenever she spoke of him, and Gallow didn't know whether it was because Jelira was still so young or because the Marroc boy was a soldier, or perhaps because that's simply how mothers were. Reddic seemed brave enough and Gallow felt churlish standing in the way of any happiness at a time like this and so he let it go and sat quietly with his Arda. They didn't say much, even if they hadn't seen each other for most of the last three years. Somehow talking seemed a waste of the little time they had left.

He slipped slowly out of his reverie to see Oribas and Achista coming across the yard with Valaric hobbling and limping beside them. Arda squeezed his hand, a little warning – a reminder of what he'd promised, perhaps, but she needn't have worried. She looked up as Valaric reached them. 'You look terrible, Mournful.'

'Shut it, woman, or I'll throw you at the forkbeards. Might do a sight better than throwing rocks at them. Rocks just come at you the once.' He looked half-dead. 'And no, Foxbeard, before you ask: I don't want a plough fixed or an axe sharpened.' He tossed a belt and a scabbard and the red sword onto the ground at Gallow's feet. 'You were supposed to take this away from me.'

'I did.'

Oribas glared at him. 'You know very well I meant you to carry it, not simply leave it lying on the floor.'

'I don't want it.'

Valaric lowered himself painfully to his knees and sat down beside Gallow, breathing hard. 'Well who else? I'm done, as you can see. Your wizard says I'll fall down and die if I try to fight any more. So I can't use it so I'm not giving you a choice.'

Oribas hissed between his teeth. 'You should not even be walking. Lying still! Perhaps, Gallow, you can tell him that. Gods know I've tried enough times to make him understand!'

'Oh please stop, you clucking old hen!' Valaric leaned into Gallow. 'Four gates fell today, Truesword. That leaves two. With their shadewalkers and those iron devils, two gates won't last us long.' He glanced again at Oribas. 'The wizard says someone has to take this sword to Witches' Reach and kill the creature Sixfingers keeps there.'

Arda still held his hand. He felt it tighten again but she didn't speak. Valaric's fingers closed on Gallow's shoulder, digging deep. 'Sixfingers is killing us. Go to Witches' Reach. Take your cursed sword. The wizard has a way out of the castle. He hasn't seen fit to share it so for all I know he means to fly, but he says it can be done. There's a Marroc as can take you through the mountains past the forkbeards. Paths your sort don't know. You can be there in a couple of days, maybe three. We'll hold as long as we can but, for the love of Modris, be quick! The wizard says you're a killer of monsters, Foxbeard, so kill whatever it is

Sixfingers has under Witches' Reach and do it soon. I can't spare you any men, but if you happen upon Sixfingers while you're out and about, you're very welcome to him.'

'Killing Medrin won't make any difference, not now.'

Valaric pushed hard on Gallow's shoulder, levering himself up again. 'Have some time with your wife before you go, Foxbeard. I'll never hear the end of it anyway but you might as well.'

He limped away, leaning on Oribas, arguing with him about arrows and some such. After they were gone Arda let go of Gallow's hand and turned his face to look at her. 'Promise me,' she said with eyes as wide as mountains. 'Promise me that when this is done you'll give away that sword and you'll come back and we'll live in old Nadric's house and make wire and nails. Promise me that and I'll be glad I came all this way to find you again. Promise me, if that wizard's got a way out, you'll take us all away when you've done this thing, and never mind anything else. Promise me that too.'

Gallow cupped her face in his hands and kissed her. 'I already did.' Somehow it was easy this time. 'When Medrin's dead they won't be looking for us any more.'

'And you'll leave Valaric to his war and come back home and sod the Vathen too?'

'I made you an oath, Arda. A forkbeard blood oath. I mean to keep it.'

'Good.' A hint of a smile twitched the corner of her mouth. 'And you'll fix the roof in the barn?'

'Leaking again?'

She wrinkled her face and nodded. 'You never did it before you left and Nadric was next to useless, and even your old friend Loudmouth couldn't make it right. Stayed good for a bit but now it needs fixing again.'

'First thing I'll do.'

'Promise? Most important promise of all?'

He laughed and smiled and took her in his arms. 'I promise.'

For a moment she let him. Then she pulled away and glared. 'Actually no, I do have an even bigger and more important promise for you. Promise you stay alive. Promise me you send these forkbeards and their shadewalkers and their iron devils all to the Isset and into the sea. Promise me you win, Gallow Truesword.' Her eyes were aflame.

'You know I can't promise those things.' He reached for her again and again she kept her distance.

'You can try.'

'That I can, Arda, that I can. I can promise that much'

She let out a snort and then a shrug and then let him hold her. 'Well, then I suppose that'll have to do.' She took his hand and started to lead him away. 'Come on. Your children would like to see you before some forkbeard monster puts an end to you. Let them know why it was all worth it. Work hard on that one, Gallow. Maybe if they believe you then I might too.'

But Gallow stayed where he was. 'I made an oath, Arda. I said I'd stay, and so I will.'

'And I release you from it for this one thing. I don't want to, but Valaric's too proud to ask if he thought there was someone else. And I know you, Gallow Truesword. You want this.'

Gallow shook his head and held out the red sword in its sheath and then dropped it in the dirt and took Arda in his arms instead. 'I do. But I want this more. If I'm going to die fighting Medrin, I'll die here, on the walls, with you near me. I'm not going to Witches' Reach, Arda. This time I'm staying here with you.'

She held him tight. 'Valaric's going to blame me for this, you know. You tell him it wasn't my fault.'

Gallow buried his face in her hair. 'Valaric's wrong – there *is* someone else. Not that he'll like it when I tell him who it is.'

Later, outside a cell not far from the one where Valaric had held Gallow, Oribas and Valaric stopped. Valaric shook his head. 'I still don't like this, wizard, not at all.'

'I know.' Oribas smiled.

'She's a Vathan.'

'It's me who must trust her, not you.'

'You say that and then you ask me to give the Sword of the Weeping God to her? To a Vathan?' Valaric opened the door. He did it carefully and with several armed Marroc guards around him. The Vathan woman glared, full of fury. She looked at Oribas and cocked her head, and Oribas felt he understood her at once. She was the same as Gallow, the same as Valaric, each of them cut from one cloth and then scattered to fall in three different lands.

'You want something,' said Oribas, and he held out the red sword and watched her face flush with wonder. She reached for it and he stepped away. 'You may have it but you must earn it. Isn't that always the way of these things?' He handed the sword back to Valaric and waved the rest of the Marroc away and sat down with Mirrahj and set to telling her, right from the start, of Witches' Reach and the shadewalkers and the ironskins and the Mother of Monsters that had made them. When he was done, he found he couldn't read her face at all, and she followed him out of the dungeons meek and quiet as a dog, and he had to keep reminding himself that she was more wolf than dog and more tiger than either.

Valaric kept asking how they were going to get past the fork-beards. To Oribas it seemed strange that he was bothered. The castle had been made by Aulians. Of course there was a secret way out and of course he'd found it. The wonder was that he hadn't found more.

28

THE HUNTRESS

No one knew who started the rumour but it spread through the castle like a plague: Sixfingers was dead, that was why the forkbeards had pulled back. Not that it meant they'd leave, but for now the Marroc cheered and drank and sang songs and threw taunts down the mountainside to where the forkbeards were building wooden shields to protect the lower tiers from Marroc stones and arrows. Gallow watched. If Medrin was dead then the Lhosir would make the mother of all pyres for him. They might just burn the whole of Varyxhun. They'd speak him out for days too, one after the other, those who knew him telling of his deeds over and over as he walked the Herenian Marches to the Maker-Devourer's cauldron. And maybe it was all true, and Gallow did see many pyres when he looked down from the castle to the city, but none near big enough for a king. Even so, the Marroc paraded Reddic around the castle walls: the hero who'd put an arrow into the forkbeard king – and maybe he had, and Medrin was just slow to die.

The Marroc had seen Gallow fight too. They'd seen him stand up to the shadewalkers and stand up to the forkbeards at Valaric's side. Foxbeard they called him now, and quietly put aside what he was though he made no effort now to hide the fork growing in his beard. The ones who'd seen him hold the shield wall behind the fourth gate all remembered Andhun now as though they'd never forgotten how he and the red sword had turned Medrin Twelvefingers into Medrin Six.

Oribas found him staring out over the valley as he always did at sunset. Everywhere else it seemed the Marroc were waiting for the Lhosir to give up and go home. But the Lhosir weren't like that, although no one wanted to hear it and even Valaric called Gallow a sour old man who preferred fighting to being with his family.

'I leave for Witches' Reach tonight,' said Oribas quietly. 'The quicker it's done, the sooner the ironskins will trouble you no more.' He looked furtively around as though afraid they might be overheard. 'I wish you would come with me. It's not that I don't trust this Vathan, but ...'

Gallow slipped the belt from his waist, slid the scabbard from the loops that held it there and handed it to Oribas. 'Take it. Let her keep it, Oribas, no matter what happens.'

'Hunting a monster again. It'll be strange not to have you at my side. I've searched the library but there's nothing. Salt will bind it, I think, but to make an end ...' He nodded to the sword. 'The Edge of Sorrows. If anything can.'

Gallow put a finger to his lips. 'Do your best, Oribas. No one will fault you. Now take a moment to be quiet and watch the sun go down.'

Oribas sidled closer. 'Sixfingers isn't dead. I know this.' Gallow turned sharply, but before he could speak Oribas leaned in and whispered in his ear, 'There were always ways in and out of this castle, my friend. Aulian ways. Achista has been to the Lhosir camp. I will tell you where. Decide when it is right for others to know.' He stepped back and shook his head. 'There is still a secret to this place, old friend. Something I haven't found. I feel it. Look for it if you can while I'm gone.'

'You can't wait to go. Why?'

Oribas shrugged. 'Since I came here, I have watched men fight one another. I have led many to shameful deaths and I am made small by what I have done. This creature, though? It gives me an honest purpose once more.'

For a while Gallow said nothing. They stood together and watched the sun set until the last brilliant crescent of orange slipped behind the mountains on the far side of the valley. As that last light died, Oribas nodded and turned to Gallow and clasped his arm. 'And so now I go. Farewell, friend. We each have our monster to face.'

Gallow took his arm and held it fiercely. 'And we'll slay them, wizard, and I'll see you again, if not here then in Middislet, a little past the Crackmarsh in Nadric's forge. Look for me there.' He smiled. 'But if you want your welcome to be a warm one then come filled with stories and not more adventures! Fare well, Aulian.'

'Fare well, Lhosir. I vow I will not die first.'

'Aye and so do I, and that's one of us an oath breaker right here.' Gallow pushed him away and watched him go, then turned back to the darkening sky across the valley. After a little while he left that too to be with the people who mattered most of all.

A quiet fell over the castle after sunset. Men slept or kept watch. The forkbeards were skulking at the foot of the mountain and Addic was limping his way to the kitchens. He went there every night after dusk and struggled his way to the cool caves deep in the mountainside that passed for pantries and cellars. He leaned on a staff that had once been the shaft of his spear but now had a crook on the top from which he hung a lantern. Short of sitting on the battlements dropping rocks on forkbeards, there wasn't much else he could do. So he came every night and counted the sacks of grain and the barrels of onions and beans and the hams to make sure all was as it should be. They had food for weeks and everyone had full bellies but he liked to be sure. And to be useful.

Now he caught the flash of a lantern ahead, quickly hidden, and stopped. That people might take to stealing food was why he came to do his counting; but that he might catch them at it was something he hadn't imagined and now he wished he had – that, and that the shaft of his spear still had a point on the end instead of a lantern and that he could still walk without it.

He took another step. 'Who's there?'

The lantern ahead flared into life again and started bobbing towards him. The air was cool after the stuffy warmth of the evening outside, although night would swiftly bring its chill. 'Addic?'

'Achista?' He stopped as she came into the circle of his light and he saw her. 'What are you doing here?' He smiled. 'You're not stealing food, are you?'

Achista came closer and stopped in front of him. 'How's the leg today?'

'Like it's on fire, just like it was when you asked this morning.'

'Oribas says you should rest it. You should listen to him.'

'Oribas says that to Valaric too. Do you see *him* listening?'

She smiled but he could see that something was wrong. 'Pig-headedness a disease now, is it? Suppose it must be.'

There was a rustle and a scrape from the caves further on and then the glow of another lantern, and slowly two more figures emerged from the shadow – Oribas, who spent half his time in the castle library carved high into the mountainside with its balcony and its hundred long thin doors that let in a glory of light when they were opened. And then the Vathan woman. Last he'd heard she belonged in the dungeons. They both had sacks slung over their shoulders.

'What are you all doing here?'

Oribas frowned at him. 'I told you to rest that leg. Does no one in this castle listen? Do I speak the word badly? Rest? R-e-s-t. Is that not correct?'

The Vathan woman shook her head and tried to push on past but Addic hopped into her way. She glared at him. 'Getting food for our journey, Marroc.'

Ah. He looked at his sister Achista. 'What journey's that?'

Achista took the staff gently out of his hand and passed it to Oribas, then put his arm over her shoulder and led him back to the kitchens. 'Oribas has something to show you.' A spikiness crept into her voice and he knew that whatever it was, he wasn't going to like it. 'There's a passage under the gates that runs beneath the Aulian Way right to the bank of the Isset. A way out. And Sixfingers isn't dead.'

The Vathan woman growled. 'I mean to change that.'

'He keeps a monster in Witches' Reach,' said Oribas quietly. 'The mother of the iron devils. We must kill it.'

Addic almost laughed. 'I see. A wizard and a Vathan. And what, sister, will you do?'

'Someone has to show them the secret ways.'

'The Aulian knows them, or he knows enough.' But he was wasting his breath and he knew it. She was going so that she could be with him, one way or the other. To keep him alive or die by his side, and he had the sudden sense that he was never going to see her again, a horrible sickening feeling in the pit of his stomach worse than the pain in his calf when the iron devil had cut him open. And now that it mattered the most, he couldn't think of a thing to say, because nothing would change anything.

Achista led him down into the cisterns where fresh water from the tarn above the castle drained through a series of tunnels and channels. They hobbled together to the far side where the water lapped at a hole in the wall not much bigger than a man.

'The water makes its way down to the Isset.' Oribas sounded smug. 'It took me a while to work it out, but if you squeeze through the tunnel quickly widens. There are steps. I think it goes down the mountain under the gates but I suppose it hardly matters how it gets there – what matters is where it ends.' He knelt down by the hole and squeezed into it, feet first, dragging his satchels behind him. 'I told Gallow where it is before we left. Since I know you will now tell Valaric too, make sure he posts a guard here. The Lhosir may see us. It's best to be sure, and though I have not yet found them, there may be others.' He vanished into the gloom of the hole. The Vathan woman followed him. She had a sword now, Addic suddenly realised. Someone had given her a sword even though Valaric had forbidden her from carrying one. And then he looked again and saw what sword it was. He backed away and shook his head.

'What are you doing, Achista? What are you doing?'

She took his hand in both of hers. 'We go with Valaric's blessing, brother.'

Words dried up and stuck to his tongue. 'The Vathan. The sword. Does he know?' He stared at her and saw it in her face. Yes, he did. And he hadn't said a word.

Achista turned away. She'd never been able to lie to him. Then she turned back and embraced him. 'Goodbye, brother. And good luck. Modris watch over you.'

'Over you too, little sister.'

She let him go, handed back his staff and his lantern and slipped quietly into the hole without another word. Addic stayed where he was, watching long after she was gone. There were tears in his eyes.

Eventually he turned his back and hobbled up through the castle to the room that Valaric the Wolf had taken for his own.

29

THE WIZARD'S WAY

Valaric stormed around the castle. Gallow watched him hobble in a fury from one battlement to the next, taking it out on anyone who happened to be near and swearing at Gallow now and then. For his own part, Gallow shrugged it away. So the Aulian had given them a way out, so what? It was all the better, wasn't it? When Medrin broke through the last gate, maybe they could slip away.

'A fine gift,' Gallow said, which only made Valaric storm even louder, but by the evening he'd limped down to see the tunnel for himself, cursing and snapping and snarling at his injured leg.

'And what does one do with this gift, Gallow Foxbeard?' he snapped when he'd seen it. 'If I had a new leg I'd be out there in the middle of them in the small hours of the night, wreaking havoc.' His eyes narrowed. 'You know forkbeards better than any of us.'

There were plenty of Marroc who could have gone instead of Valaric, but with Addic crippled, Achista gone and Angry Jonnic dead, Valaric was in a mood for arguing. Maybe it was his way of getting his own back for Gallow refusing to go to Witches' Reach, and maybe even Arda felt a twinge of guilt for that because when Valaric told her what he wanted, she only closed her eyes and nodded. By the middle of the next night, Gallow was at the bottom of the shaft with the last of Achista's Hundred Heroes behind him, a handful of the Marroc who'd seen him fight at Witches' Reach and a few Crackmarsh men who'd heard of the Foxbeard of Andhun and believed in him enough to follow him into a fight. There should have been more, and if it had been Valaric with the red sword leading the way then every Marroc in the castle would have come. But it wasn't, and despite what he'd done in front of them all, there weren't so many Marroc ready to fight beside a forkbeard, not here in Varyxhun.

Oribas's tunnel rose higher into the mountain but it was the going down that interested Gallow. They crept through the trickle of icy water, ever lower until the tunnel ended in a hole and the trickle splashed through it into some reservoir below. There were no steps, no ladder, only a gap the height of a standing man and then ice-cold water and a darkness that seemed to eat the light of their candles. Gallow peered and lowered a lamp and looked about and then handed the lamp to a Marroc, closed his eyes and dropped. The cold was shocking. His mail and his weapons dragged him straight down, but when he found his feet and stood on the bottom, the water only reached his chest. He looked back up. The lamplight from the shaft lit up a cavern shaped like a tadpole, the tail rising up out of the water into the heart of the mountain. Where that passage went not even Oribas knew.

He waded forward. It was slow and difficult and he kept losing his footing, and the cold was like a vice gripping him ever tighter. Ahead of him the roof of the cavern dropped to the water, pushing down on him, making him duck. Oribas had said there were Aulian pictograms etched into the stone where the water would lead him out but it was too dark to see them. He ran his fingers over the rock instead, feeling until he found their notches and ridges and then took a deep breath and then another, filling his lungs one last time before he dipped his head into the freezing water. Snowmelt, he remembered, that's what Oribas had said. Water that had made its way down from the tarn above the castle. He could feel himself freezing, his arms and legs already sluggish. He reached up, hands to the stone ceiling above him and walked and fell and floundered and stood up again, pushing himself forward as quickly as he dared. His head broke the surface in a second cavern, utterly pitch black. The floor rose and the water fell away until he was out, shaking himself and his furs, jumping up and down, making his heart pump faster again. Made him wonder how people as small as Achista and Oribas had come through without freezing to death, but maybe Oribas had some potion or powder for that. *Straight ahead*, the Aulian had said. *Straight ahead until you crack your head on the wall and then veer to the right and you'll see some moonlight*. So he walked with one hand reaching ahead of him and when he felt stone he veered to the right, and half a minute later he saw moonlight reflected in the dampness of the walls. He thanked the Maker-Devourer, not that the Maker-Devourer either listened or cared, and turned back to call the rest.

Reddic dropped into the freezing water, the last Marroc to go. He squealed as the cold shocked the air out of his lungs. The Marroc ahead of him turned and glared. 'Quiet, boy.' He followed the man in the darkness through water that reached almost to his neck.

The soldiers held hands, each whispering to the man behind what was coming, pulling each other onward. Reddic ducked his head beneath the water along with the rest of them and prayed to Modris, but when he felt the stone close over his head he still knew he was going to drown; and when his head found the air again and he breathed a deep chestful of ice-cold air, he felt a relief like the moment the sun had risen after his night with Jelira and the ghuldogs. He hurried after the rest, all of them picking up speed now, keen to keep moving, shaking off the water and the cold and eager for the fight. Out of the cave they scrambled up a vicious path that twisted from the bank of the Isset up to the Aulian Way as it wound along the valley beneath Varyxhun castle. He followed the others and they crouched in the shadows of an overhang.

Reddic found he could barely meet the Foxbeard's eye. There he was, hunched over two bodies. Dead forkbeards, and somehow knowing that the Foxbeard had killed two of his own only made him even more terrible and Reddic was suddenly very aware that he'd lain with the Foxbeard's wife in the caves of the Crackmarsh and then spent the night of Shieftane staring at the moon with his daughter, or someone he thought of as his daughter. He hung back. Sarvic, Valaric's right hand now, squatted beside Gallow. Rumour had it they'd once fought together against the Vathen at Lostring Hill and that the forkbeard had saved Sarvic's life. Hard to imagine when you looked at Sarvic now.

Gallow's eyes raked them. 'Medrin and the Fateguard will be in the heart of the camp. Fateguard don't sleep. Keep away from them.'

Sarvic glanced at Reddic and Gallow's eyes followed. 'The Aulian wizard says the iron devils can't cross a line of salt. Any of you bring salt with you? Any of you keep it dry through that sump?' He bared his teeth and drew his sword and pointed it at Reddic. 'On the left, you're with the Foxbeard. You wait out of sight for a hand of the moon and come at the camp from the castle road.' Where the forkbeards' watch was sharpest and they all knew it, but Sarvic left that out. 'On the right, you follow me. We go around the other side. There are Marroc in Sixfingers' army, our own kin. We need their arrows. You see a bow, you take it. A bowstring, you cut it. Kill and fight as much as you like but remember it's the arrows that the Wolf wants from us. Watch the road and remember your path. Every man makes his own way back. We'll not wait past dawn.'

None of the Marroc spoke. Gallow rose and began to lead his men away. Reddic decided the sword must have been pointing to his right and followed Sarvic instead.

There were men here he knew, Gallow had no doubt of that. Most of Medrin's army would be younger Lhosir, men like the ones he'd seen when he'd sailed with Jyrdas One-Eye to take the Crimson Shield. But there'd be some older men too, men like him who'd fought in the Screambreaker's war and found a taste for it in their blood and never given it up. For almost twelve years he thought he'd been free of that hunger but Mirrahj had taught him he was wrong. He knew better now. He'd never be free of it. He could put it aside – for Arda he could do that much – but be free of it? No.

He took his time. When he reached the edge of the Lhosir camp he kept the Marroc down and out of sight. He watched the waning half-moon creep up through the sky, wondering how long Sarvic would need before he found where Sixfingers' archers kept their arrows. Wondering how far he, Gallow, might get among them before someone realised who he was. If he could get to Medrin himself, and if he did whether that would be enough to make them go away. But that wasn't how it worked among the brothers of the sea, and besides Sixfingers still had his ironskins. They'd spot him long before he could run a spear through Medrin's heart.

The moon crept over the top of his hand. Time enough. With a sigh and a snarl, half-regret and half-hunger, he stepped out of the shadows to where the nearest Lhosir sentry must be. 'Hoy! Filthy *nioingr!*' He couldn't see the man but he was there, and sure enough a furious Lhosir came striding out from a cluster of stones long fallen from the mountaintop.

'What flap-eared piece of—' Gallow rammed into him shield first, battering him back. The force knocked the sentry off balance, and he stumbled and fell. Gallow drove his spear through the Lhosir's neck before he could say another word.

'Gallow Foxbeard,' he hissed, 'that's who.' He stepped over the body and quickly on.

Sarvic dropped to the banks of the Isset and crept through the shadows, hidden from the moon. Reddic followed. They slipped into the fringes of Varyxhun where the river touched up against it. The Isset was flowing fast and high, still rising every day as the late spring warmth reached the deep valley snows. There were no walls here and it was easy enough to creep into the deserted streets. The emptiness put Reddic on edge. He was used to the quiet of the Crackmarsh but he'd been to towns often enough on the back of his father's cart to know they were bustling places, full of life. Varyxhun was dead, abandoned. As they crept deeper in, they began to pass the gibbets where Sixfingers had hung the Marroc who hadn't run. From the castle they hadn't seemed so many, but now Reddic saw them all. A hundred of them and more.

'Sixfingers wants his kin-traitors to remember what they're fighting for,' hissed Sarvic, and Reddic winced at the savagery in his voice. Kin-traitors. That's what the Crackmarsh men called the Marroc who fought for the forkbeards, but the forkbeards had their own word for it. *Nioingrs.*

Sarvic stopped. He waved the other Marroc into the shadows and crouched down and put a finger to his lips. Reddic strained his ears. He heard voices. Marroc voices.

Three Lhosir sat beside their fire at the edge of Varyxhun, picking dirt out of their fingernails and trading battle stories. They'd been fighting the Vathen in Andhun, and not long ago at all by the sounds of it. They heard him coming and were already up and on edge as Gallow strode towards them out of the dark. As he stepped into their circle of firelight and they saw his face, they scrambled to their feet. None of them wore mail.

'I'd be very pleased to hear more.' Blood still dripped from the tip of his spear as his arm whipped back and he threw it. It struck the middle Lhosir in the chest just beneath the breastbone. He flew back and fell, twitching, trying to raise his arm as blood poured from his mouth. Gallow hefted his axe. The other two were quick, he'd give them that, with their shields propped up by their sides and their spears leaned against their shoulders. But not quick enough. He was up close before they could bring their spears to bear and between them before they could overlap their shields; and while he barged one back, he dipped almost to his knees and swung his axe across the earth – low enough to snip the stems of spring flowers and also to snap an ankle or two. A Lhosir screamed. The last one dropped his spear and went for his sword but he was too hesitant. Gallow stood and his axe rose high and came down, over and inside the guard of the other man's shield and into the Lhosir's collarbone. It bit deep. The Lhosir clutched at Gallow. His eyes rolled like a madman. He sputtered and coughed, blood welling up in gouts in time to the last few beats of his heart and then his arms went limp. Gallow pulled his axe out of him and turned on the other. The crippled Lhosir was gasping for breath. Hopping back. He was desperately young, young like Gallow had been once when he'd first crossed the sea.

'Medrin took an arrow through his chest from a crazy Marroc when he was your age. Didn't stop him from being king.' Gallow scratched at his mangled nose, his own reminder of a first year of war. 'You know who I am?'

The Lhosir didn't answer. He had his back to the mountain now, and so to the dozen Marroc creeping up behind him out of the darkness.

'I'm the Foxbeard. I'm here for Sixfingers. Built a new ram yet?'

He caught a flash of a glance away and then perhaps the Lhosir heard a noise: he turned sharply in time to see three Marroc come out of the night to pull him down. They dragged him to the fire and pushed his face into it until he stopped screaming. Good enough a way as any to get some attention, Gallow supposed.

Sarvic waved them forward. They kept low, creeping through the fringes of the Marroc camp. A few Marroc soldiers stood around a fire in the middle, looking off to the commotion on the other side of the town. In a ring around the fire were a dozen hunting shelters, branches lashed together and draped in hides. They'd each have ten or maybe twelve Marroc inside. The arrows would be at the end near the fire in leather quivers. In the Crackmarsh they did the same.

Sarvic nodded. He pointed to three of the Crackmarsh men and then to the guards and drew a finger across his throat. They moved silently forward and then struck all at once, one hand over the mouth, pulling back the chin, the other with a knife to open the throat, the way every Crackmarsh man learned for when they met a forkbeard one day. Some guards, Reddic knew, wore mail across their throats, and this was exactly why, but Sarvic had known without looking that these Marroc wouldn't have such a thing. They were Marroc and so they only got what the forkbeards threw away.

They lowered the dead guards to the ground around the fire and Sarvic beckoned the others forward. He pointed at them and then to the shelters, made a creeping silently gesture and then another throat-cutting motion. And it took a moment before Reddic realised that he really did mean them to creep inside and kill every single Marroc here.

*

Gallow sent half his Marroc looking for the Lhosir ram. The rest scattered across the town, kicking over fires and kicking in doors, setting roofs alight, murdering forkbeards where they could get away with it. With a bit of luck they might find some place where the Lhosir kept something that mattered – food, boots, arrows, anything they could take or smash or ruin. There were Lhosir in the houses all around him, asleep, half-asleep, in the middle of waking, but few on the streets. A man stumbled out of a house – Gallow darted sideways and split his head open. The more chaos the better. Let them think they were under attack by a thousand. Keep moving, that was the key – plenty of gloom and shadow in a town at night. And noise, and while the Marroc made mayhem, Gallow ran straight and in silence with one thing on his mind: Medrin. And he almost reached the heart of Varyxhun too, the big barn-like hall beside the market square. Almost, and then Lhosir were running towards him to cut him off, and they were armed and carried shields and none of them was afraid to face him, and when they were close enough for Gallow to see their faces, he understood why. He slowed and stopped and braced himself for a fight. 'Hello again, Ironfoot.'

'Foxbeard.' Ironfoot nodded. 'Your warning about the gates of Andhun was timely. Without it my men and I would all be dead. So I thank you for that.' Ironfoot was limping. Survived then, but not without a scratch.

'I heard men talking. Medrin took Andhun and held it then, did he?'

Ironfoot nodded. 'He holds the castle and what passes for their king as a hostage. Frankly, the Vathen could help themselves to the rest any time it took their fancy, but who knows? Maybe they're like the Marroc and like to keep their kings alive.'

Gallow laughed at that. 'And you, Ironfoot? Do you want to keep yours?'

'If you had Sixfingers or old Yurlak or even the Screambreaker himself up in that castle of yours, Foxbeard, do you think I'd hesitate for even a second before I came at your walls? Would any true Lhosir?' He laughed too and shook his head. 'We're not like them, Foxbeard. Why are our shields not locked together, you and I, side by side?'

'Because you follow Medrin and Medrin is no Lhosir.'

'I disagree. He's a brother of the sea and our king.'

'Yet you wouldn't hesitate for a second if I held him?'

'Not one heartbeat.' He smiled again. 'You don't like him, find him and call him out. The old way.'

'I'm here, Ironfoot. But I don't see him, I see you.'

Ironfoot shrugged again and let out a sigh. 'You picked the wrong night, Foxbeard.'

For a moment they looked at each other, smiling and remembering how they'd fought together once, remembering the men they'd known, the mighty and the small, the noble and the craven. And then slowly a change came over Ironfoot's face and he lifted his shield another inch. His grip tightened on his spear and quietly they set to killing one another.

Reddic slipped into a shelter, easing in, careful as could be. There were quivers of arrows piled just inside. He crawled past to the first Marroc. They were pressed together, sharing their warmth, wrapped in too few furs for a mountain spring night. He slipped out the knife he was supposed to use to cut their throats. Valaric and Sarvic and a few of the others had shown him how to do it back in the Crackmarsh, how to come up behind a man and open his neck the way Sarvic had done to the guards outside. Do it so he'd bleed out in a few heartbeats and die without a sound. But here, to a man wrapped in furs, lying asleep. To a Marroc?

He slipped back outside, pulling the quivers after him. Behind him the closest of the Marroc muttered and turned in his sleep. And he'd barely got out when a shout went up and inside one of the shelters a struggle broke out. He saw the hides bulge at the side and two men roll out. Then a scream went up from another and Sarvic popped his head out of the next and looked sharply around. There was blood on his knife and blood all over the rest of him. He stank of it. He dived back in and pulled out a dozen quivers then thrust them into Reddic's arms. He glanced at Reddic's knife as he pulled away, frowned a little and then shrugged. 'Hard to kill a man in his sleep, even if he's a kin-traitor. I'll not say more. Now go!'

Other Crackmarsh men rolled out of the shelters clutching

quivers, and Sarvic sent each one scurrying away. As they ran, Marroc tumbled out after them, clenching their fists and shouting. Sarvic waited long enough to stab a few and then ran too. There seemed to be a lot of them to Reddic, so perhaps it wasn't just him who'd found it hard to kill a man in his sleep.

Ironfoot lunged with his spear at Gallow's face. The man on his right tried to hook away Gallow's shield with his axe but Gallow tipped back a couple of inches at the last moment and the Lhosir missed. For a moment his arm was open. Gallow's spear flicked up and down and sliced an exposed wrist, cutting deep; the Lhosir howled and fell back. One fewer to fight; still, that had been enough for Ironfoot to ram his spear point at Gallow again, creeping it inside the rim of his shield, straight through Gallow's sodden furs and into his mail hard enough to knock the wind out of him. Gallow lifted his shield over Ironfoot's spear and turned his body, catching the spear in his cloak. Ironfoot dropped it and stepped smartly away, pulling an axe from his belt, but Gallow kept turning, snatching up the tangled spear in his shield hand and lashing it at a third Lhosir, making his head ring under his helm, and he would have lunged with his own spear and finished him too if Ironfoot hadn't barged him away. As they staggered apart, Gallow shook the spear free. The three men eyed each other.

'I'll give you a good death,' said Ironfoot.

'I'd speak you out myself, Ironfoot, but I doubt your friends will allow me that luxury.'

'You turned your back on us, Foxbeard.'

Gallow snorted. 'We've all turned our backs. We're not what we thought we were, Ironfoot. I've travelled half the world to learn it, but really we're nothing more than a pack of savages. And whatever nobility we had – if we ever did – it's dying. Men like you and me, there won't be any more of us. Whether Medrin wins or whether I kill him, it makes no difference. Our time has gone. We'll grow old and look at the world and wonder what happened to it, and as we turn feeble, we might wonder whether it would have been better if we'd died in our prime and thought ourselves heroes and seen a little less of what was to come. But by then it'll be too late.'

Thanni Ironfoot shook his head. 'We're Lhosir, Gallow. We are what we are.'

As one, Ironfoot and the other Lhosir charged. Ironfoot went for Gallow's head. Gallow ducked and ran past, shifted his grip on his spear to take it behind the point and stabbed it into the back of the other Lhosir's neck as though driving in a knife. The Lhosir stumbled and fell and a spray of blood spattered across his shield and across Ironfoot's face. For a moment Ironfoot was blinded. Gallow kicked his shield down and rammed his spear into the hollow of Ironfoot's neck. He collapsed without a sound and Gallow stared at what he'd done. A good man. One who remembered the old ways. His shoulders slumped and with a weary sigh he levelled his spear at the Lhosir who'd gathered to watch, some in mail and some not, weapons drawn and wary but not wanting to interfere in another man's fight.

'Speak him out. Speak him out well.'

He turned his back and walked away.

30

THE FIFTH GATE

They travelled through the night and most of the day that followed and then bedded down in an old goatherd's shelter high above the Devil's Caves. Achista and Oribas wrapped themselves tightly together in their furs. The Vathan woman slept alone, haughty and cold. Achista thought they might stay there through the day too, but when she scouted the paths around the Devil's Caves she didn't see signs of any forkbeards and so they pressed on. By the middle of the afternoon they were at the mouth of the cave that led into the Reach and the shaft to the Aulian tomb. This time Oribas lit a lamp, a tiny flame that guided them as far as the water. He handed them each two satchels full of salt. 'One to sit on each hip. Keep them open. As soon as you reach the top, make sure you have a handful of it ready.' He twitched. 'I don't think there will be any Lhosir, not after what I saw last time, but the creature will be close.'

Achista looked at him, eyes big in the lamplight. 'Oribas, why didn't you kill it when you were here before?'

'I didn't know how and I was afraid. Too afraid to think clearly.'

'And you're not afraid now?'

He squeezed her hand. 'You are my courage.'

The Vathan woman rolled her eyes. Oribas smiled and started to climb. He felt slightly stupid leading the way but he did it anyway.

Three Marroc never returned to the castle. They just didn't come back, and no one would ever know if the forkbeards had got them or if they quietly ran away. Others came racing to the sump cave with forkbeards running after them. They bolted straight into the water and vanished as the forkbeards watched, bemused. Valaric supposed they'd work it out and they'd surely put a watch over the caves now, but it made him smile to think of them pulling up short at the edge of the water only to watch the Marroc going deeper and deeper until their heads went under and they never came back. It probably didn't happen like that, but that was how Valaric imagined it.

Some of those forkbeards had come back out of the cave only to find more Marroc running straight at them. And Gallow, and that had gone badly for the forkbeards by all accounts. There was a bloodiness to the Foxbeard now, a viciousness, a vengeful anger. All the things Valaric had seen in Gallow before but now unfettered. He wasn't fighting for pride or honour or glory. He was fighting to keep his wife and his children from being ripped apart and hung in bloody shreds for Varyxhun's ravens.

The forkbeards came at the castle again in the morning. Valaric limped down to the battlements over the fifth gate. All the stones he'd been planning to drop on them as they climbed up the mountain were piled up behind it now and it was hard to watch forkbeards march through the third gate and do nothing. They turned the elbow in the road at the end of the third tier and started on the fourth, and there the barrage began, every Marroc soldier in Varyxhun lining the walls above. They didn't have any great boulders here but they did have a lot more arrows now; and the Aulian might not have been with them any more, but that didn't mean they hadn't talked about the best way to keep the forkbeards at bay. For a dozen yards in front of each gate the road was covered in salt to keep the iron devils back. Not that it would work for long, but it would serve for a while, and that was the point.

The forkbeards forced their way up the fourth tier and through the sundered gates and out the other side. They broke ranks and charged, eager for the fight, as they turned the elbow to the fifth tier. The battlements of Varyxhun castle itself were above them now but no Marroc appeared to pepper them with arrows. Valaric let them come; but as the first forkbeards reached the gate he yelled the order that half his Marroc had been waiting for. Up on the battlements a hundred men leaned out and emptied a hundred burning pots and pans and bowls, and for one glorious moment the whole mountainside was draped in a curtain of fire. It didn't last but it was the most glorious thing Valaric had ever seen. He laughed and whooped and howled as he watched the forkbeards scream and burn. Arrows rained into them after the fire, their own arrows stolen the night before, and this time Valaric let his archers fire at will. As the first flames burned themselves out, he bellowed up at the castle, 'Give them a hand, lads! Put the rest out for them!' Up on the walls the Marroc returned with their pots and cauldrons now filled with boiling water. The forkbeards howled and milled around, trying to guess where the water would come. They crashed into each other, slipped over the edge and fell down the cliff to the tier below in their panic, and then Valaric slashed his sword through the air. The fifth gate swung slowly open. From behind it, Gallow and Sarvic and a hundred and fifty fighting men, the best the Crackmarsh and Varyxhun had to offer, lifted their shields and spears, cried out to Modris and hurled themselves at the forkbeards.

Even from the bottom of the shaft, Oribas could hear a tapping from the top, the ringing of metal on stone. He climbed as slowly as he dared, as quietly as he could, and when he reached the top he clenched his fingers around a fistful of salt. There was light, just a little, from the other side of the broken crypt door. Not the cold white light of the Mother of Monsters but the orange flickering of a candle. The tapping was loud now, a pick hammering at stone. With slow deliberation he climbed onto the edge and inched forward on his hands and knees until he found the line of salt he'd left before. He felt his way along it, filling it out where it seemed thin, and by the time he was done, Achista was crouched beside him and the Vathan woman too. He showed them the salt and whispered, 'Whatever you do, don't break the line.' Then he stepped over, crept to the crypt and peered through the broken stone door.

The Mother of Monsters wasn't there. The tomb was empty except for a pair of Lhosir digging at the tunnel to the crypt itself. One was inside, swearing vigorously. The other sat and watched, muttering sympathy. They had a lantern between them and a weariness too, as though they'd been there for hours. On the floor lay one of the pieces of iron armour that had reminded him so much of the Fateguard. Oribas pointed and shook his head and the Vathan woman let out a silent laugh and slipped through the broken door. She moved like a ghost until she was behind the sitting Lhosir and then reared up with a rock held in both hands and brought it down onto the Lhosir's head in time to the striking of the pick inside the tomb. She caught him with her knees as he slumped and then put down her stone and dragged him out of the way, off into the shadows, all without a sound.

The Lhosir in the tunnel said something. When he didn't get an answer he said it again. The tapping stopped. He started to shuffle out of the tunnel. The Vathan woman waited out of sight, and as soon as his head was clear she brought the other Lhosir's axe down on the back of his neck. They dragged him out of the way. The rest of the tomb was empty. No monster, no ironskins, nothing. Oribas stared at the piece of metal armour on the floor. *The back plate, was it?* He didn't know. He shook his head. He'd thought he understood. The creature – whatever it was – had come back to claim the pieces of its skin that long ago it had been forced to leave behind. But where was it then? Not far away, surely. He whispered in Achista's ear what she must do and then crawled nervously into the tunnel. The other piece of armour was still inside the crypt but all the salt he'd once left there had been meticulously brushed away.

Outside, Achista took the red sword off her back and handed it in its scabbard to the Vathan woman. 'For when it comes.'

The red mist called him. It begged and pleaded with him as he saw his kinsmen climbing over the stones and he knew he couldn't refuse. The Lhosir were battered and scalded, bruised, some of them burned. Men had died screaming all around them and men still were – friends perhaps, or brothers or cousins, fathers and sons – but these were Lhosir, unafraid, furious and ready for a fight, and who better to bring it to them? Gallow ran ahead, leaving Sarvic and his Marroc behind. A part of him knew that all he was doing was drawing it out, slowing the forkbeards down, making it harder for them to form the wall of shields and spears that would sooner or later come marching up the road. Making it easier for Sarvic when the time came. But the deeper truth was that all he wanted was to drive these men out of his home for ever by stabbing them with his spear and hitting them with his axe, and when he closed his eyes all he saw was a heap of corpses burned in the castle yard with his Arda and his children among them. That was the future if Medrin took Varyxhun. Every Marroc from the mountains to Issetbridge, butchered and burned, and he, Gallow, would not let that happen.

And so he screamed at the Lhosir stumbling over the stones that littered the road; and as they saw him they screamed right back and charged, too maddened to wait and form their wall of shields and face him as a Lhosir army should. The first to reach him was bright red in the face, scalded by boiling water and mad with rage. He roared loud enough to shake the mountain and lifted an axe in both hands. He didn't even have a shield. Gallow hurled his spear with all his strength and drove it right through him, then dashed up and pulled it out before he fell and ran straight on past to the next, kicked the man's shield and stabbed his face. Pulled back, blocked an axe, twisted inside a spear thrust and slashed open the belly of a Lhosir stupid enough to come to a battle with no iron over his skin. His next lunge skittered off mail. Another Lhosir came at him with a spear – Gallow twisted the point down into the ground and stamped on the shaft, snapping it in two.

He moved through them fast, before they could make a circle or lock their shields, sliced the hamstrings of another and ran on up to the the stones and leaped up onto the last boulder right behind the gate. A Lhosir on the other side looked up. Gallow jumped, landed on his face, and stamped on it. A man with an axe hacked at him and Gallow howled, part-rage, part-glee, part-despair, while his spear lashed out with a will of its own. He couldn't help himself. Medrin's Lhosir were swarming through the gates now and he could only take a few of them, but he killed another and another, and now the rage was fading from all of them.

Medrin's men were starting to think like soldiers again. Most got past him as best they could, scrambling through the debris to the open road where they could lock their shields. And then Gallow looked up and saw Valaric, and a moment later an iron portcullis crashed down, crushing three Lhosir into bloody smears and splitting their assault in two. Sarvic and his men came storming down the road with their shields locked and their spears low and hit the trapped Lhosir like a battering ram while Gallow turned and fell on them from behind. Out on the road on the other side of the portcullis, another sheet of flame fell like a blanket over the Lhosir on the road and finally they turned to run.

Achista emptied one of her satchels of salt into the other. She put the iron back plate into the empty one and then filled it up with salt again. Mirrahj went to the other entrance, another heavy round slab of stone that had been smashed. She stared at the remains and then stepped through and looked at the strange drawings and carvings in the wall and the stone circles that turned like wheels on the other side. She reached out to touch one, then heard voices from above, loud and full of purpose. She ran back to the tomb. 'Forkbeards coming,' she hissed. As she moved to take them from behind as they entered, she drew the red sword for the first time. It felt strange in her hand. Long and yet light. She looked at it, wondering if there was any more to it than what it seemed. Gallow called it cursed, yet the Weeping Giant had carried it and the Weeping God before him and so would it not then carry a charge? An energy? And yes, perhaps a curse if the hands that clasped its hilt weren't Vathan hands? Yet she felt nothing. Oribas's words rang in her ears. *You have to earn it.* In that moment, with the red sword in her hand, she understood: he didn't mean paying a debt to him or to Gallow or to the Marroc who'd imprisoned her. He meant to the sword itself.

Achista ran to the hole where the wizard had gone. 'Oribas! Get out!' Mirrahj didn't hear what the wizard said back. The forkbeards were coming down the steps. Earn the Comforter? How? By killing the Aulian's Mother of Monsters?

'Oribas!'

The first forkbeard ran at Achista. He didn't even see Mirrahj and so she let him go and the next one after him too, and it was the third one she took in one clean slice as he ducked through the broken door and came up the other side without a head. She kicked him in the chest as he crumpled, shoving the body back into the forkbeards behind him. Inside the tomb one of the forkbeards was grappling with Achista. The other turned to face her. She ran at the forkbeard. He raised his shield to fend her off as they always did, ready to run her through at the same time as his shield hit her. And it was kind of him to lift his guard like that because it meant he had nothing to protect his legs, and instead of crashing into him she dropped to the ground and rolled and slid past him, and as she did, Solace smashed both his shins and down he went screaming.

The wizard was pulling himself out of the tunnel. The forkbeard who had Achista smashed her head into the wall and threw her to the floor. He pulled an axe and faced Mirrahj. More forkbeards were coming through the broken door. She faced them, grinning. It was a pity Gallow wasn't here. He'd have liked this. They fought well together and they could have held this space against anyone.

And then her eyes narrowed as the real prize ducked into the tomb, carrying the Crimson Shield before him. Sixfingers himself, king of the Lhosir. She bared her teeth and hissed, 'I came to kill a monster and so I shall!' and hurled herself at him bringing Solace down with an irrevocable force. And he didn't even move except to lift his shield, didn't even try to get out of the way, but as the sword and the shield met, a pain shot through her arm so harsh and sharp that she dropped Solace and doubled up at his feet, whimpering.

Medrin's expression never changed. He looked down at her and shook his head. 'Well now, I was expecting the Foxbeard. *He'd* have known better after the last time.'

'Lhosir! Behold!' She heard the wizard but her eyes were screwed shut at the pain in her arm. A brilliant light filled the room as she opened them. The forkbeards cried out and she looked round. The wizard was there, a hand falling from his eyes. He threw the satchel with the salt and the armour inside at her. 'Take this! Take it to Gallow and our bargain is done!' He barged her aside, crashed into Medrin and knocked the Lhosir king down. A forkbeard grabbed him, half-blind, and threw him aside. Mirrahj dropped her shield, shrugged the satchel over her shoulder and picked up the red sword. She almost stayed to fight, but with only one good arm it was obvious the forkbeards would win, just a question of how many she could take with her.

'Go! Now is not your time to die!'

As soon as she had her back to the wizard, another blinding flash of light filled the tomb and for a moment she could see exactly where she was going. She ran and slid through the line of salt and over the edge and down the rungs in the walls and took them three at a time, and when the forkbeards reached the top of the shaft and started to drop things on her, her sword arm was strong enough again to lift the wizard's satchel like a shield over her head. One last cry from Oribas echoed after her. 'Tell Truesword to melt it down and forge it again with salt. Fire and salt will kill it!'

She didn't stop to see if any of the forkbeards came after her but they didn't, and when she got out of the cave and back onto the mountainside and the bright afternoon sun, she saw why. They were already pouring out of Witches' Reach and down the slopes, arrowing after her.

Valaric waited a while and then raised the portcullis, and the last few forkbeards trapped behind it turned and ran. The battle-crazed Marroc charged after them, Gallow at the front, waving his blood-drenched spear like a madman, hurling curses like slingshots. He ran on past the turn in the road to the tier below and only then had the sense to finally stop. Sarvic screamed at his soldiers to grab any arrows they could find. A few hundred in the end, but that was still a few hundred that could be fired again.

Next time the forkbeards would probably take the gates but for now it was a victory and Valaric meant to make the most of it. For the rest of the morning he and Addic limped and hobbled among the forkbeard dead, laughing and joking with each other about who was more crippled while Sarvic's men stripped the corpses of anything they could use. When they were done with that, they kept on going until the bodies were naked and then took all the clothes back up to the castle and soaked them in pitch to be set alight the next time the forkbeards came. Valaric had the corpses beheaded as Achista had done at Witches' Reach. The heads went on spikes over the fifth gate, the bodies went over the edge of the cliff, tumbling and bouncing to the tier below, arms and legs spinning; and some of them, he saw, hit the road and slid over the next edge as well. It amused Valaric to imagine a few of them bouncing and falling all the way to the bottom.

In the middle of the day the Lhosir came to take the bodies of their fallen. Valaric spread his best archers along the walls to pick off any they could. Even collecting their dead would be a misery for the forkbeards. Everything. For ever. Until they left.

But they didn't leave. A few hours passed, that was all.

From the fifth gate Gallow watched the Lhosir march up the castle road for the second time that day. There must have been a thousand of them, snaking up through the tiers, and they had huge wooden shields with them this time, peaked things like the roof of a house and almost as wide as the road itself. Not many but he could see how they'd huddle under them, hidden from the Marroc arrows and stones and even from the fire, not that Valaric had much of the precious fish oil left. Boiling water and rocks then, the two things they had in abundance, and cloth from the morning's dead, soaked in pitch and set alight. It would stick, and their wooden shields would burn.

The Lhosir turned the elbow of the road into the fourth tier. As the barrage from above began, the shields moved to the front of the column. The rest of the army stayed where it was and the shields came on like a giant armoured cockroach inching towards the gate, maybe enough to hide a hundred men if they were packed tight together.

'Is there a ram under there?' Valaric stood beside him. Gallow looked but there was no way to know. 'If your Aulian wizard was here, he'd have thought of a way to turn that against them.'

And that might have been true, but Oribas was gone. Gallow picked up a stone and waited as the shield-roof came closer. It reached the gate stuck with arrows like a hedgehog but there wasn't a single dead man left in its wake. He put the stone down. Wasted. Any minute now the ladders would come and—

'What are they doing under there?' There were no sounds, no battle cries, no axes striking the gates.

'I've never heard of—'

'The salt!' hissed Valaric. 'They're clearing the salt. They've got another iron devil under there!'

Of course they were. Gallow turned away from the battlements and looked to the rope ladder that ran down from the gatehouse to the road below. If they were clearing the salt then there'd be an ironskin in the vanguard of the Lhosir. He'd face them, and Sarvic and his Crackmarsh men would face them too, and they might die or they might not. 'Open the gates again, Valaric. The fight comes either way. We broke them once this way and we can break them again.'

'Wait.' Valaric put a hand on his shoulder. 'It's not too ... Jonnic!'

A burly Marroc had climbed between the merlons. He had an axe in each hand and he grinned at Valaric with a mad gleam in his eye. 'Tell my sister how I died, Mournful. Tell her I went well.'

'Jonnic!'

The Marroc dropped. He landed on the first of the shield roofs and slid, and then slammed first one axe and then the other into the wood and caught himself, pulled himself up and sat astride the thing. 'Throw me a rope, Mournful!' At first Gallow had no idea what Jonnic meant to do. Valaric threw him the end of a rope and the Marroc tied it around one of his axes. The shield bucked and heaved beneath him but he sat fast, grinning like a madman and beckoning for more, and now Gallow understood and so did the Marroc. They tied axes to lengths of rope and threw them down, and Jonnic struck each axe into the wood as deep as it would go. A forkbeard slipped out from underneath and tried to grab him and a dozen arrows took him down. The back of the shield dropped almost to the ground and then tipped sideways as the forkbeards tried to roll him off, but Jonnic just held on to the axes and moved on to the next and the next until the shield was held fast in a dozen places. He gestured to the men on the gatehouse to lift it up.

Valaric threw another rope. 'Get back here you stupid Marroc!' Fat Jonnic shook his head and jumped down from the shield-roof and vanished beneath it, a knife in his hand. A shout went up from the Marroc as they heaved at the ropes and the shield lurched and shifted and then suddenly tore free of the Lhosir beneath and swung away. The forkbeards were like ants nested under a rock with their shelter pulled aside. They fell under the storm of stones and arrows, but not quickly enough for Jonnic, who fell, flailing in the midst of a handful of stabbing Lhosir as the second shield roof moved forward over him.

'Drop it! Drop it on them!' Valaric was seething, and Gallow half expected him to go over the edge as Jonnic had done. But he didn't, and the Marroc pulling on their ropes let go and the first shield-roof crashed onto the front of the second and brought it down, scattering the Lhosir yet again. Yet amid the scrambling chaos Gallow glimpsed the rusted and broken remains of a Fateguard's armour lying still and empty beside the gate.

'We were too slow,' he whispered.

Further down the road the forkbeards were moving again, the first hundred of them coming forward at a run. They had a ram. Quietly Gallow turned away and climbed down the ladder to the road. When the Lhosir smashed the rusted hinges down and were swarming over the stones then he'd be there to meet them again, with Sarvic and the Marroc of the Crackmarsh, sword for sword with nowhere else to go.

The flash blinded the forkbeards a second time. For a moment Oribas was free. He shouted what must be done to Mirrahj and saw her run. Then he scrambled to Achista and lifted her head, terrified by all the blood on her face, but she moaned when he shook her and so he held her tight and cradled her in his arms and by the time he could think again the Lhosir had hauled him up and pulled them apart. Oribas supposed they meant to kill him right there and then but they didn't, and after a few moments the Lhosir King came away from the shaft and looked at Oribas. A smile pinched his lips. 'I remember you. The Aulian wizard.'

Oribas dipped his head. 'I would bow properly if your men did not hold me so tightly.'

'After we met on the road I did tell them not to kill you if they found you. I said nothing more.' Behind the smile there was strain in the Lhosir king's face. He was in pain. He held up the iron hand he wore in place of the one Gallow had taken. 'What have you done, Aulian?'

'The creature my people entombed here left behind two pieces of itself when it escaped. I have encased them in salt. A common enough preservative.'

King Sixfingers pointed. 'You. Go and see if he lies.'

A Lhosir crawled into the tunnel to the crypt and a few moments later crawled out again. 'There's one piece there. Covered in salt.' He sounded bemused, as though wondering why anyone would do such a thing. Oribas smiled.

The king cocked his head. 'And the other piece, Aulian? Where's the other piece?'

They'd seen Mirrahj go and they were neither stupid nor deaf. Oribas bowed his head. 'The Vathan woman took it. If she does as I asked then she will take it to Gallow Foxbeard who will melt it down and forge it again in salt.' He shrugged. 'The Mother of Monsters will be weakened. Perhaps together we can defeat it.' He looked about the tomb. 'I had imagined it would still be here. That is why I came. To kill it. Tell me, King of the Lhosir, do you serve the monster, or does the monster serve you?'

Sixfingers laughed and a twitch of a smile lingered on his lips. 'Come with me, Aulian wizard, and I'll show you something.' He turned away and addressed his men. 'Keep them alive. Strip the woman of her weapons and the Aulian of everything but his clothes but *don't* throw anything away.' He took a step back and then stopped and gave Oribas a queer look. 'I knew you'd come here, Aulian. But I was certain it would be Gallow who brought me the red sword. Then we might have talked some more about what you came here to do. Might even have been the three of us could have reached some accord.'

'The Edge of Sorrows is not yours, King of the Lhosir.'

Sixfingers laughed again. 'A Vathan? A woman? Alone in the valley? Shall we make a wager, Aulian, on how long it is before I have her?'

The ram smashed down the fifth gate as it had smashed the third and the fourth. Under the shelter of the gatehouse another iron devil spent itself turning the portcullis to rust and the Lhosir poured through the ruins. Gallow met them as they climbed through the debris scattered across the road. Grim-faced Marroc with spears and shields locked together stood either side of him. They'd beaten Medrin's Lhosir once today so they knew it could be done and the knowing fired their blood. When the soldier beside Gallow fell to an axe buried in his helm, another stepped up to take his place, and when he too fell, a spear stabbed through his foot, another came forward. Gallow and Sarvic held the Marroc line together and close to the rubble in the road, so close that the Lhosir had no space to make a wall of their own to face them. For every Marroc that fell, two Lhosir died.

Gallow's legs ached, his shield arm had turned to lead, his shoulders ground like broken glass, yet the arm that held his spear lunged and slashed and stabbed with the same strength it ever had. He remembered how the red sword would sing to him when he held it, softly in his head and only he would hear. It sang of the end it brought to suffering and pain and woe, of the sweet nothingness of oblivion that was its gift. He had a dozen cuts and bruises: a slash on his arm from a Lhosir spear, a throbbing in his shoulder from being hit by the Marroc beside him jerking his shield, a twinge in his ankle where he'd trodden on a stone in the fighting and turned it, but they were holding. Barely, but they were.

And then the Lhosir in front of Gallow pulled suddenly back, and out of the stones strode the iron-skinned men – Fateguard, nine of them. For a moment Gallow thought the Marroc would hold, but then the Fateguard closed on the line and spear thrusts sparked off their iron skins, swords skittered aside, axes dented but didn't slow them and they came as though they didn't care. One grabbed a Marroc from the centre of the line by the arm, pulled him out and rammed a sword though his chin before throwing him over the edge of the road to the tier below.

'Salt!' Gallow dropped his shield and threw salt from the bag at his hip into a Fateguard's face. It reeled, and he rammed the iron point of his spear through the slits of its mask. The metal split and the Fateguard fell. When Gallow looked down, he saw its face disintegrate before his eyes. There was no blood. 'Salt!' They had it – Sarvic and Gallow and dozens of others. Oribas had seen to that.

Two of the Fateguard turned on him. Around him the Marroc fought on but he felt the fear wash through them like a river in flood and then in a moment they were breaking, screaming at the men behind them to run, to flee back to the castle and safety of the sixth and last gate.

'And what then?' Gallow screamed at them. 'What when they rot that one too and smash it down like all the rest?' But the Marroc didn't hear, or couldn't, or chose not to, and now they were all running and five of the Fateguard were marching up the road, battering aside the missiles thrown at them from above. Three others had him pinned, cutting off his retreat, but they paused for a moment instead of killing him. They seemed to eye him with interest.

Suddenly a single screaming Marroc sprinted down the road, hurling fistfuls of salt into the faces of the Fateguard as he passed. He reached Gallow and two of the Fateguard lurched away, caught in clouds of the stuff, but the last stepped up and ran the Marroc through. The Fateguard and the Marroc stood together for a moment, and Gallow saw the Marroc's face and knew he'd seen this man twice before, the drowning Marroc pulled out of the Isset in Andhun three years back, and then in Varyxhun when Angry Jonnic had meant to hang him.

The Fateguard threw the dead Marroc over the edge into the road below. Gallow turned back, stabbing his spear into the salt-blinded face of the ironskin in front of him. He drew out his axe and hacked the hand off the second and then its head, but now the Lhosir had returned. Shields locked together, they swallowed the Fateguard into their ranks as they came up the road at a slow run towards the sixth gate, the last before the castle of Varyxhun itself, and Gallow retreated before them. At the open gates of the castle with the Dragon's Maw at their backs, Sarvic had managed to rally the Marroc at last.

'Salt! For the love of Modris, who carries salt?'

The Lhosir stopped a dozen yards short. The last handful of Fateguard stepped forward again. Before the Marroc behind him could break and run a second time, Gallow stepped forward too. The ironskin in the middle took another step and saluted him. 'Gallow Truesword.' He took off his helm and his mask and crown. The face underneath was as sallow and as pale as Beyard's had been.

'Do I know you?'

'You were meant to be one of us, Truesword. My brother the Screambreaker was meant to bring you to us. Fate gave him that time for that purpose.'

'Your brother? Who are you?' But the Screambreaker *had* had a brother – everyone knew that. It just wasn't possible, for the Moontongue had been drowned at sea almost twenty years past.

'You know my name, Foxbeard. All Lhosir know my name and spit upon the sound of it. I am Farri Moontongue, brother to Corvin Screambreaker, and I am dead.' He levelled his sword at Gallow's heart and came forward, and Gallow backed away because, even before someone had wrapped him in an iron skin, there was no man alive or dead except the Screambreaker himself who could beat Farri Moontongue, the thief of the Crimson Shield. Gallow caught the first blow on his shield but the Moontongue was already lunging again, and Gallow moved barely in time; and then the ironskin had an axe in his other hand, and it came so fast that Gallow hardly even saw it before it smashed into the mail over his ribs and knocked the breath out of him; and Moontongue's sword was already flashing at his face, and Gallow lunged, not caring that he was about to die as long as he might take this abomination with him.

And at that moment, in the tomb beneath Witches' Reach, Achista poured salt over the armour of the Eyes of Time, the first of the Fateguard. On the top of that same tower King Medrin dreamed that his iron hand burst into flames, while somewhere not far from there the Eyes of Time felt a pain that seared through all its creations, and on the road outside the gates to Varyxhun castle the last of the Fateguard staggered and clutched their heads and fell to their knees, and the thief of the Crimson Shield paused in the blow that would have killed Gallow but Gallow's spear did not. He drove it through Farri Moontongue's throat and twisted. There was no blood.

'I did not mean for this, Gallow Truesword,' said the creature that had once been a man, 'when I did what I did.'

Gallow's axe rose and fell, he bellowed and roared, the Marroc swarmed over the other writhing Fateguard with salt and iron and fire until the ironskins were done, and then it was the Marroc who charged, not the Lhosir, and the forkbeards who melted away, too stunned by what they'd seen to stand and fight.

31

THE EYES OF TIME

'I will tell you a story, Aulian, and then perhaps you'll tell one to me.' The king of the Lhosir rode on his new horse and Oribas rode beside him, wrists tied to his saddle. Behind them some five hundred Lhosir fighters were marching up the Aulian Way to Varyxhun. 'I don't know how the Eyes of Time came to our land. Your people brought it here, whatever *it* is. They buried it in salt. It was meant to stay here for ever.' He fixed Oribas with a look that bored into the Aulian. 'I have to imagine they didn't know how to destroy it, otherwise they would have done so, but then how is it that *you* do?'

Oribas met his eye. 'I came here to do what I could, King Medrin of the Lhosir. I had thought the Mother of Monsters had made you its slave. I see now I was wrong. It is the other way around.'

'No, Aulian, you still have that wrong. My mind is my own and always has been, though a fine battle we've had on that score, but the Eyes of Time serve a mortal?' Medrin smiled up at the sky. 'I think not.' He chuckled to himself. 'Aulian, I'll kill you if I have to, I won't pretend otherwise, but I'd prefer you alive. Maybe it lightens your thoughts to know that. You travelled with Gallow a while so I suppose he must have told you about the day he and Beyard and I entered the Temple of Fates?' His six-fingered hand tapped the Crimson Shield. 'All we wanted was to see it, not to steal it, but we were found and taken for thieves. I ran and left Beyard and Gallow behind. I don't know what happened between them – something very noble, I suppose. Somehow Gallow escaped as well. I didn't know him then, had barely even heard his name before that day, but Beyard was my friend and he was taken by the Fateguard, and

I was a coward, too afraid to own up to my part in it. When I begged my father the king to save my friend, he told me I must do it myself. And he was right, and I should have gone to the temple and given myself to them. Both of us should, Gallow too, but neither of us did. No one else knew, of course. To this day no one else does. Beyard took our names with him to his pyre.' He looked across at Oribas from the back of his horse. 'Gallow was only there because his father was a smith. We needed helms that made us look like the Fateguard and someone who could climb the temple walls, and he could give us both.'

For a long time the Lhosir king stared into the distance, into the past. There was shame in his face, Oribas thought, and pain and regret and perhaps a little longing, and it took a while before he shook himself and came back. 'After Beyard was gone I came across the sea to fight with the Screambreaker. I asked him for his help. I thought, after the Fateguard had stolen King Tane's shield from him, he might harbour a grudge, but he only looked at me with scorn and shook his head. I fought beside him anyway, with the passion of a shamed man and in due course I found the punishment I was looking for.' He patted his ribs. 'It was a bad wound. I didn't even see what did it. They say it was a spear, but whatever it was, it punched through my mail and ripped me open. The wound went bad. My flesh started to rot. If I'd been anyone else they would have let me die and burned me and that would have been the end, and if an honest man who knew the truth had spoken me out, they'd have said that I'd abandoned a friend to die and remorse drove me to follow him. The Maker-Devourer doesn't take a man like that for his cauldron, Aulian. Deeds are what matter, not remorse.'

Medrin stopped as another rider drew alongside, and for a while Oribas rode between silent guards while the king did whatever it was that kings did when they rode to war. He let the sights of the valley wash through him. The sky was blue without a cloud in sight and the sun was already warm. Not hot like the desert and it never would be, but almost pleasant – he might even sweat later – and then he wondered whether that helped the Marroc of Varyxhun or the forkbeards or made no difference at all. In the morning the castle was in the shadow of the mountain. The forkbeards would prefer to fight in the mornings then.

His eyes drifted to the river. This far down the valley the Aulian Way ran a little away from the Isset, carved into the lower slopes of the mountains that channelled the water. Between the river and the road lay a steady succession of abandoned Marroc farms, most of them burned. The river ran fast and high; now and then whole trees washed by. The fields were littered with stray boulders, even the trunk of one colossal Varyxhun pine, swept down by the spring floods of years before when the river burst its banks. The Aulians had carefully built their road where the floods wouldn't reach, carving notches into the mountains where they had to, building bridges over the sharp-sided ravines and valleys between. The Aulians had always liked to dig and they'd liked to build too. The streams under the bridges rushed and hissed and foamed. The winter snows were melting, and it was a pity, Oribas thought, that he wasn't going to live to see the valley in summer. It was probably a pretty sight.

It wasn't until the middle of the afternoon that Medrin came back, and when he did he looked annoyed. 'Tell me your name, Aulian.'

'I am Oribas, O King.'

'And that Vathan woman?'

'Mirrahj Bashar.'

The king laughed. 'Bashar is a title, Oribas of Aulia. Thank you.' The more Oribas studied the king, the more he knew he was wrong about something. The king had been vexed by Mirrahj's escape and the loss of the red sword, but no more. 'I wish I'd met you back then, Aulian. So much might have been different. Do you know how to cure flesh rot?'

'You must cut out the rot. All of it.'

Medrin laughed again and shook his head. 'I was the son of a king. No one dared. They took me to Sithhun flat on my back in a cart. The Screambreaker thought it was bad luck to have his prince die in the middle of the army and so he sent me away to die alone instead. Oh, he said he was sending me back to my father but I knew better. Away, that was all that mattered. Flat on my back, and I a proud Lhosir prince.' He snorted. 'In

Sithhun there was an Aulian wizard. A man like you.' He turned and looked down at Oribas and smiled. 'He said I couldn't be saved but he did his best anyway. I was close to my end. He made potions – I don't know what they were – and had me drink them. I was delirious. He talked to me as he worked and I told him about Beyard. I don't know why. Because it preyed on me and because I thought I was dying. I remember how he changed when I spoke of the Eyes of Time. His face, his voice, everything about him, as though he was suddenly a different person. We were in Sithhun among the Marroc. The Fateguard had crossed the sea and taken the Crimson Shield and so they *had* been seen, but this Aulian knew them by another name, one I'd never heard.'

Oribas didn't try to hide his curiosity. 'Another name?'

'He spoke it but I was delirious and didn't properly remember it, only that he said it.' Medrin spat. 'The Aulian opened my wound and drained it. I remember the stench. It made me want to retch and I thought it was one of his potions and then I realised it was me. I can't tell you how it feels to smell such a terrible thing and know it's your own putrefaction. I don't remember much after that. As far as I can put it together, the few friends I had left heard my screams and ran into the room. When they saw what the Aulian had done they murdered him on the spot.' He shook his head. 'We are not reasonable people, Oribas. Perhaps you've seen this already. I think what saved me in the end was that they thought that I too was dead. The Aulian had filled my wound with maggots and honey. Do you understand?'

'To eat away the bad flesh.' Oribas looked up. He'd seen no sign of Achista and not knowing what had happened to her was wearing him down. For all he knew she'd been hanged before they even left. 'Mighty king, You told your soldiers I should not be killed. You did this for a reason. For the knowledge I—'

'Are you trying to bargain with me, Aulian? After everything you've done? Perhaps I want you kept for a very special death.'

Oribas bowed his head. 'I do not take you for a wasteful man, King of the Lhosir.' He took a deep breath. 'The Marroc woman from the tomb. She was nothing but a guide. I will give—'

'Don't lie to me!' Medrin bared his teeth. 'You've been in that tomb before and have no need of a guide, and besides which she was with you when we met on the road and you turned back my ironskins with your circle of salt. I know exactly who she is, and you'd failed before we even spoke if you meant to hide what she means to you. You'll give me all your knowledge but only if I let her go, was that it? But I won't, and you'll give it anyway if that's what I want from you. I'll keep her. Cage her and never hurt her but always let you be very sure how thin is the thread of her life. Yes. And you are right, of course: maggots to eat away the bad flesh. My stupid friends couldn't bring themselves to touch me and so the creatures were allowed to do their work. For two days I lay there, pickled in the Aulian's potions and eaten by his creatures but by the end the rot was gone. I didn't die. I suppose I started to recover, though it hardly felt it at the time. It took a very long time before I could even walk without gasping for breath.' He patted his side, just under his left breast. 'It's not a pretty sight. It had spread a long way.

'When I could speak again, I asked after the Aulian who'd cured me. When I had the answer I sent the men who'd killed him to seek out his family, but he had none. Later, when I looked for myself, I learned this Aulian was not such a pleasant fellow after all. He had a fine house in Sithhun. A palace almost, yet none of the Marroc would go near it. They said he was a witch. In time I went to his house myself and there were strange things there – few that I understood – and even now no one goes to that Aulian's palace unless I say they must. I heard he had a woman, a wife perhaps, and I heard that she fled after he died and that the Marroc caught her and tore her to pieces. I don't know if that's true but I never did find her – either in one piece or many. What I remembered, though, was how he'd changed when I spoke of the Fateguard. How he asked questions about them, about where they came from. He even spoke the name of Witches' Reach, although it wasn't until years later that I learned of the fortress that guards the Aulian Way. I spent a long time in Sithhun in that Aulian's palace. The Screambreaker was off fighting his war and I was recovering my strength from a wound that should have killed me, and when I had that strength again, I found I had no desire to fight beside a man who'd sent me away to die alone. So I stayed in Sithhun until I had my answers, and when I thought I understood how to destroy the Eyes of Time, I went home.'

Oribas looked up sharply and found Medrin was looking at him again, smiling faintly. 'That never occurred to you, did it, Aulian? Not once. Admit it. Not that I once wanted the same as you want now.' He smiled wryly at some private memory and nodded. 'One thing for which I thank my father – that he forced me to learn to read a little Aulian as well as our own tongue. The Aulian's books called it the Edge of Sorrows, and so that's what I looked for, Oribas of Aulia, and found nothing because I knew only its Aulian name. Other matters occupied me: the Screambreaker and his war, my father falling ill, the Screambreaker eyeing his throne.' He was laughing out loud now, shaking his head. 'And then after Andhun and the Vathen I found to my amazement that someone had walked this path before me. No less than Farri Moontongue, the Screambreaker's big brother.'

He might have said more, but that was when a shout made them both look up and back to where a Lhosir was pointing up the mountain. When Oribas squinted, he picked out a lone figure leading a horse along a trail hundreds of feet above them. It took a moment to realise that the figure was standing still, looking down at them, and a moment more to realise that the figure had a bow.

King Medrin snorted. 'From all the way up there? He can't possibly hope to hit anything.'

Oribas judged the angles and wasn't so sure. The archer was a long way away but he was a long way up too.

'What's he shooting at? Us?' Medrin had stopped to look. He didn't sound at all concerned.

'I can't see, O King.'

'He's shooting at something in the road ahead but I can't see what. Look.' Medrin pointed. A moment later Oribas saw a puff of dust from the middle of the road some fifty yards ahead of them. 'What *is* he doing?'

'That is Mirrahj,' said Oribas, too quietly for Medrin to hear, 'and she is finding her range.'

32

MOONTONGUE

'Farri Moontongue.' Gallow lay slumped in the castle yard, too tired to even yelp with pain as Arda washed his wounds and bound them. The yard was full of exhausted and battered Marroc, some still bleeding but all savouring the evening quiet. A moment of bliss. A moment to make peace with Modris, a moment to laugh, to remember or perhaps to forget. Some men stared, eyes far away. Others wept.

'People will remember us for what we did today.' Valaric sat beside Gallow, trading bawdy jokes with Sarvic and a few of his Crackmarsh men. 'We turned the forkbeards back. We slew the iron devils, every one of them, and when they come tomorrow the sixth gate will stand closed and that's how it stays. And you're sitting there thinking of some old forkbeard dead the best part of twenty years?'

Gallow said nothing. He'd seen the Moontongue once. He'd been ten summers old and there was no way to tell whether the dead thing he'd killed today had been the same man. The Moontongue he remembered had been a thundercloud filled with storms and lightning but also with laughter.

'All I know is he stole the Crimson Shield from your iron devils and then sank into the sea. Pity I can't say the same for the rest of you.'

'He was the Screambreaker's brother and they were the bitterest rivals. Yurlak favoured the Screambreaker and Moontongue thought he was better. That's about as much as I know. I only saw him the once before I crossed the sea but that was enough. He wasn't the sort of man you forget.'

'I heard he was tight with Neveric the Black. Neveric would turn on Tane and then the two of them would turn on you forkbeards and Neveric would sit on the throne of Sithhun and the Moontongue would be king across the sea. So Moontongue stole the shield and then Neveric turned on him and they all died and good riddance to the lot of them.' Valaric snorted. 'Neveric was always a bastard. Still, it's easy to tell tales of the dead. If it's all the same to you I'll keep my mind on thinking what tales they'll be telling of us.'

Gallow flinched as Arda poked a graze on his shoulder. 'Doesn't need stitches but I'll be dropping some brandy on that.'

'No, you won't!' said Valaric and Gallow at once.

Arda snorted and did it anyway. 'It's what your wizard would have done.'

The next arrow came straight at Medrin. The first Oribas knew of it was when the Crimson Shield suddenly shifted and the king jerked in his saddle. For a moment Oribas thought Medrin had been hit.

'Maker-Devourer!' When Medrin lowered the shield Oribas saw the arrow. Medrin looked at it. 'That's a Vathan arrow meant to pierce mail.' He laughed. 'No, wizard! This is some trick of yours. I'll not believe your Vathan woman is up there with a bow now, already ahead of us! No.' He pulled the arrow out of the shield and closed on Oribas. 'This arrow isn't real. And the archer on the mountain? Not real either. What are you doing, wizard?' He grabbed Oribas by the shoulder and stabbed him with the arrow's tip. Not deep or hard but enough to draw blood. His face changed: the smile fell away and left a cold hardness beneath. He shook his head. 'No, Aulian. Not your Vathan woman. Just some Marroc.' He kicked his horse to a canter and sped away, a dozen Lhosir at his heels while more began to climb the slope towards the archer. A soldier took the reins of Oribas's horse and led him away too. The last time Oribas looked back he saw several Lhosir still labouring up the slope. The archer hadn't moved. He had no doubt at all that it was Mirrahj.

They slept in the open that night. Oribas dozed now and then, wondering what the Lhosir king had done with Achista. Twice he jerked awake to shouted alarms from the Lhosir sentries but the commotion never came any closer. In the morning they dragged him to his feet and hauled him back to his horse, and then Medrin took him to the edge of the camp to where a gang of surly Lhosir soldiers were dragging a bound Marroc by a rope. The king shouted at them to stop, and it dismayed Oribas how his heart jumped when he realised who the Marroc must be even before he saw her face. She glared at King Sixfingers and spat into the dirt in front of his horse. Medrin laughed.

'See, Aulian, she still has all her arms and legs and most of her blood on the good side of her skin. She has nothing I want, so how long she stays that way lies with you.' He turned to the Lhosir. 'Beat her though, for her disrespect. Aulian, you may stay and watch or ride with me now, as you prefer.' Oribas didn't want to watch but he knew he had to, and so he stayed as the Lhosir punched his Achista to the ground and then kicked her half to death.

'It was the Aulian of Sithhun who set me on the path, and you're an Aulian too. That's really the only reason I haven't made ravens out of both of you.' When the army was ready to march, Oribas found himself led to Medrin's side once more. 'You deserve it for what you did. Burning men like that, their bodies sunk into water where no one will ever speak them out.' He spat. 'You think I want the red sword, don't you? Three years ago I wanted it more than anything. Not any more.' He shook his head. 'The Vathen came and my father was too old and fat to lead an army. It fell to me to go to Andhun, to be the king of the Lhosir across the sea whether I liked it or not. In Andhun I learned that the sword the Vathen carried to war was the Edge of Sorrows. I learned, at last, its other names.' He chuckled again. 'I wanted that sword, Aulian, and if Gallow had ever stopped to wonder why, if he'd ever asked me, perhaps all of this might have been different, perhaps we might have sailed side by side to the frozen wastes and the Iron Palace amid the Ice Wraiths and put an end to the Eyes of Time, each of us with one hand on the sword together. I just wanted to avenge Beyard and if he'd known, he'd have had a piece of that too, I think.' He laughed bitterly. 'I never even knew the Eyes of Time had made an ironskin of Beyard. I just thought he was dead all those long years ago.'

He unbuckled the Crimson Shield from his arm and held up his iron hand. 'For running away that day in the Temple of Fates, Gallow cut off my hand with that sword in Andhun. I was Medrin Twelvefingers before. Now I'm Sixfingers, Medrin Ironhand. I should have died. Gallow should have killed me, or the wound he gave me should have done it. But for a second time I lived.' He tapped the shield and strapped it back to his arm. 'The Vathen took Andhun and everything east of the Isset. My men took me back home. Yurlak took one look at me, flew into a rage and rushed across the sea to put down the filthy Vathen or Marroc or whoever had had the audacity to damage his son.' Medrin spat again and there was an edge of bitterness to his words. 'Never mind that it had been a Lhosir, never mind that I might die, he crossed the sea and got away from the sight of me as fast as he could. He died within the year and I shed no tears. He'd done what was needed. He'd outlived the Moontongue and the Screambreaker and that was all I was ever going to get from him. And while everyone else was fighting, I spent my time at the Temple of Fates and looking for the Screambreaker's fortune.' His face wrinkled into a suppressed smile. 'All those years of fighting and winning should have made him as rich as a king but he never took much. He did it for ...' Medrin shrugged. 'I really don't know. But by the end of my looking it was the Moontongue I came to understand. They say the Moontongue stole the Crimson Shield as a gift to Neveric the Black of the Marroc, that he meant to betray his brother and his king and that Neveric betrayed him in turn, but Moontongue had a sea more ambition to him than that. When I understood, Aulian, for a moment I was in such awe of him that I forgot to breathe. I had found a Lhosir I could finally truly admire, safe in the knowledge that he was dead. You see, the Moontongue stole the Crimson Shield for himself, not for some Marroc, and he stole it because he believed it could make the Eyes of Time into his servant. He believed he would see the future, know all things before they came to pass, and with that knowledge he would crush Yurlak, grind his brother to dust and lead a conquest the like of which the world hasn't seen since the glorious days of

Aulia. He wasn't killed by some renegade Marroc. It was iron-skins who sank his ship.'

He sighed. 'I took salt with me, Aulian, and other things, and I took the Crimson Shield. I took the knowledge I found in the house of the wizard of Sithhun and in the secret letters of the Moontongue.' He smiled again, although his smiles never touched his ice-blue eyes. 'Of course, nothing was what I thought. I was more careful than the Moontongue perhaps, but still ignorant.' The king lifted his iron hand. The fingers flexed and Oribas jerked in his saddle.

'How …?'

'The Eyes of Time made this hand for me. Through it the Fateguard obey me. I learned quickly enough why I was so favoured. I did the same as you – I threw salt. Now when I do that, I burn too.' Medrin slipped the shield back over his arm. 'I keep it hidden. I already have a finger more than most men and there are limits to how much witchery a brave Lhosir warrior will take. I found I couldn't make the Eyes of Time my slave, but with the shield nor could I be easily dismissed. We bargained. In the end, for this hand I gave my blood oath that I would search for two pieces of iron armour, lost for hundreds of years somewhere near the mountain crossing to Aulia. I knew, as I gave it, that I would never find them.'

He reined in his horse abruptly and turned in the saddle to face Oribas. 'And then you came. You and Gallow, whom everyone thought was dead, and the Edge of Sorrows, and I have to wonder what is coincidence and what is fate. That the Fateguard I unwittingly sent to Varyxhun was Beyard? That he had the red sword in his hand and Gallow in his grasp and did nothing? That you found the two pieces of iron? Coincidence or fate, Aulian? I must believe that the Eyes of Time knew, as we struck our bargain, that these things would come to pass.'

Oribas looked away. 'King of the Lhosir, my people do not believe in fate.'

'But mine do.' Medrin rounded on Oribas and now his voice took on a sharpness. 'What did your people entomb out here so very far from their home? What will it become if it's made whole? Answer me that and answer in truth and I'll give you that palace in Sithhun and everything in it. You can live out your days there in service to me. You can have your Marroc woman too, as long as she never leaves the walls of your house. Otherwise I make her into a raven and you will watch every moment of her agony.'

'What will it become?' Oribas shrugged. 'What it already is – a monster.' He looked at the river, at the rushing water still rising. A man who looked for it could see how the water was higher today than it had been yesterday.

Night after night Gallow and Valaric stood on the walls and watched the forkbeards at the bottom of the mountain. Sometimes Addic came and stood beside them and sometimes Arda. Sometimes Gallow brought the children, Tathic and Feya and Jelira and even little Pursic. He showed them the Lhosir and told them that these were his people. Then Arda told them stories, Marroc stories of men who were more than men, slow to anger and reluctant to lift their swords yet who fought with a relentless fury when evil came, protecting the folk around them until the bitter end. In Arda's stories they always won but at a terrible cost, so they died in the end.

And then Gallow told his own stories, the ones he'd learned as a child, and his too were of men who were more than men, and sometimes they too protected the weak who looked to them for shelter, but more often they fought against those who claimed to be strong and did it for no better reason than it was there to be done, and sometimes they won and sometimes they died, and often they lost a hand or a foot or an eye and none of it ever for any reason but to see who was the better man. They weren't Marroc stories and they didn't follow the Marroc way, and when Tathic asked which was better, Gallow only shrugged. 'All our stories say one thing. That a man must speak his heart and speak the truth he finds there. That he must defend both with his life if he has to.' He pointed down the mountain. 'I'm here beside you and my people are down there, and soon we'll fight because our hearts follow different songs. But I'll tell you this and they would tell you too: a man who lies, a man who gives his word freely and without thought or meaning, is a man who is worthless. This is what my people mean when they say *nioingr*. A traitor to his kin, but worst of all a traitor to himself. It's not our nature to be kind or merciful. Those are Marroc ways and my brothers of the sea sneer at them, but even so only our beards are forked, never our tongues. That is what it means to be Lhosir.'

In the afternoon, Oribas was with the first riders as they came into Varyxhun and suddenly King Medrin was beside him again. They walked their horses off the Aulian Way and through the town and into streets filled with Lhosir soldiers. Medrin led the way to the edge of the river and stopped there. 'So, Oribas of Aulia. I keep seeing your eyes stray to the water as we talk. Will it flood and wash us away? Do you know the answer or do you simply wonder?'

Oribas let out a deep breath. 'I do not know the answer, O King of the Lhosir. Perhaps the mountains are angered or perhaps they are not.'

Medrin shook his head. 'The river is a river and does what every mountain river does: rises in spring. Yet Varyxhun is not washed away and rebuilt each summer. The river will not save your Marroc friends. So ... the Eyes of Time. Do you have an answer for me?'

'Beyard was Gallow's friend and yours. Make your peace with Gallow. Whatever the creature is, he will destroy it. He will help you. I will see to it.'

'Make peace with him?' Sixfingers held up his metal hand, almost shouting in his outrage, 'He took my hand, Aulian, and Beyard is dead now.' He stared across the river and up the valley to the mountains that towered over the distant Aulian Way. 'I'll crush the Vathen if I must but my heart lies across these mountains now. The Lhosir will build Aulia once more.'

'I do not think it can be done.' Oribas shook his head. 'Not by any king, no matter how great he might be.'

'Nothing is done that is not tried. Isn't that an Aulian saying? And should it *not* be tried?' His hand swept up the valley to the castle of Varyxhun. 'Look at what you made, Aulian. Look at what you were!'

'But we were not wise, King of the Lhosir. We dug until we found something we could not contain and should not have found and with a stroke it brought everything to ruin. Nothing is done that is not tried does not mean all that there is *should* be tried. That is a saying of my people too.'

'What did your people bury here, Aulian?'

'I do not know, O King. The libraries of the castle do not say. I do not know why it was brought here and nor do I know what will happen if it is whole again. It is something unique in its danger. Perhaps in this palace of which you speak there is more ...'

Medrin nodded. 'You disappoint me, Oribas of Aulia, but I thank you for your honesty.'

He left Oribas at the side of the river staring at the water, filled with thoughts about the castle that the Aulians had called the Water Castle and the legends which spoke of a dragon who would drown any army who broke the sixth gate. Filled with the knowledge of his ancestors and their craft and their cunning and the certain understanding that he'd missed something. But filled most of all with thoughts of Achista.

Later, the Lhosir led him into the heart of the town. As the evening drew in they took him to what had once been the market, where a dozen carpenters were hard at work building what looked like wooden shelters, each as long as a hanging shed but with no walls. Sixfingers was walking among them and he smiled when he saw Oribas. 'It seems my Fateguard are all gone.' He held up his iron hand and looked at it. 'A precious gift this, once, but now it burns and serves no purpose. Thanks to you, Aulian, and so I won't be so sad to lose it again. I should have known, of course, that every gift would come with a price. I'm sure *you* would have known that.' He looked at the road leading up to Varyxhun castle, at the Lhosir moving about on the lower tiers and then across the market square where a bedraggled band of Marroc were being herded. He stood and watched as the Marroc were beaten and forced onto the wooden frames and tied there, hand and foot; and when it was done he looked at Oribas. He stayed silent but his eyes asked if Oribas understood, and Oribas bowed his head and nodded, because yes, he understood perfectly. The Lhosir would carry these human shields over their heads when they attacked the gates once more and Achista was among them.

'What do you want?' He could hardly speak.

The Lhosir king nodded slightly. Arms gripped Oribas and forced him down, holding him helpless while others tied him to the wooden frame. 'Oribas of Aulia, you came to Witches' Reach filled with purpose, yet you say you know nothing?' He shook his head. 'The Eyes of Time is here, not far away at all. Do you not feel the presence? The Fateguard are gone, the pieces of iron are found, and so our bargain is done. I fear we have become adversaries once more and so my patience for your knowledge has become frayed. Perhaps a night out here will help your memory.'

A wave of despair shook Oribas. 'I would tell you what I knew if I had the knowledge to share. Why would I not?' Desperation filled every word. Not for him, but for his love. 'The red sword. Salt and fire and salt and ice and last of all iron. There is nothing more to know! That is enough! It is all I have to give!'

But Medrin was shaking his head. 'Tomorrow I'll take the last gate of Varyxhun. I might go alone, if you convince me. Otherwise we all go together.' The king squatted beside him. 'In the morning I'll let you go. You can walk beside me. You can carry the shield for me.' He chuckled. 'If it was the other way round, we both know she'd let you die. But it isn't.' He held out his arm with its iron hand and cut the skin above his wrist with a knife. 'The Eyes of Time. My blood oath, Aulian. Tell me its secrets and I'll keep your woman from harm. Otherwise what use are you to me? What use are either of you? Think on it. You have until the morning.'

He walked away. Oribas watched him go and felt his heart turn to lead, for there were no secrets to share.

33

THE SIXTH GATE

Somewhere far away the sun began to rise. Oribas watched the snow-painted tips of the mountains across the river light up in orange fire and listened to the morning watchmen as they shuffled into the market square, yawning and rubbing their eyes. The Lhosir who'd stood guard through the night slunk away to doze before the morning battle began.

'Guard! Guard! I have something to say to your king!' Because if what Medrin needed was to hear a story about the Eyes of Time then a story he could have. It wasn't an easy thing to lie, not for one like Oribas, but he'd done far worse since he'd crossed the mountains.

The nearest watchman laughed and spat at him. 'If Ironhand wants to hear your begging for mercy, he'll come in his own good time.' He walked away. Oribas looked across the yard for Achista but he hadn't seen where the Lhosir had tied her, and when he called out the Lhosir kicked him until he was quiet. His eyes flickered about the square, searching for inspiration. He could only see two Lhosir now, not the three who'd first come into the square, but then he spied the third again, slipping out of some alley, and one of the Marroc must have said something for the Lhosir suddenly started kicking and snarling like an animal. The second watchman went over to him and the other spun around and smacked him in the face with such violence that even Oribas winced. The two fell to the ground wrestling. The first ran over, and then suddenly the third Lhosir was up again, sword drawn, and the next thing Oribas knew the other two were being murdered right in front of him. It was brutally quick and happened almost without a sound. The Lhosir dragged the two bodies under the wooden shields and ran to Oribas and crouched down beside him, and at last Oribas saw her face.

'I have to kill a monster,' she said in her singsong Vathan voice. 'So I will kill this Lhosir king.' She cut the ropes that held him. Across the square he saw another figure rise and crouch down again.

'Achista?'

Mirrahj helped him to his feet. 'Run and hide. Get away. I want the Lhosir king.'

Yes, he could do that. Or they could get back into the castle the same way they got out. And he found himself thinking of the shaft that ran up under the gates and into the cisterns and on up into the mountain, and finally his eyes flickered up to the castle and to the tarn above it, brimming full of snowmelt. He gripped Mirrahj's hand. 'No!' Across the square Achista was freeing the other Marroc. Oribas pulled Mirrahj after him. 'I know how he means to break through the last gate.' He stared at the rushing waters of the Isset, full and ready to burst its banks. 'I have to go back. I know why they call it the water castle. I know its secret. I know how to stop him. He will lead his army himself this time, I know it. You can be there, waiting for him.'

Mirrahj seemed to think on this for a moment and then nodded and handed him his precious satchel. 'Then you might want this.'

Once again the Lhosir climbed the mountain road and once again Gallow watched them. They came with a banner in their midst this time, the banner Reddic and Jonnic had seen before. Valaric looked at him. 'Are there any iron devils left, or was that all of them?'

As far as Gallow knew no one had ever counted the Fateguard or known how many they were. Not many, that was sure. He shook his head. 'Someone had better tell Reddic that Sixfingers is coming back for seconds.'

The Lhosir wound steadily closer and Valaric left to stand over the sixth gate. The Lhosir had the big wooden screens they carried over their heads again and Gallow wondered how many more Fat Jonnics there were among the Marroc. Not many.

Sarvic quietly came and stood beside him. 'Sixfingers must

think he's going to win. He wouldn't be here otherwise. So there's more iron devils after all. Must be.'

'Maybe Valaric will shout the right words into the Dragon's Maw and draw out the beast to eat them all.'

They both laughed at that. Sarvic shook his head. 'Never thought I'd see you again, forkbeard, after Lostring Hill. You saved my life from the Vathen. A Marroc saved by a forkbeard. I hated you for that. When they were going to hang you here, I paid you back.' He drew off his gauntlet and pulled the knife from his belt and cut his arm. 'Yours today, forkbeard, and freely given. I'm proud to stand with you.'

Gallow did the same. They clasped arms, their blood mingling. 'You're not the man I remember, Sarvic. If all Marroc were like you and Valaric, the Screambreaker would have turned back at the sea.'

Sarvic laughed. 'I wish that were true.'

'Watch over my Arda and my sons. If Sixfingers breaches the gates and takes the castle then he won't be kind. Don't let him take them.'

'If I still bleed I'll defend them with my life.'

'Just let Reddic get them out, Sarvic. He knows the way. You should get out too. It doesn't have to be the end here.'

'For most of us it does, Foxbeard. For most of us it does.'

The Lhosir came on up the road through the smashed lower gates. They marched along the fourth tier and Valaric loosed a single volley of precious arrows to remind Medrin's men that they weren't safe, not ever. After that the Marroc watched as the Lhosir marched under their sea of shields and their wooden roofs and turned the corner to the last tier, to the broken fifth gate and then, at the road's end, the sixth. All the oil was gone and also most of the stones piled up behind the gates to hold them shut and brace them against the inevitable ram. Shouts started up, taunts and insults raining down, but even as the Lhosir came up to the sixth gate, the Marroc held back their last precious arrows. Then a shout went up from Valaric on the gates and all along the battlements the Marroc rose. Stones crashed on the forkbeards' wooden roofs, knocking them askew. Arrows flew through the gaps. Boiling water rained over them, though it was hard to see whether it ever scalded Lhosir skin. Men snapped off the icicles that had formed overnight and threw them like spears. Gallow smiled as he saw that. Oribas would have done the same.

'No ram,' said Sarvic beside him, and Gallow saw it was true. The Lhosir had come up the mountain road with their shields but nothing else. So Sarvic was right. They had more ironskins after all. He looked at the sacks of salt lined up along the battlements and slit one open.

'Give me a hand with this?'

Sarvic nodded. The first Lhosir were at the sixth gate now, arrows thudding into their shields, and Valaric had his own sacks of salt and all manner of other things to throw down on them. Medrin and his banner were moving up under their own wooden roof. It looked different, but it took a moment for Gallow to realise why.

There were people tied to it.

As the sun crept down the mountains across the Isset, Mirrahj swore softly under her breath in her own tongue. When Achista and Oribas were finally done freeing the rest, she grabbed them both and hauled them away into the darkest shadows she could find.

'Look!' Two forkbeards stumbled bleary-eyed out of a house across the street. 'They're waking.'

'They mean to attack again this morning. King Sixfingers told me this.'

The alley where they hid ran between a jumble of yards to a wide street by the river, the obvious place to go. If they reached a boat, the current would take them and the forkbeards would never catch up on foot, but they'd need to be quick. The other freed Marroc were trying to slip away. One of them, at least, would be seen. The hue and cry would go up at any moment and forkbeards would come swarming from everywhere.

Mirrahj fingered the sword hilt at her belt. Maybe Sixfingers would come to see for himself – now there was a thought. But Oribas wanted to go back to the castle, so Mirrahj pulled him and Achista into a yard instead, and then through the back door of a house. A place to hide.

Three forkbeards looked up at them as they burst in. They were sitting in a circle on the floor. The one staring right at her froze mid-yawn. The nearest had his back to her. She kicked that one in the head, jumped on his back, drove the red sword through the one who was still yawning and then swung a backhand slash that cut open the face of the third. The one she'd kicked had time to let out an angry grunt and turn and look up and go all wide-eyed before she drove Solace through his heart. Two spears leaned against the wall. Achista snatched one. Oribas went for the other door but Mirrahj pulled him back. 'We wait here.'

Achista laughed. 'Shall we fight the whole of Sixfingers' horde?'

As a shout went up outside, the first of the fleeing Marroc seen, Mirrahj gripped Achista. 'They expect us to run! Perhaps they won't look so close. And yes, little Marroc, if we have to then we fight every forkbeard in this valley. Isn't that what you came here for?'

Oribas pulled a fur off the floor. He wrapped himself in it and lay down.

'What are you doing?'

'What if there were six forkbeards here, not three, and all had been killed? Who would know any better? Who ever thinks to look closely at the dead?'

More shouts and then one right outside: 'Marroc! Marroc!' Another shout: 'Ironhand wants them alive!'

The Aulian shifted so that his eyes were on the door but the dead forkbeards hid his face. 'Lie in the back in the darkest shadows with your weapons close and ready. Sixfingers plans to take the castle today. He has a way through the last gate and he won't wait. They won't look for long, I promise you. The castle is his prize today, not us.'

And he was right. Mirrahj settled uneasily into the far corner of the room and slumped against the wall, the red sword close to hand. When a pair of forkbeards burst in on them, she stayed very still as they stopped with the sunlight streaming behind them and squinted into the gloom and shook their heads. They left the door open and so now and then she saw others hurry past, back and forth for a while with noise and commotion all about, and then the noise faded and no forkbeards came past any more, and when the three of them finally emerged, hours after dawn, the army was all gone, marching up to the castle and Varyxhun was almost empty. Mirrahj led them from house to house, shadow to shadow, until she reached the edge of the river, and there Oribas stopped her. He looked up to the column of forkbeards steadily climbing the mountain road. 'Find a rope.' He looked her up and down and then poked her in the hip. 'And a stout piece of wood that stands this high off the ground. And be quick.'

Sarvic drew back his bow and took aim. 'Don't say a word, forkbeard. Not a word.' His voice was harsh and hoarse. He let the first arrow fly and it struck one of the Marroc in the chest. Sarvic drew another. Medrin was climbing the last tier now, about to pass through the fifth gate and in range of the boiling water and the stones, yet nothing was hitting his human shield. At least there was no hearing the screams over the shouts of the Lhosir and the Marroc on the walls.

Sarvic shot another arrow. It struck a second Marroc in the throat. A good clean kill. Gallow squinted, trying to see if Achista or Mirrahj or Oribas was a part of Medrin's shield. Under the rags and the dirt and the crusted blood it was hard to be sure.

Sarvic fired again. As Medrin's banner passed beneath he killed the last of the screaming Marroc, threw down his bow and ran along the battlements, howling at the top of his lungs, 'There! Down there! Sixfingers! Never mind the rest of them, he's the one! Kill him! Kill the forkbeard king. Look at him! *Look!*' He picked up a stone as big as his head and staggered under its weight, hefted it up to a merlon over Medrin's banner and tipped it over. It bounced off the wall and smashed into a corner of the shield. For a moment the back end wavered and sank. 'Kill him! Use everything!'

The Marroc went wild. Arrows flew at every opening, no matter how small. Men ran up and down the battlements with stones and pots of boiling water, slopping it, burning their hands and scalding their feet but they didn't care. A torrent came over the wall down onto Medrin's roof and banner. Another great stone hit square in the middle and snapped the beam that held the shield together. Smaller stones pinged off the sides and it was riddled with arrows. As Gallow watched, the roof began to break apart. The Marroc cheered but now Gallow wasn't looking at Medrin's banner, he was looking everywhere else. There was too little Lhosir in Medrin to stand beneath his own banner come what may, and yet just enough for him to be here somewhere. And he was looking for the Fateguard too because there had to be one. He could see small rams carried under the following roofs. Nothing big enough for the gates of the castle as they were, but rust their hinges to dust and ...

Another whoop and a cheer went up from the Marroc on the sixth gate and a cloud of grey showered down. The roof at the front of the Lhosir army tipped sideways and lay on its edge, about to topple over the cliff onto the tier below. Lhosir soldiers hastily lifted their shields and cowered. Medrin's roof was almost at the front of them now, bent in the middle and sagging but still carried onward. Sacks and sacks came over the gatehouse, each of them ripped before they went. The air was suddenly thick with salt but still Medrin's banner came on. Then with a great shout from the gate, a stone block the size of a man toppled from the wall. Gallow watched it plunge into the front of what was left of Medrin's roof, shattering it. The spear flying his banner snapped and exploded into shards. The roof disintegrated, the Lhosir crushed beneath it trapped screaming while others scurried for shelter, pressing themselves against the walls. Everywhere the Marroc cheered and hooted. 'For King Tane!' 'Go back to your sheep, forkbeards!'

Gallow peered frantically among the forkbeards who'd come up behind Medrin's banner, looking for the one Fateguard who had to be among them to rust the last gate. Looking and not seeing, and then he caught a glimpse: Medrin. A flash of him almost at the front, with his helm and the Crimson Shield in his hand, and then he was gone again, hidden among the press of men.

'He's not dead!' He pulled Sarvic to the edge of the wall and pointed. 'He's not dead, Sarvic. He's there.'

They looked, both of them, but all they saw now were Lhosir shields, and then three Lhosir ran for the gates and behind them the rest began to move again. 'There!' In the middle of the three. Medrin.

Sarvic let fly. His arrow hit the Crimson Shield. He tried again but it was as though each time Medrin saw the arrow coming and lifted his shield to catch it even though he never once looked up. He reached the gate, crouched down and raised a hand to touch it, the iron hand that the Eyes of Time had given him, and the shields of the Lhosir closed around him. Almost at once a cry went up from the men in the castle yard. 'The gates! It's happening!'

'Stop him!'

But how? The Marroc had thrown all their stones and the Lhosir had Medrin wrapped in shields to catch their arrows and the ground was already white with salt and their oil had gone. Gallow bowed his head. He gripped Sarvic's shoulder. 'Stay here, friend, with your bow and the best archers you have. When the gates fall they may drop their guard in their rush to kill us. Use your arrows well and then come. I'll hold a place in the line for you.' His lip curled. 'I promise there will be plenty of them left.'

He left the battlements and walked with a steady stride down into the yard, to where the Marroc soldiers waited with their shields and their spears for the gate to fall. When they did, the Lhosir would be there, and Medrin would be at the front and Gallow would call him out, and Medrin would have no choice, in front of all his men, but to accept.

Oribas and Mirrahj and Achista ran along the banks of the Isset. The forkbeards were up on the road, marching on the last gate, and the rain of stones and arrows from the Marroc had already started. Oribas could hear the shouts wafting from the mountain on the breeze. He bounded down the path with Achista behind him. Mirrahj followed, carrying their rope and the piece of wood. He ran into the cave and the winding tunnel, and if there were any forkbeards watching then he never saw them. He reached the water and ducked under the surface and felt his way through to the inner cave.

It was dark, utterly dark, and so it took a long time and a great deal of cursing before they found the hole in the roof of the cave and poked their stick through and stuck it fast. Mirrahj shinned up the rope and then Achista, then Oribas last of all, hauled up by the others. They started to climb the shaft.

'Where's Sarvic?' A runner from the gates looked up at him. Sarvic looked back.

'Here.'

The runner gave him an arrow. 'Valaric says this is for you.' The runner darted away again. Sarvic looked at the arrow and then peered more closely at the tip.

The arrowhead had Medrin's name scratched into it.

34

THE CRIMSON SHIELD

'I understand it!' In the blackness Oribas scrambled up the shaft, feeling his way one hand at a time. Achista and Mirrahj climbed behind him. 'The Dragon's Maw behind the bars. The gates that no one can enter!'

'That cave has a dragon?' Mirrahj snorted with derision.

'Yes! A *water* dragon.'

'I don't understand.' Achista kept grabbing at his feet. He was slower than either of them.

'The stories! When the Aulians built the castle, they dug into the mountain and awoke the dragon, and the dragon in its anger flooded the valley and the river rose to the walls of the castle itself and wiped everything away. And the dragon will come again to devour whoever breaks the sixth gate!'

'There are no such things as dragons.' Mirrahj spoke with a flat certainty.

'No, but—'

'My people killed them.'

Oribas cackled to himself. 'No no, there's no dragon hiding here that no one has seen for two hundred years, that is true. But what if the water was real? What if there really was a flood?'

It was Achista's turn now: 'The Isset rises every spring, but up to the castle walls? That's not possible!'

'But what if it was not the river!' Oribas was shaking with excitement. 'What if it was ...'

'The lake!'

'Yes. The tarn above the castle.' He felt the change in them after that, both of them, as the possibility coursed through their thoughts. Aulians had built the castle. Aulians liked to dig. They'd burrowed into the mountain and they'd dug their tunnels, tunnels like this one. But somehow they'd hit the underside of the lake or some flooded cave beneath it and the waters had rushed out of the Dragon's Maw and through the sixth gate and down the mountainside and washed away everything in their path. The whole lake, emptied into the Isset in one single torrent. And because they were Aulians, they went back into their tunnel after the waters had subsided and they built a wall. And slowly the lake had filled again. He could see it all as though he'd been there.

The sixth gate shuddered under the blows of the ram and with each one the rusted iron flaked and cracked. Gallow stood tense and ready. When the gates finally broke and fell they might tumble onto the Lhosir. In that moment of confusion the Marroc would fall on them, charging out of Varyxhun castle before Medrin's warriors could form their wall of shields.

The pounding stopped. The gates still stood, a haze of dust clouded behind them. At Gallow's back lay the cave, with its bars too thick to break and too close for a man to enter. He'd have given a lot to put some Marroc archers inside that cave and never mind the dragon of stories. He stood with his spear poised and waited. On the battlements above, the Marroc fell quiet. The gates creaked and groaned and one seemed to sag a little. A tension seized them – even the Lhosir fell silent now. The gates groaned again and then one of them began to fall, twisting under its own weight. The bars that held them closed caught it for a moment, but then the rusted iron that held the bars wrenched and tore and split. Corroded metal shattered in bangs and puffs of dust and retorts that Gallow felt through his feet and then the first gate hit the ground. The second was already falling, and outside on the road he saw that the Lhosir had moved back and had already formed their wall of shields and spears. One man alone stood in front of them. Medrin raised the Crimson Shield high and Gallow could see that the arm that held it ended in a ragged stump – the shield was not held but was strapped to his arm. Medrin looked right at him. 'See this, Foxbeard?' he cried. 'You did this.' He gestured at the castle, a sweep of his arm that took in Marroc and Lhosir alike. 'You did all of this.'

An arrow flew at him. Medrin caught it on the shield. Then he lifted his spear and lowered his head and started to run, and behind him the other Lhosir ran too and a great howl went up from them. The Marroc on the battlements screamed and threw their remaining stones and Gallow roared a battle cry of his own, and all around him the Marroc of the Crackmarsh lowered their spears and braced their shields to receive Medrin's charge.

Warm distant light poured into the shaft like liquid honey. Mirrahj knew at once where they were – the cisterns of Varyxhun. The Aulian was a slow climber and the ascent felt as if it had taken the whole morning though she knew it must be far less. The light drew closer. The shaft reached the cisterns and went on past, rising steadily into the mountain. Oribas kept on climbing. Mirrahj stopped. 'Aulian, where are you going?'

'To the water dragon, Vathan.'

Mirrahj shook her head. 'There's no dragon, Aulian. Only stories and their ghosts.'

'Wait and see.'

'I have a creature of my own to kill. One that's real.' She turned and pulled herself through the hole where the cisterns drained. Medrin Sixfingers was near. The sword knew it.

They took the Lhosir charge and met it, staggering a half-pace back under the crashing impact. The Lhosir pressed with a frenzied strength and the Marroc fought back with the wild abandon of men with nowhere left to run. Gallow looked for Medrin in the press of shields but the crush of bodies was too thick. He lunged with his spear and sliced open a man's arm and then stabbed him in the face. He barged with his shield and reversed his spear and stabbed the next Lhosir in the foot. But the Marroc, for all their heart, never fought together as a wall of men like this. When Gallow tore a shield aside, no spear thrust came from behind to finish the man he fought, yet when the Lhosir did the same, that thrust came fast and deadly. The Marroc to Gallow's right had his shield hooked by a Lhosir axe and pulled down and instantly a spear slashed his neck. The Marroc on the other side lifted his shield to hold off a barrage of blows and a spear plunged into his knee. He lurched, screaming, and another took him in the throat. Slowly the Marroc line fell back.

A shout went up from the sixth gate and another rain of missiles fell on the Lhosir from Valaric's Marroc, stones and arrows and boiling water and the last sacks of salt. The Lhosir fought with mad desperation to press away from the gate and for a moment the Marroc found a new heart. Gallow lost his spear, bitten in two by a Lhosir hatchet. He drew his own axe and rained blow after blow on the enemy before him, battering them back, beating them to death beneath their mail and shields. Another Marroc fell beside him. For a moment he felt something give, the whole line falter. He stumbled, forced by the press of the Lhosir to step back, and for a moment he felt the Marroc about to turn and rout – but then a cry went up: 'The Wolf! The Wolf!' And though Gallow couldn't see, he knew that Valaric, crippled or not, had come down from the gates to pick up his sword, and at the sound of his name the Marroc found their courage again. They held with bitter resolve while the Lhosir pressed like a storm. And now, at last, Gallow saw Medrin, sword raised high, driving it into the Marroc ahead of him, blow after blow after blow.

'Medrin! *Nioingr!*'

Over the noise of screams and howls Medrin turned and saw him, and then each pressed towards the other, pushing and shoving friend and foe alike aside until they were close enough for their swords to touch.

Oribas barely noticed Mirrahj go. He climbed on because he was an Aulian and he knew how an Aulian thought, and what an Aulian thought was that any good thing served more than one purpose. The tunnel from the cisterns was a way for men to escape, and that was one thing, but why then tunnel up as well as down? The anticipation gave wings to his thoughts. It was a way for water to escape without flooding the castle and so it must be that the water that might make that flood would lie at its top. And when he reached that top he stopped and tried to see, but there was no light at all, not the tiniest bit of it. With a reluctant huff he reached into his satchel and fumbled for his lamp. Nothing was where it was supposed to be – Medrin had clearly gone through his powders while they'd been riding – but eventually he found it and lit it and held it high so that he and Achista could see what they'd found, and it was enough to make Achista sigh with wonder in his ear. A rift ran up and down the inside of the mountain before them, too deep for his light to penetrate, wrinkled twists of tunnels and chasms vanishing in all directions. From where he stood, steps carved hundreds of years ago climbed the wall of the cave. From somewhere ahead he heard the hiss of water. The air was damp.

Achista rested a hand on his shoulder. 'Is it here?'

'I think so.' He started to climb the steps, creeping on his hands and feet.

'Oribas, if it is, I have to go. Valaric needs to know.'

He turned awkwardly and held her briefly. In the darkness he grinned. 'Tell him his dragon waits for him.' He watched her go and then returned to the steps. They wound around the edge of the cave wall, carved into it, narrow and old and slippery, and then spiralled up into an inverted funnel. The sound of hissing water grew stronger. Now and then he felt a waft of spray on his face. The steps took him to a ledge where the stone above closed into a narrow shaft clearly carved by men. Its walls were flat and slick and as he stepped closer, dripping water spattered his face, so much that he had to shield his lamp. Down beneath his feet was nothing but a dark void. He looked up. Above, at the limit of his light, the shaft was blocked shut. Stone blocks pressed against one another so tight that no knife blade would slip between them, and yet from the cracks ran a steady trickle of water, drips in some places but in others tight hissing jets of it as though squeezed through the very stone itself by an irresistible pressure from above.

He giggled. So there it was. The Aulians had tunnelled into the mountain and struck the bed of the lake that lay above the castle. And after the flood they'd sealed the hole the way only Aulians understood, with an arrangement of stones that would only grow stronger as more and more weight piled onto it. And as with the gatehouse he'd described to Valaric back when the Lhosir had first come, somewhere would be a single stone that held it together. A single stone that, if it was pulled away, would cause the entire structure to collapse.

His eyes gleamed. There would be a chain. And there was, hanging right down in front of him, and that was when he remembered the other part of the story he'd told to Valaric.

The fighting stopped around them. Gallow and Medrin faced each other amid a ring of men, half Marroc, half Lhosir. In the middle of the fiercest battle they would ever see men set on killing each other stepped away to make space and lowered their blades.

Medrin cocked his head and lifted the Crimson Shield. 'Marroc! Look at me! You call upon your god Modris to protect you, yet here is his shield. *His* shield! I am your king and I am your protector, and yet you've turned your back on me and so Modris spurns your names.' He looked at Gallow and bared his teeth. 'And you, Foxbeard! You were supposed to be here waiting for me with the Sword of the Weeping God! With Solace, the Comforter, the Peacebringer, the Edge of Sorrows. Our clash would have been of titans, a myth made flesh. But no, you sent the sword away with some Vathan. Was that to spite me?' He cut an arc with his sword, pointing at the Marroc around Gallow. 'I came to Varyxhun not for some strange blade, nor for some faithless *nioingr*. I came to crush these men to bloody dust so that all Marroc might understand that we are now one. One kingdom, one crown, one people.' He smiled. 'You! Look at you, Gallow Foxbeard! A Lhosir living among the Marroc, and you fight me, and yet that is what I offer: Lhosir and Marroc together, side by side. Why not?'

'We'll not be ruled by a forkbeard!' shouted Valaric, and the Marroc cheered.

Medrin threw back his head and roared with laughter. 'You'll be ruled by a king! What difference does it make whether he's born on this side of the sea or that? He might as well be an Aulian for all the difference it makes. A king is a king is a king, and kings do what kings do and whether their beards are forked or straight or they have none at all, it makes not a whit of difference. *I* am your king, no more and no less, and you are traitors, every one of you, and so you will die.'

Gallow let out a deep sigh. 'Thank you, brother of the sea.'
He drew his sword. 'Thank you for letting this be clear. Because
you're right: it's not about your beard, it's simply that as kings
go, you're a bad one.'

He lunged, and the Crimson Shield swung down and caught
his blow.

For a long long time Oribas stared at the chain. It was right in
front of him, a massive thing of iron links each the size of his
fist. He could reach out and touch it. It hung straight down from
the clot of stones above his head and ran into the darkness of
the void below. When he looked down, he could just about see a
piece of stone the size of a man dangling from its end.

He wondered what to do. Such a massive chain and such a
weight hanging from it and such a weight pushing down from
above, what difference could one man possibly make? But then
he peered more closely and saw that not all links in the chain
were alike. At the level of his eye was a single link of a different
colour, and Oribas understood. This was not iron but a milky
glassy stone, stained by years of rust from the links above but
definitely different, and he knew this stone, a kind of glass
sometimes found in rough round nuggets in the fields of old
Aulia itself, stronger than iron yet brittle. One good sharp blow
would shatter it. And when he rubbed away at the stains to be
sure, he found it marked with pictograms that left no room for
doubt. Air and earth, water and the dragon. The chain would
snap and the weight would fall. Earth would become air and
water would become the dragon. It wasn't about pulling the
chain but about snapping it.

He looked up. He couldn't see how it worked but maybe that
didn't matter. A counterweight mechanism perhaps. The intent
was clear enough.

His first problem was having no hammer to shatter the brittle
link, but that wasn't much of a problem at all because there
were loose stones right at his feet. His second problem was a
bit harder. How not to die when a ton of stone and a lakeful of
water crashed down on his head. And he was still pondering
that one and realising that it probably didn't have an answer

when he heard Achista's desperate cry echo through the caves. 'Oribas! The sixth gate is shattered! The forkbeards come! If you've found your dragon then let it out! Let it out!'

Gallow charged into Medrin like an angry boar, crashing into him, shield on shield. Medrin was smaller, weaker, sure to buckle and fall, and yet it was Gallow who reeled away as though he'd run headlong into a wall of stone. He charged again and Medrin simply stood unmoved as though he barely noticed. Breathing heavily, Gallow faced him more warily. 'What sorcery is this, Sixfingers? Has the witch you keep put a spell on you and made you into iron?'

Medrin's eyes never left him. 'I carry the shield of a god, Foxbeard. What did you expect?'

Gallow shook his head. 'It's just a shield.'

'So it is.' Medrin came at him then, slow and sure, his sword swinging in a steady barrage of blows. Gallow took them on his shield and struck back, yet Medrin caught Gallow's sword on the Crimson Shield each time with ease. 'Shall we see who tires first?' He snorted. 'A dull fight this is for our men to see. How about this? If I beat you, all your Marroc will throw down their arms and I'll let one in every four go free, chosen by chance. One in four, Gallow. Better odds than I offer with my army. And if you beat me, then what shall we say? One in three? *If* they throw down their arms, that is.' He cackled with glee. 'I'll make it sweeter. If you beat me, one in three may live, most chosen by chance but you may choose a dozen of them. Got any friends here, Foxbeard? Or family?' Then he looked at his six-fingered hand and at his stump behind his shield. 'No. We shall say six, not twelve.'

Gallow spat at Medrin's feet. 'I will cut you down, prince of cowards, and the men behind you too while the rest of your army turn to their heels!'

'No, Gallow Foxbeard.' Medrin smiled back at him. 'That's not how it will be and you very well know it.' And he jumped forward and barged into Gallow with the Crimson Shield and it was like the kick of a horse, a battering that would have shaken even old Jyrdas One-Eye in his prime. Gallow reeled and before he could do more than stay on his feet, Medrin hit him again, another hammer blow, and another, and with each blow Gallow staggered back and the Marroc behind him withdrew to make space, and Medrin and the Lhosir advanced beyond the gates and the Dragon's Maw and into the castle yard, until on the fifth blow Gallow stumbled and there was no time to recover, and when the shield of Modris struck him again, he fell exhausted and beaten. King Medrin Sixfingers pointed his sword at Gallow's face. He wasn't even breathing hard.

'Do you not see? Do you not understand? *Just* a shield? It's the shield of a god, Foxbeard. A *god!*'

'Oribas! *Oribas!*' For a moment he froze, too terrified and torn, but then he heard the sound of feet on stone and knew she was climbing the steps.

'Achista! Wait!' If he let her come she'd die beside him.

'Oribas! The forkbeards are in the yard!'

'I have the dragon. I've found it! Go! Turn back and I will release it!'

He closed his eyes and picked up a stone, and when he opened them again there were tears on his cheek. Not for himself but for her, for the years, for the hours, for the minutes they wouldn't have. It was a cruel trap these long-dead Aulians had made.

'Oribas!'

'Do not be angry, my love,' and roundly and loudly he cursed every god he knew as he drew back his rock to smash the brittle link and snap the chain in two.

Gallow felt as if he'd been trampled by a herd of wild horses. He tried to get to his feet but it was so hard and then Medrin kicked him back down. The Lhosir king walked towards the Marroc soldiers, lifting his shield high so they all could see it. He shouted at them, 'The shield of your god! Modris!' Wherever he approached they quailed and backed further away.

As he lay on the stone, Gallow felt the mountain quiver beneath him. A whisper of a rumble breathed from the Dragon's Maw, too quiet to be heard over the noise of Medrin roaring at the soldiers around him. 'Lay down your swords and your shields and sink to your knees and bow your heads, Marroc. One in four will live, that was my promise. Or fight and you can all die. Here I stand! Who will face—'

'More than happy to kill you, Sixfingers.' Valaric limped out from amid the Marroc, swinging a sword in his hand. Gallow pulled himself to his hands and knees. 'Shame my spear missed you in Andhun but I'll be happy to—'

Medrin moved like quicksilver. He barged Valaric, shield on shield, and Gallow saw Valaric's face as he reeled back, the shock and surprise as if Medrin was not one man but ten. The Wolf crashed into the Marroc behind him and slowly picked himself up. Medrin turned his back. Valaric took a deep breath and picked up his sword and this time, Gallow knew, Medrin would kill him. Valaric probably knew it too, but that wasn't going to stop him.

'I'll fight you, King Sixfingers.'

Mirrahj. She pushed her way through the Marroc. She carried no shield, but in one hand was an axe and in the other the long rust-red blade of the Edge of Sorrows. Medrin opened his arms to welcome her. 'Good for you, Vathan. About time someone with a proper sword came to this fight.'

The glass-stone link in the chain exploded. Shards like knives stung his face. Something hit him in the eye – a bright burning pain. The upper part of the chain flicked like a whip, lashing with all its pent-up energy into the stone above Oribas's head. The bottom of it plunged into the dark. He heard the crash as the stone at its end hit the floor of the cave somewhere below. Then something else came hurtling down the shaft. Another stone on the end of another chain. It jerked to a halt right in front of him and he understood. The counterweight. Somewhere above, the force of its arrest would jerk something free. He closed his eyes, waiting to die under the deluge of stone and water, but none came.

'Oribas!'

He opened one eye, the one that would still open. His face had blood on it.

'*Oribas!*'

He was alive. The dragon had failed and now he didn't know what to do. 'It didn't work.' He swore. Then he swore louder. 'It didn't work. Stupid ...' How old was it? Stuck? Rust? He didn't know. Didn't know what to do.

'Oribas, the gate is breached! The forkbeards come! Do it!'

He nodded, not that Achista could see him. 'Then we have to leave. The way we came. There is no dragon after all. It did not work. I am sorry, my love, but it is dead from age.'

'No!'

He squeezed his fists as though he could somehow squeeze an idea out from between his fingers. Only a fool gave up at the first attempt. Maybe there was another ... He froze. Cocked his head to listen.

'Oribas! What are you—'

'Be quiet!'

The hiss of the water pushing out from between the stones had changed. Very slightly, but it wasn't the same sound it had been when Oribas had come. He looked at the chain and the stone dangling in front of him. Water ran down it now, trickling off in a steady stream. It hadn't done that before. And it had come down after the first stone had hit the cave floor. The mechanism was higher up the shaft than he'd thought.

As if to answer him, a rumble shivered down the shaft – stones falling somewhere above. Awe ran cold across his skin.

'Run, Achista. Just run!'

The hole the Aulians had filled and left behind them wasn't big, easily large enough for a man to climb through but little more. Yet the pressure of water from the lake above was as though every Lhosir assaulting the walls of Varyxhun was hammering in that one place. And in that elaborate working of stones upon stones, as Oribas released the chain, something high above had shifted, and it was enough.

The rumbling grew louder. The shaft shook suddenly, right above his head. The stones that blocked it trembled. He could hardly see, and all he had was his tiny lamp in all this darkness and one eye still burned and wouldn't open and he had no idea how long he had. A few seconds perhaps. Or perhaps for ever. But either way he ran, scampering down the stairs, dancing from step to step with the crazy grace of desperation and dreadful fear and unexpected hope. A sharp crack sounded behind him. He felt it through the walls of the cave and heard a sudden spray of water, and then another crack and a terrible crashing roar as the weight of the lake at last crushed its way into the cavern. The Aulian stones plummeted past him and smashed into a thousand fragments and behind them came such a torrent of water that for a moment the whole mountain shook and almost threw him off its walls. A shock of air rushed and tugged at his limbs. He felt the mountain quake and heard its drawn-out rumble, and then he was at the top of the passage down to the cisterns and Achista was there and her arms were around him, dragging him in, hauling him to somewhere safe, and he clasped her hand and hugged her tight and kissed her while the great roar of water thrummed in his ears and the air filled with soaking spray.

'The dragon,' he whispered in her ear. 'It seems it was only sleeping after all.'

Up on the battlements Sarvic felt the mountain quiver too. He looked at his last arrow, the one Valaric had given him. The one with Medrin's name scratched into its iron head. With exaggerated care he rested it against his bowstring and drew it back and took aim. The back of Sixfingers' neck, that would do. But then a shout came from the gates, and then another and then more, and he heard Lhosir cries full of fearful warning and he couldn't help but turn to look. Water rushed from the Dragon's Maw and, even as he watched, the river became a torrent, so hard and fast with such force that all the forkbeards in the gate were swept back onto the road, and the ones on the road shouted out as the water tore over them, rising around their ankles and sucking at their feet.

Medrin waited. The Vathan woman danced around him, twirling her sword and her axe. She raised the Edge of Sorrows as if to swing it at his head and he lifted the Crimson Shield and smiled. From the corner of his eye he saw Gallow stumble to his feet and open his mouth to shout a warning. Three years ago in Andhun Gallow had struck the shield of Modris with the Sword of the Weeping God and learned a hard lesson. But this Marroc had learned it too, in the tomb under Witches' Reach. The red sword slid through the air past the Crimson Shield, turning away at the last moment as the Vathan woman struck at him with her axe instead, then drove the point of the sword low, too fast for the shield to follow but still not quick enough. Medrin saw and jumped away.

A rumble came from behind him, from the gates. He heard his Lhosir cry out. The Vathan swung again, backhanded, axe and sword at once, striking for the head and for the knees, and he saw what it was she was trying to do – to strike two blows at once so that the shield couldn't possibly deflect both.

He smiled a last smile. Too ambitious by far. Her axe struck the Crimson Shield and stuck fast, torn out of her hand. Medrin caught the red sword on his own blade, which shattered, leaving him holding a jagged stump of iron. He threw it away as they stepped apart, breathing hard. The Vathan woman looked past him, up to the castle walls, but Medrin only shook his head. 'Do you think I'm so easy to fool?' And then it seemed to Medrin that the Vathan closed her eyes and something came over her. She took the red sword in both hands, lifted it high and brought it down straight at his head, and it was the easiest thing in the world to lift the Crimson Shield.

Sarvic watched in awe. A flood like the Isset in all its rage was sweeping down the road now, washing the forkbeards away. They dropped their weapons and clung to the cliffs, climbed the walls, scrambled for any high ground they could find, for any handhold they could reach, but for every forkbeard who found safety Sarvic saw another plucked from his feet and tossed by the waters over the cliffs.

He shook himself. Laughed and then turned away because glorious as it was, he had other business. He looked back to the yard and Sixfingers and lifted his bow again. Sixfingers and the Vathan woman had stepped apart. She'd broken his sword but she'd lost her axe. He raised his bow and saw her look up, right at him, and it seemed that a glimmer of understanding passed between them. Then she looked away and lifted the red sword to split the Lhosir king in two. Sarvic took aim and his fingers released the bowstring.

Gallow watched as Solace struck the Crimson Shield. Mirrahj screamed in agony and dropped the blade. Medrin screamed too. He lurched bizarrely and half spun, eyes wild, the shield slicing down behind him at nothing at all while Mirrahj staggered away, clutching her arm to her side, doubled up in pain. Gallow was the first to move. He sprinted the few yards between them and snatched up the red sword. He turned on Medrin, ready to make an end of it, but the king was already dead. He tipped over and fell face first in front of Gallow, lying still, and it took an age for Gallow to see the arrow sticking out from the back of Medrin's neck.

35

KING OF THE VALLEY

Valaric stood on the sixth gate and looked at what was left of the valley below. The five tiers of the road from the castle to the Aulian Way. The five gates below him, all gaping holes scoured clear by the flood. And down in the valley the forkbeards' camp washed away and half of Varyxhun with it. All vanished in a lake of mud and rubble.

The Lhosir weren't all dead, not by any means, but the ones who hadn't been washed away had still gone. Maybe they were at Witches' Reach by now, licking their wounds, choosing their new king. More still were crossing the Aulian Bridge from Tarkhun. Maybe in a few days they'd be back again. Or maybe they'd had enough and they'd keep on walking, all the way to the sea and beyond, back to their homes.

He'd sent Medrin's body down on a mule. Chased it off after the last forkbeards along the Aulian Way for the forkbeards to do whatever forkbeards did. He hadn't liked doing it – what he'd wanted was to take Sixfingers' head and hang him by his feet from the gates but Gallow wouldn't let him, and his leg was giving him grief again, and in the end it had just been easier to let the crazy forkbeard have his way.

When he looked away from the valley and back into the castle, he saw that Gallow was coming to bother him again. He was with the Vathan woman and one of his Crackmarsh men, the one who thought he'd killed Medrin for a day or so. They seemed to take it in turns to make sure he had no peace. If it wasn't Gallow then it was the Aulian, or the worst of them all, Arda.

'Well? What now?'

'I came to say goodbye.'

'I need a smith.'

Gallow clapped him on the shoulder which made him stagger, and that made his leg hurt. 'Goodbye, Valaric. Come see me if you need your horse shod or a new blade for your scythe.'

Valaric winced and growled, 'So that's it? You just go now. After all this, you just go?'

'I'm going home, Valaric.'

'Well I do need a smith, but I shan't be sad to see the back of your wife so I suppose it evens out.'

'I'm taking Reddic too. Forge could do with another hand.'

'Yeah.' Valaric smirked. Reddic and Arda's firstborn. Half the Marroc in the castle knew by now. 'Anything else you want? Maybe to cut off my arms and legs too, before you go?'

Gallow held out the red sword in its scabbard.

'Taking that, are you?'

Gallow shook his head. 'In Andhun you told me it was cursed. You were right.' He cocked his head at Valaric and then handed the sword to the Vathan woman. 'This goes back where it belongs. Do we agree?'

For a moment Valaric remembered how it had felt to hold the Comforter. How strong and powerful he'd seemed. He bowed his head. 'Go on then, Vathan. Take it.' He tapped the Crimson Shield, which now hung from his arm. 'Don't bring it back, mind. You know what happens if you do. So just go home.'

Later he watched them go, picking their way down the castle road on their mules, Gallow and Arda and their children, Nadric and Reddic and the Vathen. Off to the Devil's Caves and the Crackmarsh and then their separate ways, and he wondered quietly if they'd all get home and find there what they wanted. He supposed he'd never know. And he was still wondering when Sarvic came and stood beside him and did that lurking thing again, shuffling closer and closer, except this time he managed to spit it out before Valaric hit him. 'I think you'd better come,' he said. 'Your soldiers have made something for you.'

'What's that, then? A list of demands?'

'No.'

'Gates? Is it new gates? Because we could really do with some new gates.'

'Just come and see. And don't mind me if I can't stop laughing if you ask me to start calling you Your Majesty.' He sniggered.

There was one other person to see before he left, and Gallow went to see him alone. He clasped arms with Oribas long and hard and it seemed that his hands didn't want to let go. Then Oribas closed his eyes and took a deep breath, and it felt to Gallow as though the Aulian was letting go of everything between them. Or at least perhaps loosening it a little. 'I have climbed to the lake, Gallow. Under the water my people built something. Something that was meant to stay hidden. I wonder now if it was no accident that they drained it. I have not told any other. Should I leave it be, Gallow, or should I see what lies beneath?'

Gallow smiled and shook his head. 'You know very well to leave it be, old friend.'

'I will seal the hole as my ancestors did before me. The snows are melting. It will be hidden again before long.' He bowed and then picked up a heavy satchel filled with salt and handed it to Gallow. A corner of iron poked out. 'I have one thing for you to take, Gallow.' He laughed and shook his head. 'I would shower you with gifts if I had any to give, but instead I have only this burden.'

'My hunting days are done, Oribas. I gave the sword to Mirrahj.'

But Oribas pressed the satchel into his hands anyway. 'Just this one thing, Gallow. Take it with you. Take it to your fire. Melt the iron down and forge it again with salt. Then throw it away, far from where you live. Or send it back, or drown it in the Isset, or lose it in the Crackmarsh, or hurl it into the sea. Whatever you like – just be rid of it.'

Gallow took a deep breath and then took the satchel. 'Make it work, Oribas. Make it work.' And he didn't know whether he meant Valaric's kingdom, which he was about to find he had, or holding off the Lhosir if they came again, or simply being married to a wilful Marroc woman – and the Maker-Devourer himself knew how hard *that* could be.

'I will do my best, old friend. I will do my best.'

EPILOGUE

The Vathen rode slowly through the ruins of the village. There was little left. Burned-out huts, not much else. They stopped at the edge, at what had once been a forge. One of them dismounted and poked through the rubble. Whatever had been done here, it had been a while ago.

'The forkbeards call themselves men of fate.' She said it without much feeling one way or the other, as if noting that the clouds had turned a little darker and perhaps more rain was on the way.

'This is a Marroc village,' said one of the others, with a voice that was keen to push on.

'Yes,' said the first. 'But a forkbeard lived here once. They called him Gallow. Gallow the Foxbeard.'

THE FALL OF AULIA

Phorbas Evistimacchus, Imperial Subterranean Architect. The Imperial Palace, Aulia.

In which your devoted pupil wishes to inform you of an unexpected discovery beneath the imperial palaces and begs the wisdom of his former mentor Bassus.

Bassus! Old friend! How I've missed your dry sensibility these last few days. I've no time and can only be brief to the point of scandal, but I simply must inform you of our recent momentous discovery. Would you have thought this possible, I wonder, ten years ago? It seems such a distant time and so many who work here have long lost any thought or memory as to why we do what we do. You must ask yourself, I'm sure, how could any forget that terrible day when the news came of the Emperor's wife and daughters lost at sea. I remember the look on your face when you told me his command to you which I later inherited, to delve ever deeper into the mountain until we reached the underworld itself to bring them back. Impossible? I know we both thought so, yet so we were commanded. How can any forget? Yet they do, Bassus, and I'll tell you why – it's because I'm almost the only one left here who began this with you.

But I forget myself. Three days ago we broke through to a shaft that descends deep into the mountain. It's round like a tunnel and glassy smooth and too steep to walk down without risk and we lost two men to their own enthusiasm on the first day when we broke into it. But it's exactly as you said we'd find it! Is it an entrance to the underworld itself? Could it be? The emperor is convinced. For my own part, I'm less sure. Honestly, Bassus, I don't know what to think save that I wish you were here to see this discovery for yourself.

Bassus Orichalum, Prefect of Cthonic Engineering. Varyxhun.

In which your former but long-surpassed tutor is thankful for any wisdom you may consider to have come from him and wishes very much that he might share in the triumph of Phorbas Evistimacchus.

Phorbas, I cannot begin to describe both my excitement and my apprehension on hearing of your discovery, nor can I express how dearly I wish I could be with you at this time. You know I have long predicted such tunnels delving deep into the heart of Mount Aulos. In my feeble efforts to help, I remind you of the dangers of choking gasses so deep under the ground and to be warned of places where the walls become unaccountably warm. I am, however, quite sure that my meagre wisdom is entirely unnecessary and also will arrive far to late to be of any use. I hope that by now you've explored your new tunnel to a great extent and look forward very much to learning what marvellous discoveries you've undoubtedly made. I suppose I must express my doubts that the underworld itself will open before you. If it does then I both envy you and am quite glad to be far away. If it does not, then I hope the disappointment of the Emperor will be tolerable.

My own situation is far more unenviable. This accursed land is cold and wet and thoroughly uncomfortable and I'm yet to find a single Aulian content to be stationed here. You're aware of what our predecessors carried here and and why, and that much of the work required was completed long before I arrived. A skeleton garrison remains in the fortress and in the secondary tomb, but the few natives who dwell in these parts are wild and ignorant men and their superstitions are quite enough to keep them away, thank goodness. I completed work on plugging the lake floor two years ago and have had little to amuse myself since that time other than to watch it slowly refill. I can report that the spring melt has now ended and that the dam holds fast. Phorbas, I wish you could be here to see my work. Although a paltry trifle when placed against your own, I'm really quite proud of it. The garrison commander is as eager to leave as I am, I think, and so when we see there is no leakage for another month or two, I imagine that will be enough. The tomb will remain drowned forever and I can finally come home. I hope it will be to rejoin you in Aulia itself and bask in the glow of your many marvellous discoveries.

Phorbas Evistimacchus, Imperial Subterranean Architect. The Imperial Palace, Aulia.

In which your devoted and yet frustrated pupil can report only very meagre progress and wishes you well and a speedy return.

Yes, yes, yes, choking air, I know all about choking air, Bassus. Your lessons on that point were very practical ones as I remember, and I thank you for how very firmly they've kept the danger at the forefront of my mind. It has indeed been an almost insurmountable problem, as the foulness appears content to lurk in the depths of the tunnel, refusing to emerge. The air is uncommonly warm too, as you predicted. All in all the situation is entirely unsatisfactory to me and vastly more so to His Imperial meddlesomeness. I do wish you were here if only so that one of us could get on with things while the other attends to his constant summonses. You must remember the Smoljani? He has his clanking iron-clad guards supervising us constantly and they do nothing but get in the way and badger us with constant questions. I have a scholar from the desert here with me now who thinks he has a solution to the problem of the air. We shall see.

Postscript: I've now arranged for you to find this delivered with an urgent summons carrying the Emperor's seal for you to return to the capital, as surely your work in the barbarian land is complete. I hope this pleases you.

Bassus Orichalum, Prefect of Cthonic Engineering. Some gods-forsaken place in the middle of nowhere.

In which your former but surely long-surpassed tutor is thankful beyond measure.

Well we're finally on our way, though not as quickly as either you or I would have liked. The commander of the castle has taken the Emperor's order as being an end to his entire mission here and so we've all left, every single one of us, which I can tell you took a goodly more time than if I'd left on my own and so I'm afraid I'll be a month later than otherwise might have been the case. It did however mean I had an escort of two hundred guardsmen to watch over me across these blasted mountains and just as well, for as we emerged into the hills on the other side, our vanguard was set upon by bandits and our main force was barely able to catch up in time to drive them off. I tell you, out here on the fringes of the empire it gets worse every year and I wouldn't be surprised to see outright insurrection before much longer. So I can say in all honesty that this has been the most exciting journey I've ever undertaken and I look forward very much to returning home, though I might suppose this in part stems from what I hope to see when I arrive.

Phorbas Evistimacchus, Imperial Subterranean Architect. The Imperial Palace, Aulia.

In which your devoted pupil begs you proceed with all speed home.

Bassus, you should see the contraption this desert man has made – didn't I once tell you they were by far the best scholars and inventors in the empire? We all wear iron masks now – I must say they make the Smoljani look like monsters – and drag great bladders full of air behind us into the depths of the tunnel. Together we've devised a pulley system that constantly moves new bladders from the top of the shaft to the bottom and returns the spent ones from below. With this system finally working, I've plumbed the depths of the shaft and made a most remarkable discovery. Towards its end, the tunnel grows wider and ends in a dome-like protrusion. The texture of the rock is even more like glass, more so than I've ever seen, and it's quite clearly hollow. When I stand there, I have visions of a vast subterranean cathedral beneath my feet. I've kept this discovery to myself for now, old friend. I was hoping you might be here when we open it. Travel in haste!

Phorbas Evistimacchus, Imperial Subterranean Architect. The Imperial Palace, Aulia.

In which your devoted pupil begs your forgiveness.

I'm sorry, Bassus. I wish I could wait for you, but the Emperor is constantly informed of our progress from the Smoljani he places among us and someone has explained our discovery to them. I've tried to advise caution but the Emperor will accept no delay. He's convinced we've found the entrance, at last, to the underworld. In truth I'm every bit as excited. It's absurd, but I'm starting to wonder if he might even be right. Tomorrow I shall break through and we shall see. Come with all speed, old friend. I'm sorry I couldn't wait for you.

ACKNOWLEDGEMENTS

Thanks go to Simon Spanton, who commissioned this and to Marcus Gipps, who edited it, and to all the people who put together the wonderful covers these books have had. They go to the copy-editors and proofreaders and booksellers and the marketeers and everyone who makes books possible. They go to you, for reading this.

And thanks, still, to all the crazy people who think the best way to spend a week in February is to strut though York in mail carrying an axe.

As always, if you liked this story, please tell others who might like it too. And if you did like it, there are other stories out there that you might like too, ones that had a touch in shaping these stories or ones that I read afterwards and wished I'd read before, including:

Legend by David Gemmell (Varyxhun castle has six gates after the six walls of Dros Delnoch);

Wolfsangel by M. D. Lachlan (I can still smell the blood and the iron); and

The Ten Thousand by Paul Kearney (The fight scenes – ouch!).

GALLOW

will return in:

THE ANVIL

SOLACE

DRAGON'S REACH

Ebook only short stories by Nathan Hawke,
available from all good eBook retailers